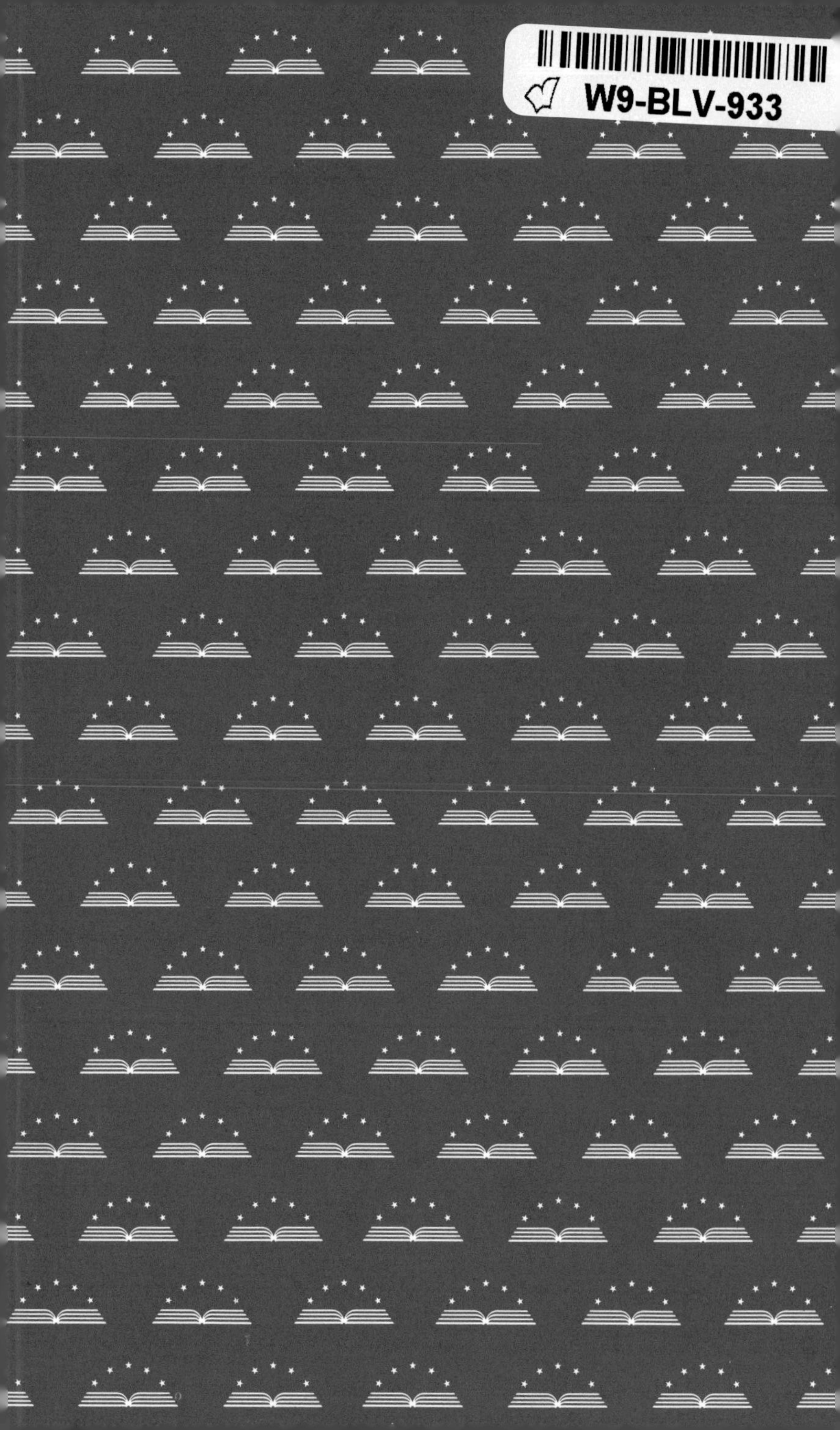
W9-BLV-933

Henry Wadsworth Longfellow

POEMS AND OTHER WRITINGS

THE LIBRARY OF AMERICA

The paper used in this publication meets the minimum requirements of the American National Standard for Information Sciences—Permanence of Paper for Printed Library Materials, ANSI Z39.48—1984.

Distributed to the trade in the United States by Penguin Putnam Inc.
and in Canada by Penguin Books Canada Ltd.

Library of Congress Catalog Number: 00-026678
For cataloging information, see end of Index.
ISBN 1-883011-85-X

First Printing
The Library of America—118

Manufactured in the United States of America

J. D. McClatchy

SELECTED THE CONTENTS AND WROTE THE NOTES FOR THIS VOLUME

Contents

HENRY WADSWORTH LONGFELLOW

from

THE VOICES OF THE NIGHT

The Spirit of Poetry

There is a quiet spirit in these woods,
That dwells where'er the gentle south-wind blows;
Where, underneath the white-thorn, in the glade,
The wild flowers bloom, or, kissing the soft air,
The leaves above their sunny palms outspread.
With what a tender and impassioned voice
It fills the nice and delicate ear of thought,
When the fast ushering star of morning comes
O'er-riding the gray hills with golden scarf;
Or when the cowled and dusky-sandalled Eve,
In mourning weeds, from out the western gate,
Departs with silent pace! That spirit moves
In the green valley, where the silver brook,
From its full laver, pours the white cascade;
And, babbling low amid the tangled woods,
Slips down through moss-grown stones with endless
  laughter.
And frequent, on the everlasting hills,
Its feet go forth, when it doth wrap itself
In all the dark embroidery of the storm,
And shouts the stern, strong wind. And here, amid
The silent majesty of these deep woods,
Its presence shall uplift thy thoughts from earth,
As to the sunshine and the pure, bright air
Their tops the green trees lift. Hence gifted bards
Have ever loved the calm and quiet shades.
For them there was an eloquent voice in all
The sylvan pomp of woods, the golden sun,
The flowers, the leaves, the river on its way,
Blue skies, and silver clouds, and gentle winds,
The swelling upland, where the sidelong sun
Aslant the wooded slope, at evening, goes,
Groves, through whose broken roof the sky looks in,
Mountain, and shattered cliff, and sunny vale,

The distant lake, fountains, and mighty trees,
In many a lazy syllable, repeating
Their old poetic legends to the wind.

And this is the sweet spirit, that doth fill
The world; and, in these wayward days of youth,
My busy fancy oft embodies it,
As a bright image of the light and beauty
That dwell in nature; of the heavenly forms
We worship in our dreams, and the soft hues
That stain the wild bird's wing, and flush the clouds
When the sun sets. Within her tender eye
The heaven of April, with its changing light,
And when it wears the blue of May, is hung,
And on her lip the rich, red rose. Her hair
Is like the summer tresses of the trees,
When twilight makes them brown, and on her cheek
Blushes the richness of an autumn sky,
With ever-shifting beauty. Then her breath,
It is so like the gentle air of Spring,
As, from the morning's dewy flowers, it comes
Full of their fragrance, that it is a joy
To have it round us, and her silver voice
Is the rich music of a summer bird,
Heard in the still night, with its passionate cadence.

Hymn to the Night

'Ασπασίη, τρίλλιστος.

I heard the trailing garments of the Night
  Sweep through her marble halls!
I saw her sable skirts all fringed with light
  From the celestial walls!

I felt her presence, by its spell of might,
  Stoop o'er me from above;
The calm, majestic presence of the Night,
  As of the one I love.

I heard the sounds of sorrow and delight,
The manifold, soft chimes,
That fill the haunted chambers of the Night,
Like some old poet's rhymes.

From the cool cisterns of the midnight air
My spirit drank repose;
The fountain of perpetual peace flows there,—
From those deep cisterns flows.

O holy Night! from thee I learn to bear
What man has borne before!
Thou layest thy finger on the lips of Care,
And they complain no more.

Peace! Peace! Orestes-like I breathe this prayer!
Descend with broad-winged flight,
The welcome, the thrice-prayed for, the most fair,
The best-beloved Night!

A Psalm of Life

Tell me not, in mournful numbers,
Life is but an empty dream!—
For the soul is dead that slumbers,
And things are not what they seem.

Life is real! Life is earnest!
And the grave is not its goal;
Dust thou art, to dust returnest,
Was not spoken of the soul.

Not enjoyment, and not sorrow,
Is our destined end or way;
But to act, that each to-morrow
Find us farther than to-day.

Art is long, and Time is fleeting,
And our hearts, though stout and brave,
Still, like muffled drums, are beating
Funeral marches to the grave.

In the world's broad field of battle,
In the bivouac of Life,
Be not like dumb, driven cattle!
Be a hero in the strife!

Trust no Future, howe'er pleasant!
Let the dead Past bury its dead!
Act,—act in the living Present!
Heart within, and God o'erhead!

Lives of great men all remind us
We can make our lives sublime,
And, departing, leave behind us
Footprints on the sands of time;

Footprints, that perhaps another,
Sailing o'er life's solemn main,
A forlorn and shipwrecked brother,
Seeing, shall take heart again.

Let us, then, be up and doing,
With a heart for any fate;
Still achieving, still pursuing,
Learn to labor and to wait.

The Light of Stars

The night is come, but not too soon;
And sinking silently,
All silently, the little moon
Drops down behind the sky.

There is no light in earth or heaven
  But the cold light of stars;
And the first watch of night is given
  To the red planet Mars.

Is it the tender star of love?
  The star of love and dreams?
Oh no! from that blue tent above
  A hero's armor gleams.

And earnest thoughts within me rise,
  When I behold afar,
Suspended in the evening skies,
  The shield of that red star.

O star of strength! I see thee stand
  And smile upon my pain;
Thou beckonest with thy mailed hand,
  And I am strong again.

Within my breast there is no light
  But the cold light of stars;
I give the first watch of the night
  To the red planet Mars.

The star of the unconquered will,
  He rises in my breast,
Serene, and resolute, and still,
  And calm, and self-possessed.

And thou, too, whosoe'er thou art,
  That readest this brief psalm,
As one by one thy hopes depart,
  Be resolute and calm.

Oh, fear not in a world like this,
  And thou shalt know erelong,
Know how sublime a thing it is
  To suffer and be strong.

Footsteps of Angels

When the hours of Day are numbered,
   And the voices of the Night
Wake the better soul, that slumbered,
   To a holy, calm delight;

Ere the evening lamps are lighted,
   And, like phantoms grim and tall,
Shadows from the fitful firelight
   Dance upon the parlor wall;

Then the forms of the departed
   Enter at the open door;
The beloved, the true-hearted,
   Come to visit me once more;

He, the young and strong, who cherished
   Noble longings for the strife,
By the roadside fell and perished,
   Weary with the march of life!

They, the holy ones and weakly,
   Who the cross of suffering bore,
Folded their pale hands so meekly,
   Spake with us on earth no more!

And with them the Being Beauteous,
   Who unto my youth was given,
More than all things else to love me,
   And is now a saint in heaven.

With a slow and noiseless footstep
   Comes that messenger divine,
Takes the vacant chair beside me,
   Lays her gentle hand in mine.

And she sits and gazes at me
  With those deep and tender eyes,
Like the stars, so still and saint-like,
  Looking downward from the skies.

Uttered not, yet comprehended,
  Is the spirit's voiceless prayer,
Soft rebukes, in blessings ended,
  Breathing from her lips of air.

Oh, though oft depressed and lonely,
  All my fears are laid aside,
If I but remember only
  Such as these have lived and died!

from

BALLADS AND OTHER POEMS

The Skeleton in Armor

"Speak! speak! thou fearful guest!
Who, with thy hollow breast
Still in rude armor drest,
   Comest to daunt me!
Wrapt not in Eastern balms,
But with thy fleshless palms
Stretched, as if asking alms,
   Why dost thou haunt me?"

Then, from those cavernous eyes
Pale flashes seemed to rise,
As when the Northern skies
   Gleam in December;
And, like the water's flow
Under December's snow,
Came a dull voice of woe
   From the heart's chamber.

"I was a Viking old!
My deeds, though manifold,
No Skald in song has told,
   No Saga taught thee!
Take heed, that in thy verse
Thou dost the tale rehearse,
Else dread a dead man's curse;
   For this I sought thee.

"Far in the Northern Land,
By the wild Baltic's strand,
I, with my childish hand,
   Tamed the gerfalcon;
And, with my skates fast-bound,
Skimmed the half-frozen Sound,

That the poor whimpering hound
   Trembled to walk on.

"Oft to his frozen lair
Tracked I the grisly bear,
While from my path the hare
   Fled like a shadow;
Oft through the forest dark
Followed the were-wolf's bark,
Until the soaring lark
   Sang from the meadow.

"But when I older grew,
Joining a corsair's crew,
O'er the dark sea I flew
   With the marauders.
Wild was the life we led;
Many the souls that sped,
Many the hearts that bled,
   By our stern orders.

"Many a wassail-bout
Wore the long Winter out;
Often our midnight shout
   Set the cocks crowing,
As we the Berserk's tale
Measured in cups of ale,
Draining the oaken pail,
   Filled to o'erflowing.

"Once as I told in glee
Tales of the stormy sea,
Soft eyes did gaze on me,
   Burning yet tender;
And as the white stars shine
On the dark Norway pine,
On that dark heart of mine
   Fell their soft splendor.

"I wooed the blue-eyed maid,
Yielding, yet half afraid,
And in the forest's shade
  Our vows were plighted.
Under its loosened vest
Fluttered her little breast,
Like birds within their nest
  By the hawk frighted.

"Bright in her father's hall
Shields gleamed upon the wall,
Loud sang the minstrels all,
  Chanting his glory;
When of old Hildebrand
I asked his daughter's hand,
Mute did the minstrels stand
  To hear my story.

"While the brown ale he quaffed,
Loud then the champion laughed,
And as the wind-gusts waft
  The sea-foam brightly,
So the loud laugh of scorn,
Out of those lips unshorn,
From the deep drinking-horn
  Blew the foam lightly.

"She was a Prince's child,
I but a Viking wild,
And though she blushed and smiled,
  I was discarded!
Should not the dove so white
Follow the sea-mew's flight,
Why did they leave that night
  Her nest unguarded?

"Scarce had I put to sea,
Bearing the maid with me,
Fairest of all was she
  Among the Norsemen!

When on the white sea-strand,
Waving his armed hand,
Saw we old Hildebrand,
With twenty horsemen.

"Then launched they to the blast,
Bent like a reed each mast,
Yet we were gaining fast,
When the wind failed us;
And with a sudden flaw
Came round the gusty Skaw,
So that our foe we saw
Laugh as he hailed us.

"And as to catch the gale
Round veered the flapping sail,
'Death!' was the helmsman's hail,
'Death without quarter!'
Mid-ships with iron keel
Struck we her ribs of steel;
Down her black hulk did reel
Through the black water!

"As with his wings aslant,
Sails the fierce cormorant,
Seeking some rocky haunt,
With his prey laden,—
So toward the open main,
Beating to sea again,
Through the wild hurricane,
Bore I the maiden.

"Three weeks we westward bore,
And when the storm was o'er,
Cloud-like we saw the shore
Stretching to leeward;
There for my lady's bower
Built I the lofty tower,
Which, to this very hour,
Stands looking seaward.

"There lived we many years;
Time dried the maiden's tears;
She had forgot her fears,
  She was a mother;
Death closed her mild blue eyes,
Under that tower she lies;
Ne'er shall the sun arise
  On such another!

"Still grew my bosom then,
Still as a stagnant fen!
Hateful to me were men,
  The sunlight hateful!
In the vast forest here,
Clad in my warlike gear,
Fell I upon my spear,
  Oh, death was grateful!

"Thus, seamed with many scars,
Bursting these prison bars,
Up to its native stars
  My soul ascended!
There from the flowing bowl
Deep drinks the warrior's soul,
Skoal! to the Northland! *skoal!*"
  Thus the tale ended.

The Wreck of the Hesperus

It was the schooner Hesperus,
  That sailed the wintry sea;
And the skipper had taken his little daughtèr,
  To bear him company.

Blue were her eyes as the fairy-flax,
  Her cheeks like the dawn of day,
And her bosom white as the hawthorn buds,
  That ope in the month of May.

The skipper he stood beside the helm,
  His pipe was in his mouth,
And he watched how the veering flaw did blow
  The smoke now West, now South.

Then up and spake an old Sailòr,
  Had sailed to the Spanish Main,
"I pray thee, put into yonder port,
  For I fear a hurricane.

"Last night, the moon had a golden ring,
  And to-night no moon we see!"
The skipper, he blew a whiff from his pipe,
  And a scornful laugh laughed he.

Colder and louder blew the wind,
  A gale from the Northeast,
The snow fell hissing in the brine,
  And the billows frothed like yeast.

Down came the storm, and smote amain
  The vessel in its strength;
She shuddered and paused, like a frighted steed,
  Then leaped her cable's length.

"Come hither! come hither! my little daughtèr,
  And do not tremble so;
For I can weather the roughest gale
  That ever wind did blow."

He wrapped her warm in his seaman's coat
  Against the stinging blast;
He cut a rope from a broken spar,
  And bound her to the mast.

"O father! I hear the church-bells ring,
  Oh say, what may it be?"
" 'T is a fog-bell on a rock-bound coast!"—
  And he steered for the open sea.

"O father! I hear the sound of guns,
Oh say, what may it be?"
"Some ship in distress, that cannot live
In such an angry sea!"

"O father! I see a gleaming light,
Oh say, what may it be?"
But the father answered never a word,
A frozen corpse was he.

Lashed to the helm, all stiff and stark,
With his face turned to the skies,
The lantern gleamed through the gleaming snow
On his fixed and glassy eyes.

Then the maiden clasped her hands and prayed
That savèd she might be;
And she thought of Christ, who stilled the wave,
On the Lake of Galilee.

And fast through the midnight dark and drear,
Through the whistling sleet and snow,
Like a sheeted ghost, the vessel swept
Tow'rds the reef of Norman's Woe.

And ever the fitful gusts between
A sound came from the land;
It was the sound of the trampling surf
On the rocks and the hard sea-sand.

The breakers were right beneath her bows,
She drifted a dreary wreck,
And a whooping billow swept the crew
Like icicles from her deck.

She struck where the white and fleecy waves
Looked soft as carded wool,
But the cruel rocks, they gored her side
Like the horns of an angry bull.

Her rattling shrouds, all sheathed in ice,
  With the masts went by the board;
Like a vessel of glass, she stove and sank,
  Ho! ho! the breakers roared!

At daybreak, on the bleak sea-beach,
  A fisherman stood aghast,
To see the form of a maiden fair,
  Lashed close to a drifting mast.

The salt sea was frozen on her breast,
  The salt tears in her eyes;
And he saw her hair, like the brown sea-weed,
  On the billows fall and rise.

Such was the wreck of the Hesperus,
  In the midnight and the snow!
Christ save us all from a death like this,
  On the reef of Norman's Woe!

The Village Blacksmith

Under a spreading chestnut-tree
  The village smithy stands;
The smith, a mighty man is he,
  With large and sinewy hands;
And the muscles of his brawny arms
  Are strong as iron bands.

His hair is crisp, and black, and long,
  His face is like the tan;
His brow is wet with honest sweat,
  He earns whate'er he can,
And looks the whole world in the face,
  For he owes not any man.

Week in, week out, from morn till night,
  You can hear his bellows blow;

You can hear him swing his heavy sledge,
  With measured beat and slow,
Like a sexton ringing the village bell,
  When the evening sun is low.

And children coming home from school
  Look in at the open door;
They love to see the flaming forge,
  And hear the bellows roar,
And catch the burning sparks that fly
  Like chaff from a threshing-floor.

He goes on Sunday to the church,
  And sits among his boys;
He hears the parson pray and preach,
  He hears his daughter's voice,
Singing in the village choir,
  And it makes his heart rejoice.

It sounds to him like her mother's voice,
  Singing in Paradise!
He needs must think of her once more,
  How in the grave she lies;
And with his hard, rough hand he wipes
  A tear out of his eyes.

Toiling,—rejoicing,—sorrowing,
  Onward through life he goes;
Each morning sees some task begin,
  Each evening sees it close;
Something attempted, something done,
  Has earned a night's repose.

Thanks, thanks to thee, my worthy friend,
  For the lesson thou hast taught!
Thus at the flaming forge of life
  Our fortunes must be wrought;
Thus on its sounding anvil shaped
  Each burning deed and thought.

It Is Not Always May

No hay pájaros en los nidos de antaño.
Spanish Proverb.

The sun is bright,—the air is clear,
  The darting swallows soar and sing,
And from the stately elms I hear
  The bluebird prophesying Spring.

So blue yon winding river flows,
  It seems an outlet from the sky,
Where, waiting till the west wind blows,
  The freighted clouds at anchor lie.

All things are new;—the buds, the leaves,
  That gild the elm-tree's nodding crest,
And even the nest beneath the eaves;—
  There are no birds in last year's nest!

All things rejoice in youth and love,
  The fulness of their first delight!
And learn from the soft heavens above
  The melting tenderness of night.

Maiden, that read'st this simple rhyme,
  Enjoy thy youth, it will not stay;
Enjoy the fragrance of thy prime,
  For oh, it is not always May!

Enjoy the Spring of Love and Youth,
  To some good angel leave the rest;
For Time will teach thee soon the truth,
  There are no birds in last year's nest!

The Rainy Day

The day is cold, and dark, and dreary;
It rains, and the wind is never weary;
The vine still clings to the mouldering wall,
But at every gust the dead leaves fall,
 And the day is dark and dreary.

My life is cold, and dark, and dreary;
It rains, and the wind is never weary;
My thoughts still cling to the mouldering Past,
But the hopes of youth fall thick in the blast,
 And the days are dark and dreary.

Be still, sad heart! and cease repining;
Behind the clouds is the sun still shining;
Thy fate is the common fate of all,
Into each life some rain must fall,
 Some days must be dark and dreary.

God's-Acre

I like that ancient Saxon phrase, which calls
 The burial-ground God's-Acre! It is just;
It consecrates each grave within its walls,
 And breathes a benison o'er the sleeping dust.

God's-Acre! Yes, that blessed name imparts
 Comfort to those who in the grave have sown
The seed that they had garnered in their hearts,
 Their bread of life, alas! no more their own.

Into its furrows shall we all be cast,
 In the sure faith, that we shall rise again
At the great harvest, when the archangel's blast
 Shall winnow, like a fan, the chaff and grain.

Then shall the good stand in immortal bloom,
  In the fair gardens of that second birth;
And each bright blossom mingle its perfume
  With that of flowers, which never bloomed on earth.

With thy rude ploughshare, Death, turn up the sod,
  And spread the furrow for the seed we sow;
This is the field and Acre of our God,
  This is the place where human harvests grow.

To the River Charles

River! that in silence windest
  Through the meadows, bright and free,
Till at length thy rest thou findest
  In the bosom of the sea!

Four long years of mingled feeling,
  Half in rest, and half in strife,
I have seen thy waters stealing
  Onward, like the stream of life.

Thou hast taught me, Silent River!
  Many a lesson, deep and long;
Thou hast been a generous giver;
  I can give thee but a song.

Oft in sadness and in illness,
  I have watched thy current glide,
Till the beauty of its stillness
  Overflowed me, like a tide.

And in better hours and brighter,
  When I saw thy waters gleam,
I have felt my heart beat lighter,
  And leap onward with thy stream.

Not for this alone I love thee,
  Nor because thy waves of blue
From celestial seas above thee
  Take their own celestial hue.

Where yon shadowy woodlands hide thee,
  And thy waters disappear,
Friends I love have dwelt beside thee,
  And have made thy margin dear.

More than this;—thy name reminds me
  Of three friends, all true and tried;
And that name, like magic, binds me
  Closer, closer to thy side.

Friends my soul with joy remembers!
  How like quivering flames they start,
When I fan the living embers
  On the hearth-stone of my heart!

'T is for this, thou Silent River!
  That my spirit leans to thee;
Thou hast been a generous giver,
  Take this idle song from me.

The Goblet of Life

Filled is Life's goblet to the brim;
And though my eyes with tears are dim,
I see its sparkling bubbles swim,
And chant a melancholy hymn
  With solemn voice and slow.

No purple flowers,—no garlands green,
Conceal the goblet's shade or sheen,
Nor maddening draughts of Hippocrene,
Like gleams of sunshine, flash between
  Thick leaves of mistletoe.

This goblet, wrought with curious art,
Is filled with waters, that upstart,
When the deep fountains of the heart,
By strong convulsions rent apart,
  Are running all to waste.

And as it mantling passes round,
With fennel is it wreathed and crowned,
Whose seed and foliage sun-imbrowned
Are in its waters steeped and drowned,
  And give a bitter taste.

Above the lowly plants it towers,
The fennel, with its yellow flowers,
And in an earlier age than ours
Was gifted with the wondrous powers,
  Lost vision to restore.

It gave new strength, and fearless mood;
And gladiators, fierce and rude,
Mingled it in their daily food;
And he who battled and subdued,
  A wreath of fennel wore.

Then in Life's goblet freely press,
The leaves that give it bitterness,
Nor prize the colored waters less,
For in thy darkness and distress
  New light and strength they give!

And he who has not learned to know
How false its sparkling bubbles show,
How bitter are the drops of woe,
With which its brim may overflow,
  He has not learned to live.

The prayer of Ajax was for light;
Through all that dark and desperate fight,
The blackness of that noonday night,
He asked but the return of sight,
  To see his foeman's face.

Let our unceasing, earnest prayer
Be, too, for light,—for strength to bear
Our portion of the weight of care,
That crushes into dumb despair
   One half the human race.

O suffering, sad humanity!
O ye afflicted ones, who lie
Steeped to the lips in misery,
Longing, and yet afraid to die,
   Patient, though sorely tried!

I pledge you in this cup of grief,
Where floats the fennel's bitter leaf!
The Battle of our Life is brief,
The alarm,—the struggle,—the relief,
   Then sleep we side by side.

Excelsior

The shades of night were falling fast,
As through an Alpine village passed
A youth, who bore, 'mid snow and ice,
A banner with the strange device,
                    Excelsior!

His brow was sad; his eye beneath,
Flashed like a falchion from its sheath,
And like a silver clarion rung
The accents of that unknown tongue,
                    Excelsior!

In happy homes he saw the light
Of household fires gleam warm and bright;
Above, the spectral glaciers shone,
And from his lips escaped a groan,
                    Excelsior!

"Try not the Pass!" the old man said;
"Dark lowers the tempest overhead,
The roaring torrent is deep and wide!"
And loud that clarion voice replied,
Excelsior!

"Oh stay," the maiden said, "and rest
Thy weary head upon this breast!"
A tear stood in his bright blue eye,
But still he answered, with a sigh,
Excelsior!

"Beware the pine-tree's withered branch!
Beware the awful avalanche!"
This was the peasant's last Good-night,
A voice replied, far up the height,
Excelsior!

At break of day, as heavenward
The pious monks of Saint Bernard
Uttered the oft-repeated prayer,
A voice cried through the startled air,
Excelsior!

A traveller, by the faithful hound,
Half-buried in the snow was found,
Still grasping in his hand of ice
That banner with the strange device,
Excelsior!

There in the twilight cold and gray,
Lifeless, but beautiful, he lay,
And from the sky, serene and far,
A voice fell, like a falling star,
Excelsior!

from

POEMS ON SLAVERY

The Slave's Dream

Beside the ungathered rice he lay,
  His sickle in his hand;
His breast was bare, his matted hair
  Was buried in the sand.
Again, in the mist and shadow of sleep,
  He saw his Native Land.

Wide through the landscape of his dreams
  The lordly Niger flowed;
Beneath the palm-trees on the plain
  Once more a king he strode;
And heard the tinkling caravans
  Descend the mountain road.

He saw once more his dark-eyed queen
  Among her children stand;
They clasped his neck, they kissed his cheeks,
  They held him by the hand!—
A tear burst from the sleeper's lids
  And fell into the sand.

And then at furious speed he rode
  Along the Niger's bank;
His bridle-reins were golden chains,
  And, with a martial clank,
At each leap he could feel his scabbard of steel
  Smiting his stallion's flank.

Before him, like a blood-red flag,
  The bright flamingoes flew;
From morn till night he followed their flight,
  O'er plains where the tamarind grew,
Till he saw the roofs of Caffre huts,
  And the ocean rose to view.

At night he heard the lion roar,
  And the hyena scream,
And the river-horse, as he crushed the reeds
  Beside some hidden stream;
And it passed, like a glorious roll of drums,
  Through the triumph of his dream.

The forests, with their myriad tongues,
  Shouted of liberty;
And the Blast of the Desert cried aloud,
  With a voice so wild and free,
That he started in his sleep and smiled
  At their tempestuous glee.

He did not feel the driver's whip,
  Nor the burning heat of day;
For Death had illumined the Land of Sleep,
  And his lifeless body lay
A worn-out fetter, that the soul
  Had broken and thrown away!

The Slave Singing at Midnight

Loud he sang the psalm of David!
He, a Negro and enslaved,
Sang of Israel's victory,
Sang of Zion, bright and free.

In that hour, when night is calmest,
Sang he from the Hebrew Psalmist,
In a voice so sweet and clear
That I could not choose but hear,

Songs of triumph, and ascriptions,
Such as reached the swart Egyptians,
When upon the Red Sea coast
Perished Pharaoh and his host.

And the voice of his devotion
Filled my soul with strange emotion;
For its tones by turns were glad,
Sweetly solemn, wildly sad.

Paul and Silas, in their prison,
Sang of Christ, the Lord arisen.
And an earthquake's arm of might
Broke their dungeon-gates at night.

But, alas! what holy angel
Brings the Slave this glad evangel?
And what earthquake's arm of might
Breaks his dungeon-gates at night?

The Witnesses

In Ocean's wide domains,
  Half buried in the sands,
Lie skeletons in chains,
  With shackled feet and hands.

Beyond the fall of dews,
  Deeper than plummet lies,
Float ships, with all their crews,
  No more to sink nor rise.

There the black Slave-ship swims,
  Freighted with human forms,
Whose fettered, fleshless limbs
  Are not the sport of storms.

These are the bones of Slaves;
  They gleam from the abyss;
They cry, from yawning waves,
  "We are the Witnesses!"

Within Earth's wide domains
  Are markets for men's lives;
Their necks are galled with chains,
  Their wrists are cramped with gyves.

Dead bodies, that the kite
  In deserts makes its prey;
Murders, that with affright
  Scare school-boys from their play!

All evil thoughts and deeds;
  Anger, and lust, and pride;
The foulest, rankest weeds,
  That choke Life's groaning tide!

These are the woes of Slaves;
  They glare from the abyss;
They cry, from unknown graves,
  "We are the Witnesses!"

The Warning

Beware! The Israelite of old, who tore
  The lion in his path,—when, poor and blind,
He saw the blessed light of heaven no more,
  Shorn of his noble strength and forced to grind
In prison, and at last led forth to be
A pander to Philistine revelry,—

Upon the pillars of the temple laid
  His desperate hands, and in its overthrow
Destroyed himself, and with him those who made
  A cruel mockery of his sightless woe;
The poor, blind Slave, the scoff and jest of all,
Expired, and thousands perished in the fall!

There is a poor, blind Samson in this land,
   Shorn of his strength and bound in bonds of steel,
Who may, in some grim revel, raise his hand,
   And shake the pillars of this Commonweal,
Till the vast Temple of our liberties
A shapeless mass of wreck and rubbish lies.

from
THE BELFRY OF BRUGES AND OTHER POEMS

The Belfry of Bruges

In the market-place of Bruges stands the belfry old and
brown;
Thrice consumed and thrice rebuilded, still it watches o'er the
town.

As the summer morn was breaking, on that lofty tower I
stood,
And the world threw off the darkness, like the weeds of
widowhood.

Thick with towns and hamlets studded, and with streams and
vapors gray,
Like a shield embossed with silver, round and vast the
landscape lay.

At my feet the city slumbered. From its chimneys, here and
there,
Wreaths of snow-white smoke, ascending, vanished, ghost-
like, into air.

Not a sound rose from the city at that early morning hour,
But I heard a heart of iron beating in the ancient tower.

From their nests beneath the rafters sang the swallows wild
and high;
And the world, beneath me sleeping, seemed more distant
than the sky.

Then most musical and solemn, bringing back the olden
times,
With their strange, unearthly changes rang the melancholy
chimes,

Like the psalms from some old cloister, when the nuns sing in
the choir;
And the great bell tolled among them, like the chanting of a
friar.

Visions of the days departed, shadowy phantoms filled my
brain;
They who live in history only seemed to walk the earth again;

All the Foresters of Flanders,—mighty Baldwin Bras de Fer,
Lyderick du Bucq and Cressy, Philip, Guy de Dampierre.

I beheld the pageants splendid that adorned those days of
old;
Stately dames, like queens attended, knights who bore the
Fleece of Gold;

Lombard and Venetian merchants with deep-laden argosies;
Ministers from twenty nations; more than royal pomp and
ease.

I beheld proud Maximilian, kneeling humbly on the ground;
I beheld the gentle Mary, hunting with her hawk and hound;

And her lighted bridal-chamber, where a duke slept with the
queen,
And the armed guard around them, and the sword
unsheathed between.

I beheld the Flemish weavers, with Namur and Juliers bold,
Marching homeward from the bloody battle of the Spurs of
Gold;

Saw the fight at Minnewater, saw the White Hoods moving
west,
Saw great Artevelde victorious scale the Golden Dragon's
nest.

And again the whiskered Spaniard all the land with terror
smote;
And again the wild alarum sounded from the tocsin's throat;

Till the bell of Ghent responded o'er lagoon and dike of
sand,
"I am Roland! I am Roland! there is victory in the land!"

Then the sound of drums aroused me. The awakened city's
roar
Chased the phantoms I had summoned back into their graves
once more.

Hours had passed away like minutes; and, before I was aware,
Lo! the shadow of the belfry crossed the sun-illumined square.

A Gleam of Sunshine

This is the place. Stand still, my steed,
Let me review the scene,
And summon from the shadowy Past
The forms that once have been.

The Past and Present here unite
Beneath Time's flowing tide,
Like footprints hidden by a brook,
But seen on either side.

Here runs the highway to the town;
There the green lane descends,
Through which I walked to church with thee,
O gentlest of my friends!

The shadow of the linden trees
Lay moving on the grass;
Between them and the moving boughs,
A shadow, thou didst pass.

Thy dress was like the lilies,
  And thy heart as pure as they:
One of God's holy messengers
  Did walk with me that day.

I saw the branches of the trees
  Bend down thy touch to meet,
The clover-blossoms in the grass
  Rise up to kiss thy feet.

"Sleep, sleep to-day, tormenting cares,
  Of earth and folly born!"
Solemnly sang the village choir
  On that sweet Sabbath morn.

Through the closed blinds the golden sun
  Poured in a dusty beam,
Like the celestial ladder seen
  By Jacob in his dream.

And ever and anon, the wind
  Sweet-scented with the hay,
Turned o'er the hymn-book's fluttering leaves
  That on the window lay.

Long was the good man's sermon,
  Yet it seemed not so to me;
For he spake of Ruth the beautiful,
  And still I thought of thee.

Long was the prayer he uttered,
  Yet it seemed not so to me;
For in my heart I prayed with him,
  And still I thought of thee.

But now, alas! the place seems changed;
  Thou art no longer here:
Part of the sunshine of the scene
  With thee did disappear.

Though thoughts, deep-rooted in my heart,
  Like pine trees dark and high,
Subdue the light of noon, and breathe
  A low and ceaseless sigh;

This memory brightens o'er the past,
  As when the sun, concealed
Behind some cloud that near us hangs,
  Shines on a distant field.

The Arsenal at Springfield

This is the Arsenal. From floor to ceiling,
  Like a huge organ, rise the burnished arms;
But from their silent pipes no anthem pealing
  Startles the villages with strange alarms.

Ah! what a sound will rise, how wild and dreary,
  When the death-angel touches those swift keys!
What loud lament and dismal Miserere
  Will mingle with their awful symphonies!

I hear even now the infinite fierce chorus,
  The cries of agony, the endless groan,
Which, through the ages that have gone before us,
  In long reverberations reach our own.

On helm and harness rings the Saxon hammer,
  Through Cimbric forest roars the Norseman's song,
And loud, amid the universal clamor,
  O'er distant deserts sounds the Tartar gong.

I hear the Florentine, who from his palace
  Wheels out his battle-bell with dreadful din,
And Aztec priests upon their teocallis
  Beat the wild war-drums made of serpent's skin;

The tumult of each sacked and burning village;
  The shout that every prayer for mercy drowns;
The soldiers' revels in the midst of pillage;
  The wail of famine in beleaguered towns;

The bursting shell, the gateway wrenched asunder,
  The rattling musketry, the clashing blade;
And ever and anon, in tones of thunder
  The diapason of the cannonade.

Is it, O man, with such discordant noises,
  With such accursed instruments as these,
Thou drownest Nature's sweet and kindly voices,
  And jarrest the celestial harmonies?

Were half the power, that fills the world with terror,
  Were half the wealth bestowed on camps and courts,
Given to redeem the human mind from error,
  There were no need of arsenals or forts:

The warrior's name would be a name abhorred!
  And every nation, that should lift again
Its hand against a brother, on its forehead
  Would wear forevermore the curse of Cain!

Down the dark future, through long generations,
  The echoing sounds grow fainter and then cease;
And like a bell, with solemn, sweet vibrations,
  I hear once more the voice of Christ say, "Peace!"

Peace! and no longer from its brazen portals
  The blast of War's great organ shakes the skies!
But beautiful as songs of the immortals,
  The holy melodies of love arise.

Rain in Summer

How beautiful is the rain!
After the dust and heat,
In the broad and fiery street,
In the narrow lane,
How beautiful is the rain!

How it clatters along the roofs,
Like the tramp of hoofs!
How it gushes and struggles out
From the throat of the overflowing spout!

Across the window-pane
It pours and pours;
And swift and wide,
With a muddy tide,
Like a river down the gutter roars
The rain, the welcome rain!

The sick man from his chamber looks
At the twisted brooks;
He can feel the cool
Breath of each little pool;
His fevered brain
Grows calm again,
And he breathes a blessing on the rain.

From the neighboring school
Come the boys,
With more than their wonted noise
And commotion;
And down the wet streets
Sail their mimic fleets,
Till the treacherous pool
Ingulfs them in its whirling
And turbulent ocean.

In the country, on every side,
Where far and wide,

Like a leopard's tawny and spotted hide,
Stretches the plain,
To the dry grass and the drier grain
How welcome is the rain!

In the furrowed land
The toilsome and patient oxen stand;
Lifting the yoke-encumbered head,
With their dilated nostrils spread,
They silently inhale
The clover-scented gale,
And the vapors that arise
From the well-watered and smoking soil.
For this rest in the furrow after toil
Their large and lustrous eyes
Seem to thank the Lord,
More than man's spoken word.

Near at hand,
From under the sheltering trees,
The farmer sees
His pastures, and his fields of grain,
As they bend their tops
To the numberless beating drops
Of the incessant rain.
He counts it as no sin
That he sees therein
Only his own thrift and gain.

These, and far more than these,
The Poet sees!
He can behold
Aquarius old
Walking the fenceless fields of air;
And from each ample fold
Of the clouds about him rolled
Scattering everywhere
The showery rain,
As the farmer scatters his grain.

He can behold
Things manifold
That have not yet been wholly told,—
Have not been wholly sung nor said.
For his thought, that never stops,
Follows the water-drops
Down to the graves of the dead,
Down through chasms and gulfs profound,
To the dreary fountain-head
Of lakes and rivers under ground;
And sees them, when the rain is done,
On the bridge of colors seven
Climbing up once more to heaven,
Opposite the setting sun.

Thus the Seer,
With vision clear,
Sees forms appear and disappear,
In the perpetual round of strange,
Mysterious change
From birth to death, from death to birth,
From earth to heaven, from heaven to earth;
Till glimpses more sublime
Of things, unseen before
Unto his wondering eyes reveal
The Universe, as an immeasurable wheel
Turning forevermore
In the rapid and rushing river of Time.

To a Child

Dear child! how radiant on thy mother's knee,
With merry-making eyes and jocund smiles,
Thou gazest at the painted tiles,
Whose figures grace,
With many a grotesque form and face,
The ancient chimney of thy nursery!
The lady with the gay macaw,

The dancing girl, the grave bashaw
With bearded lip and chin;
And, leaning idly o'er his gate,
Beneath the imperial fan of state,
The Chinese mandarin.

With what a look of proud command
Thou shakest in thy little hand
The coral rattle with its silver bells,
Making a merry tune!
Thousands of years in Indian seas
That coral grew, by slow degrees,
Until some deadly and wild monsoon
Dashed it on Coromandel's sand!
Those silver bells
Reposed of yore,
As shapeless ore,
Far down in the deep-sunken wells
Of darksome mines,
In some obscure and sunless place,
Beneath huge Chimborazo's base,
Or Potosí's o'erhanging pines!
And thus for thee, O little child,
Through many a danger and escape,
The tall ships passed the stormy cape;
For thee in foreign lands remote,
Beneath a burning, tropic clime,
The Indian peasant, chasing the wild goat,
Himself as swift and wild,
In falling, clutched the frail arbute,
The fibres of whose shallow root,
Uplifted from the soil, betrayed
The silver veins beneath it laid,
The buried treasures of the miser, Time.

But, lo! thy door is left ajar!
Thou hearest footsteps from afar!
And, at the sound,
Thou turnest round
With quick and questioning eyes,

Like one, who, in a foreign land,
Beholds on every hand
Some source of wonder and surprise!
And, restlessly, impatiently,
Thou strivest, strugglest, to be free.

The four walls of thy nursery
Are now like prison walls to thee.
No more thy mother's smiles,
No more the painted tiles,
Delight thee, nor the playthings on the floor,
That won thy little, beating heart before;
Thou strugglest for the open door.

Through these once solitary halls
Thy pattering footstep falls.
The sound of thy merry voice
Makes the old walls
Jubilant, and they rejoice
With the joy of thy young heart,
O'er the light of whose gladness
No shadows of sadness
From the sombre background of memory start.

Once, ah, once, within these walls,
One whom memory oft recalls,
The Father of his Country, dwelt.
And yonder meadows broad and damp
The fires of the besieging camp
Encircled with a burning belt.
Up and down these echoing stairs,
Heavy with the weight of cares,
Sounded his majestic tread;
Yes, within this very room
Sat he in those hours of gloom,
Weary both in heart and head.

But what are these grave thoughts to thee?
Out, out! into the open air!
Thy only dream is liberty,

Thou carest little how or where.
I see thee eager at thy play,
Now shouting to the apples on the tree,
With cheeks as round and red as they;
And now among the yellow stalks,
Among the flowering shrubs and plants,
As restless as the bee.
Along the garden walks,
The tracks of thy small carriage-wheels I trace;
And see at every turn how they efface
Whole villages of sand-roofed tents,
That rise like golden domes
Above the cavernous and secret homes
Of wandering and nomadic tribes of ants.
Ah, cruel little Tamerlane,
Who, with thy dreadful reign,
Dost persecute and overwhelm
These hapless Troglodytes of thy realm!

What! tired already! with those suppliant looks,
And voice more beautiful than a poet's books
Or murmuring sound of water as it flows,
Thou comest back to parley with repose!
This rustic seat in the old apple-tree,
With its o'erhanging golden canopy
Of leaves illuminate with autumnal hues,
And shining with the argent light of dews,
Shall for a season be our place of rest.
Beneath us, like an oriole's pendent nest,
From which the laughing birds have taken wing,
By thee abandoned, hangs thy vacant swing.
Dream-like the waters of the river gleam;
A sailless vessel drops adown the stream,
And like it, to a sea as wide and deep,
Thou driftest gently down the tides of sleep.

O child! O new-born denizen
Of life's great city! on thy head
The glory of the morn is shed,
Like a celestial benison!

Here at the portal thou dost stand,
And with thy little hand
Thou openest the mysterious gate
Into the future's undiscovered land.
I see its valves expand,
As at the touch of Fate!
Into those realms of love and hate,
Into that darkness blank and drear,
By some prophetic feeling taught,
I launch the bold, adventurous thought,
Freighted with hope and fear;
As upon subterranean streams,
In caverns unexplored and dark,
Men sometimes launch a fragile bark,
Laden with flickering fire,
And watch its swift-receding beams,
Until at length they disappear,
And in the distant dark expire.

By what astrology of fear or hope
Dare I to cast thy horoscope!
Like the new moon thy life appears;
A little strip of silver light,
And widening outward into night
The shadowy disk of future years;
And yet upon its outer rim,
A luminous circle, faint and dim,
And scarcely visible to us here,
Rounds and completes the perfect sphere;
A prophecy and intimation,
A pale and feeble adumbration,
Of the great world of light, that lies
Behind all human destinies.

Ah! if thy fate, with anguish fraught,
Should be to wet the dusty soil
With the hot tears and sweat of toil,—
To struggle with imperious thought,
Until the overburdened brain,
Weary with labor, faint with pain,

Like a jarred pendulum, retain
Only its motion, not its power,—
Remember, in that perilous hour,
When most afflicted and oppressed,
From labor there shall come forth rest.

And if a more auspicious fate
On thy advancing steps await,
Still let it ever be thy pride
To linger by the laborer's side;
With words of sympathy or song
To cheer the dreary march along
Of the great army of the poor,
O'er desert sand, o'er dangerous moor.
Nor to thyself the task shall be
Without reward; for thou shalt learn
The wisdom early to discern
True beauty in utility;
As great Pythagoras of yore,
Standing beside the blacksmith's door,
And hearing the hammers, as they smote
The anvils with a different note,
Stole from the varying tones, that hung
Vibrant on every iron tongue,
The secret of the sounding wire,
And formed the seven-chorded lyre.

Enough! I will not play the Seer;
I will no longer strive to ope
The mystic volume, where appear
The herald Hope, forerunning Fear,
And Fear, the pursuivant of Hope.
Thy destiny remains untold;
For, like Acestes' shaft of old,
The swift thought kindles as it flies,
And burns to ashes in the skies.

The Occultation of Orion

I saw, as in a dream sublime,
The balance in the hand of Time.
O'er East and West its beam impended;
And Day, with all its hours of light,
Was slowly sinking out of sight,
While, opposite, the scale of Night
Silently with the stars ascended.

Like the astrologers of eld,
In that bright vision I beheld
Greater and deeper mysteries.
I saw, with its celestial keys,
Its chords of air, its frets of fire,
The Samian's great Æolian lyre,
Rising through all its sevenfold bars,
From earth unto the fixed stars.
And through the dewy atmosphere,
Not only could I see, but hear,
Its wondrous and harmonious strings,
In sweet vibration, sphere by sphere,
From Dian's circle light and near,
Onward to vaster and wider rings,
Where, chanting through his beard of snows,
Majestic, mournful, Saturn goes,
And down the sunless realms of space
Reverberates the thunder of his bass.

Beneath the sky's triumphal arch
This music sounded like a march,
And with its chorus seemed to be
Preluding some great tragedy.
Sirius was rising in the east;
And, slow ascending one by one,
The kindling constellations shone.
Begirt with many a blazing star,
Stood the great giant Algebar,
Orion, hunter of the beast!
His sword hung gleaming by his side,
And, on his arm, the lion's hide

Scattered across the midnight air
The golden radiance of its hair.

The moon was pallid, but not faint;
And beautiful as some fair saint,
Serenely moving on her way
In hours of trial and dismay.
As if she heard the voice of God,
Unharmed with naked feet she trod
Upon the hot and burning stars,
As on the glowing coals and bars,
That were to prove her strength and try
Her holiness and her purity.

Thus moving on, with silent pace,
And triumph in her sweet, pale face,
She reached the station of Orion.
Aghast he stood in strange alarm!
And suddenly from his outstretched arm
Down fell the red skin of the lion
Into the river at his feet.
His mighty club no longer beat
The forehead of the bull; but he
Reeled as of yore beside the sea,
When, blinded by Œnopion,
He sought the blacksmith at his forge,
And, climbing up the mountain gorge,
Fixed his blank eyes upon the sun.

Then, through the silence overhead,
An angel with a trumpet said,
"Forevermore, forevermore,
The reign of violence is o'er!"
And, like an instrument that flings
Its music on another's strings,
The trumpet of the angel cast
Upon the heavenly lyre its blast,
And on from sphere to sphere the words
Reëchoed down the burning chords,—
"Forevermore, forevermore,
The reign of violence is o'er!"

The Bridge

I stood on the bridge at midnight,
   As the clocks were striking the hour,
And the moon rose o'er the city,
   Behind the dark church-tower.

I saw her bright reflection
   In the waters under me,
Like a golden goblet falling
   And sinking into the sea.

And far in the hazy distance
   Of that lovely night in June,
The blaze of the flaming furnace
   Gleamed redder than the moon.

Among the long, black rafters
   The wavering shadows lay,
And the current that came from the ocean
   Seemed to lift and bear them away;

As, sweeping and eddying through them,
   Rose the belated tide,
And, streaming into the moonlight,
   The seaweed floated wide.

And like those waters rushing
   Among the wooden piers,
A flood of thoughts came o'er me
   That filled my eyes with tears.

How often, oh how often,
   In the days that had gone by,
I had stood on that bridge at midnight
   And gazed on that wave and sky!

How often, oh how often,
   I had wished that the ebbing tide
Would bear me away on its bosom
   O'er the ocean wild and wide!

For my heart was hot and restless,
  And my life was full of care,
And the burden laid upon me
  Seemed greater than I could bear.

But now it has fallen from me,
  It is buried in the sea;
And only the sorrow of others
  Throws its shadow over me.

Yet whenever I cross the river
  On its bridge with wooden piers,
Like the odor of brine from the ocean
  Comes the thought of other years.

And I think how many thousands
  Of care-encumbered men,
Each bearing his burden of sorrow,
  Have crossed the bridge since then.

I see the long procession
  Still passing to and fro,
The young heart hot and restless,
  And the old subdued and slow!

And forever and forever,
  As long as the river flows,
As long as the heart has passions,
  As long as life has woes;

The moon and its broken reflection
  And its shadows shall appear,
As the symbol of love in heaven,
  And its wavering image here.

To the Driving Cloud

Gloomy and dark art thou, O chief of the mighty Omahas;
Gloomy and dark as the driving cloud, whose name thou hast
taken!
Wrapped in thy scarlet blanket, I see thee stalk through the
city's
Narrow and populous streets, as once by the margin of rivers
Stalked those birds unknown, that have left us only their
footprints.
What, in a few short years, will remain of thy race but the
footprints?

How canst thou walk these streets, who hast trod the green
turf of the prairies?
How canst thou breathe this air, who hast breathed the sweet
air of the mountains?
Ah! 'tis in vain that with lordly looks of disdain thou dost
challenge
Looks of disdain in return, and question these walls and these
pavements,
Claiming the soil for thy hunting-grounds, while down-
trodden millions
Starve in the garrets of Europe, and cry from its caverns that
they, too,
Have been created heirs of the earth, and claim its division!

Back, then, back to thy woods in the regions west of the
Wabash!
There as a monarch thou reignest. In autumn the leaves of
the maple
Pave the floors of thy palace-halls with gold, and in summer
Pine-trees waft through its chambers the odorous breath of
their branches.
There thou art strong and great, a hero, a tamer of horses!
There thou chasest the stately stag on the banks of the
Elkhorn,
Or by the roar of the Running-Water, or where the Omaha
Calls thee, and leaps through the wild ravine like a brave of
the Blackfeet!

Hark! what murmurs arise from the heart of those mountainous deserts?
Is it the cry of the Foxes and Crows, or the mighty Behemoth,
Who, unharmed, on his tusks once caught the bolts of the thunder,
And now lurks in his lair to destroy the race of the red man?
Far more fatal to thee and thy race than the Crows and the Foxes,
Far more fatal to thee and thy race than the tread of Behemoth,
Lo! the big thunder-canoe, that steadily breasts the Missouri's
Merciless current! and yonder, afar on the prairies, the camp-fires
Gleam through the night; and the cloud of dust in the gray of the daybreak
Marks not the buffalo's track, nor the Mandan's dexterous horse-race;
It is a caravan, whitening the desert where dwell the Camanches!
Ha! how the breath of these Saxons and Celts, like the blast of the east-wind,
Drifts evermore to the west the scanty smokes of thy wigwams!

The Day Is Done

The day is done, and the darkness
Falls from the wings of Night,
As a feather is wafted downward
From an eagle in his flight.

I see the lights of the village
Gleam through the rain and the mist,
And a feeling of sadness comes o'er me
That my soul cannot resist:

A feeling of sadness and longing,
That is not akin to pain,
And resembles sorrow only
As the mist resembles the rain.

Come, read to me some poem,
  Some simple and heartfelt lay,
That shall soothe this restless feeling,
  And banish the thoughts of day.

Not from the grand old masters,
  Not from the bards sublime,
Whose distant footsteps echo
  Through the corridors of Time.

For, like strains of martial music,
  Their mighty thoughts suggest
Life's endless toil and endeavor;
  And to-night I long for rest.

Read from some humbler poet,
  Whose songs gushed from his heart,
As showers from the clouds of summer,
  Or tears from the eyelids start;

Who, through long days of labor,
  And nights devoid of ease,
Still heard in his soul the music
  Of wonderful melodies.

Such songs have power to quiet
  The restless pulse of care,
And come like the benediction
  That follows after prayer.

Then read from the treasured volume
  The poem of thy choice,
And lend to the rhyme of the poet
  The beauty of thy voice.

And the night shall be filled with music,
  And the cares, that infest the day,
Shall fold their tents, like the Arabs,
  And as silently steal away.

Afternoon in February

The day is ending,
The night is descending;
The marsh is frozen,
  The river dead.

Through clouds like ashes
The red sun flashes
On village windows
  That glimmer red.

The snow recommences;
The buried fences
Mark no longer
  The road o'er the plain;

While through the meadows,
Like fearful shadows,
Slowly passes
  A funeral train.

The bell is pealing,
And every feeling
Within me responds
  To the dismal knell;

Shadows are trailing,
My heart is bewailing
And tolling within
  Like a funeral bell.

The Old Clock on the Stairs

Somewhat back from the village street
Stands the old-fashioned country-seat.
Across its antique portico
Tall poplar-trees their shadows throw;
And from its station in the hall
An ancient timepiece says to all,—
"Forever—never!
Never—forever!"

Half-way up the stairs it stands,
And points and beckons with its hands
From its case of massive oak,
Like a monk, who, under his cloak,
Crosses himself, and sighs, alas!
With sorrowful voice to all who pass,—
"Forever—never!
Never—forever!"

By day its voice is low and light;
But in the silent dead of night,
Distinct as a passing footstep's fall,
It echoes along the vacant hall,
Along the ceiling, along the floor,
And seems to say, at each chamber-door,—
"Forever—never!
Never—forever!"

Through days of sorrow and of mirth,
Through days of death and days of birth,
Through every swift vicissitude
Of changeful time, unchanged it has stood,
And as if, like God, it all things saw,
It calmly repeats those words of awe,—
"Forever—never!
Never—forever!"

In that mansion used to be
Free-hearted Hospitality;
His great fires up the chimney roared;
The stranger feasted at his board;
But, like the skeleton at the feast,
That warning timepiece never ceased,—
"Forever—never!
Never—forever!"

There groups of merry children played,
There youths and maidens dreaming strayed;
O precious hours! O golden prime,
And affluence of love and time!
Even as a miser counts his gold,
Those hours the ancient timepiece told,—
"Forever—never!
Never—forever!"

From that chamber, clothed in white,
The bride came forth on her wedding night;
There, in that silent room below,
The dead lay in his shroud of snow;
And in the hush that followed the prayer,
Was heard the old clock on the stair,—
"Forever—never!
Never—forever!"

All are scattered now and fled,
Some are married, some are dead;
And when I ask, with throbs of pain,
"Ah! when shall they all meet again?"
As in the days long since gone by,
The ancient timepiece makes reply,—
"Forever—never!
Never—forever!"

Never here, forever there,
Where all parting, pain, and care,
And death, and time shall disappear,—

Forever there, but never here!
The horologe of Eternity
Sayeth this incessantly,—
"Forever—never!
Never—forever!"

The Arrow and the Song

I shot an arrow into the air,
It fell to earth, I knew not where;
For, so swiftly it flew, the sight
Could not follow it in its flight.

I breathed a song into the air,
It fell to earth, I knew not where;
For who has sight so keen and strong,
That it can follow the flight of song?

Long, long afterward, in an oak
I found the arrow, still unbroke;
And the song, from beginning to end,
I found again in the heart of a friend.

The Evening Star

Lo! in the painted oriel of the West,
Whose panes the sunken sun incarnadines,
Like a fair lady at her casement, shines
The evening star, the star of love and rest!
And then anon she doth herself divest
Of all her radiant garments, and reclines
Behind the sombre screen of yonder pines,
With slumber and soft dreams of love oppressed.
O my beloved, my sweet Hesperus!
My morning and my evening star of love!
My best and gentlest lady! even thus,

As that fair planet in the sky above,
  Dost thou retire unto thy rest at night,
  And from thy darkened window fades the light.

Autumn

Thou comest, Autumn, heralded by the rain,
  With banners, by great gales incessant fanned,
  Brighter than brightest silks of Samarcand,
  And stately oxen harnessed to thy wain!
Thou standest, like imperial Charlemagne,
  Upon thy bridge of gold; thy royal hand
  Outstretched with benedictions o'er the land,
  Blessing the farms through all thy vast domain!
Thy shield is the red harvest moon, suspended
  So long beneath the heaven's o'erhanging eaves;
  Thy steps are by the farmer's prayers attended;
Like flames upon an altar shine the sheaves;
  And, following thee, in thy ovation splendid,
  Thine almoner, the wind, scatters the golden leaves!

Dante

Tuscan, that wanderest through the realms of gloom,
  With thoughtful pace, and sad, majestic eyes,
  Stern thoughts and awful from thy soul arise,
  Like Farinata from his fiery tomb.
Thy sacred song is like the trump of doom;
  Yet in thy heart what human sympathies,
  What soft compassion glows, as in the skies
  The tender stars their clouded lamps relume!
Methinks I see thee stand with pallid cheeks
  By Fra Hilario in his diocese,
  As up the convent-walls, in golden streaks,
The ascending sunbeams mark the day's decrease;
  And, as he asks what there the stranger seeks,
  Thy voice along the cloister whispers "Peace!"

Curfew

I.

Solemnly, mournfully,
  Dealing its dole,
The Curfew Bell
  Is beginning to toll.

Cover the embers,
  And put out the light;
Toil comes with the morning,
  And rest with the night.

Dark grow the windows,
  And quenched is the fire;
Sound fades into silence,—
  All footsteps retire.

No voice in the chambers,
  No sound in the hall!
Sleep and oblivion
  Reign over all!

II.

The book is completed,
  And closed, like the day;
And the hand that has written it
  Lays it away.

Dim grow its fancies;
  Forgotten they lie;
Like coals in the ashes,
  They darken and die.

Song sinks into silence,
   The story is told,
The windows are darkened,
   The hearth-stone is cold.

Darker and darker
   The black shadows fall;
Sleep and oblivion
   Reign over all.

EVANGELINE

A TALE OF ACADIE

This is the forest primeval. The murmuring pines and the hemlocks,
Bearded with moss, and in garments green, indistinct in the twilight,
Stand like Druids of eld, with voices sad and prophetic,
Stand like harpers hoar, with beards that rest on their bosoms.
Loud from its rocky caverns, the deep-voiced neighboring ocean
Speaks, and in accents disconsolate answers the wail of the forest.

This is the forest primeval; but where are the hearts that beneath it
Leaped like the roe, when he hears in the woodland the voice of the huntsman?
Where is the thatch-roofed village, the home of Acadian farmers,—
Men whose lives glided on like rivers that water the woodlands,
Darkened by shadows of earth, but reflecting an image of heaven?
Waste are those pleasant farms, and the farmers forever departed!
Scattered like dust and leaves, when the mighty blasts of October
Seize them, and whirl them aloft, and sprinkle them far o'er the ocean.
Naught but tradition remains of the beautiful village of Grand-Pré.

Ye who believe in affection that hopes, and endures, and is patient,
Ye who believe in the beauty and strength of woman's devotion,

List to the mournful tradition, still sung by the pines of the forest;
List to a Tale of Love in Acadie, home of the happy.

PART THE FIRST

I.

In the Acadian land, on the shores of the Basin of Minas,
Distant, secluded, still, the little village of Grand-Pré
Lay in the fruitful valley. Vast meadows stretched to the eastward,
Giving the village its name, and pasture to flocks without number.
Dikes, that the hands of the farmers had raised with labor incessant,
Shut out the turbulent tides; but at stated seasons the flood-gates
Opened, and welcomed the sea to wander at will o'er the meadows.
West and south there were fields of flax, and orchards and cornfields
Spreading afar and unfenced o'er the plain; and away to the northward
Blomidon rose, and the forests old, and aloft on the mountains
Sea-fogs pitched their tents, and mists from the mighty Atlantic
Looked on the happy valley, but ne'er from their station descended.
There, in the midst of its farms, reposed the Acadian village.
Strongly built were the houses, with frames of oak and of hemlock,
Such as the peasants of Normandy built in the reign of the Henries.
Thatched were the roofs, with dormer-windows; and gables projecting
Over the basement below protected and shaded the doorway.
There in the tranquil evenings of summer, when brightly the sunset

Lighted the village street, and gilded the vanes on the chimneys,
Matrons and maidens sat in snow-white caps and in kirtles
Scarlet and blue and green, with distaffs spinning the golden
Flax for the gossiping looms, whose noisy shuttles within doors
Mingled their sounds with the whir of the wheels and the songs of the maidens.
Solemnly down the street came the parish priest, and the children
Paused in their play to kiss the hand he extended to bless them.
Reverend walked he among them; and up rose matrons and maidens,
Hailing his slow approach with words of affectionate welcome.
Then came the laborers home from the field, and serenely the sun sank
Down to his rest, and twilight prevailed. Anon from the belfry
Softly the Angelus sounded, and over the roofs of the village
Columns of pale blue smoke, like clouds of incense ascending,
Rose from a hundred hearths, the homes of peace and contentment.
Thus dwelt together in love these simple Acadian farmers, —
Dwelt in the love of God and of man. Alike were they free from
Fear, that reigns with the tyrant, and envy, the vice of republics.
Neither locks had they to their doors, nor bars to their windows;
But their dwellings were open as day and the hearts of the owners;
There the richest was poor, and the poorest lived in abundance.

Somewhat apart from the village, and nearer the Basin of Minas,
Benedict Bellefontaine, the wealthiest farmer of Grand-Pré,

Dwelt on his goodly acres; and with him, directing his household,
Gentle Evangeline lived, his child, and the pride of the village.
Stalworth and stately in form was the man of seventy winters;
Hearty and hale was he, an oak that is covered with snow-flakes;
White as the snow were his locks, and his cheeks as brown as the oak-leaves.
Fair was she to behold, that maiden of seventeen summers.
Black were her eyes as the berry that grows on the thorn by the wayside,
Black, yet how softly they gleamed beneath the brown shade of her tresses!
Sweet was her breath as the breath of kine that feed in the meadows.
When in the harvest heat she bore to the reapers at noontide
Flagons of home-brewed ale, ah! fair in sooth was the maiden.
Fairer was she when, on Sunday morn, while the bell from its turret
Sprinkled with holy sounds the air, as the priest with his hyssop
Sprinkles the congregation, and scatters blessings upon them,
Down the long street she passed, with her chaplet of beads and her missal,
Wearing her Norman cap, and her kirtle of blue, and the ear-rings,
Brought in the olden time from France, and since, as an heirloom,
Handed down from mother to child, through long generations.
But a celestial brightness—a more ethereal beauty—
Shone on her face and encircled her form, when, after confession,
Homeward serenely she walked with God's benediction upon her.
When she had passed, it seemed like the ceasing of exquisite music.

Firmly builded with rafters of oak, the house of the farmer
Stood on the side of a hill commanding the sea; and a shady
Sycamore grew by the door, with a woodbine wreathing around it.
Rudely carved was the porch, with seats beneath; and a footpath
Led through an orchard wide, and disappeared in the meadow.
Under the sycamore-tree were hives overhung by a penthouse,
Such as the traveller sees in regions remote by the roadside,
Built o'er a box for the poor, or the blessed image of Mary.
Farther down, on the slope of the hill, was the well with its moss-grown
Bucket, fastened with iron, and near it a trough for the horses.
Shielding the house from storms, on the north, were the barns and the farm-yard.
There stood the broad-wheeled wains and the antique ploughs and the harrows;
There were the folds for the sheep; and there, in his feathered seraglio,
Strutted the lordly turkey, and crowed the cock, with the selfsame
Voice that in ages of old had startled the penitent Peter.
Bursting with hay were the barns, themselves a village. In each one
Far o'er the gable projected a roof of thatch; and a staircase,
Under the sheltering eaves, led up to the odorous corn-loft.
There too the dove-cot stood, with its meek and innocent inmates
Murmuring ever of love; while above in the variant breezes
Numberless noisy weathercocks rattled and sang of mutation.

Thus, at peace with God and the world, the farmer of Grand-Pré
Lived on his sunny farm, and Evangeline governed his household.
Many a youth, as he knelt in church and opened his missal,

Fixed his eyes upon her as the saint of his deepest devotion;
Happy was he who might touch her hand or the hem of her
garment!
Many a suitor came to her door, by the darkness befriended,
And, as he knocked and waited to hear the sound of her
footsteps,
Knew not which beat the louder, his heart or the knocker of
iron;
Or at the joyous feast of the Patron Saint of the village,
Bolder grew, and pressed her hand in the dance as he
whispered
Hurried words of love, that seemed a part of the music.
But, among all who came, young Gabriel only was welcome;
Gabriel Lajeunesse, the son of Basil the blacksmith,
Who was a mighty man in the village, and honored of all
men;
For, since the birth of time, throughout all ages and nations,
Has the craft of the smith been held in repute by the people.
Basil was Benedict's friend. Their children from earliest
childhood
Grew up together as brother and sister; and Father Felician,
Priest and pedagogue both in the village, had taught them
their letters
Out of the selfsame book, with the hymns of the church and
the plain-song.
But when the hymn was sung, and the daily lesson
completed,
Swiftly they hurried away to the forge of Basil the blacksmith.
There at the door they stood, with wondering eyes to behold
him
Take in his leathern lap the hoof of the horse as a plaything,
Nailing the shoe in its place; while near him the tire of the
cart-wheel
Lay like a fiery snake, coiled round in a circle of cinders.
Oft on autumnal eves, when without in the gathering
darkness
Bursting with light seemed the smithy, through every cranny
and crevice,
Warm by the forge within they watched the laboring bellows,
And as its panting ceased, and the sparks expired in the ashes,

Merrily laughed, and said they were nuns going into the chapel.
Oft on sledges in winter, as swift as the swoop of the eagle,
Down the hillside bounding, they glided away o'er the meadow.
Oft in the barns they climbed to the populous nests on the rafters,
Seeking with eager eyes that wondrous stone, which the swallow
Brings from the shore of the sea to restore the sight of its fledglings;
Lucky was he who found that stone in the nest of the swallow!
Thus passed a few swift years, and they no longer were children.
He was a valiant youth, and his face, like the face of the morning,
Gladdened the earth with its light, and ripened thought into action.
She was a woman now, with the heart and hopes of a woman.
"Sunshine of Saint Eulalie" was she called; for that was the sunshine
Which, as the farmers believed, would load their orchards with apples;
She, too, would bring to her husband's house delight and abundance,
Filling it with love and the ruddy faces of children.

II.

Now had the season returned, when the nights grow colder and longer,
And the retreating sun the sign of the Scorpion enters.
Birds of passage sailed through the leaden air, from the ice-bound,
Desolate northern bays to the shores of tropical islands.
Harvests were gathered in; and wild with the winds of September
Wrestled the trees of the forest, as Jacob of old with the angel.

All the signs foretold a winter long and inclement.
Bees, with prophetic instinct of want, had hoarded their honey
Till the hives overflowed; and the Indian hunters asserted
Cold would the winter be, for thick was the fur of the foxes.
Such was the advent of autumn. Then followed that beautiful season,
Called by the pious Acadian peasants the Summer of All-Saints!
Filled was the air with a dreamy and magical light; and the landscape
Lay as if new-created in all the freshness of childhood.
Peace seemed to reign upon earth, and the restless heart of the ocean
Was for a moment consoled. All sounds were in harmony blended.
Voices of children at play, the crowing of cocks in the farm-yards,
Whir of wings in the drowsy air, and the cooing of pigeons,
All were subdued and low as the murmurs of love, and the great sun
Looked with the eye of love through the golden vapors around him;
While arrayed in its robes of russet and scarlet and yellow,
Bright with the sheen of the dew, each glittering tree of the forest
Flashed like the plane-tree the Persian adorned with mantles and jewels.

Now recommenced the reign of rest and affection and stillness.
Day with its burden and heat had departed, and twilight descending
Brought back the evening star to the sky, and the herds to the homestead.
Pawing the ground they came, and resting their necks on each other,
And with their nostrils distended inhaling the freshness of evening.
Foremost, bearing the bell, Evangeline's beautiful heifer,

Proud of her snow-white hide, and the ribbon that waved
from her collar,
Quietly paced and slow, as if conscious of human affection.
Then came the shepherd back with his bleating flocks from
the seaside,
Where was their favorite pasture. Behind them followed the
watch-dog,
Patient, full of importance, and grand in the pride of his
instinct,
Walking from side to side with a lordly air, and superbly
Waving his bushy tail, and urging forward the stragglers;
Regent of flocks was he when the shepherd slept; their
protector,
When from the forest at night, through the starry silence the
wolves howled.
Late, with the rising moon, returned the wains from the
marshes,
Laden with briny hay, that filled the air with its odor.
Cheerily neighed the steeds, with dew on their manes and
their fetlocks,
While aloft on their shoulders the wooden and ponderous
saddles,
Painted with brilliant dyes, and adorned with tassels of
crimson,
Nodded in bright array, like hollyhocks heavy with blossoms.
Patiently stood the cows meanwhile, and yielded their udders
Unto the milkmaid's hand; whilst loud and in regular cadence
Into the sounding pails the foaming streamlets descended.
Lowing of cattle and peals of laughter were heard in the farm-
yard,
Echoed back by the barns. Anon they sank into stillness;
Heavily closed, with a jarring sound, the valves of the barn-
doors,
Rattled the wooden bars, and all for a season was silent.

In-doors, warm by the wide-mouthed fireplace, idly the
farmer
Sat in his elbow-chair and watched how the flames and the
smoke-wreaths
Struggled together like foes in a burning city. Behind him,

Nodding and mocking along the wall, with gestures fantastic,
Darted his own huge shadow, and vanished away into darkness.
Faces, clumsily carved in oak, on the back of his arm-chair
Laughed in the flickering light; and the pewter plates on the dresser
Caught and reflected the flame, as shields of armies the sunshine.
Fragments of song the old man sang, and carols of Christmas,
Such as at home, in the olden time, his fathers before him
Sang in their Norman orchards and bright Burgundian vineyards.
Close at her father's side was the gentle Evangeline seated,
Spinning flax for the loom, that stood in the corner behind her,
Silent awhile were its treadles, at rest was its diligent shuttle,
While the monotonous drone of the wheel, like the drone of a bagpipe,
Followed the old man's song and united the fragments together.
As in a church, when the chant of the choir at intervals ceases,
Footfalls are heard in the aisles, or words of the priest at the altar,
So, in each pause of the song, with measured motion the clock clicked.

Thus as they sat, there were footsteps heard, and, suddenly lifted,
Sounded the wooden latch, and the door swung back on its hinges.
Benedict knew by the hob-nailed shoes it was Basil the blacksmith,
And by her beating heart Evangeline knew who was with him.
"Welcome!" the farmer exclaimed, as their footsteps paused on the threshold,
"Welcome, Basil, my friend! Come, take thy place on the settle
Close by the chimney-side, which is always empty without thee;

Take from the shelf overhead thy pipe and the box of tobacco;
Never so much thyself art thou as when through the curling
Smoke of the pipe or the forge thy friendly and jovial face gleams
Round and red as the harvest moon through the mist of the marshes."
Then, with a smile of content, thus answered Basil the blacksmith,
Taking with easy air the accustomed seat by the fireside:—
"Benedict Bellefontaine, thou hast ever thy jest and thy ballad!
Ever in cheerfullest mood art thou, when others are filled with
Gloomy forebodings of ill, and see only ruin before them.
Happy art thou, as if every day thou hadst picked up a horseshoe."
Pausing a moment, to take the pipe that Evangeline brought him,
And with a coal from the embers had lighted, he slowly continued:—
"Four days now are passed since the English ships at their anchors
Ride in the Gaspereau's mouth, with their cannon pointed against us.
What their design may be is unknown; but all are commanded
On the morrow to meet in the church, where his Majesty's mandate
Will be proclaimed as law in the land. Alas! in the mean time
Many surmises of evil alarm the hearts of the people."
Then made answer the farmer: "Perhaps some friendlier purpose
Brings these ships to our shores. Perhaps the harvests in England
By untimely rains or untimelier heat have been blighted,
And from our bursting barns they would feed their cattle and children."
"Not so thinketh the folk in the village," said, warmly, the blacksmith,

Shaking his head, as in doubt; then, heaving a sigh, he continued:—
"Louisburg is not forgotten, nor Beau Séjour, nor Port Royal.
Many already have fled to the forest, and lurk on its outskirts,
Waiting with anxious hearts the dubious fate of to-morrow.
Arms have been taken from us, and warlike weapons of all kinds;
Nothing is left but the blacksmith's sledge and the scythe of the mower."
Then with a pleasant smile made answer the jovial farmer:—
"Safer are we unarmed, in the midst of our flocks and our cornfields,
Safer within these peaceful dikes, besieged by the ocean,
Than our fathers in forts, besieged by the enemy's cannon.
Fear no evil, my friend, and to-night may no shadow of sorrow
Fall on this house and hearth; for this is the night of the contract.
Built are the house and the barn. The merry lads of the village
Strongly have built them and well; and, breaking the glebe round about them,
Filled the barn with hay, and the house with food for a twelvemonth.
René Leblanc will be here anon, with his papers and inkhorn.
Shall we not then be glad, and rejoice in the joy of our children?"
As apart by the window she stood, with her hand in her lover's,
Blushing Evangeline heard the words that her father had spoken,
And, as they died on his lips, the worthy notary entered.

III.

Bent like a laboring oar, that toils in the surf of the ocean,
Bent, but not broken, by age was the form of the notary public;
Shocks of yellow hair, like the silken floss of the maize, hung

Over his shoulders; his forehead was high; and glasses with horn bows
Sat astride on his nose, with a look of wisdom supernal.
Father of twenty children was he, and more than a hundred
Children's children rode on his knee, and heard his great watch tick.
Four long years in the times of the war had he languished a captive,
Suffering much in an old French fort as the friend of the English.
Now, though warier grown, without all guile or suspicion,
Ripe in wisdom was he, but patient, and simple, and childlike.
He was beloved by all, and most of all by the children;
For he told them tales of the Loup-garou in the forest,
And of the goblin that came in the night to water the horses,
And of the white Létiche, the ghost of a child who unchristened
Died, and was doomed to haunt unseen the chambers of children;
And how on Christmas eve the oxen talked in the stable,
And how the fever was cured by a spider shut up in a nutshell,
And of the marvellous powers of four-leaved clover and horseshoes,
With whatsoever else was writ in the lore of the village.
Then up rose from his seat by the fireside Basil the blacksmith,
Knocked from his pipe the ashes, and slowly extending his right hand,
"Father Leblanc," he exclaimed, "thou hast heard the talk in the village,
And, perchance, canst tell us some news of these ships and their errand."
Then with modest demeanor made answer the notary public,—
"Gossip enough have I heard, in sooth, yet am never the wiser;
And what their errand may be I know not better than others.
Yet am I not of those who imagine some evil intention

Brings them here, for we are at peace; and why then molest us?"
"God's name!" shouted the hasty and somewhat irascible blacksmith;
"Must we in all things look for the how, and the why, and the wherefore?
Daily injustice is done, and might is the right of the strongest!"
But without heeding his warmth, continued the notary public,—
"Man is unjust, but God is just; and finally justice
Triumphs; and well I remember a story, that often consoled me,
When as a captive I lay in the old French fort at Port Royal."
This was the old man's favorite tale, and he loved to repeat it
When his neighbors complained that any injustice was done them.
"Once in an ancient city, whose name I no longer remember,
Raised aloft on a column, a brazen statue of Justice
Stood in the public square, upholding the scales in its left hand,
And in its right a sword, as an emblem that justice presided
Over the laws of the land, and the hearts and homes of the people.
Even the birds had built their nests in the scales of the balance,
Having no fear of the sword that flashed in the sunshine above them.
But in the course of time the laws of the land were corrupted;
Might took the place of right, and the weak were oppressed, and the mighty
Ruled with an iron rod. Then it chanced in a nobleman's palace
That a necklace of pearls was lost, and erelong a suspicion
Fell on an orphan girl who lived as a maid in the household.
She, after form of trial condemned to die on the scaffold,
Patiently met her doom at the foot of the statue of Justice.
As to her Father in heaven her innocent spirit ascended,
Lo! o'er the city a tempest rose; and the bolts of the thunder

Smote the statue of bronze, and hurled in wrath from its left hand
Down on the pavement below the clattering scales of the balance,
And in the hollow thereof was found the nest of a magpie,
Into whose clay-built walls the necklace of pearls was inwoven."
Silenced, but not convinced, when the story was ended, the blacksmith
Stood like a man who fain would speak, but findeth no language;
All his thoughts were congealed into lines on his face, as the vapors
Freeze in fantastic shapes on the window-panes in the winter.

Then Evangeline lighted the brazen lamp on the table,
Filled, till it overflowed, the pewter tankard with home-brewed
Nut-brown ale, that was famed for its strength in the village of Grand-Pré;
While from his pocket the notary drew his papers and inkhorn,
Wrote with a steady hand the date and the age of the parties,
Naming the dower of the bride in flocks of sheep and in cattle.
Orderly all things proceeded, and duly and well were completed,
And the great seal of the law was set like a sun on the margin.
Then from his leathern pouch the farmer threw on the table
Three times the old man's fee in solid pieces of silver;
And the notary rising, and blessing the bride and the bridegroom,
Lifted aloft the tankard of ale and drank to their welfare.
Wiping the foam from his lip, he solemnly bowed and departed,
While in silence the others sat and mused by the fireside,
Till Evangeline brought the draught-board out of its corner.

Soon was the game begun. In friendly contention the old men
Laughed at each lucky hit, or unsuccessful manœuvre,
Laughed when a man was crowned, or a breach was made in the king-row.
Meanwhile apart, in the twilight gloom of a window's embrasure,
Sat the lovers, and whispered together, beholding the moon rise
Over the pallid sea, and the silvery mists of the meadows.
Silently one by one, in the infinite meadows of heaven,
Blossomed the lovely stars, the forget-me-nots of the angels.

Thus was the evening passed. Anon the bell from the belfry
Rang out the hour of nine, the village curfew, and straightway
Rose the guests and departed; and silence reigned in the household.
Many a farewell word and sweet good-night on the door-step
Lingered long in Evangeline's heart, and filled it with gladness.
Carefully then were covered the embers that glowed on the hearth-stone,
And on the oaken stairs resounded the tread of the farmer.
Soon with a soundless step the foot of Evangeline followed.
Up the staircase moved a luminous space in the darkness,
Lighted less by the lamp than the shining face of the maiden.
Silent she passed the hall, and entered the door of her chamber.
Simple that chamber was, with its curtains of white, and its clothes-press
Ample and high, on whose spacious shelves were carefully folded
Linen and woollen stuffs, by the hand of Evangeline woven.
This was the precious dower she would bring to her husband in marriage,
Better than flocks and herds, being proofs of her skill as a housewife.
Soon she extinguished her lamp, for the mellow and radiant moonlight

Streamed through the windows, and lighted the room, till the heart of the maiden
Swelled and obeyed its power, like the tremulous tides of the ocean.
Ah! she was fair, exceeding fair to behold, as she stood with
Naked snow-white feet on the gleaming floor of her chamber!
Little she dreamed that below, among the trees of the orchard,
Waited her lover and watched for the gleam of her lamp and her shadow.
Yet were her thoughts of him, and at times a feeling of sadness
Passed o'er her soul, as the sailing shade of clouds in the moonlight
Flitted across the floor and darkened the room for a moment.
And, as she gazed from the window, she saw serenely the moon pass
Forth from the folds of a cloud, and one star follow her footsteps,
As out of Abraham's tent young Ishmael wandered with Hagar!

IV.

Pleasantly rose next morn the sun on the village of Grand-Pré.
Pleasantly gleamed in the soft, sweet air the Basin of Minas,
Where the ships, with their wavering shadows, were riding at anchor.
Life had long been astir in the village, and clamorous labor
Knocked with its hundred hands at the golden gates of the morning.
Now from the country around, from the farms and neighboring hamlets,
Came in their holiday dresses the blithe Acadian peasants.
Many a glad good-morrow and jocund laugh from the young folk
Made the bright air brighter, as up from the numerous meadows,

Where no path could be seen but the track of wheels in the greensward,
Group after group appeared, and joined, or passed on the highway.
Long ere noon, in the village all sounds of labor were silenced.
Thronged were the streets with people; and noisy groups at the house-doors
Sat in the cheerful sun, and rejoiced and gossiped together.
Every house was an inn, where all were welcomed and feasted;
For with this simple people, who lived like brothers together,
All things were held in common, and what one had was another's.
Yet under Benedict's roof hospitality seemed more abundant:
For Evangeline stood among the guests of her father;
Bright was her face with smiles, and words of welcome and gladness
Fell from her beautiful lips, and blessed the cup as she gave it.

Under the open sky, in the odorous air of the orchard,
Stript of its golden fruit, was spread the feast of betrothal.
There in the shade of the porch were the priest and the notary seated;
There good Benedict sat, and sturdy Basil the blacksmith.
Not far withdrawn from these, by the cider-press and the beehives,
Michael the fiddler was placed, with the gayest of hearts and of waistcoats.
Shadow and light from the leaves alternately played on his snow-white
Hair, as it waved in the wind; and the jolly face of the fiddler
Glowed like a living coal when the ashes are blown from the embers.
Gayly the old man sang to the vibrant sound of his fiddle,
Tous les Bourgeois de Chartres, and *Le Carillon de Dunquerque*,
And anon with his wooden shoes beat time to the music.
Merrily, merrily whirled the wheels of the dizzying dances

Under the orchard-trees and down the path to the meadows;
Old folk and young together, and children mingled among them.
Fairest of all the maids was Evangeline, Benedict's daughter!
Noblest of all the youths was Gabriel, son of the blacksmith!

So passed the morning away. And lo! with a summons sonorous
Sounded the bell from its tower, and over the meadows a drum beat.
Thronged erelong was the church with men. Without, in the churchyard,
Waited the women. They stood by the graves, and hung on the headstones
Garlands of autumn-leaves and evergreens fresh from the forest.
Then came the guard from the ships, and marching proudly among them
Entered the sacred portal. With loud and dissonant clangor
Echoed the sound of their brazen drums from ceiling and casement, —
Echoed a moment only, and slowly the ponderous portal
Closed, and in silence the crowd awaited the will of the soldiers.
Then uprose their commander, and spake from the steps of the altar,
Holding aloft in his hands, with its seals, the royal commission.
"You are convened this day," he said, "by his Majesty's orders.
Clement and kind has he been; but how you have answered his kindness,
Let your own hearts reply! To my natural make and my temper
Painful the task is I do, which to you I know must be grievous.
Yet must I bow and obey, and deliver the will of our monarch;
Namely, that all your lands, and dwellings, and cattle of all kinds

Forfeited be to the crown; and that you yourselves from this province
Be transported to other lands. God grant you may dwell there
Ever as faithful subjects, a happy and peaceable people!
Prisoners now I declare you; for such is his Majesty's pleasure!"
As, when the air is serene in sultry solstice of summer,
Suddenly gathers a storm, and the deadly sling of the hailstones
Beats down the farmer's corn in the field and shatters his windows,
Hiding the sun, and strewing the ground with thatch from the house-roofs,
Bellowing fly the herds, and seek to break their enclosures;
So on the hearts of the people descended the words of the speaker.
Silent a moment they stood in speechless wonder, and then rose
Louder and ever louder a wail of sorrow and anger,
And, by one impulse moved, they madly rushed to the door-way.
Vain was the hope of escape; and cries and fierce imprecations
Rang through the house of prayer; and high o'er the heads of the others
Rose, with his arms uplifted, the figure of Basil the blacksmith,
As, on a stormy sea, a spar is tossed by the billows.
Flushed was his face and distorted with passion; and wildly he shouted,—
"Down with the tyrants of England! we never have sworn them allegiance!
Death to these foreign soldiers, who seize on our homes and our harvests!"
More he fain would have said, but the merciless hand of a soldier
Smote him upon the mouth, and dragged him down to the pavement.

In the midst of the strife and tumult of angry contention,
Lo! the door of the chancel opened, and Father Felician

Entered, with serious mien, and ascended the steps of the altar.
Raising his reverend hand, with a gesture he awed into silence
All that clamorous throng; and thus he spake to his people;
Deep were his tones and solemn; in accents measured and mournful
Spake he, as, after the tocsin's alarum, distinctly the clock strikes.
"What is this that ye do, my children? what madness has seized you?
Forty years of my life have I labored among you, and taught you,
Not in word alone, but in deed, to love one another?
Is this the fruit of my toils, of my vigils and prayers and privations?
Have you so soon forgotten all lessons of love and forgiveness?
This is the house of the Prince of Peace, and would you profane it
Thus with violent deeds and hearts overflowing with hatred?
Lo! where the crucified Christ from his cross is gazing upon you!
See! in those sorrowful eyes what meekness and holy compassion!
Hark! how those lips still repeat the prayer, 'O Father, forgive them!'
Let us repeat that prayer in the hour when the wicked assail us,
Let us repeat it now, and say, 'O Father, forgive them!' "
Few were his words of rebuke, but deep in the hearts of his people
Sank they, and sobs of contrition succeeded the passionate outbreak,
While they repeated his prayer, and said, "O Father, forgive them!"

Then came the evening service. The tapers gleamed from the altar.
Fervent and deep was the voice of the priest, and the people responded,

Not with their lips alone, but their hearts; and the Ave Maria
Sang they, and fell on their knees, and their souls, with devotion translated,
Rose on the ardor of prayer, like Elijah ascending to heaven.

Meanwhile had spread in the village the tidings of ill, and on all sides
Wandered, wailing, from house to house the women and children.
Long at her father's door Evangeline stood, with her right hand
Shielding her eyes from the level rays of the sun, that, descending,
Lighted the village street with mysterious splendor, and roofed each
Peasant's cottage with golden thatch, and emblazoned its windows.
Long within had been spread the snow-white cloth on the table;
There stood the wheaten loaf, and the honey fragrant with wild-flowers;
There stood the tankard of ale, and the cheese fresh brought from the dairy,
And, at the head of the board, the great arm-chair of the farmer.
Thus did Evangeline wait at her father's door, as the sunset
Threw the long shadows of trees o'er the broad ambrosial meadows.
Ah! on her spirit within a deeper shadow had fallen,
And from the fields of her soul a fragrance celestial ascended,—
Charity, meekness, love, and hope, and forgiveness, and patience!
Then, all-forgetful of self, she wandered into the village,
Cheering with looks and words the mournful hearts of the women,
As o'er the darkening fields with lingering steps they departed,
Urged by their household cares, and the weary feet of their children.

Down sank the great red sun, and in golden, glimmering vapors
Veiled the light of his face, like the Prophet descending from Sinai.
Sweetly over the village the bell of the Angelus sounded.

Meanwhile, amid the gloom, by the church Evangeline lingered.
All was silent within; and in vain at the door and the windows
Stood she, and listened and looked, till, overcome by emotion,
"Gabriel!" cried she aloud with tremulous voice; but no answer
Came from the graves of the dead, nor the gloomier grave of the living.
Slowly at length she returned to the tenantless house of her father.
Smouldered the fire on the hearth, on the board was the supper untasted,
Empty and drear was each room, and haunted with phantoms of terror.
Sadly echoed her step on the stair and the floor of her chamber.
In the dead of the night she heard the disconsolate rain fall
Loud on the withered leaves of the sycamore-tree by the window.
Keenly the lightning flashed; and the voice of the echoing thunder
Told her that God was in heaven, and governed the world he created!
Then she remembered the tale she had heard of the justice of Heaven;
Soothed was her troubled soul, and she peacefully slumbered till morning.

V.

Four times the sun had risen and set; and now on the fifth day
Cheerily called the cock to the sleeping maids of the farm-house.

Soon o'er the yellow fields, in silent and mournful procession,
Came from the neighboring hamlets and farms the Acadian women,
Driving in ponderous wains their household goods to the sea-shore,
Pausing and looking back to gaze once more on their dwellings,
Ere they were shut from sight by the winding road and the woodland.
Close at their sides their children ran, and urged on the oxen,
While in their little hands they clasped some fragments of playthings.

Thus to the Gaspereau's mouth they hurried; and there on the sea-beach
Piled in confusion lay the household goods of the peasants.
All day long between the shore and the ships did the boats ply;
All day long the wains came laboring down from the village.
Late in the afternoon, when the sun was near to his setting,
Echoed far o'er the fields came the roll of drums from the churchyard.
Thither the women and children thronged. On a sudden the church-doors
Opened, and forth came the guard, and marching in gloomy procession
Followed the long-imprisoned, but patient, Acadian farmers.
Even as pilgrims, who journey afar from their homes and their country,
Sing as they go, and in singing forget they are weary and wayworn,
So with songs on their lips the Acadian peasants descended
Down from the church to the shore, amid their wives and their daughters.
Foremost the young men came; and, raising together their voices,
Sang with tremulous lips a chant of the Catholic Missions:—
"Sacred heart of the Saviour! O inexhaustible fountain!
Fill our hearts this day with strength and submission and patience!"

Then the old men, as they marched, and the women that stood by the wayside
Joined in the sacred psalm, and the birds in the sunshine above them
Mingled their notes therewith, like voices of spirits departed.

Half-way down to the shore Evangeline waited in silence,
Not overcome with grief, but strong in the hour of affliction,—
Calmly and sadly she waited, until the procession approached her,
And she beheld the face of Gabriel pale with emotion.
Tears then filled her eyes, and, eagerly running to meet him,
Clasped she his hands, and laid her head on his shoulder, and whispered,—
"Gabriel! be of good cheer! for if we love one another
Nothing, in truth, can harm us, whatever mischances may happen!"
Smiling she spake these words; then suddenly paused, for her father
Saw she slowly advancing. Alas! how changed was his aspect!
Gone was the glow from his cheek, and the fire from his eye, and his footstep
Heavier seemed with the weight of the heavy heart in his bosom.
But with a smile and a sigh, she clasped his neck and embraced him,
Speaking words of endearment where words of comfort availed not.
Thus to the Gaspereau's mouth moved on that mournful procession.

There disorder prevailed, and the tumult and stir of embarking.
Busily plied the freighted boats; and in the confusion
Wives were torn from their husbands, and mothers, too late, saw their children
Left on the land, extending their arms, with wildest entreaties.
So unto separate ships were Basil and Gabriel carried,

While in despair on the shore Evangeline stood with her
father.
Half the task was not done when the sun went down, and the
twilight
Deepened and darkened around; and in haste the refluent
ocean
Fled away from the shore, and left the line of the sand-beach
Covered with waifs of the tide, with kelp and the slippery sea-
weed.
Farther back in the midst of the household goods and the
wagons,
Like to a gypsy camp, or a leaguer after a battle,
All escape cut off by the sea, and the sentinels near them,
Lay encamped for the night the houseless Acadian farmers.
Back to its nethermost caves retreated the bellowing ocean,
Dragging adown the beach the rattling pebbles, and leaving
Inland and far up the shore the stranded boats of the sailors.
Then, as the night descended, the herds returned from their
pastures;
Sweet was the moist still air with the odor of milk from their
udders;
Lowing they waited, and long, at the well-known bars of the
farm-yard,—
Waited and looked in vain for the voice and the hand of the
milk-maid.
Silence reigned in the streets; from the church no Angelus
sounded,
Rose no smoke from the roofs, and gleamed no lights from
the windows.

But on the shores meanwhile the evening fires had been
kindled,
Built of the drift-wood thrown on the sands from wrecks in
the tempest.
Round them shapes of gloom and sorrowful faces were
gathered,
Voices of women were heard, and of men, and the crying of
children.
Onward from fire to fire, as from hearth to hearth in his
parish,

Wandered the faithful priest, consoling and blessing and cheering,
Like unto shipwrecked Paul on Melita's desolate sea-shore.
Thus he approached the place where Evangeline sat with her father,
And in the flickering light beheld the face of the old man,
Haggard and hollow and wan, and without either thought or emotion,
E'en as the face of a clock from which the hands have been taken.
Vainly Evangeline strove with words and caresses to cheer him,
Vainly offered him food; yet he moved not, he looked not, he spake not,
But, with a vacant stare, ever gazed at the flickering fire-light.
"Benedicite!" murmured the priest, in tones of compassion.
More he fain would have said, but his heart was full, and his accents
Faltered and paused on his lips, as the feet of a child on the threshold,
Hushed by the scene he beholds, and the awful presence of sorrow.
Silently, therefore, he laid his hand on the head of the maiden,
Raising his tearful eyes to the silent stars that above them
Moved on their way, unperturbed by the wrongs and sorrows of mortals.
Then sat he down at her side, and they wept together in silence.

Suddenly rose from the south a light, as in autumn the blood-red
Moon climbs the crystal walls of heaven, and o'er the horizon
Titan-like stretches its hundred hands upon the mountain and meadow,
Seizing the rocks and the rivers, and piling huge shadows together.
Broader and ever broader it gleamed on the roofs of the village,

Gleamed on the sky and sea, and the ships that lay in the roadstead.
Columns of shining smoke uprose, and flashes of flame were
Thrust through their folds and withdrawn, like the quivering hands of a martyr.
Then as the wind seized the gleeds and the burning thatch, and, uplifting,
Whirled them aloft through the air, at once from a hundred house-tops
Started the sheeted smoke with flashes of flame intermingled.

These things beheld in dismay the crowd on the shore and on shipboard.
Speechless at first they stood, then cried aloud in their anguish,
"We shall behold no more our homes in the village of Grand-Pré!"
Loud on a sudden the cocks began to crow in the farm-yards,
Thinking the day had dawned; and anon the lowing of cattle
Came on the evening breeze, by the barking of dogs interrupted.
Then rose a sound of dread, such as startles the sleeping encampments
Far in the western prairies or forests that skirt the Nebraska,
When the wild horses affrighted sweep by with the speed of the whirlwind,
Or the loud bellowing herds of buffaloes rush to the river.
Such was the sound that arose on the night, as the herds and the horses
Broke through their folds and fences, and madly rushed o'er the meadows.

Overwhelmed with the sight, yet speechless, the priest and the maiden
Gazed on the scene of terror that reddened and widened before them;
And as they turned at length to speak to their silent companion,
Lo! from his seat he had fallen, and stretched abroad on the sea-shore

Motionless lay his form, from which the soul had departed.
Slowly the priest uplifted the lifeless head, and the maiden
Knelt at her father's side, and wailed aloud in her terror.
Then in a swoon she sank, and lay with her head on his bosom.
Through the long night she lay in deep, oblivious slumber;
And when she awoke from the trance, she beheld a multitude near her.
Faces of friends she beheld, that were mournfully gazing upon her,
Pallid, with tearful eyes, and looks of saddest compassion.
Still the blaze of the burning village illumined the landscape,
Reddened the sky overhead, and gleamed on the faces around her,
And like the day of doom it seemed to her wavering senses.
Then a familiar voice she heard, as it said to the people, —
"Let us bury him here by the sea. When a happier season
Brings us again to our homes from the unknown land of our exile,
Then shall his sacred dust be piously laid in the churchyard."
Such were the words of the priest. And there in haste by the sea-side,
Having the glare of the burning village for funeral torches,
But without bell or book, they buried the farmer of Grand-Pré.
And as the voice of the priest repeated the service of sorrow,
Lo! with a mournful sound, like the voice of a vast congregation,
Solemnly answered the sea, and mingled its roar with the dirges.
'T was the returning tide, that afar from the waste of the ocean,
With the first dawn of the day, came heaving and hurrying landward.
Then recommenced once more the stir and noise of embarking;
And with the ebb of the tide the ships sailed out of the harbor,
Leaving behind them the dead on the shore, and the village in ruins.

PART THE SECOND

I.

Many a weary year had passed since the burning of Grand-Pré,
When on the falling tide the freighted vessels departed,
Bearing a nation, with all its household gods, into exile,
Exile without an end, and without an example in story.
Far asunder, on separate coasts, the Acadians landed;
Scattered were they, like flakes of snow, when the wind from the northeast
Strikes aslant through the fogs that darken the Banks of Newfoundland.
Friendless, homeless, hopeless, they wandered from city to city,
From the cold lakes of the North to sultry Southern savannas,—
From the bleak shores of the sea to the lands where the Father of Waters
Seizes the hills in his hands, and drags them down to the ocean,
Deep in their sands to bury the scattered bones of the mammoth.
Friends they sought and homes; and many, despairing, heart-broken,
Asked of the earth but a grave, and no longer a friend nor a fireside.
Written their history stands on tablets of stone in the churchyards.
Long among them was seen a maiden who waited and wandered,
Lowly and meek in spirit, and patiently suffering all things.
Fair was she and young: but, alas! before her extended,
Dreary and vast and silent, the desert of life, with its pathway
Marked by the graves of those who had sorrowed and suffered before her,
Passions long extinguished, and hopes long dead and abandoned,
As the emigrant's way o'er the Western desert is marked by

Camp-fires long consumed, and bones that bleach in the sunshine.
Something there was in her life incomplete, imperfect, unfinished;
As if a morning of June, with all its music and sunshine,
Suddenly paused in the sky, and, fading, slowly descended
Into the east again, from whence it late had arisen.
Sometimes she lingered in towns, till, urged by the fever within her,
Urged by a restless longing, the hunger and thirst of the spirit,
She would commence again her endless search and endeavor;
Sometimes in churchyards strayed, and gazed on the crosses and tombstones,
Sat by some nameless grave, and thought that perhaps in its bosom
He was already at rest, and she longed to slumber beside him.
Sometimes a rumor, a hearsay, an inarticulate whisper,
Came with its airy hand to point and beckon her forward.
Sometimes she spake with those who had seen her beloved and known him,
But it was long ago, in some far-off place or forgotten.
"Gabriel Lajeunesse!" they said; "Oh yes! we have seen him.
He was with Basil the blacksmith, and both have gone to the prairies;
Coureurs-des-Bois are they, and famous hunters and trappers."
"Gabriel Lajeunesse!" said others; "Oh yes! we have seen him.
He is a Voyageur in the lowlands of Louisiana."
Then would they say, "Dear child! why dream and wait for him longer?
Are there not other youths as fair as Gabriel? others
Who have hearts as tender and true, and spirits as loyal?
Here is Baptiste Leblanc, the notary's son, who has loved thee
Many a tedious year; come, give him thy hand and be happy!
Thou art too fair to be left to braid St. Catherine's tresses."
Then would Evangeline answer, serenely but sadly, "I cannot!

Whither my heart has gone, there follows my hand, and not elsewhere.
For when the heart goes before, like a lamp, and illumines the pathway,
Many things are made clear, that else lie hidden in darkness."
Thereupon the priest, her friend and father-confessor,
Said, with a smile, "O daughter! thy God thus speaketh within thee!
Talk not of wasted affection, affection never was wasted;
If it enrich not the heart of another, its waters, returning
Back to their springs, like the rain, shall fill them full of refreshment;
That which the fountain sends forth returns again to the fountain.
Patience; accomplish thy labor; accomplish thy work of affection!
Sorrow and silence are strong, and patient endurance is godlike.
Therefore accomplish thy labor of love, till the heart is made godlike,
Purified, strengthened, perfected, and rendered more worthy of heaven!"
Cheered by the good man's words, Evangeline labored and waited.
Still in her heart she heard the funeral dirge of the ocean,
But with its sound there was mingled a voice that whispered, "Despair not!"
Thus did that poor soul wander in want and cheerless discomfort,
Bleeding, barefooted, over the shards and thorns of existence.
Let me essay, O Muse! to follow the wanderer's footsteps;—
Not through each devious path, each changeful year of existence,
But as a traveller follows a streamlet's course through the valley:
Far from its margin at times, and seeing the gleam of its water
Here and there, in some open space, and at intervals only;
Then drawing nearer its banks, through sylvan glooms that conceal it,

Though he behold it not, he can hear its continuous murmur;
Happy, at length, if he find the spot where it reaches an
outlet.

II.

It was the month of May. Far down the Beautiful River,
Past the Ohio shore and past the mouth of the Wabash,
Into the golden stream of the broad and swift Mississippi,
Floated a cumbrous boat, that was rowed by Acadian
boatmen.
It was a band of exiles: a raft, as it were, from the shipwrecked
Nation, scattered along the coast, now floating together,
Bound by the bonds of a common belief and a common
misfortune;
Men and women and children, who, guided by hope or by
hearsay,
Sought for their kith and their kin among the few-acred
farmers
On the Acadian coast, and the prairies of fair Opelousas.
With them Evangeline went, and her guide, the Father
Felician.
Onward o'er sunken sands, through a wilderness sombre with
forests,
Day after day they glided adown the turbulent river;
Night after night, by their blazing fires, encamped on its
borders.
Now through rushing chutes, among green islands, where
plumelike
Cotton-trees nodded their shadowy crests, they swept with
the current,
Then emerged into broad lagoons, where silvery sand-bars
Lay in the stream, and along the wimpling waves of their
margin,
Shining with snow-white plumes, large flocks of pelicans
waded.
Level the landscape grew, and along the shores of the river,
Shaded by china-trees, in the midst of luxuriant gardens,
Stood the houses of planters, with negro-cabins and dove-
cots.

They were approaching the region where reigns perpetual summer,
Where through the Golden Coast, and groves of orange and citron,
Sweeps with majestic curve the river away to the eastward.
They, too, swerved from their course; and, entering the Bayou of Plaquemine,
Soon were lost in a maze of sluggish and devious waters,
Which, like a network of steel, extended in every direction.
Over their heads the towering and tenebrous boughs of the cypress
Met in a dusky arch, and trailing mosses in mid-air
Waved like banners that hang on the walls of ancient cathedrals.
Deathlike the silence seemed, and unbroken, save by the herons
Home to their roosts in the cedar-trees returning at sunset,
Or by the owl, as he greeted the moon with demoniac laughter.
Lovely the moonlight was as it glanced and gleamed on the water,
Gleamed on the columns of cypress and cedar sustaining the arches,
Down through whose broken vaults it fell as through chinks in a ruin.
Dreamlike, and indistinct, and strange were all things around them;
And o'er their spirits there came a feeling of wonder and sadness,—
Strange forebodings of ill, unseen and that cannot be compassed.
As, at the tramp of a horse's hoof on the turf of the prairies,
Far in advance are closed the leaves of the shrinking mimosa,
So, at the hoof-beats of fate, with sad forebodings of evil,
Shrinks and closes the heart, ere the stroke of doom has attained it.
But Evangeline's heart was sustained by a vision, that faintly
Floated before her eyes, and beckoned her on through the moonlight.

It was the thought of her brain that assumed the shape of a phantom.
Through those shadowy aisles had Gabriel wandered before her,
And every stroke of the oar now brought him nearer and nearer.

Then in his place, at the prow of the boat, rose one of the oarsmen,
And, as a signal sound, if others like them peradventure
Sailed on those gloomy and midnight streams, blew a blast on his bugle.
Wild through the dark colonnades and corridors leafy the blast rang,
Breaking the seal of silence, and giving tongues to the forest.
Soundless above them the banners of moss just stirred to the music.
Multitudinous echoes awoke and died in the distance,
Over the watery floor, and beneath the reverberant branches;
But not a voice replied; no answer came from the darkness;
And, when the echoes had ceased, like a sense of pain was the silence.
Then Evangeline slept; but the boatmen rowed through the midnight,
Silent at times, then singing familiar Canadian boat-songs,
Such as they sang of old on their own Acadian rivers,
While through the night were heard the mysterious sounds of the desert,
Far off,—indistinct,—as of wave or wind in the forest,
Mixed with the whoop of the crane and the roar of the grim alligator.

Thus ere another noon they emerged from the shades; and before them
Lay, in the golden sun, the lakes of the Atchafalaya.
Water-lilies in myriads rocked on the slight undulations
Made by the passing oars, and, resplendent in beauty, the lotus
Lifted her golden crown above the heads of the boatmen.

Faint was the air with the odorous breath of magnolia blossoms,
And with the heat of noon; and numberless sylvan islands,
Fragrant and thickly embowered with blossoming hedges of roses,
Near to whose shores they glided along, invited to slumber.
Soon by the fairest of these their weary oars were suspended.
Under the boughs of Wachita willows, that grew by the margin,
Safely their boat was moored; and scattered about on the greensward,
Tired with their midnight toil, the weary travellers slumbered.
Over them vast and high extended the cope of a cedar.
Swinging from its great arms, the trumpet-flower and the grapevine
Hung their ladder of ropes aloft like the ladder of Jacob,
On whose pendulous stairs the angels ascending, descending,
Were the swift humming-birds, that flitted from blossom to blossom.
Such was the vision Evangeline saw as she slumbered beneath it.
Filled was her heart with love, and the dawn of an opening heaven
Lighted her soul in sleep with the glory of regions celestial.

Nearer, and ever nearer, among the numberless islands,
Darted a light, swift boat, that sped away o'er the water,
Urged on its course by the sinewy arms of hunters and trappers.
Northward its prow was turned, to the land of the bison and beaver.
At the helm sat a youth, with countenance thoughtful and careworn.
Dark and neglected locks overshadowed his brow, and a sadness
Somewhat beyond his years on his face was legibly written.
Gabriel was it, who, weary with waiting, unhappy and restless,
Sought in the Western wilds oblivion of self and of sorrow.
Swiftly they glided along, close under the lee of the island,
But by the opposite bank, and behind a screen of palmettos,

So that they saw not the boat, where it lay concealed in the willows;
All undisturbed by the dash of their oars, and unseen, were the sleepers.
Angel of God was there none to awaken the slumbering maiden.
Swiftly they glided away, like the shade of a cloud on the prairie.
After the sound of their oars on the tholes had died in the distance,
As from a magic trance the sleepers awoke, and the maiden
Said with a sigh to the friendly priest, "O Father Felician!
Something says in my heart that near me Gabriel wanders.
Is it a foolish dream, an idle and vague superstition?
Or has an angel passed, and revealed the truth to my spirit?"
Then, with a blush, she added, "Alas for my credulous fancy!
Unto ears like thine such words as these have no meaning."
But made answer the reverend man, and he smiled as he answered, —
"Daughter, thy words are not idle; nor are they to me without meaning.
Feeling is deep and still; and the word that floats on the surface
Is as the tossing buoy, that betrays where the anchor is hidden.
Therefore trust to thy heart, and to what the world calls illusions.
Gabriel truly is near thee; for not far away to the southward,
On the banks of the Têche, are the towns of St. Maur and St. Martin.
There the long-wandering bride shall be given again to her bridegroom,
There the long-absent pastor regain his flock and his sheepfold.
Beautiful is the land, with its prairies and forests of fruit-trees;
Under the feet a garden of flowers, and the bluest of heavens
Bending above, and resting its dome on the walls of the forest.
They who dwell there have named it the Eden of Louisiana!"

With these words of cheer they arose and continued their journey.
Softly the evening came. The sun from the western horizon
Like a magician extended his golden wand o'er the landscape;
Twinkling vapors arose; and sky and water and forest
Seemed all on fire at the touch, and melted and mingled together.
Hanging between two skies, a cloud with edges of silver,
Floated the boat, with its dripping oars, on the motionless water.
Filled was Evangeline's heart with inexpressible sweetness.
Touched by the magic spell, the sacred fountains of feeling
Glowed with the light of love, as the skies and waters around her.
Then from a neighboring thicket the mocking-bird, wildest of singers,
Swinging aloft on a willow spray that hung o'er the water,
Shook from his little throat such floods of delirious music,
That the whole air and the woods and the waves seemed silent to listen.
Plaintive at first were the tones and sad: then soaring to madness
Seemed they to follow or guide the revel of frenzied Bacchantes.
Single notes were then heard, in sorrowful, low lamentation;
Till, having gathered them all, he flung them abroad in derision,
As when, after a storm, a gust of wind through the tree-tops
Shakes down the rattling rain in a crystal shower on the branches.
With such a prelude as this, and hearts that throbbed with emotion,
Slowly they entered the Têche, where it flows through the green Opelousas,
And, through the amber air, above the crest of the woodland,
Saw the column of smoke that arose from a neighboring dwelling;—
Sounds of a horn they heard, and the distant lowing of cattle.

III.

Near to the bank of the river, o'ershadowed by oaks, from whose branches
Garlands of Spanish moss and of mystic mistletoe flaunted,
Such as the Druids cut down with golden hatchets at Yule-tide,
Stood, secluded and still, the house of the herdsman. A garden
Girded it round about with a belt of luxuriant blossoms,
Filling the air with fragrance. The house itself was of timbers
Hewn from the cypress-tree, and carefully fitted together.
Large and low was the roof; and on slender columns supported,
Rose-wreathed, vine-encircled, a broad and spacious veranda,
Haunt of the humming-bird and the bee, extended around it.
At each end of the house, amid the flowers of the garden,
Stationed the dove-cots were, as love's perpetual symbol,
Scenes of endless wooing, and endless contentions of rivals.
Silence reigned o'er the place. The line of shadow and sunshine
Ran near the tops of the trees; but the house itself was in shadow,
And from its chimney-top, ascending and slowly expanding
Into the evening air, a thin blue column of smoke rose.
In the rear of the house, from the garden gate, ran a pathway
Through the great groves of oak to the skirts of the limitless prairie,
Into whose sea of flowers the sun was slowly descending.
Full in his track of light, like ships with shadowy canvas
Hanging loose from their spars in a motionless calm in the tropics,
Stood a cluster of trees, with tangled cordage of grape-vines.

Just where the woodlands met the flowery surf of the prairie,
Mounted upon his horse, with Spanish saddle and stirrups,
Sat a herdsman, arrayed in gaiters and doublet of deerskin.

Broad and brown was the face that from under the Spanish sombrero
Gazed on the peaceful scene, with the lordly look of its master.
Round about him were numberless herds of kine, that were grazing
Quietly in the meadows, and breathing the vapory freshness
That uprose from the river, and spread itself over the landscape.
Slowly lifting the horn that hung at his side, and expanding
Fully his broad, deep chest, he blew a blast, that resounded
Wildly and sweet and far, through the still damp air of the evening.
Suddenly out of the grass the long white horns of the cattle
Rose like flakes of foam on the adverse currents of ocean.
Silent a moment they gazed, then bellowing rushed o'er the prairie,
And the whole mass became a cloud, a shade in the distance.
Then, as the herdsman turned to the house, through the gate of the garden
Saw he the forms of the priest and the maiden advancing to meet him.
Suddenly down from his horse he sprang in amazement, and forward
Rushed with extended arms and exclamations of wonder;
When they beheld his face, they recognized Basil the Blacksmith.
Hearty his welcome was, as he led his guests to the garden.
There in an arbor of roses with endless question and answer
Gave they vent to their hearts, and renewed their friendly embraces,
Laughing and weeping by turns, or sitting silent and thoughtful.
Thoughtful, for Gabriel came not; and now dark doubts and misgivings
Stole o'er the maiden's heart; and Basil, somewhat embarrassed,
Broke the silence and said, "If you came by the Atchafalaya,
How have you nowhere encountered my Gabriel's boat on the bayous?"

Over Evangeline's face at the words of Basil a shade passed.
Tears came into her eyes, and she said, with a tremulous accent,
"Gone? is Gabriel gone?" and, concealing her face on his shoulder,
All her o'erburdened heart gave way, and she wept and lamented.
Then the good Basil said,—and his voice grew blithe as he said it,—
"Be of good cheer, my child; it is only to-day he departed.
Foolish boy! he has left me alone with my herds and my horses.
Moody and restless grown, and tried and troubled, his spirit
Could no longer endure the calm of this quiet existence.
Thinking ever of thee, uncertain and sorrowful ever,
Ever silent, or speaking only of thee and his troubles,
He at length had become so tedious to men and to maidens,
Tedious even to me, that at length I bethought me, and sent him
Unto the town of Adayes to trade for mules with the Spaniards.
Thence he will follow the Indian trails to the Ozark Mountains,
Hunting for furs in the forests, on rivers trapping the beaver.
Therefore be of good cheer; we will follow the fugitive lover;
He is not far on his way, and the Fates and the streams are against him.
Up and away to-morrow, and through the red dew of the morning
We will follow him fast, and bring him back to his prison."

Then glad voices were heard, and up from the banks of the river,
Borne aloft on his comrades' arms, came Michael the fiddler.
Long under Basil's roof had he lived like a god on Olympus,
Having no other care than dispensing music to mortals.
Far renowned was he for his silver locks and his fiddle.
"Long live Michael," they cried, "our brave Acadian minstrel!"

As they bore him aloft in triumphal procession; and straightway
Father Felician advanced with Evangeline, greeting the old man
Kindly and oft, and recalling the past, while Basil, enraptured,
Hailed with hilarious joy his old companions and gossips,
Laughing loud and long, and embracing mothers and daughters.
Much they marvelled to see the wealth of the ci-devant blacksmith,
All his domains and his herds, and his patriarchal demeanor;
Much they marvelled to hear his tales of the soil and the climate,
And of the prairies, whose numberless herds were his who would take them;
Each one thought in his heart, that he, too, would go and do likewise.
Thus they ascended the steps, and crossing the breezy veranda,
Entered the hall of the house, where already the supper of Basil
Waited his late return; and they rested and feasted together.

Over the joyous feast the sudden darkness descended.
All was silent without, and, illuming the landscape with silver,
Fair rose the dewy moon and the myriad stars; but within doors,
Brighter than these, shone the faces of friends in the glimmering lamplight.
Then from his station aloft, at the head of the table, the herdsman
Poured forth his heart and his wine together in endless profusion.
Lighting his pipe, that was filled with sweet Natchitoches tobacco,
Thus he spake to his guests, who listened, and smiled as they listened: —
"Welcome once more, my friends, who long have been friendless and homeless,

Welcome once more to a home, that is better perchance than the old one!
Here no hungry winter congeals our blood like the rivers;
Here no stony ground provokes the wrath of the farmer.
Smoothly the ploughshare runs through the soil, as a keel through the water.
All the year round the orange-groves are in blossom; and grass grows
More in a single night than a whole Canadian summer.
Here, too, numberless herds run wild and unclaimed in the prairies;
Here, too, lands may be had for the asking, and forests of timber
With a few blows of the axe are hewn and framed into houses.
After your houses are built, and your fields are yellow with harvests,
No King George of England shall drive you away from your homesteads,
Burning your dwellings and barns, and stealing your farms and your cattle."
Speaking these words, he blew a wrathful cloud from his nostrils,
While his huge, brown hand came thundering down on the table,
So that the guests all started; and Father Felician, astounded,
Suddenly paused, with a pinch of snuff half-way to his nostrils.
But the brave Basil resumed, and his words were milder and gayer: —
"Only beware of the fever, my friends, beware of the fever!
For it is not like that of our cold Acadian climate,
Cured by wearing a spider hung round one's neck in a nutshell!"
Then there were voices heard at the door, and footsteps approaching
Sounded upon the stairs and the floor of the breezy veranda.
It was the neighboring Creoles and small Acadian planters,
Who had been summoned all to the house of Basil the Herdsman.

Merry the meeting was of ancient comrades and neighbors:
Friend clasped friend in his arms; and they who before were as strangers,
Meeting in exile, became straightway as friends to each other,
Drawn by the gentle bond of a common country together.
But in the neighboring hall a strain of music, proceeding
From the accordant strings of Michael's melodious fiddle,
Broke up all further speech. Away, like children delighted,
All things forgotten beside, they gave themselves to the maddening
Whirl of the giddy dance, as it swept and swayed to the music,
Dreamlike, with beaming eyes and the rush of fluttering garments.

Meanwhile, apart, at the head of the hall, the priest and the herdsman
Sat, conversing together of past and present and future;
While Evangeline stood like one entranced, for within her
Olden memories rose, and loud in the midst of the music
Heard she the sound of the sea, and an irrepressible sadness
Came o'er her heart, and unseen she stole forth into the garden.
Beautiful was the night. Behind the black wall of the forest,
Tipping its summit with silver, arose the moon. On the river
Fell here and there through the branches a tremulous gleam of the moonlight,
Like the sweet thoughts of love on a darkened and devious spirit.
Nearer and round about her, the manifold flowers of the garden
Poured out their souls in odors, that were their prayers and confessions
Unto the night, as it went its way, like a silent Carthusian.
Fuller of fragrance than they, and as heavy with shadows and night-dews,
Hung the heart of the maiden. The calm and the magical moonlight
Seemed to inundate her soul with indefinable longings,

As, through the garden-gate, and beneath the shade of the oak-trees,
Passed she along the path to the edge of the measureless prairie.
Silent it lay, with a silvery haze upon it, and fireflies
Gleamed and floated away in mingled and infinite numbers.
Over her head the stars, the thoughts of God in the heavens,
Shone on the eyes of man, who had ceased to marvel and worship,
Save when a blazing comet was seen on the walls of that temple,
As if a hand had appeared and written upon them, "Upharsin."
And the soul of the maiden, between the stars and the fireflies,
Wandered alone, and she cried, "O Gabriel! O my beloved!
Art thou so near unto me, and yet I cannot behold thee?
Art thou so near unto me, and yet thy voice does not reach me?
Ah! how often thy feet have trod this path to the prairie!
Ah! how often thine eyes have looked on the woodlands around me!
Ah! how often beneath this oak, returning from labor,
Thou hast lain down to rest, and to dream of me in thy slumbers!
When shall these eyes behold, these arms be folded about thee?"
Loud and sudden and near the notes of a whippoorwill sounded
Like a flute in the woods; and anon, through the neighboring thickets,
Farther and farther away it floated and dropped into silence.
"Patience!" whispered the oaks from oracular caverns of darkness:
And, from the moonlit meadow, a sigh responded, "To-morrow!"

Bright rose the sun next day; and all the flowers of the garden
Bathed his shining feet with their tears, and anointed his tresses

With the delicious balm that they bore in their vases of crystal.
"Farewell!" said the priest, as he stood at the shadowy threshold;
"See that you bring us the Prodigal Son from his fasting and famine,
And, too, the Foolish Virgin, who slept when the bridegroom was coming."
"Farewell!" answered the maiden, and, smiling, with Basil descended
Down to the river's brink, where the boatmen already were waiting.
Thus beginning their journey with morning, and sunshine, and gladness,
Swiftly they followed the flight of him who was speeding before them,
Blown by the blast of fate like a dead leaf over the desert.
Not that day, nor the next, nor yet the day that succeeded,
Found they the trace of his course, in lake or forest or river,
Nor, after many days, had they found him; but vague and uncertain
Rumors alone were their guides through a wild and desolate country;
Till, at the little inn of the Spanish town of Adayes,
Weary and worn, they alighted, and learned from the garrulous landlord,
That on the day before, with horses and guides and companions,
Gabriel left the village, and took the road of the prairies.

IV.

Far in the West there lies a desert land, where the mountains
Lift, through perpetual snows, their lofty and luminous summits.
Down from their jagged, deep ravines, where the gorge, like a gateway,
Opens a passage rude to the wheels of the emigrant's wagon,
Westward the Oregon flows and the Walleway and Owyhee.

Eastward, with devious course, among the Wind-river Mountains,
Through the Sweet-water Valley precipitate leaps the Nebraska;
And to the south, from Fontaine-qui-bout and the Spanish sierras,
Fretted with sands and rocks, and swept by the wind of the desert,
Numberless torrents, with ceaseless sound, descend to the ocean,
Like the great chords of a harp, in loud and solemn vibrations.
Spreading between these streams are the wondrous, beautiful prairies;
Billowy bays of grass ever rolling in shadow and sunshine,
Bright with luxuriant clusters of roses and purple amorphas.
Over them wandered the buffalo herds, and the elk and the roebuck;
Over them wandered the wolves, and herds of riderless horses;
Fires that blast and blight, and winds that are weary with travel;
Over them wander the scattered tribes of Ishmael's children,
Staining the desert with blood; and above their terrible war-trails
Circles and sails aloft, on pinions majestic, the vulture,
Like the implacable soul of a chieftain slaughtered in battle,
By invisible stairs ascending and scaling the heavens.
Here and there rise smokes from the camps of these savage marauders;
Here and there rise groves from the margins of swift-running rivers;
And the grim, taciturn bear, the anchorite monk of the desert,
Climbs down their dark ravines to dig for roots by the brook-side,
And over all is the sky, the clear and crystalline heaven,
Like the protecting hand of God inverted above them.

Into this wonderful land, at the base of the Ozark Mountains,

Gabriel far had entered, with hunters and trappers behind him.
Day after day, with their Indian guides, the maiden and Basil
Followed his flying steps, and thought each day to o'ertake him.
Sometimes they saw, or thought they saw, the smoke of his camp-fire
Rise in the morning air from the distant plain; but at nightfall,
When they had reached the place, they found only embers and ashes.
And, though their hearts were sad at times and their bodies were weary,
Hope still guided them on, as the magic Fata Morgana
Showed them her lakes of light, that retreated and vanished before them.

Once, as they sat by their evening fire, there silently entered
Into their little camp an Indian woman, whose features
Wore deep traces of sorrow, and patience as great as her sorrow.
She was a Shawnee woman returning home to her people,
From the far-off hunting-grounds of the cruel Camanches,
Where her Canadian husband, a Coureur-des-Bois, had been murdered.
Touched were their hearts at her story, and warmest and friendliest welcome
Gave they, with words of cheer, and she sat and feasted among them
On the buffalo-meat and the venison cooked on the embers.
But when their meal was done, and Basil and all his companions,
Worn with the long day's march and the chase of the deer and the bison,
Stretched themselves on the ground, and slept where the quivering fire-light
Flashed on their swarthy cheeks, and their forms wrapped up in their blankets,
Then at the door of Evangeline's tent she sat and repeated

Slowly, with soft, low voice, and the charm of her Indian accent,
All the tale of her love, with its pleasures, and pains, and reverses.
Much Evangeline wept at the tale, and to know that another
Hapless heart like her own had loved and had been disappointed.
Moved to the depths of her soul by pity and woman's compassion,
Yet in her sorrow pleased that one who had suffered was near her,
She in turn related her love and all its disasters.
Mute with wonder the Shawnee sat, and when she had ended
Still was mute; but at length, as if a mysterious horror
Passed through her brain, she spake, and repeated the tale of the Mowis;
Mowis, the bridegroom of snow, who won and wedded a maiden,
But, when the morning came, arose and passed from the wigwam,
Fading and melting away and dissolving into the sunshine,
Till she beheld him no more, though she followed far into the forest.
Then, in those sweet, low tones, that seemed like a weird incantation,
Told she the tale of the fair Lilinau, who was wooed by a phantom,
That through the pines o'er her father's lodge, in the hush of the twilight,
Breathed like the evening wind, and whispered love to the maiden,
Till she followed his green and waving plume through the forest,
And nevermore returned, nor was seen again by her people.
Silent with wonder and strange surprise, Evangeline listened
To the soft flow of her magical words, till the region around her
Seemed like enchanted ground, and her swarthy guest the enchantress.
Slowly over the tops of the Ozark Mountains the moon rose,

Lighting the little tent, and with a mysterious splendor
Touching the sombre leaves, and embracing and filling the woodland.
With a delicious sound the brook rushed by, and the branches
Swayed and sighed overhead in scarcely audible whispers.
Filled with the thoughts of love was Evangeline's heart, but a secret,
Subtile sense crept in of pain and indefinite terror,
As the cold, poisonous snake creeps into the nest of the swallow.
It was no earthly fear. A breath from the region of spirits
Seemed to float in the air of night; and she felt for a moment
That, like the Indian maid, she, too, was pursuing a phantom.
With this thought she slept, and the fear and the phantom had vanished.

Early upon the morrow the march was resumed; and the Shawnee
Said, as they journeyed along, "On the western slope of these mountains
Dwells in his little village the Black Robe chief of the Mission.
Much he teaches the people, and tells them of Mary and Jesus.
Loud laugh their hearts with joy, and weep with pain, as they hear him."
Then, with a sudden and secret emotion, Evangeline answered,
"Let us go to the Mission, for there good tidings await us!"
Thither they turned their steeds; and behind a spur of the mountains,
Just as the sun went down, they heard a murmur of voices,
And in a meadow green and broad, by the bank of a river,
Saw the tents of the Christians, the tents of the Jesuit Mission.
Under a towering oak, that stood in the midst of the village,
Knelt the Black Robe chief with his children. A crucifix fastened
High on the trunk of the tree, and overshadowed by grape-vines,
Looked with its agonized face on the multitude kneeling beneath it.

This was their rural chapel. Aloft, through the intricate arches
Of its aerial roof, arose the chant of their vespers,
Mingling its notes with the soft susurrus and sighs of the branches.
Silent, with heads uncovered, the travellers, nearer approaching,
Knelt on the swarded floor, and joined in the evening devotions.
But when the service was done, and the benediction had fallen
Forth from the hands of the priest, like seed from the hands of the sower,
Slowly the reverend man advanced to the strangers, and bade them
Welcome; and when they replied, he smiled with benignant expression,
Hearing the homelike sounds of his mother-tongue in the forest,
And, with words of kindness, conducted them into his wigwam.
There upon mats and skins they reposed, and on cakes of the maize-ear
Feasted, and slaked their thirst from the water-gourd of the teacher.
Soon was their story told; and the priest with solemnity answered: —
"Not six suns have risen and set since Gabriel, seated
On this mat by my side, where now the maiden reposes,
Told me this same sad tale; then arose and continued his journey!"
Soft was the voice of the priest, and he spake with an accent of kindness;
But on Evangeline's heart fell his words as in winter the snow-flakes
Fall into some lone nest from which the birds have departed.
"Far to the north he has gone," continued the priest; "but in autumn,
When the chase is done, will return again to the Mission."
Then Evangeline said, and her voice was meek and submissive,

"Let me remain with thee, for my soul is sad and afflicted."
So seemed it wise and well unto all; and betimes on the morrow,
Mounting his Mexican steed, with his Indian guides and companions,
Homeward Basil returned, and Evangeline stayed at the Mission.

Slowly, slowly, slowly the days succeeded each other,—
Days and weeks and months; and the fields of maize that were springing
Green from the ground when a stranger she came, now waving above her,
Lifted their slender shafts, with leaves interlacing, and forming
Cloisters for mendicant crows and granaries pillaged by squirrels.
Then in the golden weather the maize was husked, and the maidens
Blushed at each blood-red ear, for that betokened a lover,
But at the crooked laughed, and called it a thief in the corn-field.
Even the blood-red ear to Evangeline brought not her lover.
"Patience!" the priest would say; "have faith, and thy prayer will be answered!
Look at this vigorous plant that lifts its head from the meadow,
See how its leaves are turned to the north, as true as the magnet;
This is the compass-flower, that the finger of God has planted
Here in the houseless wild, to direct the traveller's journey
Over the sea-like, pathless, limitless waste of the desert.
Such in the soul of man is faith. The blossoms of passion,
Gay and luxuriant flowers, are brighter and fuller of fragrance,
But they beguile us, and lead us astray, and their odor is deadly.
Only this humble plant can guide us here, and hereafter
Crown us with asphodel flowers, that are wet with the dews of nepenthe."

So came the autumn, and passed, and the winter,—yet Gabriel came not;
Blossomed the opening spring, and the notes of the robin and bluebird
Sounded sweet upon wold and in wood, yet Gabriel came not.
But on the breath of the summer winds a rumor was wafted
Sweeter than song of bird, or hue or odor of blossom.
Far to the north and east, it said, in the Michigan forests,
Gabriel had his lodge by the banks of the Saginaw River.
And, with returning guides, that sought the lakes of St. Lawrence,
Saying a sad farewell, Evangeline went from the Mission.
When over weary ways, by long and perilous marches,
She had attained at length the depths of the Michigan forests,
Found she the hunter's lodge deserted and fallen to ruin!

Thus did the long sad years glide on, and in seasons and places
Divers and distant far was seen the wandering maiden;—
Now in the Tents of Grace of the meek Moravian Missions,
Now in the noisy camps and the battle-fields of the army,
Now in secluded hamlets, in towns and populous cities.
Like a phantom she came, and passed away unremembered.
Fair was she and young, when in hope began the long journey;
Faded was she and old, when in disappointment it ended.
Each succeeding year stole something away from her beauty,
Leaving behind it, broader and deeper, the gloom and the shadow.
Then there appeared and spread faint streaks of gray o'er her forehead,
Dawn of another life, that broke o'er her earthly horizon,
As in the eastern sky the first faint streaks of the morning.

V.

In that delightful land which is washed by the Delaware's waters,
Guarding in sylvan shades the name of Penn the apostle,

Stands on the banks of its beautiful stream the city he founded.
There all the air is balm, and the peach is the emblem of beauty,
And the streets still reëcho the names of the trees of the forest,
As if they fain would appease the Dryads whose haunts they molested.
There from the troubled sea had Evangeline landed, an exile,
Finding among the children of Penn a home and a country.
There old René Leblanc had died; and when he departed,
Saw at his side only one of all his hundred descendants.
Something at least there was in the friendly streets of the city,
Something that spake to her heart, and made her no longer a stranger;
And her ear was pleased with the Thee and Thou of the Quakers,
For it recalled the past, the old Acadian country,
Where all men were equal, and all were brothers and sisters.
So, when the fruitless search, the disappointed endeavor,
Ended, to recommence no more upon earth, uncomplaining,
Thither, as leaves to the light, were turned her thoughts and her footsteps.
As from the mountain's top the rainy mists of the morning
Roll away, and afar we behold the landscape below us,
Sun-illumined, with shining rivers and cities and hamlets,
So fell the mists from her mind, and she saw the world far below her,
Dark no longer, but all illumined with love; and the pathway
Which she had climbed so far, lying smooth and fair in the distance.
Gabriel was not forgotten. Within her heart was his image,
Clothed in the beauty of love and youth, as last she beheld him,
Only more beautiful made by his death-like silence and absence.
Into her thoughts of him time entered not, for it was not.
Over him years had no power; he was not changed, but transfigured;

He had become to her heart as one who is dead, and not
absent;
Patience and abnegation of self, and devotion to others,
This was the lesson a life of trial and sorrow had taught her.
So was her love diffused, but, like to some odorous spices,
Suffered no waste nor loss, though filling the air with aroma.
Other hope had she none, nor wish in life, but to follow
Meekly, with reverent steps, the sacred feet of her Saviour.
Thus many years she lived as a Sister of Mercy; frequenting
Lonely and wretched roofs in the crowded lanes of the city,
Where distress and want concealed themselves from the
sunlight,
Where disease and sorrow in garrets languished neglected.
Night after night, when the world was asleep, as the
watchman repeated
Loud, through the gusty streets, that all was well in the city,
High at some lonely window he saw the light of her taper.
Day after day, in the gray of the dawn, as slow through the
suburbs
Plodded the German farmer, with flowers and fruits for the
market,
Met he that meek, pale face, returning home from its
watchings.

Then it came to pass that a pestilence fell on the city,
Presaged by wondrous signs, and mostly by flocks of wild
pigeons,
Darkening the sun in their flight, with naught in their craws
but an acorn.
And, as the tides of the sea arise in the month of September,
Flooding some silver stream, till it spreads to a lake in the
meadow,
So death flooded life, and, o'erflowing its natural margin,
Spread to a brackish lake, the silver stream of existence.
Wealth had no power to bribe, nor beauty to charm, the
oppressor;
But all perished alike beneath the scourge of his anger;—
Only, alas! the poor, who had neither friends nor attendants,
Crept away to die in the almshouse, home of the homeless.

Then in the suburbs it stood, in the midst of meadows and woodlands;—
Now the city surrounds it; but still, with its gateway and wicket
Meek, in the midst of splendor, its humble walls seem to echo
Softly the words of the Lord: "The poor ye always have with you."
Thither, by night and by day, came the Sister of Mercy. The dying
Looked up into her face, and thought, indeed, to behold there
Gleams of celestial light encircle her forehead with splendor,
Such as the artist paints o'er the brows of saints and apostles,
Or such as hangs by night o'er a city seen at a distance.
Unto their eyes it seemed the lamps of the city celestial,
Into whose shining gates erelong their spirits would enter.

Thus, on a Sabbath morn, through the streets, deserted and silent,
Wending her quiet way, she entered the door of the almshouse.
Sweet on the summer air was the odor of flowers in the garden;
And she paused on her way to gather the fairest among them,
That the dying once more might rejoice in their fragrance and beauty.
Then, as she mounted the stairs to the corridors, cooled by the east-wind,
Distant and soft on her ear fell the chimes from the belfry of Christ Church,
While, intermingled with these, across the meadows were wafted
Sounds of psalms, that were sung by the Swedes in their church at Wicaco.
Soft as descending wings fell the calm of the hour on her spirit:
Something within her said, "At length thy trials are ended";
And, with light in her looks, she entered the chambers of sickness.
Noiselessly moved about the assiduous, careful attendants,

Moistening the feverish lip, and the aching brow, and in silence
Closing the sightless eyes of the dead, and concealing their faces,
Where on their pallets they lay, like drifts of snow by the roadside.
Many a languid head, upraised as Evangeline entered,
Turned on its pillow of pain to gaze while she passed, for her presence
Fell on their hearts like a ray of the sun on the walls of a prison.
And, as she looked around, she saw how Death, the consoler,
Laying his hand upon many a heart, had healed it forever.
Many familiar forms had disappeared in the night time;
Vacant their places were, or filled already by strangers.

Suddenly, as if arrested by fear or a feeling of wonder,
Still she stood, with her colorless lips apart, while a shudder
Ran through her frame, and, forgotten, the flowerets dropped from her fingers,
And from her eyes and cheeks the light and bloom of the morning.
Then there escaped from her lips a cry of such terrible anguish,
That the dying heard it, and started up from their pillows.
On the pallet before her was stretched the form of an old man.
Long, and thin, and gray were the locks that shaded his temples;
But, as he lay in the morning light, his face for a moment
Seemed to assume once more the forms of its earlier manhood;
So are wont to be changed the faces of those who are dying.
Hot and red on his lips still burned the flush of the fever,
As if life, like the Hebrew, with blood had besprinkled its portals,
That the Angel of Death might see the sign, and pass over.
Motionless, senseless, dying, he lay, and his spirit exhausted
Seemed to be sinking down through infinite depths in the darkness,

Darkness of slumber and death, forever sinking and sinking.
Then through those realms of shade, in multiplied
reverberations,
Heard he that cry of pain, and through the hush that
succeeded
Whispered a gentle voice, in accents tender and saint-like,
"Gabriel! O my beloved!" and died away into silence.
Then he beheld, in a dream, once more the home of his
childhood;
Green Acadian meadows, with sylvan rivers among them,
Village, and mountain, and woodlands; and, walking under
their shadow,
As in the days of her youth, Evangeline rose in his vision.
Tears came into his eyes; and as slowly he lifted his eyelids,
Vanished the vision away, but Evangeline knelt by his bedside.
Vainly he strove to whisper her name, for the accents
unuttered
Died on his lips, and their motion revealed what his tongue
would have spoken.
Vainly he strove to rise; and Evangeline, kneeling beside him,
Kissed his dying lips, and laid his head on her bosom.
Sweet was the light of his eyes; but it suddenly sank into
darkness,
As when a lamp is blown out by a gust of wind at a casement.

All was ended now, the hope, and the fear, and the sorrow,
All the aching of heart, the restless, unsatisfied longing,
All the dull, deep pain, and constant anguish of patience!
And, as she pressed once more the lifeless head to her bosom,
Meekly she bowed her own, and murmured, "Father I thank
thee!"

Still stands the forest primeval; but far away from its shadow,
Side by side, in their nameless graves, the lovers are sleeping.
Under the humble walls of the little Catholic churchyard,
In the heart of the city, they lie, unknown and unnoticed.
Daily the tides of life go ebbing and flowing beside them,

Thousands of throbbing hearts, where theirs are at rest and forever,
Thousands of aching brains, where theirs no longer are busy,
Thousands of toiling hands, where theirs have ceased from their labors,
Thousands of weary feet, where theirs have completed their journey!

Still stands the forest primeval; but under the shade of its branches
Dwells another race, with other customs and language.
Only along the shore of the mournful and misty Atlantic
Linger a few Acadian peasants, whose fathers from exile
Wandered back to their native land to die in its bosom.
In the fisherman's cot the wheel and the loom are still busy;
Maidens still wear their Norman caps and their kirtles of homespun,
And by the evening fire repeat Evangeline's story,
While from its rocky caverns the deep-voiced, neighboring ocean
Speaks, and in accents disconsolate answers the wail of the forest.

from

THE SEASIDE AND THE FIRESIDE

The Building of the Ship

"Build me straight, O worthy Master!
  Stanch and strong, a goodly vessel,
That shall laugh at all disaster,
  And with wave and whirlwind wrestle!"

The merchant's word
Delighted the Master heard;
For his heart was in his work, and the heart
Giveth grace unto every Art.
A quiet smile played round his lips,
As the eddies and dimples of the tide
Play round the bows of ships,
That steadily at anchor ride.
And with a voice that was full of glee,
He answered, "Erelong we will launch
A vessel as goodly, and strong, and stanch,
As ever weathered a wintry sea!"
And first with nicest skill and art,
Perfect and finished in every part,
A little model the Master wrought,
Which should be to the larger plan
What the child is to the man,
Its counterpart in miniature;
That with a hand more swift and sure
The greater labor might be brought
To answer to his inward thought.
And as he labored, his mind ran o'er
The various ships that were built of yore,
And above them all, and strangest of all
Towered the Great Harry, crank and tall,
Whose picture was hanging on the wall,
With bows and stern raised high in air,
And balconies hanging here and there,

And signal lanterns and flags afloat,
And eight round towers, like those that frown
From some old castle, looking down
Upon the drawbridge and the moat.
And he said with a smile, "Our ship, I wis,
Shall be of another form than this!"
It was of another form, indeed;
Built for freight, and yet for speed,
A beautiful and gallant craft;
Broad in the beam, that the stress of the blast,
Pressing down upon sail and mast,
Might not the sharp bows overwhelm;
Broad in the beam, but sloping aft
With graceful curve and slow degrees,
That she might be docile to the helm,
And that the currents of parted seas,
Closing behind, with mighty force,
Might aid and not impede her course.

In the ship-yard stood the Master,
With the model of the vessel,
That should laugh at all disaster,
And with wave and whirlwind wrestle!
Covering many a rood of ground,
Lay the timber piled around;
Timber of chestnut, and elm, and oak,
And scattered here and there, with these,
The knarred and crooked cedar knees;
Brought from regions far away,
From Pascagoula's sunny bay,
And the banks of the roaring Roanoke!
Ah! what a wondrous thing it is
To note how many wheels of toil
One thought, one word, can set in motion!
There's not a ship that sails the ocean,
But every climate, every soil,
Must bring its tribute, great or small,
And help to build the wooden wall!

The sun was rising o'er the sea,
And long the level shadows lay,
As if they, too, the beams would be
Of some great, airy argosy,
Framed and launched in a single day.
That silent architect, the sun,
Had hewn and laid them every one,
Ere the work of man was yet begun.
Beside the Master, when he spoke,
A youth, against an anchor leaning,
Listened, to catch his slightest meaning.
Only the long waves, as they broke
In ripples on the pebbly beach,
Interrupted the old man's speech.
Beautiful they were, in sooth,
The old man and the fiery youth!
The old man, in whose busy brain
Many a ship that sailed the main
Was modelled o'er and o'er again;—
The fiery youth, who was to be
The heir of his dexterity,
The heir of his house, and his daughter's hand,
When he had built and launched from land
What the elder head had planned.

"Thus," said he, "will we build this ship!
Lay square the blocks upon the slip,
And follow well this plan of mine.
Choose the timbers with greatest care;
Of all that is unsound beware;
For only what is sound and strong
To this vessel shall belong.
Cedar of Maine and Georgia pine
Here together shall combine.
A goodly frame, and a goodly fame,
And the UNION be her name!
For the day that gives her to the sea
Shall give my daughter unto thee!"

The Master's word
Enraptured the young man heard;
And as he turned his face aside,
With a look of joy and a thrill of pride
Standing before
Her father's door,
He saw the form of his promised bride.
The sun shone on her golden hair,
And her cheek was glowing fresh and fair,
With the breath of morn and the soft sea air.
Like a beauteous barge was she,
Still at rest on the sandy beach,
Just beyond the billow's reach;
But he
Was the restless, seething, stormy sea!
Ah, how skilful grows the hand
That obeyeth Love's command!
It is the heart, and not the brain,
That to the highest doth attain,
And he who followeth Love's behest
Far excelleth all the rest!

Thus with the rising of the sun
Was the noble task begun,
And soon throughout the ship-yard's bounds
Were heard the intermingled sounds
Of axes and of mallets, plied
With vigorous arms on every side;
Plied so deftly and so well,
That, ere the shadows of evening fell,
The keel of oak for a noble ship,
Scarfed and bolted, straight and strong,
Was lying ready, and stretched along
The blocks, well placed upon the slip.
Happy, thrice happy, every one
Who sees his labor well begun,
And not perplexed and multiplied,
By idly waiting for time and tide!

And when the hot, long day was o'er,
The young man at the Master's door
Sat with the maiden calm and still,
And within the porch, a little more
Removed beyond the evening chill,
The father sat, and told them tales
Of wrecks in the great September gales,
Of pirates coasting the Spanish Main,
And ships that never came back again,
The chance and change of a sailor's life,
Want and plenty, rest and strife,
His roving fancy, like the wind,
That nothing can stay and nothing can bind,
And the magic charm of foreign lands,
With shadows of palms, and shining sands,
Where the tumbling surf,
O'er the coral reefs of Madagascar,
Washes the feet of the swarthy Lascar,
As he lies alone and asleep on the turf.
And the trembling maiden held her breath
At the tales of that awful, pitiless sea,
With all its terror and mystery,
The dim, dark sea, so like unto Death,
That divides and yet unites mankind!
And whenever the old man paused, a gleam
From the bowl of his pipe would awhile illume
The silent group in the twilight gloom,
And thoughtful faces, as in a dream;
And for a moment one might mark
What had been hidden by the dark,
That the head of the maiden lay at rest,
Tenderly, on the young man's breast!

Day by day the vessel grew,
With timbers fashioned strong and true,
Stemson and keelson and sternson-knee,
Till, framed with perfect symmetry,
A skeleton ship rose up to view!
And around the bows and along the side
The heavy hammers and mallets plied,

Till after many a week, at length,
Wonderful for form and strength,
Sublime in its enormous bulk,
Loomed aloft the shadowy hulk!
And around it columns of smoke, upwreathing,
Rose from the boiling, bubbling, seething
Caldron, that glowed,
And overflowed
With the black tar, heated for the sheathing.
And amid the clamors
Of clattering hammers,
He who listened heard now and then
The song of the Master and his men:—

"Build me straight, O worthy Master,
  Staunch and strong, a goodly vessel,
That shall laugh at all disaster,
  And with wave and whirlwind wrestle!"

With oaken brace and copper band,
Lay the rudder on the sand,
That, like a thought, should have control
Over the movement of the whole;
And near it the anchor, whose giant hand
Would reach down and grapple with the land,
And immovable and fast
Hold the great ship against the bellowing blast!
And at the bows an image stood,
By a cunning artist carved in wood,
With robes of white, that far behind
Seemed to be fluttering in the wind.
It was not shaped in a classic mould,
Not like a Nymph or Goddess of old,
Or Naiad rising from the water,
But modelled from the Master's daughter!
On many a dreary and misty night,
'T will be seen by the rays of the signal light,
Speeding along through the rain and the dark,
Like a ghost in its snow-white sark,
The pilot of some phantom bark,

Guiding the vessel, in its flight,
By a path none other knows aright!

Behold, at last,
Each tall and tapering mast
Is swung into its place;
Shrouds and stays
Holding it firm and fast!

Long ago,
In the deer-haunted forests of Maine,
When upon mountain and plain
Lay the snow,
They fell,—those lordly pines!
Those grand, majestic pines!
'Mid shouts and cheers
The jaded steers,
Panting beneath the goad,
Dragged down the weary, winding road
Those captive kings so straight and tall,
To be shorn of their streaming hair,
And naked and bare,
To feel the stress and the strain
Of the wind and the reeling main,
Whose roar
Would remind them forevermore
Of their native forests they should not see again.

And everywhere
The slender, graceful spars
Poise aloft in the air,
And at the mast-head,
White, blue, and red,
A flag unrolls the stripes and stars.
Ah! when the wanderer, lonely, friendless,
In foreign harbors shall behold
That flag unrolled,
'T will be as a friendly hand
Stretched out from his native land,
Filling his heart with memories sweet and endless!

All is finished! and at length
Has come the bridal day
Of beauty and of strength.
To-day the vessel shall be launched!
With fleecy clouds the sky is blanched,
And o'er the bay,
Slowly, in all his splendors dight,
The great sun rises to behold the sight.

The ocean old,
Centuries old,
Strong as youth, and as uncontrolled,
Paces restless to and fro,
Up and down the sands of gold.
His beating heart is not at rest;
And far and wide,
With ceaseless flow,
His beard of snow
Heaves with the heaving of his breast.
He waits impatient for his bride.
There she stands,
With her foot upon the sands,
Decked with flags and streamers gay,
In honor of her marriage day,
Her snow-white signals fluttering, blending,
Round her like a veil descending,
Ready to be
The bride of the gray old sea.

On the deck another bride
Is standing by her lover's side.
Shadows from the flags and shrouds,
Like the shadows cast by clouds,
Broken by many a sunny fleck,
Fall around them on the deck.

The prayer is said,
The service read,
The joyous bridegroom bows his head;
And in tears the good old Master

Shakes the brown hand of his son,
Kisses his daughter's glowing cheek
In silence, for he cannot speak,
And ever faster
Down his own the tears begin to run.
The worthy pastor—
The shepherd of that wandering flock,
That has the ocean for its wold,
That has the vessel for its fold,
Leaping ever from rock to rock—
Spake, with accents mild and clear,
Words of warning, words of cheer,
But tedious to the bridegroom's ear.
He knew the chart
Of the sailor's heart,
All its pleasures and its griefs,
All its shallows and rocky reefs,
All those secret currents, that flow
With such resistless undertow,
And lift and drift, with terrible force,
The will from its moorings and its course.
Therefore he spake, and thus said he:—

"Like unto ships far off at sea,
Outward or homeward bound, are we.
Before, behind, and all around,
Floats and swings the horizon's bound,
Seems at its distant rim to rise
And climb the crystal wall of the skies,
And then again to turn and sink,
As if we could slide from its outer brink.
Ah! it is not the sea,
It is not the sea that sinks and shelves,
But ourselves
That rock and rise
With endless and uneasy motion,
Now touching the very skies,
Now sinking into the depths of ocean.
Ah! if our souls but poise and swing
Like the compass in its brazen ring,

Ever level and ever true
To the toil and the task we have to do,
We shall sail securely, and safely reach
The Fortunate Isles, on whose shining beach
The sights we see, and the sounds we hear,
Will be those of joy and not of fear!"

Then the Master,
With a gesture of command,
Waved his hand;
And at the word,
Loud and sudden there was heard,
All around them and below,
The sound of hammers, blow on blow,
Knocking away the shores and spurs.
And see! she stirs!
She starts,—she moves,—she seems to feel
The thrill of life along her keel,
And, spurning with her foot the ground,
With one exulting, joyous bound,
She leaps into the ocean's arms!

And lo! from the assembled crowd
There rose a shout, prolonged and loud,
That to the ocean seemed to say,
"Take her, O bridegroom, old and gray,
Take her to thy protecting arms,
With all her youth and all her charms!"

How beautiful she is! How fair
She lies within those arms, that press
Her form with many a soft caress
Of tenderness and watchful care!
Sail forth into the sea, O ship!
Through wind and wave, right onward steer!
The moistened eye, the trembling lip,
Are not the signs of doubt or fear.

Sail forth into the sea of life,
O gentle, loving, trusting wife,

And safe from all adversity
Upon the bosom of that sea
Thy comings and thy goings be!
For gentleness and love and trust
Prevail o'er angry wave and gust;
And in the wreck of noble lives
Something immortal still survives!

Thou, too, sail on, O Ship of State!
Sail on, O UNION, strong and great!
Humanity with all its fears,
With all the hopes of future years,
Is hanging breathless on thy fate!
We know what Master laid thy keel,
What Workmen wrought thy ribs of steel,
Who made each mast, and sail, and rope,
What anvils rang, what hammers beat,
In what a forge and what a heat
Were shaped the anchors of thy hope!
Fear not each sudden sound and shock,
'T is of the wave and not the rock;
'T is but the flapping of the sail,
And not a rent made by the gale!
In spite of rock and tempest's roar,
In spite of false lights on the shore,
Sail on, nor fear to breast the sea!
Our hearts, our hopes, are all with thee,
Our hearts, our hopes, our prayers, our tears,
Our faith triumphant o'er our fears,
Are all with thee,—are all with thee!

Seaweed

When descends on the Atlantic
  The gigantic
Storm-wind of the equinox,
Landward in his wrath he scourges
  The toiling surges,
Laden with seaweed from the rocks:

From Bermuda's reefs; from edges
  Of sunken ledges,
In some far-off, bright Azore;
From Bahama, and the dashing,
  Silver-flashing
Surges of San Salvador;

From the tumbling surf, that buries
  The Orkneyan skerries,
Answering the hoarse Hebrides;
And from wrecks of ships, and drifting
  Spars, uplifting
On the desolate, rainy seas;—

Ever drifting, drifting, drifting
  On the shifting
Currents of the restless main;
Till in sheltered coves, and reaches
  Of sandy beaches,
All have found repose again.

So when storms of wild emotion
  Strike the ocean
Of the poet's soul, erelong
From each cave and rocky fastness,
  In its vastness,
Floats some fragment of a song:

From the far-off isles enchanted,
  Heaven has planted
With the golden fruit of Truth;

From the flashing surf, whose vision
Gleams Elysian
In the tropic clime of Youth;

From the strong Will, and the Endeavor
That forever
Wrestle with the tides of Fate;
From the wreck of Hopes far-scattered,
Tempest-shattered,
Floating waste and desolate;—

Ever drifting, drifting, drifting
On the shifting
Currents of the restless heart;
Till at length in books recorded,
They, like hoarded
Household words, no more depart.

Chrysaor

Just above yon sandy bar,
As the day grows fainter and dimmer,
Lonely and lovely, a single star
Lights the air with a dusky glimmer.

Into the ocean faint and far
Falls the trail of its golden splendor,
And the gleam of that single star
Is ever refulgent, soft, and tender.

Chrysaor, rising out of the sea,
Showed thus glorious and thus emulous,
Leaving the arms of Callirrhoe,
Forever tender, soft, and tremulous.

Thus o'er the ocean faint and far
Trailed the gleam of his falchion brightly;
Is it a God, or is it a star
That, entranced, I gaze on nightly!

Twilight

The twilight is sad and cloudy,
  The wind blows wild and free,
And like the wings of sea-birds
  Flash the white caps of the sea.

But in the fisherman's cottage
  There shines a ruddier light,
And a little face at the window
  Peers out into the night.

Close, close it is pressed to the window,
  As if those childish eyes
Were looking into the darkness
  To see some form arise.

And a woman's waving shadow
  Is passing to and fro,
Now rising to the ceiling,
  Now bowing and bending low.

What tale do the roaring ocean,
  And the night-wind, bleak and wild,
As they beat at the crazy casement,
  Tell to that little child?

And why do the roaring ocean,
  And the night-wind, wild and bleak,
As they beat at the heart of the mother
  Drive the color from her cheek?

Sir Humphrey Gilbert

Southward with fleet of ice
  Sailed the corsair Death;
Wild and fast blew the blast,
  And the east-wind was his breath.

His lordly ships of ice
  Glisten in the sun;
On each side, like pennons wide,
  Flashing crystal streamlets run.

His sails of white sea-mist
  Dripped with silver rain;
But where he passed there were cast
  Leaden shadows o'er the main.

Eastward from Campobello
  Sir Humphrey Gilbert sailed;
Three days or more seaward he bore,
  Then, alas! the land-wind failed.

Alas! the land-wind failed,
  And ice-cold grew the night;
And nevermore, on sea or shore,
  Should Sir Humphrey see the light.

He sat upon the deck,
  The Book was in his hand;
"Do not fear! Heaven is as near,"
  He said, "by water as by land!"

In the first watch of the night,
  Without a signal's sound,
Out of the sea, mysteriously,
  The fleet of Death rose all around.

The moon and the evening star
  Were hanging in the shrouds;
Every mast, as it passed,
  Seemed to rake the passing clouds.

They grappled with their prize,
At midnight black and cold!
As of a rock was the shock;
Heavily the ground-swell rolled.

Southward through day and dark,
They drift in close embrace,
With mist and rain, o'er the open main;
Yet there seems no change of place.

Southward, forever southward,
They drift through dark and day;
And like a dream, in the Gulf-Stream
Sinking, vanish all away.

The Lighthouse

The rocky ledge runs far into the sea,
And on its outer point, some miles away,
The Lighthouse lifts its massive masonry,
A pillar of fire by night, of cloud by day.

Even at this distance I can see the tides,
Upheaving, break unheard along its base,
A speechless wrath, that rises and subsides
In the white lip and tremor of the face.

And as the evening darkens, lo! how bright,
Through the deep purple of the twilight air,
Beams forth the sudden radiance of its light
With strange, unearthly splendor in the glare!

Not one alone; from each projecting cape
And perilous reef along the ocean's verge,
Starts into life a dim, gigantic shape,
Holding its lantern o'er the restless surge.

Like the great giant Christopher it stands
  Upon the brink of the tempestuous wave,
Wading far out among the rocks and sands,
  The night-o'ertaken mariner to save.

And the great ships sail outward and return,
  Bending and bowing o'er the billowy swells,
And ever joyful, as they see it burn,
  They wave their silent welcomes and farewells.

They come forth from the darkness, and their sails
  Gleam for a moment only in the blaze,
And eager faces, as the light unveils,
  Gaze at the tower, and vanish while they gaze.

The mariner remembers when a child,
  On his first voyage, he saw it fade and sink;
And when, returning from adventures wild,
  He saw it rise again o'er ocean's brink.

Steadfast, serene, immovable, the same
  Year after year, through all the silent night
Burns on forevermore that quenchless flame,
  Shines on that inextinguishable light!

It sees the ocean to its bosom clasp
  The rocks and sea-sand with the kiss of peace;
It sees the wild winds lift it in their grasp,
  And hold it up, and shake it like a fleece.

The startled waves leap over it; the storm
  Smites it with all the scourges of the rain,
And steadily against its solid form
  Press the great shoulders of the hurricane.

The sea-bird wheeling round it, with the din
  Of wings and winds and solitary cries,
Blinded and maddened by the light within,
  Dashes himself against the glare, and dies.

A new Prometheus, chained upon the rock,
  Still grasping in his hand the fire of Jove,
It does not hear the cry, nor heed the shock,
  But hails the mariner with words of love.

"Sail on!" it says, "sail on, ye stately ships!
  And with your floating bridge the ocean span;
Be mine to guard this light from all eclipse,
  Be yours to bring man nearer unto man!"

The Fire of Drift-Wood

We sat within the farm-house old,
  Whose windows, looking o'er the bay,
Gave to the sea-breeze damp and cold,
  An easy entrance, night and day.

Not far away we saw the port,
  The strange, old-fashioned, silent town,
The lighthouse, the dismantled fort,
  The wooden houses, quaint and brown.

We sat and talked until the night,
  Descending, filled the little room;
Our faces faded from the sight,
  Our voices only broke the gloom.

We spake of many a vanished scene,
  Of what we once had thought and said,
Of what had been, and might have been,
  And who was changed, and who was dead;

And all that fills the hearts of friends,
  When first they feel, with secret pain,
Their lives thenceforth have separate ends,
  And never can be one again;

The first slight swerving of the heart,
  That words are powerless to express,
And leave it still unsaid in part,
  Or say it in too great excess.

The very tones in which we spake
  Had something strange, I could but mark;
The leaves of memory seemed to make
  A mournful rustling in the dark.

Oft died the words upon our lips,
  As suddenly, from out the fire
Built of the wreck of stranded ships,
  The flames would leap and then expire.

And, as their splendor flashed and failed,
  We thought of wrecks upon the main,
Of ships dismasted, that were hailed
  And sent no answer back again.

The windows, rattling in their frames,
  The ocean, roaring up the beach,
The gusty blast, the bickering flames,
  All mingled vaguely in our speech;

Until they made themselves a part
  Of fancies floating through the brain,
The long-lost ventures of the heart,
  That send no answers back again.

O flames that glowed! O hearts that yearned!
  They were indeed too much akin,
The drift-wood fire without that burned,
  The thoughts that burned and glowed within.

Resignation

There is no flock, however watched and tended,
  But one dead lamb is there!
There is no fireside, howsoe'er defended,
  But has one vacant chair!

The air is full of farewells to the dying,
  And mournings for the dead;
The heart of Rachel, for her children crying
  Will not be comforted!

Let us be patient! These severe afflictions
  Not from the ground arise,
But oftentimes celestial benedictions
  Assume this dark disguise.

We see but dimly through the mists and vapors;
  Amid these earthly damps
What seem to us but sad, funereal tapers
  May be heaven's distant lamps.

There is no Death! What seems so is transition;
  This life of mortal breath
Is but a suburb of the life elysian,
  Whose portal we call Death.

She is not dead,—the child of our affection,—
  But gone unto that school
Where she no longer needs our poor protection,
  And Christ himself doth rule.

In that great cloister's stillness and seclusion,
  By guardian angels led,
Safe from temptation, safe from sin's pollution,
  She lives, whom we call dead.

Day after day we think what she is doing
  In those bright realms of air;
Year after year, her tender steps pursuing,
  Behold her grown more fair.

Thus do we walk with her, and keep unbroken
  The bond which nature gives,
Thinking that our remembrance, though unspoken,
  May reach her where she lives.

Not as a child shall we again behold her;
  For when with raptures wild
In our embraces we again enfold her,
  She will not be a child;

But a fair maiden, in her Father's mansion,
  Clothed with celestial grace;
And beautiful with all the soul's expansion
  Shall we behold her face.

And though at times impetuous with emotion
  And anguish long suppressed,
The swelling heart heaves moaning like the ocean,
  That cannot be at rest,—

We will be patient, and assuage the feeling
  We may not wholly stay;
By silence sanctifying, not concealing,
  The grief that must have way.

The Builders

All are architects of Fate,
  Working in these walls of Time;
Some with massive deeds and great,
  Some with ornaments of rhyme.

Nothing useless is, or low;
  Each thing in its place is best;
And what seems but idle show
  Strengthens and supports the rest.

For the structure that we raise,
Time is with materials filled;
Our to-days and yesterdays
Are the blocks with which we build.

Truly shape and fashion these;
Leave no yawning gaps between;
Think not, because no man sees,
Such things will remain unseen.

In the elder days of Art,
Builders wrought with greatest care
Each minute and unseen part;
For the Gods see everywhere.

Let us do our work as well,
Both the unseen and the seen;
Make the house, where Gods may dwell,
Beautiful, entire, and clean.

Else our lives are incomplete,
Standing in these walls of Time,
Broken stairways, where the feet
Stumble as they seek to climb.

Build to-day, then, strong and sure,
With a firm and ample base;
And ascending and secure
Shall to-morrow find its place.

Thus alone can we attain
To those turrets, where the eye
Sees the world as one vast plain,
And one boundless reach of sky.

Sand of the Desert in an Hour-Glass

A handful of red sand, from the hot clime
Of Arab deserts brought,
Within this glass becomes the spy of Time,
The minister of Thought.

How many weary centuries has it been
About those deserts blown!
How many strange vicissitudes has seen,
How many histories known!

Perhaps the camels of the Ishmaelite
Trampled and passed it o'er,
When into Egypt from the patriarch's sight
His favorite son they bore.

Perhaps the feet of Moses, burnt and bare,
Crushed it beneath their tread,
Or Pharaoh's flashing wheels into the air
Scattered it as they sped;

Or Mary, with the Christ of Nazareth
Held close in her caress,
Whose pilgrimage of hope and love and faith
Illumed the wilderness;

Or anchorites beneath Engaddi's palms
Pacing the Dead Sea beach,
And singing slow their old Armenian psalms
In half-articulate speech;

Or caravans, that from Bassora's gate
With westward steps depart;
Or Mecca's pilgrims, confident of Fate,
And resolute in heart!

These have passed over it, or may have passed!
Now in this crystal tower
Imprisoned by some curious hand at last,
It counts the passing hour.

And as I gaze, these narrow walls expand;—
  Before my dreamy eye
Stretches the desert with its shifting sand,
  Its unimpeded sky.

And borne aloft by the sustaining blast,
  This little golden thread
Dilates into a column high and vast,
  A form of fear and dread.

And onward, and across the setting sun,
  Across the boundless plain,
The column and its broader shadow run,
  Till thought pursues in vain.

The vision vanishes! These walls again
  Shut out the lurid sun,
Shut out the hot, immeasurable plain;
  The half-hour's sand is run!

The Open Window

The old house by the lindens
  Stood silent in the shade,
And on the gravelled pathway
  The light and shadow played.

I saw the nursery windows
  Wide open to the air;
But the faces of the children,
  They were no longer there.

The large Newfoundland house-dog
  Was standing by the door;
He looked for his little playmates,
  Who would return no more.

They walked not under the lindens,
They played not in the hall;
But shadow, and silence, and sadness
Were hanging over all.

The birds sang in the branches,
With sweet, familiar tone;
But the voices of the children
Will be heard in dreams alone!

And the boy that walked beside me,
He could not understand
Why closer in mine, ah! closer,
I pressed his warm, soft hand!

THE SONG OF HIAWATHA

INTRODUCTION

Should you ask me, whence these stories?
Whence these legends and traditions,
With the odors of the forest,
With the dew and damp of meadows,
With the curling smoke of wigwams,
With the rushing of great rivers,
With their frequent repetitions,
And their wild reverberations,
As of thunder in the mountains?
  I should answer, I should tell you,
"From the forests and the prairies,
From the great lakes of the Northland,
From the land of the Ojibways,
From the land of the Dacotahs,
From the mountains, moors, and fen-lands
Where the heron, the Shuh-shuh-gah,
Feeds among the reeds and rushes.
I repeat them as I heard them
From the lips of Nawadaha,
The musician, the sweet singer."
  Should you ask where Nawadaha
Found these songs so wild and wayward,
Found these legends and traditions,
I should answer, I should tell you,
"In the bird's-nests of the forest,
In the lodges of the beaver,
In the hoof-prints of the bison,
In the eyry of the eagle!
  "All the wild-fowl sang them to him,
In the moorlands and the fen-lands,
In the melancholy marshes;
Chetowaik, the plover, sang them,
Mahng, the loon, the wild-goose, Wawa,
The blue heron, the Shuh-shuh-gah,
And the grouse, the Mushkodasa!"

If still further you should ask me,
Saying, "Who was Nawadaha?
Tell us of this Nawadaha,"
I should answer your inquiries
Straightway in such words as follow.

"In the vale of Tawasentha,
In the green and silent valley,
By the pleasant water-courses,
Dwelt the singer Nawadaha.
Round about the Indian village
Spread the meadows and the corn-fields,
And beyond them stood the forest,
Stood the groves of singing pine-trees,
Green in Summer, white in Winter,
Ever sighing, ever singing.

"And the pleasant water-courses,
You could trace them through the valley,
By the rushing in the Spring-time,
By the alders in the Summer,
By the white fog in the Autumn,
By the black line in the Winter;
And beside them dwelt the singer,
In the vale of Tawasentha,
In the green and silent valley.

"There he sang of Hiawatha,
Sang the Song of Hiawatha,
Sang his wondrous birth and being,
How he prayed and how he fasted,
How he lived, and toiled, and suffered,
That the tribes of men might prosper,
That he might advance his people!"

Ye who love the haunts of Nature,
Love the sunshine of the meadow,
Love the shadow of the forest,
Love the wind among the branches,
And the rain-shower and the snow-storm,
And the rushing of great rivers
Through their palisades of pine-trees,
And the thunder in the mountains,
Whose innumerable echoes

Flap like eagles in their eyries;—
Listen to these wild traditions,
To this Song of Hiawatha!
  Ye who love a nation's legends,
Love the ballads of a people,
That like voices from afar off
Call to us to pause and listen,
Speak in tones so plain and childlike,
Scarcely can the ear distinguish
Whether they are sung or spoken;—
Listen to this Indian Legend,
To this Song of Hiawatha!
  Ye whose hearts are fresh and simple,
Who have faith in God and Nature,
Who believe, that in all ages
Every human heart is human,
That in even savage bosoms
There are longings, yearnings, strivings
For the good they comprehend not,
That the feeble hands and helpless,
Groping blindly in the darkness,
Touch God's right hand in that darkness
And are lifted up and strengthened;—
Listen to this simple story,
To this Song of Hiawatha!
  Ye, who sometimes, in your rambles
Through the green lanes of the country,
Where the tangled barberry-bushes
Hang their tufts of crimson berries
Over stone walls gray with mosses,
Pause by some neglected graveyard,
For a while to muse, and ponder
On a half-effaced inscription,
Written with little skill of song-craft,
Homely phrases, but each letter
Full of hope and yet of heart-break,
Full of all the tender pathos
Of the Here and the Hereafter;—
Stay and read this rude inscription,
Read this Song of Hiawatha!

I

THE PEACE-PIPE

On the Mountains of the Prairie,
On the great Red Pipe-stone Quarry,
Gitche Manito, the mighty,
He the Master of Life, descending,
On the red crags of the quarry
Stood erect, and called the nations,
Called the tribes of men together.
From his footprints flowed a river,
Leaped into the light of morning,
O'er the precipice plunging downward
Gleamed like Ishkoodah, the comet.
And the Spirit, stooping earthward,
With his finger on the meadow
Traced a winding pathway for it,
Saying to it, "Run in this way!"
From the red stone of the quarry
With his hand he broke a fragment,
Moulded it into a pipe-head,
Shaped and fashioned it with figures;
From the margin of the river
Took a long reed for a pipe-stem,
With its dark green leaves upon it;
Filled the pipe with bark of willow,
With the bark of the red willow;
Breathed upon the neighboring forest,
Made its great boughs chafe together,
Till in flame they burst and kindled;
And erect upon the mountains,
Gitche Manito, the mighty,
Smoked the calumet, the Peace-Pipe,
As a signal to the nations.
And the smoke rose slowly, slowly,
Through the tranquil air of morning,
First a single line of darkness,
Then a denser, bluer vapor,
Then a snow-white cloud unfolding,

Like the tree-tops of the forest,
Ever rising, rising, rising,
Till it touched the top of heaven,
Till it broke against the heaven,
And rolled outward all around it.
From the Vale of Tawasentha,
From the Valley of Wyoming,
From the groves of Tuscaloosa,
From the far-off Rocky Mountains,
From the Northern lakes and rivers
All the tribes beheld the signal,
Saw the distant smoke ascending,
The Pukwana of the Peace-Pipe.
And the Prophets of the nations
Said: "Behold it, the Pukwana!
By this signal from afar off,
Bending like a wand of willow,
Waving like a hand that beckons,
Gitche Manito, the mighty,
Calls the tribes of men together,
Calls the warriors to his council!"
Down the rivers, o'er the prairies,
Came the warriors of the nations,
Came the Delawares and Mohawks,
Came the Choctaws and Camanches,
Came the Shoshonies and Blackfeet,
Came the Pawnees and Omahas,
Came the Mandans and Dacotahs,
Came the Hurons and Ojibways,
All the warriors drawn together
By the signal of the Peace-Pipe,
To the Mountains of the Prairie,
To the great Red Pipe-stone Quarry.
And they stood there on the meadow,
With their weapons and their war-gear,
Painted like the leaves of Autumn,
Painted like the sky of morning,
Wildly glaring at each other;
In their faces stern defiance,
In their hearts the feuds of ages,

The hereditary hatred,
The ancestral thirst of vengeance.
  Gitche Manito, the mighty,
The creator of the nations,
Looked upon them with compassion,
With paternal love and pity;
Looked upon their wrath and wrangling
But as quarrels among children,
But as feuds and fights of children!
  Over them he stretched his right hand,
To subdue their stubborn natures,
To allay their thirst and fever,
By the shadow of his right hand;
Spake to them with voice majestic
As the sound of far-off waters,
Falling into deep abysses,
Warning, chiding, spake in this wise:—
  "O my children! my poor children!
Listen to the words of wisdom,
Listen to the words of warning,
From the lips of the Great Spirit,
From the Master of Life, who made you!
  "I have given you lands to hunt in,
I have given you streams to fish in,
I have given you bear and bison,
I have given you roe and reindeer,
I have given you brant and beaver,
Filled the marshes full of wild-fowl,
Filled the rivers full of fishes;
Why then are you not contented?
Why then will you hunt each other?
  "I am weary of your quarrels,
Weary of your wars and bloodshed,
Weary of your prayers for vengeance,
Of your wranglings and dissensions;
All your strength is in your union,
All your danger is in discord;
Therefore be at peace henceforward,
And as brothers live together.
  "I will send a Prophet to you,

A Deliverer of the nations,
Who shall guide you and shall teach you,
Who shall toil and suffer with you.
If you listen to his counsels,
You will multiply and prosper;
If his warnings pass unheeded,
You will fade away and perish!
"Bathe now in the stream before you,
Wash the war-paint from your faces,
Wash the blood-stains from your fingers,
Bury your war-clubs and your weapons,
Break the red stone from this quarry,
Mould and make it into Peace-Pipes,
Take the reeds that grow beside you,
Deck them with your brightest feathers,
Smoke the calumet together,
And as brothers live henceforward!"
Then upon the ground the warriors
Threw their cloaks and shirts of deer-skin,
Threw their weapons and their war-gear,
Leaped into the rushing river,
Washed the war-paint from their faces.
Clear above them flowed the water,
Clear and limpid from the footprints
Of the Master of Life descending;
Dark below them flowed the water,
Soiled and stained with streaks of crimson,
As if blood were mingled with it!
From the river came the warriors,
Clean and washed from all their war-paint;
On the banks their clubs they buried,
Buried all their warlike weapons.
Gitche Manito, the mighty,
The Great Spirit, the creator,
Smiled upon his helpless children!
And in silence all the warriors
Broke the red stone of the quarry,
Smoothed and formed it into Peace-Pipes,
Broke the long reeds by the river,
Decked them with their brightest feathers,

And departed each one homeward,
While the Master of Life, ascending,
Through the opening of cloud-curtains,
Through the doorways of the heaven,
Vanished from before their faces,
In the smoke that rolled around him,
The Pukwana of the Peace-Pipe!

II

THE FOUR WINDS

"Honor be to Mudjekeewis!"
Cried the warriors, cried the old men,
When he came in triumph homeward
With the sacred Belt of Wampum,
From the regions of the North-Wind,
From the kingdom of Wabasso,
From the land of the White Rabbit.
He had stolen the Belt of Wampum
From the neck of Mishe-Mokwa,
From the Great Bear of the mountains,
From the terror of the nations,
As he lay asleep and cumbrous
On the summit of the mountains,
Like a rock with mosses on it,
Spotted brown and gray with mosses.
Silently he stole upon him
Till the red nails of the monster
Almost touched him, almost scared him,
Till the hot breath of his nostrils
Warmed the hands of Mudjekeewis,
As he drew the Belt of Wampum
Over the round ears, that heard not,
Over the small eyes, that saw not,
Over the long nose and nostrils,
The black muffle of the nostrils,
Out of which the heavy breathing
Warmed the hands of Mudjekeewis.
Then he swung aloft his war-club,

Shouted loud and long his war-cry,
Smote the mighty Mishe-Mokwa
In the middle of the forehead,
Right between the eyes he smote him.
With the heavy blow bewildered,
Rose the Great Bear of the mountains;
But his knees beneath him trembled,
And he whimpered like a woman,
As he reeled and staggered forward,
As he sat upon his haunches;
And the mighty Mudjekeewis,
Standing fearlessly before him,
Taunted him in loud derision,
Spake disdainfully in this wise:—
"Hark you, Bear! you are a coward,
And no Brave, as you pretended;
Else you would not cry and whimper
Like a miserable woman!
Bear! you know our tribes are hostile,
Long have been at war together;
Now you find that we are strongest,
You go sneaking in the forest,
You go hiding in the mountains!
Had you conquered me in battle
Not a groan would I have uttered;
But you, Bear! sit here and whimper,
And disgrace your tribe by crying,
Like a wretched Shaugodaya,
Like a cowardly old woman!"
Then again he raised his war-club,
Smote again the Mishe-Mokwa
In the middle of his forehead,
Broke his skull, as ice is broken
When one goes to fish in Winter.
Thus was slain the Mishe-Mokwa,
He the Great Bear of the mountains,
He the terror of the nations.
"Honor be to Mudjekeewis!"
With a shout exclaimed the people,
"Honor be to Mudjekeewis!

Henceforth he shall be the West-Wind,
And hereafter and forever
Shall he hold supreme dominion
Over all the winds of heaven.
Call him no more Mudjekeewis,
Call him Kabeyun, the West-Wind!"
  Thus was Mudjekeewis chosen
Father of the Winds of Heaven.
For himself he kept the West-Wind,
Gave the others to his children;
Unto Wabun gave the East-Wind,
Gave the South to Shawondasee,
And the North-Wind, wild and cruel,
To the fierce Kabibonokka.
  Young and beautiful was Wabun;
He it was who brought the morning,
He it was whose silver arrows
Chased the dark o'er hill and valley;
He it was whose cheeks were painted
With the brightest streaks of crimson,
And whose voice awoke the village,
Called the deer, and called the hunter.
  Lonely in the sky was Wabun;
Though the birds sang gayly to him,
Though the wild-flowers of the meadow
Filled the air with odors for him;
Though the forests and the rivers
Sang and shouted at his coming,
Still his heart was sad within him,
For he was alone in heaven.
  But one morning, gazing earthward,
While the village still was sleeping,
And the fog lay on the river,
Like a ghost, that goes at sunrise,
He beheld a maiden walking
All alone upon a meadow,
Gathering water-flags and rushes
By a river in the meadow.
  Every morning, gazing earthward,
Still the first thing he beheld there

Was her blue eyes looking at him,
Two blue lakes among the rushes.
And he loved the lonely maiden,
Who thus waited for his coming;
For they both were solitary,
She on earth and he in heaven.
  And he wooed her with caresses,
Wooed her with his smile of sunshine,
With his flattering words he wooed her,
With his sighing and his singing,
Gentlest whispers in the branches,
Softest music, sweetest odors,
Till he drew her to his bosom,
Folded in his robes of crimson,
Till into a star he changed her,
Trembling still upon his bosom;
And forever in the heavens
They are seen together walking,
Wabun and the Wabun-Annung,
Wabun and the Star of Morning.
  But the fierce Kabibonokka
Had his dwelling among icebergs,
In the everlasting snow-drifts,
In the kingdom of Wabasso,
In the land of the White Rabbit.
He it was whose hand in Autumn
Painted all the trees with scarlet,
Stained the leaves with red and yellow;
He it was who sent the snow-flakes,
Sifting, hissing through the forest,
Froze the ponds, the lakes, the rivers,
Drove the loon and sea-gull southward,
Drove the cormorant and curlew
To their nests of sedge and sea-tang
In the realms of Shawondasee.
  Once the fierce Kabibonokka
Issued from his lodge of snow-drifts,
From his home among the icebergs,
And his hair, with snow besprinkled,
Streamed behind him like a river,

Like a black and wintry river,
As he howled and hurried southward,
Over frozen lakes and moorlands.
  There among the reeds and rushes
Found he Shingebis, the diver,
Trailing strings of fish behind him,
O'er the frozen fens and moorlands,
Lingering still among the moorlands,
Though his tribe had long departed
To the land of Shawondasee.
  Cried the fierce Kabibonokka,
"Who is this that dares to brave me?
Dares to stay in my dominions,
When the Wawa has departed,
When the wild-goose has gone southward,
And the heron, the Shuh-shuh-gah,
Long ago departed southward?
I will go into his wigwam,
I will put his smouldering fire out!"
  And at night Kabibonokka
To the lodge came wild and wailing,
Heaped the snow in drifts about it,
Shouted down into the smoke-flue,
Shook the lodge-poles in his fury,
Flapped the curtain of the door-way.
Shingebis, the diver, feared not,
Shingebis, the diver, cared not;
Four great logs had he for firewood,
One for each moon of the winter,
And for food the fishes served him.
By his blazing fire he sat there,
Warm and merry, eating, laughing,
Singing, "O Kabibonokka,
You are but my fellow-mortal!"
  Then Kabibonokka entered,
And though Shingebis, the diver,
Felt his presence by the coldness,
Felt his icy breath upon him,
Still he did not cease his singing,
Still he did not leave his laughing,

Only turned the log a little,
Only made the fire burn brighter,
Made the sparks fly up the smoke-flue.
  From Kabibonokka's forehead,
From his snow-besprinkled tresses,
Drops of sweat fell fast and heavy,
Making dints upon the ashes,
As along the eaves of lodges,
As from drooping boughs of hemlock,
Drips the melting snow in spring-time,
Making hollows in the snow-drifts.
  Till at last he rose defeated,
Could not bear the heat and laughter,
Could not bear the merry singing,
But rushed headlong through the door way,
Stamped upon the crusted snow-drifts,
Stamped upon the lakes and rivers,
Made the snow upon them harder,
Made the ice upon them thicker,
Challenged Shingebis, the diver,
To come forth and wrestle with him,
To come forth and wrestle naked
On the frozen fens and moorlands.
  Forth went Shingebis, the diver,
Wrestled all night with the North-Wind,
Wrestled naked on the moorlands
With the fierce Kabibonokka,
Till his panting breath grew fainter,
Till his frozen grasp grew feebler,
Till he reeled and staggered backward,
And retreated, baffled, beaten,
To the kingdom of Wabasso,
To the land of the White Rabbit,
Hearing still the gusty laughter,
Hearing Shingebis, the diver,
Singing, "O Kabibonokka,
You are but my fellow-mortal!"
  Shawondasee, fat and lazy,
Had his dwelling far to southward,
In the drowsy, dreamy sunshine,

In the never-ending Summer.
He it was who sent the wood-birds,
Sent the robin, the Opechee,
Sent the blue-bird, the Owaissa,
Sent the Shawshaw, sent the swallow,
Sent the wild-goose, Wawa, northward,
Sent the melons and tobacco,
And the grapes in purple clusters.
  From his pipe the smoke ascending
Filled the sky with haze and vapor,
Filled the air with dreamy softness,
Gave a twinkle to the water,
Touched the rugged hills with smoothness,
Brought the tender Indian Summer
To the melancholy north-land,
In the dreary Moon of Snow-shoes.
  Listless, careless Shawondasee!
In his life he had one shadow,
In his heart one sorrow had he.
Once, as he was gazing northward,
Far away upon a prairie
He beheld a maiden standing,
Saw a tall and slender maiden
All alone upon a prairie;
Brightest green were all her garments,
And her hair was like the sunshine.
  Day by day he gazed upon her,
Day by day he sighed with passion,
Day by day his heart within him
Grew more hot with love and longing
For the maid with yellow tresses.
But he was too fat and lazy
To bestir himself and woo her.
Yes, too indolent and easy
To pursue her and persuade her;
So he only gazed upon her,
Only sat and sighed with passion
For the maiden of the prairie.
  Till one morning, looking northward,

He beheld her yellow tresses
Changed and covered o'er with whiteness,
Covered as with whitest snow-flakes.
"Ah! my brother from the North-land,
From the kingdom of Wabasso,
From the land of the White Rabbit!
You have stolen the maiden from me,
You have laid your hand upon her,
You have wooed and won my maiden,
With your stories of the North-land!"
  Thus the wretched Shawondasee
Breathed into the air his sorrow;
And the South-Wind o'er the prairie
Wandered warm with sighs of passion,
With the sighs of Shawondasee,
Till the air seemed full of snow-flakes,
Full of thistle-down the prairie,
And the maid with hair like sunshine
Vanished from his sight forever;
Never more did Shawondasee
See the maid with yellow tresses!
  Poor, deluded Shawondasee!
'T was no woman that you gazed at,
'T was no maiden that you sighed for,
'T was the prairie dandelion
That through all the dreamy Summer
You had gazed at with such longing,
You had sighed for with such passion,
And had puffed away forever,
Blown into the air with sighing.
Ah! deluded Shawondasee!
  Thus the Four Winds were divided;
Thus the sons of Mudjekeewis
Had their stations in the heavens,
At the corners of the heavens;
For himself the West-Wind only
Kept the mighty Mudjekeewis.

III

HIAWATHA'S CHILDHOOD

Downward through the evening twilight,
In the days that are forgotten,
In the unremembered ages,
From the full moon fell Nokomis,
Fell the beautiful Nokomis,
She a wife, but not a mother.
  She was sporting with her women,
Swinging in a swing of grape-vines,
When her rival the rejected,
Full of jealousy and hatred,
Cut the leafy swing asunder,
Cut in twain the twisted grape-vines,
And Nokomis fell affrighted
Downward through the evening twilight,
On the Muskoday, the meadow,
On the prairie full of blossoms.
"See! a star falls!" said the people;
"From the sky a star is falling!"
  There among the ferns and mosses,
There among the prairie lilies,
On the Muskoday, the meadow,
In the moonlight and the starlight,
Fair Nokomis bore a daughter.
And she called her name Wenonah,
As the first-born of her daughters.
And the daughter of Nokomis
Grew up like the prairie lilies,
Grew a tall and slender maiden,
With the beauty of the moonlight,
With the beauty of the starlight.
  And Nokomis warned her often,
Saying oft, and oft repeating,
"Oh, beware of Mudjekeewis,
Of the West-Wind, Mudjekeewis;
Listen not to what he tells you;
Lie not down upon the meadow,

Stoop not down among the lilies,
Lest the West-Wind come and harm you!"
But she heeded not the warning,
Heeded not those words of wisdom,
And the West-Wind came at evening,
Walking lightly o'er the prairie,
Whispering to the leaves and blossoms,
Bending low the flowers and grasses,
Found the beautiful Wenonah,
Lying there among the lilies,
Wooed her with his words of sweetness,
Wooed her with his soft caresses,
Till she bore a son in sorrow,
Bore a son of love and sorrow.
Thus was born my Hiawatha,
Thus was born the child of wonder;
But the daughter of Nokomis,
Hiawatha's gentle mother,
In her anguish died deserted
By the West-Wind, false and faithless,
By the heartless Mudjekeewis.
For her daughter long and loudly
Wailed and wept the sad Nokomis;
"Oh that I were dead!" she murmured,
"Oh that I were dead, as thou art!
No more work, and no more weeping,
Wahonowin! Wahonowin!"
By the shores of Gitche Gumee,
By the shining Big-Sea-Water,
Stood the wigwam of Nokomis,
Daughter of the Moon, Nokomis.
Dark behind it rose the forest,
Rose the black and gloomy pine-trees,
Rose the firs with cones upon them;
Bright before it beat the water,
Beat the clear and sunny water,
Beat the shining Big-Sea-Water.
There the wrinkled old Nokomis
Nursed the little Hiawatha,
Rocked him in his linden cradle,

Bedded soft in moss and rushes,
Safely bound with reindeer sinews;
Stilled his fretful wail by saying,
"Hush! the Naked Bear will hear thee!"
Lulled him into slumber, singing,
"Ewa-yea! my little owlet!
Who is this, that lights the wigwam?
With his great eyes lights the wigwam?
Ewa-yea! my little owlet!"
  Many things Nokomis taught him
Of the stars that shine in heaven;
Showed him Ishkoodah, the comet,
Ishkoodah, with fiery tresses;
Showed the Death-Dance of the spirits,
Warriors with their plumes and war-clubs,
Flaring far away to northward
In the frosty nights of Winter;
Showed the broad white road in heaven,
Pathway of the ghosts, the shadows,
Running straight across the heavens,
Crowded with the ghosts, the shadows.
  At the door on summer evenings
Sat the little Hiawatha;
Heard the whispering of the pine-trees,
Heard the lapping of the waters,
Sounds of music, words of wonder;
"Minne-wawa!" said the pine-trees,
"Mudway-aushka!" said the water.
  Saw the fire-fly, Wah-wah-taysee,
Flitting through the dusk of evening,
With the twinkle of its candle
Lighting up the brakes and bushes,
And he sang the song of children,
Sang the song Nokomis taught him:
"Wah-wah-taysee, little fire-fly,
Little, flitting, white-fire insect,
Little, dancing, white-fire creature,
Light me with your little candle,
Ere upon my bed I lay me,
Ere in sleep I close my eyelids!"

Saw the moon rise from the water
Rippling, rounding from the water,
Saw the flecks and shadows on it,
Whispered, "What is that, Nokomis?"
And the good Nokomis answered:
"Once a warrior, very angry,
Seized his grandmother, and threw her
Up into the sky at midnight;
Right against the moon he threw her;
'T is her body that you see there."
Saw the rainbow in the heaven,
In the eastern sky, the rainbow,
Whispered, "What is that, Nokomis?"
And the good Nokomis answered:
" 'T is the heaven of flowers you see there;
All the wild-flowers of the forest,
All the lilies of the prairie,
When on earth they fade and perish,
Blossom in that heaven above us."
When he heard the owls at midnight,
Hooting, laughing in the forest,
"What is that?" he cried in terror,
"What is that," he said, "Nokomis?"
And the good Nokomis answered:
"That is but the owl and owlet,
Talking in their native language,
Talking, scolding at each other."
Then the little Hiawatha
Learned of every bird its language,
Learned their names and all their secrets,
How they built their nests in Summer,
Where they hid themselves in Winter,
Talked with them whene'er he met them,
Called them "Hiawatha's Chickens."
Of all beasts he learned the language,
Learned their names and all their secrets,
How the beavers built their lodges,
Where the squirrels hid their acorns,
How the reindeer ran so swiftly,
Why the rabbit was so timid,

Talked with them whene'er he met them,
Called them "Hiawatha's Brothers."
Then Iagoo, the great boaster,
He the marvellous story-teller,
He the traveller and the talker,
He the friend of old Nokomis,
Made a bow for Hiawatha;
From a branch of ash he made it,
From an oak-bough made the arrows,
Tipped with flint, and winged with feathers,
And the cord he made of deer-skin.
Then he said to Hiawatha:
"Go, my son, into the forest,
Where the red deer herd together,
Kill for us a famous roebuck,
Kill for us a deer with antlers!"
Forth into the forest straightway
All alone walked Hiawatha
Proudly, with his bow and arrows;
And the birds sang round him, o'er him,
"Do not shoot us, Hiawatha!"
Sang the robin, the Opechee,
Sang the bluebird, the Owaissa,
"Do not shoot us, Hiawatha!"
Up the oak-tree, close beside him,
Sprang the squirrel, Adjidaumo,
In and out among the branches,
Coughed and chattered from the oak-tree,
Laughed, and said between his laughing,
"Do not shoot me, Hiawatha!"
And the rabbit from his pathway
Leaped aside, and at a distance
Sat erect upon his haunches,
Half in fear and half in frolic,
Saying to the little hunter,
"Do not shoot me, Hiawatha!"
But he heeded not, nor heard them,
For his thoughts were with the red deer;
On their tracks his eyes were fastened,
Leading downward to the river,

To the ford across the river,
And as one in slumber walked he.
  Hidden in the alder-bushes,
There he waited till the deer came,
Till he saw two antlers lifted,
Saw two eyes look from the thicket,
Saw two nostrils point to windward,
And a deer came down the pathway,
Flecked with leafy light and shadow.
And his heart within him fluttered,
Trembled like the leaves above him,
Like the birch-leaf palpitated,
As the deer came down the pathway.
  Then, upon one knee uprising,
Hiawatha aimed an arrow;
Scarce a twig moved with his motion,
Scarce a leaf was stirred or rustled,
But the wary roebuck started,
Stamped with all his hoofs together,
Listened with one foot uplifted,
Leaped as if to meet the arrow;
Ah! the singing, fatal arrow,
Like a wasp it buzzed and stung him!
  Dead he lay there in the forest,
By the ford across the river;
Beat his timid heart no longer,
But the heart of Hiawatha
Throbbed and shouted and exulted,
As he bore the red deer homeward,
And Iagoo and Nokomis
Hailed his coming with applauses.
  From the red deer's hide Nokomis
Made a cloak for Hiawatha,
From the red deer's flesh Nokomis
Made a banquet to his honor.
All the village came and feasted,
All the guests praised Hiawatha,
Called him Strong-Heart, Soan-ge-taha!
Called him Loon-Heart, Mahn-go-taysee!

IV

HIAWATHA AND MUDJEKEEWIS

Out of childhood into manhood
Now had grown my Hiawatha,
Skilled in all the craft of hunters,
Learned in all the lore of old men,
In all youthful sports and pastimes,
In all manly arts and labors.
Swift of foot was Hiawatha;
He could shoot an arrow from him,
And run forward with such fleetness,
That the arrow fell behind him!
Strong of arm was Hiawatha;
He could shoot ten arrows upward,
Shoot them with such strength and swiftness,
That the tenth had left the bow-string
Ere the first to earth had fallen!
He had mittens, Minjekahwun,
Magic mittens made of deer-skin;
When upon his hands he wore them,
He could smite the rocks asunder,
He could grind them into powder.
He had moccasins enchanted,
Magic moccasins of deer-skin;
When he bound them round his ankles,
When upon his feet he tied them,
At each stride a mile he measured!
Much he questioned old Nokomis
Of his father Mudjekeewis;
Learned from her the fatal secret
Of the beauty of his mother,
Of the falsehood of his father;
And his heart was hot within him,
Like a living coal his heart was.
Then he said to old Nokomis,
"I will go to Mudjekeewis,
See how fares it with my father,

At the doorways of the West-Wind,
At the portals of the Sunset!"
From his lodge went Hiawatha,
Dressed for travel, armed for hunting;
Dressed in deer-skin shirt and leggings,
Richly wrought with quills and wampum;
On his head his eagle-feathers,
Round his waist his belt of wampum,
In his hand his bow of ash-wood,
Strung with sinews of the reindeer;
In his quiver oaken arrows,
Tipped with jasper, winged with feathers;
With his mittens, Minjekahwun,
With his moccasins enchanted.
Warning said the old Nokomis,
"Go not forth, O Hiawatha!
To the kingdom of the West-Wind,
To the realms of Mudjekeewis,
Lest he harm you with his magic,
Lest he kill you with his cunning!"
But the fearless Hiawatha
Heeded not her woman's warning;
Forth he strode into the forest,
At each stride a mile he measured;
Lurid seemed the sky above him,
Lurid seemed the earth beneath him,
Hot and close the air around him,
Filled with smoke and fiery vapors,
As of burning woods and prairies,
For his heart was hot within him,
Like a living coal his heart was.
So he journeyed westward, westward,
Left the fleetest deer behind him,
Left the antelope and bison;
Crossed the rushing Esconaba,
Crossed the mighty Mississippi,
Passed the Mountains of the Prairie,
Passed the land of Crows and Foxes,
Passed the dwellings of the Blackfeet,

Came unto the Rocky Mountains,
To the kingdom of the West-Wind,
Where upon the gusty summits
Sat the ancient Mudjekeewis,
Ruler of the winds of heaven.
  Filled with awe was Hiawatha
At the aspect of his father.
On the air about him wildly
Tossed and streamed his cloudy tresses,
Gleamed like drifting snow his tresses,
Glared like Ishkoodah, the comet,
Like the star with fiery tresses.
  Filled with joy was Mudjekeewis
When he looked on Hiawatha,
Saw his youth rise up before him
In the face of Hiawatha,
Saw the beauty of Wenonah
From the grave rise up before him.
  "Welcome!" said he, "Hiawatha,
To the kingdom of the West-Wind!
Long have I been waiting for you!
Youth is lovely, age is lonely,
Youth is fiery, age is frosty;
You bring back the days departed,
You bring back my youth of passion,
And the beautiful Wenonah!"
  Many days they talked together,
Questioned, listened, waited, answered;
Much the mighty Mudjekeewis
Boasted of his ancient prowess,
Of his perilous adventures,
His indomitable courage,
His invulnerable body.
  Patiently sat Hiawatha,
Listening to his father's boasting;
With a smile he sat and listened,
Uttered neither threat nor menace,
Neither word nor look betrayed him,
But his heart was hot within him,
Like a living coal his heart was.

Then he said, "O Mudjekeewis,
Is there nothing that can harm you?
Nothing that you are afraid of?"
And the mighty Mudjekeewis,
Grand and gracious in his boasting,
Answered, saying, "There is nothing,
Nothing but the black rock yonder,
Nothing but the fatal Wawbeek!"
And he looked at Hiawatha
With a wise look and benignant,
With a countenance paternal,
Looked with pride upon the beauty
Of his tall and graceful figure,
Saying, "O my Hiawatha!
Is there anything can harm you?
Anything you are afraid of?"
But the wary Hiawatha
Paused awhile, as if uncertain,
Held his peace, as if resolving,
And then answered, "There is nothing,
Nothing but the bulrush yonder,
Nothing but the great Apukwa!"
And as Mudjekeewis, rising,
Stretched his hand to pluck the bulrush,
Hiawatha cried in terror,
Cried in well-dissembled terror,
"Kago! kago! do not touch it!"
"Ah, kaween!" said Mudjekeewis,
"No indeed, I will not touch it!"
Then they talked of other matters;
First of Hiawatha's brothers,
First of Wabun, of the East-Wind,
Of the South-Wind, Shawondasee,
Of the North, Kabibonokka;
Then of Hiawatha's mother,
Of the beautiful Wenonah,
Of her birth upon the meadow,
Of her death, as old Nokomis
Had remembered and related.
And he cried, "O Mudjekeewis,

It was you who killed Wenonah,
Took her young life and her beauty,
Broke the Lily of the Prairie,
Trampled it beneath your footsteps;
You confess it! you confess it!"
And the mighty Mudjekeewis
Tossed upon the wind his tresses,
Bowed his hoary head in anguish,
With a silent nod assented.
  Then up started Hiawatha,
And with threatening look and gesture
Laid his hand upon the black rock,
On the fatal Wawbeek laid it,
With his mittens, Minjekahwun,
Rent the jutting crag asunder,
Smote and crushed it into fragments,
Hurled them madly at his father,
The remorseful Mudjekeewis,
For his heart was hot within him,
Like a living coal his heart was.
  But the ruler of the West-Wind
Blew the fragments backward from him,
With the breathing of his nostrils,
With the tempest of his anger,
Blew them back at his assailant;
Seized the bulrush, the Apukwa,
Dragged it with its roots and fibres
From the margin of the meadow,
From its ooze the giant bulrush;
Long and loud laughed Hiawatha!
  Then began the deadly conflict,
Hand to hand among the mountains;
From his eyry screamed the eagle,
The Keneu, the great war-eagle,
Sat upon the crags around them,
Wheeling flapped his wings above them.
  Like a tall tree in the tempest
Bent and lashed the giant bulrush;
And in masses huge and heavy

Crashing fell the fatal Wawbeek;
Till the earth shook with the tumult
And confusion of the battle,
And the air was full of shoutings,
And the thunder of the mountains,
Starting, answered, "Baim-wawa!"
  Back retreated Mudjekeewis,
Rushing westward o'er the mountains,
Stumbling westward down the mountains,
Three whole days retreated fighting,
Still pursued by Hiawatha
To the doorways of the West-Wind,
To the portals of the Sunset,
To the earth's remotest border,
Where into the empty spaces
Sinks the sun, as a flamingo
Drops into her nest at nightfall
In the melancholy marshes.
  "Hold!" at length cried Mudjekeewis,
"Hold, my son, my Hiawatha!
'T is impossible to kill me,
For you cannot kill the immortal.
I have put you to this trial,
But to know and prove your courage;
Now receive the prize of valor!
  "Go back to your home and people,
Live among them, toil among them,
Cleanse the earth from all that harms it,
Clear the fishing-grounds and rivers,
Slay all monsters and magicians,
All the Wendigoes, the giants,
All the serpents, the Kenabeeks,
As I slew the Mishe-Mokwa,
Slew the Great Bear of the mountains.
  "And at last when Death draws near you,
When the awful eyes of Pauguk
Glare upon you in the darkness,
I will share my kingdom with you,
Ruler shall you be thenceforward

Of the Northwest-Wind, Keewaydin,
Of the home-wind, the Keewaydin."
  Thus was fought that famous battle
In the dreadful days of Shah-shah,
In the days long since departed,
In the kingdom of the West-Wind.
Still the hunter sees its traces
Scattered far o'er hill and valley;
Sees the giant bulrush growing
By the ponds and water-courses,
Sees the masses of the Wawbeek
Lying still in every valley.
  Homeward now went Hiawatha;
Pleasant was the landscape round him,
Pleasant was the air above him,
For the bitterness of anger
Had departed wholly from him,
From his brain the thought of vengeance,
From his heart the burning fever.
  Only once his pace he slackened,
Only once he paused or halted,
Paused to purchase heads of arrows
Of the ancient Arrow-maker,
In the land of the Dacotahs,
Where the Falls of Minnehaha
Flash and gleam among the oak-trees,
Laugh and leap into the valley.
  There the ancient Arrow-maker
Made his arrow-heads of sandstone,
Arrow-heads of chalcedony,
Arrow-heads of flint and jasper,
Smoothed and sharpened at the edges,
Hard and polished, keen and costly.
  With him dwelt his dark-eyed daughter,
Wayward as the Minnehaha,
With her moods of shade and sunshine,
Eyes that smiled and frowned alternate,
Feet as rapid as the river,
Tresses flowing like the water,
And as musical a laughter:

And he named her from the river,
From the water-fall he named her,
Minnehaha, Laughing Water.
  Was it then for heads of arrows,
Arrow-heads of chalcedony,
Arrow-heads of flint and jasper,
That my Hiawatha halted
In the land of the Dacotahs?
  Was it not to see the maiden,
See the face of Laughing Water
Peeping from behind the curtain,
Hear the rustling of her garments
From behind the waving curtain,
As one sees the Minnehaha
Gleaming, glancing through the branches,
As one hears the Laughing Water
From behind its screen of branches?
  Who shall say what thoughts and visions
Fill the fiery brains of young men?
Who shall say what dreams of beauty
Filled the heart of Hiawatha?
All he told to old Nokomis,
When he reached the lodge at sunset,
Was the meeting with his father,
Was his fight with Mudjekeewis;
Not a word he said of arrows,
Not a word of Laughing Water.

V

HIAWATHA'S FASTING

You shall hear how Hiawatha
Prayed and fasted in the forest,
Not for greater skill in hunting,
Not for greater craft in fishing,
Not for triumphs in the battle,
And renown among the warriors,
But for profit of the people,
For advantage of the nations.

First he built a lodge for fasting,
Built a wigwam in the forest,
By the shining Big-Sea-Water,
In the blithe and pleasant Spring-time,
In the Moon of Leaves he built it,
And, with dreams and visions many,
Seven whole days and nights he fasted.
On the first day of his fasting
Through the leafy woods he wandered;
Saw the deer start from the thicket,
Saw the rabbit in his burrow,
Heard the pheasant, Bena, drumming,
Heard the squirrel, Adjidaumo,
Rattling in his hoard of acorns,
Saw the pigeon, the Omeme,
Building nests among the pine-trees,
And in flocks the wild-goose, Wawa,
Flying to the fen-lands northward,
Whirring, wailing far above him.
"Master of Life!" he cried, desponding,
"Must our lives depend on these things?"
On the next day of his fasting
By the river's brink he wandered,
Through the Muskoday, the meadow,
Saw the wild rice, Mahnomonee,
Saw the blueberry, Meenahga,
And the strawberry, Odahmin,
And the gooseberry, Shahbomin,
And the grape-vine, the Bemahgut,
Trailing o'er the alder-branches,
Filling all the air with fragrance!
"Master of Life!" he cried, desponding,
"Must our lives depend on these things?"
On the third day of his fasting
By the lake he sat and pondered,
By the still, transparent water;
Saw the sturgeon, Nahma, leaping,
Scattering drops like beads of wampum,
Saw the yellow perch, the Sahwa,
Like a sunbeam in the water,

Saw the pike, the Maskenozha,
And the herring, Okahahwis,
And the Shawgashee, the craw-fish!
"Master of Life!" he cried, desponding,
"Must our lives depend on these things?"
On the fourth day of his fasting
In his lodge he lay exhausted;
From his couch of leaves and branches
Gazing with half-open eyelids,
Full of shadowy dreams and visions,
On the dizzy, swimming landscape,
On the gleaming of the water,
On the splendor of the sunset.
And he saw a youth approaching,
Dressed in garments green and yellow,
Coming through the purple twilight,
Through the splendor of the sunset;
Plumes of green bent o'er his forehead,
And his hair was soft and golden.
Standing at the open doorway,
Long he looked at Hiawatha,
Looked with pity and compassion
On his wasted form and features,
And, in accents like the sighing
Of the South-Wind in the tree-tops,
Said he, "O my Hiawatha!
All your prayers are heard in heaven,
For you pray not like the others;
Not for greater skill in hunting,
Not for greater craft in fishing,
Not for triumph in the battle,
Nor renown among the warriors,
But for profit of the people,
For advantage of the nations.
"From the Master of Life descending,
I, the friend of man, Mondamin,
Come to warn you and instruct you,
How by struggle and by labor
You shall gain what you have prayed for.
Rise up from your bed of branches,

Rise, O youth, and wrestle with me!"
  Faint with famine, Hiawatha
Started from his bed of branches,
From the twilight of his wigwam
Forth into the flush of sunset
Came, and wrestled with Mondamin;
At his touch he felt new courage
Throbbing in his brain and bosom,
Felt new life and hope and vigor
Run through every nerve and fibre.
  So they wrestled there together
In the glory of the sunset,
And the more they strove and struggled,
Stronger still grew Hiawatha;
Till the darkness fell around them,
And the heron, the Shuh-shuh-gah,
From her nest among the pine-trees,
Gave a cry of lamentation,
Gave a scream of pain and famine.
  " 'T is enough!" then said Mondamin,
Smiling upon Hiawatha,
"But to-morrow, when the sun sets,
I will come again to try you."
And he vanished, and was seen not;
Whether sinking as the rain sinks,
Whether rising as the mists rise,
Hiawatha saw not, knew not,
Only saw that he had vanished,
Leaving him alone and fainting,
With the misty lake below him,
And the reeling stars above him.
  On the morrow and the next day,
When the sun through heaven descending,
Like a red and burning cinder
From the hearth of the Great Spirit,
Fell into the western waters,
Came Mondamin for the trial,
For the strife with Hiawatha;
Came as silent as the dew comes,
From the empty air appearing,

Into empty air returning,
Taking shape when earth it touches,
But invisible to all men
In its coming and its going.
  Thrice they wrestled there together
In the glory of the sunset,
Till the darkness fell around them,
Till the heron, the Shuh-shuh-gah,
From her nest among the pine-trees,
Uttered her loud cry of famine,
And Mondamin paused to listen.
  Tall and beautiful he stood there,
In his garments green and yellow;
To and fro his plumes above him
Waved and nodded with his breathing,
And the sweat of the encounter
Stood like drops of dew upon him.
  And he cried, "O Hiawatha!
Bravely have you wrestled with me,
Thrice have wrestled stoutly with me,
And the Master of Life, who sees us,
He will give to you the triumph!"
  Then he smiled, and said: "To-morrow
Is the last day of your conflict,
Is the last day of your fasting.
You will conquer and o'ercome me;
Make a bed for me to lie in,
Where the rain may fall upon me,
Where the sun may come and warm me;
Strip these garments, green and yellow,
Strip this nodding plumage from me,
Lay me in the earth, and make it
Soft and loose and light above me.
  "Let no hand disturb my slumber,
Let no weed nor worm molest me,
Let not Kahgahgee, the raven,
Come to haunt me and molest me,
Only come yourself to watch me,
Till I wake, and start, and quicken,
Till I leap into the sunshine."

And thus saying, he departed;
Peacefully slept Hiawatha,
But he heard the Wawonaissa,
Heard the whippoorwill complaining,
Perched upon his lonely wigwam;
Heard the rushing Sebowisha,
Heard the rivulet rippling near him,
Talking to the darksome forest;
Heard the sighing of the branches,
As they lifted and subsided
At the passing of the night-wind,
Heard them, as one hears in slumber
Far-off murmurs, dreamy whispers:
Peacefully slept Hiawatha.

On the morrow came Nokomis,
On the seventh day of his fasting,
Came with food for Hiawatha,
Came imploring and bewailing,
Lest his hunger should o'ercome him,
Lest his fasting should be fatal.

But he tasted not, and touched not,
Only said to her, "Nokomis,
Wait until the sun is setting,
Till the darkness falls around us,
Till the heron, the Shuh-shuh-gah,
Crying from the desolate marshes,
Tells us that the day is ended."

Homeward weeping went Nokomis,
Sorrowing for her Hiawatha,
Fearing lest his strength should fail him,
Lest his fasting should be fatal.
He meanwhile sat weary waiting
For the coming of Mondamin,
Till the shadows, pointing eastward,
Lengthened over field and forest,
Till the sun dropped from the heaven,
Floating on the waters westward,
As a red leaf in the Autumn
Falls and floats upon the water,
Falls and sinks into its bosom.

And behold! the young Mondamin,
With his soft and shining tresses,
With his garments green and yellow,
With his long and glossy plumage,
Stood and beckoned at the doorway.
And as one in slumber walking,
Pale and haggard, but undaunted,
From the wigwam Hiawatha
Came and wrestled with Mondamin.
Round about him spun the landscape,
Sky and forest reeled together,
And his strong heart leaped within him,
As the sturgeon leaps and struggles
In a net to break its meshes.
Like a ring of fire around him
Blazed and flared the red horizon,
And a hundred suns seemed looking
At the combat of the wrestlers.
Suddenly upon the greensward
All alone stood Hiawatha,
Panting with his wild exertion,
Palpitating with the struggle;
And before him breathless, lifeless,
Lay the youth, with hair dishevelled,
Plumage torn, and garments tattered,
Dead he lay there in the sunset.
And victorious Hiawatha
Made the grave as he commanded,
Stripped the garments from Mondamin,
Stripped his tattered plumage from him,
Laid him in the earth, and made it
Soft and loose and light above him;
And the heron, the Shuh-shuh-gah,
From the melancholy moorlands,
Gave a cry of lamentation,
Gave a cry of pain and anguish!
Homeward then went Hiawatha
To the lodge of old Nokomis,
And the seven days of his fasting
Were accomplished and completed.

But the place was not forgotten
Where he wrestled with Mondamin;
Nor forgotten nor neglected
Was the grave where lay Mondamin,
Sleeping in the rain and sunshine,
Where his scattered plumes and garments
Faded in the rain and sunshine.
  Day by day did Hiawatha
Go to wait and watch beside it;
Kept the dark mould soft above it,
Kept it clean from weeds and insects,
Drove away, with scoffs and shoutings,
Kahgahgee, the king of ravens.
  Till at length a small green feather
From the earth shot slowly upward,
Then another and another,
And before the Summer ended
Stood the maize in all its beauty,
With its shining robes about it,
And its long, soft, yellow tresses;
And in rapture Hiawatha
Cried aloud, "It is Mondamin!
Yes, the friend of man, Mondamin!"
  Then he called to old Nokomis
And Iagoo, the great boaster,
Showed them where the maize was growing,
Told them of his wondrous vision,
Of his wrestling and his triumph,
Of this new gift to the nations,
Which should be their food forever.
  And still later, when the Autumn
Changed the long, green leaves to yellow,
And the soft and juicy kernels
Grew like wampum hard and yellow,
Then the ripened ears he gathered,
Stripped the withered husks from off them,
As he once had stripped the wrestler,
Gave the first Feast of Mondamin,
And made known unto the people
This new gift of the Great Spirit.

VI

HIAWATHA'S FRIENDS

Two good friends had Hiawatha,
Singled out from all the others,
Bound to him in closest union,
And to whom he gave the right hand
Of his heart, in joy and sorrow;
Chibiabos, the musician,
And the very strong man, Kwasind.
  Straight between them ran the pathway,
Never grew the grass upon it;
Singing birds, that utter falsehoods,
Story-tellers, mischief-makers,
Found no eager ear to listen,
Could not breed ill-will between them,
For they kept each other's counsel,
Spake with naked hearts together,
Pondering much and much contriving
How the tribes of men might prosper.
  Most beloved by Hiawatha
Was the gentle Chibiabos,
He the best of all musicians,
He the sweetest of all singers.
Beautiful and childlike was he,
Brave as man is, soft as woman,
Pliant as a wand of willow,
Stately as a deer with antlers.
  When he sang, the village listened;
All the warriors gathered round him,
All the women came to hear him;
Now he stirred their souls to passion,
Now he melted them to pity.
  From the hollow reeds he fashioned
Flutes so musical and mellow,
That the brook, the Sebowisha,
Ceased to murmur in the woodland,
That the wood-birds ceased from singing,
And the squirrel, Adjidaumo,
Ceased his chatter in the oak-tree,

And the rabbit, the Wabasso,
Sat upright to look and listen.
Yes, the brook, the Sebowisha,
Pausing, said, "O Chibiabos,
Teach my waves to flow in music,
Softly as your words in singing!"
Yes, the bluebird, the Owaissa,
Envious, said, "O Chibiabos,
Teach me tones as wild and wayward,
Teach me songs as full of frenzy!"
Yes, the robin, the Opechee,
Joyous, said, "O Chibiabos,
Teach me tones as sweet and tender,
Teach me songs as full of gladness!"
And the whippoorwill, Wawonaissa,
Sobbing, said, "O Chibiabos,
Teach me tones as melancholy,
Teach me songs as full of sadness!"
All the many sounds of nature
Borrowed sweetness from his singing;
All the hearts of men were softened
By the pathos of his music;
For he sang of peace and freedom,
Sang of beauty, love, and longing;
Sang of death, and life undying
In the Islands of the Blessed,
In the kingdom of Ponemah,
In the land of the Hereafter.
Very dear to Hiawatha
Was the gentle Chibiabos,
He the best of all musicians,
He the sweetest of all singers;
For his gentleness he loved him,
And the magic of his singing.
Dear, too, unto Hiawatha
Was the very strong man, Kwasind,
He the strongest of all mortals,
He the mightiest among many;
For his very strength he loved him,
For his strength allied to goodness.

Idle in his youth was Kwasind,
Very listless, dull, and dreamy,
Never played with other children,
Never fished and never hunted,
Not like other children was he;
But they saw that much he fasted,
Much his Manito entreated,
Much besought his Guardian Spirit.
"Lazy Kwasind!" said his mother,
"In my work you never help me!
In the Summer you are roaming
Idly in the fields and forests;
In the Winter you are cowering
O'er the firebrands in the wigwam!
In the coldest days of Winter
I must break the ice for fishing;
With my nets you never help me!
At the door my nets are hanging,
Dripping, freezing with the water;
Go and wring them, Yenadizze!
Go and dry them in the sunshine!"
Slowly, from the ashes, Kwasind
Rose, but made no angry answer;
From the lodge went forth in silence,
Took the nets, that hung together,
Dripping, freezing at the doorway;
Like a wisp of straw he wrung them,
Like a wisp of straw he broke them,
Could not wring them without breaking,
Such the strength was in his fingers.
"Lazy Kwasind!" said his father,
"In the hunt you never help me;
Every bow you touch is broken,
Snapped asunder every arrow;
Yet come with me to the forest,
You shall bring the hunting homeward."
Down a narrow pass they wandered,
Where a brooklet led them onward,
Where the trail of deer and bison
Marked the soft mud on the margin,

Till they found all further passage
Shut against them, barred securely
By the trunks of trees uprooted,
Lying lengthwise, lying crosswise,
And forbidding further passage.
"We must go back," said the old man,
"O'er these logs we cannot clamber;
Not a woodchuck could get through them,
Not a squirrel clamber o'er them!"
And straightway his pipe he lighted,
And sat down to smoke and ponder.
But before his pipe was finished,
Lo! the path was cleared before him;
All the trunks had Kwasind lifted,
To the right hand, to the left hand,
Shot the pine-trees swift as arrows,
Hurled the cedars light as lances.
"Lazy Kwasind!" said the young men,
As they sported in the meadow:
"Why stand idly looking at us,
Leaning on the rock behind you?
Come and wrestle with the others,
Let us pitch the quoit together!"
Lazy Kwasind made no answer,
To their challenge made no answer,
Only rose, and slowly turning,
Seized the huge rock in his fingers,
Tore it from its deep foundation,
Poised it in the air a moment,
Pitched it sheer into the river,
Sheer into the swift Pauwating,
Where it still is seen in Summer.
Once as down that foaming river,
Down the rapids of Pauwating,
Kwasind sailed with his companions,
In the stream he saw a beaver,
Saw Ahmeek, the King of Beavers,
Struggling with the rushing currents,
Rising, sinking in the water.
Without speaking, without pausing,

Kwasind leaped into the river,
Plunged beneath the bubbling surface,
Through the whirlpools chased the beaver,
Followed him among the islands,
Stayed so long beneath the water,
That his terrified companions
Cried, "Alas! good-by to Kwasind!
We shall never more see Kwasind!"
But he reappeared triumphant,
And upon his shining shoulders
Brought the beaver, dead and dripping,
Brought the King of all the Beavers.
And these two, as I have told you,
Were the friends of Hiawatha,
Chibiabos, the musician,
And the very strong man, Kwasind.
Long they lived in peace together,
Spake with naked hearts together,
Pondering much and much contriving
How the tribes of men might prosper.

VII

HIAWATHA'S SAILING

"Give me of your bark, O Birch-tree!
Of your yellow bark, O Birch-tree!
Growing by the rushing river,
Tall and stately in the valley!
I a light canoe will build me,
Build a swift Cheemaun for sailing,
That shall float upon the river,
Like a yellow leaf in Autumn,
Like a yellow water-lily!
"Lay aside your cloak, O Birch-tree!
Lay aside your white-skin wrapper,
For the Summer-time is coming,
And the sun is warm in heaven,
And you need no white-skin wrapper!"
Thus aloud cried Hiawatha

In the solitary forest,
By the rushing Taquamenaw,
When the birds were singing gayly,
In the Moon of Leaves were singing,
And the sun, from sleep awaking,
Started up and said, "Behold me!
Gheezis, the great Sun, behold me!"
  And the tree with all its branches
Rustled in the breeze of morning,
Saying, with a sigh of patience,
"Take my cloak, O Hiawatha!"
  With his knife the tree he girdled;
Just beneath its lowest branches,
Just above the roots, he cut it,
Till the sap came oozing outward;
Down the trunk, from top to bottom,
Sheer he cleft the bark asunder,
With a wooden wedge he raised it,
Stripped it from the trunk unbroken.
  "Give me of your boughs, O Cedar!
Of your strong and pliant branches,
My canoe to make more steady,
Make more strong and firm beneath me!"
  Through the summit of the Cedar
Went a sound, a cry of horror,
Went a murmur of resistance;
But it whispered, bending downward,
"Take my boughs, O Hiawatha!"
  Down he hewed the boughs of cedar,
Shaped them straightway to a frame-work,
Like two bows he formed and shaped them,
Like two bended bows together.
  "Give me of your roots, O Tamarack!
Of your fibrous roots, O Larch-tree!
My canoe to bind together,
So to bind the ends together
That the water may not enter,
That the river may not wet me!"
  And the Larch, with all its fibres,
Shivered in the air of morning,

Touched his forehead with its tassels,
Said, with one long sigh of sorrow,
"Take them all, O Hiawatha!"
  From the earth he tore the fibres,
Tore the tough roots of the Larch-tree,
Closely sewed the bark together,
Bound it closely to the frame-work.
  "Give me of your balm, O Fir-tree!
Of your balsam and your resin,
So to close the seams together
That the water may not enter,
That the river may not wet me!"
  And the Fir-tree, tall and sombre,
Sobbed through all its robes of darkness,
Rattled like a shore with pebbles,
Answered wailing, answered weeping,
"Take my balm, O Hiawatha!"
  And he took the tears of balsam,
Took the resin of the Fir-tree,
Smeared therewith each seam and fissure,
Made each crevice safe from water.
  "Give me of your quills, O Hedgehog!
All your quills, O Kagh, the Hedgehog!
I will make a necklace of them,
Make a girdle for my beauty,
And two stars to deck her bosom!"
  From a hollow tree the Hedgehog
With his sleepy eyes looked at him,
Shot his shining quills, like arrows,
Saying with a drowsy murmur,
Through the tangle of his whiskers,
"Take my quills, O Hiawatha!"
  From the ground the quills he gathered,
All the little shining arrows,
Stained them red and blue and yellow,
With the juice of roots and berries;
Into his canoe he wrought them,
Round its waist a shining girdle,
Round its bows a gleaming necklace,
On its breast two stars resplendent.

Thus the Birch Canoe was builded
In the valley, by the river,
In the bosom of the forest;
And the forest's life was in it,
All its mystery and its magic,
All the lightness of the birch-tree,
All the toughness of the cedar,
All the larch's supple sinews;
And it floated on the river
Like a yellow leaf in Autumn,
Like a yellow water-lily.
Paddles none had Hiawatha,
Paddles none he had or needed,
For his thoughts as paddles served him,
And his wishes served to guide him;
Swift or slow at will he glided,
Veered to right or left at pleasure.
Then he called aloud to Kwasind,
To his friend, the strong man, Kwasind,
Saying, "Help me clear this river
Of its sunken logs and sand-bars."
Straight into the river Kwasind
Plunged as if he were an otter,
Dived as if he were a beaver,
Stood up to his waist in water,
To his arm-pits in the river,
Swam and shouted in the river,
Tugged at sunken logs and branches,
With his hands he scooped the sand-bars,
With his feet the ooze and tangle.
And thus sailed my Hiawatha
Down the rushing Taquamenaw,
Sailed through all its bends and windings,
Sailed through all its deeps and shallows,
While his friend, the strong man, Kwasind,
Swam the deeps, the shallows waded.
Up and down the river went they,
In and out among its islands,
Cleared its bed of root and sand-bar,
Dragged the dead trees from its channel,

Made its passage safe and certain,
Made a pathway for the people,
From its springs among the mountains,
To the waters of Pauwating,
To the bay of Taquamenaw.

VIII

HIAWATHA'S FISHING

Forth upon the Gitche Gumee,
On the shining Big-Sea-Water,
With his fishing-line of cedar,
Of the twisted bark of cedar,
Forth to catch the sturgeon Nahma,
Mishe-Nahma, King of Fishes,
In his birch canoe exulting
All alone went Hiawatha.
  Through the clear, transparent water
He could see the fishes swimming
Far down in the depths below him;
See the yellow perch, the Sahwa,
Like a sunbeam in the water,
See the Shawgashee, the craw-fish,
Like a spider on the bottom,
On the white and sandy bottom.
  At the stern sat Hiawatha,
With his fishing-line of cedar;
In his plumes the breeze of morning
Played as in the hemlock branches;
On the bows, with tail erected,
Sat the squirrel, Adjidaumo;
In his fur the breeze of morning
Played as in the prairie grasses.
  On the white sand of the bottom
Lay the monster Mishe-Nahma,
Lay the sturgeon, King of Fishes;
Through his gills he breathed the water,
With his fins he fanned and winnowed,
With his tail he swept the sand-floor.

There he lay in all his armor;
On each side a shield to guard him,
Plates of bone upon his forehead,
Down his sides and back and shoulders
Plates of bone with spines projecting!
Painted was he with his war-paints,
Stripes of yellow, red, and azure,
Spots of brown and spots of sable;
And he lay there on the bottom,
Fanning with his fins of purple,
As above him Hiawatha
In his birch canoe came sailing,
With his fishing-line of cedar.
"Take my bait," cried Hiawatha,
Down into the depths beneath him,
"Take my bait, O Sturgeon, Nahma!
Come up from below the water,
Let us see which is the stronger!"
And he dropped his line of cedar
Through the clear, transparent water,
Waited vainly for an answer,
Long sat waiting for an answer,
And repeating loud and louder,
"Take my bait, O King of Fishes!"
Quiet lay the sturgeon, Nahma,
Fanning slowly in the water,
Looking up at Hiawatha,
Listening to his call and clamor,
His unnecessary tumult,
Till he wearied of the shouting;
And he said to the Kenozha,
To the pike, the Maskenozha,
"Take the bait of this rude fellow,
Break the line of Hiawatha!"
In his fingers Hiawatha
Felt the loose line jerk and tighten;
As he drew it in, it tugged so
That the birch canoe stood endwise,
Like a birch log in the water,
With the squirrel, Adjidaumo,

Perched and frisking on the summit.
   Full of scorn was Hiawatha
When he saw the fish rise upward,
Saw the pike, the Maskenozha,
Coming nearer, nearer to him,
And he shouted through the water,
"Esa! esa! shame upon you!
You are but the pike, Kenozha,
You are not the fish I wanted,
You are not the King of Fishes!"
   Reeling downward to the bottom
Sank the pike in great confusion,
And the mighty sturgeon, Nahma,
Said to Ugudwash, the sun-fish,
To the bream, with scales of crimson,
"Take the bait of this great boaster,
Break the line of Hiawatha!"
   Slowly upward, wavering, gleaming,
Rose the Ugudwash, the sun-fish,
Seized the line of Hiawatha,
Swung with all his weight upon it,
Made a whirlpool in the water,
Whirled the birch canoe in circles,
Round and round in gurgling eddies,
Till the circles in the water
Reached the far-off sandy beaches,
Till the water-flags and rushes
Nodded on the distant margins.
   But when Hiawatha saw him
Slowly rising through the water,
Lifting up his disk refulgent,
Loud he shouted in derision,
"Esa! esa! shame upon you!
You are Ugudwash, the sun-fish,
You are not the fish I wanted,
You are not the King of Fishes!"
   Slowly downward, wavering, gleaming,
Sank the Ugudwash, the sun-fish,
And again the sturgeon, Nahma,
Heard the shout of Hiawatha,

Heard his challenge of defiance,
The unnecessary tumult,
Ringing far across the water.
From the white sand of the bottom
Up he rose with angry gesture,
Quivering in each nerve and fibre,
Clashing all his plates of armor,
Gleaming bright with all his war-paint;
In his wrath he darted upward,
Flashing leaped into the sunshine,
Opened his great jaws, and swallowed
Both canoe and Hiawatha.
Down into that darksome cavern
Plunged the headlong Hiawatha,
As a log on some black river
Shoots and plunges down the rapids,
Found himself in utter darkness,
Groped about in helpless wonder,
Till he felt a great heart beating,
Throbbing in that utter darkness.
And he smote it in his anger,
With his fist, the heart of Nahma,
Felt the mighty King of Fishes
Shudder through each nerve and fibre,
Heard the water gurgle round him
As he leaped and staggered through it,
Sick at heart, and faint and weary.
Crosswise then did Hiawatha
Drag his birch-canoe for safety,
Lest from out the jaws of Nahma,
In the turmoil and confusion,
Forth he might be hurled and perish.
And the squirrel, Adjidaumo,
Frisked and chatted very gayly,
Toiled and tugged with Hiawatha
Till the labor was completed.
Then said Hiawatha to him,
"O my little friend, the squirrel,
Bravely have you toiled to help me;
Take the thanks of Hiawatha,

And the name which now he gives you;
For hereafter and forever
Boys shall call you Adjidaumo,
Tail-in-air the boys shall call you!"
And again the sturgeon, Nahma,
Gasped and quivered in the water,
Then was still, and drifted landward
Till he grated on the pebbles,
Till the listening Hiawatha
Heard him grate upon the margin,
Felt him strand upon the pebbles,
Knew that Nahma, King of Fishes,
Lay there dead upon the margin.
Then he heard a clang and flapping,
As of many wings assembling,
Heard a screaming and confusion,
As of birds of prey contending,
Saw a gleam of light above him,
Shining through the ribs of Nahma,
Saw the glittering eyes of sea-gulls,
Of Kayoshk, the sea-gulls, peering,
Gazing at him through the opening,
Heard them saying to each other,
" 'T is our brother, Hiawatha!"
And he shouted from below them,
Cried exulting from the caverns:
"O ye sea-gulls! O my brothers!
I have slain the sturgeon, Nahma;
Make the rifts a little larger,
With your claws the openings widen,
Set me free from this dark prison,
And henceforward and forever
Men shall speak of your achievements,
Calling you Kayoshk, the sea-gulls,
Yes, Kayoshk, the Noble Scratchers!"
And the wild and clamorous sea-gulls
Toiled with beak and claws together,
Made the rifts and openings wider
In the mighty ribs of Nahma,
And from peril and from prison,

From the body of the sturgeon,
From the peril of the water,
They released my Hiawatha.
He was standing near his wigwam,
On the margin of the water,
And he called to old Nokomis,
Called and beckoned to Nokomis,
Pointed to the sturgeon, Nahma,
Lying lifeless on the pebbles,
With the sea-gulls feeding on him.
"I have slain the Mishe-Nahma,
Slain the King of Fishes!" said he;
"Look! the sea-gulls feed upon him,
Yes, my friends Kayoshk, the sea-gulls;
Drive them not away, Nokomis,
They have saved me from great peril
In the body of the sturgeon,
Wait until their meal is ended,
Till their craws are full with feasting,
Till they homeward fly, at sunset,
To their nests among the marshes;
Then bring all your pots and kettles,
And make oil for us in Winter."
And she waited till the sun set,
Till the pallid moon, the Night-sun,
Rose above the tranquil water,
Till Kayoshk, the sated sea-gulls,
From their banquet rose with clamor,
And across the fiery sunset
Winged their way to far-off islands,
To their nests among the rushes.
To his sleep went Hiawatha,
And Nokomis to her labor,
Toiling patient in the moonlight,
Till the sun and moon changed places,
Till the sky was red with sunrise,
And Kayoshk, the hungry sea-gulls,
Came back from the reedy islands,
Clamorous for their morning banquet.

Three whole days and nights alternate
Old Nokomis and the sea-gulls
Stripped the oily flesh of Nahma,
Till the waves washed through the rib-bones,
Till the sea-gulls came no longer,
And upon the sands lay nothing
But the skeleton of Nahma.

IX

HIAWATHA AND THE PEARL-FEATHER

On the shores of Gitche Gumee,
Of the shining Big-Sea-Water,
Stood Nokomis, the old woman,
Pointing with her finger westward,
O'er the water pointing westward,
To the purple clouds of sunset.
Fiercely the red sun descending
Burned his way along the heavens,
Set the sky on fire behind him,
As war-parties, when retreating,
Burn the prairies on their war-trail;
And the moon, the Night-sun, eastward,
Suddenly starting from his ambush,
Followed fast those bloody footprints,
Followed in that fiery war-trail,
With its glare upon his features.
And Nokomis, the old woman,
Pointing with her finger westward,
Spake these words to Hiawatha:
"Yonder dwells the great Pearl-Feather,
Megissogwon, the Magician,
Manito of Wealth and Wampum,
Guarded by his fiery serpents,
Guarded by the black pitch-water.
You can see his fiery serpents,
The Kenabeek, the great serpents,
Coiling, playing in the water;

You can see the black pitch-water
Stretching far away beyond them,
To the purple clouds of sunset!
  "He it was who slew my father,
By his wicked wiles and cunning,
When he from the moon descended,
When he came on earth to seek me.
He, the mightiest of Magicians,
Sends the fever from the marshes,
Sends the pestilential vapors,
Sends the poisonous exhalations,
Sends the white fog from the fen-lands,
Sends disease and death among us!
  "Take your bow, O Hiawatha,
Take your arrows, jasper-headed,
Take your war-club, Puggawaugun,
And your mittens, Minjekahwun,
And your birch-canoe for sailing,
And the oil of Mishe-Nahma,
So to smear its sides, that swiftly
You may pass the black pitch-water;
Slay this merciless magician,
Save the people from the fever
That he breathes across the fen-lands,
And avenge my father's murder!"
  Straightway then my Hiawatha
Armed himself with all his war-gear,
Launched his birch-canoe for sailing;
With his palm its sides he patted,
Said with glee, "Cheemaun, my darling,
O my Birch-canoe! leap forward,
Where you see the fiery serpents,
Where you see the black pitch-water!"
  Forward leaped Cheemaun exulting,
And the noble Hiawatha
Sang his war-song wild and woful,
And above him the war-eagle,
The Keneu, the great war-eagle,
Master of all fowls with feathers,
Screamed and hurtled through the heavens.

Soon he reached the fiery serpents,
The Kenabeek, the great serpents,
Lying huge upon the water,
Sparkling, rippling in the water,
Lying coiled across the passage,
With their blazing crests uplifted,
Breathing fiery fogs and vapors,
So that none could pass beyond them.
But the fearless Hiawatha
Cried aloud, and spake in this wise:
"Let me pass my way, Kenabeek,
Let me go upon my journey!"
And they answered, hissing fiercely,
With their fiery breath made answer:
"Back, go back! O Shaugodaya!
Back to old Nokomis, Faint-heart!"
Then the angry Hiawatha
Raised his mighty bow of ash-tree,
Seized his arrows, jasper-headed,
Shot them fast among the serpents;
Every twanging of the bow-string
Was a war-cry and a death-cry,
Every whizzing of an arrow
Was a death-song of Kenabeek.
Weltering in the bloody water,
Dead lay all the fiery serpents,
And among them Hiawatha
Harmless sailed, and cried exulting:
"Onward, O Cheemaun, my darling!
Onward to the black pitch-water!"
Then he took the oil of Nahma,
And the bows and sides anointed,
Smeared them well with oil, that swiftly
He might pass the black pitch-water.
All night long he sailed upon it,
Sailed upon that sluggish water,
Covered with its mould of ages,
Black with rotting water-rushes,
Rank with flags and leaves of lilies,
Stagnant, lifeless, dreary, dismal,

Lighted by the shimmering moonlight,
And by will-o'-the-wisps illumined,
Fires by ghosts of dead men kindled,
In their weary night-encampments.
  All the air was white with moonlight,
All the water black with shadow,
And around him the Suggema,
The mosquito, sang his war-song,
And the fire-flies, Wah-wah-taysee,
Waved their torches to mislead him;
And the bull-frog, the Dahinda,
Thrust his head into the moonlight,
Fixed his yellow eyes upon him,
Sobbed and sank beneath the surface;
And anon a thousand whistles,
Answered over all the fen-lands,
And the heron, the Shuh-shuh-gah,
Far off on the reedy margin,
Heralded the hero's coming.
  Westward thus fared Hiawatha,
Toward the realm of Megissogwon,
Toward the land of the Pearl-Feather,
Till the level moon stared at him,
In his face stared pale and haggard,
Till the sun was hot behind him,
Till it burned upon his shoulders,
And before him on the upland
He could see the Shining Wigwam
Of the Manito of Wampum,
Of the mightiest of Magicians.
  Then once more Cheemaun he patted,
To his birch-canoe said, "Onward!"
And it stirred in all its fibres,
And with one great bound of triumph
Leaped across the water-lilies,
Leaped through tangled flags and rushes,
And upon the beach beyond them
Dry-shod landed Hiawatha.
  Straight he took his bow of ash-tree,
On the sand one end he rested,

With his knee he pressed the middle,
Stretched the faithful bow-string tighter,
Took an arrow, jasper-headed,
Shot it at the Shining Wigwam,
Sent it singing as a herald,
As a bearer of his message,
Of his challenge loud and lofty:
"Come forth from your lodge, Pearl-Feather!
Hiawatha waits your coming!"
  Straightway from the Shining Wigwam
Came the mighty Megissogwon,
Tall of stature, broad of shoulder,
Dark and terrible in aspect,
Clad from head to foot in wampum,
Armed with all his warlike weapons,
Painted like the sky of morning,
Streaked with crimson, blue, and yellow,
Crested with great eagle-feathers,
Streaming upward, streaming outward.
  "Well I know you, Hiawatha!"
Cried he in a voice of thunder,
In a tone of loud derision.
"Hasten back, O Shaugodaya!
Hasten back among the women,
Back to old Nokomis, Faint-heart!
I will slay you as you stand there,
As of old I slew her father!"
  But my Hiawatha answered,
Nothing daunted, fearing nothing:
"Big words do not smite like war-clubs,
Boastful breath is not a bow-string,
Taunts are not so sharp as arrows,
Deeds are better things than words are,
Actions mightier than boastings!"
  Then began the greatest battle
That the sun had ever looked on,
That the war-birds ever witnessed.
All a Summer's day it lasted,
From the sunrise to the sunset;
For the shafts of Hiawatha

Harmless hit the shirt of wampum,
Harmless fell the blows he dealt it
With his mittens, Minjekahwun,
Harmless fell the heavy war-club;
It could dash the rocks asunder,
But it could not break the meshes
Of that magic shirt of wampum.
  Till at sunset Hiawatha,
Leaning on his bow of ash-tree,
Wounded, weary, and desponding,
With his mighty war-club broken,
With his mittens torn and tattered,
And three useless arrows only,
Paused to rest beneath a pine-tree,
From whose branches trailed the mosses,
And whose trunk was coated over
With the Dead-man's Moccasin-leather,
With the fungus white and yellow.
  Suddenly from the boughs above him
Sang the Mama, the woodpecker:
"Aim your arrows, Hiawatha,
At the head of Megissogwon,
Strike the tuft of hair upon it,
At their roots the long black tresses;
There alone can he be wounded!"
  Winged with feathers, tipped with jasper,
Swift flew Hiawatha's arrow,
Just as Megissogwon, stooping,
Raised a heavy stone to throw it.
Full upon the crown it struck him,
At the roots of his long tresses,
And he reeled and staggered forward,
Plunging like a wounded bison,
Yes, like Pezhekee, the bison,
When the snow is on the prairie.
  Swifter flew the second arrow,
In the pathway of the other,
Piercing deeper than the other,
Wounding sorer than the other;
And the knees of Megissogwon

Shook like windy reeds beneath him,
Bent and trembled like the rushes.
  But the third and latest arrow
Swiftest flew, and wounded sorest,
And the mighty Megissogwon
Saw the fiery eyes of Pauguk,
Saw the eyes of Death glare at him,
Heard his voice call in the darkness;
At the feet of Hiawatha
Lifeless lay the great Pearl-Feather,
Lay the mightiest of Magicians.
  Then the grateful Hiawatha
Called the Mama, the woodpecker,
From his perch among the branches
Of the melancholy pine-tree,
And, in honor of his service,
Stained with blood the tuft of feathers
On the little head of Mama;
Even to this day he wears it,
Wears the tuft of crimson feathers,
As a symbol of his service.
  Then he stripped the shirt of wampum
From the back of Megissogwon,
As a trophy of the battle,
As a signal of his conquest.
On the shore he left the body,
Half on land and half in water,
In the sand his feet were buried,
And his face was in the water.
And above him, wheeled and clamored
The Keneu, the great war-eagle,
Sailing round in narrower circles,
Hovering nearer, nearer, nearer.
  From the wigwam Hiawatha
Bore the wealth of Megissogwon,
All his wealth of skins and wampum,
Furs of bison and of beaver,
Furs of sable and of ermine,
Wampum belts and strings and pouches,
Quivers wrought with beads of wampum,

Filled with arrows, silver-headed.
  Homeward then he sailed exulting,
Homeward through the black pitch-water,
Homeward through the weltering serpents,
With the trophies of the battle,
With a shout and song of triumph.
  On the shore stood old Nokomis,
On the shore stood Chibiabos,
And the very strong man, Kwasind,
Waiting for the hero's coming,
Listening to his songs of triumph.
And the people of the village
Welcomed him with songs and dances,
Made a joyous feast, and shouted:
"Honor be to Hiawatha!
He has slain the great Pearl-Feather,
Slain the mightiest of magicians,
Him, who sent the fiery fever,
Sent the white fog from the fen-lands,
Sent disease and death among us!"
  Ever dear to Hiawatha
Was the memory of Mama!
And in token of his friendship,
As a mark of his remembrance,
He adorned and decked his pipe-stem
With the crimson tuft of feathers,
With the blood-red crest of Mama.
But the wealth of Megissogwon,
All the trophies of the battle,
He divided with his people,
Shared it equally among them.

X

HIAWATHA'S WOOING

"As unto the bow the cord is,
So unto the man is woman,
Though she bends him, she obeys him,
Though she draws him, yet she follows,

Useless each without the other!"
   Thus the youthful Hiawatha
Said within himself and pondered,
Much perplexed by various feelings,
Listless, longing, hoping, fearing,
Dreaming still of Minnehaha,
Of the lovely Laughing Water,
In the land of the Dacotahs.
   "Wed a maiden of your people,"
Warning said the old Nokomis;
"Go not eastward, go not westward,
For a stranger, whom we know not!
Like a fire upon the hearth-stone
Is a neighbor's homely daughter,
Like the starlight or the moonlight
Is the handsomest of strangers!"
   Thus dissuading spake Nokomis,
And my Hiawatha answered
Only this: "Dear old Nokomis,
Very pleasant is the firelight,
But I like the starlight better,
Better do I like the moonlight!"
   Gravely then said old Nokomis:
"Bring not here an idle maiden,
Bring not here a useless woman,
Hands unskilful, feet unwilling;
Bring a wife with nimble fingers,
Heart and hand that move together,
Feet that run on willing errands!"
   Smiling answered Hiawatha:
"In the land of the Dacotahs
Lives the Arrow-maker's daughter,
Minnehaha, Laughing Water,
Handsomest of all the women.
I will bring her to your wigwam,
She shall run upon your errands,
Be your starlight, moonlight, firelight,
Be the sunlight of my people!"
   Still dissuading said Nokomis:
"Bring not to my lodge a stranger

From the land of the Dacotahs!
Very fierce are the Dacotahs,
Often is there war between us,
There are feuds yet unforgotten,
Wounds that ache and still may open!"
  Laughing answered Hiawatha:
"For that reason, if no other,
Would I wed the fair Dacotah,
That our tribes might be united,
That old feuds might be forgotten,
And old wounds be healed forever!"
  Thus departed Hiawatha
To the land of the Dacotahs,
To the land of handsome women;
Striding over moor and meadow,
Through interminable forests,
Through uninterrupted silence.
  With his moccasins of magic,
At each stride a mile he measured;
Yet the way seemed long before him,
And his heart outran his footsteps;
And he journeyed without resting,
Till he heard the cataract's laughter,
Heard the Falls of Minnehaha
Calling to him through the silence.
"Pleasant is the sound!" he murmured,
"Pleasant is the voice that calls me!"
  On the outskirts of the forests,
'Twixt the shadow and the sunshine,
Herds of fallow deer were feeding,
But they saw not Hiawatha;
To his bow he whispered, "Fail not!"
To his arrow whispered, "Swerve not!"
Sent it singing on its errand,
To the red heart of the roebuck;
Threw the deer across his shoulder,
And sped forward without pausing.
  At the doorway of his wigwam
Sat the ancient Arrow-maker,
In the land of the Dacotahs,

Making arrow-heads of jasper,
Arrow-heads of chalcedony.
At his side, in all her beauty,
Sat the lovely Minnehaha,
Sat his daughter, Laughing Water,
Plaiting mats of flags and rushes;
Of the past the old man's thoughts were,
And the maiden's of the future.

He was thinking, as he sat there,
Of the days when with such arrows
He had struck the deer and bison,
On the Muskoday, the meadow;
Shot the wild goose, flying southward,
On the wing, the clamorous Wawa;
Thinking of the great war-parties,
How they came to buy his arrows,
Could not fight without his arrows.
Ah, no more such noble warriors
Could be found on earth as they were!
Now the men were all like women,
Only used their tongues for weapons!

She was thinking of a hunter,
From another tribe and country,
Young and tall and very handsome,
Who one morning, in the Spring-time,
Came to buy her father's arrows,
Sat and rested in the wigwam,
Lingered long about the doorway,
Looking back as he departed.
She had heard her father praise him,
Praise his courage and his wisdom;
Would he come again for arrows
To the Falls of Minnehaha?
On the mat her hands lay idle,
And her eyes were very dreamy.

Through their thoughts they heard a footstep,
Heard a rustling in the branches,
And with glowing cheek and forehead,
With the deer upon his shoulders,
Suddenly from out the woodlands

Hiawatha stood before them.
  Straight the ancient Arrow-maker
Looked up gravely from his labor,
Laid aside the unfinished arrow,
Bade him enter at the doorway,
Saying, as he rose to meet him,
"Hiawatha, you are welcome!"
  At the feet of Laughing Water
Hiawatha laid his burden,
Threw the red deer from his shoulders;
And the maiden looked up at him,
Looked up from her mat of rushes,
Said with gentle look and accent,
"You are welcome, Hiawatha!"
  Very spacious was the wigwam,
Made of deer-skins dressed and whitened,
With the Gods of the Dacotahs
Drawn and painted on its curtains,
And so tall the doorway, hardly
Hiawatha stooped to enter,
Hardly touched his eagle-feathers
As he entered at the doorway.
  Then uprose the Laughing Water,
From the ground fair Minnehaha,
Laid aside her mat unfinished,
Brought forth food and set before them,
Water brought them from the brooklet,
Gave them food in earthen vessels,
Gave them drink in bowls of bass-wood,
Listened while the guest was speaking,
Listened while her father answered,
But not once her lips she opened,
Not a single word she uttered.
  Yes, as in a dream she listened
To the words of Hiawatha,
As he talked of old Nokomis,
Who had nursed him in his childhood,
As he told of his companions,
Chibiabos, the musician,
And the very strong man, Kwasind,

And of happiness and plenty
In the land of the Ojibways,
In the pleasant land and peaceful.
"After many years of warfare,
Many years of strife and bloodshed,
There is peace between the Ojibways
And the tribe of the Dacotahs."
Thus continued Hiawatha,
And then added, speaking slowly,
"That this peace may last forever,
And our hands be clasped more closely,
And our hearts be more united,
Give me as my wife this maiden,
Minnehaha, Laughing Water,
Loveliest of Dacotah women!"
And the ancient Arrow-maker
Paused a moment ere he answered,
Smoked a little while in silence,
Looked at Hiawatha proudly,
Fondly looked at Laughing Water,
And made answer very gravely:
"Yes, if Minnehaha wishes;
Let your heart speak, Minnehaha!"
And the lovely Laughing Water
Seemed more lovely as she stood there,
Neither willing nor reluctant,
As she went to Hiawatha,
Softly took the seat beside him,
While she said, and blushed to say it,
"I will follow you, my husband!"
This was Hiawatha's wooing!
Thus it was he won the daughter
Of the ancient Arrow-maker,
In the land of the Dacotahs!
From the wigwam he departed,
Leading with him Laughing Water;
Hand in hand they went together,
Through the woodland and the meadow,
Left the old man standing lonely
At the doorway of his wigwam,

Heard the Falls of Minnehaha
Calling to them from the distance,
Crying to them from afar off,
"Fare thee well, O Minnehaha!"
  And the ancient Arrow-maker
Turned again unto his labor,
Sat down by his sunny doorway,
Murmuring to himself, and saying:
"Thus it is our daughters leave us,
Those we love, and those who love us!
Just when they have learned to help us,
When we are old and lean upon them,
Comes a youth with flaunting feathers,
With his flute of reeds, a stranger
Wanders piping through the village,
Beckons to the fairest maiden,
And she follows where he leads her,
Leaving all things for the stranger!"
  Pleasant was the journey homeward,
Through interminable forests,
Over meadow, over mountain,
Over river, hill, and hollow.
Short it seemed to Hiawatha,
Though they journeyed very slowly,
Though his pace he checked and slackened
To the steps of Laughing Water.
  Over wide and rushing rivers
In his arms he bore the maiden;
Light he thought her as a feather,
As the plume upon his head-gear;
Cleared the tangled pathway for her,
Bent aside the swaying branches,
Made at night a lodge of branches,
And a bed with boughs of hemlock,
And a fire before the doorway
With the dry cones of the pine-tree.
  All the travelling winds went with them,
O'er the meadows, through the forest;
All the stars of night looked at them,
Watched with sleepless eyes their slumber;

From his ambush in the oak-tree
Peeped the squirrel, Adjidaumo,
Watched with eager eyes the lovers;
And the rabbit, the Wabasso,
Scampered from the path before them,
Peering, peeping from his burrow,
Sat erect upon his haunches,
Watched with curious eyes the lovers.

Pleasant was the journey homeward!
All the birds sang loud and sweetly
Songs of happiness and heart's-ease;
Sang the bluebird, the Owaissa,
"Happy are you, Hiawatha,
Having such a wife to love you!"
Sang the robin, the Opechee,
"Happy are you, Laughing Water,
Having such a noble husband!"

From the sky the sun benignant
Looked upon them through the branches,
Saying to them, "O my children,
Love is sunshine, hate is shadow,
Life is checkered shade and sunshine,
Rule by love, O Hiawatha!"

From the sky the moon looked at them,
Filled the lodge with mystic splendors,
Whispered to them, "O my children,
Day is restless; night is quiet,
Man imperious, woman feeble;
Half is mine, although I follow;
Rule by patience, Laughing Water!"

Thus it was they journeyed homeward;
Thus it was that Hiawatha
To the lodge of old Nokomis
Brought the moonlight, starlight, firelight,
Brought the sunshine of his people,
Minnehaha, Laughing Water,
Handsomest of all the women
In the land of the Dacotahs,
In the land of handsome women.

XI

HIAWATHA'S WEDDING-FEAST

You shall hear how Pau-Puk-Keewis,
How the handsome Yenadizze
Danced at Hiawatha's wedding;
How the gentle Chibiabos,
He the sweetest of musicians,
Sang his songs of love and longing;
How Iagoo, the great boaster,
He the marvellous story-teller,
Told his tales of strange adventure,
That the feast might be more joyous,
That the time might pass more gayly,
And the guests be more contented.
  Sumptuous was the feast Nokomis
Made at Hiawatha's wedding;
All the bowls were made of bass-wood,
White and polished very smoothly,
All the spoons of horn of bison,
Black and polished very smoothly.
  She had sent through all the village
Messengers with wands of willow,
As a sign of invitation,
As a token of the feasting;
And the wedding guests assembled,
Clad in all their richest raiment,
Robes of fur and belts of wampum,
Splendid with their paint and plumage,
Beautiful with beads and tassels.
  First they ate the sturgeon, Nahma,
And the pike, the Maskenozha,
Caught and cooked by old Nokomis;
Then on pemican they feasted,
Pemican and buffalo marrow,
Haunch of deer and hump of bison,
Yellow cakes of the Mondamin,
And the wild rice of the river.
  But the gracious Hiawatha,
And the lovely Laughing Water,

And the careful old Nokomis,
Tasted not the food before them,
Only waited on the others,
Only served their guests in silence.
And when all the guests had finished,
Old Nokomis, brisk and busy,
From an ample pouch of otter,
Filled the red-stone pipes for smoking
With tobacco from the South-land,
Mixed with bark of the red willow,
And with herbs and leaves of fragrance.
Then she said, "O Pau-Puk-Keewis,
Dance for us your merry dances,
Dance the Beggar's Dance to please us,
That the feast may be more joyous,
That the time may pass more gayly,
And our guests be more contented!"
Then the handsome Pau-Puk-Keewis,
He the idle Yenadizze,
He the merry mischief-maker,
Whom the people called the Storm-Fool,
Rose among the guests assembled.
Skilled was he in sports and pastimes,
In the merry dance of snow-shoes,
In the play of quoits and ball-play;
Skilled was he in games of hazard,
In all games of skill and hazard,
Pugasaing, the Bowl and Counters,
Kuntassoo, the Game of Plum-stones.
Though the warriors called him Faint-Heart,
Called him coward, Shaugodaya,
Idler, gambler, Yenadizze,
Little heeded he their jesting,
Little cared he for their insults,
For the women and the maidens
Loved the handsome Pau-Puk-Keewis.
He was dressed in shirt of doeskin,
White and soft, and fringed with ermine,
All inwrought with beads of wampum;
He was dressed in deer-skin leggings,

Fringed with hedgehog quills and ermine,
And in moccasins of buck-skin,
Thick with quills and beads embroidered.
On his head were plumes of swan's down,
On his heels were tails of foxes,
In one hand a fan of feathers,
And a pipe was in the other.
  Barred with streaks of red and yellow,
Streaks of blue and bright vermilion,
Shone the face of Pau-Puk-Keewis.
From his forehead fell his tresses,
Smooth, and parted like a woman's,
Shining bright with oil, and plaited,
Hung with braids of scented grasses,
As among the guests assembled,
To the sound of flutes and singing,
To the sound of drums and voices,
Rose the handsome Pau-Puk-Keewis,
And began his mystic dances.
  First he danced a solemn measure,
Very slow in step and gesture,
In and out among the pine-trees,
Through the shadows and the sunshine,
Treading softly like a panther.
Then more swiftly and still swifter,
Whirling, spinning round in circles,
Leaping o'er the guests assembled,
Eddying round and round the wigwam,
Till the leaves went whirling with him,
Till the dust and wind together
Swept in eddies round about him.
  Then along the sandy margin
Of the lake, the Big-Sea-Water,
On he sped with frenzied gestures,
Stamped upon the sand, and tossed it
Wildly in the air around him;
Till the wind became a whirlwind,
Till the sand was blown and sifted
Like great snowdrifts o'er the landscape,
Heaping all the shores with Sand Dunes,

Sand Hills of the Nagow Wudjoo!
Thus the merry Pau-Puk-Keewis
Danced his Beggar's Dance to please them,
And, returning, sat down laughing
There among the guests assembled,
Sat and fanned himself serenely
With his fan of turkey-feathers.
Then they said to Chibiabos,
To the friend of Hiawatha,
To the sweetest of all singers,
To the best of all musicians,
"Sing to us, O Chibiabos!
Songs of love and songs of longing,
That the feast may be more joyous,
That the time may pass more gayly,
And our guests be more contented!"
And the gentle Chibiabos
Sang in accents sweet and tender,
Sang in tones of deep emotion,
Songs of love and songs of longing;
Looking still at Hiawatha,
Looking at fair Laughing Water,
Sang he softly, sang in this wise:
"Onaway! Awake, beloved!
Thou the wild-flower of the forest!
Thou the wild-bird of the prairie!
Thou with eyes so soft and fawn-like!
"If thou only lookest at me,
I am happy, I am happy,
As the lilies of the prairie,
When they feel the dew upon them!
"Sweet thy breath is as the fragrance
Of the wild-flowers in the morning,
As their fragrance is at evening,
In the Moon when leaves are falling.
"Does not all the blood within me
Leap to meet thee, leap to meet thee,
As the springs to meet the sunshine,
In the Moon when nights are brightest?
"Onaway! my heart sings to thee,

Sings with joy when thou art near me,
As the sighing, singing branches
In the pleasant Moon of Strawberries!
"When thou art not pleased, beloved,
Then my heart is sad and darkened,
As the shining river darkens
When the clouds drop shadows on it!
"When thou smilest, my beloved,
Then my troubled heart is brightened,
As in sunshine gleam the ripples
That the cold wind makes in rivers.
"Smiles the earth, and smile the waters,
Smile the cloudless skies above us,
But I lose the way of smiling
When thou art no longer near me!
"I myself, myself! behold me!
Blood of my beating heart, behold me!
Oh awake, awake, beloved!
Onaway! awake, beloved!"
Thus the gentle Chibiabos
Sang his song of love and longing;
And Iagoo, the great boaster,
He the marvellous story-teller,
He the friend of old Nokomis,
Jealous of the sweet musician,
Jealous of the applause they gave him,
Saw in all the eyes around him,
Saw in all their looks and gestures,
That the wedding guests assembled
Longed to hear his pleasant stories,
His immeasurable falsehoods.
Very boastful was Iagoo;
Never heard he an adventure
But himself had met a greater;
Never any deed of daring
But himself had done a bolder;
Never any marvellous story
But himself could tell a stranger.
Would you listen to his boasting,
Would you only give him credence,

No one ever shot an arrow
Half so far and high as he had;
Ever caught so many fishes,
Ever killed so many reindeer,
Ever trapped so many beaver!
None could run so fast as he could,
None could dive so deep as he could,
None could swim so far as he could;
None had made so many journeys,
None had seen so many wonders,
As this wonderful Iagoo,
As this marvellous story-teller!
Thus his name became a by-word
And a jest among the people;
And whene'er a boastful hunter
Praised his own address too highly,
Or a warrior, home returning,
Talked too much of his achievements,
All his hearers cried, "Iagoo!
Here's Iagoo come among us!"
He it was who carved the cradle
Of the little Hiawatha,
Carved its framework out of linden,
Bound it strong with reindeer sinews;
He it was who taught him later
How to make his bows and arrows,
How to make the bows of ash-tree,
And the arrows of the oak-tree.
So among the guests assembled
At my Hiawatha's wedding
Sat Iagoo, old and ugly,
Sat the marvellous story-teller.
And they said, "O good Iagoo,
Tell us now a tale of wonder,
Tell us of some strange adventure,
That the feast may be more joyous,
That the time may pass more gayly,
And our guests be more contented!"
And Iagoo answered straightway,
"You shall hear a tale of wonder,

You shall hear the strange adventures
Of Osseo, the Magician,
From the Evening Star descended."

XII

THE SON OF THE EVENING STAR

Can it be the sun descending
O'er the level plain of water?
Or the Red Swan floating, flying,
Wounded by the magic arrow,
Staining all the waves with crimson,
With the crimson of its life-blood,
Filling all the air with splendor,
With the splendor of its plumage?
Yes; it is the sun descending,
Sinking down into the water;
All the sky is stained with purple,
All the water flushed with crimson!
No; it is the Red Swan floating,
Diving down beneath the water;
To the sky its wings are lifted,
With its blood the waves are reddened!
Over it the Star of Evening
Melts and trembles through the purple,
Hangs suspended in the twilight.
No; it is a bead of wampum
On the robes of the Great Spirit
As he passes through the twilight,
Walks in silence through the heavens.
This with joy beheld Iagoo
And he said in haste: "Behold it!
See the sacred Star of Evening!
You shall hear a tale of wonder,
Hear the story of Osseo,
Son of the Evening Star, Osseo!
"Once, in days no more remembered,
Ages nearer the beginning,
When the heavens were closer to us,

And the Gods were more familiar,
In the North-land lived a hunter,
With ten young and comely daughters,
Tall and lithe as wands of willow;
Only Oweenee, the youngest,
She the wilful and the wayward,
She the silent, dreamy maiden,
Was the fairest of the sisters.
"All these women married warriors,
Married brave and haughty husbands;
Only Oweenee, the youngest,
Laughed and flouted all her lovers,
All her young and handsome suitors,
And then married old Osseo,
Old Osseo, poor and ugly,
Broken with age and weak with coughing,
Always coughing like a squirrel.
"Ah, but beautiful within him
Was the spirit of Osseo,
From the Evening Star descended,
Star of Evening, Star of Woman,
Star of tenderness and passion!
All its fire was in his bosom,
All its beauty in his spirit,
All its mystery in his being,
All its splendor in his language!
"And her lovers, the rejected,
Handsome men with belts of wampum,
Handsome men with paint and feathers,
Pointed at her in derision,
Followed her with jest and laughter.
But she said: 'I care not for you,
Care not for your belts of wampum,
Care not for your paint and feathers,
Care not for your jests and laughter;
I am happy with Osseo!'
"Once to some great feast invited,
Through the damp and dusk of evening,
Walked together the ten sisters,
Walked together with their husbands;

Slowly followed old Osseo,
With fair Oweenee beside him;
All the others chatted gayly,
These two only walked in silence.
  "At the western sky Osseo
Gazed intent, as if imploring,
Often stopped and gazed imploring
At the trembling Star of Evening,
At the tender Star of Woman;
And they heard him murmur softly,
'*Ah, showain nemeshin, Nosa!*
Pity, pity me, my father!'
  " 'Listen!' said the eldest sister,
'He is praying to his father!
What a pity that the old man
Does not stumble in the pathway,
Does not break his neck by falling!'
And they laughed till all the forest
Rang with their unseemly laughter.
  "On their pathway through the woodlands
Lay an oak, by storms uprooted,
Lay the great trunk of an oak-tree,
Buried half in leaves and mosses,
Mouldering, crumbling, huge and hollow.
And Osseo, when he saw it,
Gave a shout, a cry of anguish,
Leaped into its yawning cavern,
At one end went in an old man,
Wasted, wrinkled, old, and ugly;
From the other came a young man,
Tall and straight and strong and handsome.
  "Thus Osseo was transfigured,
Thus restored to youth and beauty;
But, alas for good Osseo,
And for Oweenee, the faithful!
Strangely, too, was she transfigured.
Changed into a weak old woman,
With a staff she tottered onward,
Wasted, wrinkled, old, and ugly!
And the sisters and their husbands

Laughed until the echoing forest
Rang with their unseemly laughter.
"But Osseo turned not from her,
Walked with slower step beside her,
Took her hand, as brown and withered
As an oak-leaf is in Winter,
Called her sweetheart, Nenemoosha,
Soothed her with soft words of kindness,
Till they reached the lodge of feasting,
Till they sat down in the wigwam,
Sacred to the Star of Evening,
To the tender Star of Woman.
"Wrapt in visions, lost in dreaming,
At the banquet sat Osseo;
All were merry, all were happy,
All were joyous but Osseo.
Neither food nor drink he tasted,
Neither did he speak nor listen,
But as one bewildered sat he,
Looking dreamily and sadly,
First at Oweenee, then upward
At the gleaming sky above them.
"Then a voice was heard, a whisper,
Coming from the starry distance,
Coming from the empty vastness,
Low, and musical, and tender;
And the voice said: 'O Osseo!
O my son, my best beloved!
Broken are the spells that bound you,
All the charms of the magician,
All the magic powers of evil;
Come to me; ascend, Osseo!
" 'Taste the food that stands before you:
It is blessed and enchanted,
It has magic virtues in it,
It will change you to a spirit.
All your bowls and all your kettles
Shall be wood and clay no longer;
But the bowls be changed to wampum,
And the kettles shall be silver;

They shall shine like shells of scarlet,
Like the fire shall gleam and glimmer.
" 'And the women shall no longer
Bear the dreary doom of labor,
But be changed to birds, and glisten
With the beauty of the starlight,
Painted with the dusky splendors
Of the skies and clouds of evening!'
"What Osseo heard as whispers,
What as words he comprehended,
Was but music to the others,
Music as of birds afar off,
Of the whippoorwill afar off,
Of the lonely Wawonaissa
Singing in the darksome forest.
"Then the lodge began to tremble,
Straight began to shake and tremble,
And they felt it rising, rising,
Slowly through the air ascending,
From the darkness of the tree-tops
Forth into the dewy starlight,
Till it passed the topmost branches;
And behold! the wooden dishes
All were changed to shells of scarlet!
And behold! the earthen kettles
All were changed to bowls of silver!
And the roof-poles of the wigwam
Were as glittering rods of silver,
And the roof of bark upon them
As the shining shards of beetles.
"Then Osseo gazed around him,
And he saw the nine fair sisters,
All the sisters and their husbands,
Changed to birds of various plumage.
Some were jays and some were magpies,
Others thrushes, others blackbirds;
And they hopped, and sang, and twittered,
Perked and fluttered all their feathers,
Strutted in their shining plumage,
And their tails like fans unfolded.

"Only Oweenee, the youngest,
Was not changed, but sat in silence,
Wasted, wrinkled, old, and ugly,
Looking sadly at the others;
Till Osseo, gazing upward,
Gave another cry of anguish,
Such a cry as he had uttered
By the oak-tree in the forest.
"Then returned her youth and beauty,
And her soiled and tattered garments
Were transformed to robes of ermine,
And her staff became a feather,
Yes, a shining silver feather!
"And again the wigwam trembled,
Swayed and rushed through airy currents,
Through transparent cloud and vapor,
And amid celestial splendors
On the Evening Star alighted,
As a snow-flake falls on snow-flake,
As a leaf drops on a river,
As the thistle-down on water.
"Forth with cheerful words of welcome
Came the father of Osseo,
He with radiant locks of silver,
He with eyes serene and tender.
And he said: 'My son, Osseo,
Hang the cage of birds you bring there,
Hang the cage with rods of silver,
And the birds with glistening feathers,
At the doorway of my wigwam.'
"At the door he hung the bird-cage,
And they entered in and gladly
Listened to Osseo's father,
Ruler of the Star of Evening,
As he said: 'O my Osseo!
I have had compassion on you,
Given you back your youth and beauty,
Into birds of various plumage
Changed your sisters and their husbands;
Changed them thus because they mocked you

In the figure of the old man,
In that aspect sad and wrinkled,
Could not see your heart of passion,
Could not see your youth immortal;
Only Oweenee, the faithful,
Saw your naked heart and loved you.
“ ‘In the lodge that glimmers yonder,
In the little star that twinkles
Through the vapors, on the left hand,
Lives the envious Evil Spirit,
The Wabeno, the magician,
Who transformed you to an old man.
Take heed lest his beams fall on you,
For the rays he darts around him
Are the power of his enchantment,
Are the arrows that he uses.’
“Many years, in peace and quiet,
On the peaceful Star of Evening
Dwelt Osseo with his father;
Many years, in song and flutter,
At the doorway of the wigwam,
Hung the cage with rods of silver,
And fair Oweenee, the faithful,
Bore a son unto Osseo,
With the beauty of his mother,
With the courage of his father.
“And the boy grew up and prospered,
And Osseo, to delight him,
Made him little bows and arrows,
Opened the great cage of silver,
And let loose his aunts and uncles,
All those birds with glossy feathers,
For his little son to shoot at.
“Round and round they wheeled and darted,
Filled the Evening Star with music,
With their songs of joy and freedom;
Filled the Evening Star with splendor,
With the fluttering of their plumage;
Till the boy, the little hunter,
Bent his bow and shot an arrow,

Shot a swift and fatal arrow,
And a bird, with shining feathers,
At his feet fell wounded sorely.
"But, O wondrous transformation!
'T was no bird he saw before him,
'T was a beautiful young woman,
With the arrow in her bosom!
"When her blood fell on the planet,
On the sacred Star of Evening,
Broken was the spell of magic,
Powerless was the strange enchantment,
And the youth, the fearless bowman,
Suddenly felt himself descending,
Held by unseen hands, but sinking
Downward through the empty spaces,
Downward through the clouds and vapors,
Till he rested on an island,
On an island, green and grassy,
Yonder in the Big-Sea-Water.
"After him he saw descending
All the birds with shining feathers,
Fluttering, falling, wafted downward,
Like the painted leaves of Autumn;
And the lodge with poles of silver,
With its roof like wings of beetles,
Like the shining shards of beetles,
By the winds of heaven uplifted,
Slowly sank upon the island,
Bringing back the good Osseo,
Bringing Oweenee, the faithful.
"Then the birds, again transfigured,
Reassumed the shape of mortals,
Took their shape, but not their stature;
They remained as Little People,
Like the pygmies, the Puk-Wudjies,
And on pleasant nights of Summer,
When the Evening Star was shining,
Hand in hand they danced together
On the island's craggy headlands,
On the sand-beach low and level.

"Still their glittering lodge is seen there,
On the tranquil Summer evenings,
And upon the shore the fisher
Sometimes hears their happy voices,
Sees them dancing in the starlight!"
When the story was completed,
When the wondrous tale was ended,
Looking round upon his listeners,
Solemnly Iagoo added:
'There are great men, I have known such,
Whom their people understand not,
Whom they even make a jest of,
Scoff and jeer at in derision.
From the story of Osseo
Let us learn the fate of jesters!"
All the wedding guests delighted
Listened to the marvellous story,
Listened laughing and applauding,
And they whispered to each other:
"Does he mean himself, I wonder?
And are we the aunts and uncles?"
Then again sang Chibiabos,
Sang a song of love and longing,
In those accents sweet and tender,
In those tones of pensive sadness,
Sang a maiden's lamentation
For her lover, her Algonquin.
"When I think of my beloved,
Ah me! think of my beloved,
When my heart is thinking of him,
O my sweetheart, my Algonquin!
"Ah me! when I parted from him,
Round my neck he hung the wampum,
As a pledge, the snow-white wampum,
O my sweetheart, my Algonquin!
"I will go with you, he whispered,
Ah me! to your native country;
Let me go with you, he whispered,
O my sweetheart, my Algonquin!
"Far away, away, I answered,

Very far away, I answered,
Ah me! is my native country,
O my sweetheart, my Algonquin!
"When I looked back to behold him,
Where we parted, to behold him,
After me he still was gazing,
O my sweetheart, my Algonquin!
"By the tree he still was standing,
By the fallen tree was standing,
That had dropped into the water,
O my sweetheart, my Algonquin!
"When I think of my beloved,
Ah me! think of my beloved,
When my heart is thinking of him,
O my sweetheart, my Algonquin!"
Such was Hiawatha's Wedding,
Such the dance of Pau-Puk-Keewis,
Such the story of Iagoo,
Such the songs of Chibiabos;
Thus the wedding banquet ended,
And the wedding guests departed,
Leaving Hiawatha happy
With the night and Minnehaha.

XIII

BLESSING THE CORNFIELDS

Sing, O Song of Hiawatha,
Of the happy days that followed,
In the land of the Ojibways,
In the pleasant land and peaceful!
Sing the mysteries of Mondamin,
Sing the Blessing of the Cornfields!
Buried was the bloody hatchet,
Buried was the dreadful war-club,
Buried were all warlike weapons,
And the war-cry was forgotten.
There was peace among the nations;
Unmolested roved the hunters,

Built the birch canoe for sailing,
Caught the fish in lake and river,
Shot the deer and trapped the beaver;
Unmolested worked the women,
Made their sugar from the maple,
Gathered wild rice in the meadows,
Dressed the skins of deer and beaver.
All around the happy village
Stood the maize-fields, green and shining,
Waved the green plumes of Mondamin,
Waved his soft and sunny tresses,
Filling all the land with plenty.
'T was the women who in Spring-time
Planted the broad fields and fruitful,
Buried in the earth Mondamin;
'T was the women who in Autumn
Stripped the yellow husks of harvest,
Stripped the garments from Mondamin,
Even as Hiawatha taught them.
Once, when all the maize was planted,
Hiawatha, wise and thoughtful,
Spake and said to Minnehaha,
To his wife, the Laughing Water:
"You shall bless to-night the cornfields,
Draw a magic circle round them,
To protect them from destruction,
Blast of mildew, blight of insect,
Wagemin, the thief of cornfields,
Paimosaid, who steals the maize-ear!
"In the night, when all is silence,
In the night, when all is darkness,
When the Spirit of Sleep, Nepahwin,
Shuts the doors of all the wigwams,
So that not an ear can hear you,
So that not an eye can see you,
Rise up from your bed in silence,
Lay aside your garments wholly,
Walk around the fields you planted,
Round the borders of the cornfields,
Covered by your tresses only,

Robed with darkness as a garment.
  "Thus the fields shall be more fruitful,
And the passing of your footsteps
Draw a magic circle round them,
So that neither blight nor mildew,
Neither burrowing worm nor insect,
Shall pass o'er the magic circle;
Not the dragon-fly, Kwo-ne-she,
Nor the spider, Subbekashe,
Nor the grasshopper, Pah-puk-keena,
Nor the mighty caterpillar,
Way-muk-kwana, with the bear-skin,
King of all the caterpillars!"
  On the tree-tops near the cornfields
Sat the hungry crows and ravens,
Kahgahgee, the King of Ravens,
With his band of black marauders.
And they laughed at Hiawatha,
Till the tree-tops shook with laughter,
With their melancholy laughter,
At the words of Hiawatha.
"Hear him!" said they; "hear the Wise Man,
Hear the plots of Hiawatha!"
  When the noiseless night descended
Broad and dark o'er field and forest,
When the mournful Wawonaissa,
Sorrowing sang among the hemlocks,
And the Spirit of Sleep, Nepahwin,
Shut the doors of all the wigwams,
From her bed rose Laughing Water,
Laid aside her garments wholly,
And with darkness clothed and guarded,
Unashamed and unaffrighted,
Walked securely round the cornfields,
Drew the sacred, magic circle
Of her footprints round the cornfields.
  No one but the Midnight only
Saw her beauty in the darkness,
No one but the Wawonaissa
Heard the panting of her bosom;

Guskewau, the darkness, wrapped her
Closely in his sacred mantle,
So that none might see her beauty,
So that none might boast, "I saw her!"
  On the morrow, as the day dawned,
Kahgahgee, the King of Ravens,
Gathered all his black marauders,
Crows and blackbirds, jays and ravens,
Clamorous on the dusky tree-tops,
And descended, fast and fearless,
On the fields of Hiawatha,
On the grave of the Mondamin.
  "We will drag Mondamin," said they,
"From the grave where he is buried,
Spite of all the magic circles
Laughing Water draws around it,
Spite of all the sacred footprints
Minnehaha stamps upon it!"
  But the wary Hiawatha,
Ever thoughtful, careful, watchful,
Had o'erheard the scornful laughter
When they mocked him from the tree-tops.
"Kaw!" he said, "my friends the ravens!
Kahgahgee, my King of Ravens!
I will teach you all a lesson
That shall not be soon forgotten!"
  He had risen before the daybreak,
He had spread o'er all the cornfields
Snares to catch the black marauders,
And was lying now in ambush
In the neighboring grove of pine-trees,
Waiting for the crows and blackbirds,
Waiting for the jays and ravens.
  Soon they came with caw and clamor,
Rush of wings and cry of voices,
To their work of devastation,
Settling down upon the cornfields,
Delving deep with beak and talon,
For the body of Mondamin.
And with all their craft and cunning,

All their skill in wiles of warfare,
They perceived no danger near them,
Till their claws became entangled,
Till they found themselves imprisoned
In the snares of Hiawatha.
From his place of ambush came he,
Striding terrible among them,
And so awful was his aspect
That the bravest quailed with terror.
Without mercy he destroyed them
Right and left, by tens and twenties,
And their wretched, lifeless bodies
Hung aloft on poles for scarecrows
Round the consecrated cornfields,
As a signal of his vengeance,
As a warning to marauders.
Only Kahgahgee, the leader,
Kahgahgee, the King of Ravens,
He alone was spared among them
As a hostage for his people.
With his prisoner-string he bound him,
Led him captive to his wigwam,
Tied him fast with cords of elm-bark
To the ridge-pole of his wigwam.
"Kahgahgee, my raven!" said he,
"You the leader of the robbers,
You the plotter of this mischief,
The contriver of this outrage,
I will keep you, I will hold you,
As a hostage for your people,
As a pledge of good behavior!"
And he left him, grim and sulky,
Sitting in the morning sunshine
On the summit of the wigwam,
Croaking fiercely his displeasure,
Flapping his great sable pinions,
Vainly struggling for his freedom,
Vainly calling on his people!
Summer passed, and Shawondasee
Breathed his sighs o'er all the landscape,

From the South-land sent his ardors,
Wafted kisses warm and tender;
And the maize-field grew and ripened,
Till it stood in all the splendor
Of its garments green and yellow,
Of its tassels and its plumage,
And the maize-ears full and shining
Gleamed from bursting sheaths of verdure.
  Then Nokomis, the old woman,
Spake, and said to Minnehaha:
" 'T is the Moon when leaves are falling;
All the wild rice has been gathered,
And the maize is ripe and ready;
Let us gather in the harvest,
Let us wrestle with Mondamin,
Strip him of his plumes and tassels,
Of his garments green and yellow!"
  And the merry Laughing Water
Went rejoicing from the Wigwam,
With Nokomis, old and wrinkled,
And they called the women round them,
Called the young men and the maidens,
To the harvest of the cornfields,
To the husking of the maize-ear.
  On the border of the forest,
Underneath the fragrant pine-trees,
Sat the old men and the warriors
Smoking in the pleasant shadow.
In uninterrupted silence
Looked they at the gamesome labor
Of the young men and the women;
Listened to their noisy talking,
To their laughter and their singing,
Heard them chattering like the magpies,
Heard them laughing like the blue-jays,
Heard them singing like the robins.
  And whene'er some lucky maiden
Found a red ear in the husking,
Found a maize-ear red as blood is,
"Nushka!" cried they all together,

"Nushka! you shall have a sweetheart,
You shall have a handsome husband!"
"Ugh!" the old men all responded
From their seats beneath the pine-trees.
  And whene'er a youth or maiden
Found a crooked ear in husking,
Found a maize-ear in the husking
Blighted, mildewed, or misshapen,
Then they laughed and sang together,
Crept and limped about the cornfields,
Mimicked in their gait and gestures
Some old man, bent almost double,
Singing singly or together:
"Wagemin, the thief of cornfields!
Paimosaid, who steals the maize-ear!"
  Till the cornfields rang with laughter,
Till from Hiawatha's wigwam
Kahgahgee, the King of Ravens,
Screamed and quivered in his anger,
And from all the neighboring tree-tops
Cawed and croaked the black marauders.
"Ugh!" the old men all responded,
From their seats beneath the pine-trees!

XIV

PICTURE-WRITING

In those days said Hiawatha,
"Lo! how all things fade and perish!
From the memory of the old men
Pass away the great traditions,
The achievements of the warriors,
The adventures of the hunters,
All the wisdom of the Medas,
All the craft of the Wabenos,
All the marvellous dreams and visions
Of the Jossakeeds, the Prophets!
  "Great men die and are forgotten,
Wise men speak; their words of wisdom

Perish in the ears that hear them,
Do not reach the generations
That, as yet unborn, are waiting
In the great, mysterious darkness
Of the speechless days that shall be!
"On the grave-posts of our fathers
Are no signs, no figures painted;
Who are in those graves we know not,
Only know they are our fathers.
Of what kith they are and kindred,
From what old, ancestral Totem,
Be it Eagle, Bear, or Beaver,
They descended, this we know not,
Only know they are our fathers.
"Face to face we speak together,
But we cannot speak when absent,
Cannot send our voices from us
To the friends that dwell afar off;
Cannot send a secret message,
But the bearer learns our secret,
May pervert it, may betray it,
May reveal it unto others."
Thus said Hiawatha, walking
In the solitary forest,
Pondering, musing in the forest,
On the welfare of his people.
From his pouch he took his colors,
Took his paints of different colors,
On the smooth bark of a birch-tree
Painted many shapes and figures,
Wonderful and mystic figures,
And each figure had a meaning,
Each some word or thought suggested.
Gitche Manito the Mighty,
He, the Master of Life, was painted
As an egg, with points projecting
To the four winds of the heavens.
Everywhere is the Great Spirit,
Was the meaning of this symbol.
Mitche Manito the Mighty,

He the dreadful Spirit of Evil,
As a serpent was depicted,
As Kenabeek, the great serpent.
Very crafty, very cunning,
Is the creeping Spirit of Evil,
Was the meaning of this symbol.
   Life and Death he drew as circles,
Life was white, but Death was darkened;
Sun and moon and stars he painted,
Man and beast, and fish and reptile,
Forests, mountains, lakes, and rivers.
   For the earth he drew a straight line,
For the sky a bow above it;
White the space between for daytime,
Filled with little stars for night-time;
On the left a point for sunrise,
On the right a point for sunset,
On the top a point for noontide,
And for rain and cloudy weather
Waving lines descending from it.
   Footprints pointing towards a wigwam
Were a sign of invitation,
Were a sign of guests assembling;
Bloody hands with palms uplifted
Were a symbol of destruction,
Were a hostile sign and symbol.
   All these things did Hiawatha
Show unto his wondering people,
And interpreted their meaning,
And he said: "Behold, your grave-posts
Have no mark, no sign, nor symbol.
Go and paint them all with figures;
Each one with its household symbol,
With its own ancestral Totem;
So that those who follow after
May distinguish them and know them."
   And they painted on the grave-posts
On the graves yet unforgotten,
Each his own ancestral Totem,
Each the symbol of his household;

Figures of the Bear and Reindeer,
Of the Turtle, Crane, and Beaver,
Each inverted as a token
That the owner was departed,
That the chief who bore the symbol
Lay beneath in dust and ashes.
And the Jossakeeds, the Prophets,
The Wabenos, the Magicians,
And the Medicine-men, the Medas,
Painted upon bark and deer-skin
Figures for the songs they chanted,
For each song a separate symbol,
Figures mystical and awful,
Figures strange and brightly colored;
And each figure had its meaning,
Each some magic song suggested.
The Great Spirit, the Creator,
Flashing light through all the heaven;
The Great Serpent, the Kenabeek,
With his bloody crest erected,
Creeping, looking into heaven;
In the sky the sun, that listens,
And the moon eclipsed and dying;
Owl and eagle, crane and hen-hawk,
And the cormorant, bird of magic;
Headless men, that walk the heavens,
Bodies lying pierced with arrows,
Bloody hands of death uplifted,
Flags on graves, and great war-captains
Grasping both the earth and heaven!
Such as these the shapes they painted
On the birch-bark and the deer-skin;
Songs of war and songs of hunting,
Songs of medicine and of magic,
All were written in these figures,
For each figure had its meaning,
Each its separate song recorded.
Nor forgotten was the Love-Song,
The most subtle of all medicines,
The most potent spell of magic,

Dangerous more than war or hunting!
Thus the Love-Song was recorded,
Symbol and interpretation.
  First a human figure standing,
Painted in the brightest scarlet;
'T is the lover, the musician,
And the meaning is, "My painting
Makes me powerful over others."
  Then the figure seated, singing,
Playing on a drum of magic,
And the interpretation, "Listen!
'T is my voice you hear, my singing!"
  Then the same red figure seated
In the shelter of a wigwam,
And the meaning of the symbol,
"I will come and sit beside you
In the mystery of my passion!"
  Then two figures, man and woman,
Standing hand in hand together
With their hands so clasped together
That they seemed in one united,
And the words thus represented
Are, "I see your heart within you,
And your cheeks are red with blushes!"
  Next the maiden on an island,
In the centre of an island;
And the song this shape suggested
Was, "Though you were at a distance,
Were upon some far-off island,
Such the spell I cast upon you,
Such the magic power of passion,
I could straightway draw you to me!"
  Then the figure of the maiden
Sleeping, and the lover near her,
Whispering to her in her slumbers,
Saying, "Though you were far from me
In the land of Sleep and Silence,
Still the voice of love would reach you!"
  And the last of all the figures
Was a heart within a circle,

Drawn within a magic circle;
And the image had this meaning:
"Naked lies your heart before me,
To your naked heart I whisper!"
  Thus it was that Hiawatha,
In his wisdom, taught the people
All the mysteries of painting,
All the art of Picture-Writing,
On the smooth bark of the birch-tree,
On the white skin of the reindeer,
On the grave-posts of the village.

XV

HIAWATHA'S LAMENTATION

In those days the Evil Spirits,
All the Manitos of mischief,
Fearing Hiawatha's wisdom,
And his love for Chibiabos,
Jealous of their faithful friendship,
And their noble words and actions,
Made at length a league against them,
To molest them and destroy them.
  Hiawatha, wise and wary,
Often said to Chibiabos,
"O my brother! do not leave me,
Lest the Evil Spirits harm you!"
Chibiabos, young and heedless,
Laughing shook his coal-black tresses,
Answered ever sweet and childlike,
"Do not fear for me, O brother!
Harm and evil come not near me!"
  Once when Peboan, the Winter,
Roofed with ice the Big-Sea-Water,
When the snow-flakes, whirling downward,
Hissed among the withered oak-leaves,
Changed the pine-trees into wigwams,
Covered all the earth with silence,—
Armed with arrows, shod with snow-shoes,

Heeding not his brother's warning,
Fearing not the Evil Spirits,
Forth to hunt the deer with antlers
All alone went Chibiabos.
Right across the Big-Sea-Water
Sprang with speed the deer before him.
With the wind and snow he followed,
O'er the treacherous ice he followed,
Wild with all the fierce commotion
And the rapture of the hunting.
  But beneath, the Evil Spirits
Lay in ambush, waiting for him,
Broke the treacherous ice beneath him,
Dragged him downward to the bottom,
Buried in the sand his body.
Unktahee, the god of water,
He the god of the Dacotahs,
Drowned him in the deep abysses
Of the lake of Gitche Gumee.
  From the headlands Hiawatha
Sent forth such a wail of anguish,
Such a fearful lamentation,
That the bison paused to listen,
And the wolves howled from the prairies,
And the thunder in the distance
Starting answered "Baim-wawa!"
  Then his face with black he painted,
With his robe his head he covered,
In his wigwam sat lamenting,
Seven long weeks he sat lamenting,
Uttering still this moan of sorrow:—
  "He is dead, the sweet musician!
He the sweetest of all singers!
He has gone from us forever,
He has moved a little nearer
To the Master of all music,
To the Master of all singing!
O my brother, Chibiabos!"
  And the melancholy fir-trees
Waved their dark green fans above him,

Waved their purple cones above him,
Sighing with him to console him,
Mingling with his lamentation
Their complaining, their lamenting.
  Came the Spring, and all the forest
Looked in vain for Chibiabos;
Sighed the rivulet, Sebowisha,
Sighed the rushes in the meadow.
  From the tree-tops sang the bluebird,
Sang the bluebird, the Owaissa,
"Chibiabos! Chibiabos!
He is dead, the sweet musician!"
  From the wigwam sang the robin,
Sang the robin, the Opechee,
"Chibiabos! Chibiabos!
He is dead, the sweetest singer!"
  And at night through all the forest
Went the whippoorwill complaining,
Wailing went the Wawonaissa,
"Chibiabos! Chibiabos!
He is dead, the sweet musician!
He the sweetest of all singers!"
  Then the medicine-men, the Medas,
The magicians, the Wabenos,
And the Jossakeeds, the Prophets,
Came to visit Hiawatha;
Built a Sacred Lodge beside him,
To appease him, to console him,
Walked in silent, grave procession,
Bearing each a pouch of healing,
Skin of beaver, lynx, or otter,
Filled with magic roots and simples,
Filled with very potent medicines.
  When he heard their steps approaching,
Hiawatha ceased lamenting,
Called no more on Chibiabos;
Naught he questioned, naught he answered,
But his mournful head uncovered,
From his face the mourning colors
Washed he slowly and in silence,

Slowly and in silence followed
Onward to the Sacred Wigwam.
  There a magic drink they gave him,
Made of Nahma-wusk, the spearmint,
And Wabeno-wusk, the yarrow,
Roots of power, and herbs of healing;
Beat their drums, and shook their rattles;
Chanted singly and in chorus,
Mystic songs like these, they chanted.
  "I myself, myself! behold me!
'T is the great Gray Eagle talking;
Come, ye white crows, come and hear him!
The loud-speaking thunder helps me;
All the unseen spirits help me;
I can hear their voices calling,
All around the sky I hear them!
I can blow you strong, my brother,
I can heal you, Hiawatha!"
  "Hi-au-ha!" replied the chorus,
"Way-ha-way!" the mystic chorus.
  "Friends of mine are all the serpents!
Hear me shake my skin of hen-hawk!
Mahng, the white loon, I can kill him;
I can shoot your heart and kill it!
I can blow you strong, my brother,
I can heal you, Hiawatha!"
  "Hi-au-ha!" replied the chorus.
"Way-ha-way!" the mystic chorus.
  "I myself, myself! the prophet!
When I speak the wigwam trembles,
Shakes the Sacred Lodge with terror,
Hands unseen begin to shake it!
When I walk, the sky I tread on
Bends and makes a noise beneath me!
I can blow you strong, my brother!
Rise and speak, O Hiawatha!"
  "Hi-au-ha!" replied the chorus,
"Way-ha-way!" the mystic chorus.
  Then they shook their medicine-pouches
O'er the head of Hiawatha,

Danced their medicine-dance around him;
And upstarting wild and haggard,
Like a man from dreams awakened,
He was healed of all his madness.
As the clouds are swept from heaven,
Straightway from his brain departed
All his moody melancholy;
As the ice is swept from rivers,
Straightway from his heart departed
All his sorrow and affliction.
Then they summoned Chibiabos
From his grave beneath the waters,
From the sands of Gitche Gumee
Summoned Hiawatha's brother.
And so mighty was the magic
Of that cry and invocation,
That he heard it as he lay there
Underneath the Big-Sea-Water;
From the sand he rose and listened,
Heard the music and the singing,
Came, obedient to the summons,
To the doorway of the wigwam,
But to enter they forbade him.
Through a chink a coal they gave him,
Through the door a burning fire-brand;
Ruler in the Land of Spirits,
Ruler o'er the dead, they made him,
Telling him a fire to kindle
For all those that died thereafter,
Camp-fires for their night encampments
On their solitary journey
To the kingdom of Ponemah,
To the land of the Hereafter.
From the village of his childhood,
From the homes of those who knew him,
Passing silent through the forest,
Like a smoke-wreath wafted sideways,
Slowly vanished Chibiabos!
Where he passed, the branches moved not,
Where he trod, the grasses bent not,

And the fallen leaves of last year
Made no sound beneath his footsteps.
  Four whole days he journeyed onward
Down the pathway of the dead men;
On the dead-man's strawberry feasted,
Crossed the melancholy river,
On the swinging log he crossed it,
Came unto the Lake of Silver,
In the Stone Canoe was carried
To the Islands of the Blessed,
To the land of ghosts and shadows.
  On that journey, moving slowly,
Many weary spirits saw he,
Panting under heavy burdens,
Laden with war-clubs, bows and arrows,
Robes of fur, and pots and kettles,
And with food that friends had given
For that solitary journey.
  "Ay! why do the living," said they,
"Lay such heavy burdens on us!
Better were it to go naked,
Better were it to go fasting,
Than to bear such heavy burdens
On our long and weary journey!"
  Forth then issued Hiawatha,
Wandered eastward, wandered westward,
Teaching men the use of simples
And the antidotes for poisons,
And the cure of all diseases.
Thus was first made known to mortals
All the mystery of Medamin,
All the sacred art of healing.

XVI

PAU-PUK-KEEWIS

You shall hear how Pau-Puk-Keewis
He, the handsome Yenadizze,
Whom the people called the Storm-Fool,

Vexed the village with disturbance;
You shall hear of all his mischief,
And his flight from Hiawatha,
And his wondrous transmigrations,
And the end of his adventures.
  On the shores of Gitche Gumee,
On the dunes of Nagow Wudjoo,
By the shining Big-Sea-Water
Stood the lodge of Pau-Puk-Keewis.
It was he who in his frenzy
Whirled these drifting sands together,
On the dunes of Nagow Wudjoo,
When, among the guests assembled,
He so merrily and madly
Danced at Hiawatha's wedding,
Danced the Beggar's Dance to please them.
  Now, in search of new adventures,
From his lodge went Pau-Puk-Keewis,
Came with speed into the village,
Found the young men all assembled
In the lodge of old Iagoo,
Listening to his monstrous stories,
To his wonderful adventures.
  He was telling them the story
Of Ojeeg, the Summer-Maker,
How he made a hole in heaven,
How he climbed up into heaven,
And let out the summer-weather,
The perpetual, pleasant Summer;
How the Otter first essayed it;
How the Beaver, Lynx, and Badger
Tried in turn the great achievement,
From the summit of the mountain
Smote their fists against the heavens,
Smote against the sky their foreheads,
Cracked the sky, but could not break it;
How the Wolverine, uprising,
Made him ready for the encounter,
Bent his knees down, like a squirrel,
Drew his arms back, like a cricket.

"Once he leaped," said old Iagoo,
"Once he leaped, and lo! above him
Bent the sky, as ice in rivers
When the waters rise beneath it;
Twice he leaped, and lo! above him
Cracked the sky, as ice in rivers
When the freshet is at highest!
Thrice he leaped, and lo! above him
Broke the shattered sky asunder,
And he disappeared within it,
And Ojeeg, the Fisher Weasel,
With a bound went in behind him!"

"Hark you!" shouted Pau-Puk-Keewis
As he entered at the doorway;
"I am tired of all this talking,
Tired of old Iagoo's stories,
Tired of Hiawatha's wisdom.
Here is something to amuse you,
Better than this endless talking."

Then from out his pouch of wolf-skin
Forth he drew, with solemn manner,
All the game of Bowl and Counters,
Pugasaing, with thirteen pieces.
White on one side were they painted,
And vermilion on the other;
Two Kenabeeks or great serpents,
Two Ininewug or wedge-men,
One great war-club, Pugamaugun,
And one slender fish, the Keego,
Four round pieces, Ozawabeeks,
And three Sheshebwug or ducklings.
All were made of bone and painted,
All except the Ozawabeeks;
These were brass, on one side burnished,
And were black upon the other.

In a wooden bowl he placed them,
Shook and jostled them together,
Threw them on the ground before him.
Thus exclaiming and explaining:
"Red side up are all the pieces,

And one great Kenabeek standing
On the bright side of a brass piece,
On a burnished Ozawabeek;
Thirteen tens and eight are counted."
Then again he shook the pieces,
Shook and jostled them together,
Threw them on the ground before him,
Still exclaiming and explaining:
"White are both the great Kenabeeks,
White the Ininewug, the wedge-men,
Red are all the other pieces;
Five tens and an eight are counted."
Thus he taught the game of hazard,
Thus displayed it and explained it,
Running through its various chances,
Various changes, various meanings:
Twenty curious eyes stared at him.
Full of eagerness stared at him.
"Many games," said old Iagoo,
"Many games of skill and hazard
Have I seen in different nations,
Have I played in different countries.
He who plays with old Iagoo
Must have very nimble fingers;
Though you think yourself so skilful
I can beat you, Pau-Puk-Keewis,
I can even give you lessons
In your game of Bowl and Counters!"
So they sat and played together,
All the old men and the young men,
Played for dresses, weapons, wampum,
Played till midnight, played till morning,
Played until the Yenadizze,
Till the cunning Pau-Puk-Keewis,
Of their treasures had despoiled them,
Of the best of all their dresses,
Shirts of deer-skin, robes of ermine,
Belts of wampum, crests of feathers,
Warlike weapons, pipes and pouches.
Twenty eyes glared wildly at him,

Like the eyes of wolves glared at him.
  Said the lucky Pau-Puk-Keewis:
"In my wigwam I am lonely,
In my wanderings and adventures
I have need of a companion,
Fain would have a Meshinauwa,
An attendant and pipe-bearer.
I will venture all these winnings,
All these garments heaped about me,
All this wampum, all these feathers,
On a single throw will venture
All against the young man yonder!"
'T was a youth of sixteen summers,
'T was a nephew of Iagoo;
Face-in-a-Mist, the people called him.
  As the fire burns in a pipe-head
Dusky red beneath the ashes,
So beneath his shaggy eyebrows
Glowed the eyes of old Iagoo.
"Ugh!" he answered very fiercely;
"Ugh!" they answered all and each one.
  Seized the wooden bowl the old man,
Closely in his bony fingers
Clutched the fatal bowl, Onagon,
Shook it fiercely and with fury,
Made the pieces ring together
As he threw them down before him.
  Red were both the great Kenabeeks,
Red the Ininewug, the wedge-men,
Red the Sheshebwug, the ducklings,
Black the four brass Ozawabeeks,
White alone the fish, the Keego;
Only five the pieces counted!
  Then the smiling Pau-Puk-Keewis
Shook the bowl and threw the pieces;
Lightly in the air he tossed them,
And they fell about him scattered;
Dark and bright the Ozawabeeks,
Red and white the other pieces,
And upright among the others

One Ininewug was standing,
Even as crafty Pau-Puk-Keewis
Stood alone among the players,
Saying, "Five tens! mine the game is!"
Twenty eyes glared at him fiercely,
Like the eyes of wolves glared at him,
As he turned and left the wigwam,
Followed by his Meshinauwa,
By the nephew of Iagoo,
By the tall and graceful stripling,
Bearing in his arms the winnings,
Shirts of deer-skin, robes of ermine,
Belts of wampum, pipes and weapons.
"Carry them," said Pau-Puk-Keewis,
Pointing with his fan of feathers,
"To my wigwam far to eastward,
On the dunes of Nagow Wudjoo!"
Hot and red with smoke and gambling
Were the eyes of Pau-Puk-Keewis
As he came forth to the freshness
Of the pleasant Summer morning.
All the birds were singing gayly,
All the streamlets flowing swiftly,
And the heart of Pau-Puk-Keewis
Sang with pleasure as the birds sing,
Beat with triumph like the streamlets,
As he wandered through the village,
In the early gray of morning,
With his fan of turkey-feathers,
With his plumes and tufts of swan's down,
Till he reached the farthest wigwam,
Reached the lodge of Hiawatha.
Silent was it and deserted;
No one met him at the doorway,
No one came to bid him welcome;
But the birds were singing round it,
In and out and round the doorway,
Hopping, singing, fluttering, feeding,
And aloft upon the ridge-pole
Kahgahgee, the King of Ravens,

Sat with fiery eyes, and, screaming,
Flapped his wings at Pau-Puk-Keewis.
"All are gone! the lodge is empty!"
Thus it was spake Pau-Puk-Keewis,
In his heart resolving mischief;—
"Gone is wary Hiawatha,
Gone the silly Laughing Water,
Gone Nokomis, the old woman,
And the lodge is left unguarded!"
By the neck he seized the raven,
Whirled it round him like a rattle,
Like a medicine-pouch he shook it,
Strangled Kahgahgee, the raven,
From the ridge-pole of the wigwam
Left its lifeless body hanging,
As an insult to its master,
As a taunt to Hiawatha.
With a stealthy step he entered,
Round the lodge in wild disorder
Threw the household things about him,
Piled together in confusion
Bowls of wood and earthen kettles,
Robes of buffalo and beaver,
Skins of otter, lynx, and ermine,
As an insult to Nokomis,
As a taunt to Minnehaha.
Then departed Pau-Puk-Keewis,
Whistling, singing through the forest,
Whistling gayly to the squirrels,
Who from hollow boughs above him
Dropped their acorn-shells upon him,
Singing gayly to the wood birds,
Who from out the leafy darkness
Answered with a song as merry.
Then he climbed the rocky headlands,
Looking o'er the Gitche Gumee,
Perched himself upon their summit,
Waiting full of mirth and mischief
The return of Hiawatha.
Stretched upon his back he lay there;

Far below him plashed the waters,
Plashed and washed the dreamy waters;
Far above him swam the heavens,
Swam the dizzy, dreamy heavens;
Round him hovered, fluttered, rustled,
Hiawatha's mountain chickens,
Flock-wise swept and wheeled about him,
Almost brushed him with their pinions.
  And he killed them as he lay there,
Slaughtered them by tens and twenties,
Threw their bodies down the headland,
Threw them on the beach below him,
Till at length Kayoshk, the sea-gull,
Perched upon a crag above them,
Shouted: "It is Pau-Puk-Keewis!
He is slaying us by hundreds!
Send a message to our brother,
Tidings send to Hiawatha!"

XVII

THE HUNTING OF PAU-PUK-KEEWIS

Full of wrath was Hiawatha
When he came into the village,
Found the people in confusion,
Heard of all the misdemeanors,
All the malice and the mischief,
Of the cunning Pau-Puk-Keewis.
  Hard his breath came through his nostrils,
Through his teeth he buzzed and muttered
Words of anger and resentment,
Hot and humming, like a hornet.
"I will slay this Pau-Puk-Keewis,
Slay this mischief-maker!" said he.
"Not so long and wide the world is,
Not so rude and rough the way is,
That my wrath shall not attain him,
That my vengeance shall not reach him!"
  Then in swift pursuit departed

Hiawatha and the hunters
On the trail of Pau-Puk-Keewis,
Through the forest, where he passed it,
To the headlands where he rested;
But they found not Pau-Puk-Keewis,
Only in the trampled grasses,
In the whortleberry-bushes,
Found the couch where he had rested,
Found the impress of his body.

From the lowlands far beneath them,
From the Muskoday, the meadow,
Pau-Puk-Keewis, turning backward,
Made a gesture of defiance,
Made a gesture of derision;
And aloud cried Hiawatha,
From the summit of the mountains:
"Not so long and wide the world is,
Not so rude and rough the way is,
But my wrath shall overtake you,
And my vengeance shall attain you!"

Over rock and over river,
Thorough bush, and brake, and forest,
Ran the cunning Pau-Puk-Keewis;
Like an antelope he bounded,
Till he came unto a streamlet
In the middle of the forest,
To a streamlet still and tranquil,
That had overflowed its margin,
To a dam made by the beavers,
To a pond of quiet water,
Where knee-deep the trees were standing,
Where the water-lilies floated,
Where the rushes waved and whispered.

On the dam stood Pau-Puk-Keewis,
On the dam of trunks and branches,
Through whose chinks the water spouted,
O'er whose summit flowed the streamlet.
From the bottom rose the beaver,
Looked with two great eyes of wonder,
Eyes that seemed to ask a question,

At the stranger, Pau-Puk-Keewis.
  On the dam stood Pau-Puk-Keewis,
O'er his ankles flowed the streamlet,
Flowed the bright and silvery water,
And he spake unto the beaver,
With a smile he spake in this wise:
  "O my friend Ahmeek, the beaver,
Cool and pleasant is the water;
Let me dive into the water,
Let me rest there in your lodges;
Change me, too, into a beaver!"
  Cautiously replied the beaver,
With reserve he thus made answer:
"Let me first consult the others,
Let me ask the other beavers."
Down he sank into the water,
Heavily sank he, as a stone sinks,
Down among the leaves and branches,
Brown and matted at the bottom.
  On the dam stood Pau-Puk-Keewis,
O'er his ankles flowed the streamlet,
Spouted through the chinks below him,
Dashed upon the stones beneath him,
Spread serene and calm before him,
And the sunshine and the shadows
Fell in flecks and gleams upon him,
Fell in little shining patches,
Through the waving, rustling branches.
  From the bottom rose the beavers,
Silently above the surface
Rose one head and then another,
Till the pond seemed full of beavers,
Full of black and shining faces.
  To the beavers Pau-Puk-Keewis
Spake entreating, said in this wise:
"Very pleasant is your dwelling,
O my friends! and safe from danger;
Can you not with all your cunning,
All your wisdom and contrivance,
Change me, too, into a beaver?"

"Yes!" replied Ahmeek, the beaver,
He the King of all the beavers,
"Let yourself slide down among us,
Down into the tranquil water."
Down into the pond among them
Silently sank Pau-Puk-Keewis;
Black became his shirt of deer-skin,
Black his moccasins and leggings,
In a broad black tail behind him
Spread his fox-tails and his fringes;
He was changed into a beaver.
"Make me large," said Pau-Puk-Keewis,
"Make me large and make me larger,
Larger than the other beavers."
"Yes," the beaver chief responded,
"When our lodge below you enter,
In our wigwam we will make you
Ten times larger than the others."
Thus into the clear, brown water
Silently sank Pau-Puk-Keewis:
Found the bottom covered over
With the trunks of trees and branches,
Hoards of food against the winter,
Piles and heaps against the famine;
Found the lodge with arching doorway,
Leading into spacious chambers.
Here they made him large and larger,
Made him largest of the beavers,
Ten times larger than the others.
"You shall be our ruler," said they;
"Chief and King of all the beavers."
But not long had Pau-Puk-Keewis
Sat in state among the beavers,
When there came a voice of warning
From the watchman at his station
In the water-flags and lilies,
Saying, "Here is Hiawatha!
Hiawatha with his hunters!"
Then they heard a cry above them,
Heard a shouting and a tramping,

Heard a crashing and a rushing,
And the water round and o'er them
Sank and sucked away in eddies,
And they knew their dam was broken.
  On the lodge's roof the hunters
Leaped, and broke it all asunder;
Streamed the sunshine through the crevice,
Sprang the beavers through the doorway,
Hid themselves in deeper water,
In the channel of the streamlet;
But the mighty Pau-Puk-Keewis
Could not pass beneath the doorway;
He was puffed with pride and feeding,
He was swollen like a bladder.
  Through the roof looked Hiawatha,
Cried aloud, "O Pau-Puk-Keewis!
Vain are all your craft and cunning,
Vain your manifold disguises!
Well I know you, Pau-Puk-Keewis!"
With their clubs they beat and bruised him,
Beat to death poor Pau-Puk-Keewis,
Pounded him as maize is pounded,
Till his skull was crushed to pieces.
  Six tall hunters, lithe and limber,
Bore him home on poles and branches,
Bore the body of the beaver;
But the ghost, the Jeebi in him,
Thought and felt as Pau-Puk-Keewis,
Still lived on as Pau-Puk-Keewis.
  And it fluttered, strove, and struggled,
Waving hither, waving thither,
As the curtains of a wigwam
Struggle with their thongs of deer-skin,
When the wintry wind is blowing;
Till it drew itself together,
Till it rose up from the body,
Till it took the form and features
Of the cunning Pau-Puk-Keewis
Vanishing into the forest.
  But the wary Hiawatha

Saw the figure ere it vanished,
Saw the form of Pau-Puk-Keewis
Glide into the soft blue shadow
Of the pine-trees of the forest;
Toward the squares of white beyond it,
Toward an opening in the forest,
Like a wind it rushed and panted,
Bending all the boughs before it,
And behind it, as the rain comes,
Came the steps of Hiawatha.
To a lake with many islands
Came the breathless Pau-Puk-Keewis,
Where among the water-lilies
Pishnekuh, the brant, were sailing;
Through the tufts of rushes floating,
Steering through the reedy islands.
Now their broad black beaks they lifted,
Now they plunged beneath the water,
Now they darkened in the shadow,
Now they brightened in the sunshine.
"Pishnekuh!" cried Pau-Puk-Keewis,
"Pishnekuh! my brothers!" said he,
"Change me to a brant with plumage,
With a shining neck and feathers,
Make me large, and make me larger,
Ten times larger than the others."
Straightway to a brant they changed him,
With two huge and dusky pinions,
With a bosom smooth and rounded,
With a bill like two great paddles,
Made him larger than the others,
Ten times larger than the largest,
Just as, shouting from the forest,
On the shore stood Hiawatha.
Up they rose with cry and clamor,
With a whir and beat of pinions,
Rose up from the reedy islands,
From the water-flags and lilies.
And they said to Pau-Puk-Keewis:
"In your flying, look not downward,

Take good heed, and look not downward,
Lest some strange mischance should happen,
Lest some great mishap befall you!"
  Fast and far they fled to northward,
Fast and far through mist and sunshine,
Fed among the moors and fen-lands,
Slept among the reeds and rushes.
  On the morrow as they journeyed,
Buoyed and lifted by the South-wind,
Wafted onward by the South-wind,
Blowing fresh and strong behind them,
Rose a sound of human voices,
Rose a clamor from beneath them,
From the lodges of a village,
From the people miles beneath them.
  For the people of the village
Saw the flock of brant with wonder,
Saw the wings of Pau-Puk-Keewis
Flapping far up in the ether,
Broader than two doorway curtains.
  Pau-Puk-Keewis heard the shouting,
Knew the voice of Hiawatha,
Knew the outcry of Iagoo,
And forgetful of the warning,
Drew his neck in, and looked downward,
And the wind that blew behind him
Caught his mighty fan of feathers,
Sent him wheeling, whirling downward!
  All in vain did Pau-Puk-Keewis
Struggle to regain his balance!
Whirling round and round and downward,
He beheld in turn the village
And in turn the flock above him,
Saw the village coming nearer,
And the flock receding farther,
Heard the voices growing louder,
Heard the shouting and the laughter;
Saw no more the flock above him,
Only saw the earth beneath him;
Dead out of the empty heaven,

Dead among the shouting people,
With a heavy sound and sullen,
Fell the brant with broken pinions.
  But his soul, his ghost, his shadow,
Still survived as Pau-Puk-Keewis,
Took again the form and features
Of the handsome Yenadizze,
And again went rushing onward,
Followed fast by Hiawatha,
Crying: "Not so wide the world is,
Not so long and rough the way is,
But my wrath shall overtake you,
But my vengeance shall attain you!"
  And so near he came, so near him,
That his hand was stretched to seize him,
His right hand to seize and hold him,
When the cunning Pau-Puk-Keewis
Whirled and spun about in circles,
Fanned the air into a whirlwind,
Danced the dust and leaves about him,
And amid the whirling eddies
Sprang into a hollow oak-tree,
Changed himself into a serpent,
Gliding out through root and rubbish.
  With his right hand Hiawatha
Smote amain the hollow oak-tree,
Rent it into shreds and splinters,
Left it lying there in fragments.
But in vain; for Pau-Puk-Keewis,
Once again in human figure,
Full in sight ran on before him,
Sped away in gust and whirlwind,
On the shores of Gitche Gumee,
Westward by the Big-Sea-Water,
Came unto the rocky headlands,
To the Pictured Rocks of sandstone,
Looking over lake and landscape.
  And the Old Man of the Mountain,
He the Manito of Mountains,
Opened wide his rocky doorways,

Opened wide his deep abysses,
Giving Pau-Puk-Keewis shelter
In his caverns dark and dreary,
Bidding Pau-Puk-Keewis welcome
To his gloomy lodge of sandstone.
There without stood Hiawatha,
Found the doorways closed against him,
With his mittens, Minjekahwun,
Smote great caverns in the sandstone,
Cried aloud in tones of thunder,
"Open! I am Hiawatha!"
But the Old Man of the Mountain
Opened not, and made no answer
From the silent crags of sandstone,
From the gloomy rock abysses.
Then he raised his hands to heaven,
Called imploring on the tempest,
Called Waywassimo, the lightning,
And the thunder, Annemeekee;
And they came with night and darkness,
Sweeping down the Big-Sea-Water
From the distant Thunder Mountains;
And the trembling Pau-Puk-Keewis
Heard the footsteps of the thunder,
Saw the red eyes of the lightning,
Was afraid, and crouched and trembled.
Then Waywassimo, the lightning,
Smote the doorways of the caverns,
With his war-club smote the doorways,
Smote the jutting crags of sandstone,
And the thunder, Annemeekee,
Shouted down into the caverns,
Saying, "Where is Pau-Puk-Keewis!"
And the crags fell, and beneath them
Dead among the rocky ruins
Lay the cunning Pau-Puk-Keewis,
Lay the handsome Yenadizze,
Slain in his own human figure.
Ended were his wild adventures,
Ended were his tricks and gambols,

Ended all his craft and cunning,
Ended all his mischief-making,
All his gambling and his dancing,
All his wooing of the maidens.
  Then the noble Hiawatha
Took his soul, his ghost, his shadow,
Spake and said: "O Pau-Puk-Keewis,
Never more in human figure
Shall you search for new adventures;
Never more with jest and laughter
Dance the dust and leaves in whirlwinds;
But above there in the heavens
You shall soar and sail in circles;
I will change you to an eagle,
To Keneu, the great war-eagle,
Chief of all the fowls with feathers,
Chief of Hiawatha's chickens."
  And the name of Pau-Puk-Keewis
Lingers still among the people,
Lingers still among the singers,
And among the story-tellers;
And in Winter, when the snow-flakes
Whirl in eddies round the lodges,
When the wind in gusty tumult
O'er the smoke-flue pipes and whistles,
"There," they cry, "comes Pau-Puk-Keewis;
He is dancing through the village,
He is gathering in his harvest!"

XVIII

THE DEATH OF KWASIND

Far and wide among the nations
Spread the name and fame of Kwasind;
No man dared to strive with Kwasind,
No man could compete with Kwasind.
But the mischievous Puk-Wudjies,
They the envious Little People,
They the fairies and the pygmies,
Plotted and conspired against him.

"If this hateful Kwasind," said they,
"If this great, outrageous fellow
Goes on thus a little longer,
Tearing everything he touches,
Rending everything to pieces,
Filling all the world with wonder,
What becomes of the Puk-Wudjies?
Who will care for the Puk-Wudjies?
He will tread us down like mushrooms,
Drive us all into the water,
Give our bodies to be eaten
By the wicked Nee-ba-naw-baigs,
By the Spirits of the water!"
So the angry Little People
All conspired against the Strong Man,
All conspired to murder Kwasind,
Yes, to rid the world of Kwasind,
The audacious, overbearing,
Heartless, haughty, dangerous Kwasind!
Now this wondrous strength of Kwasind
In his crown alone was seated;
In his crown too was his weakness;
There alone could he be wounded,
Nowhere else could weapon pierce him,
Nowhere else could weapon harm him.
Even there the only weapon
That could wound him, that could slay him,
Was the seed-cone of the pine-tree,
Was the blue cone of the fir-tree.
This was Kwasind's fatal secret,
Known to no man among mortals;
But the cunning Little People,
The Puk-Wudjees, knew the secret,
Knew the only way to kill him.
So they gathered cones together,
Gathered seed-cones of the pine-tree,
Gathered blue cones of the fir-tree,
In the woods by Taquamenaw,
Brought them to the river's margin,
Heaped them in great piles together,

Where the red rocks from the margin
Jutting overhang the river.
There they lay in wait for Kwasind,
The malicious Little People.
'T was an afternoon in Summer;
Very hot and still the air was,
Very smooth the gliding river,
Motionless the sleeping shadows:
Insects glistened in the sunshine,
Insects skated on the water,
Filled the drowsy air with buzzing,
With a far resounding war-cry.
Down the river came the Strong Man,
In his birch canoe came Kwasind,
Floating slowly down the current
Of the sluggish Taquamenaw,
Very languid with the weather,
Very sleepy with the silence.
From the overhanging branches,
From the tassels of the birch-trees,
Soft the Spirit of Sleep descended;
By his airy hosts surrounded,
His invisible attendants,
Came the Spirit of Sleep, Nepahwin;
Like the burnished Dush-kwo-ne-she,
Like a dragon-fly, he hovered
O'er the drowsy head of Kwasind.
To his ear there came a murmur
As of waves upon a sea-shore,
As of far-off tumbling waters,
As of winds among the pine-trees;
And he felt upon his forehead
Blows of little airy war-clubs,
Wielded by the slumbrous legions
Of the Spirit of Sleep, Nepahwin,
As of some one breathing on him.
At the first blow of their war-clubs,
Fell a drowsiness on Kwasind;
At the second blow they smote him,
Motionless his paddle rested;

At the third, before his vision
Reeled the landscape into darkness,
Very sound asleep was Kwasind.
 So he floated down the river,
Like a blind man seated upright,
Floated down the Taquamenaw,
Underneath the trembling birch-trees,
Underneath the wooded headlands,
Underneath the war encampment
Of the pygmies, the Puk-Wudjies.
 There they stood, all armed and waiting,
Hurled the pine-cones down upon him,
Struck him on his brawny shoulders,
On his crown defenceless struck him.
"Death to Kwasind!" was the sudden
War-cry of the Little People.
 And he sideways swayed and tumbled,
Sideways fell into the river,
Plunged beneath the sluggish water
Headlong, as an otter plunges;
And the birch canoe, abandoned,
Drifted empty down the river,
Bottom upward swerved and drifted:
Nothing more was seen of Kwasind.
 But the memory of the Strong Man
Lingered long among the people,
And whenever through the forest
Raged and roared the wintry tempest,
And the branches, tossed and troubled,
Creaked and groaned and split asunder,
"Kwasind!" cried they; "that is Kwasind!
He is gathering in his fire-wood!"

XIX

THE GHOSTS

Never stoops the soaring vulture
On his quarry in the desert,
On the sick or wounded bison,
But another vulture, watching

From his high aerial look-out,
Sees the downward plunge, and follows;
And a third pursues the second,
Coming from the invisible ether,
First a speck, and then a vulture,
Till the air is dark with pinions.
So disasters come not singly;
But as if they watched and waited,
Scanning one another's motions,
When the first descends, the others
Follow, follow, gathering flock-wise
Round their victim, sick and wounded,
First a shadow, then a sorrow,
Till the air is dark with anguish.
Now, o'er all the dreary North-land,
Mighty Peboan, the Winter,
Breathing on the lakes and rivers,
Into stone had changed their waters.
From his hair he shook the snow-flakes,
Till the plains were strewn with whiteness,
One uninterrupted level,
As if, stooping, the Creator
With his hand had smoothed them over.
Through the forest, wide and wailing,
Roamed the hunter on his snow-shoes;
In the village worked the women,
Pounded maize, or dressed the deer-skin;
And the young men played together
On the ice the noisy ball-play,
On the plain the dance of snow-shoes.
One dark evening, after sundown,
In her wigwam Laughing Water
Sat with old Nokomis, waiting
For the steps of Hiawatha
Homeward from the hunt returning.
On their faces gleamed the fire-light,
Painting them with streaks of crimson,
In the eyes of old Nokomis
Glimmered like the watery moonlight,
In the eyes of Laughing Water

Glistened like the sun in water;
And behind them crouched their shadows
In the corners of the wigwam,
And the smoke in wreaths above them
Climbed and crowded through the smoke-flue.
  Then the curtain of the doorway
From without was slowly lifted;
Brighter glowed the fire a moment,
And a moment swerved the smoke-wreath,
As two women entered softly,
Passed the doorway uninvited,
Without word of salutation,
Without sign of recognition,
Sat down in the farthest corner,
Crouching low among the shadows.
  From their aspect and their garments,
Strangers seemed they in the village;
Very pale and haggard were they,
As they sat there sad and silent,
Trembling, cowering with the shadows.
  Was it the wind above the smoke-flue,
Muttering down into the wigwam?
Was it the owl, the Koko-koho,
Hooting from the dismal forest?
Sure a voice said in the silence:
"These are corpses clad in garments,
These are ghosts that come to haunt you,
From the kingdom of Ponemah,
From the land of the Hereafter!"
  Homeward now came Hiawatha
From his hunting in the forest,
With the snow upon his tresses,
And the red deer on his shoulders.
At the feet of Laughing Water
Down he threw his lifeless burden;
Nobler, handsomer she thought him,
Than when first he came to woo her,
First threw down the deer before her,
As a token of his wishes,
As a promise of the future.

Then he turned and saw the strangers,
Cowering, crouching with the shadows;
Said within himself, "Who are they?
What strange guests has Minnehaha?"
But he questioned not the strangers,
Only spake to bid them welcome
To his lodge, his food, his fireside.
When the evening meal was ready,
And the deer had been divided,
Both the pallid guests, the strangers,
Springing from among the shadows,
Seized upon the choicest portions,
Seized the white fat of the roebuck,
Set apart for Laughing Water,
For the wife of Hiawatha;
Without asking, without thanking,
Eagerly devoured the morsels,
Flitted back among the shadows
In the corner of the wigwam.
Not a word spake Hiawatha,
Not a motion made Nokomis,
Not a gesture Laughing Water;
Not a change came o'er their features;
Only Minnehaha softly
Whispered, saying, "They are famished;
Let them do what best delights them;
Let them eat, for they are famished."
Many a daylight dawned and darkened,
Many a night shook off the daylight
As the pine shakes off the snow-flakes
From the midnight of its branches;
Day by day the guests unmoving
Sat there silent in the wigwam;
But by night, in storm or starlight,
Forth they went into the forest,
Bringing fire-wood to the wigwam,
Bringing pine-cones for the burning,
Always sad and always silent.
And whenever Hiawatha
Came from fishing or from hunting,

When the evening meal was ready,
And the food had been divided,
Gliding from their darksome corner,
Came the pallid guests, the strangers,
Seized upon the choicest portions
Set aside for Laughing Water,
And without rebuke or question
Flitted back among the shadows.
  Never once had Hiawatha
By a word or look reproved them;
Never once had old Nokomis
Made a gesture of impatience;
Never once had Laughing Water
Shown resentment at the outrage.
All had they endured in silence,
That the rights of guest and stranger,
That the virtue of free-giving,
By a look might not be lessened,
By a word might not be broken.
  Once at midnight Hiawatha,
Ever wakeful, ever watchful,
In the wigwam, dimly lighted
By the brands that still were burning,
By the glimmering, flickering fire-light,
Heard a sighing, oft repeated,
Heard a sobbing, as of sorrow.
  From his couch rose Hiawatha,
From his shaggy hides of bison,
Pushed aside the deer-skin curtain,
Saw the pallid guests, the shadows,
Sitting upright on their couches,
Weeping in the silent midnight.
  And he said: "O guests! why is it
That your hearts are so afflicted,
That you sob so in the midnight?
Has perchance the old Nokomis,
Has my wife, my Minnehaha,
Wronged or grieved you by unkindness,
Failed in hospitable duties?"
  Then the shadows ceased from weeping,

Ceased from sobbing and lamenting,
And they said, with gentle voices:
"We are ghosts of the departed,
Souls of those who once were with you.
From the realms of Chibiabos
Hither have we come to try you,
Hither have we come to warn you.
"Cries of grief and lamentation
Reach us in the Blessed Islands;
Cries of anguish from the living,
Calling back their friends departed,
Sadden us with useless sorrow.
Therefore have we come to try you;
No one knows us, no one heeds us.
We are but a burden to you,
And we see that the departed
Have no place among the living.
"Think of this, O Hiawatha!
Speak of it to all the people,
That henceforward and forever
They no more with lamentations
Sadden the souls of the departed
In the Islands of the Blessed.
"Do not lay such heavy burdens
In the graves of those you bury,
Not such weight of furs and wampum,
Not such weight of pots and kettles,
For the spirits faint beneath them.
Only give them food to carry,
Only give them fire to light them.
"Four days is the spirit's journey
To the land of ghosts and shadows,
Four its lonely night encampments;
Four times must their fires be lighted.
Therefore, when the dead are buried,
Let a fire, as night approaches,
Four times on the grave be kindled,
That the soul upon its journey
May not lack the cheerful fire-light,
May not grope about in darkness.

"Farewell, noble Hiawatha!
We have put you to the trial,
To the proof have put your patience,
By the insult of our presence,
By the outrage of our actions.
We have found you great and noble.
Fail not in the greater trial,
Faint not in the harder struggle."
When they ceased, a sudden darkness
Fell and filled the silent wigwam.
Hiawatha heard a rustle
As of garments trailing by him,
Heard the curtain of the doorway
Lifted by a hand he saw not,
Felt the cold breath of the night air,
For a moment saw the star-light;
But he saw the ghosts no longer,
Saw no more the wandering spirits
From the kingdom of Ponemah,
From the land of the Hereafter.

XX

THE FAMINE

Oh, the long and dreary Winter!
Oh, the cold and cruel Winter!
Ever thicker, thicker, thicker
Froze the ice on lake and river,
Ever deeper, deeper, deeper
Fell the snow o'er all the landscape,
Fell the covering snow, and drifted
Through the forest, round the village.
Hardly from his buried wigwam
Could the hunter force a passage;
With his mittens and his snow-shoes
Vainly walked he through the forest,
Sought for bird or beast and found none,
Saw no track of deer or rabbit,
In the snow beheld no footprints,

In the ghastly, gleaming forest
Fell, and could not rise from weakness,
Perished there from cold and hunger.
  Oh the famine and the fever!
Oh the wasting of the famine!
Oh the blasting of the fever!
Oh the wailing of the children!
Oh the anguish of the women!
  All the earth was sick and famished;
Hungry was the air around them,
Hungry was the sky above them,
And the hungry stars in heaven
Like the eyes of wolves glared at them!
  Into Hiawatha's wigwam
Came two other guests, as silent
As the ghosts were, and as gloomy,
Waited not to be invited,
Did not parley at the doorway,
Sat there without word of welcome
In the seat of Laughing Water;
Looked with haggard eyes and hollow
At the face of Laughing Water.
  And the foremost said: "Behold me!
I am Famine, Bukadawin!"
And the other said: "Behold me!
I am Fever, Ahkosewin!"
  And the lovely Minnehaha
Shuddered as they looked upon her,
Shuddered at the words they uttered,
Lay down on her bed in silence,
Hid her face, but made no answer;
Lay there trembling, freezing, burning
At the looks they cast upon her,
At the fearful words they uttered.
  Forth into the empty forest
Rushed the maddened Hiawatha;
In his heart was deadly sorrow,
In his face a stony firmness;
On his brow the sweat of anguish
Started, but it froze and fell not.

Wrapped in furs and armed for hunting,
With his mighty bow of ash-tree,
With his quiver full of arrows,
With his mittens, Minjekahwun,
Into the vast and vacant forest
On his snow-shoes strode he forward.
"Gitche Manito, the Mighty!"
Cried he with his face uplifted
In that bitter hour of anguish,
"Give your children food, O father!
Give us food, or we must perish!
Give me food for Minnehaha,
For my dying Minnehaha!"
Through the far-resounding forest,
Through the forest vast and vacant
Rang that cry of desolation,
But there came no other answer
Than the echo of his crying,
Than the echo of the woodlands,
"Minnehaha! Minnehaha!"
All day long roved Hiawatha
In that melancholy forest,
Through the shadow of whose thickets,
In the pleasant days of Summer,
Of that ne'er forgotten Summer,
He had brought his young wife homeward
From the land of the Dacotahs;
When the birds sang in the thickets,
And the streamlets laughed and glistened,
And the air was full of fragrance,
And the lovely Laughing Water
Said with voice that did not tremble,
"I will follow you, my husband!"
In the wigwam with Nokomis,
With those gloomy guests, that watched her,
With the Famine and the Fever,
She was lying, the Beloved,
She the dying Minnehaha.
"Hark!" she said; "I hear a rushing,
Hear a roaring and a rushing,

Hear the Falls of Minnehaha
Calling to me from a distance!"
"No, my child!" said old Nokomis,
" 'T is the night-wind in the pine-trees!"
"Look!" she said; "I see my father
Standing lonely at his doorway,
Beckoning to me from his wigwam
In the land of the Dacotahs!"
"No, my child!" said old Nokomis,
" 'T is the smoke, that waves and beckons!"
"Ah!" said she, "the eyes of Pauguk
Glare upon me in the darkness,
I can feel his icy fingers
Clasping mine amid the darkness!
Hiawatha! Hiawatha!"
And the desolate Hiawatha,
Far away amid the forest,
Miles away among the mountains,
Heard that sudden cry of anguish,
Heard the voice of Minnehaha
Calling to him in the darkness,
"Hiawatha! Hiawatha!"
Over snow-fields waste and pathless,
Under snow-encumbered branches,
Homeward hurried Hiawatha,
Empty-handed, heavy-hearted,
Heard Nokomis moaning, wailing:
"Wahonowin! Wahonowin!
Would that I had perished for you,
Would that I were dead as you are!
Wahonowin! Wahonowin!"
And he rushed into the wigwam,
Saw the old Nokomis slowly
Rocking to and fro and moaning,
Saw his lovely Minnehaha
Lying dead and cold before him,
And his bursting heart within him
Uttered such a cry of anguish,
That the forest moaned and shuddered,
That the very stars in heaven

Shook and trembled with his anguish.
  Then he sat down, still and speechless,
On the bed of Minnehaha,
At the feet of Laughing Water,
At those willing feet, that never
More would lightly run to meet him,
Never more would lightly follow.
  With both hands his face he covered,
Seven long days and nights he sat there,
As if in a swoon he sat there,
Speechless, motionless, unconscious
Of the daylight or the darkness.
  Then they buried Minnehaha;
In the snow a grave they made her,
In the forest deep and darksome,
Underneath the moaning hemlocks;
Clothed her in her richest garments,
Wrapped her in her robes of ermine,
Covered her with snow, like ermine;
Thus they buried Minnehaha.
  And at night a fire was lighted,
On her grave four times was kindled,
For her soul upon its journey
To the Islands of the Blessed.
From his doorway Hiawatha
Saw it burning in the forest,
Lighting up the gloomy hemlocks;
From his sleepless bed uprising,
From the bed of Minnehaha,
Stood and watched it at the doorway,
That it might not be extinguished,
Might not leave her in the darkness.
  "Farewell!" said he, "Minnehaha!
Farewell, O my Laughing Water!
All my heart is buried with you,
All my thoughts go onward with you!
Come not back again to labor,
Come not back again to suffer,
Where the Famine and the Fever
Wear the heart and waste the body.

Soon my task will be completed,
Soon your footsteps I shall follow
To the Islands of the Blessed,
To the Kingdom of Ponemah,
To the land of the Hereafter!"

XXI

THE WHITE MAN'S FOOT

In his lodge beside a river,
Close beside a frozen river,
Sat an old man, sad and lonely.
White his hair was as a snow-drift;
Dull and low his fire was burning,
And the old man shook and trembled,
Folded in his Waubewyon,
In his tattered white-skin-wrapper,
Hearing nothing but the tempest
As it roared along the forest,
Seeing nothing but the snow-storm,
As it whirled and hissed and drifted.
All the coals were white with ashes,
And the fire was slowly dying,
As a young man, walking lightly,
At the open doorway entered.
Red with blood of youth his cheeks were,
Soft his eyes, as stars in Spring-time,
Bound his forehead was with grasses;
Bound and plumed with scented grasses,
On his lips a smile of beauty,
Filling all the lodge with sunshine,
In his hand a bunch of blossoms
Filling all the lodge with sweetness.
"Ah, my son!" exclaimed the old man,
"Happy are my eyes to see you.
Sit here on the mat beside me,
Sit here by the dying embers,
Let us pass the night together.
Tell me of your strange adventures,

Of the lands where you have travelled;
I will tell you of my prowess,
Of my many deeds of wonder."
  From his pouch he drew his peace-pipe,
Very old and strangely fashioned;
Made of red stone was the pipe-head,
And the stem a reed with feathers;
Filled the pipe with bark of willow,
Placed a burning coal upon it,
Gave it to his guest, the stranger,
And began to speak in this wise:
"When I blow my breath about me,
When I breathe upon the landscape,
Motionless are all the rivers,
Hard as stone becomes the water!"
  And the young man answered, smiling:
"When I blow my breath about me,
When I breathe upon the landscape,
Flowers spring up o'er all the meadows,
Singing, onward rush the rivers!"
  "When I shake my hoary tresses,"
Said the old man darkly frowning,
"All the land with snow is covered;
All the leaves from all the branches
Fall and fade and die and wither,
For I breathe, and lo! they are not.
From the waters and the marshes
Rise the wild goose and the heron,
Fly away to distant regions,
For I speak, and lo! they are not.
And where'er my footsteps wander,
All the wild beasts of the forest
Hide themselves in holes and caverns,
And the earth becomes as flintstone!"
  "When I shake my flowing ringlets,"
Said the young man, softly laughing,
"Showers of rain fall warm and welcome,
Plants lift up their heads rejoicing,
Back into their lakes and marshes

Come the wild goose and the heron,
Homeward shoots the arrowy swallow,
Sing the bluebird and the robin,
And where'er my footsteps wander,
All the meadows wave with blossoms,
All the woodlands ring with music,
All the trees are dark with foliage!"
While they spake, the night departed:
From the distant realms of Wabun,
From his shining lodge of silver,
Like a warrior robed and painted,
Came the sun, and said, "Behold me!
Gheezis, the great sun, behold me!"
Then the old man's tongue was speechless
And the air grew warm and pleasant,
And upon the wigwam sweetly
Sang the bluebird and the robin,
And the stream began to murmur,
And a scent of growing grasses
Through the lodge was gently wafted.
And Segwun, the youthful stranger,
More distinctly in the daylight
Saw the icy face before him;
It was Peboan, the Winter!
From his eyes the tears were flowing,
As from melting lakes the streamlets,
And his body shrunk and dwindled
As the shouting sun ascended,
Till into the air it faded,
Till into the ground it vanished,
And the young man saw before him,
On the hearth-stone of the wigwam,
Where the fire had smoked and smouldered,
Saw the earliest flower of Spring-time,
Saw the Beauty of the Spring-time,
Saw the Miskodeed in blossom.
Thus it was that in the North-land
After that unheard-of coldness,
That intolerable Winter,

Came the Spring with all its splendor,
All its birds and all its blossoms,
All its flowers and leaves and grasses.
  Sailing on the wind to northward,
Flying in great flocks, like arrows,
Like huge arrows shot through heaven,
Passed the swan, the Mahnahbezee,
Speaking almost as a man speaks;
And in long lines waving, bending
Like a bow-string snapped asunder,
Came the white goose, Waw-be-wawa;
And in pairs, or singly flying,
Mahng the loon, with clangorous pinions,
The blue heron, the Shuh-shuh-gah,
And the grouse, the Mushkodasa.
  In the thickets and the meadows
Piped the bluebird, the Owaissa,
On the summit of the lodges
Sang the robin, the Opechee,
In the covert of the pine-trees
Cooed the pigeon, the Omemee,
And the sorrowing Hiawatha,
Speechless in his infinite sorrow,
Heard their voices calling to him,
Went forth from his gloomy doorway,
Stood and gazed into the heaven,
Gazed upon the earth and waters.
  From his wanderings far to eastward,
From the regions of the morning,
From the shining land of Wabun,
Homeward now returned Iagoo,
The great traveller, the great boaster,
Full of new and strange adventures,
Marvels many and many wonders.
  And the people of the village
Listened to him as he told them
Of his marvellous adventures,
Laughing answered him in this wise:
"Ugh! it is indeed Iagoo!
No one else beholds such wonders!"

He had seen, he said, a water
Bigger than the Big-Sea-Water,
Broader than the Gitche Gumee,
Bitter so that none could drink it!
At each other looked the warriors,
Looked the women at each other,
Smiled, and said, "It cannot be so!
Kaw!" they said, "it cannot be so!"
O'er it, said he, o'er this water
Came a great canoe with pinions,
A canoe with wings came flying,
Bigger than a grove of pine-trees,
Taller than the tallest tree-tops!
And the old men and the women
Looked and tittered at each other;
"Kaw!" they said, "we don't believe it!"
From its mouth, he said, to greet him,
Came Waywassimo, the lightning,
Came the thunder, Annemeekee!
And the warriors and the women
Laughed aloud at poor Iagoo;
"Kaw!" they said, "what tales you tell us!"
In it, said he, came a people,
In the great canoe with pinions
Came, he said, a hundred warriors;
Painted white were all their faces
And with hair their chins were covered!
And the warriors and the women
Laughed and shouted in derision,
Like the ravens on the tree-tops,
Like the crows upon the hemlocks.
"Kaw!" they said, "what lies you tell us!
Do not think that we believe them!"
Only Hiawatha laughed not,
But he gravely spake and answered
To their jeering and their jesting:
"True is all Iagoo tells us;
I have seen it in a vision,
Seen the great canoe with pinions,
Seen the people with white faces,

Seen the coming of this bearded
People of the wooden vessel
From the regions of the morning,
From the shining land of Wabun.
"Gitche Manito, the Mighty,
The Great Spirit, the Creator,
Sends them hither on his errand,
Sends them to us with his message.
Wheresoe'er they move, before them
Swarms the stinging fly, the Ahmo,
Swarms the bee, the honey-maker;
Wheresoe'er they tread, beneath them
Springs a flower unknown among us,
Springs the White-man's Foot in blossom.
"Let us welcome, then, the strangers,
Hail them as our friends and brothers,
And the heart's right hand of friendship
Give them when they come to see us.
Gitche Manito, the Mighty,
Said this to me in my vision.
"I beheld, too, in that vision
All the secrets of the future,
Of the distant days that shall be.
I beheld the westward marches
Of the unknown, crowded nations.
All the land was full of people,
Restless, struggling, toiling, striving,
Speaking many tongues, yet feeling
But one heart-beat in their bosoms.
In the woodlands rang their axes,
Smoked their towns in all the valleys,
Over all the lakes and rivers
Rushed their great canoes of thunder.
"Then a darker, drearier vision
Passed before me, vague and cloud-like;
I beheld our nation scattered,
All forgetful of my counsels,
Weakened, warring with each other:
Saw the remnants of our people

Sweeping westward, wild and woful,
Like the cloud-rack of a tempest,
Like the withered leaves of Autumn!"

XXII

HIAWATHA'S DEPARTURE

By the shore of Gitche Gumee,
By the shining Big-Sea-Water,
At the doorway of his wigwam,
In the pleasant Summer morning,
Hiawatha stood and waited.
All the air was full of freshness,
All the earth was bright and joyous,
And before him, through the sunshine,
Westward toward the neighboring forest
Passed in golden swarms the Ahmo,
Passed the bees, the honey-makers,
Burning, singing in the sunshine.
  Bright above him shone the heavens,
Level spread the lake before him;
From its bosom leaped the sturgeon,
Sparkling, flashing in the sunshine;
On its margin the great forest
Stood reflected in the water,
Every tree-top had its shadow,
Motionless beneath the water.
  From the brow of Hiawatha
Gone was every trace of sorrow,
As the fog from off the water,
As the mist from off the meadow.
With a smile of joy and triumph,
With a look of exultation,
As of one who in a vision
Sees what is to be, but is not,
Stood and waited Hiawatha.
  Toward the sun his hands were lifted,
Both the palms spread out against it,
And between the parted fingers

Fell the sunshine on his features,
Flecked with light his naked shoulders,
As it falls and flecks on oak-tree
Through the rifted leaves and branches.
O'er the water floating, flying,
Something in the hazy distance,
Something in the mists of morning,
Loomed and lifted from the water,
Now seemed floating, now seemed flying,
Coming nearer, nearer, nearer.
Was it Shingebis the diver?
Or the pelican, the Shada?
Or the heron, the Shuh-shuh-gah?
Or the white goose, Waw-be-wawa,
With the water dripping, flashing,
From its glossy neck and feathers?
It was neither goose nor diver,
Neither pelican nor heron,
O'er the water floating, flying,
Through the shining mist of morning,
But a birch canoe with paddles,
Rising, sinking on the water,
Dripping, flashing in the sunshine;
And within it came a people
From the distant land of Wabun,
From the farthest realms of morning
Came the Black-Robe chief, the Prophet,
He the Priest of Prayer, the Pale-face,
With his guides and his companions.
And the noble Hiawatha,
With his hands aloft extended,
Held aloft in sign of welcome,
Waited, full of exultation,
Till the birch canoe with paddles
Grated on the shining pebbles,
Stranded on the sandy margin,
Till the Black-Robe chief, the Pale-face,
With the cross upon his bosom,
Landed on the sandy margin.

Then the joyous Hiawatha
Cried aloud and spake in this wise:
"Beautiful is the sun, O strangers,
When you come so far to see us!
All our town in peace awaits you,
All our doors stand open for you;
You shall enter all our wigwams,
For the heart's right hand we give you.
"Never bloomed the earth so gayly,
Never shone the sun so brightly,
As to-day they shine and blossom
When you come so far to see us!
Never was our lake so tranquil,
Nor so free from rocks and sand-bars;
For your birch canoe in passing
Has removed both rock and sand-bar.
"Never before had our tobacco
Such a sweet and pleasant flavor,
Never the broad leaves of our cornfields
Were so beautiful to look on,
As they seem to us this morning,
When you come so far to see us!"
And the Black-Robe chief made answer,
Stammered in his speech a little,
Speaking words yet unfamiliar:
"Peace be with you, Hiawatha,
Peace be with you and your people,
Peace of prayer, and peace of pardon,
Peace of Christ, and joy of Mary!"
Then the generous Hiawatha
Led the strangers to his wigwam,
Seated them on skins of bison,
Seated them on skins of ermine,
And the careful old Nokomis
Brought them food in bowls of basswood,
Water brought in birchen dippers,
And the calumet, the peace-pipe,
Filled and lighted for their smoking.
All the old men of the village,

All the warriors of the nation,
All the Jossakeeds, the Prophets,
The magicians, the Wabenos,
And the medicine-men, the Medas,
Came to bid the strangers welcome;
"It is well," they said, "O brothers,
That you come so far to see us!"
In a circle round the doorway,
With their pipes they sat in silence,
Waiting to behold the strangers,
Waiting to receive their message;
Till the Black-Robe chief, the Pale-face,
From the wigwam came to greet them,
Stammering in his speech a little,
Speaking words yet unfamiliar;
"It is well," they said, "O brother,
That you come so far to see us!"
Then the Black-Robe chief, the Prophet,
Told his message to the people,
Told the purport of his mission,
Told them of the Virgin Mary,
And her blessed Son, the Saviour,
How in distant lands and ages
He had lived on earth as we do;
How he fasted, prayed, and labored;
How the Jews, the tribe accursed,
Mocked him, scourged him, crucified him;
How he rose from where they laid him,
Walked again with his disciples,
And ascended into heaven.
And the chiefs made answer, saying:
"We have listened to your message,
We have heard your words of wisdom,
We will think on what you tell us.
It is well for us, O brothers,
That you come so far to see us!"
Then they rose up and departed
Each one homeward to his wigwam,
To the young men and the women
Told the story of the strangers

Whom the Master of Life had sent them
From the shining land of Wabun.
   Heavy with the heat and silence
Grew the afternoon of Summer;
With a drowsy sound the forest
Whispered round the sultry wigwam,
With a sound of sleep the water
Rippled on the beach below it;
From the cornfields shrill and ceaseless
Sang the grasshopper, Pah-puk-keena;
And the guests of Hiawatha,
Weary with the heat of Summer,
Slumbered in the sultry wigwam.
   Slowly o'er the simmering landscape
Fell the evening's dusk and coolness,
And the long and level sunbeams
Shot their spears into the forest,
Breaking through its shields of shadow,
Rushed into each secret ambush,
Searched each thicket, dingle, hollow;
Still the guests of Hiawatha
Slumbered in the silent wigwam.
   From his place rose Hiawatha,
Bade farewell to old Nokomis,
Spake in whispers, spake in this wise,
Did not wake the guests, that slumbered:
   "I am going, O Nokomis,
On a long and distant journey,
To the portals of the Sunset,
To the regions of the home-wind,
Of the Northwest-Wind, Keewaydin.
But these guests I leave behind me,
In your watch and ward I leave them;
See that never harm comes near them,
See that never fear molests them,
Never danger nor suspicion,
Never want of food or shelter,
In the lodge of Hiawatha!"
   Forth into the village went he,
Bade farewell to all the warriors,

Bade farewell to all the young men,
Spake persuading, spake in this wise:
"I am going, O my people,
On a long and distant journey;
Many moons and many winters
Will have come, and will have vanished,
Ere I come again to see you.
But my guests I leave behind me;
Listen to their words of wisdom,
Listen to the truth they tell you,
For the Master of Life has sent them
From the land of light and morning!"
On the shore stood Hiawatha,
Turned and waved his hand at parting;
On the clear and luminous water
Launched his birch canoe for sailing,
From the pebbles of the margin
Shoved it forth into the water;
Whispered to it, "Westward! westward!"
And with speed it darted forward.
And the evening sun descending
Set the clouds on fire with redness,
Burned the broad sky, like a prairie,
Left upon the level water
One long track and trail of splendor,
Down whose stream, as down a river,
Westward, westward Hiawatha
Sailed into the fiery sunset,
Sailed into the purple vapors,
Sailed into the dusk of evening.
And the people from the margin
Watched him floating, rising, sinking,
Till the birch canoe seemed lifted
High into that sea of splendor,
Till it sank into the vapors
Like the new moon slowly, slowly
Sinking in the purple distance.
And they said, "Farewell forever!"
Said, "Farewell, O Hiawatha!"
And the forests, dark and lonely,

Moved through all their depths of darkness,
Sighed, "Farewell, O Hiawatha!"
And the waves upon the margin
Rising, rippling on the pebbles,
Sobbed, "Farewell, O Hiawatha!"
And the heron, the Shuh-shuh-gah,
From her haunts among the fen-lands,
Screamed, "Farewell, O Hiawatha!"
  Thus departed Hiawatha,
Hiawatha the Beloved,
In the glory of the sunset,
In the purple mists of evening,
To the regions of the home-wind,
Of the Northwest-Wind, Keewaydin,
To the Islands of the Blessed,
To the kingdom of Ponemah,
To the land of the Hereafter!

from

THE COURTSHIP OF MILES STANDISH AND OTHER POEMS

The Courtship of Miles Standish

I.

MILES STANDISH.

In the Old Colony days, in Plymouth the land of the Pilgrims,
To and fro in a room of his simple and primitive dwelling,
Clad in doublet and hose, and boots of Cordovan leather,
Strode, with a martial air, Miles Standish the Puritan Captain.
Buried in thought he seemed, with his hands behind him, and pausing
Ever and anon to behold his glittering weapons of warfare,
Hanging in shining array along the walls of the chamber,—
Cutlass and corselet of steel, and his trusty sword of Damascus,
Curved at the point and inscribed with its mystical Arabic sentence,
While underneath, in a corner, were fowling-piece, musket, and matchlock.
Short of stature he was, but strongly built and athletic,
Broad in the shoulders, deep-chested, with muscles and sinews of iron;
Brown as a nut was his face, but his russet beard was already
Flaked with patches of snow, as hedges sometimes in November.
Near him was seated John Alden, his friend, and household companion,
Writing with diligent speed at a table of pine by the window;
Fair-haired, azure-eyed, with delicate Saxon complexion,
Having the dew of his youth, and the beauty thereof, as the captives
Whom Saint Gregory saw, and exclaimed, "Not Angles, but Angels."

Youngest of all was he of the men who came in the Mayflower.

Suddenly breaking the silence, the diligent scribe interrupting,
Spake, in the pride of his heart, Miles Standish the Captain of Plymouth.
"Look at these arms," he said, "the warlike weapons that hang here
Burnished and bright and clean, as if for parade or inspection!
This is the sword of Damascus I fought with in Flanders; this breastplate,
Well I remember the day! once saved my life in a skirmish;
Here in front you can see the very dint of the bullet
Fired point-blank at my heart by a Spanish arcabucero.
Had it not been of sheer steel, the forgotten bones of Miles Standish
Would at this moment be mould, in their grave in the Flemish morasses."
Thereupon answered John Alden, but looked not up from his writing:
"Truly the breath of the Lord hath slackened the speed of the bullet;
He in his mercy preserved you, to be our shield and our weapon!"
Still the Captain continued, unheeding the words of the stripling:
"See, how bright they are burnished, as if in an arsenal hanging;
That is because I have done it myself, and not left it to others.
Serve yourself, would you be well served, is an excellent adage;
So I take care of my arms, as you of your pens and your inkhorn.
Then, too, there are my soldiers, my great, invincible army,
Twelve men, all equipped, having each his rest and his matchlock,
Eighteen shillings a month, together with diet and pillage,
And, like Cæsar, I know the name of each of my soldiers!"
This he said with a smile, that danced in his eyes, as the sunbeams

Dance on the waves of the sea, and vanish again in a moment.
Alden laughed as he wrote, and still the Captain continued:
"Look! you can see from this window my brazen howitzer planted
High on the roof of the church, a preacher who speaks to the purpose,
Steady, straightforward, and strong, with irresistible logic,
Orthodox, flashing conviction right into the hearts of the heathen.
Now we are ready, I think, for any assault of the Indians;
Let them come, if they like, and the sooner they try it the better,—
Let them come, if they like, be it sagamore, sachem, or pow-wow,
Aspinet, Samoset, Corbitant, Squanto, or Tokamahamon!"

Long at the window he stood, and wistfully gazed on the landscape,
Washed with a cold gray mist, the vapory breath of the east-wind,
Forest and meadow and hill, and the steel-blue rim of the ocean,
Lying silent and sad, in the afternoon shadows and sunshine.
Over his countenance flitted a shadow like those on the landscape,
Gloom intermingled with light; and his voice was subdued with emotion,
Tenderness, pity, regret, as after a pause he proceeded:
"Yonder there, on the hill by the sea, lies buried Rose Standish;
Beautiful rose of love, that bloomed for me by the wayside!
She was the first to die of all who came in the Mayflower!
Green above her is growing the field of wheat we have sown there,
Better to hide from the Indian scouts the graves of our people,
Lest they should count them and see how many already have perished!"
Sadly his face he averted, and strode up and down, and was thoughtful.

Fixed to the opposite wall was a shelf of books, and among them
Prominent three, distinguished alike for bulk and for binding;
Bariffe's Artillery Guide, and the Commentaries of Cæsar
Out of the Latin translated by Arthur Goldinge of London,
And, as if guarded by these, between them was standing the Bible.
Musing a moment before them, Miles Standish paused, as if doubtful
Which of the three he should choose for his consolation and comfort,
Whether the wars of the Hebrews, the famous campaigns of the Romans,
Or the Artillery practice, designed for belligerent Christians.
Finally down from its shelf he dragged the ponderous Roman,
Seated himself at the window, and opened the book, and in silence
Turned o'er the well-worn leaves, where thumb-marks thick on the margin,
Like the trample of feet, proclaimed the battle was hottest.
Nothing was heard in the room but the hurrying pen of the stripling,
Busily writing epistles important, to go by the Mayflower,
Ready to sail on the morrow, or next day at latest, God willing!
Homeward bound with the tidings of all that terrible winter,
Letters written by Alden, and full of the name of Priscilla!
Full of the name and the fame of the Puritan maiden Priscilla!

II.

LOVE AND FRIENDSHIP.

Nothing was heard in the room but the hurrying pen of the stripling,
Or an occasional sigh from the laboring heart of the Captain,
Reading the marvellous words and achievements of Julius Cæsar.

After a while he exclaimed, as he smote with his hand, palm downwards,
Heavily on the page: "A wonderful man was this Cæsar!
You are a writer, and I am a fighter, but here is a fellow
Who could both write and fight, and in both was equally skilful!"
Straightway answered and spake John Alden, the comely, the youthful:
"Yes, he was equally skilled, as you say, with his pen and his weapons.
Somewhere have I read, but where I forget, he could dictate
Seven letters at once, at the same time writing his memoirs."
"Truly," continued the Captain, not heeding or hearing the other,
"Truly a wonderful man was Caius Julius Cæsar!
Better be first, he said, in a little Iberian village,
Than be second in Rome, and I think he was right when he said it.
Twice was he married before he was twenty, and many times after;
Battles five hundred he fought, and a thousand cities he conquered;
He, too, fought in Flanders, as he himself has recorded;
Finally he was stabbed by his friend, the orator Brutus!
Now, do you know what he did on a certain occasion in Flanders,
When the rear-guard of his army retreated, the front giving way too,
And the immortal Twelfth Legion was crowded so closely together
There was no room for their swords? Why, he seized a shield from a soldier,
Put himself straight at the head of his troops, and commanded the captains,
Calling on each by his name, to order forward the ensigns;
Then to widen the ranks, and give more room for their weapons;
So he won the day, the battle of something-or-other.
That's what I always say; if you wish a thing to be well done,
You must do it yourself, you must not leave it to others!"

All was silent again; the Captain continued his reading.
Nothing was heard in the room but the hurrying pen of the stripling
Writing epistles important to go next day by the Mayflower,
Filled with the name and the fame of the Puritan maiden Priscilla;
Every sentence began or closed with the name of Priscilla,
Till the treacherous pen, to which he confided the secret,
Strove to betray it by singing and shouting the name of Priscilla!
Finally closing his book, with a bang of the ponderous cover,
Sudden and loud as the sound of a soldier grounding his musket,
Thus to the young man spake Miles Standish the Captain of Plymouth:
"When you have finished your work, I have something important to tell you.
Be not however in haste; I can wait; I shall not be impatient!"
Straightway Alden replied, as he folded the last of his letters,
Pushing his papers aside, and giving respectful attention:
"Speak; for whenever you speak, I am always ready to listen,
Always ready to hear whatever pertains to Miles Standish."
Thereupon answered the Captain, embarrassed, and culling his phrases:
" 'T is not good for a man to be alone, say the Scriptures.
This I have said before, and again and again I repeat it;
Every hour in the day, I think it, and feel it, and say it.
Since Rose Standish died, my life has been weary and dreary;
Sick at heart have I been, beyond the healing of friendship;
Oft in my lonely hours have I thought of the maiden Priscilla.
She is alone in the world; her father and mother and brother
Died in the winter together; I saw her going and coming,
Now to the grave of the dead, and now to the bed of the dying,
Patient, courageous, and strong, and said to myself, that if ever
There were angels on earth, as there are angels in heaven,
Two have I seen and known; and the angel whose name is Priscilla
Holds in my desolate life the place which the other abandoned.

Long have I cherished the thought, but never have dared to reveal it,
Being a coward in this, though valiant enough for the most part.
Go to the damsel Priscilla, the loveliest maiden of Plymouth,
Say that a blunt old Captain, a man not of words but of actions,
Offers his hand and his heart, the hand and heart of a soldier.
Not in these words, you know, but this in short is my meaning;
I am a maker of war, and not a maker of phrases.
You, who are bred as a scholar, can say it in elegant language,
Such as you read in your books of the pleadings and wooings of lovers,
Such as you think best adapted to win the heart of a maiden."

When he had spoken, John Alden, the fair-haired, taciturn stripling,
All aghast at his words, surprised, embarrassed, bewildered,
Trying to mask his dismay by treating the subject with lightness,
Trying to smile, and yet feeling his heart stand still in his bosom,
Just as a timepiece stops in a house that is stricken by lightning,
Thus made answer and spake, or rather stammered than answered:
"Such a message as that, I am sure I should mangle and mar it;
If you would have it well done,—I am only repeating your maxim,—
You must do it yourself, you must not leave it to others!"
But with the air of a man whom nothing can turn from his purpose,
Gravely shaking his head, made answer the Captain of Plymouth:
"Truly the maxim is good, and I do not mean to gainsay it;
But we must use it discreetly, and not waste powder for nothing.
Now, as I said before, I was never a maker of phrases.

I can march up to a fortress and summon the place to
surrender,
But march up to a woman with such a proposal, I dare not.
I'm not afraid of bullets, nor shot from the mouth of a
cannon,
But of a thundering 'No!' point-blank from the mouth of a
woman,
That I confess I'm afraid of, nor am I ashamed to confess it!
So you must grant my request, for you are an elegant scholar,
Having the graces of speech, and skill in the turning of
phrases."
Taking the hand of his friend, who still was reluctant and
doubtful,
Holding it long in his own, and pressing it kindly, he added:
"Though I have spoken thus lightly, yet deep is the feeling
that prompts me;
Surely you cannot refuse what I ask in the name of our
friendship!"
Then made answer John Alden: "The name of friendship is
sacred;
What you demand in that name, I have not the power to
deny you!"
So the strong will prevailed, subduing and moulding the
gentler,
Friendship prevailed over love, and Alden went on his errand.

III.

THE LOVER'S ERRAND.

So the strong will prevailed, and Alden went on his errand,
Out of the street of the village, and into the paths of the
forest,
Into the tranquil woods, where bluebirds and robins were
building
Towns in the populous trees, with hanging gardens of
verdure,
Peaceful, aerial cities of joy and affection and freedom.
All around him was calm, but within him commotion and
conflict,

Love contending with friendship, and self with each generous
impulse.
To and fro in his breast his thoughts were heaving and
dashing,
As in a foundering ship, with every roll of the vessel,
Washes the bitter sea, the merciless surge of the ocean!
"Must I relinquish it all," he cried with a wild lamentation,—
"Must I relinquish it all, the joy, the hope, the illusion?
Was it for this I have loved, and waited, and worshipped in
silence?
Was it for this I have followed the flying feet and the shadow
Over the wintry sea, to the desolate shores of New England?
Truly the heart is deceitful, and out of its depths of
corruption
Rise, like an exhalation, the misty phantoms of passion;
Angels of light they seem, but are only delusions of Satan.
All is clear to me now; I feel it, I see it distinctly!
This is the hand of the Lord; it is laid upon me in anger,
For I have followed too much the heart's desires and
devices,
Worshipping Astaroth blindly, and impious idols of Baal.
This is the cross I must bear; the sin and the swift
retribution."

So through the Plymouth woods John Alden went on his
errand;
Crossing the brook at the ford, where it brawled over pebble
and shallow,
Gathering still, as he went, the May-flowers blooming around
him,
Fragrant, filling the air with a strange and wonderful
sweetness,
Children lost in the woods, and covered with leaves in their
slumber.
"Puritan flowers," he said, "and the type of Puritan maidens,
Modest and simple and sweet, the very type of Priscilla!
So I will take them to her; to Priscilla the Mayflower of
Plymouth,
Modest and simple and sweet, as a parting gift will I take
them;

Breathing their silent farewells, as they fade and wither and perish,
Soon to be thrown away as is the heart of the giver."
So through the Plymouth woods John Alden went on his errand;
Came to an open space, and saw the disk of the ocean,
Sailless, sombre and cold with the comfortless breath of the east-wind;
Saw the new-built house, and people at work in a meadow;
Heard, as he drew near the door, the musical voice of Priscilla
Singing the hundredth Psalm, the grand old Puritan anthem,
Music that Luther sang to the sacred words of the Psalmist,
Full of the breath of the Lord, consoling and comforting many.
Then, as he opened the door, he beheld the form of the maiden
Seated beside her wheel, and the carded wool like a snow-drift
Piled at her knee, her white hands feeding the ravenous spindle,
While with her foot on the treadle she guided the wheel in its motion.
Open wide on her lap lay the well-worn psalm-book of Ainsworth,
Printed in Amsterdam, the words and the music together,
Rough-hewn, angular notes, like stones in the wall of a churchyard,
Darkened and overhung by the running vine of the verses.
Such was the book from whose pages she sang the old Puritan anthem,
She, the Puritan girl, in the solitude of the forest,
Making the humble house and the modest apparel of home-spun
Beautiful with her beauty, and rich with the wealth of her being!
Over him rushed, like a wind that is keen and cold and relentless,
Thoughts of what might have been, and the weight and woe of his errand;

All the dreams that had faded, and all the hopes that had vanished,
All his life henceforth a dreary and tenantless mansion,
Haunted by vain regrets, and pallid, sorrowful faces.
Still he said to himself, and almost fiercely he said it,
"Let not him that putteth his hand to the plough look backwards;
Though the ploughshare cut through the flowers of life to its fountains,
Though it pass o'er the graves of the dead and the hearths of the living,
It is the will of the Lord; and his mercy endureth forever!"

So he entered the house: and the hum of the wheel and the singing
Suddenly ceased; for Priscilla, aroused by his step on the threshold,
Rose as he entered, and gave him her hand, in signal of welcome,
Saying, "I knew it was you, when I heard your step in the passage;
For I was thinking of you, as I sat there singing and spinning."
Awkward and dumb with delight, that a thought of him had been mingled
Thus in the sacred psalm, that came from the heart of the maiden,
Silent before her he stood, and gave her the flowers for an answer,
Finding no words for his thought. He remembered that day in the winter,
After the first great snow, when he broke a path from the village,
Reeling and plunging along through the drifts that encumbered the doorway,
Stamping the snow from his feet as he entered the house, and Priscilla
Laughed at his snowy locks, and gave him a seat by the fireside,

Grateful and pleased to know he had thought of her in the
snow-storm.
Had he but spoken then! perhaps not in vain had he spoken;
Now it was all too late; the golden moment had vanished!
So he stood there abashed, and gave her the flowers for an
answer.

Then they sat down and talked of the birds and the
beautiful Spring-time,
Talked of their friends at home, and the Mayflower that sailed
on the morrow.
"I have been thinking all day," said gently the Puritan
maiden,
"Dreaming all night, and thinking all day, of the hedge-rows
of England,—
They are in blossom now, and the country is all like a garden;
Thinking of lanes and fields, and the song of the lark and the
linnet,
Seeing the village street, and familiar faces of neighbors
Going about as of old, and stopping to gossip together,
And, at the end of the street, the village church, with the ivy
Climbing the old gray tower, and the quiet graves in the
churchyard.
Kind are the people I live with, and dear to me my religion;
Still my heart is so sad, that I wish myself back in Old
England.
You will say it is wrong, but I cannot help it: I almost
Wish myself back in Old England, I feel so lonely and
wretched."

Thereupon answered the youth: "Indeed I do not
condemn you;
Stouter hearts than a woman's have quailed in this terrible
winter.
Yours is tender and trusting, and needs a stronger to lean on;
So I have come to you now, with an offer and proffer of
marriage
Made by a good man and true, Miles Standish the Captain of
Plymouth!"

Thus he delivered his message, the dexterous writer of letters,—
Did not embellish the theme, nor array it in beautiful phrases,
But came straight to the point, and blurted it out like a school-boy;
Even the Captain himself could hardly have said it more bluntly.
Mute with amazement and sorrow, Priscilla the Puritan maiden
Looked into Alden's face, her eyes dilated with wonder,
Feeling his words like a blow, that stunned her and rendered her speechless;
Till at length she exclaimed, interrupting the ominous silence:
"If the great Captain of Plymouth is so very eager to wed me,
Why does he not come himself, and take the trouble to woo me?
If I am not worth the wooing, I surely am not worth the winning!"
Then John Alden began explaining and smoothing the matter,
Making it worse as he went, by saying the Captain was busy,—
Had no time for such things;—such things! the words grating harshly
Fell on the ear of Priscilla; and swift as a flash she made answer:
"Has he no time for such things, as you call it, before he is married,
Would he be likely to find it, or make it, after the wedding?
That is the way with you men; you don't understand us, you cannot.
When you have made up your minds, after thinking of this one and that one,
Choosing, selecting, rejecting, comparing one with another,
Then you make known your desire, with abrupt and sudden avowal,
And are offended and hurt, and indignant perhaps, that a woman
Does not respond at once to a love that she never suspected,
Does not attain at a bound the height to which you have been climbing.

This is not right nor just: for surely a woman's affection
Is not a thing to be asked for, and had for only the asking.
When one is truly in love, one not only says it, but shows it.
Had he but waited awhile, had he only showed that he loved
me,
Even this Captain of yours—who knows?—at last might have
won me,
Old and rough as he is; but now it never can happen."

Still John Alden went on, unheeding the words of Priscilla,
Urging the suit of his friend, explaining, persuading,
expanding;
Spoke of his courage and skill, and of all his battles in
Flanders,
How with the people of God he had chosen to suffer
affliction;
How, in return for his zeal, they had made him Captain of
Plymouth;
He was a gentleman born, could trace his pedigree plainly
Back to Hugh Standish of Duxbury Hall, in Lancashire,
England,
Who was the son of Ralph, and the grandson of Thurston de
Standish;
Heir unto vast estates, of which he was basely defrauded,
Still bore the family arms, and had for his crest a cock
argent
Combed and wattled gules, and all the rest of the blazon.
He was a man of honor, of noble and generous nature;
Though he was rough, he was kindly; she knew how during
the winter
He had attended the sick, with a hand as gentle as woman's;
Somewhat hasty and hot, he could not deny it, and
headstrong,
Stern as a soldier might be, but hearty, and placable always,
Not to be laughed at and scorned, because he was little of
stature;
For he was great of heart, magnanimous, courtly, courageous;
Any woman in Plymouth, nay, any woman in England,
Might be happy and proud to be called the wife of Miles
Standish!

But as he warmed and glowed, in his simple and eloquent language,
Quite forgetful of self, and full of the praise of his rival,
Archly the maiden smiled, and, with eyes overrunning with laughter,
Said, in a tremulous voice, "Why don't you speak for yourself, John?"

IV.

JOHN ALDEN.

Into the open air John Alden, perplexed and bewildered,
Rushed like a man insane, and wandered alone by the sea-side;
Paced up and down the sands, and bared his head to the east-wind,
Cooling his heated brow, and the fire and fever within him.
Slowly as out of the heavens, with apocalyptical splendors,
Sank the City of God, in the vision of John the Apostle,
So, with its cloudy walls of chrysolite, jasper, and sapphire,
Sank the broad red sun, and over its turrets uplifted
Glimmered the golden reed of the angel who measured the city.

"Welcome, O wind of the East!" he exclaimed in his wild exultation,
"Welcome, O wind of the East, from the caves of the misty Atlantic!
Blowing o'er fields of dulse, and measureless meadows of sea-grass,
Blowing o'er rocky wastes, and the grottos and gardens of ocean!
Lay thy cold, moist hand on my burning forehead, and wrap me
Close in thy garments of mist, to allay the fever within me!"

Like an awakened conscience, the sea was moaning and tossing,
Beating remorseful and loud the mutable sands of the sea-shore.

Fierce in his soul was the struggle and tumult of passions contending;
Love triumphant and crowned, and friendship wounded and bleeding,
Passionate cries of desire, and importunate pleadings of duty!
"Is it my fault," he said, "that the maiden has chosen between us?
Is it my fault that he failed,—my fault that I am the victor?"
Then within him there thundered a voice, like the voice of the Prophet:
"It hath displeased the Lord!"—and he thought of David's transgression,
Bathsheba's beautiful face, and his friend in the front of the battle!
Shame and confusion of guilt, and abasement and self-condemnation,
Overwhelmed him at once; and he cried in the deepest contrition:
"It hath displeased the Lord! It is the temptation of Satan!"

Then, uplifting his head, he looked at the sea, and beheld there
Dimly the shadowy form of the Mayflower riding at anchor,
Rocked on the rising tide, and ready to sail on the morrow;
Heard the voices of men through the mist, the rattle of cordage
Thrown on the deck, the shouts of the mate, and the sailors' "Ay, ay, Sir!"
Clear and distinct, but not loud, in the dripping air of the twilight.
Still for a moment he stood, and listened, and stared at the vessel,
Then went hurriedly on, as one who, seeing a phantom,
Stops, then quickens his pace, and follows the beckoning shadow.
"Yes, it is plain to me now," he murmured; "the hand of the Lord is
Leading me out of the land of darkness, the bondage of error,
Through the sea, that shall lift the walls of its waters around me,

Hiding me, cutting me off, from the cruel thoughts that pursue me.
Back will I go o'er the ocean, this dreary land will abandon,
Her whom I may not love, and him whom my heart has offended.
Better to be in my grave in the green old churchyard in England,
Close by my mother's side, and among the dust of my kindred;
Better be dead and forgotten, than living in shame and dishonor;
Sacred and safe and unseen, in the dark of the narrow chamber
With me my secret shall lie, like a buried jewel that glimmers
Bright on the hand that is dust, in the chambers of silence and darkness,—
Yes, as the marriage ring of the great espousal hereafter!"

Thus as he spake, he turned, in the strength of his strong resolution,
Leaving behind him the shore, and hurried along in the twilight,
Through the congenial gloom of the forest silent and sombre,
Till he beheld the lights in the seven houses of Plymouth,
Shining like seven stars in the dusk and mist of the evening.
Soon he entered his door, and found the redoubtable Captain
Sitting alone, and absorbed in the martial pages of Cæsar,
Fighting some great campaign in Hainault or Brabant or Flanders.
"Long have you been on your errand," he said with a cheery demeanor,
Even as one who is waiting an answer, and fears not the issue.
"Not far off is the house, although the woods are between us;
But you have lingered so long, that while you were going and coming
I have fought ten battles and sacked and demolished a city.
Come, sit down, and in order relate to me all that has happened."

Then John Alden spake, and related the wondrous adventure,
From beginning to end, minutely, just as it happened;

How he had seen Priscilla, and how he had sped in his courtship,
Only smoothing a little, and softening down her refusal.
But when he came at length to the words Priscilla had spoken,
Words so tender and cruel: "Why don't you speak for yourself, John?"
Up leaped the Captain of Plymouth, and stamped on the floor, till his armor
Clanged on the wall, where it hung, with a sound of sinister omen.
All his pent-up wrath burst forth in a sudden explosion,
E'en as a hand-grenade, that scatters destruction around it.
Wildly he shouted, and loud: "John Alden! you have betrayed me!
Me, Miles Standish, your friend! have supplanted, defrauded, betrayed me!
One of my ancestors ran his sword through the heart of Wat Tyler;
Who shall prevent me from running my own through the heart of a traitor?
Yours is the greater treason, for yours is a treason to friendship!
You, who lived under my roof, whom I cherished and loved as a brother;
You, who have fed at my board, and drunk at my cup, to whose keeping
I have intrusted my honor, my thoughts the most sacred and secret,—
You too, Brutus! ah woe to the name of friendship hereafter!
Brutus was Cæsar's friend, and you were mine, but henceforward
Let there be nothing between us save war, and implacable hatred!"

So spake the Captain of Plymouth, and strode about in the chamber,
Chafing and choking with rage; like cords were the veins on his temples.
But in the midst of his anger a man appeared at the doorway,

Bringing in uttermost haste a message of urgent importance,
Rumors of danger and war and hostile incursions of Indians
Straightway the Captain paused, and, without further question or parley,
Took from the nail on the wall his sword with its scabbard of iron,
Buckled the belt round his waist, and, frowning fiercely, departed.
Alden was left alone. He heard the clank of the scabbard
Growing fainter and fainter, and dying away in the distance.
Then he arose from his seat, and looked forth into the darkness,
Felt the cool air blow on his cheek, that was hot with the insult,
Lifted his eyes to the heavens, and, folding his hands as in childhood,
Prayed in the silence of night to the Father who seeth in secret.

Meanwhile the choleric Captain strode wrathful away to the council,
Found it already assembled, impatiently waiting his coming;
Men in the middle of life, austere and grave in deportment,
Only one of them old, the hill that was nearest to heaven,
Covered with snow, but erect, the excellent Elder of Plymouth.
God had sifted three kingdoms to find the wheat for this planting,
Then had sifted the wheat, as the living seed of a nation;
So say the chronicles old, and such is the faith of the people!
Near them was standing an Indian, in attitude stern and defiant,
Naked down to the waist, and grim and ferocious in aspect;
While on the table before them was lying unopened a Bible,
Ponderous, bound in leather, brass-studded, printed in Holland,
And beside it outstretched the skin of a rattlesnake glittered,
Filled, like a quiver, with arrows; a signal and challenge of warfare,
Brought by the Indian, and speaking with arrowy tongues of defiance.

This Miles Standish beheld, as he entered, and heard them debating
What were an answer befitting the hostile message and menace,
Talking of this and of that, contriving, suggesting, objecting;
One voice only for peace, and that the voice of the Elder,
Judging it wise and well that some at least were converted,
Rather than any were slain, for this was but Christian behavior!
Then out spake Miles Standish, the stalwart Captain of Plymouth,
Muttering deep in his throat, for his voice was husky with anger,
"What! do you mean to make war with milk and the water of roses?
Is it to shoot red squirrels you have your howitzer planted
There on the roof of the church, or is it to shoot red devils?
Truly the only tongue that is understood by a savage
Must be the tongue of fire that speaks from the mouth of the cannon!"
Thereupon answered and said the excellent Elder of Plymouth,
Somewhat amazed and alarmed at this irreverent language:
"Not so thought St. Paul, nor yet the other Apostles;
Not from the cannon's mouth were the tongues of fire they spake with!"
But unheeded fell this mild rebuke on the Captain,
Who had advanced to the table, and thus continued discoursing:
"Leave this matter to me, for to me by right it pertaineth.
War is a terrible trade; but in the cause that is righteous,
Sweet is the smell of powder; and thus I answer the challenge!"

Then from the rattlesnake's skin, with a sudden, contemptuous gesture,
Jerking the Indian arrows, he filled it with powder and bullets
Full to the very jaws, and handed it back to the savage,
Saying, in thundering tones: "Here, take it! this is your answer!"

Silently out of the room then glided the glistening savage,
Bearing the serpent's skin, and seeming himself like a serpent,
Winding his sinuous way in the dark to the depths of the forest.

V.

THE SAILING OF THE MAYFLOWER.

Just in the gray of the dawn, as the mists uprose from the meadows,
There was a stir and a sound in the slumbering village of Plymouth;
Clanging and clicking of arms, and the order imperative, "Forward!"
Given in tone suppressed, a tramp of feet, and then silence.
Figures ten, in the mist, marched slowly out of the village.
Standish the stalwart it was, with eight of his valorous army,
Led by their Indian guide, by Hobomok, friend of the white men,
Northward marching to quell the sudden revolt of the savage.
Giants they seemed in the mist, or the mighty men of King David;
Giants in heart they were, who believed in God and the Bible,—
Ay, who believed in the smiting of Midianites and Philistines.
Over them gleamed far off the crimson banners of morning;
Under them loud on the sands, the serried billows, advancing,
Fired along the line, and in regular order retreated.

Many a mile had they marched, when at length the village of Plymouth
Woke from its sleep, and arose, intent on its manifold labors.
Sweet was the air and soft; and slowly the smoke from the chimneys
Rose over roofs of thatch, and pointed steadily eastward;
Men came forth from the doors, and paused and talked of the weather,
Said that the wind had changed, and was blowing fair for the Mayflower;

Talked of their Captain's departure, and all the dangers that menaced,
He being gone, the town, and what should be done in his absence.
Merrily sang the birds, and the tender voices of women
Consecrated with hymns the common cares of the household.
Out of the sea rose the sun, and the billows rejoiced at his coming;
Beautiful were his feet on the purple tops of the mountains;
Beautiful on the sails of the Mayflower riding at anchor,
Battered and blackened and worn by all the storms of the winter.
Loosely against her masts was hanging and flapping her canvas,
Rent by so many gales, and patched by the hands of the sailors.
Suddenly from her side, as the sun rose over the ocean,
Darted a puff of smoke, and floated seaward; anon rang
Loud over field and forest the cannon's roar, and the echoes
Heard and repeated the sound, the signal-gun of departure!
Ah! but with louder echoes replied the hearts of the people!
Meekly, in voices subdued, the chapter was read from the Bible,
Meekly the prayer was begun, but ended in fervent entreaty!
Then from their houses in haste came forth the Pilgrims of Plymouth,
Men and women and children, all hurrying down to the sea-shore,
Eager, with tearful eyes, to say farewell to the Mayflower,
Homeward bound o'er the sea, and leaving them here in the desert.

Foremost among them was Alden. All night he had lain without slumber,
Turning and tossing about in the heat and unrest of his fever.
He had beheld Miles Standish, who came back late from the council,
Stalking into the room, and heard him mutter and murmur,
Sometimes it seemed a prayer, and sometimes it sounded like swearing.

Once he had come to the bed, and stood there a moment in silence;
Then he had turned away, and said: "I will not awake him;
Let him sleep on, it is best; for what is the use of more talking!"
Then he extinguished the light, and threw himself down on his pallet,
Dressed as he was, and ready to start at the break of the morning,—
Covered himself with the cloak he had worn in his campaigns in Flanders,—
Slept as a soldier sleeps in his bivouac, ready for action.
But with the dawn he arose; in the twilight Alden beheld him
Put on his corselet of steel, and all the rest of his armor,
Buckle about his waist his trusty blade of Damascus,
Take from the corner his musket, and so stride out of the chamber.
Often the heart of the youth had burned and yearned to embrace him,
Often his lips had essayed to speak, imploring for pardon;
All the old friendship came back, with its tender and grateful emotions;
But his pride overmastered the nobler nature within him,—
Pride, and the sense of his wrong, and the burning fire of the insult.
So he beheld his friend departing in anger, but spake not,
Saw him go forth to danger, perhaps to death, and he spake not!
Then he arose from his bed, and heard what the people were saying,
Joined in the talk at the door, with Stephen and Richard and Gilbert,
Joined in the morning prayer, and in the reading of Scripture,
And, with the others, in haste went hurrying down to the sea-shore,
Down to the Plymouth Rock, that had been to their feet as a doorstep
Into a world unknown,—the corner-stone of a nation!

There with his boat was the Master, already a little impatient
Lest he should lose the tide, or the wind might shift to the eastward,
Square-built, hearty, and strong, with an odor of ocean about him,
Speaking with this one and that, and cramming letters and parcels
Into his pockets capacious, and messages mingled together
Into his narrow brain, till at last he was wholly bewildered.
Nearer the boat stood Alden, with one foot placed on the gunwale,
One still firm on the rock, and talking at times with the sailors,
Seated erect on the thwarts, all ready and eager for starting.
He too was eager to go, and thus put an end to his anguish,
Thinking to fly from despair, that swifter than keel is or canvas,
Thinking to drown in the sea the ghost that would rise and pursue him.
But as he gazed on the crowd, he beheld the form of Priscilla
Standing dejected among them, unconscious of all that was passing.
Fixed were her eyes upon his, as if she divined his intention,
Fixed with a look so sad, so reproachful, imploring, and patient,
That with a sudden revulsion his heart recoiled from its purpose,
As from the verge of a crag, where one step more is destruction.
Strange is the heart of man, with its quick, mysterious instincts!
Strange is the life of man, and fatal or fated are moments,
Whereupon turn, as on hinges, the gates of the wall adamantine!
"Here I remain!" he exclaimed, as he looked at the heavens above him,
Thanking the Lord whose breath had scattered the mist and the madness,
Wherein, blind and lost, to death he was staggering headlong.

"Yonder snow-white cloud, that floats in the ether above me,
Seems like a hand that is pointing and beckoning over the ocean.
There is another hand, that is not so spectral and ghost-like,
Holding me, drawing me back, and clasping mine for protection.
Float, O hand of cloud, and vanish away in the ether!
Roll thyself up like a fist, to threaten and daunt me; I heed not
Either your warning or menace, or any omen of evil!
There is no land so sacred, no air so pure and so wholesome,
As is the air she breathes, and the soil that is pressed by her footsteps.
Here for her sake will I stay, and like an invisible presence
Hover around her forever, protecting, supporting her weakness;
Yes! as my foot was the first that stepped on this rock at the landing,
So, with the blessing of God, shall it be the last at the leaving!"

Meanwhile the Master alert, but with dignified air and important,
Scanning with watchful eye the tide and the wind and the weather,
Walked about on the sands, and the people crowded around him
Saying a few last words, and enforcing his careful remembrance.
Then, taking each by the hand, as if he were grasping a tiller,
Into the boat he sprang, and in haste shoved off to his vessel,
Glad in his heart to get rid of all this worry and flurry,
Glad to be gone from a land of sand and sickness and sorrow,
Short allowance of victual, and plenty of nothing but Gospel!
Lost in the sound of the oars was the last farewell of the Pilgrims.
O strong hearts and true! not one went back in the Mayflower!
No, not one looked back, who had set his hand to this ploughing!

Soon were heard on board the shouts and songs of the sailors
Heaving the windlass round, and hoisting the ponderous anchor.
Then the yards were braced, and all sails set to the west-wind,
Blowing steady and strong; and the Mayflower sailed from the harbor,
Rounded the point of the Gurnet, and leaving far to the southward
Island and cape of sand, and the Field of the First Encounter,
Took the wind on her quarter, and stood for the open Atlantic,
Borne on the send of the sea, and the swelling hearts of the Pilgrims.

Long in silence they watched the receding sail of the vessel,
Much endeared to them all, as something living and human;
Then, as if filled with the spirit, and wrapt in a vision prophetic,
Baring his hoary head, the excellent Elder of Plymouth
Said, "Let us pray!" and they prayed, and thanked the Lord and took courage.
Mournfully sobbed the waves at the base of the rock, and above them
Bowed and whispered the wheat on the hill of death, and their kindred
Seemed to awake in their graves, and to join in the prayer that they uttered.
Sun-illumined and white, on the eastern verge of the ocean
Gleamed the departing sail, like a marble slab in a graveyard;
Buried beneath it lay forever all hope of escaping.
Lo! as they turned to depart, they saw the form of an Indian,
Watching them from the hill; but while they spake with each other,
Pointing with outstretched hands, and saying, "Look!" he had vanished.
So they returned to their homes; but Alden lingered a little,
Musing alone on the shore, and watching the wash of the billows
Round the base of the rock, and the sparkle and flash of the sunshine,
Like the spirit of God, moving visibly over the waters.

VI.

PRISCILLA.

Thus for a while he stood, and mused by the shore of the ocean,
Thinking of many things, and most of all of Priscilla;
And as if thought had the power to draw to itself, like the loadstone,
Whatsoever it touches, by subtile laws of its nature,
Lo! as he turned to depart, Priscilla was standing beside him.

"Are you so much offended, you will not speak to me?" said she.
"Am I so much to blame, that yesterday, when you were pleading
Warmly the cause of another, my heart, impulsive and wayward,
Pleaded your own, and spake out, forgetful perhaps of decorum?
Certainly you can forgive me for speaking so frankly, for saying
What I ought not to have said, yet now I can never unsay it;
For there are moments in life, when the heart is so full of emotion,
That if by chance it be shaken, or into its depths like a pebble
Drops some careless word, it overflows, and its secret,
Spilt on the ground like water, can never be gathered together.
Yesterday I was shocked, when I heard you speak of Miles Standish,
Praising his virtues, transforming his very defects into virtues,
Praising his courage and strength, and even his fighting in Flanders,
As if by fighting alone you could win the heart of a woman,
Quite overlooking yourself and the rest, in exalting your hero.
Therefore I spake as I did, by an irresistible impulse.
You will forgive me, I hope, for the sake of the friendship between us,
Which is too true and too sacred to be so easily broken!"

Thereupon answered John Alden, the scholar, the friend of Miles Standish:
"I was not angry with you, with myself alone I was angry,
Seeing how badly I managed the matter I had in my keeping."
"No!" interrupted the maiden, with answer prompt and decisive;
"No; you were angry with me, for speaking so frankly and freely.
It was wrong, I acknowledge; for it is the fate of a woman
Long to be patient and silent, to wait like a ghost that is speechless,
Till some questioning voice dissolves the spell of its silence.
Hence is the inner life of so many suffering women
Sunless and silent and deep, like subterranean rivers
Running through caverns of darkness, unheard, unseen, and unfruitful,
Chafing their channels of stone, with endless and profitless murmurs."
Thereupon answered John Alden, the young man, the lover of women:
"Heaven forbid it, Priscilla; and truly they seem to me always
More like the beautiful rivers that watered the garden of Eden,
More like the river Euphrates, through deserts of Havilah flowing,
Filling the land with delight, and memories sweet of the garden!"
"Ah, by these words, I can see," again interrupted the maiden,
"How very little you prize me, or care for what I am saying.
When from the depths of my heart, in pain and with secret misgiving,
Frankly I speak to you, asking for sympathy only and kindness,
Straightway you take up my words, that are plain and direct and in earnest,
Turn them away from their meaning, and answer with flattering phrases.
This is not right, is not just, is not true to the best that is in you;

For I know and esteem you, and feel that your nature is noble,
Lifting mine up to a higher, a more ethereal level.
Therefore I value your friendship, and feel it perhaps the more keenly
If you say aught that implies I am only as one among many,
If you make use of those common and complimentary phrases
Most men think so fine, in dealing and speaking with women,
But which women reject as insipid, if not as insulting."

Mute and amazed was Alden; and listened and looked at Priscilla,
Thinking he never had seen her more fair, more divine in her beauty.
He who but yesterday pleaded so glibly the cause of another,
Stood there embarrassed and silent, and seeking in vain for an answer.
So the maiden went on, and little divined or imagined
What was at work in his heart, that made him so awkward and speechless.
"Let us, then, be what we are, and speak what we think, and in all things
Keep ourselves loyal to truth, and the sacred professions of friendship.
It is no secret I tell you, nor am I ashamed to declare it:
I have liked to be with you, to see you, to speak with you always.
So I was hurt at your words, and a little affronted to hear you
Urge me to marry your friend, though he were the Captain Miles Standish.
For I must tell you the truth: much more to me is your friendship
Than all the love he could give, were he twice the hero you think him."
Then she extended her hand, and Alden, who eagerly grasped it,
Felt all the wounds in his heart, that were aching and bleeding so sorely,
Healed by the touch of that hand, and he said, with a voice full of feeling:

"Yes, we must ever be friends; and of all who offer you friendship
Let me be ever the first, the truest, the nearest and dearest!"

Casting a farewell look at the glimmering sail of the Mayflower,
Distant, but still in sight, and sinking below the horizon,
Homeward together they walked, with a strange, indefinite feeling,
That all the rest had departed and left them alone in the desert.
But, as they went through the fields in the blessing and smile of the sunshine,
Lighter grew their hearts, and Priscilla said very archly:
"Now that our terrible Captain has gone in pursuit of the Indians,
Where he is happier far than he would be commanding a household,
You may speak boldly, and tell me of all that happened between you,
When you returned last night, and said how ungrateful you found me."
Thereupon answered John Alden, and told her the whole of the story,—
Told her his own despair, and the direful wrath of Miles Standish.
Whereat the maiden smiled, and said between laughing and earnest,
"He is a little chimney, and heated hot in a moment!"
But as he gently rebuked her, and told her how he had suffered,—
How he had even determined to sail that day in the Mayflower,
And had remained for her sake, on hearing the dangers that threatened,—
All her manner was changed, and she said with a faltering accent,
"Truly I thank you for this: how good you have been to me always!"

Thus, as a pilgrim devout, who toward Jerusalem journeys,
Taking three steps in advance, and one reluctantly backward,
Urged by importunate zeal, and withheld by pangs of contrition;
Slowly but steadily onward, receding yet ever advancing,
Journeyed this Puritan youth to the Holy Land of his longings,
Urged by the fervor of love, and withheld by remorseful misgivings.

VII.

THE MARCH OF MILES STANDISH.

Meanwhile the stalwart Miles Standish was marching steadily northward,
Winding through forest and swamp, and along the trend of the sea-shore,
All day long, with hardly a halt, the fire of his anger
Burning and crackling within, and the sulphurous odor of powder
Seeming more sweet to his nostrils than all the scents of the forest.
Silent and moody he went, and much he revolved his discomfort;
He who was used to success, and to easy victories always,
Thus to be flouted, rejected, and laughed to scorn by a maiden,
Thus to be mocked and betrayed by the friend whom most he had trusted!
Ah! 't was too much to be borne, and he fretted and chafed in his armor!

"I alone am to blame," he muttered, "for mine was the folly.
What has a rough old soldier, grown grim and gray in the harness,
Used to the camp and its ways, to do with the wooing of maidens?
'T was but a dream,—let it pass,—let it vanish like so many others!

What I thought was a flower, is only a weed, and is worthless;
Out of my heart will I pluck it, and throw it away, and henceforward
Be but a fighter of battles, a lover and wooer of dangers!"
Thus he revolved in his mind his sorry defeat and discomfort,
While he was marching by day or lying at night in the forest,
Looking up at the trees, and the constellations beyond them.

After a three days' march he came to an Indian encampment
Pitched on the edge of a meadow, between the sea and the forest;
Women at work by the tents, and warriors, horrid with war-paint,
Seated about a fire, and smoking and talking together;
Who, when they saw from afar the sudden approach of the white men,
Saw the flash of the sun on breastplate and sabre and musket,
Straightway leaped to their feet, and two, from among them advancing,
Came to parley with Standish, and offer him furs as a present;
Friendship was in their looks, but in their hearts there was hatred.
Braves of the tribe were these, and brothers, gigantic in stature,
Huge as Goliath of Gath, or the terrible Og, king of Bashan;
One was Pecksuot named, and the other was called Wattawamat.
Round their necks were suspended their knives in scabbards of wampum,
Two-edged, trenchant knives, with points as sharp as a needle.
Other arms had they none, for they were cunning and crafty.
"Welcome, English!" they said,—these words they had learned from the traders
Touching at times on the coast, to barter and chaffer for peltries.
Then in their native tongue they began to parley with Standish,

Through his guide and interpreter, Hobomok, friend of the white man,
Begging for blankets and knives, but mostly for muskets and powder,
Kept by the white man, they said, concealed, with the plague, in his cellars,
Ready to be let loose, and destroy his brother the red man!
But when Standish refused, and said he would give them the Bible,
Suddenly changing their tone, they began to boast and to bluster.
Then Wattawamat advanced with a stride in front of the other,
And, with a lofty demeanor, thus vauntingly spake to the Captain:
"Now Wattawamat can see, by the fiery eyes of the Captain,
Angry is he in his heart; but the heart of the brave Wattawamat
Is not afraid at the sight. He was not born of a woman,
But on a mountain at night, from an oak-tree riven by lightning,
Forth he sprang at a bound, with all his weapons about him,
Shouting, 'Who is there here to fight with the brave Wattawamat?' "
Then he unsheathed his knife, and, whetting the blade on his left hand,
Held it aloft and displayed a woman's face on the handle;
Saying, with bitter expression and look of sinister meaning:
"I have another at home, with the face of a man on the handle;
By and by they shall marry; and there will be plenty of children!"

Then stood Pecksuot forth, self-vaunting, insulting Miles Standish:
While with his fingers he patted the knife that hung at his bosom,
Drawing it half from its sheath, and plunging it back, as he muttered,
"By and by it shall see; it shall eat; ah, ha! but shall speak not!

This is the mighty Captain the white men have sent to destroy us!
He is a little man; let him go and work with the women!"

Meanwhile Standish had noted the faces and figures of Indians
Peeping and creeping about from bush to tree in the forest,
Feigning to look for game, with arrows set on their bow-strings,
Drawing about him still closer and closer the net of their ambush.
But undaunted he stood, and dissembled and treated them smoothly;
So the old chronicles say, that were writ in the days of the fathers.
But when he heard their defiance, the boast, the taunt, and the insult,
All the hot blood of his race, of Sir Hugh and of Thurston de Standish,
Boiled and beat in his heart, and swelled in the veins of his temples.
Headlong he leaped on the boaster, and, snatching his knife from its scabbard,
Plunged it into his heart, and, reeling backward, the savage
Fell with his face to the sky, and a fiendlike fierceness upon it.
Straight there arose from the forest the awful sound of the war-whoop,
And, like a flurry of snow on the whistling wind of December,
Swift and sudden and keen came a flight of feathery arrows.
Then came a cloud of smoke, and out of the cloud came the lightning,
Out of the lightning thunder; and death unseen ran before it.
Frightened the savages fled for shelter in swamp and in thicket,
Hotly pursued and beset; but their sachem, the brave Wattawamat,
Fled not; he was dead. Unswerving and swift had a bullet
Passed through his brain, and he fell with both hands clutching the greensward,

Seeming in death to hold back from his foe the land of his fathers.

There on the flowers of the meadow the warriors lay, and above them,
Silent, with folded arms, stood Hobomok, friend of the white man.
Smiling at length he exclaimed to the stalwart Captain of Plymouth:—
"Pecksuot bragged very loud, of his courage, his strength, and his stature,—
Mocked the great Captain, and called him a little man; but I see now
Big enough have you been to lay him speechless before you!"

Thus the first battle was fought and won by the stalwart Miles Standish.
When the tidings thereof were brought to the village of Plymouth,
And as a trophy of war the head of the brave Wattawamat
Scowled from the roof of the fort, which at once was a church and a fortress,
All who beheld it rejoiced, and praised the Lord, and took courage.
Only Priscilla averted her face from this spectre of terror,
Thanking God in her heart that she had not married Miles Standish;
Shrinking, fearing almost, lest, coming home from his battles,
He should lay claim to her hand, as the prize and reward of his valor.

VIII.

THE SPINNING-WHEEL.

Month after month passed away, and in Autumn the ships of the merchants
Came with kindred and friends, with cattle and corn for the Pilgrims.
All in the village was peace; the men were intent on their labors,

Busy with hewing and building, with garden-plot and with merestead,
Busy with breaking the glebe, and mowing the grass in the meadows,
Searching the sea for its fish, and hunting the deer in the forest.
All in the village was peace; but at times the rumor of warfare
Filled the air with alarm, and the apprehension of danger.
Bravely the stalwart Standish was scouring the land with his forces,
Waxing valiant in fight and defeating the alien armies,
Till his name had become a sound of fear to the nations.
Anger was still in his heart, but at times the remorse and contrition
Which in all noble natures succeed the passionate outbreak,
Came like a rising tide, that encounters the rush of a river,
Staying its current awhile, but making it bitter and brackish.

Meanwhile Alden at home had built him a new habitation,
Solid, substantial, of timber rough-hewn from the firs of the forest.
Wooden-barred was the door, and the roof was covered with rushes;
Latticed the windows were, and the window-panes were of paper,
Oiled to admit the light, while wind and rain were excluded.
There too he dug a well, and around it planted an orchard:
Still may be seen to this day some trace of the well and the orchard.
Close to the house was the stall, where, safe and secure from annoyance,
Raghorn, the snow-white bull, that had fallen to Alden's allotment
In the division of cattle, might ruminate in the night-time
Over the pastures he cropped, made fragrant by sweet pennyroyal.

Oft when his labor was finished, with eager feet would the dreamer
Follow the pathway that ran through the woods to the house of Priscilla,

Led by illusions romantic and subtile deceptions of fancy,
Pleasure disguised as duty, and love in the semblance of friendship.
Ever of her he thought, when he fashioned the walls of his dwelling;
Ever of her he thought, when he delved in the soil of his garden;
Ever of her he thought, when he read in his Bible on Sunday
Praise of the virtuous woman, as she is described in the Proverbs,—
How the heart of her husband doth safely trust in her always,
How all the days of her life she will do him good, and not evil,
How she seeketh the wool and the flax and worketh with gladness,
How she layeth her hand to the spindle and holdeth the distaff,
How she is not afraid of the snow for herself or her household,
Knowing her household are clothed with the scarlet cloth of her weaving!

So as she sat at her wheel one afternoon in the Autumn,
Alden, who opposite sat, and was watching her dexterous fingers,
As if the thread she was spinning were that of his life and his fortune,
After a pause in their talk, thus spake to the sound of the spindle.
"Truly, Priscilla," he said, "when I see you spinning and spinning,
Never idle a moment, but thrifty and thoughtful of others,
Suddenly you are transformed, are visibly changed in a moment;
You are no longer Priscilla, but Bertha the Beautiful Spinner."
Here the light foot on the treadle grew swifter and swifter; the spindle
Uttered an angry snarl, and the thread snapped short in her fingers;
While the impetuous speaker, not heeding the mischief, continued:

"You are the beautiful Bertha, the spinner, the queen of Helvetia;
She whose story I read at a stall in the streets of Southampton,
Who, as she rode on her palfrey, o'er valley and meadow and mountain,
Ever was spinning her thread from a distaff fixed to her saddle.
She was so thrifty and good, that her name passed into a proverb.
So shall it be with your own, when the spinning-wheel shall no longer
Hum in the house of the farmer, and fill its chambers with music.
Then shall the mothers, reproving, relate how it was in their childhood,
Praising the good old times, and the days of Priscilla the spinner!"
Straight uprose from her wheel the beautiful Puritan maiden,
Pleased with the praise of her thrift from him whose praise was the sweetest,
Drew from the reel on the table a snowy skein of her spinning,
Thus making answer, meanwhile, to the flattering phrases of Alden:
"Come, you must not be idle; if I am a pattern for housewives,
Show yourself equally worthy of being the model of husbands.
Hold this skein on your hands, while I wind it, ready for knitting;
Then who knows but hereafter, when fashions have changed and the manners,
Fathers may talk to their sons of the good old times of John Alden!"
Thus, with a jest and a laugh, the skein on his hands she adjusted,
He sitting awkwardly there, with his arms extended before him,
She standing graceful, erect, and winding the thread from his fingers,

Sometimes chiding a little his clumsy manner of holding,
Sometimes touching his hands, as she disentangled expertly
Twist or knot in the yarn, unawares—for how could she help it?—
Sending electrical thrills through every nerve in his body.

Lo! in the midst of this scene, a breathless messenger entered,
Bringing in hurry and heat the terrible news from the village.
Yes; Miles Standish was dead!—an Indian had brought them the tidings,—
Slain by a poisoned arrow, shot down in the front of the battle,
Into an ambush beguiled, cut off with the whole of his forces;
All the town would be burned, and all the people be murdered!
Such were the tidings of evil that burst on the hearts of the hearers.
Silent and statue-like stood Priscilla, her face looking backward
Still at the face of the speaker, her arms uplifted in horror;
But John Alden, upstarting, as if the barb of the arrow
Piercing the heart of his friend had struck his own, and had sundered
Once and forever the bonds that held him bound as a captive
Wild with excess of sensation, the awful delight of his freedom,
Mingled with pain and regret, unconscious of what he was doing,
Clasped, almost with a groan, the motionless form of Priscilla,
Pressing her close to his heart, as forever his own, and exclaiming:
"Those whom the Lord hath united, let no man put them asunder!"

Even as rivulets twain, from distant and separate sources,
Seeing each other afar, as they leap from the rocks, and pursuing
Each one its devious path, but drawing nearer and nearer,
Rush together at last, at their trysting-place in the forest;
So these lives that had run thus far in separate channels,
Coming in sight of each other, then swerving and flowing asunder,

Parted by barriers strong, but drawing nearer and nearer,
Rushed together at last, and one was lost in the other.

IX.

THE WEDDING-DAY.

Forth from the curtain of clouds, from the tent of purple and scarlet,
Issued the sun, the great High-Priest, in his garments resplendent,
Holiness unto the Lord, in letters of light, on his forehead,
Round the hem of his robe the golden bells and pomegranates.
Blessing the world he came, and the bars of vapor beneath him
Gleamed like a grate of brass, and the sea at his feet was a laver!

This was the wedding morn of Priscilla the Puritan maiden.
Friends were assembled together; the Elder and Magistrate also
Graced the scene with their presence, and stood like the Law and the Gospel,
One with the sanction of earth and one with the blessing of heaven.
Simple and brief was the wedding, as that of Ruth and of Boaz.
Softly the youth and the maiden repeated the words of betrothal,
Taking each other for husband and wife in the Magistrate's presence,
After the Puritan way, and the laudable custom of Holland.
Fervently then, and devoutly, the excellent Elder of Plymouth
Prayed for the hearth and the home, that were founded that day in affection,
Speaking of life and of death, and imploring Divine benedictions.

Lo! when the service was ended, a form appeared on the threshold,

Clad in armor of steel, a sombre and sorrowful figure!
Why does the bridegroom start and stare at the strange apparition?
Why does the bride turn pale, and hide her face on his shoulder?
Is it a phantom of air,—a bodiless, spectral illusion?
Is it a ghost from the grave, that has come to forbid the betrothal?
Long had it stood there unseen, a guest uninvited, unwelcomed;
Over its clouded eyes there had passed at times an expression
Softening the gloom and revealing the warm heart hidden beneath them,
As when across the sky the driving rack of the rain-cloud
Grows for a moment thin, and betrays the sun by its brightness.
Once it had lifted its hand, and moved its lips, but was silent,
As if an iron will had mastered the fleeting intention.
But when were ended the troth and the prayer and the last benediction,
Into the room it strode, and the people beheld with amazement
Bodily there in his armor Miles Standish, the Captain of Plymouth!
Grasping the bridegroom's hand, he said with emotion, "Forgive me!
I have been angry and hurt,—too long have I cherished the feeling;
I have been cruel and hard, but now, thank God! it is ended.
Mine is the same hot blood that leaped in the veins of Hugh Standish,
Sensitive, swift to resent, but as swift in atoning for error.
Never so much as now was Miles Standish the friend of John Alden."
Thereupon answered the bridegroom: "Let all be forgotten between us,—
All save the dear, old friendship, and that shall grow older and dearer!"
Then the Captain advanced, and, bowing, saluted Priscilla,

Gravely, and after the manner of old-fashioned gentry in
England,
Something of camp and of court, of town and of country,
commingled,
Wishing her joy of her wedding, and loudly lauding her
husband.
Then he said with a smile: "I should have remembered the
adage,—
If you would be well served, you must serve yourself; and
moreover,
No man can gather cherries in Kent at the season of
Christmas!"

Great was the people's amazement, and greater yet their
rejoicing,
Thus to behold once more the sunburnt face of their Captain,
Whom they had mourned as dead; and they gathered and
crowded about him,
Eager to see him and hear him, forgetful of bride and of
bridegroom,
Questioning, answering, laughing, and each interrupting the
other,
Till the good Captain declared, being quite overpowered and
bewildered,
He had rather by far break into an Indian encampment,
Than come again to a wedding to which he had not been
invited.

Meanwhile the bridegroom went forth and stood with the
bride at the doorway,
Breathing the perfumed air of that warm and beautiful
morning.
Touched with autumnal tints, but lonely and sad in the
sunshine,
Lay extended before them the land of toil and privation;
There were the graves of the dead, and the barren waste of
the sea-shore,
There the familiar fields, the groves of pine, and the
meadows;

But to their eyes transfigured, it seemed as the Garden of
Eden,
Filled with the presence of God, whose voice was the sound
of the ocean.

Soon was their vision disturbed by the noise and stir of
departure,
Friends coming forth from the house, and impatient of
longer delaying,
Each with his plan for the day, and the work that was left
uncompleted.
Then from a stall near at hand, amid exclamations of wonder,
Alden the thoughtful, the careful, so happy, so proud of
Priscilla,
Brought out his snow-white bull, obeying the hand of its
master,
Led by a cord that was tied to an iron ring in its nostrils,
Covered with crimson cloth, and a cushion placed for a
saddle.
She should not walk, he said, through the dust and heat of
the noonday;
Nay, she should ride like a queen, not plod along like a
peasant.
Somewhat alarmed at first, but reassured by the others,
Placing her hand on the cushion, her foot in the hand of her
husband,
Gayly, with joyous laugh, Priscilla mounted her palfrey.
"Nothing is wanting now," he said with a smile, "but the
distaff;
Then you would be in truth my queen, my beautiful Bertha!"

Onward the bridal procession now moved to their new
habitation,
Happy husband and wife, and friends conversing together.
Pleasantly murmured the brook, as they crossed the ford in
the forest,
Pleased with the image that passed, like a dream of love
through its bosom,
Tremulous, floating in air, o'er the depths of the azure
abysses.

Down through the golden leaves the sun was pouring his
splendors,
Gleaming on purple grapes, that, from branches above them
suspended,
Mingled their odorous breath with the balm of the pine and
the fir-tree,
Wild and sweet as the clusters that grew in the valley of
Eschol.
Like a picture it seemed of the primitive, pastoral ages,
Fresh with the youth of the world, and recalling Rebecca and
Isaac,
Old and yet ever new, and simple and beautiful always,
Love immortal and young in the endless succession of lovers.
So through the Plymouth woods passed onward the bridal
procession.

Birds of Passage

Black shadows fall
From the lindens tall,
That lift aloft their massive wall
Against the southern sky;

And from the realms
Of the shadowy elms
A tide-like darkness overwhelms
The fields that round us lie.

But the night is fair,
And everywhere
A warm, soft vapor fills the air,
And distant sounds seem near;

And above, in the light
Of the star-lit night,
Swift birds of passage wing their flight
Through the dewy atmosphere.

I hear the beat
Of their pinions fleet,
As from the land of snow and sleet
 They seek a southern lea.

I hear the cry
Of their voices high
Falling dreamily through the sky,
 But their forms I cannot see.

Oh, say not so!
Those sounds that flow
In murmurs of delight and woe
 Come not from wings of birds.

They are the throngs
Of the poet's songs,
Murmurs of pleasures, and pains, and wrongs,
 The sound of winged words.

This is the cry
Of souls, that high
On toiling, beating pinions, fly,
 Seeking a warmer clime.

From their distant flight
Through realms of light
It falls into our world of night,
 With the murmuring sound of rhyme.

The Ladder of St. Augustine

Saint Augustine! well hast thou said,
 That of our vices we can frame
A ladder, if we will but tread
 Beneath our feet each deed of shame!

All common things, each day's events,
 That with the hour begin and end,

Our pleasures and our discontents,
   Are rounds by which we may ascend.

The low desire, the base design,
   That makes another's virtues less;
The revel of the ruddy wine,
   And all occasions of excess;

The longing for ignoble things;
   The strife for triumph more than truth;
The hardening of the heart, that brings
   Irreverence for the dreams of youth;

All thoughts of ill; all evil deeds,
   That have their root in thoughts of ill;
Whatever hinders or impedes
   The action of the nobler will;—

All these must first be trampled down
   Beneath our feet, if we would gain
In the bright fields of fair renown
   The right of eminent domain.

We have not wings, we cannot soar;
   But we have feet to scale and climb
By slow degrees, by more and more,
   The cloudy summits of our time.

Thy mighty pyramids of stone
   That wedge-like cleave the desert airs,
When nearer seen, and better known,
   Are but gigantic flights of stairs.

The distant mountains, that uprear
   Their solid bastions to the skies,
Are crossed by pathways, that appear
   As we to higher levels rise.

The heights by great men reached and kept
   Were not attained by sudden flight,

But they, while their companions slept,
Were toiling upward in the night.

Standing on what too long we bore
With shoulders bent and downcast eyes,
We may discern—unseen before—
A path to higher destinies,

Nor deem the irrevocable Past
As wholly wasted, wholly vain,
If, rising on its wrecks, at last
To something nobler we attain.

The Phantom Ship

In Mather's Magnalia Christi,
Of the old colonial time,
May be found in prose the legend
That is here set down in rhyme.

A ship sailed from New Haven,
And the keen and frosty airs,
That filled her sails at parting,
Were heavy with good men's prayers.

"O Lord! if it be thy pleasure"—
Thus prayed the old divine—
"To bury our friends in the ocean,
Take them, for they are thine!"

But Master Lamberton muttered,
And under his breath said he,
"This ship is so crank and walty,
I fear our grave she will be!"

And the ships that came from England,
When the winter months were gone,
Brought no tidings of this vessel
Nor of Master Lamberton.

This put the people to praying
  That the Lord would let them hear
What in his greater wisdom
  He had done with friends so dear.

And at last their prayers were answered:
  It was in the month of June,
An hour before the sunset
  Of a windy afternoon,

When, steadily steering landward,
  A ship was seen below,
And they knew it was Lamberton, Master,
  Who sailed so long ago.

On she came, with a cloud of canvas,
  Right against the wind that blew,
Until the eye could distinguish
  The faces of the crew.

Then fell her straining topmasts,
  Hanging tangled in the shrouds,
And her sails were loosened and lifted,
  And blown away like clouds.

And the masts, with all their rigging,
  Fell slowly, one by one,
And the hulk dilated and vanished,
  As a sea-mist in the sun!

And the people who saw this marvel
  Each said unto his friend,
That this was the mould of their vessel,
  And thus her tragic end.

And the pastor of the village
  Gave thanks to God in prayer,
That, to quiet their troubled spirits,
  He had sent this Ship of Air.

The Warden of the Cinque Ports

A mist was driving down the British Channel,
    The day was just begun,
And through the window-panes, on floor and panel,
    Streamed the red autumn sun.

It glanced on flowing flag and rippling pennon,
    And the white sails of ships;
And, from the frowning rampart, the black cannon
    Hailed it with feverish lips.

Sandwich and Romney, Hastings, Hithe, and Dover
    Were all alert that day,
To see the French war-steamers speeding over,
    When the fog cleared away.

Sullen and silent, and like couchant lions,
    Their cannon, through the night,
Holding their breath, had watched, in grim defiance,
    The sea-coast opposite.

And now they roared at drum-beat from their stations
    On every citadel;
Each answering each, with morning salutations,
    That all was well.

And down the coast, all taking up the burden,
    Replied the distant forts,
As if to summon from his sleep the Warden
    And Lord of the Cinque Ports.

Him shall no sunshine from the fields of azure,
    No drum-beat from the wall,
No morning gun from the black fort's embrasure,
    Awaken with its call!

No more, surveying with an eye impartial
    The long line of the coast,
Shall the gaunt figure of the old Field Marshal
    Be seen upon his post!

For in the night, unseen, a single warrior,
In sombre harness mailed,
Dreaded of man, and surnamed the Destroyer,
The rampart wall had scaled.

He passed into the chamber of the sleeper,
The dark and silent room,
And as he entered, darker grew, and deeper,
The silence and the gloom.

He did not pause to parley or dissemble,
But smote the Warden hoar;
Ah! what a blow! that made all England tremble
And groan from shore to shore.

Meanwhile, without, the surly cannon waited,
The sun rose bright o'erhead;
Nothing in Nature's aspect intimated
That a great man was dead.

Haunted Houses

All houses wherein men have lived and died
Are haunted houses. Through the open doors
The harmless phantoms on their errands glide,
With feet that make no sound upon the floors.

We meet them at the doorway, on the stair,
Along the passages they come and go,
Impalpable impressions on the air,
A sense of something moving to and fro.

There are more guests at table, than the hosts
Invited; the illuminated hall
Is thronged with quiet, inoffensive ghosts,
As silent as the pictures on the wall.

The stranger at my fireside cannot see
The forms I see, nor hear the sounds I hear;

He but perceives what is; while unto me
   All that has been is visible and clear.

We have no title-deeds to house or lands;
   Owners and occupants of earlier dates
From graves forgotten stretch their dusty hands,
   And hold in mortmain still their old estates.

The spirit-world around this world of sense
   Floats like an atmosphere, and everywhere
Wafts through these earthly mists and vapors dense
   A vital breath of more ethereal air.

Our little lives are kept in equipoise
   By opposite attractions and desires;
The struggle of the instinct that enjoys,
   And the more noble instinct that aspires.

These perturbations, this perpetual jar
   Of earthly wants and aspirations high,
Come from the influence of an unseen star,
   An undiscovered planet in our sky.

And as the moon from some dark gate of cloud
   Throws o'er the sea a floating bridge of light,
Across whose trembling planks our fancies crowd
   Into the realm of mystery and night,—

So from the world of spirits there descends
   A bridge of light, connecting it with this,
O'er whose unsteady floor, that sways and bends,
   Wander our thoughts above the dark abyss.

In the Churchyard at Cambridge

In the village churchyard she lies,
Dust is in her beautiful eyes,
  No more she breathes, nor feels, nor stirs;
At her feet and at her head
Lies a slave to attend the dead,
  But their dust is white as hers.

Was she, a lady of high degree,
So much in love with the vanity
  And foolish pomp of this world of ours?
Or was it Christian charity,
And lowliness and humility,
  The richest and rarest of all dowers?

Who shall tell us? No one speaks;
No color shoots into those cheeks,
  Either of anger or of pride,
At the rude question we have asked;
Nor will the mystery be unmasked
  By those who are sleeping at her side.

Hereafter?—And do you think to look
On the terrible pages of that Book
  To find her failings, faults, and errors?
Ah, you will then have other cares,
In your own shortcomings and despairs,
  In your own secret sins and terrors!

The Emperor's Bird's-Nest

Once the Emperor Charles of Spain,
  With his swarthy, grave commanders,
I forget in what campaign,
Long besieged, in mud and rain,
  Some old frontier town of Flanders.

Up and down the dreary camp,
   In great boots of Spanish leather,
Striding with a measured tramp,
These Hidalgos, dull and damp,
   Cursed the Frenchmen, cursed the weather.

Thus as to and fro they went
   Over upland and through hollow,
Giving their impatience vent,
Perched upon the Emperor's tent,
   In her nest, they spied a swallow.

Yes, it was a swallow's nest,
   Built of clay and hair of horses,
Mane, or tail, or dragoon's crest,
Found on hedge-rows east and west,
   After skirmish of the forces.

Then an old Hidalgo said,
   As he twirled his gray mustachio,
"Sure this swallow overhead
Thinks the Emperor's tent a shed,
   And the Emperor but a Macho!"

Hearing his imperial name
   Coupled with those words of malice,
Half in anger, half in shame,
Forth the great campaigner came
   Slowly from his canvas palace.

"Let no hand the bird molest,"
   Said he solemnly, "nor hurt her!"
Adding then, by way of jest,
"Golondrina is my guest,
   'T is the wife of some deserter!"

Swift as bowstring speeds a shaft,
   Through the camp was spread the rumor,
And the soldiers, as they quaffed
Flemish beer at dinner, laughed
   At the Emperor's pleasant humor.

So unharmed and unafraid
   Sat the swallow still and brooded,
Till the constant cannonade
Through the walls a breach had made,
   And the siege was thus concluded.

Then the army, elsewhere bent,
   Struck its tents as if disbanding,
Only not the Emperor's tent,
For he ordered, ere he went,
   Very curtly, "Leave it standing!"

So it stood there all alone,
   Loosely flapping, torn and tattered,
Till the brood was fledged and flown,
Singing o'er those walls of stone
   Which the cannon-shot had shattered.

The Two Angels

Two angels, one of Life and one of Death,
   Passed o'er our village as the morning broke;
The dawn was on their faces, and beneath,
   The sombre houses hearsed with plumes of smoke.

Their attitude and aspect were the same,
   Alike their features and their robes of white;
But one was crowned with amaranth, as with flame,
   And one with asphodels, like flakes of light.

I saw them pause on their celestial way;
   Then said I, with deep fear and doubt oppressed,
"Beat not so loud, my heart, lest thou betray
   The place where thy beloved are at rest!"

And he who wore the crown of asphodels,
   Descending, at my door began to knock,
And my soul sank within me, as in wells
   The waters sink before an earthquake's shock.

I recognized the nameless agony,
The terror and the tremor and the pain,
That oft before had filled or haunted me,
And now returned with threefold strength again.

The door I opened to my heavenly guest,
And listened, for I thought I heard God's voice;
And, knowing whatsoe'er he sent was best,
Dared neither to lament nor to rejoice.

Then with a smile, that filled the house with light,
"My errand is not Death, but Life," he said;
And ere I answered, passing out of sight,
On his celestial embassy he sped.

'T was at thy door, O friend! and not at mine,
The angel with the amaranthine wreath,
Pausing, descended, and with voice divine
Whispered a word that had a sound like Death.

Then fell upon the house a sudden gloom,
A shadow on those features fair and thin;
And softly, from that hushed and darkened room,
Two angels issued, where but one went in.

All is of God! If he but wave his hand,
The mists collect, the rain falls thick and loud,
Till, with a smile of light on sea and land,
Lo! he looks back from the departing cloud.

Angels of Life and Death alike are his;
Without his leave they pass no threshold o'er;
Who, then, would wish or dare, believing this,
Against his messengers to shut the door?

Daylight and Moonlight

In broad daylight, and at noon,
Yesterday I saw the moon
Sailing high, but faint and white,
As a school-boy's paper kite.

In broad daylight, yesterday,
I read a Poet's mystic lay;
And it seemed to me at most
As a phantom, or a ghost.

But at length the feverish day
Like a passion died away,
And the night, serene and still,
Fell on village, vale, and hill.

Then the moon, in all her pride,
Like a spirit glorified,
Filled and overflowed the night
With revelations of her light.

And the Poet's song again
Passed like music through my brain;
Night interpreted to me
All its grace and mystery.

The Jewish Cemetery at Newport

How strange it seems! These Hebrews in their graves,
  Close by the street of this fair seaport town,
Silent beside the never-silent waves,
  At rest in all this moving up and down!

The trees are white with dust, that o'er their sleep
  Wave their broad curtains in the south-wind's breath,
While underneath these leafy tents they keep
  The long, mysterious Exodus of Death.

And these sepulchral stones, so old and brown,
That pave with level flags their burial-place,
Seem like the tablets of the Law, thrown down
And broken by Moses at the mountain's base.

The very names recorded here are strange,
Of foreign accent, and of different climes;
Alvares and Rivera interchange
With Abraham and Jacob of old times.

"Blessed be God! for he created Death!"
The mourners said, "and Death is rest and peace;"
Then added, in the certainty of faith,
"And giveth Life that nevermore shall cease."

Closed are the portals of their Synagogue,
No Psalms of David now the silence break,
No Rabbi reads the ancient Decalogue
In the grand dialect the Prophets spake.

Gone are the living, but the dead remain,
And not neglected; for a hand unseen,
Scattering its bounty, like a summer rain,
Still keeps their graves and their remembrance green.

How came they here? What burst of Christian hate,
What persecution, merciless and blind,
Drove o'er the sea—that desert desolate—
These Ishmaels and Hagars of mankind?

They lived in narrow streets and lanes obscure,
Ghetto and Judenstrass, in mirk and mire;
Taught in the school of patience to endure
The life of anguish and the death of fire.

All their lives long, with the unleavened bread
And bitter herbs of exile and its fears,
The wasting famine of the heart they fed,
And slaked its thirst with marah of their tears.

Anathema maranatha! was the cry
  That rang from town to town, from street to street;
At every gate the accursed Mordecai
  Was mocked and jeered, and spurned by Christian feet.

Pride and humiliation hand in hand
  Walked with them through the world where'er they went;
Trampled and beaten were they as the sand,
  And yet unshaken as the continent.

For in the background figures vague and vast
  Of patriarchs and of prophets rose sublime,
And all the great traditions of the Past
  They saw reflected in the coming time.

And thus forever with reverted look
  The mystic volume of the world they read,
Spelling it backward, like a Hebrew book,
  Till life became a Legend of the Dead.

But ah! what once has been shall be no more!
  The groaning earth in travail and in pain
Brings forth its races, but does not restore,
  And the dead nations never rise again.

My Lost Youth

Often I think of the beautiful town
  That is seated by the sea;
Often in thought go up and down
The pleasant streets of that dear old town,
  And my youth comes back to me.
    And a verse of a Lapland song
    Is haunting my memory still:
  "A boy's will is the wind's will,
And the thoughts of youth are long, long thoughts."

I can see the shadowy lines of its trees,
  And catch, in sudden gleams,
The sheen of the far-surrounding seas,
And islands that were the Hesperides
  Of all my boyish dreams.
    And the burden of that old song,
    It murmurs and whispers still:
  "A boy's will is the wind's will,
And the thoughts of youth are long, long thoughts."

I remember the black wharves and the slips,
  And the sea-tides tossing free;
And Spanish sailors with bearded lips,
And the beauty and mystery of the ships,
  And the magic of the sea.
    And the voice of that wayward song
    Is singing and saying still:
  "A boy's will is the wind's will,
And the thoughts of youth are long, long thoughts."

I remember the bulwarks by the shore,
  And the fort upon the hill;
The sunrise gun, with its hollow roar,
The drum-beat repeated o'er and o'er,
  And the bugle wild and shrill.
    And the music of that old song
    Throbs in my memory still:
  "A boy's will is the wind's will,
And the thoughts of youth are long, long thoughts."

I remember the sea-fight far away,
  How it thundered o'er the tide!
And the dead captains, as they lay
In their graves, o'erlooking the tranquil bay,
  Where they in battle died.
    And the sound of that mournful song
    Goes through me with a thrill:
  "A boy's will is the wind's will,
And the thoughts of youth are long, long thoughts."

I can see the breezy dome of groves,
The shadows of Deering's Woods;
And the friendships old and the early loves
Come back with a Sabbath sound, as of doves
In quiet neighborhoods.
And the verse of that sweet old song,
It flutters and murmurs still:
"A boy's will is the wind's will,
And the thoughts of youth are long, long thoughts."

I remember the gleams and glooms that dart
Across the school-boy's brain;
The song and the silence in the heart,
That in part are prophecies, and in part
Are longings wild and vain.
And the voice of that fitful song
Sings on, and is never still:
"A boy's will is the wind's will,
And the thoughts of youth are long, long thoughts."

There are things of which I may not speak;
There are dreams that cannot die;
There are thoughts that make the strong heart weak,
And bring a pallor into the cheek,
And a mist before the eye.
And the words of that fatal song
Come over me like a chill:
"A boy's will is the wind's will,
And the thoughts of youth are long, long thoughts."

Strange to me now are the forms I meet
When I visit the dear old town;
But the native air is pure and sweet,
And the trees that o'ershadow each well-known street,
As they balance up and down,
Are singing the beautiful song,
Are sighing and whispering still:
"A boy's will is the wind's will,
And the thoughts of youth are long, long thoughts."

And Deering's Woods are fresh and fair,
  And with joy that is almost pain
My heart goes back to wander there,
And among the dreams of the days that were,
  I find my lost youth again.
    And the strange and beautiful song,
    The groves are repeating it still:
  "A boy's will is the wind's will,
And the thoughts of youth are long, long thoughts."

The Ropewalk

In that building, long and low,
With its windows all a-row,
  Like the port-holes of a hulk,
Human spiders spin and spin,
Backward down their threads so thin
  Dropping, each a hempen bulk.

At the end, an open door;
Squares of sunshine on the floor
  Light the long and dusky lane;
And the whirring of a wheel,
Dull and drowsy, makes me feel
  All its spokes are in my brain.

As the spinners to the end
Downward go and reascend,
  Gleam the long threads in the sun;
While within this brain of mine
Cobwebs brighter and more fine
  By the busy wheel are spun.

Two fair maidens in a swing,
Like white doves upon the wing,
  First before my vision pass;
Laughing, as their gentle hands
Closely clasp the twisted strands,
  At their shadow on the grass.

Then a booth of mountebanks,
With its smell of tan and planks,
  And a girl poised high in air
On a cord, in spangled dress,
With a faded loveliness,
  And a weary look of care.

Then a homestead among farms,
And a woman with bare arms
  Drawing water from a well;
As the bucket mounts apace,
With it mounts her own fair face,
  As at some magician's spell.

Then an old man in a tower,
Ringing loud the noontide hour,
  While the rope coils round and round
Like a serpent at his feet,
And again, in swift retreat,
  Nearly lifts him from the ground.

Then within a prison-yard,
Faces fixed, and stern, and hard,
  Laughter and indecent mirth;
Ah! it is the gallows-tree!
Breath of Christian charity,
  Blow, and sweep it from the earth!

Then a school-boy, with his kite
Gleaming in a sky of light,
  And an eager, upward look;
Steeds pursued through lane and field;
Fowlers with their snares concealed;
  And an angler by a brook.

Ships rejoicing in the breeze,
Wrecks that float o'er unknown seas,
  Anchors dragged through faithless sand;
Sea-fog drifting overhead,
And, with lessening line and lead,
  Sailors feeling for the land.

All these scenes do I behold,
These, and many left untold,
  In that building long and low;
While the wheel goes round and round,
With a drowsy, dreamy sound,
  And the spinners backward go.

Daybreak

A wind came up out of the sea,
And said, "O mists, make room for me."

It hailed the ships, and cried, "Sail on,
Ye mariners, the night is gone."

And hurried landward far away,
Crying, "Awake! it is the day."

It said unto the forest, "Shout!
Hang all your leafy banners out!"

It touched the wood-bird's folded wing,
And said, "O bird, awake and sing."

And o'er the farms, "O chanticleer,
Your clarion blow; the day is near."

It whispered to the fields of corn,
"Bow down, and hail the coming morn."

It shouted through the belfry-tower,
"Awake, O bell! proclaim the hour."

It crossed the churchyard with a sigh,
And said, "Not yet! in quiet lie."

The Fiftieth Birthday of Agassiz

May 28, 1857

It was fifty years ago
   In the pleasant month of May,
In the beautiful Pays de Vaud,
   A child in its cradle lay.

And Nature, the old nurse, took
   The child upon her knee,
Saying: "Here is a story-book
   Thy Father has written for thee."

"Come, wander with me," she said,
   "Into regions yet untrod;
And read what is still unread
   In the manuscripts of God."

And he wandered away and away
   With Nature, the dear old nurse,
Who sang to him night and day
   The rhymes of the universe.

And whenever the way seemed long,
   Or his heart began to fail,
She would sing a more wonderful song,
   Or tell a more marvellous tale.

So she keeps him still a child,
   And will not let him go,
Though at times his heart beats wild
   For the beautiful Pays de Vaud;

Though at times he hears in his dreams
   The Ranz des Vaches of old,
And the rush of mountain streams
   From glaciers clear and cold;

And the mother at home says, "Hark!
   For his voice I listen and yearn;
It is growing late and dark,
   And my boy does not return!"

Children

Come to me, O ye children!
For I hear you at your play,
And the questions that perplexed me
Have vanished quite away.

Ye open the eastern windows,
That look towards the sun,
Where thoughts are singing swallows
And the brooks of morning run.

In your hearts are the birds and the sunshine,
In your thoughts the brooklet's flow,
But in mine is the wind of Autumn
And the first fall of the snow.

Ah! what would the world be to us
If the children were no more?
We should dread the desert behind us
Worse than the dark before.

What the leaves are to the forest,
With light and air for food,
Ere their sweet and tender juices
Have been hardened into wood,—

That to the world are children;
Through them it feels the glow
Of a brighter and sunnier climate
Than reaches the trunks below.

Come to me, O ye children!
And whisper in my ear
What the birds and the winds are singing
In your sunny atmosphere.

For what are all our contrivings,
  And the wisdom of our books,
When compared with your caresses,
  And the gladness of your looks?

Ye are better than all the ballads
  That ever were sung or said;
For ye are living poems,
  And all the rest are dead.

Sandalphon

Have you read in the Talmud of old,
In the Legends the Rabbins have told
  Of the limitless realms of the air,
Have you read it,—the marvellous story
Of Sandalphon, the Angel of Glory,
  Sandalphon, the Angel of Prayer?

How, erect, at the outermost gates
Of the City Celestial he waits,
  With his feet on the ladder of light,
That, crowded with angels unnumbered,
By Jacob was seen, as he slumbered
  Alone in the desert at night?

The Angels of Wind and of Fire
Chant only one hymn, and expire
  With the song's irresistible stress;
Expire in their rapture and wonder,
As harp-strings are broken asunder
  By music they throb to express.

But serene in the rapturous throng,
Unmoved by the rush of the song,
  With eyes unimpassioned and slow,
Among the dead angels, the deathless
Sandalphon stands listening breathless
  To sounds that ascend from below;—

From the spirits on earth that adore,
From the souls that entreat and implore
  In the fervor and passion of prayer;
From the hearts that are broken with losses,
And weary with dragging the crosses
  Too heavy for mortals to bear.

And he gathers the prayers as he stands,
And they change into flowers in his hands,
  Into garlands of purple and red;
And beneath the great arch of the portal,
Through the streets of the City Immortal
  Is wafted the fragrance they shed.

It is but a legend, I know,—
A fable, a phantom, a show,
  Of the ancient Rabbinical lore;
Yet the old mediæval tradition,
The beautiful, strange superstition,
  But haunts me and holds me the more.

When I look from my window at night,
And the welkin above is all white,
  All throbbing and panting with stars,
Among them majestic is standing
Sandalphon the angel, expanding
  His pinions in nebulous bars.

And the legend, I feel, is a part
Of the hunger and thirst of the heart,
  The frenzy and fire of the brain,
That grasps at the fruitage forbidden,
The golden pomegranates of Eden,
  To quiet its fever and pain.

POEMS 1859–1863

The Children's Hour

Between the dark and the daylight,
  When the night is beginning to lower,
Comes a pause in the day's occupations,
  That is known as the Children's Hour.

I hear in the chamber above me
  The patter of little feet,
The sound of a door that is opened,
  And voices soft and sweet.

From my study I see in the lamplight,
  Descending the broad hall stair,
Grave Alice, and laughing Allegra,
  And Edith with golden hair.

A whisper, and then a silence:
  Yet I know by their merry eyes
They are plotting and planning together
  To take me by surprise.

A sudden rush from the stairway,
  A sudden raid from the hall!
By three doors left unguarded
  They enter my castle wall!

They climb up into my turret
  O'er the arms and back of my chair;
If I try to escape, they surround me;
  They seem to be everywhere.

They almost devour me with kisses,
  Their arms about me entwine,
Till I think of the Bishop of Bingen
  In his Mouse-Tower on the Rhine!

Do you think, O blue-eyed banditti,
  Because you have scaled the wall,
Such an old mustache as I am
  Is not a match for you all!

I have you fast in my fortress,
  And will not let you depart,
But put you down into the dungeon
  In the round-tower of my heart.

And there will I keep you forever,
  Yes, forever and a day,
Till the walls shall crumble to ruin,
  And moulder in dust away!

Enceladus

Under Mount Etna he lies,
  It is slumber, it is not death;
For he struggles at times to arise
And above him the lurid skies
  Are hot with his fiery breath.

The crags are piled on his breast,
  The earth is heaped on his head;
But the groans of his wild unrest,
Though smothered and half suppressed,
  Are heard, and he is not dead.

And the nations far away
  Are watching with eager eyes;
They talk together and say,
"To-morrow, perhaps to-day,
  Enceladus will arise!"

And the old gods, the austere
  Oppressors in their strength,
Stand aghast and white with fear

At the ominous sounds they hear,
  And tremble, and mutter, "At length!"

Ah me! for the land that is sown
  With the harvest of despair!
Where the burning cinders, blown
From the lips of the overthrown
  Enceladus, fill the air.

Where ashes are heaped in drifts
  Over vineyard and field and town,
Whenever he starts and lifts
His head through the blackened rifts
  Of the crags that keep him down.

See, see! the red light shines!
  'T is the glare of his awful eyes!
    And the storm-wind shouts through the pines
Of Alps and of Apennines,
  "Enceladus, arise!"

The Cumberland

At anchor in Hampton Roads we lay,
  On board of the Cumberland, sloop-of-war;
And at times from the fortress across the bay
    The alarum of drums swept past,
    Or a bugle blast
  From the camp on the shore.

Then far away to the south uprose
  A little feather of snow-white smoke,
And we knew that the iron ship of our foes
    Was steadily steering its course
    To try the force
  Of our ribs of oak.

Down upon us heavily runs,
   Silent and sullen, the floating fort;
Then comes a puff of smoke from her guns,
      And leaps the terrible death,
      With fiery breath,
   From each open port.

We are not idle, but send her straight
   Defiance back in a full broadside!
As hail rebounds from a roof of slate,
      Rebounds our heavier hail
      From each iron scale
   Of the monster's hide.

"Strike your flag!" the rebel cries,
   In his arrogant old plantation strain.
"Never!" our gallant Morris replies;
      "It is better to sink than to yield!"
      And the whole air pealed
   With the cheers of our men.

Then, like a kraken huge and black,
   She crushed our ribs in her iron grasp!
Down went the Cumberland all a wrack,
      With a sudden shudder of death,
      And the cannon's breath
   For her dying gasp.

Next morn, as the sun rose over the bay,
   Still floated our flag at the mainmast head.
Lord, how beautiful was Thy day!
      Every waft of the air
      Was a whisper of prayer,
   Or a dirge for the dead.

Ho! brave hearts that went down in the seas!
   Ye are at peace in the troubled stream;
Ho! brave land! with hearts like these,
      Thy flag, that is rent in twain,
      Shall be one again,
   And without a seam!

Snow-Flakes

Out of the bosom of the Air,
Out of the cloud-folds of her garments shaken,
Over the woodlands brown and bare,
Over the harvest-fields forsaken,
Silent, and soft, and slow
Descends the snow.

Even as our cloudy fancies take
Suddenly shape in some divine expression,
Even as the troubled heart doth make
In the white countenance confession,
The troubled sky reveals
The grief it feels.

This is the poem of the air,
Slowly in silent syllables recorded;
This is the secret of despair,
Long in its cloudy bosom hoarded,
Now whispered and revealed
To wood and field.

A Day of Sunshine

O gift of God! O perfect day:
Whereon shall no man work, but play;
Whereon it is enough for me,
Not to be doing, but to be!

Through every fibre of my brain,
Through every nerve, through every vein,
I feel the electric thrill, the touch
Of life, that seems almost too much.

I hear the wind among the trees
Playing celestial symphonies;
I see the branches downward bent,
Like keys of some great instrument.

And over me unrolls on high
The splendid scenery of the sky,
Where through a sapphire sea the sun
Sails like a golden galleon,

Towards yonder cloud-land in the West,
Towards yonder Islands of the Blest,
Whose steep sierra far uplifts
Its craggy summits white with drifts.

Blow, winds! and waft through all the rooms
The snow-flakes of the cherry-blooms!
Blow, winds! and bend within my reach
The fiery blossoms of the peach!

O Life and Love! O happy throng
Of thoughts, whose only speech is song!
O heart of man! canst thou not be
Blithe as the air is, and as free?

Something Left Undone

Labor with what zeal we will,
  Something still remains undone,
Something uncompleted still
  Waits the rising of the sun.

By the bedside, on the stair,
  At the threshold, near the gates,
With its menace or its prayer,
  Like a mendicant it waits;

Waits, and will not go away;
  Waits, and will not be gainsaid;
By the cares of yesterday
  Each to-day is heavier made;

Till at length the burden seems
  Greater than our strength can bear,
Heavy as the weight of dreams,
  Pressing on us everywhere.

And we stand from day to day,
  Like the dwarfs of times gone by,
Who, as Northern legends say,
  On their shoulders held the sky.

Weariness

O little feet! that such long years
Must wander on through hopes and fears,
  Must ache and bleed beneath your load;
I, nearer to the wayside inn
Where toil shall cease and rest begin,
  Am weary, thinking of your road!

O little hands! that, weak or strong,
Have still to serve or rule so long,
  Have still so long to give or ask;
I, who so much with book and pen
Have toiled among my fellow-men,
  Am weary, thinking of your task.

O little hearts! that throb and beat
With such impatient, feverish heat,
  Such limitless and strong desires;
Mine, that so long has glowed and burned,
With passions into ashes turned,
  Now covers and conceals its fires.

O little souls! as pure and white
And crystalline as rays of light
  Direct from heaven, their source divine;
Refracted through the mist of years,
How red my setting sun appears,
  How lurid looks this soul of mine!

from

TALES OF A WAYSIDE INN

PART FIRST

Prelude

THE WAYSIDE INN

One Autumn night, in Sudbury town,
Across the meadows bare and brown,
The windows of the wayside inn
Gleamed red with fire-light through the leaves
Of woodbine, hanging from the eaves
Their crimson curtains rent and thin.

As ancient is this hostelry
As any in the land may be,
Built in the old Colonial day,
When men lived in a grander way,
With ampler hospitality;
A kind of old Hobgoblin Hall,
Now somewhat fallen to decay,
With weather-stains upon the wall,
And stairways worn, and crazy doors,
And creaking and uneven floors,
And chimneys huge, and tiled and tall.

A region of repose it seems,
A place of slumber and of dreams,
Remote among the wooded hills!
For there no noisy railway speeds,
Its torch-race scattering smoke and gleeds;
But noon and night, the panting teams
Stop under the great oaks, that throw
Tangles of light and shade below,
On roofs and doors and window-sills.
Across the road the barns display

Their lines of stalls, their mows of hay,
Through the wide doors the breezes blow,
The wattled cocks strut to and fro,
And, half effaced by rain and shine,
The Red Horse prances on the sign.
Round this old-fashioned, quaint abode
Deep silence reigned, save when a gust
Went rushing down the county road,
And skeletons of leaves, and dust,
A moment quickened by its breath,
Shuddered and danced their dance of death,
And through the ancient oaks o'erhead
Mysterious voices moaned and fled.

But from the parlor of the inn
A pleasant murmur smote the ear,
Like water rushing through a weir:
Oft interrupted by the din
Of laughter and of loud applause,
And, in each intervening pause,
The music of a violin.
The fire-light, shedding over all
The splendor of its ruddy glow,
Filled the whole parlor large and low;
It gleamed on wainscot and on wall,
It touched with more than wonted grace
Fair Princess Mary's pictured face;
It bronzed the rafters overhead,
On the old spinet's ivory keys
It played inaudible melodies,
It crowned the sombre clock with flame,
The hands, the hours, the maker's name,
And painted with a livelier red
The Landlord's coat-of-arms again;
And, flashing on the window-pane,
Emblazoned with its light and shade
The jovial rhymes, that still remain,
Writ near a century ago,
By the great Major Molineaux,
Whom Hawthorne has immortal made.

Before the blazing fire of wood
Erect the rapt musician stood;
And ever and anon he bent
His head upon his instrument,
And seemed to listen, till he caught
Confessions of its secret thought,—
The joy, the triumph, the lament,
The exultation and the pain;
Then, by the magic of his art,
He soothed the throbbings of its heart,
And lulled it into peace again.

Around the fireside at their ease
There sat a group of friends, entranced
With the delicious melodies;
Who from the far-off noisy town
Had to the wayside inn come down,
To rest beneath its old oak trees.
The fire-light on their faces glanced,
Their shadows on the wainscot danced,
And, though of different lands and speech,
Each had his tale to tell, and each
Was anxious to be pleased and please.
And while the sweet musician plays,
Let me in outline sketch them all,
Perchance uncouthly as the blaze
With its uncertain touch portrays
Their shadowy semblance on the wall.

But first the Landlord will I trace;
Grave in his aspect and attire;
A man of ancient pedigree,
A Justice of the Peace was he,
Known in all Sudbury as "The Squire."
Proud was he of his name and race,
Of old Sir William and Sir Hugh,
And in the parlor, full in view,
His coat-of-arms, well framed and glazed,
Upon the wall in colors blazed;
He beareth gules upon his shield,

A chevron argent in the field,
With three wolf's heads, and for the crest
A Wyvern part-per-pale addressed
Upon a helmet barred; below
The scroll reads, "By the name of Howe."
And over this, no longer bright,
Though glimmering with a latent light,
Was hung the sword his grandsire bore
In the rebellious days of yore,
Down there at Concord in the fight.

A youth was there, of quiet ways,
A Student of old books and days,
To whom all tongues and lands were known,
And yet a lover of his own;
With many a social virtue graced,
And yet a friend of solitude;
A man of such a genial mood
The heart of all things he embraced,
And yet of such fastidious taste,
He never found the best too good.
Books were his passion and delight,
And in his upper room at home
Stood many a rare and sumptuous tome,
In vellum bound, with gold bedight,
Great volumes garmented in white,
Recalling Florence, Pisa, Rome.
He loved the twilight that surrounds
The border-land of old romance;
Where glitter hauberk, helm, and lance,
And banner waves, and trumpet sounds,
And ladies ride with hawk on wrist,
And mighty warriors sweep along,
Magnified by the purple mist,
The dusk of centuries and of song.
The chronicles of Charlemagne,
Of Merlin and the Mort d'Arthure,
Mingled together in his brain
With tales of Flores and Blanchefleur,
Sir Ferumbras, Sir Eglamour,

Sir Launcelot, Sir Morgadour,
Sir Guy, Sir Bevis, Sir Gawain.

A young Sicilian, too, was there;
In sight of Etna born and bred,
Some breath of its volcanic air
Was glowing in his heart and brain,
And, being rebellious to his liege,
After Palermo's fatal siege,
Across the western seas he fled,
In good King Bomba's happy reign.
His face was like a summer night,
All flooded with a dusky light;
His hands were small; his teeth shone white
As sea-shells, when he smiled or spoke;
His sinews supple and strong as oak;
Clean shaven was he as a priest,
Who at the mass on Sunday sings,
Save that upon his upper lip
His beard, a good palm's length at least,
Level and pointed at the tip,
Shot sideways, like a swallow's wings.
The poets read he o'er and o'er,
And most of all the Immortal Four
Of Italy; and next to those,
The story-telling bard of prose,
Who wrote the joyous Tuscan tales
Of the Decameron, that make
Fiesole's green hills and vales
Remembered for Boccaccio's sake.
Much too of music was his thought;
The melodies and measures fraught
With sunshine and the open air,
Of vineyards and the singing sea
Of his beloved Sicily;
And much it pleased him to peruse
The songs of the Sicilian muse,—
Bucolic songs by Meli sung
In the familiar peasant tongue,
That made men say, "Behold! once more

The pitying gods to earth restore
Theocritus of Syracuse!"

A Spanish Jew from Alicant
With aspect grand and grave was there;
Vender of silks and fabrics rare,
And attar of rose from the Levant.
Like an old Patriarch he appeared,
Abraham or Isaac, or at least
Some later Prophet or High-Priest;
With lustrous eyes, and olive skin,
And, wildly tossed from cheeks and chin,
The tumbling cataract of his beard.
His garments breathed a spicy scent
Of cinnamon and sandal blent,
Like the soft aromatic gales
That meet the mariner, who sails
Through the Moluccas, and the seas
That wash the shores of Celebes.
All stories that recorded are
By Pierre Alphonse he knew by heart,
And it was rumored he could say
The Parables of Sandabar,
And all the Fables of Pilpay,
Or if not all, the greater part!
Well versed was he in Hebrew books,
Talmud and Targum, and the lore
Of Kabala; and evermore
There was a mystery in his looks;
His eyes seemed gazing far away,
As if in vision or in trance
He heard the solemn sackbut play,
And saw the Jewish maidens dance.

A Theologian, from the school
Of Cambridge on the Charles, was there;
Skilful alike with tongue and pen,
He preached to all men everywhere
The Gospel of the Golden Rule,
The New Commandment given to men,

Thinking the deed, and not the creed,
Would help us in our utmost need.
With reverent feet the earth he trod,
Nor banished nature from his plan,
But studied still with deep research
To build the Universal Church,
Lofty as in the love of God,
And ample as the wants of man.

A Poet, too, was there, whose verse
Was tender, musical, and terse;
The inspiration, the delight,
The gleam, the glory, the swift flight,
Of thoughts so sudden, that they seem
The revelations of a dream,
All these were his; but with them came
No envy of another's fame;
He did not find his sleep less sweet
For music in some neighboring street,
Nor rustling hear in every breeze
The laurels of Miltiades.
Honor and blessings on his head
While living, good report when dead,
Who, not too eager for renown,
Accepts, but does not clutch, the crown!

Last the Musician, as he stood
Illumined by that fire of wood;
Fair-haired, blue-eyed, his aspect blithe,
His figure tall and straight and lithe,
And every feature of his face
Revealing his Norwegian race;
A radiance, streaming from within,
Around his eyes and forehead beamed,
The Angel with the violin,
Painted by Raphael, he seemed.
He lived in that ideal world
Whose language is not speech, but song;
Around him evermore the throng
Of elves and sprites their dances whirled;

The Strömkarl sang, the cataract hurled
Its headlong waters from the height;
And mingled in the wild delight
The scream of sea-birds in their flight,
The rumor of the forest trees,
The plunge of the implacable seas,
The tumult of the wind at night,
Voices of eld, like trumpets blowing,
Old ballads, and wild melodies
Through mist and darkness pouring forth,
Like Elivagar's river flowing
Out of the glaciers of the North.

The instrument on which he played
Was in Cremona's workshops made,
By a great master of the past,
Ere yet was lost the art divine;
Fashioned of maple and of pine,
That in Tyrolean forests vast
Had rocked and wrestled with the blast:
Exquisite was it in design,
Perfect in each minutest part,
A marvel of the lutist's art;
And in its hollow chamber, thus,
The maker from whose hands it came
Had written his unrivalled name,—
"Antonius Stradivarius."

And when he played, the atmosphere
Was filled with magic, and the ear
Caught echoes of that Harp of Gold,
Whose music had so weird a sound,
The hunted stag forgot to bound,
The leaping rivulet backward rolled,
The birds came down from bush and tree,
The dead came from beneath the sea,
The maiden to the harper's knee!

The music ceased; the applause was loud,
The pleased musician smiled and bowed;

The wood-fire clapped its hands of flame,
The shadows on the wainscot stirred,
And from the harpsichord there came
A ghostly murmur of acclaim,
A sound like that sent down at night
By birds of passage in their flight,
From the remotest distance heard.

Then silence followed; then began
A clamor for the Landlord's tale,—
The story promised them of old,
They said, but always left untold;
And he, although a bashful man,
And all his courage seemed to fail,
Finding excuse of no avail,
Yielded; and thus the story ran.

The Landlord's Tale

PAUL REVERE'S RIDE

Listen, my children, and you shall hear
Of the midnight ride of Paul Revere,
On the eighteenth of April, in Seventy-five;
Hardly a man is now alive
Who remembers that famous day and year.

He said to his friend, "If the British march
By land or sea from the town to-night,
Hang a lantern aloft in the belfry arch
Of the North Church tower as a signal light,—
One, if by land, and two, if by sea;
And I on the opposite shore will be,
Ready to ride and spread the alarm
Through every Middlesex village and farm,
For the country folk to be up and to arm."
Then he said, "Good night!" and with muffled oar
Silently rowed to the Charlestown shore,

Just as the moon rose over the bay,
Where swinging wide at her moorings lay
The Somerset, British man-of-war;
A phantom ship, with each mast and spar
Across the moon like a prison bar,
And a huge black hulk, that was magnified
By its own reflection in the tide.

Meanwhile, his friend, through alley and street,
Wanders and watches with eager ears,
Till in the silence around him he hears
The muster of men at the barrack door,
The sound of arms, and the tramp of feet,
And the measured tread of the grenadiers,
Marching down to their boats on the shore.

Then he climbed the tower of the Old North Church,
By the wooden stairs, with stealthy tread,
To the belfry-chamber overhead,
And startled the pigeons from their perch
On the sombre rafters, that round him made
Masses and moving shapes of shade,—
By the trembling ladder, steep and tall,
To the highest window in the wall,
Where he paused to listen and look down
A moment on the roofs of the town,
And the moonlight flowing over all.
Beneath, in the churchyard, lay the dead,
In their night-encampment on the hill,
Wrapped in silence so deep and still
That he could hear, like a sentinel's tread,
The watchful night-wind, as it went
Creeping along from tent to tent,
And seeming to whisper, "All is well!"
A moment only he feels the spell
Of the place and the hour, and the secret dread
Of the lonely belfry and the dead;
For suddenly all his thoughts are bent
On a shadowy something far away,
Where the river widens to meet the bay,—

A line of black that bends and floats
On the rising tide, like a bridge of boats.

Meanwhile, impatient to mount and ride,
Booted and spurred, with a heavy stride
On the opposite shore walked Paul Revere.
Now he patted his horse's side,
Now gazed at the landscape far and near,
Then, impetuous, stamped the earth,
And turned and tightened his saddle girth;
But mostly he watched with eager search
The belfry-tower of the Old North Church,
As it rose above the graves on the hill,
Lonely and spectral and sombre and still.
And lo! as he looks, on the belfry's height
A glimmer, and then a gleam of light!
He springs to the saddle, the bridle he turns,
But lingers and gazes, till full on his sight
A second lamp in the belfry burns!

A hurry of hoofs in a village street,
A shape in the moonlight, a bulk in the dark,
And beneath, from the pebbles, in passing, a spark
Struck out by a steed flying fearless and fleet:
That was all! And yet, through the gloom and the light,
The fate of a nation was riding that night;
And the spark struck out by that steed, in his flight,
Kindled the land into flame with its heat.
He has left the village and mounted the steep,
And beneath him, tranquil and broad and deep,
Is the Mystic, meeting the ocean tides;
And under the alders, that skirt its edge,
Now soft on the sand, now loud on the ledge,
Is heard the tramp of his steed as he rides.

It was twelve by the village clock,
When he crossed the bridge into Medford town.
He heard the crowing of the cock,
And the barking of the farmer's dog,
And felt the damp of the river fog,
That rises after the sun goes down.

It was one by the village clock,
When he galloped into Lexington.
He saw the gilded weathercock
Swim in the moonlight as he passed,
And the meeting-house windows, blank and bare,
Gaze at him with a spectral glare,
As if they already stood aghast
At the bloody work they would look upon.

It was two by the village clock,
When he came to the bridge in Concord town.
He heard the bleating of the flock,
And the twitter of birds among the trees,
And felt the breath of the morning breeze
Blowing over the meadows brown.
And one was safe and asleep in his bed
Who at the bridge would be first to fall,
Who that day would be lying dead,
Pierced by a British musket-ball.

You know the rest. In the books you have read,
How the British Regulars fired and fled,—
How the farmers gave them ball for ball,
From behind each fence and farm-yard wall,
Chasing the red-coats down the lane,
Then crossing the fields to emerge again
Under the trees at the turn of the road,
And only pausing to fire and load.

So through the night rode Paul Revere;
And so through the night went his cry of alarm
To every Middlesex village and farm,—
A cry of defiance and not of fear,
A voice in the darkness, a knock at the door,
And a word that shall echo forevermore!
For, borne on the night-wind of the Past,
Through all our history, to the last,
In the hour of darkness and peril and need,
The people will waken and listen to hear
The hurrying hoof-beats of that steed,
And the midnight message of Paul Revere.

Interlude

The Landlord ended thus his tale,
Then rising took down from its nail
The sword that hung there, dim with dust,
And cleaving to its sheath with rust,
And said, "This sword was in the fight."
The Poet seized it, and exclaimed,
"It is the sword of a good knight,
Though homespun was his coat-of-mail;
What matter if it be not named
Joyeuse, Colada, Durindale,
Excalibar, or Aroundight,
Or other name the books record?
Your ancestor, who bore this sword
As Colonel of the Volunteers,
Mounted upon his old gray mare,
Seen here and there and everywhere,
To me a grander shape appears
Than old Sir William, or what not,
Clinking about in foreign lands
With iron gauntlets on his hands,
And on his head an iron pot!"

All laughed; the Landlord's face grew red
As his escutcheon on the wall;
He could not comprehend at all
The drift of what the Poet said;
For those who had been longest dead
Were always greatest in his eyes;
And he was speechless with surprise
To see Sir William's plumed head
Brought to a level with the rest,
And made the subject of a jest.
And this perceiving, to appease
The Landlord's wrath, the others' fears,
The Student said, with careless ease,
"The ladies and the cavaliers,
The arms, the loves, the courtesies,
The deeds of high emprise, I sing!

Thus Ariosto says, in words
That have the stately stride and ring
Of armed knights and clashing swords.
Now listen to the tale I bring;
Listen! though not to me belong
The flowing draperies of his song,
The words that rouse, the voice that charms.
The Landlord's tale was one of arms,
Only a tale of love is mine,
Blending the human and divine,
A tale of the Decameron, told
In Palmieri's garden old,
By Fiametta, laurel-crowned,
While her companions lay around,
And heard the intermingled sound
Of airs that on their errands sped,
And wild birds gossiping overhead,
And lisp of leaves, and fountain's fall,
And her own voice more sweet than all,
Telling the tale, which, wanting these,
Perchance may lose its power to please."

The Student's Tale

THE FALCON OF SER FEDERIGO

One summer morning, when the sun was hot,
Weary with labor in his garden-plot,
On a rude bench beneath his cottage eaves,
Ser Federigo sat among the leaves
Of a huge vine, that, with its arms outspread,
Hung its delicious clusters overhead.
Below him, through the lovely valley, flowed
The river Arno, like a winding road,
And from its banks were lifted high in air
The spires and roofs of Florence called the Fair;
To him a marble tomb, that rose above
His wasted fortunes and his buried love.

For there, in banquet and in tournament,
His wealth had lavished been, his substance spent,
To woo and lose, since ill his wooing sped,
Monna Giovanna, who his rival wed,
Yet ever in his fancy reigned supreme,
The ideal woman of a young man's dream.

Then he withdrew, in poverty and pain,
To this small farm, the last of his domain,
His only comfort and his only care
To prune his vines, and plant the fig and pear;
His only forester and only guest
His falcon, faithful to him, when the rest,
Whose willing hands had found so light of yore
The brazen knocker of his palace door,
Had now no strength to lift the wooden latch,
That entrance gave beneath a roof of thatch.
Companion of his solitary ways,
Purveyor of his feasts on holidays,
On him this melancholy man bestowed
The love with which his nature overflowed.

And so the empty-handed years went round,
Vacant, though voiceful with prophetic sound,
And so, that summer morn, he sat and mused
With folded, patient hands, as he was used,
And dreamily before his half-closed sight
Floated the vision of his lost delight.
Beside him, motionless, the drowsy bird
Dreamed of the chase, and in his slumber heard
The sudden, scythe-like sweep of wings, that dare
The headlong plunge through eddying gulfs of air,
Then, starting broad awake upon his perch,
Tinkled his bells, like mass-bells in a church,
And looking at his master, seemed to say,
"Ser Federigo, shall we hunt to-day?"

Ser Federigo thought not of the chase;
The tender vision of her lovely face,
I will not say he seems to see, he sees

In the leaf-shadows of the trellises,
Herself, yet not herself; a lovely child
With flowing tresses, and eyes wide and wild,
Coming undaunted up the garden walk,
And looking not at him, but at the hawk.
"Beautiful falcon!" said he, "would that I
Might hold thee on my wrist, or see thee fly!"
The voice was hers, and made strange echoes start
Through all the haunted chambers of his heart,
As an æolian harp through gusty doors
Of some old ruin its wild music pours.

"Who is thy mother, my fair boy?" he said,
His hand laid softly on that shining head.
"Monna Giovanna. Will you let me stay
A little while, and with your falcon play?
We live there, just beyond your garden wall,
In the great house behind the poplars tall."

So he spake on; and Federigo heard
As from afar each softly uttered word,
And drifted onward through the golden gleams
And shadows of the misty sea of dreams,
As mariners becalmed through vapors drift,
And feel the sea beneath them sink and lift,
And hear far off the mournful breakers roar,
And voices calling faintly from the shore!
Then waking from his pleasant reveries,
He took the little boy upon his knees,
And told him stories of his gallant bird,
Till in their friendship he became a third.

Monna Giovanna, widowed in her prime,
Had come with friends to pass the summer time
In her grand villa, half-way up the hill,
O'erlooking Florence, but retired and still;
With iron gates, that opened through long lines
Of sacred ilex and centennial pines,
And terraced gardens, and broad steps of stone,
And sylvan deities, with moss o'ergrown,

And fountains palpitating in the heat,
And all Val d'Arno stretched beneath its feet.
Here in seclusion, as a widow may,
The lovely lady whiled the hours away,
Pacing in sable robes the statued hall,
Herself the stateliest statue among all,
And seeing more and more, with secret joy,
Her husband risen and living in her boy,
Till the lost sense of life returned again,
Not as delight, but as relief from pain.
Meanwhile the boy, rejoicing in his strength,
Stormed down the terraces from length to length;
The screaming peacock chased in hot pursuit,
And climbed the garden trellises for fruit.
But his chief pastime was to watch the flight
Of a gerfalcon, soaring into sight,
Beyond the trees that fringed the garden wall,
Then downward stooping at some distant call;
And as he gazed full often wondered he
Who might the master of the falcon be,
Until that happy morning, when he found
Master and falcon in the cottage ground.

And now a shadow and a terror fell
On the great house, as if a passing-bell
Tolled from the tower, and filled each spacious room
With secret awe and preternatural gloom;
The petted boy grew ill, and day by day
Pined with mysterious malady away.
The mother's heart would not be comforted;
Her darling seemed to her already dead,
And often, sitting by the sufferer's side,
"What can I do to comfort thee?" she cried.
At first the silent lips made no reply,
But, moved at length by her importunate cry,
"Give me," he answered, with imploring tone,
"Ser Federigo's falcon for my own!"

No answer could the astonished mother make;
How could she ask, e'en for her darling's sake,

Such favor at a luckless lover's hand,
Well knowing that to ask was to command?
Well knowing, what all falconers confessed,
In all the land that falcon was the best,
The master's pride and passion and delight,
And the sole pursuivant of this poor knight.
But yet, for her child's sake, she could no less
Than give assent, to soothe his restlessness,
So promised, and then promising to keep
Her promise sacred, saw him fall asleep.

The morrow was a bright September morn;
The earth was beautiful as if new-born;
There was that nameless splendor everywhere,
That wild exhilaration in the air,
Which makes the passers in the city street
Congratulate each other as they meet.
Two lovely ladies, clothed in cloak and hood,
Passed through the garden gate into the wood,
Under the lustrous leaves, and through the sheen
Of dewy sunshine showering down between.
The one, close-hooded, had the attractive grace
Which sorrow sometimes lends a woman's face;
Her dark eyes moistened with the mists that roll
From the gulf-stream of passion in the soul;
The other with her hood thrown back, her hair
Making a golden glory in the air,
Her cheeks suffused with an auroral blush,
Her young heart singing louder than the thrush.
So walked, that morn, through mingled light and shade,
Each by the other's presence lovelier made,
Monna Giovanna and her bosom friend,
Intent upon their errand and its end.

They found Ser Federigo at his toil,
Like banished Adam, delving in the soil;
And when he looked and these fair women spied,
The garden suddenly was glorified;
His long-lost Eden was restored again,
And the strange river winding through the plain

No longer was the Arno to his eyes,
But the Euphrates watering Paradise!

Monna Giovanna raised her stately head,
And with fair words of salutation said:
"Ser Federigo, we come here as friends,
Hoping in this to make some poor amends
For past unkindness. I who ne'er before
Would even cross the threshold of your door,
I who in happier days such pride maintained,
Refused your banquets, and your gifts disdained,
This morning come, a self-invited guest,
To put your generous nature to the test,
And breakfast with you under your own vine."
To which he answered: "Poor desert of mine,
Not your unkindness call it, for if aught
Is good in me of feeling or of thought,
From you it comes, and this last grace outweighs
All sorrows, all regrets of other days."

And after further compliment and talk,
Among the asters in the garden walk
He left his guests; and to his cottage turned,
And as he entered for a moment yearned
For the lost splendors of the days of old,
The ruby glass, the silver and the gold,
And felt how piercing is the sting of pride,
By want embittered and intensified.
He looked about him for some means or way
To keep this unexpected holiday;
Searched every cupboard, and then searched again,
Summoned the maid, who came, but came in vain;
"The Signor did not hunt to-day," she said,
"There 's nothing in the house but wine and bread."
Then suddenly the drowsy falcon shook
His little bells, with that sagacious look,
Which said, as plain as language to the ear,
If anything is wanting, I am here!"
Yes, everything is wanting, gallant bird!
The master seized thee without further word.

Like thine own lure, he whirled thee round; ah me!
The pomp and flutter of brave falconry,
The bells, the jesses, the bright scarlet hood,
The flight and the pursuit o'er field and wood,
All these forevermore are ended now;
No longer victor, but the victim thou!

Then on the board a snow-white cloth he spread,
Laid on its wooden dish the loaf of bread,
Brought purple grapes with autumn sunshine hot,
The fragrant peach, the juicy bergamot;
Then in the midst a flask of wine he placed
And with autumnal flowers the banquet graced.
Ser Federigo, would not these suffice
Without thy falcon stuffed with cloves and spice?

When all was ready, and the courtly dame
With her companion to the cottage came,
Upon Ser Federigo's brain there fell
The wild enchantment of a magic spell!
The room they entered, mean and low and small,
Was changed into a sumptuous banquet-hall,
With fanfares by aerial trumpets blown;
The rustic chair she sat on was a throne;
He ate celestial food, and a divine
Flavor was given to his country wine,
And the poor falcon, fragrant with his spice,
A peacock was, or bird of paradise!

When the repast was ended, they arose
And passed again into the garden-close.
Then said the lady, "Far too well I know,
Remembering still the days of long ago,
Though you betray it not, with what surprise
You see me here in this familiar wise.
You have no children, and you cannot guess
What anguish, what unspeakable distress
A mother feels, whose child is lying ill,
Nor how her heart anticipates his will.
And yet for this, you see me lay aside

All womanly reserve and check of pride,
And ask the thing most precious in your sight,
Your falcon, your sole comfort and delight,
Which if you find it in your heart to give,
My poor, unhappy boy perchance may live."

Ser Federigo listens, and replies,
With tears of love and pity in his eyes:
"Alas, dear lady! there can be no task
So sweet to me, as giving when you ask.
One little hour ago, if I had known
This wish of yours, it would have been my own.
But thinking in what manner I could best
Do honor to the presence of my guest,
I deemed that nothing worthier could be
Than what most dear and precious was to me;
And so my gallant falcon breathed his last
To furnish forth this morning our repast."

In mute contrition, mingled with dismay,
The gentle lady turned her eyes away,
Grieving that he such sacrifice should make
And kill his falcon for a woman's sake,
Yet feeling in her heart a woman's pride,
That nothing she could ask for was denied;
Then took her leave, and passed out at the gate
With footstep slow and soul disconsolate.

Three days went by, and lo! a passing-bell
Tolled from the little chapel in the dell;
Ten strokes Ser Federigo heard, and said,
Breathing a prayer, "Alas! her child is dead!"
Three months went by; and lo! a merrier chime
Rang from the chapel bells at Christmas-time;
The cottage was deserted, and no more
Ser Federigo sat beside its door,
But now, with servitors to do his will,
In the grand villa, half-way up the hill,
Sat at the Christmas feast, and at his side
Monna Giovanna, his beloved bride,

Never so beautiful, so kind, so fair,
Enthroned once more in the old rustic chair,
High-perched upon the back of which there stood
The image of a falcon carved in wood,
And underneath the inscription, with a date,
"All things come round to him who will but wait."

Interlude

Soon as the story reached its end,
One, over eager to commend,
Crowned it with injudicious praise;
And then the voice of blame found vent,
And fanned the embers of dissent
Into a somewhat lively blaze.

The Theologian shook his head;
"These old Italian tales," he said,
"From the much-praised Decameron down
Through all the rabble of the rest,
Are either trifling, dull, or lewd;
The gossip of a neighborhood
In some remote provincial town,
A scandalous chronicle at best!
They seem to me a stagnant fen,
Grown rank with rushes and with reeds,
Where a white lily, now and then,
Blooms in the midst of noxious weeds
And deadly nightshade on its banks!"

To this the Student straight replied,
"For the white lily, many thanks!
One should not say, with too much pride,
Fountain, I will not drink of thee!
Nor were it grateful to forget
That from these reservoirs and tanks
Even imperial Shakespeare drew
His Moor of Venice, and the Jew,

And Romeo and Juliet,
And many a famous comedy."

Then a long pause; till some one said,
"An Angel is flying overhead!"
At these words spake the Spanish Jew,
And murmured with an inward breath:
"God grant, if what you say be true,
It may not be the Angel of Death!"
And then another pause; and then,
Stroking his beard, he said again:
"This brings back to my memory
A story in the Talmud told,
That book of gems, that book of gold,
Of wonders many and manifold,
A tale that often comes to me,
And fills my heart, and haunts my brain,
And never wearies nor grows old."

The Spanish Jew's Tale

THE LEGEND OF RABBI BEN LEVI

Rabbi Ben Levi, on the Sabbath, read
A volume of the Law, in which it said,
"No man shall look upon my face and live."
And as he read, he prayed that God would give
His faithful servant grace with mortal eye
To look upon His face and yet not die.

Then fell a sudden shadow on the page,
And, lifting up his eyes, grown dim with age,
He saw the Angel of Death before him stand,
Holding a naked sword in his right hand.
Rabbi Ben Levi was a righteous man,
Yet through his veins a chill of terror ran.
With trembling voice he said, "What wilt thou here?"
The angel answered, "Lo! the time draws near

When thou must die; yet first, by God's decree,
Whate'er thou askest shall be granted thee."
Replied the Rabbi, "Let these living eyes
First look upon my place in Paradise."

Then said the Angel, "Come with me and look."
Rabbi Ben Levi closed the sacred book,
And rising, and uplifting his gray head,
"Give me thy sword," he to the Angel said,
"Lest thou shouldst fall upon me by the way."
The angel smiled and hastened to obey,
Then led him forth to the Celestial Town,
And set him on the wall, whence, gazing down,
Rabbi Ben Levi, with his living eyes,
Might look upon his place in Paradise.

Then straight into the city of the Lord
The Rabbi leaped with the Death-Angel's sword,
And through the streets there swept a sudden breath
Of something there unknown, which men call death.
Meanwhile the Angel stayed without, and cried,
"Come back!" To which the Rabbi's voice replied,
"No! in the name of God, whom I adore,
I swear that hence I will depart no more!"

Then all the Angels cried, "O Holy One,
See what the son of Levi here hath done!
The kingdom of Heaven he takes by violence,
And in Thy name refuses to go hence!"
The Lord replied, "My Angels, be not wroth;
Did e'er the son of Levi break his oath?
Let him remain; for he with mortal eye
Shall look upon my face and yet not die."

Beyond the outer wall the Angel of Death
Heard the great voice, and said, with panting breath,
"Give back the sword, and let me go my way."
Whereat the Rabbi paused, and answered, "Nay!
Anguish enough already hath it caused
Among the sons of men." And while he paused

He heard the awful mandate of the Lord
Resounding through the air, "Give back the sword!"

The Rabbi bowed his head in silent prayer;
Then said he to the dreadful Angel, "Swear
No human eye shall look on it again;
But when thou takest away the souls of men,
Thyself unseen, and with an unseen sword,
Thou wilt perform the bidding of the Lord."
The Angel took the sword again, and swore,
And walks on earth unseen forevermore.

Interlude

He ended: and a kind of spell
Upon the silent listeners fell.
His solemn manner and his words
Had touched the deep, mysterious chords
That vibrate in each human breast
Alike, but not alike confessed.
The spiritual world seemed near;
And close above them, full of fear,
Its awful adumbration passed,
A luminous shadow, vague and vast.
They almost feared to look, lest there,
Embodied from the impalpable air,
They might behold the Angel stand,
Holding the sword in his right hand.

At last, but in a voice subdued,
Not to disturb their dreamy mood,
Said the Sicilian: "While you spoke,
Telling your legend marvellous,
Suddenly in my memory woke
The thought of one, now gone from us, —
An old Abate, meek and mild,
My friend and teacher, when a child,
Who sometimes in those days of old

The legend of an Angel told,
Which ran, as I remember, thus."

The Sicilian's Tale

KING ROBERT OF SICILY

Robert of Sicily, brother of Pope Urbane
And Valmond, Emperor of Allemaine,
Apparelled in magnificent attire,
With retinue of many a knight and squire,
On St. John's eve, at vespers, proudly sat
And heard the priests chant the Magnificat.
And as he listened, o'er and o'er again
Repeated, like a burden or refrain,
He caught the words, "*Deposuit potentes*
De sede, et exaltavit humiles;"
And slowly lifting up his kingly head
He to a learned clerk beside him said,
"What mean these words?" The clerk made answer meet,
"He has put down the mighty from their seat,
And has exalted them of low degree."
Thereat King Robert muttered scornfully,
" 'T is well that such seditious words are sung
Only by priests and in the Latin tongue;
For unto priests and people be it known,
There is no power can push me from my throne!"
And leaning back, he yawned and fell asleep,
Lulled by the chant monotonous and deep.

When he awoke, it was already night;
The church was empty, and there was no light,
Save where the lamps, that glimmered few and faint,
Lighted a little space before some saint.
He started from his seat and gazed around,
But saw no living thing and heard no sound.
He groped towards the door, but it was locked;
He cried aloud, and listened, and then knocked,

And uttered awful threatenings and complaints,
And imprecations upon men and saints.
The sounds reëchoed from the roof and walls
As if dead priests were laughing in their stalls.

At length the sexton, hearing from without
The tumult of the knocking and the shout,
And thinking thieves were in the house of prayer,
Came with his lantern, asking, "Who is there?"
Half choked with rage, King Robert fiercely said,
"Open: 't is I, the King! Art thou afraid?"
The frightened sexton, muttering, with a curse,
"This is some drunken vagabond, or worse!"
Turned the great key and flung the portal wide;
A man rushed by him at a single stride,
Haggard, half naked, without hat or cloak,
Who neither turned, nor looked at him, nor spoke,
But leaped into the blackness of the night,
And vanished like a spectre from his sight.

Robert of Sicily, brother of Pope Urbane
And Valmond, Emperor of Allemaine,
Despoiled of his magnificent attire,
Bareheaded, breathless, and besprent with mire,
With sense of wrong and outrage desperate,
Strode on and thundered at the palace gate;
Rushed through the courtyard, thrusting in his rage
To right and left each seneschal and page,
And hurried up the broad and sounding stair,
His white face ghastly in the torches' glare.
From hall to hall he passed with breathless speed;
Voices and cries he heard, but did not heed,
Until at last he reached the banquet-room,
Blazing with light, and breathing with perfume.

There on the dais sat another king,
Wearing his robes, his crown, his signet-ring,
King Robert's self in features, form, and height,
But all transfigured with angelic light!
It was an Angel; and his presence there

With a divine effulgence filled the air,
An exaltation, piercing the disguise,
Though none the hidden Angel recognize.

A moment speechless, motionless, amazed,
The throneless monarch on the Angel gazed,
Who met his look of anger and surprise
With the divine compassion of his eyes;
Then said, "Who art thou? and why com'st thou here?"
To which King Robert answered with a sneer,
"I am the King, and come to claim my own
From an impostor, who usurps my throne!"
And suddenly, at these audacious words,
Up sprang the angry guests, and drew their swords;
The Angel answered, with unruffled brow,
"Nay, not the King, but the King's Jester, thou
Henceforth shalt wear the bells and scalloped cape,
And for thy counsellor shalt lead an ape;
Thou shalt obey my servants when they call,
And wait upon my henchmen in the hall!"

Deaf to King Robert's threats and cries and prayers,
They thrust him from the hall and down the stairs;
A group of tittering pages ran before,
And as they opened wide the folding-door,
His heart failed, for he heard, with strange alarms,
The boisterous laughter of the men-at-arms,
And all the vaulted chamber roar and ring
With the mock plaudits of "Long live the King!"

Next morning, waking with the day's first beam,
He said within himself, "It was a dream!"
But the straw rustled as he turned his head,
There were the cap and bells beside his bed,
Around him rose the bare, discolored walls,
Close by, the steeds were champing in their stalls,
And in the corner, a revolting shape,
Shivering and chattering sat the wretched ape.
It was no dream; the world he loved so much
Had turned to dust and ashes at his touch!

Days came and went; and now returned again
To Sicily the old Saturnian reign;
Under the Angel's governance benign
The happy island danced with corn and wine,
And deep within the mountain's burning breast
Enceladus, the giant, was at rest.

Meanwhile King Robert yielded to his fate,
Sullen and silent and disconsolate.
Dressed in the motley garb that Jesters wear,
With look bewildered and a vacant stare,
Close shaven above the ears, as monks are shorn,
By courtiers mocked, by pages laughed to scorn,
His only friend the ape, his only food
What others left,—he still was unsubdued.
And when the Angel met him on his way,
And half in earnest, half in jest, would say,
Sternly, though tenderly, that he might feel
The velvet scabbard held a sword of steel,
"Art thou the King?" the passion of his woe
Burst from him in resistless overflow,
And, lifting high his forehead, he would fling
The haughty answer back, "I am, I am the King!"

Almost three years were ended; when there came
Ambassadors of great repute and name
From Valmond, Emperor of Allemaine,
Unto King Robert, saying that Pope Urbane
By letter summoned them forthwith to come
On Holy Thursday to his city of Rome.
The Angel with great joy received his guests,
And gave them presents of embroidered vests,
And velvet mantles with rich ermine lined,
And rings and jewels of the rarest kind.
Then he departed with them o'er the sea
Into the lovely land of Italy,
Whose loveliness was more resplendent made
By the mere passing of that cavalcade,
With plumes, and cloaks, and housings, and the stir
Of jewelled bridle and of golden spur.

And lo! among the menials, in mock state,
Upon a piebald steed, with shambling gait,
His cloak of fox-tails flapping in the wind,
The solemn ape demurely perched behind,
King Robert rode, making huge merriment
In all the country towns through which they went.

The Pope received them with great pomp and blare
Of bannered trumpets, on Saint Peter's square,
Giving his benediction and embrace,
Fervent, and full of apostolic grace.
While with congratulations and with prayers
He entertained the Angel unawares,
Robert, the Jester, bursting through the crowd,
Into their presence rushed, and cried aloud,
"I am the King! Look, and behold in me
Robert, your brother, King of Sicily!
This man, who wears my semblance to your eyes,
Is an impostor in a king's disguise.
Do you not know me? does no voice within
Answer my cry, and say we are akin?"
The Pope in silence, but with troubled mien,
Gazed at the Angel's countenance serene;
The Emperor, laughing, said, "It is strange sport
To keep a madman for thy Fool at court!"
And the poor, baffled Jester in disgrace
Was hustled back among the populace.

In solemn state the Holy Week went by,
And Easter Sunday gleamed upon the sky;
The presence of the Angel, with its light,
Before the sun rose, made the city bright,
And with new fervor filled the hearts of men,
Who felt that Christ indeed had risen again.
Even the Jester, on his bed of straw,
With haggard eyes the unwonted splendor saw,
He felt within a power unfelt before,
And, kneeling humbly on his chamber floor,
He heard the rushing garments of the Lord
Sweep through the silent air, ascending heavenward.

And now the visit ending, and once more
Valmond returning to the Danube's shore,
Homeward the Angel journeyed, and again
The land was made resplendent with his train,
Flashing along the towns of Italy
Unto Salerno, and from thence by sea.
And when once more within Palermo's wall,
And, seated on the throne in his great hall,
He heard the Angelus from convent towers,
As if the better world conversed with ours,
He beckoned to King Robert to draw nigher,
And with a gesture bade the rest retire;
And when they were alone, the Angel said,
"Art thou the King?" Then, bowing down his head,
King Robert crossed both hands upon his breast,
And meekly answered him: "Thou knowest best!
My sins as scarlet are; let me go hence,
And in some cloister's school of penitence,
Across those stones, that pave the way to heaven,
Walk barefoot, till my guilty soul be shriven!"

The Angel smiled, and from his radiant face
A holy light illumined all the place,
And through the open window, loud and clear,
They heard the monks chant in the chapel near,
Above the stir and tumult of the street:
"He has put down the mighty from their seat,
And has exalted them of low degree!"
And through the chant a second melody
Rose like the throbbing of a single string:
"I am an Angel, and thou art the King!"

King Robert, who was standing near the throne,
Lifted his eyes, and lo! he was alone!
But all apparelled as in days of old,
With ermined mantle and with cloth of gold;
And when his courtiers came, they found him there
Kneeling upon the floor, absorbed in silent prayer.

Interlude

And then the blue-eyed Norseman told
A Saga of the days of old.
"There is," said he, "a wondrous book
Of Legends in the old Norse tongue,
Of the dead kings of Norroway,—
Legends that once were told or sung
In many a smoky fireside nook
Of Iceland, in the ancient day,
By wandering Saga-man or Scald;
'Heimskringla' is the volume called;
And he who looks may find therein
The story that I now begin."

And in each pause the story made
Upon his violin he played,
As an appropriate interlude,
Fragments of old Norwegian tunes
That bound in one the separate runes,
And held the mind in perfect mood,
Entwining and encircling all
The strange and antiquated rhymes
With melodies of olden times;
As over some half-ruined wall,
Disjointed and about to fall,
Fresh woodbines climb and interlace,
And keep the loosened stones in place.

The Musician's Tale

THE SAGA OF KING OLAF

I

The Challenge of Thor

I am the God Thor,
I am the War God,
I am the Thunderer!
Here in my Northland,
My fastness and fortress,
Reign I forever!

Here amid icebergs
Rule I the nations;
This is my hammer,
Miölner the mighty;
Giants and sorcerers
Cannot withstand it!

These are the gauntlets
Wherewith I wield it,
And hurl it afar off;
This is my girdle;
Whenever I brace it,
Strength is redoubled!

The light thou beholdest
Stream through the heavens,
In flashes of crimson,
Is but my red beard
Blown by the night-wind,
Affrighting the nations!

Jove is my brother;
Mine eyes are the lightning;
The wheels of my chariot
Roll in the thunder,
The blows of my hammer
Ring in the earthquake!

Force rules the world still,
Has ruled it, shall rule it;
Meekness is weakness,
Strength is triumphant,
Over the whole earth
Still is it Thor's-Day!

Thou art a God too,
O Galilean!
And thus single-handed
Unto the combat,
Gauntlet or Gospel,
Here I defy thee!

II

King Olaf's Return

And King Olaf heard the cry,
Saw the red light in the sky,
  Laid his hand upon his sword,
As he leaned upon the railing,
And his ships went sailing, sailing
  Northward into Drontheim fiord.

There he stood as one who dreamed;
And the red light glanced and gleamed
  On the armor that he wore;
And he shouted, as the rifted
Streamers o'er him shook and shifted,
  "I accept thy challenge, Thor!"

To avenge his father slain,
And reconquer realm and reign,
  Came the youthful Olaf home,
Through the midnight sailing, sailing,
Listening to the wild wind's wailing,
  And the dashing of the foam.

To his thoughts the sacred name
Of his mother Astrid came,

And the tale she oft had told
Of her flight by secret passes
Through the mountains and morasses,
To the home of Hakon old.

Then strange memories crowded back
Of Queen Gunhild's wrath and wrack,
And a hurried flight by sea;
Of grim Vikings, and the rapture
Of the sea-fight, and the capture,
And the life of slavery.

How a stranger watched his face
In the Esthonian market-place,
Scanned his features one by one,
Saying, "We should know each other;
I am Sigurd, Astrid's brother,
Thou art Olaf, Astrid's son!"

Then as Queen Allogia's page,
Old in honors, young in age,
Chief of all her men-at-arms;
Till vague whispers, and mysterious,
Reached King Valdemar, the imperious,
Filling him with strange alarms.

Then his cruisings o'er the seas,
Westward to the Hebrides
And to Scilly's rocky shore;
And the hermit's cavern dismal,
Christ's great name and rites baptismal
In the ocean's rush and roar.

All these thoughts of love and strife
Glimmered through his lurid life,
As the stars' intenser light
Through the red flames o'er him trailing,
As his ships went sailing, sailing
Northward in the summer night.

Trained for either camp or court,
Skilful in each manly sport,
   Young and beautiful and tall;
Art of warfare, craft of chases,
Swimming, skating, snow-shoe races,
   Excellent alike in all.

When at sea, with all his rowers,
He along the bending oars
   Outside of his ship could run.
He the Smalsor Horn ascended,
And his shining shield suspended
   On its summit, like a sun.

On the ship-rails he could stand,
Wield his sword with either hand,
   And at once two javelins throw;
At all feasts where ale was strongest
Sat the merry monarch longest,
   First to come and last to go.

Norway never yet had seen
One so beautiful of mien,
   One so royal in attire,
When in arms completely furnished,
Harness gold-inlaid and burnished,
   Mantle like a flame of fire.

Thus came Olaf to his own,
When upon the night-wind blown
   Passed that cry along the shore;
And he answered, while the rifted
Streamers o'er him shook and shifted,
   "I accept thy challenge, Thor!"

III

Thora of Rimol

"Thora of Rimol! hide me! hide me!
Danger and shame and death betide me!
For Olaf the King is hunting me down
Through field and forest, through thorp and town!"
    Thus cried Jarl Hakon
    To Thora, the fairest of women.

"Hakon Jarl! for the love I bear thee
Neither shall shame nor death come near thee!
But the hiding-place wherein thou must lie
Is the cave underneath the swine in the sty."
    Thus to Jarl Hakon
    Said Thora, the fairest of women.

So Hakon Jarl and his base thrall Karker
Crouched in the cave, than a dungeon darker,
As Olaf came riding, with men in mail,
Through the forest roads into Orkadale,
    Demanding Jarl Hakon
    Of Thora, the fairest of women.

"Rich and honored shall be whoever
The head of Hakon Jarl shall dissever!"
Hakon heard him, and Karker the slave,
Through the breathing-holes of the darksome cave.
    Alone in her chamber
    Wept Thora, the fairest of women.

Said Karker, the crafty, "I will not slay thee!
For all the king's gold I will never betray thee!"
"Then why dost thou turn so pale, O churl,
And then again black as the earth?" said the Earl.
    More pale and more faithful
    Was Thora, the fairest of women.

From a dream in the night the thrall started, saying,
"Round my neck a gold ring King Olaf was laying!"

And Hakon answered, "Beware of the king!
He will lay round thy neck a blood-red ring."
    At the ring on her finger
    Gazed Thora, the fairest of women.

At daybreak slept Hakon, with sorrows encumbered,
But screamed and drew up his feet as he slumbered;
The thrall in the darkness plunged with his knife,
And the Earl awakened no more in this life.
    But wakeful and weeping
    Sat Thora, the fairest of women.

At Nidarholm the priests are all singing,
Two ghastly heads on the gibbet are swinging;
One is Jarl Hakon's and one is his thrall's,
And the people are shouting from windows and walls;
    While alone in her chamber
    Swoons Thora, the fairest of women.

IV

Queen Sigrid the Haughty

Queen Sigrid the Haughty sat proud and aloft
In her chamber, that looked over meadow and croft.
    Heart's dearest,
    Why dost thou sorrow so?

The floor with tassels of fir was besprent,
Filling the room with their fragrant scent.

She heard the birds sing, she saw the sun shine,
The air of summer was sweeter than wine.

Like a sword without scabbard the bright river lay
Between her own kingdom and Norroway.

But Olaf the King had sued for her hand,
The sword would be sheathed, the river be spanned.

Her maidens were seated around her knee,
Working bright figures in tapestry.

And one was singing the ancient rune
Of Brynhilda's love and the wrath of Gudrun.

And through it, and round it, and over it all
Sounded incessant the waterfall.

The Queen in her hand held a ring of gold,
From the door of Ladé's Temple old.

King Olaf had sent her this wedding gift,
But her thoughts as arrows were keen and swift.

She had given the ring to her goldsmiths twain,
Who smiled, as they handed it back again.

And Sigrid the Queen, in her haughty way,
Said, "Why do you smile, my goldsmiths, say?"

And they answered: "O Queen! if the truth must be told,
The ring is of copper, and not of gold!"

The lightning flashed o'er her forehead and cheek,
She only murmured, she did not speak:

"If in his gifts he can faithless be,
There will be no gold in his love to me."

A footstep was heard on the outer stair,
And in strode King Olaf with royal air.

He kissed the Queen's hand, and he whispered of love,
And swore to be true as the stars are above.

But she smiled with contempt as she answered: "O King,
Will you swear it, as Odin once swore, on the ring?"

And the King: "Oh speak not of Odin to me,
The wife of King Olaf a Christian must be."

Looking straight at the King, with her level brows,
She said, "I keep true to my faith and my vows."

Then the face of King Olaf was darkened with gloom,
He rose in his anger and strode through the room.

"Why, then, should I care to have thee?" he said,—
"A faded old woman, a heathenish jade!"

His zeal was stronger than fear or love,
And he struck the Queen in the face with his glove.

Then forth from the chamber in anger he fled,
And the wooden stairway shook with his tread.

Queen Sigrid the Haughty said under her breath,
"This insult, King Olaf, shall be thy death!"
        Heart's dearest,
        Why dost thou sorrow so?

V

The Skerry of Shrieks

Now from all King Olaf's farms
        His men-at-arms
Gathered on the Eve of Easter;
To his house at Angvalds-ness
        Fast they press,
Drinking with the royal feaster.

Loudly through the wide-flung door
        Came the roar
Of the sea upon the Skerry;
And its thunder loud and near
        Reached the ear,
Mingling with their voices merry.

"Hark!" said Olaf to his Scald,
Halfred the Bald,
"Listen to that song, and learn it!
Half my kingdom would I give,
As I live,
If by such songs you would earn it!

"For of all the runes and rhymes
Of all times,
Best I like the ocean's dirges,
When the old harper heaves and rocks,
His hoary locks
Flowing and flashing in the surges!"

Halfred answered: "I am called
The Unappalled!
Nothing hinders me or daunts me.
Hearken to me, then, O King,
While I sing
The great Ocean Song that haunts me."

"I will hear your song sublime
Some other time,"
Says the drowsy monarch, yawning,
And retires; each laughing guest
Applauds the jest;
Then they sleep till day is dawning.

Pacing up and down the yard,
King Olaf's guard
Saw the sea-mist slowly creeping
O'er the sands, and up the hill,
Gathering still
Round the house where they were sleeping.

It was not the fog he saw,
Nor misty flaw,
That above the landscape brooded;
It was Eyvind Kallda's crew
Of warlocks blue
With their caps of darkness hooded!

Round and round the house they go,
  Weaving slow
Magic circles to encumber
And imprison in their ring
  Olaf the King,
As he helpless lies in slumber.

Then athwart the vapors dun
  The Easter sun
Streamed with one broad track of splendor!
In their real forms appeared
  The warlocks weird,
Awful as the Witch of Endor.

Blinded by the light that glared,
  They groped and stared,
Round about with steps unsteady;
From his window Olaf gazed,
  And, amazed,
"Who are these strange people?" said he.

"Eyvind Kallda and his men!"
  Answered then
From the yard a sturdy farmer;
While the men-at-arms apace
  Filled the place,
Busily buckling on their armor.

From the gates they sallied forth,
  South and north,
Scoured the island coast around them,
Seizing all the warlock band,
  Foot and hand
On the Skerry's rocks they bound them.

And at eve the king again
  Called his train,
And, with all the candles burning,
Silent sat and heard once more
  The sullen roar
Of the ocean tides returning.

Shrieks and cries of wild despair
    Filled the air,
Growing fainter as they listened;
Then the bursting surge alone
    Sounded on;—
Thus the sorcerers were christened!

"Sing, O Scald, your song sublime,
    Your ocean-rhyme,"
Cried King Olaf: "it will cheer me!"
Said the Scald, with pallid cheeks,
    "The Skerry of Shrieks
Sings too loud for you to hear me!"

VI

The Wraith of Odin

The guests were loud, the ale was strong,
King Olaf feasted late and long;
The hoary Scalds together sang;
O'erhead the smoky rafters rang.
    Dead rides Sir Morten of Fogelsang.

The door swung wide, with creak and din;
A blast of cold night-air came in,
And on the threshold shivering stood
A one-eyed guest, with cloak and hood.
    Dead rides Sir Morten of Fogelsang.

The King exclaimed, "O graybeard pale!
Come warm thee with this cup of ale."
The foaming draught the old man quaffed,
The noisy guests looked on and laughed.
    Dead rides Sir Morten of Fogelsang.

Then spake the King: "Be not afraid:
Sit here by me." The guest obeyed,
And, seated at the table, told
Tales of the sea, and Sagas old.
    Dead rides Sir Morten of Fogelsang.

And ever, when the tale was o'er,
The King demanded yet one more;
Till Sigurd the Bishop smiling said,
" 'T is late, O King, and time for bed."
Dead rides Sir Morten of Fogelsang.

The King retired; the stranger guest
Followed and entered with the rest;
The lights were out, the pages gone,
But still the garrulous guest spake on.
Dead rides Sir Morten of Fogelsang.

As one who from a volume reads,
He spake of heroes and their deeds,
Of lands and cities he had seen,
And stormy gulfs that tossed between.
Dead rides Sir Morten of Fogelsang.

Then from his lips in music rolled
The Havamal of Odin old,
With sounds mysterious as the roar
Of billows on a distant shore.
Dead rides Sir Morten of Fogelsang.

"Do we not learn from runes and rhymes
Made by the gods in elder times,
And do not still the great Scalds teach
That silence better is than speech?"
Dead rides Sir Morten of Fogelsang.

Smiling at this, the King replied,
"Thy lore is by thy tongue belied;
For never was I so enthralled
Either by Saga-man or Scald."
Dead rides Sir Morten of Fogelsang.

The Bishop said, "Late hours we keep!
Night wanes, O King! 't is time for sleep!"
Then slept the King, and when he woke
The guest was gone, the morning broke.
Dead rides Sir Morten of Fogelsang.

They found the doors securely barred,
They found the watch-dog in the yard,
There was no footprint in the grass,
And none had seen the stranger pass.
Dead rides Sir Morten of Fogelsang.

King Olaf crossed himself and said:
"I know that Odin the Great is dead;
Sure is the triumph of our Faith,
The one-eyed stranger was his wraith."
Dead rides Sir Morten of Fogelsang.

VII

Iron-Beard

Olaf the King, one summer morn,
Blew a blast on his bugle-horn,
Sending his signal through the land of Drontheim.

And to the Hus-Ting held at Mere
Gathered the farmers far and near,
With their war weapons ready to confront him.

Ploughing under the morning star,
Old Iron-Beard in Yriar
Heard the summons, chuckling with a low laugh.

He wiped the sweat-drops from his brow,
Unharnessed his horses from the plough,
And clattering came on horseback to King Olaf.

He was the churliest of the churls;
Little he cared for king or earls;
Bitter as home-brewed ale were his foaming passions.

Hodden-gray was the garb he wore,
And by the Hammer of Thor he swore;
He hated the narrow town, and all its fashions.

But he loved the freedom of his farm,
His ale at night, by the fireside warm,
Gudrun his daughter, with her flaxen tresses.

He loved his horses and his herds,
The smell of the earth, and the song of birds,
His well-filled barns, his brook with its watercresses.

Huge and cumbersome was his frame;
His beard, from which he took his name,
Frosty and fierce, like that of Hymer the Giant.

So at the Hus-Ting he appeared,
The farmer of Yriar, Iron-Beard,
On horseback, in an attitude defiant.

And to King Olaf he cried aloud,
Out of the middle of the crowd,
That tossed about him like a stormy ocean:

"Such sacrifices shalt thou bring
To Odin and to Thor, O King,
As other kings have done in their devotion!"

King Olaf answered: "I command
This land to be a Christian land;
Here is my Bishop who the folk baptizes!

"But if you ask me to restore
Your sacrifices, stained with gore,
Then will I offer human sacrifices!

"Not slaves and peasants shall they be,
But men of note and high degree,
Such men as Orm of Lyra and Kar of Gryting!"

Then to their Temple strode he in,
And loud behind him heard the din
Of his men-at-arms and the peasants fiercely fighting.

There in the Temple, carved in wood,
The image of great Odin stood,
And other gods, with Thor supreme among them.

King Olaf smote them with the blade
Of his huge war-axe, gold inlaid,
And downward shattered to the pavement flung them.

At the same moment rose without,
From the contending crowd, a shout,
A mingled sound of triumph and of wailing.

And there upon the trampled plain
The farmer Iron-Beard lay slain,
Midway between the assailed and the assailing.

King Olaf from the doorway spoke:
"Choose ye between two things, my folk,
To be baptized or given up to slaughter!"

And seeing their leader stark and dead,
The people with a murmur said,
"O King, baptize us with thy holy water."

So all the Drontheim land became
A Christian land in name and fame,
In the old gods no more believing and trusting.

And as a blood-atonement, soon
King Olaf wed the fair Gudrun;
And thus in peace ended the Drontheim Hus-Ting!

VIII

Gudrun

On King Olaf's bridal night
Shines the moon with tender light,
And across the chamber streams
Its tide of dreams.

At the fatal midnight hour,
When all evil things have power,
In the glimmer of the moon
Stands Gudrun.

Close against her heaving breast
Something in her hand is pressed;
Like an icicle, its sheen
Is cold and keen.

On the cairn are fixed her eyes
Where her murdered father lies,
And a voice remote and drear
She seems to hear.

What a bridal night is this!
Cold will be the dagger's kiss;
Laden with the chill of death
Is its breath.

Like the drifting snow she sweeps
To the couch where Olaf sleeps;
Suddenly he wakes and stirs,
His eyes meet hers.

"What is that," King Olaf said,
"Gleams so bright above my head?
Wherefore standest thou so white
In pale moonlight?"

" 'T is the bodkin that I wear
When at night I bind my hair;
It woke me falling on the floor;
'T is nothing more."

"Forests have ears, and fields have eyes;
Often treachery lurking lies
Underneath the fairest hair!
Gudrun beware!"

Ere the earliest peep of morn
Blew King Olaf's bugle-horn;
And forever sundered ride
   Bridegroom and bride!

IX

Thangbrand the Priest

Short of stature, large of limb,
   Burly face and russet beard,
All the women stared at him,
   When in Iceland he appeared.
      "Look!" they said,
      With nodding head,
"There goes Thangbrand, Olaf's Priest."

All the prayers he knew by rote,
   He could preach like Chrysostom,
From the Fathers he could quote,
   He had even been at Rome.
      A learned clerk,
      A man of mark,
Was this Thangbrand, Olaf's Priest.

He was quarrelsome and loud,
   And impatient of control,
Boisterous in the market crowd,
   Boisterous at the wassail-bowl,
      Everywhere
      Would drink and swear,
Swaggering Thangbrand, Olaf's Priest.

In his house this malcontent
   Could the King no longer bear,
So to Iceland he was sent
   To convert the heathen there,
      And away
      One summer day
Sailed this Thangbrand, Olaf's Priest.

There in Iceland, o'er their books
  Pored the people day and night,
But he did not like their looks,
  Nor the songs they used to write.
    "All this rhyme
    Is waste of time!"
Grumbled Thangbrand, Olaf's Priest.

To the alehouse, where he sat,
  Came the Scalds and Saga-men;
Is it to be wondered at
  That they quarrelled now and then,
    When o'er his beer
    Began to leer
Drunken Thangbrand, Olaf's Priest?

All the folk in Altafiord
  Boasted of their island grand;
Saying in a single word,
  "Iceland is the finest land
    That the sun
    Doth shine upon!"
Loud laughed Thangbrand, Olaf's Priest.

And he answered: "What 's the use
  Of this bragging up and down,
When three women and one goose
  Make a market in your town!"
    Every Scald
    Satires scrawled
On poor Thangbrand, Olaf's Priest.

Something worse they did than that;
  And what vexed him most of all
Was a figure in shovel hat,
  Drawn in charcoal on the wall;
    With words that go
    Sprawling below,
"This is Thangbrand, Olaf's Priest."

Hardly knowing what he did,
   Then he smote them might and main,
Thorvald Veile and Veterlid
   Lay there in the alehouse slain.
      "To-day we are gold,
      To-morrow mould!"
Muttered Thangbrand, Olaf's Priest.

Much in fear of axe and rope,
   Back to Norway sailed he then.
"O King Olaf! little hope
   Is there of these Iceland men!"
      Meekly said,
      With bending head,
Pious Thangbrand, Olaf's Priest.

X

Raud the Strong

"All the old gods are dead,
All the wild warlocks fled;
But the White Christ lives and reigns,
And throughout my wide domains
His Gospel shall be spread!"
   On the Evangelists
   Thus swore King Olaf.

But still in dreams of the night
Beheld he the crimson light,
And heard the voice that defied
Him who was crucified,
And challenged him to the fight.
   To Sigurd the Bishop
   King Olaf confessed it.

And Sigurd the Bishop said,
"The old gods are not dead,
For the great Thor still reigns,
And among the Jarls and Thanes

The old witchcraft still is spread."
    Thus to King Olaf
    Said Sigurd the Bishop.

"Far north in the Salten Fiord,
By rapine, fire, and sword,
Lives the Viking, Raud the Strong;
All the Godoe Isles belong
To him and his heathen horde."
    Thus went on speaking
    Sigurd the Bishop.

"A warlock, a wizard is he,
And lord of the wind and the sea;
And whichever way he sails,
He has ever favoring gales,
By his craft in sorcery."
    Here the sign of the cross
    Made devoutly King Olaf.

"With rites that we both abhor,
He worships Odin and Thor;
So it cannot yet be said,
That all the old gods are dead,
And the warlocks are no more,"
    Flushing with anger
    Said Sigurd the Bishop.

Then King Olaf cried aloud:
"I will talk with this mighty Raud,
And along the Salten Fiord
Preach the Gospel with my sword,
Or be brought back in my shroud!"
    So northward from Drontheim
    Sailed King Olaf!

XI

Bishop Sigurd of Salten Fiord

Loud the angry wind was wailing
As King Olaf's ships came sailing
Northward out of Drontheim haven
To the mouth of Salten Fiord.

Though the flying sea-spray drenches
Fore and aft the rowers' benches,
Not a single heart is craven
Of the champions there on board.

All without the Fiord was quiet,
But within it storm and riot,
Such as on his Viking cruises
Raud the Strong was wont to ride.

And the sea through all its tide-ways
Swept the reeling vessels sideways,
As the leaves are swept through sluices,
When the flood-gates open wide.

" 'T is the warlock! 't is the demon
Raud!" cried Sigurd to the seamen;
"But the Lord is not affrighted
By the witchcraft of his foes."

To the ship's bow he ascended,
By his choristers attended,
Round him were the tapers lighted,
And the sacred incense rose.

On the bow stood Bishop Sigurd,
In his robes, as one transfigured,
And the Crucifix he planted
High amid the rain and mist.

Then with holy water sprinkled
All the ship; the mass-bells tinkled:
Loud the monks around him chanted,
Loud he read the Evangelist.

As into the Fiord they darted,
On each side the water parted;
Down a path like silver molten
    Steadily rowed King Olaf's ships;

Steadily burned all night the tapers,
And the White Christ through the vapors
Gleamed across the Fiord of Salten,
    As through John's Apocalypse,—

Till at last they reached Raud's dwelling
On the little isle of Gelling;
Not a guard was at the doorway,
    Not a glimmer of light was seen.

But at anchor, carved and gilded,
Lay the dragon-ship he builded;
'T was the grandest ship in Norway,
    With its crest and scales of green.

Up the stairway, softly creeping,
To the loft where Raud was sleeping,
With their fists they burst asunder
    Bolt and bar that held the door.

Drunken with sleep and ale they found him,
Dragged him from his bed and bound him,
While he stared with stupid wonder
    At the look and garb they wore.

Then King Olaf said: "O Sea-King!
Little time have we for speaking,
Choose between the good and evil;
    Be baptized! or thou shalt die!"

But in scorn the heathen scoffer
Answered: "I disdain thine offer;
Neither fear I God nor Devil;
    Thee and thy Gospel I defy!"

Then between his jaws distended,
When his frantic struggles ended,
Through King Olaf's horn an adder,
Touched by fire, they forced to glide.

Sharp his tooth was as an arrow,
As he gnawed through bone and marrow;
But without a groan or shudder,
Raud the Strong blaspheming died.

Then baptized they all that region,
Swarthy Lap and fair Norwegian,
Far as swims the salmon, leaping,
Up the streams of Salten Fiord.

In their temples Thor and Odin
Lay in dust and ashes trodden,
As King Olaf, onward sweeping,
Preached the Gospel with his sword.

Then he took the carved and gilded
Dragon-ship that Raud had builded,
And the tiller single-handed
Grasping, steered into the main.

Southward sailed the sea-gulls o'er him,
Southward sailed the ship that bore him,
Till at Drontheim haven landed
Olaf and his crew again.

XII

King Olaf's Christmas

At Drontheim, Olaf the King
Heard the bells of Yule-tide ring,
As he sat in his banquet-hall,
Drinking the nut-brown ale,
With his bearded Berserks hale
And tall.

Three days his Yule-tide feasts
He held with Bishops and Priests,
 And his horn filled up to the brim;
But the ale was never too strong,
Nor the Saga-man's tale too long,
 For him.

O'er his drinking-horn, the sign
He made of the cross divine,
 As he drank, and muttered his prayers;
But the Berserks evermore
Made the sign of the Hammer of Thor
 Over theirs.

The gleams of the fire-light dance
Upon helmet and hauberk and lance,
 And laugh in the eyes of the King;
And he cries to Halfred the Scald,
Gray-bearded, wrinkled, and bald,
 "Sing!"

"Sing me a song divine,
With a sword in every line,
 And this shall be thy reward."
And he loosened the belt at his waist,
And in front of the singer placed
 His sword.

"Quern-biter of Hakon the Good,
Wherewith at a stroke he hewed
 The millstone through and through,
And Foot-breadth of Thoralf the Strong,
Were neither so broad nor so long,
 Nor so true."

Then the Scald took his harp and sang,
And loud through the music rang
 The sound of that shining word;
And the harp-strings a clangor made,
As if they were struck with the blade
 Of a sword.

And the Berserks round about
Broke forth into a shout
    That made the rafters ring:
They smote with their fists on the board,
And shouted, "Long live the Sword,
    And the King!"

But the King said, "O my son,
I miss the bright word in one
    Of thy measures and thy rhymes."
And Halfred the Scald replied,
"In another 't was multiplied
    Three times."

Then King Olaf raised the hilt
Of iron, cross-shaped and gilt,
    And said, "Do not refuse;
Count well the gain and the loss,
Thor's hammer or Christ's cross:
    Choose!"

And Halfred the Scald said, "This
In the name of the Lord I kiss,
    Who on it was crucified!"
And a shout went round the board,
"In the name of Christ the Lord,
    Who died!"

Then over the waste of snows
The noonday sun uprose,
    Through the driving mists revealed,
Like the lifting of the Host,
By incense-clouds almost
    Concealed.

On the shining wall a vast
And shadowy cross was cast
    From the hilt of the lifted sword,
And in foaming cups of ale
The Berserks drank "Was-hael!
    To the Lord!"

XIII

The Building of the Long Serpent

Thorberg Skafting, master-builder,
In his ship-yard by the sea,
Whistling, said, "It would bewilder
Any man but Thorberg Skafting,
Any man but me!"

Near him lay the Dragon stranded,
Built of old by Raud the Strong,
And King Olaf had commanded
He should build another Dragon,
Twice as large and long.

Therefore whistled Thorberg Skafting,
As he sat with half-closed eyes,
And his head turned sideways, drafting
That new vessel for King Olaf
Twice the Dragon's size.

Round him busily hewed and hammered
Mallet huge and heavy axe;
Workmen laughed and sang and clamored;
Whirred the wheels, that into rigging
Spun the shining flax!

All this tumult heard the master,—
It was music to his ear;
Fancy whispered all the faster,
"Men shall hear of Thorberg Skafting
For a hundred year!"

Workmen sweating at the forges
Fashioned iron bolt and bar,
Like a warlock's midnight orgies
Smoked and bubbled the black caldron
With the boiling tar.

Did the warlocks mingle in it,
 Thorberg Skafting, any curse?
Could you not be gone a minute
But some mischief must be doing,
 Turning bad to worse?

'T was an ill wind that came wafting
 From his homestead words of woe;
To his farm went Thorberg Skafting,
Oft repeating to his workmen,
 Build ye thus and so.

After long delays returning
 Came the master back by night;
To his ship-yard longing, yearning,
Hurried he, and did not leave it
 Till the morning's light.

"Come and see my ship, my darling!"
 On the morrow said the King;
"Finished now from keel to carling;
Never yet was seen in Norway
 Such a wondrous thing!"

In the ship-yard, idly talking,
 At the ship the workmen stared:
Some one, all their labor balking,
Down her sides had cut deep gashes,
 Not a plank was spared!

"Death be to the evil-doer!"
 With an oath King Olaf spoke;
"But rewards to his pursuer!"
And with wrath his face grew redder
 Than his scarlet cloak.

Straight the master-builder, smiling,
 Answered thus the angry King:
"Cease blaspheming and reviling,
Olaf, it was Thorberg Skafting
 Who has done this thing!"

Then he chipped and smoothed the planking,
Till the King, delighted, swore,
With much lauding and much thanking,
"Handsomer is now my Dragon
Than she was before!"

Seventy ells and four extended
On the grass the vessel's keel;
High above it, gilt and splendid,
Rose the figure-head ferocious
With its crest of steel.

Then they launched her from the tressels,
In the ship-yard by the sea;
She was the grandest of all vessels,
Never ship was built in Norway
Half so fine as she!

The Long Serpent was she christened,
'Mid the roar of cheer on cheer!
They who to the Saga listened
Heard the name of Thorberg Skafting
For a hundred year!

XIV

The Crew of the Long Serpent

Safe at anchor in Drontheim bay
King Olaf's fleet assembled lay,
And, striped with white and blue,
Downward fluttered sail and banner,
As alights the screaming lanner;
Lustily cheered, in their wild manner,
The Long Serpent's crew.

Her forecastle man was Ulf the Red;
Like a wolf's was his shaggy head,
His teeth as large and white;
His beard, of gray and russet blended,

Round as a swallow's nest descended;
As standard-bearer he defended
  Olaf's flag in the fight.

Near him Kolbiorn had his place,
Like the King in garb and face,
  So gallant and so hale;
Every cabin-boy and varlet
Wondered at his cloak of scarlet;
Like a river, frozen and star-lit,
  Gleamed his coat of mail.

By the bulkhead, tall and dark,
Stood Thrand Rame of Thelemark,
  A figure gaunt and grand;
On his hairy arm imprinted
Was an anchor, azure-tinted;
Like Thor's hammer, huge and dinted
  Was his brawny hand.

Einar Tamberskelver, bare
To the winds his golden hair,
  By the mainmast stood;
Graceful was his form, and slender,
And his eyes were deep and tender
As a woman's, in the splendor
  Of her maidenhood.

In the fore-hold Biorn and Bork
Watched the sailors at their work:
  Heavens! how they swore!
Thirty men they each commanded,
Iron-sinewed, horny-handed,
Shoulders broad, and chests expanded,
  Tugging at the oar.

These, and many more like these,
With King Olaf sailed the seas,
  Till the waters vast
Filled them with a vague devotion,

With the freedom and the motion,
With the roll and roar of ocean
  And the sounding blast.

When they landed from the fleet,
How they roared through Drontheim's street,
  Boisterous as the gale!
How they laughed and stamped and pounded,
Till the tavern roof resounded,
And the host looked on astounded
  As they drank the ale!

Never saw the wild North Sea
Such a gallant company
  Sail its billows blue!
Never, while they cruised and quarrelled,
Old King Gorm, or Blue-Tooth Harald,
Owned a ship so well apparelled,
  Boasted such a crew!

XV

A Little Bird in the Air

A little bird in the air
Is singing of Thyri the fair,
  The sister of Svend the Dane;
And the song of the garrulous bird
In the streets of the town is heard,
  And repeated again and again.
    Hoist up your sails of silk,
    And flee away from each other.

To King Burislaf, it is said,
Was the beautiful Thyri wed,
  And a sorrowful bride went she;
And after a week and a day
She has fled away and away
  From his town by the stormy sea.
    Hoist up your sails of silk,
    And flee away from each other.

They say, that through heat and through cold,
Through weald, they say, and through wold,
  By day and by night, they say,
She has fled; and the gossips report
She has come to King Olaf's court,
  And the town is all in dismay.
    Hoist up your sails of silk,
    And flee away from each other.

It is whispered King Olaf has seen,
Has talked with the beautiful Queen;
  And they wonder how it will end;
For surely, if here she remain,
It is war with King Svend the Dane,
  And King Burislaf the Vend!
    Hoist up your sails of silk,
    And flee away from each other.

Oh, greatest wonder of all!
It is published in hamlet and hall,
  It roars like a flame that is fanned!
The King—yes, Olaf the King—
Has wedded her with his ring,
  And Thyri is Queen in the land!
    Hoist up your sails of silk,
    And flee away from each other.

XVI

Queen Thyri and the Angelica Stalks

Northward over Drontheim,
Flew the clamorous sea-gulls,
Sang the lark and linnet
  From the meadows green;

Weeping in her chamber,
Lonely and unhappy,
Sat the Drottning Thyri,
  Sat King Olaf's Queen.

In at all the windows
Streamed the pleasant sunshine,
On the roof above her
  Softly cooed the dove;

But the sound she heard not,
Nor the sunshine heeded,
For the thoughts of Thyri
  Were not thoughts of love.

Then King Olaf entered,
Beautiful as morning,
Like the sun at Easter
  Shone his happy face;

In his hand he carried
Angelicas uprooted,
With delicious fragrance
  Filling all the place.

Like a rainy midnight
Sat the Drottning Thyri,
Even the smile of Olaf
  Could not cheer her gloom;

Nor the stalks he gave her
With a gracious gesture,
And with words as pleasant
  As their own perfume.

In her hands he placed them,
And her jewelled fingers
Through the green leaves glistened
  Like the dews of morn;

But she cast them from her,
Haughty and indignant,
On the floor she threw them
  With a look of scorn.

"Richer presents," said she,
"Gave King Harald Gormson
To the Queen, my mother,
Than such worthless weeds;

"When he ravaged Norway,
Laying waste the kingdom,
Seizing scatt and treasure
For her royal needs.

"But thou darest not venture
Through the Sound to Vendland,
My domains to rescue
From King Burislaf;

"Lest King Svend of Denmark,
Forked Beard, my brother,
Scatter all thy vessels
As the wind the chaff."

Then up sprang King Olaf,
Like a reindeer bounding,
With an oath he answered
Thus the luckless Queen:

"Never yet did Olaf
Fear King Svend of Denmark;
This right hand shall hale him
By his forked chin!"

Then he left the chamber,
Thundering through the doorway,
Loud his steps resounded
Down the outer stair.

Smarting with the insult,
Through the streets of Drontheim
Strode he red and wrathful,
With his stately air.

All his ships he gathered,
Summoned all his forces,
Making his war levy
In the region round.

Down the coast of Norway,
Like a flock of sea-gulls,
Sailed the fleet of Olaf
Through the Danish Sound.

With his own hand fearless
Steered he the Long Serpent,
Strained the creaking cordage,
Bent each boom and gaff;

Till in Vendland landing,
The domains of Thyri
He redeemed and rescued
From King Burislaf.

Then said Olaf, laughing,
"Not ten yoke of oxen
Have the power to draw us
Like a woman's hair!

"Now will I confess it,
Better things are jewels
Than angelica stalks are
For a queen to wear."

XVII

King Svend of the Forked Beard

Loudly the sailors cheered
Svend of the Forked Beard,
As with his fleet he steered
Southward to Vendland;
Where with their courses hauled
All were together called,
Under the Isle of Svald
Near to the mainland.

After Queen Gunhild's death,
So the old Saga saith,
Plighted King Svend his faith
  To Sigrid the Haughty;
And to avenge his bride,
Soothing her wounded pride,
Over the waters wide
  King Olaf sought he.

Still on her scornful face,
Blushing with deep disgrace,
Bore she the crimson trace
  Of Olaf's gauntlet;
Like a malignant star,
Blazing in heaven afar,
Red shone the angry scar
  Under her frontlet.

Oft to King Svend she spake,
"For thine own honor's sake
Shalt thou swift vengeance take
  On the vile coward!"
Until the King at last,
Gusty and overcast,
Like a tempestuous blast
  Threatened and lowered.

Soon as the Spring appeared,
Svend of the Forked Beard
High his red standard reared,
  Eager for battle;
While every warlike Dane,
Seizing his arms again,
Left all unsown the grain,
  Unhoused the cattle.

Likewise the Swedish King
Summoned in haste a Thing,
Weapons and men to bring
  In aid of Denmark;

Eric the Norseman, too,
As the war-tidings flew,
Sailed with a chosen crew
   From Lapland and Finmark.

So upon Easter day
Sailed the three kings away,
Out of the sheltered bay,
   In the bright season;
With them Earl Sigvald came,
Eager for spoil and fame;
Pity that such a name
   Stooped to such treason!

Safe under Svald at last,
Now were their anchors cast,
Safe from the sea and blast,
   Plotted the three kings;
While, with a base intent,
Southward Earl Sigvald went,
On a foul errand bent,
   Unto the Sea-kings.

Thence to hold on his course
Unto King Olaf's force,
Lying within the hoarse
   Mouths of Stet-haven;
Him to ensnare and bring
Unto the Danish king,
Who his dead corse would fling
   Forth to the raven!

XVIII

King Olaf and Earl Sigvald

On the gray sea-sands
King Olaf stands,
Northward and seaward
He points with his hands.

With eddy and whirl
The sea-tides curl,
Washing the sandals
Of Sigvald the Earl.

The mariners shout,
The ships swing about,
The yards are all hoisted,
The sails flutter out.

The war-horns are played,
The anchors are weighed,
Like moths in the distance
The sails flit and fade.

The sea is like lead,
The harbor lies dead,
As a corse on the sea-shore,
Whose spirit has fled!

On that fatal day,
The histories say,
Seventy vessels
Sailed out of the bay.

But soon scattered wide
O'er the billows they ride,
While Sigvald and Olaf
Sail side by side.

Cried the Earl: "Follow me!
I your pilot will be,
For I know all the channels
Where flows the deep sea!"

So into the strait
Where his foes lie in wait,
Gallant King Olaf
Sails to his fate!

Then the sea-fog veils
The ships and their sails;
Queen Sigrid the Haughty,
Thy vengeance prevails!

XIX

King Olaf's War-Horns

"Strike the sails!" King Olaf said;
"Never shall men of mine take flight;
Never away from battle I fled,
Never away from my foes!
    Let God dispose
Of my life in the fight!"

"Sound the horns!" said Olaf the King;
And suddenly through the drifting brume
The blare of the horns began to ring,
Like the terrible trumpet shock
    Of Regnarock,
On the Day of Doom!

Louder and louder the war-horns sang
Over the level floor of the flood;
All the sails came down with a clang,
And there in the midst overhead
    The sun hung red
As a drop of blood.

Drifting down on the Danish fleet
Three together the ships were lashed,
So that neither should turn and retreat;
In the midst, but in front of the rest,
    The burnished crest
Of the Serpent flashed.

King Olaf stood on the quarter-deck,
With bow of ash and arrows of oak,
His gilded shield was without a fleck,

His helmet inlaid with gold,
And in many a fold
Hung his crimson cloak.

On the forecastle Ulf the Red
Watched the lashing of the ships;
"If the Serpent lie so far ahead,
We shall have hard work of it here,"
Said he with a sneer
On his bearded lips.

King Olaf laid an arrow on string,
"Have I a coward on board?" said he.
"Shoot it another way, O King!"
Sullenly answered Ulf,
The old sea-wolf;
"You have need of me!"

In front came Svend, the King of the Danes,
Sweeping down with his fifty rowers;
To the right, the Swedish king with his thanes;
And on board of the Iron Beard
Earl Eric steered
To the left with his oars.

"These soft Danes and Swedes," said the King,
"At home with their wives had better stay,
Than come within reach of my Serpent's sting:
But where Eric the Norseman leads
Heroic deeds
Will be done to-day!"

Then as together the vessels crashed,
Eric severed the cables of hide,
With which King Olaf's ships were lashed,
And left them to drive and drift
With the currents swift
Of the outward tide.

Louder the war-horns growl and snarl,
Sharper the dragons bite and sting!

Eric the son of Hakon Jarl
A death-drink salt as the sea
   Pledges to thee,
Olaf the King!

XX

Einar Tamberskelver

It was Einar Tamberskelver
   Stood beside the mast;
From his yew-bow, tipped with silver,
   Flew the arrows fast;
Aimed at Eric unavailing,
   As he sat concealed,
Half behind the quarter-railing,
   Half behind his shield.

First an arrow struck the tiller,
   Just above his head;
"Sing, O Eyvind Skaldaspiller,"
   Then Earl Eric said.
"Sing the song of Hakon dying,
   Sing his funeral wail!"
And another arrow flying
   Grazed his coat of mail.

Turning to a Lapland yeoman,
   As the arrow passed,
Said Earl Eric, "Shoot that bowman
   Standing by the mast."
Sooner than the word was spoken
   Flew the yeoman's shaft;
Einar's bow in twain was broken,
   Einar only laughed.

"What was that?" said Olaf, standing
   On the quarter-deck.
"Something heard I like the stranding
   Of a shattered wreck."
Einar then, the arrow taking

From the loosened string,
Answered, "That was Norway breaking
From thy hand, O King!"

"Thou art but a poor diviner,"
Straightway Olaf said;
"Take my bow, and swifter, Einar,
Let thy shafts be sped."
Of his bows the fairest choosing,
Reached he from above;
Einar saw the blood-drops oozing
Through his iron glove.

But the bow was thin and narrow;
At the first assay,
O'er its head he drew the arrow,
Flung the bow away;
Said, with hot and angry temper
Flushing in his cheek,
"Olaf! for so great a Kämper
Are thy bows too weak!"

Then, with smile of joy defiant
On his beardless lip,
Scaled he, light and self-reliant,
Eric's dragon-ship.
Loose his golden locks were flowing,
Bright his armor gleamed;
Like Saint Michael overthrowing
Lucifer he seemed.

XXI

King Olaf's Death-Drink

All day has the battle raged,
All day have the ships engaged,
But not yet is assuaged
The vengeance of Eric the Earl.

The decks with blood are red,
The arrows of death are sped,
The ships are filled with the dead,
   And the spears the champions hurl.

They drift as wrecks on the tide,
The grappling-irons are plied,
The boarders climb up the side,
   The shouts are feeble and few.

Ah! never shall Norway again
See her sailors come back o'er the main;
They all lie wounded or slain,
   Or asleep in the billows blue!

On the deck stands Olaf the King,
Around him whistle and sing
The spears that the foemen fling,
   And the stones they hurl with their hands.

In the midst of the stones and the spears,
Kolbiorn, the marshal, appears,
His shield in the air he uprears,
   By the side of King Olaf he stands.

Over the slippery wreck
Of the Long Serpent's deck
Sweeps Eric with hardly a check,
   His lips with anger are pale;

He hews with his axe at the mast,
Till it falls, with the sails overcast,
Like a snow-covered pine in the vast
   Dim forests of Orkadale.

Seeking King Olaf then,
He rushes aft with his men,
As a hunter into the den
   Of the bear, when he stands at bay.

"Remember Jarl Hakon!" he cries;
When lo! on his wondering eyes,
Two kingly figures arise,
   Two Olafs in warlike array!

Then Kolbiorn speaks in the ear
Of King Olaf a word of cheer,
In a whisper that none may hear,
   With a smile on his tremulous lip;

Two shields raised high in the air,
Two flashes of golden hair,
Two scarlet meteors' glare,
   And both have leaped from the ship.

Earl Eric's men in the boats
Seize Kolbiorn's shield as it floats,
And cry, from their hairy throats,
   "See! it is Olaf the King!"

While far on the opposite side
Floats another shield on the tide,
Like a jewel set in the wide
   Sea-current's eddying ring.

There is told a wonderful tale,
How the King stripped off his mail,
Like leaves of the brown sea-kale,
   As he swam beneath the main;

But the young grew old and gray,
And never, by night or by day,
In his kingdom of Norroway
   Was King Olaf seen again!

XXII

The Nun of Nidaros

In the convent of Drontheim,
Alone in her chamber
Knelt Astrid the Abbess,
At midnight, adoring,
Beseeching, entreating
The Virgin and Mother.

She heard in the silence
The voice of one speaking,
Without in the darkness,
In gusts of the night-wind,
Now louder, now nearer,
Now lost in the distance.

The voice of a stranger
It seemed as she listened,
Of some one who answered
Beseeching, imploring,
A cry from afar off
She could not distinguish.

The voice of Saint John,
The beloved disciple,
Who wandered and waited
The Master's appearance,
Alone in the darkness,
Unsheltered and friendless.

"It is accepted,
The angry defiance,
The challenge of battle!
It is accepted,
But not with the weapons
Of war that thou wieldest!

"Cross against corselet,
Love against hatred,

Peace-cry for war-cry!
Patience is powerful;
He that o'ercometh
Hath power o'er the nations!

"As torrents in summer,
Half dried in their channels,
Suddenly rise, though the
Sky is still cloudless,
For rain has been falling
Far off at their fountains;

"So hearts that are fainting
Grow full to o'erflowing,
And they that behold it
Marvel, and know not
That God at their fountains
Far off has been raining!

"Stronger than steel
Is the sword of the Spirit;
Swifter than arrows
The light of the truth is,
Greater than anger
Is love, and subdueth!

"Thou art a phantom,
A shape of the sea-mist,
A shape of the brumal
Rain, and the darkness
Fearful and formless;
Day dawns and thou art not!

"The dawn is not distant,
Nor is the night starless;
Love is eternal!
God is still God, and
His faith shall not fail us;
Christ is eternal!"

Interlude

A strain of music closed the tale,
A low, monotonous, funeral wail,
That with its cadence, wild and sweet,
Made the long Saga more complete.

"Thank God," the Theologian said,
"The reign of violence is dead,
Or dying surely from the world;
While Love triumphant reigns instead,
And in a brighter sky o'erhead
His blessed banners are unfurled.
And most of all thank God for this:
The war and waste of clashing creeds
Now end in words, and not in deeds,
And no one suffers loss, or bleeds,
For thoughts that men call heresies.

"I stand without here in the porch,
I hear the bell's melodious din,
I hear the organ peal within,
I hear the prayer, with words that scorch
Like sparks from an inverted torch,
I hear the sermon upon sin,
With threatenings of the last account.
And all, translated in the air,
Reach me but as our dear Lord's Prayer,
And as the Sermon on the Mount.

"Must it be Calvin, and not Christ?
Must it be Athanasian creeds,
Or holy water, books, and beads?
Must struggling souls remain content
With councils and decrees of Trent?
And can it be enough for these
The Christian Church the year embalms
With evergreens and boughs of palms,
And fills the air with litanies?

"I know that yonder Pharisee
Thanks God that he is not like me;
In my humiliation dressed,
I only stand and beat my breast,
And pray for human charity.

"Not to one church alone, but seven,
The voice prophetic spake from heaven;
And unto each the promise came,
Diversified, but still the same;
For him that overcometh are
The new name written on the stone,
The raiment white, the crown, the throne,
And I will give him the Morning Star!

"Ah! to how many Faith has been
No evidence of things unseen,
But a dim shadow, that recasts
The creed of the Phantasiasts,
For whom no Man of Sorrows died,
For whom the Tragedy Divine
Was but a symbol and a sign,
And Christ a phantom crucified!

"For others a diviner creed
Is living in the life they lead.
The passing of their beautiful feet
Blesses the pavement of the street,
And all their looks and words repeat
Old Fuller's saying, wise and sweet,
Not as a vulture, but a dove,
The Holy Ghost came from above.

"And this brings back to me a tale
So sad the hearer well may quail,
And question if such things can be;
Yet in the chronicles of Spain
Down the dark pages runs this stain,
And naught can wash them white again,
So fearful is the tragedy."

The Theologian's Tale

TORQUEMADA

In the heroic days when Ferdinand
And Isabella ruled the Spanish land,
And Torquemada, with his subtle brain,
Ruled them, as Grand Inquisitor of Spain,
In a great castle near Valladolid,
Moated and high and by fair woodlands hid,
There dwelt, as from the chronicles we learn,
An old Hidalgo proud and taciturn,
Whose name has perished, with his towers of stone,
And all his actions save this one alone;
This one, so terrible, perhaps 't were best
If it, too, were forgotten with the rest;
Unless, perchance, our eyes can see therein
The martyrdom triumphant o'er the sin;
A double picture, with its gloom and glow,
The splendor overhead, the death below.

This sombre man counted each day as lost
On which his feet no sacred threshold crossed;
And when he chanced the passing Host to meet,
He knelt and prayed devoutly in the street;
Oft he confessed; and with each mutinous thought,
As with wild beasts at Ephesus, he fought.
In deep contrition scourged himself in Lent,
Walked in processions, with his head down bent,
At plays of Corpus Christi oft was seen,
And on Palm Sunday bore his bough of green.
His sole diversion was to hunt the boar
Through tangled thickets of the forest hoar,
Or with his jingling mules to hurry down
To some grand bull-fight in the neighboring town,
Or in the crowd with lighted taper stand,
When Jews were burned, or banished from the land.
Then stirred within him a tumultuous joy;
The demon whose delight is to destroy
Shook him, and shouted with a trumpet tone,
"Kill! kill! and let the Lord find out his own!"

And now, in that old castle in the wood,
His daughters, in the dawn of womanhood,
Returning from their convent school, had made
Resplendent with their bloom the forest shade,
Reminding him of their dead mother's face,
When first she came into that gloomy place,—
A memory in his heart as dim and sweet
As moonlight in a solitary street,
Where the same rays, that lift the sea, are thrown
Lovely but powerless upon walls of stone.
These two fair daughters of a mother dead
Were all the dream had left him as it fled.
A joy at first, and then a growing care,
As if a voice within him cried, "Beware!"
A vague presentiment of impending doom,
Like ghostly footsteps in a vacant room,
Haunted him day and night; a formless fear
That death to some one of his house was near,
With dark surmises of a hidden crime,
Made life itself a death before its time.
Jealous, suspicious, with no sense of shame,
A spy upon his daughters he became;
With velvet slippers, noiseless on the floors,
He glided softly through half-open doors;
Now in the room, and now upon the stair,
He stood beside them ere they were aware;
He listened in the passage when they talked,
He watched them from the casement when they walked,
He saw the gypsy haunt the river's side,
He saw the monk among the cork-trees glide;
And, tortured by the mystery and the doubt
Of some dark secret, past his finding out,
Baffled he paused; then reassured again
Pursued the flying phantom of his brain.
He watched them even when they knelt in church;
And then, descending lower in his search,
Questioned the servants, and with eager eyes
Listened incredulous to their replies;
The gypsy? none had seen her in the wood!
The monk? a mendicant in search of food!

At length the awful revelation came,
Crushing at once his pride of birth and name;
The hopes his yearning bosom forward cast
And the ancestral glories of the past,
All fell together, crumbling in disgrace,
A turret rent from battlement to base.
His daughters talking in the dead of night
In their own chamber, and without a light,
Listening, as he was wont, he overheard,
And learned the dreadful secret, word by word;
And hurrying from his castle, with a cry
He raised his hands to the unpitying sky,
Repeating one dread word, till bush and tree
Caught it, and shuddering answered, "Heresy!"

Wrapped in his cloak, his hat drawn o'er his face,
Now hurrying forward, now with lingering pace,
He walked all night the alleys of his park,
With one unseen companion in the dark,
The Demon who within him lay in wait
And by his presence turned his love to hate,
Forever muttering in an undertone,
"Kill! kill! and let the Lord find out his own!"

Upon the morrow, after early Mass,
While yet the dew was glistening on the grass,
And all the woods were musical with birds,
The old Hidalgo, uttering fearful words,
Walked homeward with the Priest, and in his room
Summoned his trembling daughters to their doom.
When questioned, with brief answers they replied,
Nor when accused evaded or denied;
Expostulations, passionate appeals,
All that the human heart most fears or feels,
In vain the Priest with earnest voice essayed;
In vain the father threatened, wept, and prayed;
Until at last he said, with haughty mien,
"The Holy Office, then, must intervene!"

And now the Grand Inquisitor of Spain,
With all the fifty horsemen of his train,
His awful name resounding, like the blast
Of funeral trumpets, as he onward passed,
Came to Valladolid, and there began
To harry the rich Jews with fire and ban.
To him the Hidalgo went, and at the gate
Demanded audience on affairs of state,
And in a secret chamber stood before
A venerable graybeard of fourscore,
Dressed in the hood and habit of a friar;
Out of his eyes flashed a consuming fire,
And in his hand the mystic horn he held,
Which poison and all noxious charms dispelled.
He heard in silence the Hidalgo's tale,
Then answered in a voice that made him quail:
"Son of the Church! when Abraham of old
To sacrifice his only son was told,
He did not pause to parley nor protest,
But hastened to obey the Lord's behest.
In him it was accounted righteousness;
The Holy Church expects of thee no less!"

A sacred frenzy seized the father's brain,
And Mercy from that hour implored in vain.
Ah! who will e'er believe the words I say?
His daughters he accused, and the same day
They both were cast into the dungeon's gloom,
That dismal antechamber of the tomb,
Arraigned, condemned, and sentenced to the flame,
The secret torture and the public shame.

Then to the Grand Inquisitor once more
The Hidalgo went more eager than before,
And said: "When Abraham offered up his son,
He clave the wood wherewith it might be done.
By his example taught, let me too bring
Wood from the forest for my offering!"
And the deep voice, without a pause, replied:
"Son of the Church! by faith now justified,

Complete thy sacrifice, even as thou wilt;
The Church absolves thy conscience from all guilt!"

Then this most wretched father went his way
Into the woods, that round his castle lay,
Where once his daughters in their childhood played
With their young mother in the sun and shade.
Now all the leaves had fallen; the branches bare
Made a perpetual moaning in the air,
And screaming from their eyries overhead
The ravens sailed athwart the sky of lead.
With his own hands he lopped the boughs and bound
Fagots, that crackled with foreboding sound,
And on his mules, caparisoned and gay
With bells and tassels, sent them on their way.

Then with his mind on one dark purpose bent,
Again to the Inquisitor he went,
And said: "Behold, the fagots I have brought,
And now, lest my atonement be as naught,
Grant me one more request, one last desire,—
With my own hand to light the funeral fire!"
And Torquemada answered from his seat,
"Son of the Church! Thine offering is complete;
Her servants through all ages shall not cease
To magnify thy deed. Depart in peace!"

Upon the market-place, builded of stone
The scaffold rose, whereon Death claimed his own.
At the four corners, in stern attitude,
Four statues of the Hebrew Prophets stood,
Gazing with calm indifference in their eyes
Upon this place of human sacrifice,
Round which was gathering fast the eager crowd,
With clamor of voices dissonant and loud,
And every roof and window was alive
With restless gazers, swarming like a hive.

The church-bells tolled, the chant of monks drew near,
Loud trumpets stammered forth their notes of fear,

A line of torches smoked along the street,
There was a stir, a rush, a tramp of feet,
And, with its banners floating in the air,
Slowly the long procession crossed the square,
And, to the statues of the Prophets bound,
The victims stood, with fagots piled around.
Then all the air a blast of trumpets shook,
And louder sang the monks with bell and book,
And the Hidalgo, lofty, stern, and proud,
Lifted his torch, and, bursting through the crowd,
Lighted in haste the fagots, and then fled,
Lest those imploring eyes should strike him dead!

O pitiless skies! why did your clouds retain
For peasants' fields their floods of hoarded rain?
O pitiless earth! why open no abyss
To bury in its chasm a crime like this?

That night, a mingled column of fire and smoke
From the dark thickets of the forest broke,
And, glaring o'er the landscape leagues away,
Made all the fields and hamlets bright as day.
Wrapped in a sheet of flame the castle blazed,
And as the villagers in terror gazed,
They saw the figure of that cruel knight
Lean from a window in the turret's height,
His ghastly face illumined with the glare,
His hands upraised above his head in prayer,
Till the floor sank beneath him, and he fell
Down the black hollow of that burning well.

Three centuries and more above his bones
Have piled the oblivious years like funeral stones;
His name has perished with him, and no trace
Remains on earth of his afflicted race;
But Torquemada's name, with clouds o'ercast,
Looms in the distant landscape of the Past,
Like a burnt tower upon a blackened heath,
Lit by the fires of burning woods beneath!

Interlude

Thus closed the tale of guilt and gloom,
That cast upon each listener's face
Its shadow, and for some brief space
Unbroken silence filled the room.
The Jew was thoughtful and distressed;
Upon his memory thronged and pressed
The persecution of his race,
Their wrongs and sufferings and disgrace;
His head was sunk upon his breast,
And from his eyes alternate came
Flashes of wrath and tears of shame.

The Student first the silence broke,
As one who long has lain in wait,
With purpose to retaliate,
And thus he dealt the avenging stroke.
"In such a company as this,
A tale so tragic seems amiss,
That by its terrible control
O'ermasters and drags down the soul
Into a fathomless abyss.
The Italian Tales that you disdain,
Some merry Night of Straparole,
Or Machiavelli's Belphagor,
Would cheer us and delight us more,
Give greater pleasure and less pain
Than your grim tragedies of Spain!"

And here the Poet raised his hand,
With such entreaty and command,
It stopped discussion at its birth,
And said: "The story I shall tell
Has meaning in it, if not mirth;
Listen, and hear what once befell
The merry birds of Killingworth!"

The Poet's Tale

THE BIRDS OF KILLINGWORTH

It was the season, when through all the land
  The merle and mavis build, and building sing
Those lovely lyrics, written by His hand,
  Whom Saxon Cædmon calls the Blithe-heart King;
When on the boughs the purple buds expand,
  The banners of the vanguard of the Spring,
And rivulets, rejoicing, rush and leap,
And wave their fluttering signals from the steep.

The robin and the bluebird, piping loud,
  Filled all the blossoming orchards with their glee;
The sparrows chirped as if they still were proud
  Their race in Holy Writ should mentioned be;
And hungry crows, assembled in a crowd,
  Clamored their piteous prayer incessantly,
Knowing who hears the ravens cry, and said:
"Give us, O Lord, this day, our daily bread!"

Across the Sound the birds of passage sailed,
  Speaking some unknown language strange and sweet
Of tropic isle remote, and passing hailed
  The village with the cheers of all their fleet;
Or quarrelling together, laughed and railed
  Like foreign sailors, landed in the street
Of seaport town, and with outlandish noise
Of oaths and gibberish frightening girls and boys.

Thus came the jocund Spring in Killingworth,
  In fabulous days, some hundred years ago;
And thrifty farmers, as they tilled the earth,
  Heard with alarm the cawing of the crow,
That mingled with the universal mirth,
  Cassandra-like, prognosticating woe;
They shook their heads, and doomed with dreadful words
To swift destruction the whole race of birds.

And a town-meeting was convened straightway
   To set a price upon the guilty heads
Of these marauders, who, in lieu of pay,
   Levied black-mail upon the garden beds
And cornfields, and beheld without dismay
   The awful scarecrow, with his fluttering shreds;
The skeleton that waited at their feast,
Whereby their sinful pleasure was increased.

Then from his house, a temple painted white,
   With fluted columns, and a roof of red,
The Squire came forth, august and splendid sight!
   Slowly descending, with majestic tread,
Three flights of steps, nor looking left nor right,
   Down the long street he walked, as one who said,
"A town that boasts inhabitants like me
Can have no lack of good society!"

The Parson, too, appeared, a man austere,
   The instinct of whose nature was to kill;
The wrath of God he preached from year to year,
   And read, with fervor, Edwards on the Will;
His favorite pastime was to slay the deer
   In Summer on some Adirondac hill;
E'en now, while walking down the rural lane,
He lopped the wayside lilies with his cane.

From the Academy, whose belfry crowned
   The hill of Science with its vane of brass,
Came the Preceptor, gazing idly round,
   Now at the clouds, and now at the green grass,
And all absorbed in reveries profound
   Of fair Almira in the upper class,
Who was, as in a sonnet he had said,
As pure as water, and as good as bread.

And next the Deacon issued from his door,
   In his voluminous neck-cloth, white as snow;
A suit of sable bombazine he wore;
   His form was ponderous, and his step was slow;

There never was so wise a man before;
He seemed the incarnate "Well, I told you so!"
And to perpetuate his great renown
There was a street named after him in town.

These came together in the new town-hall,
With sundry farmers from the region round.
The Squire presided, dignified and tall,
His air impressive and his reasoning sound;
Ill fared it with the birds, both great and small;
Hardly a friend in all that crowd they found,
But enemies enough, who every one
Charged them with all the crimes beneath the sun.

When they had ended, from his place apart
Rose the Preceptor, to redress the wrong,
And, trembling like a steed before the start,
Looked round bewildered on the expectant throng;
Then thought of fair Almira, and took heart
To speak out what was in him, clear and strong,
Alike regardless of their smile or frown,
And quite determined not to be laughed down.

"Plato, anticipating the Reviewers,
From his Republic banished without pity
The Poets; in this little town of yours,
You put to death, by means of a Committee,
The ballad-singers and the Troubadours,
The street-musicians of the heavenly city,
The birds, who make sweet music for us all
In our dark hours, as David did for Saul.

"The thrush that carols at the dawn of day
From the green steeples of the piny wood;
The oriole in the elm; the noisy jay,
Jargoning like a foreigner at his food;
The bluebird balanced on some topmost spray,
Flooding with melody the neighborhood;
Linnet and meadow-lark, and all the throng
That dwell in nests, and have the gift of song.

"You slay them all! and wherefore? for the gain
  Of a scant handful more or less of wheat,
Or rye, or barley, or some other grain,
  Scratched up at random by industrious feet,
Searching for worm or weevil after rain!
  Or a few cherries, that are not so sweet
As are the songs these uninvited guests
Sing at their feast with comfortable breasts.

"Do you ne'er think what wondrous beings these?
  Do you ne'er think who made them, and who taught
The dialect they speak, where melodies
  Alone are the interpreters of thought?
Whose household words are songs in many keys,
  Sweeter than instrument of man e'er caught!
Whose habitations in the tree-tops even
Are half-way houses on the road to heaven!

"Think, every morning when the sun peeps through
  The dim, leaf-latticed windows of the grove,
How jubilant the happy birds renew
  Their old, melodious madrigals of love!
And when you think of this, remember too
  'T is always morning somewhere, and above
The awakening continents, from shore to shore,
Somewhere the birds are singing evermore.

"Think of your woods and orchards without birds!
  Of empty nests that cling to boughs and beams
As in an idiot's brain remembered words
  Hang empty 'mid the cobwebs of his dreams!
Will bleat of flocks or bellowing of herds
  Make up for the lost music, when your teams
Drag home the stingy harvest, and no more
The feathered gleaners follow to your door?

"What! would you rather see the incessant stir
  Of insects in the windrows of the hay,
And hear the locust and the grasshopper
  Their melancholy hurdy-gurdies play?

Is this more pleasant to you than the whir
   Of meadow-lark, and her sweet roundelay,
Or twitter of little field-fares, as you take
Your nooning in the shade of bush and brake?

"You call them thieves and pillagers; but know,
   They are the winged wardens of your farms,
Who from the cornfields drive the insidious foe,
   And from your harvests keep a hundred harms;
Even the blackest of them all, the crow,
   Renders good service as your man-at-arms,
Crushing the beetle in his coat of mail,
And crying havoc on the slug and snail.

"How can I teach your children gentleness,
   And mercy to the weak, and reverence
For Life, which, in its weakness or excess,
   Is still a gleam of God's omnipotence,
Or Death, which, seeming darkness, is no less
   The selfsame light, although averted hence,
When by your laws, your actions, and your speech,
You contradict the very things I teach?"

With this he closed; and through the audience went
   A murmur, like the rustle of dead leaves;
The farmers laughed and nodded, and some bent
   Their yellow heads together like their sheaves;
Men have no faith in fine-spun sentiment
   Who put their trust in bullocks and in beeves.
The birds were doomed; and, as the record shows,
A bounty offered for the heads of crows.

There was another audience out of reach,
   Who had no voice nor vote in making laws,
But in the papers read his little speech,
   And crowned his modest temples with applause;
They made him conscious, each one more than each,
   He still was victor, vanquished in their cause.
Sweetest of all the applause he won from thee,
O fair Almira at the Academy!

And so the dreadful massacre began;
   O'er fields and orchards, and o'er woodland crests,
The ceaseless fusillade of terror ran.
   Dead fell the birds, with blood-stains on their breasts,
Or wounded crept away from sight of man,
   While the young died of famine in their nests;
A slaughter to be told in groans, not words,
The very St. Bartholomew of Birds!

The Summer came, and all the birds were dead;
   The days were like hot coals; the very ground
Was burned to ashes; in the orchards fed
   Myriads of caterpillars, and around
The cultivated fields and garden beds
   Hosts of devouring insects crawled, and found
No foe to check their march, till they had made
The land a desert without leaf or shade.

Devoured by worms, like Herod, was the town,
   Because, like Herod, it had ruthlessly
Slaughtered the Innocents. From the trees spun down
   The canker-worms upon the passers-by,
Upon each woman's bonnet, shawl, and gown,
   Who shook them off with just a little cry;
They were the terror of each favorite walk,
The endless theme of all the village talk.

The farmers grew impatient, but a few
   Confessed their error, and would not complain,
For after all, the best thing one can do
   When it is raining, is to let it rain.
Then they repealed the law, although they knew
   It would not call the dead to life again;
As school-boys, finding their mistake too late,
Draw a wet sponge across the accusing slate.

That year in Killingworth the Autumn came
   Without the light of his majestic look,
The wonder of the falling tongues of flame,
   The illumined pages of his Doom's-Day book.

A few lost leaves blushed crimson with their shame,
  And drowned themselves despairing in the brook,
While the wild wind went moaning everywhere,
Lamenting the dead children of the air!

But the next Spring a stranger sight was seen,
  A sight that never yet by bard was sung,
As great a wonder as it would have been
  If some dumb animal had found a tongue!
A wagon, overarched with evergreen,
  Upon whose boughs were wicker cages hung,
All full of singing birds, came down the street,
Filling the air with music wild and sweet.

From all the country round these birds were brought,
  By order of the town, with anxious quest,
And, loosened from their wicker prisons, sought
  In woods and fields the places they loved best,
Singing loud canticles, which many thought
  Were satires to the authorities addressed,
While others, listening in green lanes, averred
Such lovely music never had been heard!

But blither still and louder carolled they
  Upon the morrow, for they seemed to know
It was the fair Almira's wedding-day,
  And everywhere, around, above, below,
When the Preceptor bore his bride away,
  Their songs burst forth in joyous overflow,
And a new heaven bent over a new earth
Amid the sunny farms of Killingworth.

Finale

The hour was late; the fire burned low,
The Landlord's eyes were closed in sleep,
And near the story's end a deep
Sonorous sound at times was heard,

As when the distant bagpipes blow.
At this all laughed; the Landlord stirred,
As one awaking from a swound,
And, gazing anxiously around,
Protested that he had not slept,
But only shut his eyes, and kept
His ears attentive to each word.

Then all arose, and said "Good Night."
Alone remained the drowsy Squire
To rake the embers of the fire,
And quench the waning parlor light;
While from the windows, here and there,
The scattered lamps a moment gleamed,
And the illumined hostel seemed
The constellation of the Bear,
Downward, athwart the misty air,
Sinking and setting toward the sun.
Far off the village clock struck one.

from

PART SECOND

The Spanish Jew's Tale

KAMBALU

Into the city of Kambalu,
By the road that leadeth to Ispahan,
At the head of his dusty caravan,
Laden with treasure from realms afar,
Baldacca and Kelat and Kandahar,
Rode the great captain Alau.

The Khan from his palace-window gazed,
And saw in the thronging street beneath,
In the light of the setting sun, that blazed

Through the clouds of dust by the caravan raised,
The flash of harness and jewelled sheath,
And the shining scimitars of the guard,
And the weary camels that bared their teeth,
As they passed and passed through the gates unbarred
Into the shade of the palace-yard.

Thus into the city of Kambalu
Rode the great captain Alau;
And he stood before the Khan, and said:
"The enemies of my lord are dead;
All the Kalifs of all the West
Bow and obey thy least behest;
The plains are dark with the mulberry-trees,
The weavers are busy in Samarcand,
The miners are sifting the golden sand,
The divers plunging for pearls in the seas,
And peace and plenty are in the land.

"Baldacca's Kalif, and he alone,
Rose in revolt against thy throne:
His treasures are at thy palace-door,
With the swords and the shawls and the jewels he wore;
His body is dust o'er the desert blown.

"A mile outside of Baldacca's gate
I left my forces to lie in wait,
Concealed by forests and hillocks of sand,
And forward dashed with a handful of men,
To lure the old tiger from his den
Into the ambush I had planned.
Ere we reached the town the alarm was spread,
For we heard the sound of gongs from within;
And with clash of cymbals and warlike din
The gates swung wide; and we turned and fled;
And the garrison sallied forth and pursued,
With the gray old Kalif at their head,
And above them the banner of Mohammed:
So we snared them all, and the town was subdued.

"As in at the gate we rode, behold,
A tower that is called the Tower of Gold!
For there the Kalif had hidden his wealth,
Heaped and hoarded and piled on high,
Like sacks of wheat in a granary;
And thither the miser crept by stealth
To feel of the gold that gave him health,
And to gaze and gloat with his hungry eye
On jewels that gleamed like a glow-worm's spark,
Or the eyes of a panther in the dark.

"I said to the Kalif: 'Thou art old,
Thou hast no need of so much gold.
Thou shouldst not have heaped and hidden it here,
Till the breath of battle was hot and near,
But have sown through the land these useless hoards
To spring into shining blades of swords,
And keep thine honor sweet and clear.
These grains of gold are not grains of wheat;
These bars of silver thou canst not eat;
These jewels and pearls and precious stones
Cannot cure the aches in thy bones,
Nor keep the feet of Death one hour
From climbing the stairways of thy tower!'

"Then into his dungeon I locked the drone,
And left him to feed there all alone
In the honey-cells of his golden hive;
Never a prayer, nor a cry, nor a groan
Was heard from those massive walls of stone,
Nor again was the Kalif seen alive!

"When at last we unlocked the door,
We found him dead upon the floor;
The rings had dropped from his withered hands,
His teeth were like bones in the desert sands:
Still clutching his treasure he had died;
And as he lay there, he appeared
A statue of gold with a silver beard,
His arms outstretched as if crucified."

This is the story, strange and true,
That the great captain Alau
Told to his brother the Tartar Khan,
When he rode that day into Kambalu
By the road that leadeth to Ispahan.

The Student's Tale

THE COBBLER OF HAGENAU

I trust that somewhere and somehow
You all have heard of Hagenau,
A quiet, quaint,.and ancient town
Among the green Alsatian hills,
A place of valleys, streams, and mills,
Where Barbarossa's castle, brown
With rust of centuries, still looks down
On the broad, drowsy land below,—
On shadowy forests filled with game,
And the blue river winding slow
Through meadows, where the hedges grow
That give this little town its name.

It happened in the good old times,
While yet the Master-singers filled
The noisy workshop and the guild
With various melodies and rhymes,
That here in Hagenau there dwelt
A cobbler,—one who loved debate,
And, arguing from a postulate,
Would say what others only felt;
A man of forecast and of thrift,
And of a shrewd and careful mind
In this world's business, but inclined
Somewhat to let the next world drift.

Hans Sachs with vast delight he read,
And Regenbogen's rhymes of love,
For their poetic fame had spread

Even to the town of Hagenau;
And some Quick Melody of the Plough,
Or Double Harmony of the Dove
Was always running in his head.
He kept, moreover, at his side,
Among his leathers and his tools,
Reynard the Fox, the Ship of Fools,
Or Eulenspiegel, open wide;
With these he was much edified:
He thought them wiser than the Schools.

His good wife, full of godly fear,
Liked not these worldly themes to hear;
The Psalter was her book of songs;
The only music to her ear
Was that which to the Church belongs,
When the loud choir on Sunday chanted,
And the two angels carved in wood,
That by the windy organ stood,
Blew on their trumpets loud and clear,
And all the echoes, far and near,
Gibbered as if the church were haunted.

Outside his door, one afternoon,
This humble votary of the muse
Sat in the narrow strip of shade
By a projecting cornice made,
Mending the Burgomaster's shoes,
And singing a familiar tune:—

"Our ingress into the world
  Was naked and bare;
Our progress through the world
  Is trouble and care;
Our egress from the world
  Will be nobody knows where:
But if we do well here
  We shall do well there;
And I could tell you no more,
  Should I preach a whole year!"

Thus sang the cobbler at his work;
And with his gestures marked the time,
Closing together with a jerk
Of his waxed thread the stitch and rhyme.

Meanwhile his quiet little dame
Was leaning o'er the window-sill,
Eager, excited, but mouse-still,
Gazing impatiently to see
What the great throng of folk might be
That onward in procession came,
Along the unfrequented street,
With horns that blew, and drums that beat,
And banners flying, and the flame
Of tapers, and, at times, the sweet
Voices of nuns; and as they sang
Suddenly all the church-bells rang.

In a gay coach, above the crowd,
There sat a monk in ample hood,
Who with his right hand held aloft
A red and ponderous cross of wood,
To which at times he meekly bowed.
In front three horsemen rode, and oft,
With voice and air importunate,
A boisterous herald cried aloud:
"The grace of God is at your gate!"
So onward to the church they passed.

The cobbler slowly turned his last,
And, wagging his sagacious head,
Unto his kneeling housewife said:
" 'T is the monk Tetzel. I have heard
The cawings of that reverend bird.
Don't let him cheat you of your gold;
Indulgence is not bought and sold."

The church of Hagenau, that night,
Was full of people, full of light;
An odor of incense filled the air,

The priest intoned, the organ groaned
Its inarticulate despair;
The candles on the altar blazed,
And full in front of it upraised
The red cross stood against the glare.
Below, upon the altar-rail
Indulgences were set to sale,
Like ballads at a country fair.
A heavy strong-box, iron-bound
And carved with many a quaint device,
Received, with a melodious sound,
The coin that purchased Paradise.

Then from the pulpit overhead,
Tetzel the monk, with fiery glow,
Thundered upon the crowd below.
"Good people all, draw near!" he said;
"Purchase these letters, signed and sealed,
By which all sins, though unrevealed
And unrepented, are forgiven!
Count but the gain, count not the loss!
Your gold and silver are but dross,
And yet they pave the way to heaven.
I hear your mothers and your sires
Cry from their purgatorial fires,
And will ye not their ransom pay?
O senseless people! when the gate
Of heaven is open, will ye wait?
Will ye not enter in to-day?
To-morrow it will be too late;
I shall be gone upon my way.
Make haste! bring money while ye may!"

The women shuddered, and turned pale;
Allured by hope or driven by fear,
With many a sob and many a tear,
All crowded to the altar-rail.
Pieces of silver and of gold
Into the tinkling strong-box fell
Like pebbles dropped into a well;

And soon the ballads were all sold.
The cobbler's wife among the rest
Slipped into the capacious chest
A golden florin; then withdrew,
Hiding the paper in her breast;
And homeward through the darkness went
Comforted, quieted, content;
She did not walk, she rather flew,
A dove that settles to her nest,
When some appalling bird of prey
That scared her has been driven away.

The days went by, the monk was gone,
The summer passed, the winter came;
Though seasons changed, yet still the same
The daily round of life went on;
The daily round of household care,
The narrow life of toil and prayer.
But in her heart the cobbler's dame
Had now a treasure beyond price,
A secret joy without a name,
The certainty of Paradise.
Alas, alas! Dust unto dust!
Before the winter wore away,
Her body in the churchyard lay,
Her patient soul was with the Just!
After her death, among the things
That even the poor preserve with care, —
Some little trinkets and cheap rings,
A locket with her mother's hair,
Her wedding gown, the faded flowers
She wore upon her wedding day,—
Among these memories of past hours,
That so much of the heart reveal,
Carefully kept and put away,
The Letter of Indulgence lay
Folded, with signature and seal.

Meanwhile the Priest, aggrieved and pained,
Waited and wondered that no word

Of mass or requiem he heard,
As by the Holy Church ordained:
Then to the Magistrate complained,
That as this woman had been dead
A week or more, and no mass said,
It was rank heresy, or at least
Contempt of Church; thus said the Priest;
And straight the cobbler was arraigned.

He came, confiding in his cause,
But rather doubtful of the laws.
The Justice from his elbow-chair
Gave him a look that seemed to say:
"Thou standest before a Magistrate,
Therefore do not prevaricate!"
Then asked him in a business way,
Kindly but cold: "Is thy wife dead?"
The cobbler meekly bowed his head;
"She is," came struggling from his throat
Scarce audibly. The Justice wrote
The words down in a book, and then
Continued, as he raised his pen;
"She is; and hath a mass been said
For the salvation of her soul?
Come, speak the truth! confess the whole!"
The cobbler without pause replied:
"Of mass or prayer there was no need;
For at the moment when she died
Her soul was with the glorified!"
And from his pocket with all speed
He drew the priestly title-deed,
And prayed the Justice he would read.

The Justice read, amused, amazed;
And as he read his mirth increased;
At times his shaggy brows he raised,
Now wondering at the cobbler gazed,
Now archly at the angry Priest.
"From all excesses, sins, and crimes
Thou hast committed in past times

Thee I absolve! And furthermore,
Purified from all earthly taints,
To the communion of the Saints
And to the sacraments restore!
All stains of weakness, and all trace
Of shame and censure I efface;
Remit the pains thou shouldst endure,
And make thee innocent and pure,
So that in dying, unto thee
The gates of heaven shall open be!
Though long thou livest, yet this grace
Until the moment of thy death
Unchangeable continueth!"

Then said he to the Priest: "I find
This document is duly signed
Brother John Tetzel, his own hand.
At all tribunals in the land
In evidence it may be used;
Therefore acquitted is the accused."
Then to the cobbler turned: "My friend,
Pray tell me, didst thou ever read
Reynard the Fox?"—"Oh yes, indeed!"—
"I thought so. Don't forget the end."

The Theologian's Tale

THE LEGEND BEAUTIFUL

"Hadst thou stayed, I must have fled!"
That is what the Vision said.

In his chamber all alone,
Kneeling on the floor of stone,
Prayed the Monk in deep contrition
For his sins of indecision,
Prayed for greater self-denial
In temptation and in trial;

It was noonday by the dial,
And the Monk was all alone.

Suddenly, as if it lightened,
An unwonted splendor brightened
All within him and without him
In that narrow cell of stone;
And he saw the Blessed Vision
Of our Lord, with light Elysian
Like a vesture wrapped about Him,
Like a garment round Him thrown.

Not as crucified and slain,
Not in agonies of pain,
Not with bleeding hands and feet,
Did the Monk his Master see;
But as in the village street,
In the house or harvest-field,
Halt and lame and blind He healed,
When He walked in Galilee.

In an attitude imploring,
Hands upon his bosom crossed,
Wondering, worshipping, adoring,
Knelt the Monk in rapture lost.
Lord, he thought, in heaven that reignest,
Who am I, that thus thou deignest
To reveal thyself to me?
Who am I, that from the centre
Of thy glory thou shouldst enter
This poor cell, my guest to be?

Then amid his exaltation,
Loud the convent bell appalling,
From its belfry calling, calling,
Rang through court and corridor
With persistent iteration
He had never heard before.
It was now the appointed hour
When alike in shine or shower,

Winter's cold or summer's heat,
To the convent portals came
All the blind and halt and lame,
All the beggars of the street,
For their daily dole of food
Dealt them by the brotherhood;
And their almoner was he
Who upon his bended knee,
Rapt in silent ecstasy
Of divinest self-surrender,
Saw the Vision and the Splendor.
Deep distress and hesitation
Mingled with his adoration;
Should he go or should he stay?
Should he leave the poor to wait
Hungry at the convent gate,
Till the Vision passed away?
Should he slight his radiant guest,
Slight this visitant celestial,
For a crowd of ragged, bestial
Beggars at the convent gate?
Would the Vision there remain?
Would the Vision come again?
Then a voice within his breast
Whispered, audible and clear
As if to the outward ear:
"Do thy duty; that is best;
Leave unto thy Lord the rest!"

Straightway to his feet he started,
And with longing look intent
On the Blessed Vision bent,
Slowly from his cell departed,
Slowly on his errand went.

At the gate the poor were waiting,
Looking through the iron grating,
With that terror in the eye
That is only seen in those
Who amid their wants and woes

Hear the sound of doors that close,
And of feet that pass them by;
Grown familiar with disfavor,
Grown familiar with the savor
Of the bread by which men die!
But to-day, they knew not why,
Like the gate of Paradise
Seemed the convent gate to rise,
Like a sacrament divine
Seemed to them the bread and wine.
In his heart the Monk was praying,
Thinking of the homeless poor,
What they suffer and endure;
What we see not, what we see;
And the inward voice was saying:
"Whatsoever thing thou doest
To the least of mine and lowest,
That thou doest unto me!"

Unto me! but had the Vision
Come to him in beggar's clothing,
Come a mendicant imploring,
Would he then have knelt adoring,
Or have listened with derision,
And have turned away with loathing?

Thus his conscience put the question,
Full of troublesome suggestion,
As at length, with hurried pace,
Towards his cell he turned his face,
And beheld the convent bright
With a supernatural light,
Like a luminous cloud expanding
Over floor and wall and ceiling.

But he paused with awe-struck feeling
At the threshold of his door,
For the Vision still was standing
As he left it there before,
When the convent bell appalling,

From its belfry calling, calling,
Summoned him to feed the poor.
Through the long hour intervening
It had waited his return,
And he felt his bosom burn,
Comprehending all the meaning,
When the Blessed Vision said,
"Hadst thou stayed, I must have fled!"

from
PART THIRD

The Spanish Jew's Tale

AZRAEL

King Solomon, before his palace gate
At evening, on the pavement tessellate
Was walking with a stranger from the East,
Arrayed in rich attire as for a feast,
The mighty Runjeet-Sing, a learned man,
And Rajah of the realms of Hindostan.
And as they walked the guest became aware
Of a white figure in the twilight air,
Gazing intent, as one who with surprise
His form and features seemed to recognize;
And in a whisper to the king he said:
"What is yon shape, that, pallid as the dead,
Is watching me, as if he sought to trace
In the dim light the features of my face?"

The king looked, and replied: "I know him well;
It is the Angel men call Azrael,
'T is the Death Angel; what hast thou to fear?"
And the guest answered: "Lest he should come near,
And speak to me, and take away my breath!
Save me from Azrael, save me from death!

O king, that hast dominion o'er the wind,
Bid it arise and bear me hence to Ind."

The king gazed upward at the cloudless sky,
Whispered a word, and raised his hand on high,
And lo! the signet-ring of chrysoprase
On his uplifted finger seemed to blaze
With hidden fire, and rushing from the west
There came a mighty wind, and seized the guest
And lifted him from earth, and on they passed,
His shining garments streaming in the blast,
A silken banner o'er the walls upreared,
A purple cloud, that gleamed and disappeared.
Then said the Angel, smiling: "If this man
Be Rajah Runjeet-Sing of Hindostan,
Thou hast done well in listening to his prayer;
I was upon my way to seek him there."

The Sicilian's Tale

THE MONK OF CASAL-MAGGIORE

Once on a time, some centuries ago,
  In the hot sunshine two Franciscan friars
Wended their weary way, with footsteps slow,
  Back to their convent, whose white walls and spires
Gleamed on the hillside like a patch of snow;
  Covered with dust they were, and torn by briers,
And bore like sumpter-mules upon their backs
The badge of poverty, their beggar's sacks.

The first was Brother Anthony, a spare
  And silent man, with pallid cheeks and thin,
Much given to vigils, penance, fasting, prayer,
  Solemn and gray, and worn with discipline,
As if his body but white ashes were,
  Heaped on the living coals that glowed within;
A simple monk, like many of his day,
Whose instinct was to listen and obey.

A different man was Brother Timothy,
  Of larger mould and of a coarser paste;
A rubicund and stalwart monk was he,
  Broad in the shoulders, broader in the waist,
Who often filled the dull refectory
  With noise by which the convent was disgraced,
But to the mass-book gave but little heed,
By reason he had never learned to read.

Now, as they passed the outskirts of a wood,
  They saw, with mingled pleasure and surprise,
Fast tethered to a tree an ass, that stood
  Lazily winking his large, limpid eyes.
The farmer Gilbert, of that neighborhood,
  His owner was, who, looking for supplies
Of fagots, deeper in the wood had strayed,
Leaving his beast to ponder in the shade.

As soon as Brother Timothy espied
  The patient animal, he said: "Good-lack!
Thus for our needs doth Providence provide;
  We 'll lay our wallets on the creature's back."
This being done, he leisurely untied
  From head and neck the halter of the jack,
And put it round his own, and to the tree
Stood tethered fast as if the ass were he.

And, bursting forth into a merry laugh,
  He cried to Brother Anthony: "Away!
And drive the ass before you with your staff;
  And when you reach the convent you may say
You left me at a farm, half tired and half
  Ill with a fever, for a night and day,
And that the farmer lent this ass to bear
Our wallets, that are heavy with good fare."

Now Brother Anthony, who knew the pranks
  Of Brother Timothy, would not persuade
Or reason with him on his quirks and cranks,
  But, being obedient, silently obeyed;

And, smiting with his staff the ass's flanks,
Drove him before him over hill and glade,
Safe with his provend to the convent gate,
Leaving poor Brother Timothy to his fate.

Then Gilbert, laden with fagots for his fire,
Forth issued from the wood, and stood aghast
To see the ponderous body of the friar
Standing where he had left his donkey last.
Trembling he stood, and dared not venture nigher,
But stared, and gaped, and crossed himself full fast;
For, being credulous and of little wit,
He thought it was some demon from the pit.

While speechless and bewildered thus he gazed,
And dropped his load of fagots on the ground,
Quoth Brother Timothy: "Be not amazed
That where you left a donkey should be found
A poor Franciscan friar, half-starved and crazed,
Standing demure and with a halter bound;
But set me free, and hear the piteous story
Of Brother Timothy of Casal-Maggiore.

"I am a sinful man, although you see
I wear the consecrated cowl and cape;
You never owned an ass, but you owned me,
Changed and transformed from my own natural shape
All for the deadly sin of gluttony,
From which I could not otherwise escape,
Than by this penance, dieting on grass,
And being worked and beaten as an ass.

"Think of the ignominy I endured;
Think of the miserable life I led,
The toil and blows to which I was inured,
My wretched lodging in a windy shed,
My scanty fare so grudgingly procured,
The damp and musty straw that formed my bed!
But, having done this penance for my sins,
My life as man and monk again begins."

The simple Gilbert, hearing words like these,
  Was conscience-stricken, and fell down apace
Before the friar upon his bended knees,
  And with a suppliant voice implored his grace;
And the good monk, now very much at ease,
  Granted him pardon with a smiling face,
Nor could refuse to be that night his guest,
It being late, and he in need of rest.

Upon a hillside, where the olive thrives,
  With figures painted on its whitewashed walls,
The cottage stood; and near the humming hives
  Made murmurs as of far-off waterfalls;
A place where those who love secluded lives
  Might live content, and, free from noise and brawls,
Like Claudian's Old Man of Verona here
Measure by fruits the slow-revolving year.

And, coming to this cottage of content,
  They found his children, and the buxom wench
His wife, Dame Cicely, and his father, bent
  With years and labor, seated on a bench,
Repeating over some obscure event
  In the old wars of Milanese and French;
All welcomed the Franciscan, with a sense
Of sacred awe and humble reverence.

When Gilbert told them what had come to pass,
  How beyond question, cavil, or surmise,
Good Brother Timothy had been their ass,
  You should have seen the wonder in their eyes;
You should have heard them cry "Alas! alas!"
  Have heard their lamentations and their sighs!
For all believed the story, and began
To see a saint in this afflicted man.

Forthwith there was prepared a grand repast,
  To satisfy the craving of the friar
After so rigid and prolonged a fast;
  The bustling housewife stirred the kitchen fire;

Then her two barn-yard fowls, her best and last
   Were put to death, at her express desire,
And served up with a salad in a bowl,
And flasks of country wine to crown the whole.

It would not be believed should I repeat
   How hungry Brother Timothy appeared;
It was a pleasure but to see him eat,
   His white teeth flashing through his russet beard,
His face aglow and flushed with wine and meat,
   His roguish eyes that rolled and laughed and leered!
Lord! how he drank the blood-red country wine
As if the village vintage were divine!

And all the while he talked without surcease,
   And told his merry tales with jovial glee
That never flagged, but rather did increase,
   And laughed aloud as if insane were he,
And wagged his red beard, matted like a fleece,
   And cast such glances at Dame Cicely
That Gilbert now grew angry with his guest,
And thus in words his rising wrath expressed.

"Good father," said he, "easily we see
   How needful in some persons, and how right,
Mortification of the flesh may be.
   The indulgence you have given it to-night,
After long penance, clearly proves to me
   Your strength against temptation is but slight,
And shows the dreadful peril you are in
Of a relapse into your deadly sin.

"To-morrow morning, with the rising sun,
   Go back unto your convent, nor refrain
From fasting and from scourging, for you run
   Great danger to become an ass again,
Since monkish flesh and asinine are one;
   Therefore be wise, nor longer here remain,
Unless you wish the scourge should be applied
By other hands, that will not spare your hide."

When this the monk had heard, his color fled
  And then returned, like lightning in the air,
Till he was all one blush from foot to head,
  And even the bald spot in his russet hair
Turned from its usual pallor to bright red!
  The old man was asleep upon his chair.
Then all retired, and sank into the deep
And helpless imbecility of sleep.

They slept until the dawn of day drew near,
  Till the cock should have crowed, but did not crow,
For they had slain the shining chanticleer
  And eaten him for supper, as you know.
The monk was up betimes and of good cheer,
  And, having breakfasted, made haste to go,
As if he heard the distant matin bell,
And had but little time to say farewell.

Fresh was the morning as the breath of kine;
  Odors of herbs commingled with the sweet
Balsamic exhalations of the pine;
  A haze was in the air presaging heat;
Uprose the sun above the Apennine,
  And all the misty valleys at its feet
Were full of the delirious song of birds,
Voices of men, and bells, and low of herds.

All this to Brother Timothy was naught;
  He did not care for scenery, nor here
His busy fancy found the thing it sought;
  But when he saw the convent walls appear,
And smoke from kitchen chimneys upward caught
  And whirled aloft into the atmosphere,
He quickened his slow footsteps, like a beast
That scents the stable a league off at least.

And as he entered through the convent gate
  He saw there in the court the ass, who stood
Twirling his ears about, and seemed to wait,
  Just as he found him waiting in the wood;

And told the Prior that, to alleviate
  The daily labors of the brotherhood,
The owner, being a man of means and thrift,
Bestowed him on the convent as a gift.

And thereupon the Prior for many days
  Revolved this serious matter in his mind,
And turned it over many different ways,
  Hoping that some safe issue he might find;
But stood in fear of what the world would say,
  If he accepted presents of this kind,
Employing beasts of burden for the packs
That lazy monks should carry on their backs.

Then, to avoid all scandal of the sort,
  And stop the mouth of cavil, he decreed
That he would cut the tedious matter short,
  And sell the ass with all convenient speed,
Thus saving the expense of his support,
  And hoarding something for a time of need.
So he despatched him to the neighboring Fair,
And freed himself from cumber and from care.

It happened now by chance, as some might say,
  Others perhaps would call it destiny,
Gilbert was at the Fair; and heard a bray,
  And nearer came, and saw that it was he,
And whispered in his ear, "Ah, lackaday!
  Good father, the rebellious flesh, I see,
Has changed you back into an ass again,
And all my admonitions were in vain."

The ass, who felt this breathing in his ear,
  Did not turn round to look, but shook his head,
As if he were not pleased these words to hear,
  And contradicted all that had been said.
And this made Gilbert cry in voice more clear,
  "I know you well; your hair is russet-red;
Do not deny it; for you are the same
Franciscan friar, and Timothy by name."

The ass, though now the secret had come out,
  Was obstinate, and shook his head again;
Until a crowd was gathered round about
  To hear this dialogue between the twain;
And raised their voices in a noisy shout
  When Gilbert tried to make the matter plain,
And flouted him and mocked him all day long
With laughter and with jibes and scraps of song.

"If this be Brother Timothy," they cried,
  "Buy him, and feed him on the tenderest grass;
Thou canst not do too much for one so tried
  As to be twice transformed into an ass."
So simple Gilbert bought him, and untied
  His halter, and o'er mountain and morass
He led him homeward, talking as he went
Of good behavior and a mind content.

The children saw them coming, and advanced,
  Shouting with joy, and hung about his neck,—
Not Gilbert's, but the ass's,—round him danced,
  And wove green garlands wherewithal to deck
His sacred person; for again it chanced
  Their childish feelings, without rein or check,
Could not discriminate in any way
A donkey from a friar of Orders Gray.

"O Brother Timothy," the children said,
  "You have come back to us just as before;
We were afraid, and thought that you were dead,
  And we should never see you any more."
And then they kissed the white star on his head,
  That like a birth-mark or a badge he wore,
And patted him upon the neck and face,
And said a thousand things with childish grace.

Thenceforward and forever he was known
  As Brother Timothy, and led alway
A life of luxury, till he had grown
  Ungrateful, being stuffed with corn and hay,

And very vicious. Then in angry tone,
  Rousing himself, poor Gilbert said one day,
"When simple kindness is misunderstood
A little flagellation may do good."

His many vices need not here be told;
  Among them was a habit that he had
Of flinging up his heels at young and old,
  Breaking his halter, running off like mad
O'er pasture-lands and meadow, wood and wold,
  And other misdemeanors quite as bad;
But worst of all was breaking from his shed
At night, and ravaging the cabbage-bed.

So Brother Timothy went back once more
  To his old life of labor and distress;
Was beaten worse than he had been before;
  And now, instead of comfort and caress,
Came labors manifold and trials sore;
  And as his toils increased his food grew less,
Until at last the great consoler, Death,
Ended his many sufferings with his breath.

Great was the lamentation when he died;
  And mainly that he died impenitent;
Dame Cicely bewailed, the children cried,
  The old man still remembered the event
In the French war, and Gilbert magnified
  His many virtues, as he came and went,
And said: "Heaven pardon Brother Timothy,
And keep us from the sin of gluttony."

Finale

These are the tales those merry guests
Told to each other, well or ill;
Like summer birds that lift their crests
Above the borders of their nests
And twitter, and again are still.

These are the tales, or new or old,
In idle moments idly told;
Flowers of the field with petals thin,
Lilies that neither toil nor spin,
And tufts of wayside weeds and gorse
Hung in the parlor of the inn
Beneath the sign of the Red Horse.

And still, reluctant to retire,
The friends sat talking by the fire
And watched the smouldering embers burn
To ashes, and flash up again
Into a momentary glow,
Lingering like them when forced to go,
And going when they would remain;
For on the morrow they must turn
Their faces homeward, and the pain
Of parting touched with its unrest
A tender nerve in every breast.

But sleep at last the victory won;
They must be stirring with the sun,
And drowsily good night they said,
And went still gossiping to bed,
And left the parlor wrapped in gloom.
The only live thing in the room
Was the old clock, that in its pace
Kept time with the revolving spheres
And constellations in their flight,
And struck with its uplifted mace
The dark, unconscious hours of night,
To senseless and unlistening ears.

Uprose the sun; and every guest,
Uprisen, was soon equipped and dressed
For journeying home and city-ward;
The old stage-coach was at the door,
With horses harnessed, long before
The sunshine reached the withered sward

Beneath the oaks, whose branches hoar
Murmured: "Farewell forevermore."

"Farewell!" the portly Landlord cried;
"Farewell!" the parting guests replied,
But little thought that nevermore
Their feet would pass that threshold o'er;
That nevermore together there
Would they assemble, free from care,
To hear the oaks' mysterious roar,
And breathe the wholesome country air.

Where are they now? What lands and skies
Paint pictures in their friendly eyes?
What hope deludes, what promise cheers,
What pleasant voices fill their ears?
Two are beyond the salt sea waves,
And three already in their graves.
Perchance the living still may look
Into the pages of this book,
And see the days of long ago
Floating and fleeting to and fro,
As in the well-remembered brook
They saw the inverted landscape gleam,
And their own faces like a dream
Look up upon them from below.

from

FLOWER-DE-LUCE

Palingenesis

I lay upon the headland-height, and listened
To the incessant sobbing of the sea
    In caverns under me,
And watched the waves, that tossed and fled and glistened,
Until the rolling meadows of amethyst
    Melted away in mist.

Then suddenly, as one from sleep, I started;
For round about me all the sunny capes
    Seemed peopled with the shapes
Of those whom I had known in days departed,
Apparelled in the loveliness which gleams
    On faces seen in dreams.

A moment only, and the light and glory
Faded away, and the disconsolate shore
    Stood lonely as before;
And the wild-roses of the promontory
Around me shuddered in the wind, and shed
    Their petals of pale red.

There was an old belief that in the embers
Of all things their primordial form exists,
    And cunning alchemists
Could re-create the rose with all its members
From its own ashes, but without the bloom,
    Without the lost perfume.

Ah me! what wonder-working, occult science
Can from the ashes in our hearts once more
    The rose of youth restore?
What craft of alchemy can bid defiance
To time and change, and for a single hour
    Renew this phantom-flower?

"Oh, give me back," I cried, "the vanished splendors,
The breath of morn, and the exultant strife,
When the swift stream of life
Bounds o'er its rocky channel, and surrenders
The pond, with all its lilies, for the leap
Into the unknown deep!"

And the sea answered, with a lamentation,
Like some old prophet wailing, and it said,
"Alas! thy youth is dead!
It breathes no more, its heart has no pulsation;
In the dark places with the dead of old
It lies forever cold!"

Then said I, "From its consecrated cerements
I will not drag this sacred dust again,
Only to give me pain;
But, still remembering all the lost endearments,
Go on my way, like one who looks before,
And turns to weep no more."

Into what land of harvests, what plantations
Bright with autumnal foliage and the glow
Of sunsets burning low;
Beneath what midnight skies, whose constellations
Light up the spacious avenues between
This world and the unseen!

Amid what friendly greetings and caresses,
What households, though not alien, yet not mine,
What bowers of rest divine;
To what temptations in lone wildernesses,
What famine of the heart, what pain and loss,
The bearing of what cross!

I do not know; nor will I vainly question
Those pages of the mystic book which hold
The story still untold,
But without rash conjecture or suggestion
Turn its last leaves in reverence and good heed,
Until "The End" I read.

Hawthorne

How beautiful it was, that one bright day
In the long week of rain!
Though all its splendor could not chase away
The omnipresent pain.

The lovely town was white with apple-blooms,
And the great elms o'erhead
Dark shadows wove on their aerial looms
Shot through with golden thread.

Across the meadows, by the gray old manse,
The historic river flowed:
I was as one who wanders in a trance,
Unconscious of his road.

The faces of familiar friends seemed strange;
Their voices I could hear,
And yet the words they uttered seemed to change
Their meaning to my ear.

For the one face I looked for was not there,
The one low voice was mute;
Only an unseen presence filled the air,
And baffled my pursuit.

Now I look back, and meadow, manse, and stream
Dimly my thought defines;
I only see—a dream within a dream—
The hill-top hearsed with pines.

I only hear above his place of rest
Their tender undertone,
The infinite longings of a troubled breast,
The voice so like his own.

There in seclusion and remote from men
The wizard hand lies cold,
Which at its topmost speed let fall the pen,
And left the tale half told.

Ah! who shall lift that wand of magic power,
And the lost clew regain?
The unfinished window in Aladdin's tower
Unfinished must remain!

Christmas Bells

I heard the bells on Christmas Day
Their old, familiar carols play,
And wild and sweet
The words repeat
Of peace on earth, good-will to men!

And thought how, as the day had come,
The belfries of all Christendom
Had rolled along
The unbroken song
Of peace on earth, good-will to men!

Till, ringing, singing on its way,
The world revolved from night to day,
A voice, a chime,
A chant sublime
Of peace on earth, good-will to men!

Then from each black, accursed mouth
The cannon thundered in the South,
And with the sound
The carols drowned
Of peace on earth, good-will to men!

It was as if an earthquake rent
The hearth-stones of a continent,
And made forlorn
The households born
Of peace on earth, good-will to men!

And in despair I bowed my head;
"There is no peace on earth," I said;
"For hate is strong,
And mocks the song
Of peace on earth, good-will to men!"

Then pealed the bells more loud and deep:
"God is not dead; nor doth he sleep!
The Wrong shall fail,
The Right prevail,
With peace on earth, good-will to men!"

The Wind Over the Chimney

See, the fire is sinking low,
Dusky red the embers glow,
While above them still I cower,
While a moment more I linger,
Though the clock, with lifted finger,
Points beyond the midnight hour.

Sings the blackened log a tune
Learned in some forgotten June
From a school-boy at his play,
When they both were young together,
Heart of youth and summer weather
Making all their holiday.

And the night-wind rising, hark!
How above there in the dark,
In the midnight and the snow,
Ever wilder, fiercer, grander,
Like the trumpets of Iskander,
All the noisy chimneys blow!

Every quivering tongue of flame
Seems to murmur some great name,
Seems to say to me, "Aspire!"

But the night-wind answers, "Hollow
Are the visions that you follow,
  Into darkness sinks your fire!"

Then the flicker of the blaze
Gleams on volumes of old days,
  Written by masters of the art,
Loud through whose majestic pages
Rolls the melody of ages,
  Throb the harp-strings of the heart.

And again the tongues of flame
Start exulting and exclaim:
  "These are prophets, bards, and seers;
In the horoscope of nations,
Like ascendant constellations,
  They control the coming years."

But the night-wind cries: "Despair!
Those who walk with feet of air
  Leave no long-enduring marks;
At God's forges incandescent
Mighty hammers beat incessant,
  These are but the flying sparks.

"Dust are all the hands that wrought;
Books are sepulchres of thought;
  The dead laurels of the dead
Rustle for a moment only,
Like the withered leaves in lonely
  Churchyards at some passing tread."

Suddenly the flame sinks down;
Sink the rumors of renown;
  And alone the night-wind drear
Clamors louder, wilder, vaguer,—
" 'T is the brand of Meleager
  Dying on the hearth-stone here!"

And I answer,—"Though it be,
Why should that discomfort me?
  No endeavor is in vain;
Its reward is in the doing,
And the rapture of pursuing
  Is the prize the vanquished gain."

Killed at the Ford

He is dead, the beautiful youth,
The heart of honor, the tongue of truth,
He, the life and light of us all,
Whose voice was blithe as a bugle-call,
Whom all eyes followed with one consent,
The cheer of whose laugh, and whose pleasant word,
Hushed all murmurs of discontent.

Only last night, as we rode along,
Down the dark of the mountain gap,
To visit the picket-guard at the ford,
Little dreaming of any mishap,
He was humming the words of some old song:
"Two red roses he had on his cap
And another he bore at the point of his sword."

Sudden and swift a whistling ball
Came out of a wood, and the voice was still;
Something I heard in the darkness fall,
And for a moment my blood grew chill;
I spake in a whisper, as he who speaks
In a room where some one is lying dead;
But he made no answer to what I said.

We lifted him up to his saddle again,
And through the mire and the mist and the rain
Carried him back to the silent camp,
And laid him as if asleep on his bed;
And I saw by the light of the surgeon's lamp

Two white roses upon his cheeks,
And one, just over his heart, blood-red!

And I saw in a vision how far and fleet
That fatal bullet went speeding forth,
Till it reached a town in the distant North,
Till it reached a house in a sunny street,
Till it reached a heart that ceased to beat
Without a murmur, without a cry;
And a bell was tolled, in that far-off town,
For one who had passed from cross to crown,
And the neighbors wondered that she should die.

Giotto's Tower

How many lives, made beautiful and sweet
  By self-devotion and by self-restraint,
  Whose pleasure is to run without complaint
  On unknown errands of the Paraclete,
Wanting the reverence of unshodden feet,
  Fail of the nimbus which the artists paint
  Around the shining forehead of the saint,
  And are in their completeness incomplete!
In the old Tuscan town stands Giotto's tower,
  The lily of Florence blossoming in stone,—
  A vision, a delight, and a desire,—
The builder's perfect and centennial flower,
  That in the night of ages bloomed alone,
  But wanting still the glory of the spire.

Divina Commedia

I.

Oft have I seen at some cathedral door
A laborer, pausing in the dust and heat,
Lay down his burden, and with reverent feet
Enter, and cross himself, and on the floor
Kneel to repeat his paternoster o'er;
Far off the noises of the world retreat;
The loud vociferations of the street
Become an undistinguishable roar.
So, as I enter here from day to day,
And leave my burden at this minster gate,
Kneeling in prayer, and not ashamed to pray,
The tumult of the time disconsolate
To inarticulate murmurs dies away,
While the eternal ages watch and wait.

II.

How strange the sculptures that adorn these towers!
This crowd of statues, in whose folded sleeves
Birds build their nests; while canopied with leaves
Parvis and portal bloom like trellised bowers,
And the vast minster seems a cross of flowers!
But fiends and dragons on the gargoyled eaves
Watch the dead Christ between the living thieves,
And, underneath, the traitor Judas lowers!
Ah! from what agonies of heart and brain,
What exultations trampling on despair,
What tenderness, what tears, what hate of wrong,
What passionate outcry of a soul in pain,
Uprose this poem of the earth and air,
This mediæval miracle of song!

III.

I enter, and I see thee in the gloom
Of the long aisles, O poet saturnine!
And strive to make my steps keep pace with thine.
The air is filled with some unknown perfume;

The congregation of the dead make room
  For thee to pass; the votive tapers shine;
  Like rooks that haunt Ravenna's groves of pine
  The hovering echoes fly from tomb to tomb.
From the confessionals I hear arise
  Rehearsals of forgotten tragedies,
  And lamentations from the crypts below;
And then a voice celestial that begins
  With the pathetic words, "Although your sins
  As scarlet be," and ends with "as the snow."

IV.

With snow-white veil and garments as of flame,
  She stands before thee, who so long ago
  Filled thy young heart with passion and the woe
  From which thy song and all its splendors came;
And while with stern rebuke she speaks thy name,
  The ice about thy heart melts as the snow
  On mountain heights, and in swift overflow
  Comes gushing from thy lips in sobs of shame.
Thou makest full confession; and a gleam,
  As of the dawn on some dark forest cast,
  Seems on thy lifted forehead to increase;
Lethe and Eunoe—the remembered dream
  And the forgotten sorrow—bring at last
  That perfect pardon which is perfect peace.

V.

I lift mine eyes, and all the windows blaze
  With forms of Saints and holy men who died,
  Here martyred and hereafter glorified;
  And the great Rose upon its leaves displays
Christ's Triumph, and the angelic roundelays,
  With splendor upon splendor multiplied;
  And Beatrice again at Dante's side
  No more rebukes, but smiles her words of praise.
And then the organ sounds, and unseen choirs
  Sing the old Latin hymns of peace and love
  And benedictions of the Holy Ghost;

And the melodious bells among the spires
  O'er all the house-tops and through heaven above
  Proclaim the elevation of the Host!

VI.

O star of morning and of liberty!
  O bringer of the light, whose splendor shines
  Above the darkness of the Apennines,
  Forerunner of the day that is to be!
The voices of the city and the sea,
  The voices of the mountains and the pines,
  Repeat thy song, till the familiar lines
  Are footpaths for the thought of Italy!
Thy fame is blown abroad from all the heights,
  Through all the nations, and a sound is heard,
  As of a mighty wind, and men devout,
Strangers of Rome, and the new proselytes,
  In their own language hear thy wondrous word,
  And many are amazed and many doubt.

from
CHRISTUS: A MYSTERY

from
The Divine Tragedy

Mount Quarantania

I.

LUCIFER.

Not in the lightning's flash, nor in the thunder,
Not in the tempest, nor the cloudy storm,
        Will I array my form;
But part invisible these boughs asunder,
And move and murmur, as the wind upheaves
        And whispers in the leaves.

Not as a terror and a desolation,
Not in my natural shape, inspiring fear
        And dread, will I appear;
But in soft tones of sweetness and persuasion,
A sound as of the fall of mountain streams,
        Or voices heard in dreams.

He sitteth there in silence, worn and wasted
With famine, and uplifts his hollow eyes
        To the unpitying skies;
For forty days and nights he hath not tasted
Of food or drink, his parted lips are pale,
        Surely his strength must fail.

Wherefore dost thou in penitential fasting
Waste and consume the beauty of thy youth?
        Ah, if thou be in truth
The Son of the Unnamed, the Everlasting,
Command these stones beneath thy feet to be
        Changed into bread for thee!

CHRISTUS.

'T is written: Man shall not live by bread alone,
But by each word that from God's mouth proceedeth!

II.

LUCIFER.

Too weak, alas! too weak is the temptation
For one whose soul to nobler things aspires
        Than sensual desires!
Ah, could I, by some sudden aberration,
Lead and delude to suicidal death
        This Christ of Nazareth!

Unto the holy Temple on Moriah,
With its resplendent domes, and manifold
        Bright pinnacles of gold,
Where they await thy coming, O Messiah!
Lo, I have brought thee! Let thy glory here
        Be manifest and clear.

Reveal thyself by royal act and gesture
Descending with the bright triumphant host
        Of all the highermost
Archangels, and about thee as a vesture
The shining clouds, and all thy splendors show
        Unto the world below!

Cast thyself down, it is the hour appointed;
And God hath given his angels charge and care
        To keep thee and upbear
Upon their hands his only Son, the Anointed,
Lest he should dash his foot against a stone
        And die, and be unknown.

CHRISTUS.

'T is written: Thou shalt not tempt the Lord thy God!

III.

LUCIFER.

I cannot thus delude him to perdition!
But one temptation still remains untried,

The trial of his pride,
The thirst of power, the fever of ambition!
Surely by these a humble peasant's son
At last may be undone!

Above the yawning chasms and deep abysses,
Across the headlong torrents, I have brought
Thy footprints, swift as thought;
And from the highest of these precipices,
The Kingdoms of the world thine eyes behold,
Like a great map unrolled.

From far-off Lebanon, with cedars crested,
To where the waters of the Asphalt Lake
On its white pebbles break,
And the vast desert, silent, sand-invested,
These kingdoms all are mine, and thine shall be,
If thou wilt worship me!

CHRISTUS.

Get thee behind me, Satan! thou shalt worship
The Lord thy God; Him only shalt thou serve!

ANGELS MINISTRANT.

The sun goes down; the evening shadows lengthen,
The fever and the struggle of the day
Abate and pass away;
Thine Angels Ministrant, we come to strengthen
And comfort thee, and crown thee with the palm,
The silence and the calm.

The First Passover: Part II

The Tower of Magdala

MARY MAGDALENE.

Companionless, unsatisfied, forlorn,
I sit here in this lonely tower, and look
Upon the lake below me, and the hills
That swoon with heat, and see as in a vision
All my past life unroll itself before me.
The princes and the merchants come to me,
Merchants of Tyre and Princes of Damascus,

And pass, and disappear, and are no more;
But leave behind their merchandise and jewels,
Their perfumes, and their gold, and their disgust.
I loathe them, and the very memory of them
Is unto me, as thought of food to one
Cloyed with the luscious figs of Dalmanutha!
What if hereafter, in the long hereafter
Of endless joy or pain, or joy in pain,
It were my punishment to be with them
Grown hideous and decrepit in their sins,
And hear them say: Thou that hast brought us here,
Be unto us as thou hast been of old!

I look upon this raiment that I wear,
These silks, and these embroideries, and they seem
Only as cerements wrapped about my limbs!
I look upon these rings thick set with pearls,
And emerald and amethyst and jasper,
And they are burning coals upon my flesh!
This serpent on my wrist becomes alive!
Away, thou viper! and away, ye garlands,
Whose odors bring the swift remembrance back
Of the unhallowed revels in these chambers!
But yesterday,—and yet it seems to me
Something remote, like a pathetic song
Sung long ago by minstrels in the street,—
But yesterday, as from this tower I gazed,
Over the olive and the walnut trees
Upon the lake and the white ships, and wondered
Whither and whence they steered, and who was in them,
A fisher's boat drew near the landing-place
Under the oleanders, and the people
Came up from it, and passed beneath the tower,
Close under me. In front of them, as leader,
Walked one of royal aspect, clothed in white,
Who lifted up his eyes, and looked at me,
And all at once the air seemed filled and living
With a mysterious power, that streamed from him,
And overflowed me with an atmosphere
Of light and love. As one entranced I stood,

And when I woke again, lo! he was gone;
So that I said: Perhaps it is a dream.
But from that very hour the seven demons
That had their habitation in this body
Which men call beautiful, departed from me!

This morning, when the first gleam of the dawn
Made Lebanon a glory in the air,
And all below was darkness, I beheld
An angel, or a spirit glorified,
With wind-tossed garments walking on the lake.
The face I could not see, but I distinguished
The attitude and gesture, and I knew
'T was he that healed me. And the gusty wind
Brought to mine ears a voice, which seemed to say:
Be of good cheer! 'T is I! Be not afraid!
And from the darkness, scarcely heard, the answer:
If it be thou, bid me come unto thee
Upon the water! And the voice said: Come!
And then I heard a cry of fear: Lord, save me!
As of a drowning man. And then the voice:
Why didst thou doubt, O thou of little faith!
At this all vanished, and the wind was hushed,
And the great sun came up above the hills,
And the swift-flying vapors hid themselves
In caverns among the rocks! Oh, I must find him
And follow him, and be with him forever!

Thou box of alabaster, in whose walls
The souls of flowers lie pent, the precious balm
And spikenard of Arabian farms, the spirits
Of aromatic herbs, ethereal natures
Nursed by the sun and dew, not all unworthy
To bathe his consecrated feet, whose step
Makes every threshold holy that he crosses;
Let us go forth upon our pilgrimage,
Thou and I only! Let us search for him
Until we find him, and pour out our souls
Before his feet, till all that's left of us
Shall be the broken caskets that once held us!

The First Passover: Part IX

Simon Magus and Helen of Tyre

On the house-top at Endor. Night. A lighted lantern on a table.

SIMON.

Swift are the blessed Immortals to the mortal
That perseveres! So doth it stand recorded
In the divine Chaldæan Oracles
Of Zoroaster, once Ezekiel's slave,
Who in his native East betook himself
To lonely meditation, and the writing
On the dried skins of oxen the Twelve Books
Of the Avesta and the Oracles!
Therefore I persevere; and I have brought thee
From the great city of Tyre, where men deride
The things they comprehend not, to this plain
Of Esdraelon, in the Hebrew tongue
Called Armageddon, and this town of Endor,
Where men believe; where all the air is full
Of marvellous traditions, and the Enchantress
That summoned up the ghost of Samuel
Is still remembered. Thou hast seen the land;
Is it not fair to look on?

HELEN.

It is fair,
Yet not so fair as Tyre.

SIMON.

Is not Mount Tabor
As beautiful as Carmel by the Sea?

HELEN.

It is too silent and too solitary;
I miss the tumult of the streets; the sounds
Of traffic, and the going to and fro
Of people in gay attire, with cloaks of purple,
And gold and silver jewelry!

SIMON.

Inventions
Of Ahriman, the spirit of the dark,
The Evil Spirit!

HELEN.

I regret the gossip

Of friends and neighbors at the open door
On summer nights.

SIMON.

An idle waste of time.

HELEN.

The singing and the dancing, the delight
Of music and of motion. Woe is me,
To give up all these pleasures, and to lead
The life we lead!

SIMON.

Thou canst not raise thyself
Up to the level of my higher thought,
And though possessing thee, I still remain
Apart from thee, and with thee, am alone
In my high dreams.

HELEN.

Happier was I in Tyre.
Oh, I remember how the gallant ships
Came sailing in, with ivory, gold, and silver,
And apes and peacocks; and the singing sailors,
And the gay captains with their silken dresses,
Smelling of aloes, myrrh, and cinnamon!

SIMON.

But the dishonor, Helen! Let the ships
Of Tarshish howl for that!

HELEN.

And what dishonor?
Remember Rahab, and how she became
The ancestress of the great Psalmist David;
And wherefore should not I, Helen of Tyre,
Attain like honor?

SIMON.

Thou art Helen of Tyre,
And hast been Helen of Troy, and hast been Rahab,
The Queen of Sheba, and Semiramis,
And Sara of seven husbands, and Jezebel,
And other women of the like allurements;
And now thou art Minerva, the first Æon,
The Mother of Angels!

HELEN.

And the concubine
Of Simon the Magician! Is it honor
For one who has been all these noble dames,
To tramp about the dirty villages
And cities of Samaria with a juggler?
A charmer of serpents?

SIMON.

He who knows himself
Knows all things in himself. I have charmed thee,
Thou beautiful asp: yet am I no magician.
I am the Power of God, and the Beauty of God!
I am the Paraclete, the Comforter!

HELEN.

Illusions! Thou deceiver, self-deceived!
Thou dost usurp the titles of another;
Thou art not what thou sayest.

SIMON.

Am I not?
Then feel my power.

HELEN.

Would I had ne'er left Tyre!

He looks at her, and she sinks into a deep sleep.

SIMON.

Go, see it in thy dreams, fair unbeliever!
And leave me unto mine, if they be dreams,
That take such shapes before me, that I see them;
These effable and ineffable impressions
Of the mysterious world, that come to me
From the elements of Fire and Earth and Water,
And the all-nourishing Ether! It is written,
Look not on Nature, for her name is fatal!
Yet there are Principles, that make apparent
The images of unapparent things,
And the impression of vague characters
And visions most divine appear in ether.
So speak the Oracles; then wherefore fatal?
I take this orange-bough, with its five leaves,
Each equidistant on the upright stem;
And I project them on a plane below,

In the circumference of a circle drawn
About a centre where the stem is planted,
And each still equidistant from the other;
As if a thread of gossamer were drawn
Down from each leaf, and fastened with a pin.
Now if from these five points a line be traced
To each alternate point, we shall obtain
The Pentagram, or Solomon's Pentangle,
A charm against all witchcraft, and a sign,
Which on the banner of Antiochus
Drove back the fierce barbarians of the North,
Demons esteemed, and gave the Syrian King
The sacred name of Soter, or of Savior.
Thus Nature works mysteriously with man;
And from the Eternal One, as from a centre,
All things proceed, in fire, air, earth, and water,
And all are subject to one law, which broken
Even in a single point, is broken in all;
Demons rush in, and chaos comes again.

By this will I compel the stubborn spirits,
That guard the treasures, hid in caverns deep
On Gerizim, by Uzzi the High-Priest,
The ark and holy vessels, to reveal
Their secret unto me, and to restore
These precious things to the Samaritans.
A mist is rising from the plain below me,
And as I look, the vapors shape themselves
Into strange figures, as if unawares
My lips had breathed the Tetragrammaton,
And from their graves, o'er all the battle-fields
Of Armageddon, the long-buried captains
Had started, with their thousands, and ten thousands,
And rushed together to renew their wars,
Powerless, and weaponless, and without a sound!
Wake, Helen, from thy sleep! The air grows cold;
Let us go down.

HELEN, *awaking.*

Oh, would I were at home!

SIMON.

Thou sayest that I usurp another's titles.
In youth I saw the Wise Men of the East,
Magalath and Pangalath and Saracen,
Who followed the bright star, but home returned
For fear of Herod by another way.
Oh shining worlds above me! in what deep
Recesses of your realms of mystery
Lies hidden now that star? and where are they
That brought the gifts of frankincense and myrrh?

HELEN.

The Nazarene still liveth.

SIMON.

We have heard
His name in many towns, but have not seen Him.
He flits before us; tarries not; is gone
When we approach, like something unsubstantial,
Made of the air, and fading into air.
He is at Nazareth, He is at Nain,
Or at the Lovely Village on the Lake,
Or sailing on its waters.

HELEN.

So say those
Who do not wish to find Him.

SIMON.

Can this be
The King of Israel, whom the Wise Men worshipped?
Or does He fear to meet me? It would seem so.
We should soon learn which of us twain usurps
The titles of the other, as thou sayest.

They go down.

The Second Passover: Part XI

Pontius Pilate

PILATE.

Wholly incomprehensible to me,
Vainglorious, obstinate, and given up
To unintelligible old traditions,
And proud, and self-conceited are these Jews!

Not long ago, I marched the legions down
From Cæsarea to their winter-quarters
Here in Jerusalem, with the effigies
Of Cæsar on their ensigns, and a tumult
Arose among these Jews, because their Law
Forbids the making of all images!
They threw themselves upon the ground with wild
Expostulations, bared their necks, and cried
That they would sooner die than have their Law
Infringed in any manner; as if Numa
Were not as great as Moses, and the Laws
Of the Twelve Tables as their Pentateuch!

And then, again, when I desired to span
Their valley with an aqueduct, and bring
A rushing river in to wash the city
And its inhabitants,—they all rebelled
As if they had been herds of unwashed swine!
Thousands and thousands of them got together
And raised so great a clamor round my doors,
That, fearing violent outbreak, I desisted,
And left them to their wallowing in the mire.

And now here comes the reverend Sanhedrim
Of lawyers, priests, and Scribes and Pharisees,
Like old and toothless mastiffs, that can bark,
But cannot bite, howling their accusations
Against a mild enthusiast, who hath preached
I know not what new doctrine, being King
Of some vague kingdom in the other world,
That hath no more to do with Rome and Cæsar
Than I have with the patriarch Abraham!
Finding this man to be a Galilean
I sent him straight to Herod, and I hope
That is the last of it; but if it be not,
I still have power to pardon and release him,
As is the custom at the Passover,
And so accommodate the matter smoothly,
Seeming to yield to them, yet saving him;
A prudent and sagacious policy
For Roman Governors in the Provinces.

Incomprehensible, fanatic people!
Ye have a God, who seemeth like yourselves
Incomprehensible, dwelling apart,
Majestic, cloud-encompassed, clothed in darkness!
One whom ye fear, but love not; yet ye have
No Goddesses to soften your stern lives,
And make you tender unto human weakness,
While we of Rome have everywhere around us
Our amiable divinities, that haunt
The woodlands, and the waters, and frequent
Our households, with their sweet and gracious presence!
I will go in, and while these Jews are wrangling,
Read my Ovidius on the Art of Love.

The Third Passover: Part VI

Aceldama

JUDAS ISCARIOT.

Lost! lost! forever lost! I have betrayed
The innocent blood! O God! if thou art love,
Why didst thou leave me naked to the tempter?
Why didst thou not commission thy swift lightning
To strike me dead? or why did I not perish
With those by Herod slain, the innocent children
Who went with playthings in their little hands
Into the darkness of the other world,
As if to bed? Or wherefore was I born,
If thou in thy foreknowledge didst perceive
All that I am, and all that I must be?
I know I am not generous, am not gentle,
Like other men; but I have tried to be,
And I have failed. I thought by following Him
I should grow like Him; but the unclean spirit
That from my childhood up hath tortured me
Hath been too cunning and too strong for me.
Am I to blame for this? Am I to blame
Because I cannot love, and ne'er have known
The love of woman or the love of children?
It is a curse and a fatality,
A mark, that hath been set upon my forehead,

That none shall slay me, for it were a mercy
That I were dead, or never had been born.

Too late! too late! I shall not see Him more
Among the living. That sweet, patient face
Will never more rebuke me, nor those lips
Repeat the words: One of you shall betray me!
It stung me into madness. How I loved,
Yet hated Him! But in the other world!
I will be there before Him, and will wait
Until He comes, and fall down on my knees
And kiss his feet, imploring pardon, pardon!

I heard Him say: All sins shall be forgiven,
Except the sin against the Holy Ghost.
That shall not be forgiven in this world,
Nor in the world to come. Is that my sin?
Have I offended so there is no hope
Here nor hereafter? That I soon shall know.
O God, have mercy! Christ have mercy on me!
Throws himself headlong from the cliff.

The Third Passover: Part IX

from

The Golden Legend

A Covered Bridge at Lucerne.

PRINCE HENRY.

God's blessing on the architects who build
The bridges o'er swift rivers and abysses
Before impassable to human feet,
No less than on the builders of cathedrals,
Whose massive walls are bridges thrown across
The dark and terrible abyss of Death.
Well has the name of Pontifex been given
Unto the Church's head, as the chief builder
And architect of the invisible bridge
That leads from earth to heaven.

ELSIE.

How dark it grows!
What are these paintings on the walls around us?

PRINCE HENRY.

The Dance Macaber!

ELSIE.

What?

PRINCE HENRY.

The Dance of Death!
All that go to and fro must look upon it,
Mindful of what they shall be, while beneath,
Among the wooden piles, the turbulent river
Rushes, impetuous as the river of life,
With dimpling eddies, ever green and bright,
Save where the shadow of this bridge falls on it.

ELSIE.

Oh yes! I see it now!

PRINCE HENRY.

The grim musician
Leads all men through the mazes of that dance,
To different sounds in different measures moving;
Sometimes he plays a lute, sometimes a drum,
To tempt or terrify.

ELSIE.

What is this picture?

PRINCE HENRY.

It is a young man singing to a nun,
Who kneels at her devotions, but in kneeling
Turns round to look at him; and Death, meanwhile,
Is putting out the candles on the altar!

ELSIE.

Ah, what a pity 't is that she should listen
Unto such songs, when in her orisons
She might have heard in heaven the angels singing!

PRINCE HENRY.

Here he has stolen a jester's cap and bells,
And dances with the Queen.

ELSIE.

A foolish jest!

PRINCE HENRY.

And here the heart of the new-wedded wife,
Coming from church with her beloved lord,
He startles with the rattle of his drum.

ELSIE.

Ah, that is sad! And yet perhaps 't is best
That she should die, with all the sunshine on her,
And all the benedictions of the morning,
Before this affluence of golden light
Shall fade into a cold and clouded gray,
Then into darkness!

PRINCE HENRY.

Under it is written,
"Nothing but death shall separate thee and me!"

ELSIE.

And what is this, that follows close upon it?

PRINCE HENRY.

Death, playing on a dulcimer. Behind him,
A poor old woman, with a rosary,
Follows the sound, and seems to wish her feet
Were swifter to o'ertake him. Underneath,
The inscription reads, "Better is Death than Life."

ELSIE.

Better is Death than Life! Ah yes! to thousands
Death plays upon a dulcimer, and sings
That song of consolation, till the air
Rings with it, and they cannot choose but follow
Whither he leads. And not the old alone,
But the young also hear it, and are still.

PRINCE HENRY.

Yes, in their sadder moments. 'T is the sound
Of their own hearts they hear, half full of tears,
Which are like crystal cups, half filled with water,
Responding to the pressure of a finger
With music sweet and low and melancholy.
Let us go forward, and no longer stay
In this great picture-gallery of Death!
I hate it! ay, the very thought of it!

ELSIE.

Why is it hateful to you?

PRINCE HENRY.

For the reason
That life, and all that speaks of life, is lovely,
And death, and all that speaks of death, is hateful.

ELSIE.

The grave itself is but a covered bridge,
Leading from light to light, through a brief darkness!

PRINCE HENRY, *emerging from the bridge.*

I breathe again more freely! Ah, how pleasant
To come once more into the light of day,
Out of that shadow of death! To hear again
The hoof-beats of our horses on firm ground,
And not upon those hollow planks, resounding
With a sepulchral echo, like the clods
On coffins in a churchyard! Yonder lies
The Lake of the Four Forest-Towns, apparelled
In light, and lingering, like a village maiden,
Hid in the bosom of her native mountains,
Then pouring all her life into another's,
Changing her name and being! Overhead,
Shaking his cloudy tresses loose in air,
Rises Pilatus, with his windy pines.

They pass on.

THE DEVIL'S BRIDGE.

PRINCE HENRY *and* ELSIE *crossing with attendants.*

GUIDE.

This bridge is called the Devil's Bridge.
With a single arch, from ridge to ridge,
It leaps across the terrible chasm
Yawning beneath us, black and deep,
As if, in some convulsive spasm,
The summits of the hills had cracked,
And made a road for the cataract
That raves and rages down the steep!

LUCIFER, *under the bridge.*

Ha! ha!

GUIDE.

Never any bridge but this
Could stand across the wild abyss;

All the rest, of wood or stone,
By the Devil's hand were overthrown.
He toppled crags from the precipice,
And whatsoe'er was built by day
In the night was swept away;
None could stand but this alone.

LUCIFER, *under the bridge.*

Ha! ha!

GUIDE.

I showed you in the valley a bowlder
Marked with the imprint of his shoulder;
As he was bearing it up this way,
A peasant, passing, cried, "Herr Jé!"
And the Devil dropped it in his fright,
And vanished suddenly out of sight!

LUCIFER, *under the bridge*

Ha! ha!

GUIDE.

Abbot Giraldus of Einsiedel,
For pilgrims on their way to Rome,
Built this at last, with a single arch,
Under which, on its endless march,
Runs the river, white with foam,
Like a thread through the eye of a needle.
And the Devil promised to let it stand,
Under compact and condition
That the first living thing which crossed
Should be surrendered into his hand,
And be beyond redemption lost.

LUCIFER, *under the bridge.*

Ha! ha! perdition!

GUIDE.

At length, the bridge being all completed,
The Abbot, standing at its head,
Threw across it a loaf of bread,
Which a hungry dog sprang after,
And the rocks reëchoed with the peals of laughter
To see the Devil thus defeated!

They pass on.

LUCIFER, *under the bridge.*

Ha! ha! defeated!
For journeys and for crimes like this
I let the bridge stand o'er the abyss!

THE ST. GOTHARD PASS.

PRINCE HENRY.

This is the highest point. Two ways the rivers
Leap down to different seas, and as they roll
Grow deep and still, and their majestic presence
Becomes a benefaction to the towns
They visit, wandering silently among them,
Like patriarchs old among their shining tents.

ELSIE.

How bleak and bare it is! Nothing but mosses
Grow on these rocks.

PRINCE HENRY.

Yet are they not forgotten.
Beneficent Nature sends the mists to feed them.

ELSIE.

See yonder little cloud, that, borne aloft
So tenderly by the wind, floats fast away
Over the snowy peaks! It seems to me
The body of St. Catherine, borne by angels!

PRINCE HENRY.

Thou art St. Catherine, and invisible angels
Bear thee across these chasms and precipices,
Lest thou shouldst dash thy feet against a stone!

ELSIE.

Would I were borne unto my grave, as she was,
Upon angelic shoulders! Even now
I seem uplifted by them, light as air!
What sound is that?

PRINCE HENRY.

The tumbling avalanches!

ELSIE.

How awful, yet how beautiful!

PRINCE HENRY.

These are
The voices of the mountains! Thus they ope
Their snowy lips, and speak unto each other,
In the primeval language, lost to man.

ELSIE.

What land is this that spreads itself beneath us?

PRINCE HENRY.

Italy! Italy!

ELSIE.

Land of the Madonna!
How beautiful it is! It seems a garden
Of Paradise!

PRINCE HENRY.

Nay, of Gethsemane
To thee and me, of passion and of prayer!
Yet once of Paradise. Long years ago
I wandered as a youth among its bowers,
And never from my heart has faded quite
Its memory, that, like a summer sunset,
Encircles with a ring of purple light
All the horizon of my youth.

GUIDE.

O friends!
The days are short, the way before us long;
We must not linger, if we think to reach
The inn at Belinzona before vespers!

They pass on.

from Part V

The New England Tragedies

JOHN ENDICOTT

DRAMATIS PERSONÆ.

JOHN ENDICOTT	*Governor.*
JOHN ENDICOTT	*His son.*
RICHARD BELLINGHAM	*Deputy Governor.*
JOHN NORTON	*Minister of the Gospel.*
EDWARD BUTTER	*Treasurer.*
WALTER MERRY	*Tithing-man.*
NICHOLAS UPSALL	*An old citizen.*
SAMUEL COLE	*Landlord of the Three Mariners.*
SIMON KEMPTHORN RALPH GOLDSMITH	*Sea-Captains.*
WENLOCK CHRISTISON EDITH, *his daughter* EDWARD WHARTON	*Quakers.*

Assistants, Halberdiers, Marshal, etc.
The Scene is in Boston in the year 1665.

PROLOGUE.

To-night we strive to read, as we may best,
This city, like an ancient palimpsest;
And bring to light, upon the blotted page,
The mournful record of an earlier age,
That, pale and half effaced, lies hidden away
Beneath the fresher writing of to-day.

Rise, then, O buried city that hast been;
Rise up, rebuilded in the painted scene,
And let our curious eyes behold once more
The pointed gable and the pent-house door,
The Meeting-house with leaden-latticed panes,
The narrow thoroughfares, the crooked lanes!

Rise, too, ye shapes and shadows of the Past,
Rise from your long-forgotten graves at last;
Let us behold your faces, let us hear
The words ye uttered in those days of fear!
Revisit your familiar haunts again,—
The scenes of triumph, and the scenes of pain,

And leave the footprints of your bleeding feet
Once more upon the pavement of the street!

Nor let the Historian blame the Poet here,
If he perchance misdate the day or year,
And group events together, by his art,
That in the Chronicles lie far apart;
For as the double stars, though sundered far,
Seem to the naked eye a single star,
So facts of history, at a distance seen,
Into one common point of light convene.

"Why touch upon such themes?" perhaps some friend
May ask, incredulous; "and to what good end?
Why drag again into the light of day
The errors of an age long passed away?"
I answer: "For the lesson that they teach:
The tolerance of opinion and of speech.
Hope, Faith, and Charity remain,—these three;
And greatest of them all is Charity."

Let us remember, if these words be true,
That unto all men Charity is due;
Give what we ask; and pity, while we blame,
Lest we become copartners in the shame,
Lest we condemn, and yet ourselves partake,
And persecute the dead for conscience' sake.

Therefore it is the author seeks and strives
To represent the dead as in their lives,
And lets at times his characters unfold
Their thoughts in their own language, strong and bold;
He only asks of you to do the like;
To hear him first, and, if you will, then strike.

ACT I.

SCENE I.—*Sunday afternoon. The interior of the Meeting-house. On the pulpit, an hour-glass; below, a box for contributions.* JOHN NORTON *in the pulpit.* GOVERNOR ENDICOTT *in a canopied seat, attended by four halberdiers. The congregation singing.*

The Lord descended from above,
  And bowed the heavens high;
And underneath his feet He cast
  The darkness of the sky.

On Cherubim and Seraphim
  Right royally He rode,
And on the wings of mighty winds
  Came flying all abroad.

NORTON (*rising and turning the hour-glass on the pulpit*).
I heard a great voice from the temple saying
Unto the Seven Angels, Go your ways;
Pour out the vials of the wrath of God
Upon the earth. And the First Angel went
And poured his vial on the earth; and straight
There fell a noisome and a grievous sore
On them which had the birth-mark of the Beast,
And them which worshipped and adored his image.
On us hath fallen this grievous pestilence.
There is a sense of terror in the air;
And apparitions of things horrible
Are seen by many. From the sky above us
The stars fall; and beneath us the earth quakes!
The sound of drums at midnight from afar,
The sound of horsemen riding to and fro,
As if the gates of the invisible world
Were opened, and the dead came forth to warn us,—
All these are omens of some dire disaster
Impending over us, and soon to fall.
Moreover, in the language of the Prophet,
Death is again come up into our windows,
To cut off little children from without,
And young men from the streets. And in the midst
Of all these supernatural threats and warnings
Doth Heresy uplift its horrid head;
A vision of Sin more awful and appalling
Than any phantasm, ghost, or apparition,
As arguing and portending some enlargement
Of the mysterious Power of Darkness!

EDITH, *barefooted, and clad in sackcloth, with her hair hanging loose upon her shoulders, walks slowly up the aisle, followed by* WHARTON *and other Quakers. The congregation starts up in confusion.*

EDITH (*to* NORTON, *raising her hand*).

Peace!

NORTON.

Anathema maranatha! The Lord cometh!

EDITH.

Yea, verily He cometh, and shall judge
The shepherds of Israel who do feed themselves,
And leave their flocks to eat what they have trodden
Beneath their feet.

NORTON.

Be silent, babbling woman!
St. Paul commands all women to keep silence
Within the churches.

EDITH.

Yet the women prayed
And prophesied at Corinth in his day;
And, among those on whom the fiery tongues
Of Pentecost descended, some were women!

NORTON.

The Elders of the Churches, by our law,
Alone have power to open the doors of speech
And silence in the Assembly. I command you!

EDITH.

The law of God is greater than your laws!
Ye build your church with blood, your town with crime;
The heads thereof give judgment for reward;
The priests thereof teach only for their hire;
Your laws condemn the innocent to death;
And against this I bear my testimony!

NORTON.

What testimony?

EDITH.

That of the Holy Spirit,
Which, as your Calvin says, surpasseth reason.

NORTON.

The laborer is worthy of his hire.

EDITH.

Yet our great Master did not teach for hire,
And the Apostles without purse or scrip
Went forth to do his work. Behold this box
Beneath thy pulpit. Is it for the poor?
Thou canst not answer. It is for the Priest;
And against this I bear my testimony.

NORTON.

Away with all these Heretics and Quakers!
Quakers, forsooth! Because a quaking fell
On Daniel, at beholding of the Vision,
Must ye needs shake and quake? Because Isaiah
Went stripped and barefoot, must ye wail and howl?
Must ye go stripped and naked? must ye make
A wailing like the dragons, and a mourning
As of the owls? Ye verify the adage
That Satan is God's ape! Away with them!

Tumult. The Quakers are driven out with violence, EDITH *following slowly. The congregation retires in confusion.*

Thus freely do the Reprobates commit
Such measure of iniquity as fits them
For the intended measure of God's wrath,
And even in violating God's commands
Are they fulfilling the divine decree!
The will of man is but an instrument
Disposed and predetermined to its action
According unto the decree of God,
Being as much subordinate thereto
As is the axe unto the hewer's hand!

He descends from the pulpit, and joins GOVERNOR ENDICOTT, *who comes forward to meet him.*

The omens and the wonders of the time,
Famine, and fire, and shipwreck, and disease,
The blast of corn, the death of our young men,
Our sufferings in all precious, pleasant things,
Are manifestations of the wrath divine,
Signs of God's controversy with New England.
These emissaries of the Evil One,
These servants and ambassadors of Satan,

Are but commissioned executioners
Of God's vindictive and deserved displeasure.
We must receive them as the Roman Bishop
Once received Attila, saying, I rejoice
You have come safe, whom I esteem to be
The scourge of God, sent to chastise his people.
This very heresy, perchance, may serve
The purposes of God to some good end.
With you I leave it; but do not neglect
The holy tactics of the civil sword.

ENDICOTT.

And what more can be done?

NORTON.

The hand that cut
The Red Cross from the colors of the king
Can cut the red heart from this heresy.
Fear not. All blasphemies immediate
And heresies turbulent must be suppressed
By civil power.

ENDICOTT.

But in what way suppressed?

NORTON.

The Book of Deuteronomy declares
That if thy son, thy daughter, or thy wife,
Ay, or the friend which is as thine own soul,
Entice thee secretly, and say to thee,
Let us serve other gods, then shall thine eye
Not pity him, but thou shalt surely kill him,
And thine own hand shall be the first upon him
To slay him.

ENDICOTT.

Four already have been slain;
And others banished upon pain of death.
But they come back again to meet their doom,
Bringing the linen for their winding-sheets.
We must not go too far. In truth, I shrink
From shedding of more blood. The people murmur
At our severity.

NORTON.

Then let them murmur!
Truth is relentless; justice never wavers;
The greatest firmness is the greatest mercy;
The noble order of the Magistracy
Cometh immediately from God, and yet
This noble order of the Magistracy
Is by these Heretics despised and outraged.

ENDICOTT.

To-night they sleep in prison. If they die,
They cannot say that we have caused their death.
We do but guard the passage, with the sword
Pointed towards them; if they dash upon it,
Their blood will be on their own heads, not ours.

NORTON.

Enough. I ask no more. My predecessor
Coped only with the milder heresies
Of Antinomians and of Anabaptists.
He was not born to wrestle with these fiends.
Chrysostom in his pulpit; Augustine
In disputation; Timothy in his house!
The lantern of St. Botolph's ceased to burn
When from the portals of that church he came
To be a burning and a shining light
Here in the wilderness. And, as he lay
On his death-bed, he saw me in a vision
Ride on a snow-white horse into this town.
His vision was prophetic; thus I came,
A terror to the impenitent, and Death
On the pale horse of the Apocalypse
To all the accursed race of Heretics!

[*Exeunt.*

SCENE II.—*A street. On one side,* NICHOLAS UPSALL'S *house; on the other,* WALTER MERRY'S, *with a flock of pigeons on the roof.* UPSALL *seated in the porch of his house.*

UPSALL.

O day of rest! How beautiful, how fair,
How welcome to the weary and the old!
Day of the Lord! and truce to earthly cares!

Day of the Lord, as all our days should be!
Ah, why will man by his austerities
Shut out the blessed sunshine and the light,
And make of thee a dungeon of despair!

WALTER MERRY (*entering and looking round him*).

All silent as a graveyard! No one stirring;
No football in the street, no sound of voices!
By righteous punishment and perseverance,
And perseverance in that punishment,
At last I 've brought this contumacious town
To strict observance of the Sabbath day.
Those wanton gospellers, the pigeons yonder,
Are now the only Sabbath-breakers left.
I cannot put them down. As if to taunt me,
They gather every Sabbath afternoon
In noisy congregation on my roof,
Billing and cooing. Whir! take that, ye Quakers.

Throws a stone at the pigeons. Sees UPSALL.

Ah! Master Nicholas!

UPSALL.

Good afternoon,
Dear neighbor Walter.

MERRY.

Master Nicholas,
You have to-day withdrawn yourself from meeting.

UPSALL.

Yea, I have chosen rather to worship God
Sitting in silence here at my own door.

MERRY.

Worship the Devil! You this day have broken
Three of our strictest laws. First, by abstaining
From public worship. Secondly, by walking
Profanely on the Sabbath.

UPSALL.

Not one step.
I have been sitting still here, seeing the pigeons
Feed in the street and fly about the roofs.

MERRY.

You have been in the street with other intent
Than going to and from the Meeting-house.

And, thirdly, you are harboring Quakers here.
I am amazed!

UPSALL.

Men sometimes, it is said,
Entertain angels unawares.

MERRY.

Nice angels!
Angels in broad-brimmed hats and russet cloaks,
The color of the Devil's nutting-bag! They came
Into the Meeting-house this afternoon
More in the shape of devils than of angels.
The women screamed and fainted; and the boys
Made such an uproar in the gallery
I could not keep them quiet.

UPSALL.

Neighbor Walter,
Your persecution is of no avail.

MERRY.

'T is prosecution, as the Governor says,
Not persecution.

UPSALL.

Well, your prosecution;
Your hangings do no good.

MERRY.

The reason is,
We do not hang enough. But, mark my words,
We 'll scour them; yea, I warrant ye, we 'll scour them!
And now go in and entertain your angels,
And don't be seen here in the street again
Till after sundown!—There they are again!

Exit UPSALL. MERRY *throws another stone at the pigeons, and then goes into his house.*

SCENE III.—*A room in* UPSALL'S *house. Night.* EDITH, WHARTON, *and other Quakers seated at a table.* UPSALL *seated near them. Several books on the table.*

WHARTON.

William and Marmaduke, our martyred brothers,
Sleep in untimely graves, if aught untimely
Can find place in the providence of God,

Where nothing comes too early or too late.
I saw their noble death. They to the scaffold
Walked hand in hand. Two hundred armed men
And many horsemen guarded them, for fear
Of rescue by the crowd, whose hearts were stirred.

EDITH.

O holy martyrs!

WHARTON.

When they tried to speak,
Their voices by the roll of drums were drowned.
When they were dead they still looked fresh and fair,
The terror of death was not upon their faces.
Our sister Mary, likewise, the meek woman,
Has passed through martyrdom to her reward;
Exclaiming, as they led her to her death,
"These many days I 've been in Paradise."
And, when she died, Priest Wilson threw the hangman
His handkerchief, to cover the pale face
He dared not look upon.

EDITH.

As persecuted,
Yet not forsaken; as unknown, yet known;
As dying, and behold we are alive;
As sorrowful, and yet rejoicing alway;
As having nothing, yet possessing all!

WHARTON.

And Leddra, too, is dead. But from his prison,
The day before his death, he sent these words
Unto the little flock of Christ: "Whatever
May come upon the followers of the Light,—
Distress, affliction, famine, nakedness,
Or perils in the city or the sea,
Or persecution, or even death itself,—
I am persuaded that God's armor of Light,
As it is loved and lived in, will preserve you.
Yea, death itself; through which you will find entrance
Into the pleasant pastures of the fold,
Where you shall feed forever as the herds
That roam at large in the low valleys of Achor.
And as the flowing of the ocean fills

Each creek and branch thereof, and then retires,
Leaving behind a sweet and wholesome savor;
So doth the virtue and the life of God
Flow evermore into the hearts of those
Whom He hath made partakers of his nature;
And, when it but withdraws itself a little,
Leaves a sweet savor after it, that many
Can say they are made clean by every word
That He hath spoken to them in their silence."

EDITH (*rising, and breaking into a kind of chant*).

Truly we do but grope here in the dark,
Near the partition-wall of Life and Death,
At every moment dreading or desiring
To lay our hands upon the unseen door!
Let us, then, labor for an inward stillness, —
An inward stillness and an inward healing;
That perfect silence where the lips and heart
Are still, and we no longer entertain
Our own imperfect thoughts and vain opinions,
But God alone speaks in us, and we wait
In singleness of heart, that we may know
His will, and in the silence of our spirits,
That we may do His will, and do that only!

A long pause, interrupted by the sound of a drum approaching, then shouts in the street, and a loud knocking at the door.

MARSHAL.

Within there! Open the door!

MERRY.

Will no one answer?

MARSHAL.

In the King's name! Within there!

MERRY.

Open the door!

UPSALL (*from the window*).

It is not barred. Come in. Nothing prevents you.
The poor man's door is ever on the latch.
He needs no bolt nor bar to shut out thieves;
He fears no enemies, and has no friends
Importunate enough to need a key.

Enter JOHN ENDICOTT, *the* MARSHAL, MERRY, *and a crowd. Seeing the Quakers silent and unmoved, they pause, awe-struck.* ENDICOTT *opposite* EDITH.

MARSHAL.

In the King's name do I arrest you all!
Away with them to prison. Master Upsall,
You are again discovered harboring here
These ranters and disturbers of the peace.
You know the law.

UPSALL.

I know it, and am ready
To suffer yet again its penalties.

EDITH (*to* ENDICOTT).

Why dost thou persecute me, Saul of Tarsus?

ACT II.

SCENE I.—JOHN ENDICOTT'S *room. Early morning.*

JOHN ENDICOTT.

"Why dost thou persecute me, Saul of Tarsus?"
All night these words were ringing in mine ears!
A sorrowful sweet face; a look that pierced me
With meek reproach; a voice of resignation
That had a life of suffering in its tone;
And that was all! And yet I could not sleep,
Or, when I slept, I dreamed that awful dream!
I stood beneath the elm-tree on the Common
On which the Quakers have been hanged, and heard
A voice, not hers, that cried amid the darkness,
"This is Aceldama, the field of blood!
I will have mercy, and not sacrifice!"

Opens the window, and looks out.

The sun is up already; and my heart
Sickens and sinks within me when I think
How many tragedies will be enacted
Before his setting. As the earth rolls round,
It seems to me a huge Ixion's wheel,
Upon whose whirling spokes we are bound fast,
And must go with it! Ah, how bright the sun
Strikes on the sea and on the masts of vessels,
That are uplifted in the morning air,

Like crosses of some peaceable crusade!
It makes me long to sail for lands unknown,
No matter whither! Under me, in shadow,
Gloomy and narrow lies the little town,
Still sleeping, but to wake and toil awhile,
Then sleep again. How dismal looks the prison,
How grim and sombre in the sunless street,—
The prison where she sleeps, or wakes and waits
For what I dare not think of,—death, perhaps!
A word that has been said may be unsaid:
It is but air. But when a deed is done
It cannot be undone, nor can our thoughts
Reach out to all the mischiefs that may follow.
'T is time for morning prayers. I will go down.
My father, though severe, is kind and just;
And when his heart is tender with devotion,—
When from his lips have fallen the words, "Forgive us
As we forgive,"—then will I intercede
For these poor people, and perhaps may save them.

[*Exit.*

SCENE II.—*Dock Square. On one side, the tavern of the Three Mariners. In the background, a quaint building with gables; and, beyond it, wharves and shipping.* CAPTAIN KEMPTHORN *and others seated at a table before the door.* SAMUEL COLE *standing near them.*

KEMPTHORN.

Come, drink about! Remember Parson Melham,
And bless the man who first invented flip!

They drink.

COLE.

Pray, Master Kempthorn, where were you last night?

KEMPTHORN.

On board the Swallow, Simon Kempthorn, master,
Up for Barbadoes, and the Windward Islands.

COLE.

The town was in a tumult.

KEMPTHORN.

And for what?

COLE.

Your Quakers were arrested.

KEMPTHORN.

How my Quakers?

COLE.

Those you brought in your vessel from Barbadoes.
They made an uproar in the Meeting-house
Yesterday, and they 're now in prison for it.
I owe you little thanks for bringing them
To the Three Mariners.

KEMPTHORN.

They have not harmed you.
I tell you, Goodman Cole, that Quaker girl
Is precious as a sea-bream's eye. I tell you
It was a lucky day when first she set
Her little foot upon the Swallow's deck,
Bringing good luck, fair winds, and pleasant weather.

COLE.

I am a law-abiding citizen;
I have a seat in the new Meeting-house,
A cow-right on the Common; and, besides,
Am corporal in the Great Artillery.
I rid me of the vagabonds at once.

KEMPTHORN.

Why should you not have Quakers at your tavern
If you have fiddlers?

COLE.

Never! never! never!
If you want fiddling you must go elsewhere,
To the Green Dragon and the Admiral Vernon,
And other such disreputable places.
But the Three Mariners is an orderly house,
Most orderly, quiet, and respectable.
Lord Leigh said he could be as quiet here
As at the Governor's. And have I not
King Charles's Twelve Good Rules, all framed and glazed,
Hanging in my best parlor?

KEMPTHORN.

Here's a health
To good King Charles. Will you not drink the King?
Then drink confusion to old Parson Palmer.

COLE.

And who is Parson Palmer? I don't know him.

KEMPTHORN.

He had his cellar underneath his pulpit,
And so preached o'er his liquor, just as you do.

A drum within.

COLE.

Here comes the Marshal.

MERRY (*within*).

Make room for the Marshal.

KEMPTHORN.

How pompous and imposing he appears!
His great buff doublet bellying like a mainsail,
And all his streamers fluttering in the wind.
What holds he in his hand?

COLE.

A Proclamation.

Enter the MARSHAL, *with a proclamation; and* MERRY, *with a halberd. They are preceded by a drummer, and followed by the hangman, with an armful of books, and a crowd of people, among whom are* UPSALL *and* JOHN ENDICOTT. *A pile is made of the books.*

MERRY.

Silence, the drum! Good citizens, attend
To the new laws enacted by the Court.

MARSHAL (*reads*).

"Whereas a cursed sect of Heretics
Has lately risen, commonly called Quakers,
Who take upon themselves to be commissioned
Immediately of God, and furthermore
Infallibly assisted by the Spirit
To write and utter blasphemous opinions,
Despising Government and the order of God
In Church and Commonwealth, and speaking evil
Of Dignities, reproaching and reviling
The Magistrates and Ministers, and seeking
To turn the people from their faith, and thus
Gain proselytes to their pernicious ways;—
This Court, considering the premises,
And to prevent like mischief as is wrought

By their means in our land, doth hereby order,
That whatsoever master or commander
Of any ship, bark, pink, or catch shall bring
To any roadstead, harbor, creek, or cove
Within this Jurisdiction any Quakers,
Or other blasphemous Heretics, shall pay
Unto the Treasurer of the Commonwealth
One hundred pounds, and for default thereof
Be put in prison, and continue there
Till the said sum be satisfied and paid."

COLE.

Now, Simon Kempthorn, what say you to that?

KEMPTHORN.

I pray you, Cole, lend me a hundred pounds!

MARSHAL (*reads*).

"If any one within this Jurisdiction
Shall henceforth entertain, or shall conceal
Quakers, or other blasphemous Heretics,
Knowing them so to be, every such person
Shall forfeit to the country forty shillings
For each hour's entertainment or concealment,
And shall be sent to prison, as aforesaid,
Until the forfeiture be wholly paid."

Murmurs in the crowd.

KEMPTHORN.

Now, Goodman Cole, I think your turn has come!

COLE.

Knowing them so to be!

KEMPTHORN.

At forty shillings
The hour, your fine will be some forty pounds!

COLE.

Knowing them so to be! That is the law.

MARSHAL (*reads*).

"And it is further ordered and enacted,
If any Quaker or Quakers shall presume
To come henceforth into this Jurisdiction,
Every male Quaker for the first offence
Shall have one ear cut off; and shall be kept
At labor in the Workhouse, till such time

As he be sent away at his own charge.
And for the repetition of the offence
Shall have his other ear cut off, and then
Be branded in the palm of his right hand.
And every woman Quaker shall be whipt
Severely in three towns; and every Quaker,
Or he or she, that shall for a third time
Herein again offend, shall have their tongues
Bored through with a hot iron, and shall be
Sentenced to Banishment on pain of Death."

Loud murmurs. The voice of CHRISTISON *in the crowd.*

O patience of the Lord! How long, how long,
Ere thou avenge the blood of Thine Elect?

MERRY.

Silence, there, silence! Do not break the peace!

MARSHAL (*reads*).

"Every inhabitant of this Jurisdiction
Who shall defend the horrible opinions
Of Quakers, by denying due respect
To equals and superiors, and withdrawing
From Church Assemblies, and thereby approving
The abusive and destructive practices
Of this accursed sect, in opposition
To all the orthodox received opinions
Of godly men, shall be forthwith committed
Unto close prison for one month; and then
Refusing to retract and to reform
The opinions as aforesaid, he shall be
Sentenced to Banishment on pain of Death.
By the Court. Edward Rawson, Secretary."
Now, hangman, do your duty. Burn those books.

Loud murmurs in the crowd. The pile of books is lighted.

UPSALL.

I testify against these cruel laws!
Forerunners are they of some judgment on us;
And, in the love and tenderness I bear
Unto this town and people, I beseech you,
O Magistrates, take heed, lest ye be found
As fighters against God!

JOHN ENDICOTT (*taking* UPSALL'S *hand*).

Upsall, I thank you
For speaking words such as some younger man,
I, or another, should have said before you.
Such laws as these are cruel and oppressive;
A blot on this fair town, and a disgrace
To any Christian people.

MERRY (*aside, listening behind them*).

Here 's sedition!
I never thought that any good would come
Of this young popinjay, with his long hair
And his great boots, fit only for the Russians
Or barbarous Indians, as his father says!

THE VOICE.

Woe to the bloody town! And rightfully
Men call it the Lost Town! The blood of Abel
Cries from the ground, and at the final judgment
The Lord will say, "Cain, Cain! where is thy brother?"

MERRY.

Silence there in the crowd!

UPSALL (*aside*).

'T is Christison!

THE VOICE.

O foolish people, ye that think to burn
And to consume the truth of God, I tell you
That every flame is a loud tongue of fire
To publish it abroad to all the world
Louder than tongues of men!

KEMPTHORN (*springing to his feet*).

Well said, my hearty!
There 's a brave fellow! There 's a man of pluck!
A man who 's not afraid to say his say,
Though a whole town 's against him. Rain, rain, rain,
Bones of St. Botolph, and put out this fire!

The drum beats. Exeunt all but MERRY, KEMPTHORN, *and* COLE.

MERRY.

And now that matter 's ended, Goodman Cole,
Fetch me a mug of ale, your strongest ale.

KEMPTHORN (*sitting down*).

And me another mug of flip; and put
Two gills of brandy in it.

[*Exit* COLE.

MERRY.

No; no more.
Not a drop more, I say. You 've had enough.

KEMPTHORN.

And who are you, sir?

MERRY.

I 'm a Tithing-man,
And Merry is my name.

KEMPTHORN.

A merry name!
I like it; and I 'll drink your merry health
Till all is blue.

MERRY.

And then you will be clapped
Into the stocks, with the red letter D
Hung round about your neck for drunkenness.
You 're a free-drinker,—yes, and a free-thinker!

KEMPTHORN.

And you are Andrew Merry, or Merry Andrew.

MERRY.

My name is Walter Merry, and not Andrew.

KEMPTHORN.

Andrew or Walter, you 're a merry fellow;
I 'll swear to that.

MERRY.

No swearing, let me tell you.
The other day one Shorthose had his tongue
Put into a cleft stick for profane swearing.

COLE *brings the ale.*

KEMPTHORN.

Well, where 's my flip? As sure as my name 's Kempthorn —

MERRY.

Is your name Kempthorn?

KEMPTHORN.

That 's the name I go by.

MERRY.

What, Captain Simon Kempthorn of the Swallow?

KEMPTHORN.

No other.

MERRY (*touching him on the shoulder*).

Then you 're wanted. I arrest you
In the King's name.

KEMPTHORN.

And where 's your warrant?

MERRY (*unfolding a paper, and reading*).

Here.

Listen to me. "Hereby you are required,
In the King's name, to apprehend the body
Of Simon Kempthorn, mariner, and him
Safely to bring before me, there to answer
All such objections as are laid to him,
Touching the Quakers." Signed, John Endicott.

KEMPTHORN.

Has it the Governor's seal?

MERRY.

Ay, here it is.

KEMPTHORN.

Death's head and cross-bones. That 's a pirate's flag!

MERRY.

Beware how you revile the Magistrates;
You may be whipped for that.

KEMPTHORN.

Then mum 's the word.

Exeunt MERRY *and* KEMPTHORN.

COLE.

There 's mischief brewing! Sure, there 's mischief brewing!
I feel like Master Josselyn when he found
The hornet's nest, and thought it some strange fruit,
Until the seeds came out, and then he dropped it.

[*Exit.*

SCENE III.—*A room in the Governor's house. Enter* GOVERNOR ENDICOTT *and* MERRY.

ENDICOTT.

My son, you say?

MERRY.

Your Worship's eldest son.

ENDICOTT.

Speaking against the laws?

MERRY.

Ay, worshipful sir.

ENDICOTT.

And in the public market-place?

MERRY.

I saw him
With my own eyes, heard him with my own ears.

ENDICOTT.

Impossible!

MERRY.

He stood there in the crowd
With Nicholas Upsall, when the laws were read
To-day against the Quakers, and I heard him
Denounce and vilipend them as unjust,
And cruel, wicked, and abominable.

ENDICOTT.

Ungrateful son! O God! thou layest upon me
A burden heavier than I can bear!
Surely the power of Satan must be great
Upon the earth, if even the elect
Are thus deceived and fall away from grace!

MERRY.

Worshipful sir! I meant no harm —

ENDICOTT.

'T is well.
You 've done your duty, though you 've done it roughly,
And every word you 've uttered since you came
Has stabbed me to the heart!

MERRY.

I do beseech
Your Worship's pardon!

ENDICOTT.

He whom I have nurtured
And brought up in the reverence of the Lord!
The child of all my hopes and my affections!
He upon whom I leaned as a sure staff

For my old age! It is God's chastisement
For leaning upon any arm but His!

MERRY.

Your Worship!—

ENDICOTT.

And this comes from holding parley
With the delusions and deceits of Satan.
At once, forever, must they be crushed out,
Or all the land will reek with heresy!
Pray, have you any children?

MERRY.

No, not any.

ENDICOTT.

Thank God for that. He has delivered you
From a great care. Enough; my private griefs
Too long have kept me from the public service.

Exit MERRY. ENDICOTT *seats himself at the table and arranges his papers.*

The hour has come; and I am eager now
To sit in judgment on these Heretics.

A knock.

Come in. Who is it? (*Not looking up.*)

JOHN ENDICOTT.

It is I.

ENDICOTT (*restraining himself*).

Sit down!

JOHN ENDICOTT (*sitting down*).

I come to intercede for these poor people
Who are in prison, and await their trial.

ENDICOTT.

It is of them I wish to speak with you.
I have been angry with you, but 't is passed.
For when I hear your footsteps come or go,
See in your features your dead mother's face,
And in your voice detect some tone of hers,
All anger vanishes, and I remember
The days that are no more, and come no more,
When as a child you sat upon my knee,
And prattled of your playthings, and the games
You played among the pear trees in the orchard!

JOHN ENDICOTT.

Oh, let the memory of my noble mother
Plead with you to be mild and merciful!
For mercy more becomes a Magistrate
Than the vindictive wrath which men call justice!

ENDICOTT.

The sin of heresy is a deadly sin.
'T is like the falling of the snow, whose crystals
The traveller plays with, thoughtless of his danger,
Until he sees the air so full of light
That it is dark; and blindly staggering onward,
Lost, and bewildered, he sits down to rest;
There falls a pleasant drowsiness upon him,
And what he thinks is sleep, alas! is death.

JOHN ENDICOTT.

And yet who is there that has never doubted?
And doubting and believing, has not said,
"Lord, I believe; help thou my unbelief"?

ENDICOTT.

In the same way we trifle with our doubts,
Whose shining shapes are like the stars descending;
Until at last, bewildered and dismayed,
Blinded by that which seemed to give us light,
We sink to sleep, and find that it is death,

Rising.

Death to the soul through all eternity!
Alas that I should see you growing up
To man's estate, and in the admonition
And nurture of the Law, to find you now
Pleading for Heretics!

JOHN ENDICOTT (*rising*).

In the sight of God,
Perhaps all men are Heretics. Who dares
To say that he alone has found the truth?
We cannot always feel and think and act
As those who go before us. Had you done so,
You would not now be here.

ENDICOTT.

Have you forgotten
The doom of Heretics, and the fate of those

Who aid and comfort them? Have you forgotten
That in the market-place this very day
You trampled on the laws? What right have you,
An inexperienced and untravelled youth,
To sit in judgment here upon the acts
Of older men and wiser than yourself,
Thus stirring up sedition in the streets,
And making me a byword and a jest?

JOHN ENDICOTT.

Words of an inexperienced youth like me
Were powerless if the acts of older men
Went not before them. 'T is these laws themselves
Stir up sedition, not my judgment of them.

ENDICOTT.

Take heed, lest I be called, as Brutus was,
To be the judge of my own son! Begone!
When you are tired of feeding upon husks,
Return again to duty and submission,
But not till then.

JOHN ENDICOTT.

I hear and I obey!

[*Exit.*

ENDICOTT.

Oh happy, happy they who have no children!
He 's gone! I hear the hall door shut behind him.
It sends a dismal echo through my heart,
As if forever it had closed between us,
And I should look upon his face no more!
Oh, this will drag me down into my grave,—
To that eternal resting-place wherein
Man lieth down, and riseth not again!
Till the heavens be no more he shall not wake,
Nor be roused from his sleep; for Thou dost change
His countenance, and sendest him away!

[*Exit.*

ACT III.

SCENE I.—*The Court of Assistants.* ENDICOTT, BELLINGHAM, ATHERTON, *and other magistrates.* KEMPTHORN, MERRY, *and constables. Afterwards* WHARTON, EDITH, *and* CHRISTISON.

ENDICOTT.

Call Captain Simon Kempthorn.

MERRY.

Simon Kempthorn,
Come to the bar!

KEMPTHORN *comes forward.*

ENDICOTT.

You are accused of bringing
Into this Jurisdiction, from Barbadoes,
Some persons of that sort and sect of people
Known by the name of Quakers, and maintaining
Most dangerous and heretical opinions;
Purposely coming here to propagate
Their heresies and errors; bringing with them
And spreading sundry books here, which contain
Their doctrines most corrupt and blasphemous,
And contrary to the truth professed among us.
What say you to this charge?

KEMPTHORN.

I do acknowledge,
Among the passengers on board the Swallow
Were certain persons saying Thee and Thou.
They seemed a harmless people, mostways silent,
Particularly when they said their prayers.

ENDICOTT.

Harmless and silent as the pestilence!
You 'd better have brought the fever or the plague
Among us in your ship! Therefore, this Court,
For preservation of the Peace and Truth,
Hereby commands you speedily to transport,
Or cause to be transported speedily,
The aforesaid persons hence unto Barbadoes,
From whence they came; you paying all the charges
Of their imprisonment.

KEMPTHORN.

Worshipful sir,
No ship e'er prospered that has carried Quakers
Against their will! I knew a vessel once—

ENDICOTT.

And for the more effectual performance

Hereof you are to give security
In bonds amounting to one hundred pounds.
On your refusal, you will be committed
To prison till you do it.

KEMPTHORN.

But you see
I cannot do it. The law, sir, of Barbadoes
Forbids the landing Quakers on the island.

ENDICOTT.

Then you will be committed. Who comes next?

MERRY.

There is another charge against the Captain.

ENDICOTT.

What is it?

MERRY.

Profane swearing, please your Worship.
He cursed and swore from Dock Square to the Court-house.

ENDICOTT.

Then let him stand in the pillory for one hour.

[*Exit* KEMPTHORN *with constable.*

Who 's next?

MERRY.

The Quakers.

ENDICOTT.

Call them.

MERRY.

Edward Wharton,
Come to the bar!

WHARTON.

Yea, even to the bench.

ENDICOTT.

Take off your hat.

WHARTON.

My hat offendeth not.
If it offendeth any, let him take it;
For I shall not resist.

ENDICOTT.

Take off his hat.
Let him be fined ten shillings for contempt.

MERRY *takes off* WHARTON'S *hat.*

WHARTON.

What evil have I done?

ENDICOTT.

Your hair 's too long;
And in not putting off your hat to us
You 've disobeyed and broken that commandment
Which sayeth "Honor thy father and thy mother."

WHARTON.

John Endicott, thou art become too proud;
And lovest him who putteth off the hat,
And honoreth thee by bowing of the body,
And sayeth "Worshipful sir!" 'T is time for thee
To give such follies over, for thou mayest
Be drawing very near unto thy grave.

ENDICOTT.

Now, sirrah, leave your canting. Take the oath.

WHARTON.

Nay, sirrah me no sirrahs!

ENDICOTT.

Will you swear?

WHARTON.

Nay, I will not.

ENDICOTT.

You made a great disturbance
And uproar yesterday in the Meeting-house,
Having your hat on.

WHARTON.

I made no disturbance;
For peacefully I stood, like other people.
I spake no words; moved against none my hand;
But by the hair they haled me out, and dashed
Their books into my face.

ENDICOTT.

You, Edward Wharton,
On pain of death, depart this Jurisdiction
Within ten days. Such is your sentence. Go.

WHARTON.

John Endicott, it had been well for thee
If this day's doings thou hadst left undone.
But, banish me as far as thou hast power,

Beyond the guard and presence of my God
Thou canst not banish me!

ENDICOTT.

Depart the Court;
We have no time to listen to your babble.
Who 's next?

[*Exit* WHARTON.

MERRY.

This woman, for the same offence.

EDITH *comes forward.*

ENDICOTT.

What is your name?

EDITH.

'T is to the world unknown,
But written in the Book of Life.

ENDICOTT.

Take heed
It be not written in the Book of Death!
What is it?

EDITH.

Edith Christison.

ENDICOTT (*with eagerness*).

The daughter
Of Wenlock Christison?

EDITH.

I am his daughter.

ENDICOTT.

Your father hath given us trouble many times.
A bold man and a violent, who sets
At naught the authority of our Church and State,
And is in banishment on pain of death.
Where are you living?

EDITH.

In the Lord.

ENDICOTT.

Make answer
Without evasion. Where?

EDITH.

My outward being
Is in Barbadoes.

ENDICOTT.

Then why come you here?

EDITH.

I come upon an errand of the Lord.

ENDICOTT.

'T is not the business of the Lord you 're doing;
It is the Devil's. Will you take the oath?
Give her the Book.

MERRY *offers the book.*

EDITH.

You offer me this Book
To swear on; and it saith, "Swear not at all,
Neither by heaven, because it is God's Throne,
Nor by the earth, because it is his footstool!"
I dare not swear.

ENDICOTT.

You dare not? Yet you Quakers
Deny this Book of Holy Writ, the Bible,
To be the Word of God.

EDITH (*reverentially*).

Christ is the Word,
The everlasting oath of God. I dare not.

ENDICOTT.

You own yourself a Quaker,—do you not?

EDITH.

I own that in derision and reproach
I am so called.

ENDICOTT.

Then you deny the Scripture
To be the rule of life.

EDITH.

Yea, I believe
The Inner Light, and not the Written Word,
To be the rule of life.

ENDICOTT.

And you deny
That the Lord's Day is holy.

EDITH.

Every day
Is the Lord's Day. It runs through all our lives,

As through the pages of the Holy Bible,
"Thus saith the Lord."

ENDICOTT.

You are accused of making
An horrible disturbance, and affrighting
The people in the Meeting-house on Sunday.
What answer make you?

EDITH.

I do not deny
That I was present in your Steeple-house
On the First Day; but I made no disturbance.

ENDICOTT.

Why came you there?

EDITH.

Because the Lord commanded.
His word was in my heart, a burning fire
Shut up within me and consuming me,
And I was very weary with forbearing;
I could not stay.

ENDICOTT.

'T was not the Lord that sent you;
As an incarnate devil did you come!

EDITH.

On the First Day, when, seated in my chamber,
I heard the bells toll, calling you together,
The sound struck at my life, as once at his,
The holy man, our Founder, when he heard
The far-off bells toll in the Vale of Beavor.
It sounded like a market bell to call
The folk together, that the Priest might set
His wares to sale. And the Lord said within me,
"Thou must go cry aloud against that Idol,
And all the worshippers thereof." I went
Barefooted, clad in sackcloth, and I stood
And listened at the threshold; and I heard
The praying and the singing and the preaching,
Which were but outward forms, and without power.
Then rose a cry within me, and my heart
Was filled with admonitions and reproofs.
Remembering how the Prophets and Apostles

Denounced the covetous hirelings and diviners,
I entered in, and spake the words the Lord
Commanded me to speak. I could no less.

ENDICOTT.

Are you a Prophetess?

EDITH.

Is it not written,
"Upon my handmaidens will I pour out
My spirit, and they shall prophesy"?

ENDICOTT.

Enough;
For out of your own mouth are you condemned!
Need we hear further?

THE JUDGES.

We are satisfied.

ENDICOTT.

It is sufficient. Edith Christison,
The sentence of the Court is, that you be
Scourged in three towns, with forty stripes save one,
Then banished upon pain of death!

EDITH.

Your sentence
Is truly no more terrible to me
Than had you blown a feather into the air,
And, as it fell upon me, you had said,
"Take heed it hurt thee not!" God's will be done!

WENLOCK CHRISTISON (*unseen in the crowd*).

Woe to the city of blood! The stone shall cry
Out of the wall; the beam from out the timber
Shall answer it! Woe unto him that buildeth
A town with blood, and stablisheth a city
By his iniquity!

ENDICOTT.

Who is it makes
Such outcry here?

CHRISTISON (*coming forward*).

I, Wenlock Christison!

ENDICOTT.

Banished on pain of death, why come you here?

CHRISTISON.

I come to warn you that you shed no more
The blood of innocent men! It cries aloud
For vengeance to the Lord!

ENDICOTT.

Your life is forfeit
Unto the law; and you shall surely die,
And shall not live.

CHRISTISON.

Like unto Eleazer,
Maintaining the excellence of ancient years
And the honor of his gray head, I stand before you;
Like him disdaining all hypocrisy,
Lest, through desire to live a little longer,
I get a stain to my old age and name!

ENDICOTT.

Being in banishment, on pain of death,
You come now in among us in rebellion.

CHRISTISON.

I come not in among you in rebellion,
But in obedience to the Lord of Heaven.
Not in contempt to any Magistrate,
But only in the love I bear your souls,
As ye shall know hereafter, when all men
Give an account of deeds done in the body!
God's righteous judgments ye cannot escape.

ONE OF THE JUDGES.

Those who have gone before you said the same,
And yet no judgment of the Lord hath fallen
Upon us.

CHRISTISON.

He but waiteth till the measure
Of your iniquities shall be filled up,
And ye have run your race. Then will his wrath
Descend upon you to the uttermost!
For thy part, Humphrey Atherton, it hangs
Over thy head already. It shall come
Suddenly, as a thief doth in the night,
And in the hour when least thou thinkest of it!

ENDICOTT.

We have a law, and by that law you die.

CHRISTISON.

I, a free man of England and freeborn,
Appeal unto the laws of mine own nation!

ENDICOTT.

There 's no appeal to England from this Court!
What! do you think our statutes are but paper?
Are but dead leaves that rustle in the wind?
Or litter to be trampled under foot?
What say ye, Judges of the Court,—what say ye?
Shall this man suffer death? Speak your opinions.

ONE OF THE JUDGES.

I am a mortal man, and die I must,
And that erelong; and I must then appear
Before the awful judgment-seat of Christ,
To give account of deeds done in the body.
My greatest glory on that day will be,
That I have given my vote against this man.

CHRISTISON.

If, Thomas Danforth, thou hast nothing more
To glory in upon that dreadful day
Than blood of innocent people, then thy glory
Will be turned into shame! The Lord hath said it!

ANOTHER JUDGE.

I cannot give consent, while other men
Who have been banished upon pain of death
Are now in their own houses here among us.

ENDICOTT.

Ye that will not consent, make record of it.
I thank my God that I am not afraid
To give my judgment. Wenlock Christison,
You must be taken back from hence to prison,
Thence to the place of public execution,
There to be hanged till you be dead—dead—dead!

CHRISTISON.

If ye have power to take my life from me,—
Which I do question,—God hath power to raise
The principle of life in other men,
And send them here among you. There shall be

No peace unto the wicked, saith my God.
Listen, ye Magistrates, for the Lord hath said it!
The day ye put his servitors to death,
That day the Day of your own Visitation,
The Day of Wrath, shall pass above your heads,
And ye shall be accursed forevermore!

To EDITH, *embracing her.*

Cheer up, dear heart! they have not power to harm us.

[*Exeunt* CHRISTISON *and* EDITH *guarded. The Scene closes.*

SCENE II.—*A street. Enter* JOHN ENDICOTT *and* UPSALL.

JOHN ENDICOTT.

Scourged in three towns! and yet the busy people
Go up and down the streets on their affairs
Of business or of pleasure, as if nothing
Had happened to disturb them or their thoughts!
When bloody tragedies like this are acted,
The pulses of a nation should stand still;
The town should be in mourning, and the people
Speak only in low whispers to each other.

UPSALL.

I know this people; and that underneath
A cold outside there burns a secret fire
That will find vent, and will not be put out,
Till every remnant of these barbarous laws
Shall be to ashes burned, and blown away.

JOHN ENDICOTT.

Scourged in three towns! It is incredible
Such things can be! I feel the blood within me
Fast mounting in rebellion, since in vain
Have I implored compassion of my father!

UPSALL.

You know your father only as a father;
I know him better as a Magistrate.
He is a man both loving and severe;
A tender heart; a will inflexible.
None ever loved him more than I have loved him.
He is an upright man and a just man
In all things save the treatment of the Quakers.

JOHN ENDICOTT.

Yet I have found him cruel and unjust
Even as a father. He has driven me forth
Into the street; has shut his door upon me,
With words of bitterness. I am as homeless
As these poor Quakers are.

UPSALL.

Then come with me.
You shall be welcome for your father's sake,
And the old friendship that has been between us.
He will relent erelong. A father's anger
Is like a sword without a handle, piercing
Both ways alike, and wounding him that wields it
No less than him that it is pointed at.

[*Exeunt.*

SCENE III.—*The prison. Night.* EDITH *reading the Bible by a lamp.*

EDITH.

"Blessed are ye when men shall persecute you,
And shall revile you, and shall say against you
All manner of evil falsely for my sake!
Rejoice, and be exceeding glad, for great
Is your reward in heaven. For so the prophets,
Which were before you, have been persecuted."

Enter JOHN ENDICOTT.

JOHN ENDICOTT.

Edith!

EDITH.

Who is it speaketh?

JOHN ENDICOTT.

Saul of Tarsus;
As thou didst call me once.

EDITH (*coming forward*).

Yea, I remember.
Thou art the Governor's son.

JOHN ENDICOTT.

I am ashamed
Thou shouldst remember me.

EDITH.

Why comest thou

Into this dark guest-chamber in the night?
What seekest thou?

JOHN ENDICOTT.

Forgiveness!

EDITH.

I forgive
All who have injured me. What hast thou done?

JOHN ENDICOTT.

I have betrayed thee, thinking that in this
I did God service. Now, in deep contrition,
I come to rescue thee.

EDITH.

From what?

JOHN ENDICOTT.

From prison.

EDITH.

I am safe here within these gloomy walls.

JOHN ENDICOTT.

From scourging in the streets, and in three towns!

EDITH.

Remembering who was scourged for me, I shrink not
Nor shudder at the forty stripes save one.

JOHN ENDICOTT.

Perhaps from death itself!

EDITH.

I fear not death,
Knowing who died for me.

JOHN ENDICOTT (*aside*).

Surely some divine
Ambassador is speaking through those lips
And looking through those eyes! I cannot answer!

EDITH.

If all these prison doors stood opened wide
I would not cross the threshold,—not one step.
There are invisible bars I cannot break;
There are invisible doors that shut me in,
And keep me ever steadfast to my purpose.

JOHN ENDICOTT.

Thou hast the patience and the faith of Saints!

EDITH.

Thy Priest hath been with me this day to save me,
Not only from the death that comes to all,
But from the second death!

JOHN ENDICOTT.

The Pharisee!
My heart revolts against him and his creed!
Alas! the coat that was without a seam
Is rent asunder by contending sects;
Each bears away a portion of the garment,
Blindly believing that he has the whole!

EDITH.

When Death, the Healer, shall have touched our eyes
With moist clay of the grave, then shall we see
The truth as we have never yet beheld it.
But he that overcometh shall not be
Hurt of the second death. Has he forgotten
The many mansions in our father's house?

JOHN ENDICOTT.

There is no pity in his iron heart!
The hands that now bear stamped upon their palms
The burning sign of Heresy, hereafter
Shall be uplifted against such accusers,
And then the imprinted letter and its meaning
Will not be Heresy, but Holiness!

EDITH.

Remember, thou condemnest thine own father!

JOHN ENDICOTT.

I have no father! He has cast me off.
I am as homeless as the wind that moans
And wanders through the streets. Oh, come with me!
Do not delay. Thy God shall be my God,
And where thou goest I will go.

EDITH.

I cannot.
Yet will I not deny it, nor conceal it;
From the first moment I beheld thy face
I felt a tenderness in my soul towards thee.
My mind has since been inward to the Lord,
Waiting his word. It has not yet been spoken.

JOHN ENDICOTT.

I cannot wait. Trust me. Oh, come with me!

EDITH.

In the next room, my father, an old man,
Sitteth imprisoned and condemned to death,
Willing to prove his faith by martyrdom;
And thinkest thou his daughter would do less?

JOHN ENDICOTT.

Oh, life is sweet, and death is terrible!

EDITH.

I have too long walked hand in hand with death
To shudder at that pale familiar face.
But leave me now. I wish to be alone.

JOHN ENDICOTT.

Not yet. Oh, let me stay.

EDITH.

Urge me no more.

JOHN ENDICOTT.

Alas! good-night. I will not say good-by!

EDITH.

Put this temptation underneath thy feet.
To him that overcometh shall be given
The white stone with the new name written on it,
That no man knows save him that doth receive it,
And I will give thee a new name, and call thee
Paul of Damascus and not Saul of Tarsus.

[*Exit* ENDICOTT. EDITH *sits down again to read the Bible.*

ACT IV.

SCENE I.—*King Street, in front of the town-house.* KEMPTHORN *in the pillory.* MERRY *and a crowd of lookers-on.*

KEMPTHORN (*sings*).

The world is full of care,
Much like unto a bubble;
Women and care, and care and women,
And women and care and trouble.

Good Master Merry, may I say confound?

MERRY.

Ay, that you may.

KEMPTHORN.

Well, then, with your permission,
Confound the Pillory!

MERRY.

That's the very thing
The joiner said who made the Shrewsbury stocks.
He said, Confound the stocks, because they put him
Into his own. He was the first man in them.

KEMPTHORN.

For swearing, was it?

MERRY.

No, it was for charging;
He charged the town too much; and so the town,
To make things square, set him in his own stocks,
And fined him five pound sterling,—just enough
To settle his own bill.

KEMPTHORN.

And served him right;
But, Master Merry, is it not eight bells?

MERRY.

Not quite.

KEMPTHORN.

For, do you see? I 'm getting tired
Of being perched aloft here in this cro' nest
Like the first mate of a whaler, or a Middy
Mast-headed, looking out for land! Sail ho!
Here comes a heavy-laden merchantman
With the lee clews eased off, and running free
Before the wind. A solid man of Boston.
A comfortable man, with dividends,
And the first salmon, and the first green peas.

A gentleman passes.

He does not even turn his head to look.
He 's gone without a word. Here comes another,
A different kind of craft on a taut bow-line,—
Deacon Giles Firmin the apothecary,
A pious and a ponderous citizen,
Looking as rubicund and round and splendid
As the great bottle in his own shop window!

DEACON FIRMIN *passes.*

And here 's my host of the Three Mariners,
My creditor and trusty taverner,
My corporal in the Great Artillery!
He 's not a man to pass me without speaking.

COLE *looks away and passes.*

Don't yaw so; keep your luff, old hypocrite!
Respectable, ah yes, respectable,
You, with your seat in the new Meeting-house,
Your cow-right on the Common! But who's this?
I did not know the Mary Ann was in!
And yet this is my old friend, Captain Goldsmith,
As sure as I stand in the bilboes here.
Why, Ralph, my boy!

Enter RALPH GOLDSMITH.

GOLDSMITH.

Why, Simon, is it you?
Set in the bilboes?

KEMPTHORN.

Chock-a-block, you see,
And without chafing-gear.

GOLDSMITH.

And what 's it for?

KEMPTHORN.

Ask that starbowline with the boat-hook there,
That handsome man.

MERRY (*bowing*).

For swearing.

KEMPTHORN.

In this town
They put sea-captains in the stocks for swearing,
And Quakers for not swearing. So look out.

GOLDSMITH.

I pray you set him free; he meant no harm;
'T is an old habit he picked up afloat.

MERRY.

Well, as your time is out, you may come down.
The law allows you now to go at large
Like Elder Oliver's horse upon the Common.

KEMPTHORN.

Now, hearties, bear a hand! Let go and haul.

KEMPTHORN *is set free, and comes forward, shaking* GOLDSMITH'S *hand.*

KEMPTHORN.

Give me your hand, Ralph. Ah, how good it feels!
The hand of an old friend.

GOLDSMITH.

God bless you, Simon!

KEMPTHORN.

Now let us make a straight wake for the tavern
Of the Three Mariners, Samuel Cole commander;
Where we can take our ease, and see the shipping,
And talk about old times.

GOLDSMITH.

First I must pay
My duty to the Governor, and take him
His letters and despatches. Come with me.

KEMPTHORN.

I 'd rather not. I saw him yesterday.

GOLDSMITH.

Then wait for me at the Three Nuns and Comb.

KEMPTHORN.

I thank you. That 's too near to the town pump.
I will go with you to the Governor's,
And wait outside there, sailing off and on;
If I am wanted, you can hoist a signal.

MERRY.

Shall I go with you and point out the way?

GOLDSMITH.

Oh no, I thank you. I am not a stranger
Here in your crooked little town.

MERRY.

How now, sir?
Do you abuse our town? [*Exit.*

GOLDSMITH.

Oh, no offence.

KEMPTHORN.

Ralph, I am under bonds for a hundred pound.

GOLDSMITH.

Hard lines. What for?

KEMPTHORN.

To take some Quakers back
I brought here from Barbadoes in the Swallow.
And how to do it I don't clearly see,
For one of them is banished, and another
Is sentenced to be hanged! What shall I do?

GOLDSMITH.

Just slip your hawser on some cloudy night;
Sheer off, and pay it with the topsail, Simon!

[*Exeunt.*

SCENE II.—*Street in front of the prison. In the background a gateway and several flights of steps leading up terraces to the Governor's house. A pump on one side of the street.* JOHN ENDICOTT, MERRY, UPSALL, *and others. A drum beats.*

JOHN ENDICOTT.

Oh shame, shame, shame!

MERRY.

Yes, it would be a shame
But for the damnable sin of Heresy!

JOHN ENDICOTT.

A woman scourged and dragged about our streets!

MERRY.

Well, Roxbury and Dorchester must take
Their share of shame. She will be whipped in each!
Three towns, and Forty Stripes save one; that makes
Thirteen in each.

JOHN ENDICOTT.

And are we Jews or Christians?
See where she comes, amid a gaping crowd!
And she a child. Oh, pitiful! pitiful!
There's blood upon her clothes, her hands, her feet!

Enter MARSHAL *and a drummer,* EDITH, *stripped to the waist, followed by the hangman with a scourge, and a noisy crowd.*

EDITH.

Here let me rest one moment. I am tired.
Will some one give me water?

MERRY.

At his peril.

UPSALL.

Alas! that I should live to see this day!

A WOMAN.

Did I forsake my father and my mother
And come here to New England to see this?

EDITH.

I am athirst. Will no one give me water?

JOHN ENDICOTT (*making his way through the crowd with water*).

In the Lord's name!

EDITH (*drinking*).

In his name I receive it!
Sweet as the water of Samaria's well
This water tastes. I thank thee. Is it thou?
I was afraid thou hadst deserted me.

JOHN ENDICOTT.

Never will I desert thee, nor deny thee.
Be comforted.

MERRY.

O Master Endicott,
Be careful what you say.

JOHN ENDICOTT.

Peace, idle babbler!

MERRY.

You 'll rue these words!

JOHN ENDICOTT.

Art thou not better now?

EDITH.

They 've struck me as with roses.

JOHN ENDICOTT.

Ah, these wounds!
These bloody garments!

EDITH.

It is granted me
To seal my testimony with my blood.

JOHN ENDICOTT.

O blood-red seal of man's vindictive wrath!
O roses of the garden of the Lord!
I, of the household of Iscariot,
I have betrayed in thee my Lord and Master!

WENLOCK CHRISTISON *appears above, at the window of the prison, stretching out his hands through the bars.*

CHRISTISON.

Be of good courage, O my child! my child!
Blessed art thou when men shall persecute thee!
Fear not their faces, saith the Lord, fear not,
For I am with thee to deliver thee.

A CITIZEN.

Who is it crying from the prison yonder!

MERRY.

It is old Wenlock Christison.

CHRISTISON.

Remember
Him who was scourged, and mocked, and crucified!
I see his messengers attending thee.
Be steadfast, oh, be steadfast to the end!

EDITH (*with exultation*).

I cannot reach thee with these arms, O father!
But closely in my soul do I embrace thee
And hold thee. In thy dungeon and thy death
I will be with thee, and will comfort thee!

MARSHAL.

Come, put an end to this. Let the drum beat.

The drum beats. Exeunt all but JOHN ENDICOTT, UPSALL, *and* MERRY.

CHRISTISON.

Dear child, farewell! Never shall I behold
Thy face again with these bleared eyes of flesh;
And never wast thou fairer, lovelier, dearer
Than now, when scourged and bleeding, and insulted
For the truth's sake. O pitiless, pitiless town!
The wrath of God hangs over thee; and the day
Is near at hand when thou shalt be abandoned
To desolation and the breeding of nettles.
The bittern and the cormorant shall lodge
Upon thine upper lintels, and their voice
Sing in thy windows. Yea, thus saith the Lord!

JOHN ENDICOTT.

Awake! awake! ye sleepers, ere too late,
And wipe these bloody statutes from your books!

[*Exit.*

MERRY.

Take heed; the walls have ears!

UPSALL.

At last, the heart
Of every honest man must speak or break!

Enter GOVERNOR ENDICOTT *with his halberdiers.*

ENDICOTT.

What is this stir and tumult in the street?

MERRY.

Worshipful sir, the whipping of a girl,
And her old father howling from the prison.

ENDICOTT (*to his halberdiers*).

Go on.

CHRISTISON.

Antiochus! Antiochus!
O thou that slayest the Maccabees! The Lord
Shall smite thee with incurable disease,
And no man shall endure to carry thee!

MERRY.

Peace, old blasphemer!

CHRISTISON.

I both feel and see
The presence and the waft of death go forth
Against thee, and already thou dost look
Like one that 's dead!

MERRY (*pointing*).

And there is your own son,
Worshipful sir, abetting the sedition.

ENDICOTT.

Arrest him. Do not spare him.

MERRY (*aside*).

His own child!
There is some special providence takes care
That none shall be too happy in this world!
His own first-born.

ENDICOTT.

O Absalom, my son!

[*Exeunt; the Governor with his halberdiers ascending the steps of his house.*

SCENE III.—*The Governor's private room. Papers upon the table.* ENDICOTT *and* BELLINGHAM.

ENDICOTT.

There is a ship from England has come in,
Bringing despatches and much news from home.
His Majesty was at the Abbey crowned;
And when the coronation was complete
There passed a mighty tempest o'er the city,
Portentous with great thunderings and lightnings.

BELLINGHAM.

After his father's, if I well remember,
There was an earthquake, that foreboded evil.

ENDICOTT.

Ten of the Regicides have been put to death!
The bodies of Cromwell, Ireton, and Bradshaw
Have been dragged from their graves, and publicly
Hanged in their shrouds at Tyburn.

BELLINGHAM.

Horrible!

ENDICOTT.

Thus the old tyranny revives again!
Its arm is long enough to reach us here,
As you will see. For, more insulting still
Than flaunting in our faces dead men's shrouds,
Here is the King's Mandamus, taking from us,
From this day forth, all power to punish Quakers.

BELLINGHAM.

That takes from us all power; we are but puppets,
And can no longer execute our laws.

ENDICOTT.

His Majesty begins with pleasant words,
"Trusty and well-beloved, we greet you well;"
Then with a ruthless hand he strips from me
All that which makes me what I am; as if
From some old general in the field, grown gray
In service, scarred with many wounds,
Just at the hour of victory, he should strip
His badge of office and his well-gained honors,
And thrust him back into the ranks again.

Opens the Mandamus, and hands it to BELLINGHAM; *and, while he is reading,* ENDICOTT *walks up and down the room.*

Here, read it for yourself; you see his words
Are pleasant words—considerate—not reproachful—
Nothing could be more gentle—or more royal;
But then the meaning underneath the words,
Mark that. He says all people known as Quakers
Among us, now condemned to suffer death
Or any corporal punishment whatever,
Who are imprisoned, or may be obnoxious
To the like condemnation, shall be sent
Forthwith to England, to be dealt with there
In such wise as shall be agreeable
Unto the English law and their demerits.
Is it not so?

BELLINGHAM (*returning the paper*).

Ay, so the paper says.

ENDICOTT.

It means we shall no longer rule the Province;
It means farewell to law and liberty,
Authority, respect for Magistrates,
The peace and welfare of the Commonwealth.
If all the knaves upon this continent
Can make appeal to England, and so thwart
The ends of truth and justice by delay,
Our power is gone forever. We are nothing
But ciphers, valueless save when we follow
Some unit; and our unit is the King!
'T is he that gives us value.

BELLINGHAM.

I confess
Such seems to be the meaning of this paper,
But being the King's Mandamus, signed and sealed,
We must obey, or we are in rebellion.

ENDICOTT.

I tell you, Richard Bellingham,—I tell you,
That this is the beginning of a struggle
Of which no mortal can foresee the end.
I shall not live to fight the battle for you,
I am a man disgraced in every way;

This order takes from me my self-respect
And the respect of others. 'T is my doom,
Yes, my death-warrant, but must be obeyed!
Take it, and see that it is executed
So far as this, that all be set at large;
But see that none of them be sent to England
To bear false witness, and to spread reports
That might be prejudicial to ourselves.

[*Exit* BELLINGHAM.

There's a dull pain keeps knocking at my heart,
Dolefully saying, "Set thy house in order,
For thou shalt surely die, and shalt not live!"
For me the shadow on the dial-plate
Goeth not back, but on into the dark!

[*Exit.*

SCENE IV.—*The street. A crowd, reading a placard on the door of the Meeting-house.* NICHOLAS UPSALL *among them. Enter* JOHN NORTON.

NORTON.

What is this gathering here?

UPSALL.

One William Brand,
An old man like ourselves, and weak in body,
Has been so cruelly tortured in his prison,
The people are excited, and they threaten
To tear the prison down.

NORTON.

What has been done?

UPSALL.

He has been put in irons, with his neck
And heels tied close together, and so left
From five in the morning until nine at night.

NORTON.

What more was done?

UPSALL.

He has been kept five days
In prison without food, and cruelly beaten,
So that his limbs were cold, his senses stopped.

NORTON.

What more?

UPSALL.

And is this not enough?

NORTON.

Now hear me.
This William Brand of yours has tried to beat
Our Gospel Ordinances black and blue;
And, if he has been beaten in like manner,
It is but justice, and I will appear
In his behalf that did so. I suppose
That he refused to work.

UPSALL.

He was too weak.
How could an old man work, when he was starving?

NORTON.

And what is this placard?

UPSALL.

The Magistrates,
To appease the people and prevent a tumult,
Have put up these placards throughout the town,
Declaring that the jailer shall be dealt with
Impartially and sternly by the Court.

NORTON (*tearing down the placard*).

Down with this weak and cowardly concession,
This flag of truce with Satan and with Sin!
I fling it in his face! I trample it
Under my feet! It is his cunning craft,
The masterpiece of his diplomacy,
To cry and plead for boundless toleration.
But toleration is the first-born child
Of all abominations and deceits.
There is no room in Christ's triumphant army
For tolerationists. And if an Angel
Preach any other gospel unto you
Than that ye have received, God's malediction
Descend upon him! Let him be accursed!

[*Exit.*

UPSALL.

Now, go thy ways, John Norton! go thy ways,
Thou Orthodox Evangelist, as men call thee!
But even now there cometh out of England,
Like an o'ertaking and accusing conscience,
An outraged man, to call thee to account
For the unrighteous murder of his son!

[*Exit.*

SCENE V.—*The Wilderness. Enter* EDITH.

EDITH.

How beautiful are these autumnal woods!
The wilderness doth blossom like the rose,
And change into a garden of the Lord!
How silent everywhere! Alone and lost
Here in the forest, there comes over me
An inward awfulness. I recall the words
Of the Apostle Paul: "In journeyings often,
Often in perils in the wilderness,
In weariness, in painfulness, in watchings,
In hunger and thirst, in cold and nakedness;"
And I forget my weariness and pain,
My watchings, and my hunger and my thirst.
The Lord hath said that He will seek his flock
In cloudy and dark days, and they shall dwell
Securely in the wilderness, and sleep
Safe in the woods! Whichever way I turn,
I come back with my face towards the town.
Dimly I see it, and the sea beyond it.
O cruel town! I know what waits me there,
And yet I must go back; for ever louder
I hear the inward calling of the Spirit,
And must obey the voice. O woods, that wear
Your golden crown of martyrdom, blood-stained,
From you I learn a lesson of submission,
And am obedient even unto death,
If God so wills it. [*Exit.*

JOHN ENDICOTT (*within*).

Edith! Edith! Edith!

He enters.

It is in vain! I call, she answers not;
I follow, but I find no trace of her!
Blood! blood! The leaves above me and around me
Are red with blood! The pathways of the forest,
The clouds that canopy the setting sun,
And even the little river in the meadows
Are stained with it! Where'er I look, I see it!
Away, thou horrible vision! Leave me! leave me!
Alas! yon winding stream, that gropes its way
Through mist and shadow, doubling on itself,
At length will find, by the unerring law
Of nature, what it seeks. O soul of man,
Groping through mist and shadow, and recoiling
Back on thyself, are, too, thy devious ways
Subject to law? and when thou seemest to wander
The farthest from thy goal, art thou still drawing
Nearer and nearer to it, till at length
Thou findest, like the river, what thou seekest?

[*Exit.*

ACT V.

SCENE I.—*Daybreak. Street in front of* UPSALL'S *house. A light in the window. Enter* JOHN ENDICOTT.

JOHN ENDICOTT.

O silent, sombre, and deserted streets,
To me ye 're peopled with a sad procession,
And echo only to the voice of sorrow!
O houses full of peacefulness and sleep,
Far better were it to awake no more
Than wake to look upon such scenes again!
There is a light in Master Upsall's window.
The good man is already risen, for sleep
Deserts the couches of the old.

Knocks at UPSALL'S *door.*

UPSALL (*at the window*).

Who 's there?

JOHN ENDICOTT.

Am I so changed you do not know my voice?

UPSALL.

I know you. Have you heard what things have happened?

JOHN ENDICOTT.

I have heard nothing.

UPSALL.

Stay; I will come down.

JOHN ENDICOTT.

I am afraid some dreadful news awaits me!
I do not dare to ask, yet am impatient
To know the worst. Oh, I am very weary
With waiting and with watching and pursuing!

Enter UPSALL.

UPSALL.

Thank God, you have come back! I 've much to tell you.
Where have you been?

JOHN ENDICOTT.

You know that I was seized,
Fined, and released again. You know that Edith,
After her scourging in three towns, was banished
Into the wilderness, into the land
That is not sown; and there I followed her,
But found her not. Where is she?

UPSALL.

She is here.

JOHN ENDICOTT.

Oh, do not speak that word, for it means death!

UPSALL.

No, it means life. She sleeps in yonder chamber.
Listen to me. When news of Leddra's death
Reached England, Edward Burroughs, having boldly
Got access to the presence of the King,
Told him there was a vein of innocent blood
Opened in his dominions here, which threatened
To overrun them all. The King replied,
"But I will stop that vein!" and he forthwith
Sent his Mandamus to our Magistrates,
That they proceed no further in this business.
So all are pardoned, and all set at large.

JOHN ENDICOTT.

Thank God! This is a victory for truth!
Our thoughts are free. They cannot be shut up
In prison walls, nor put to death on scaffolds!

UPSALL.

Come in; the morning air blows sharp and cold
Through the damp streets.

JOHN ENDICOTT.

It is the dawn of day
That chases the old darkness from our sky,
And fills the land with liberty and light.

[*Exeunt.*

SCENE II.—*The parlor of the Three Mariners. Enter* KEMPTHORN.

KEMPTHORN.

A dull life this,—a dull life anyway!
Ready for sea; the cargo all aboard,
Cleared for Barbadoes, and a fair wind blowing
From nor'-nor'-west; and I, an idle lubber,
Laid neck and heels by that confounded bond!
I said to Ralph, says I, "What 's to be done?"
Says he: "Just slip your hawser in the night;
Sheer off, and pay it with the topsail, Simon."
But that won't do; because, you see, the owners
Somehow or other are mixed up with it.
Here are King Charles's Twelve Good Rules, that Cole
Thinks as important as the Rule of Three.

Reads.

"Make no comparisons; make no long meals."
Those are good rules and golden for a landlord
To hang in his best parlor, framed and glazed!
"Maintain no ill opinions; urge no healths."
I drink the King's, whatever he may say,
And, as to ill opinions, that depends.
Now of Ralph Goldsmith I 've a good opinion,
And of the bilboes I 've an ill opinion;
And both of these opinions I 'll maintain
As long as there 's a shot left in the locker.

Enter EDWARD BUTTER *with an ear-trumpet.*

BUTTER.

Good morning, Captain Kempthorn.

KEMPTHORN.

Sir, to you.
You 've the advantage of me. I don't know you.
What may I call your name?

BUTTER.

That 's not your name?

KEMPTHORN.

Yes, that 's my name. What 's yours?

BUTTER.

My name is Butter.
I am the treasurer of the Commonwealth.

KEMPTHORN.

Will you be seated?

BUTTER.

What say? Who 's conceited?

KEMPTHORN.

Will you sit down?

BUTTER.

Oh, thank you.

KEMPTHORN.

Spread yourself
Upon this chair, sweet Butter.

BUTTER (*sitting down*).

A fine morning.

KEMPTHORN.

Nothing 's the matter with it that I know of.
I have seen better, and I have seen worse.
The wind 's nor'west. That 's fair for them that sail.

BUTTER.

You need not speak so loud; I understand you.
You sail to-day.

KEMPTHORN.

No, I don't sail to-day.
So, be it fair or foul, it matters not.
Say, will you smoke? There 's choice tobacco here.

BUTTER.

No, thank you. It 's against the law to smoke.

KEMPTHORN.

Then, will you drink? There 's good ale at this inn.

BUTTER.

No, thank you. It 's against the law to drink.

KEMPTHORN.

Well, almost everything 's against the law
In this good town. Give a wide berth to one thing,
You 're sure to fetch up soon on something else.

BUTTER.

And so you sail to-day for dear Old England.
I am not one of those who think a sup
Of this New England air is better worth
Than a whole draught of our Old England's ale.

KEMPTHORN.

Nor I. Give me the ale and keep the air.
But, as I said, I do not sail to-day.

BUTTER.

Ah yes; you sail to-day.

KEMPTHORN.

I 'm under bonds
To take some Quakers back to the Barbadoes;
And one of them is banished, and another
Is sentenced to be hanged.

BUTTER.

No, all are pardoned,
All are set free, by order of the Court;
But some of them would fain return to England.
You must not take them. Upon that condition
Your bond is cancelled.

KEMPTHORN.

Ah, the wind has shifted!
I pray you, do you speak officially?

BUTTER.

I always speak officially. To prove it,
Here is the bond.

Rising and giving a paper.

KEMPTHORN.

And here 's my hand upon it.
And, look you, when I say I 'll do a thing
The thing is done. Am I now free to go?

BUTTER.

What say?

KEMPTHORN.

I say, confound the tedious man
With his strange speaking-trumpet! Can I go?

BUTTER.

You 're free to go, by order of the Court.
Your servant, sir. [*Exit.*

KEMPTHORN (*shouting from the window*).

Swallow, ahoy! Hallo!
If ever a man was happy to leave Boston,
That man is Simon Kempthorn of the Swallow!

Reënter BUTTER.

BUTTER.

Pray, did you call?

KEMPTHORN.

Call? Yes, I hailed the Swallow.

BUTTER.

That 's not my name. My name is Edward Butter.
You need not speak so loud.

KEMPTHORN (*shaking hands*).

Good-by! Good-by!

BUTTER.

Your servant, sir.

KEMPTHORN.

And yours a thousand times!

[*Exeunt.*

SCENE III.—GOVERNOR ENDICOTT'S *private room. An open window.* ENDICOTT *seated in an arm-chair.* BELLINGHAM *standing near.*

ENDICOTT.

O lost, O loved! wilt thou return no more?
O loved and lost, and loved the more when lost!
How many men are dragged into their graves
By their rebellious children! I now feel
The agony of a father's breaking heart
In David's cry, "O Absalom, my son!"

BELLINGHAM.

Can you not turn your thoughts a little while
To public matters? There are papers here
That need attention.

ENDICOTT.

Trouble me no more!
My business now is with another world.
Ah, Richard Bellingham! I greatly fear
That in my righteous zeal I have been led
To doing many things which, left undone,
My mind would now be easier. Did I dream it,
Or has some person told me, that John Norton
Is dead?

BELLINGHAM.

You have not dreamed it. He is dead,
And gone to his reward. It was no dream.

ENDICOTT.

Then it was very sudden; for I saw him
Standing where you now stand, not long ago.

BELLINGHAM.

By his own fireside, in the afternoon,
A faintness and a giddiness came o'er him;
And, leaning on the chimney-piece, he cried,
"The hand of God is on me!" and fell dead.

ENDICOTT.

And did not some one say, or have I dreamed it,
That Humphrey Atherton is dead?

BELLINGHAM.

Alas!
He too is gone, and by a death as sudden.
Returning home one evening, at the place
Where usually the Quakers have been scourged,
His horse took fright, and threw him to the ground,
So that his brains were dashed about the street.

ENDICOTT.

I am not superstitious, Bellingham,
And yet I tremble lest it may have been
A judgment on him.

BELLINGHAM.

So the people think.
They say his horse saw standing in the way
The ghost of William Leddra, and was frightened.
And furthermore, brave Richard Davenport,

The captain of the Castle, in the storm
Has been struck dead by lightning.

ENDICOTT.

Speak no more.
For as I listen to your voice it seems
As if the Seven Thunders uttered their voices,
And the dead bodies lay about the streets
Of the disconsolate city! Bellingham,
I did not put those wretched men to death.
I did but guard the passage with the sword
Pointed towards them, and they rushed upon it!
Yet now I would that I had taken no part
In all that bloody work.

BELLINGHAM.

The guilt of it
Be on their heads, not ours.

ENDICOTT.

Are all set free?

BELLINGHAM.

All are at large.

ENDICOTT.

And none have been sent back
To England to malign us with the King?

BELLINGHAM.

The ship that brought them sails this very hour,
But carries no one back.

A distant cannon.

ENDICOTT.

What is that gun?

BELLINGHAM.

Her parting signal. Through the window there,
Look, you can see her sails, above the roofs,
Dropping below the Castle, outward bound.

ENDICOTT.

O white, white, white! Would that my soul had wings
As spotless as those shining sails to fly with!
Now lay this cushion straight. I thank you. Hark!
I thought I heard the hall door open and shut!
I thought I heard the footsteps of my boy!

BELLINGHAM.

It was the wind. There 's no one in the passage.

ENDICOTT.

O Absalom, my son! I feel the world
Sinking beneath me, sinking, sinking, sinking!
Death knocks! I go to meet him! Welcome, Death!

Rises, and sinks back dead; his head falling aside upon his shoulder.

BELLINGHAM.

O ghastly sight! Like one who has been hanged!
Endicott! Endicott! He makes no answer!

Raises ENDICOTT'S *head.*

He breathes no more! How bright this signet-ring
Glitters upon his hand, where he has worn it
Through such long years of trouble, as if Death
Had given him this memento of affection,
And whispered in his ear, "Remember me!"
How placid and how quiet is his face,
Now that the struggle and the strife are ended!
Only the acrid spirit of the times
Corroded this true steel. Oh, rest in peace,
Courageous heart! Forever rest in peace!

GILES COREY OF THE SALEM FARMS

DRAMATIS PERSONÆ.

Giles Corey . . . . *Farmer.*
John Hathorne . . . . *Magistrate.*
Cotton Mather . . . . *Minister of the Gospel.*
Jonathan Walcot . . . . *A youth.*
Richard Gardner . . . . *Sea-Captain.*
John Gloyd . . . . *Corey's hired man.*
Martha . . . . *Wife of Giles Corey.*
Tituba . . . . *An Indian woman.*
Mary Walcot . . . . *One of the Afflicted.*

The Scene is in Salem in the year 1692.

PROLOGUE.

Delusions of the days that once have been,
Witchcraft and wonders of the world unseen,
Phantoms of air, and necromantic arts
That crushed the weak and awed the stoutest hearts,—
These are our theme to-night; and vaguely here,
Through the dim mists that crowd the atmosphere,
We draw the outlines of weird figures cast
In shadow on the background of the Past.

Who would believe that in the quiet town
Of Salem, and amid the woods that crown
The neighboring hillsides, and the sunny farms
That fold it safe in their paternal arms,—
Who would believe that in those peaceful streets,
Where the great elms shut out the summer heats,
Where quiet reigns, and breathes through brain and breast
The benediction of unbroken rest,—
Who would believe such deeds could find a place
As these whose tragic history we retrace?

'T was but a village then: the goodman ploughed
His ample acres under sun or cloud;
The goodwife at her doorstep sat and spun,
And gossiped with her neighbors in the sun;
The only men of dignity and state
Were then the Minister and the Magistrate,

Who ruled their little realm with iron rod,
Less in the love than in the fear of God;
And who believed devoutly in the Powers
Of Darkness, working in this world of ours,
In spells of Witchcraft, incantations dread,
And shrouded apparitions of the dead.

Upon this simple folk "with fire and flame,"
Saith the old Chronicle, "the Devil came;
Scattering his firebrands and his poisonous darts,
To set on fire of Hell all tongues and hearts!
And 't is no wonder; for, with all his host,
There most he rages where he hateth most,
And is most hated; so on us he brings
All these stupendous and portentous things!"

Something of this our scene to-night will show;
And ye who listen to the Tale of Woe,
Be not too swift in casting the first stone,
Nor think New England bears the guilt alone.
This sudden burst of wickedness and crime
Was but the common madness of the time,
When in all lands, that lie within the sound
Of Sabbath bells, a Witch was burned or drowned.

ACT I.

SCENE I.—*The woods near Salem Village. Enter* TITUBA, *with a basket of herbs.*

TITUBA.

Here 's monk's-hood, that breeds fever in the blood;
And deadly nightshade, that makes men see ghosts;
And henbane, that will shake them with convulsions;
And meadow-saffron and black hellebore,
That rack the nerves, and puff the skin with dropsy;
And bitter-sweet, and briony, and eye-bright,
That cause eruptions, nosebleed, rheumatisms;
I know them, and the places where they hide
In field and meadow; and I know their secrets,
And gather them because they give me power
Over all men and women. Armed with these,

I, Tituba, an Indian and a slave,
Am stronger than the captain with his sword,
Am richer than the merchant with his money,
Am wiser than the scholar with his books,
Mightier than Ministers and Magistrates,
With all the fear and reverence that attend them!
For I can fill their bones with aches and pains,
Can make them cough with asthma, shake with palsy,
Can make their daughters see and talk with ghosts,
Or fall into delirium and convulsions.
I have the Evil Eye, the Evil Hand;
A touch from me, and they are weak with pain,
A look from me, and they consume and die.
The death of cattle and the blight of corn,
The shipwreck, the tornado, and the fire,—
These are my doings, and they know it not.
Thus I work vengeance on mine enemies,
Who, while they call me slave, are slaves to me!

Exit TITUBA. *Enter* MATHER, *booted and spurred, with a riding-whip in his hand.*

MATHER.

Methinks that I have come by paths unknown
Into the land and atmosphere of Witches;
For, meditating as I journeyed on,
Lo! I have lost my way! If I remember
Rightly, it is Scribonius the learned
That tells the story of a man who, praying
For one that was possessed by Evil Spirits,
Was struck by Evil Spirits in the face;
I, journeying to circumvent the Witches
Surely by Witches have been led astray.
I am persuaded there are few affairs
In which the Devil doth not interfere.
We cannot undertake a journey even,
But Satan will be there to meddle with it
By hindering or by furthering. He hath led me
Into this thicket, struck me in the face
With branches of the trees, and so entangled
The fetlocks of my horse with vines and brambles,
That I must needs dismount, and search on foot

For the lost pathway leading to the village.

Reënter TITUBA.

What shape is this? What monstrous apparition,
Exceeding fierce, that none may pass that way?
Tell me, good woman, if you are a woman—

TITUBA.

I am a woman, but I am not good.
I am a Witch!

MATHER.

Then tell me, Witch and woman,
For you must know the pathways through this wood,
Where lieth Salem Village?

TITUBA.

Reverend sir,
The village is near by. I 'm going there
With these few herbs. I 'll lead you. Follow me.

MATHER.

First say, who are you? I am loath to follow
A stranger in this wilderness, for fear
Of being misled, and left in some morass.
Who are you?

TITUBA.

I am Tituba the Witch,
Wife of John Indian.

MATHER.

You are Tituba?
I know you then. You have renounced the Devil,
And have become a penitent confessor.
The Lord be praised! Go on, I 'll follow you.
Wait only till I fetch my horse, that stands
Tethered among the trees, not far from here.

TITUBA.

Let me get up behind you, reverend sir.

MATHER.

The Lord forbid! What would the people think,
If they should see the Reverend Cotton Mather
Ride into Salem with a Witch behind him?
The Lord forbid!

TITUBA.

I do not need a horse!
I can ride through the air upon a stick,
Above the tree-tops and above the houses,
And no one see me, no one overtake me!

[*Exeunt.*

SCENE II.—*A room at* JUSTICE HATHORNE'S. *A clock in the corner. Enter* HATHORNE *and* MATHER.

HATHORNE.

You are welcome, reverend sir, thrice welcome here
Beneath my humble roof.

MATHER.

I thank your Worship.

HATHORNE.

Pray you be seated. You must be fatigued
With your long ride through unfrequented woods.

They sit down.

MATHER.

You know the purport of my visit here,—
To be advised by you, and counsel with you,
And with the Reverend Clergy of the village,
Touching these witchcrafts that so much afflict you;
And see with mine own eyes the wonders told
Of spectres and the shadows of the dead,
That come back from their graves to speak with men.

HATHORNE.

Some men there are, I have known such, who think
That the two worlds—the seen and the unseen,
The world of matter and the world of spirit—
Are like the hemispheres upon our maps,
And touch each other only at a point.
But these two worlds are not divided thus,
Save for the purposes of common speech.
They form one globe, in which the parted seas
All flow together and are intermingled,
While the great continents remain distinct.

MATHER.

I doubt it not. The spiritual world
Lies all about us, and its avenues

Are open to the unseen feet of phantoms
That come and go, and we perceive them not,
Save by their influence, or when at times
A most mysterious Providence permits them
To manifest themselves to mortal eyes.

HATHORNE.

You, who are always welcome here among us,
Are doubly welcome now. We need your wisdom,
Your learning in these things, to be our guide.
The Devil hath come down in wrath upon us,
And ravages the land with all his hosts.

MATHER.

The Unclean Spirit said, "My name is Legion!"
Multitudes in the Valley of Destruction!
But when our fervent, well-directed prayers,
Which are the great artillery of Heaven,
Are brought into the field, I see them scattered
And driven like Autumn leaves before the wind.

HATHORNE.

You, as a Minister of God, can meet them
With spiritual weapons; but, alas!
I, as a Magistrate, must combat them
With weapons from the armory of the flesh.

MATHER.

These wonders of the world invisible,—
These spectral shapes that haunt our habitations,—
The multiplied and manifold afflictions
With which the aged and the dying saints
Have their death prefaced and their age imbittered,—
Are but prophetic trumpets that proclaim
The Second Coming of our Lord on earth.
The evening wolves will be much more abroad,
When we are near the evening of the world.

HATHORNE.

When you shall see, as I have hourly seen,
The sorceries and the witchcrafts that torment us,
See children tortured by invisible spirits,
And wasted and consumed by powers unseen,
You will confess the half has not been told you.

MATHER.

It must be so. The death-pangs of the Devil
Will make him more a Devil than before;
And Nebuchadnezzar's furnace will be heated
Seven times more hot before its putting out.

HATHORNE.

Advise me, reverend sir. I look to you
For counsel and for guidance in this matter.
What further shall we do?

MATHER.

Remember this,
That as a sparrow falls not to the ground
Without the will of God, so not a Devil
Can come down from the air without his leave.
We must inquire.

HATHORNE.

Dear sir, we have inquired;
Sifted the matter thoroughly through and through,
And then resifted it.

MATHER.

If God permits
These Evil Spirits from the unseen regions
To visit us with surprising informations,
We must inquire what cause there is for this,
But not receive the testimony borne
By spectres as conclusive proof of guilt
In the accused.

HATHORNE.

Upon such evidence
We do not rest our case. The ways are many
In which the guilty do betray themselves.

MATHER.

Be careful. Carry the knife with such exactness,
That on one side no innocent blood be shed
By too excessive zeal, and, on the other
No shelter given to any work of darkness.

HATHORNE.

For one, I do not fear excess of zeal.
What do we gain by parleying with the Devil?
You reason, but you hesitate to act!

Ah, reverend sir! believe me, in such cases
The only safety is in acting promptly.
'T is not the part of wisdom to delay
In things where not to do is still to do
A deed more fatal than the deed we shrink from.
You are a man of books and meditation,
But I am one who acts.

MATHER.

God give us wisdom
In the directing of this thorny business,
And guide us, lest New England should become
Of an unsavory and sulphurous odor
In the opinion of the world abroad!

The clock strikes.

I never hear the striking of a clock
Without a warning and an admonition
That time is on the wing, and we must quicken
Our tardy pace in journeying Heavenward,
As Israel did in journeying Canaan-ward!

They rise.

HATHORNE.

Then let us make all haste; and I will show you
In what disguises and what fearful shapes
The Unclean Spirits haunt this neighborhood,
And you will pardon my excess of zeal.

MATHER.

Ah, poor New England! He who hurricanoed
The house of Job is making now on thee
One last assault, more deadly and more snarled
With unintelligible circumstances
Than any thou hast hitherto encountered!

[*Exeunt.*

SCENE III.—*A room in* WALCOT'S *house.* MARY WALCOT *seated in an arm-chair.* TITUBA *with a mirror.*

MARY.

Tell me another story, Tituba.
A drowsiness is stealing over me
Which is not sleep; for, though I close mine eyes,
I am awake, and in another world.

Dim faces of the dead and of the absent
Come floating up before me,—floating, fading,
And disappearing.

TITUBA.

Look into this glass.
What see you?

MARY.

Nothing but a golden vapor.
Yes, something more. An island, with the sea
Breaking all round it, like a blooming hedge.
What land is this?

TITUBA.

It is San Salvador,
Where Tituba was born. What see you now?

MARY.

A man all black and fierce.

TITUBA.

That is my father.
He was an Obi man, and taught me magic,—
Taught me the use of herbs and images.
What is he doing?

MARY.

Holding in his hand
A waxen figure. He is melting it
Slowly before a fire.

TITUBA.

And now what see you?

MARY.

A woman lying on a bed of leaves,
Wasted and worn away. Ah, she is dying!

TITUBA.

That is the way the Obi men destroy
The people they dislike! That is the way
Some one is wasting and consuming you.

MARY.

You terrify me, Tituba! Oh, save me
From those who make me pine and waste away!
Who are they? Tell me.

TITUBA.

That I do not know,
But you will see them. They will come to you.

MARY.

No, do not let them come! I cannot bear it!
I am too weak to bear it! I am dying.

Falls into a trance.

TITUBA.

Hark! there is some one coming!

Enter HATHORNE, MATHER, *and* WALCOT.

WALCOT.

There she lies,
Wasted and worn by devilish incantations!
O my poor sister!

MATHER.

Is she always thus?

WALCOT.

Nay, she is sometimes tortured by convulsions.

MATHER.

Poor child! How thin she is! How wan and wasted!

HATHORNE.

Observe her. She is troubled in her sleep.

MATHER.

Some fearful vision haunts her.

HATHORNE.

You now see
With your own eyes, and touch with your own hands,
The mysteries of this Witchcraft.

MATHER.

One would need
The hands of Briareus and the eyes of Argus
To see and touch them all.

HATHORNE.

You now have entered
The realm of ghosts and phantoms,—the vast realm
Of the unknown and the invisible,
Through whose wide-open gates there blows a wind
From the dark valley of the shadow of Death,
That freezes us with horror.

MARY (*starting*).

Take her hence!
Take her away from me. I see her there!
She 's coming to torment me!

WALCOT (*taking her hand*).

O my sister!
What frightens you? She neither hears nor sees me.
She 's in a trance.

MARY.

Do you not see her there?

TITUBA.

My child, who is it?

MARY.

Ah, I do not know.
I cannot see her face.

TITUBA.

How is she clad?

MARY.

She wears a crimson bodice. In her hand
She holds an image, and is pinching it
Between her fingers. Ah, she tortures me!
I see her face now. It is Goodwife Bishop!
Why does she torture me? I never harmed her!
And now she strikes me with an iron rod!
Oh, I am beaten!

MATHER.

This is wonderful!
I can see nothing! Is this apparition
Visibly there, and yet we cannot see it?

HATHORNE.

It is. The spectre is invisible
Unto our grosser senses, but she sees it.

MARY.

Look! look! there is another clad in gray!
She holds a spindle in her hand, and threatens
To stab me with it! It is Goodwife Corey!
Keep her away! Now she is coming at me!
O mercy! mercy!

WALCOT (*thrusting with his sword*).
There is nothing there!
MATHER (*to* HATHORNE).
Do you see anything?
HATHORNE.
The laws that govern
The spiritual world prevent our seeing
Things palpable and visible to her.
These spectres are to us as if they were not.
Mark her; she wakes.
TITUBA *touches her, and she awakes.*
MARY.
Who are these gentlemen?
WALCOT.
They are our friends. Dear Mary, are you better?
MARY.
Weak, very weak.
Taking a spindle from her lap, and holding it up.
How came this spindle here?
TITUBA.
You wrenched it from the hand of Goodwife Corey
When she rushed at you.
HATHORNE.
Mark that, reverend sir!
MATHER.
It is most marvellous, most inexplicable!
TITUBA (*picking up a bit of gray cloth from the floor*).
And here, too, is a bit of her gray dress,
That the sword cut away.
MATHER.
Beholding this,
It were indeed by far more credulous
To be incredulous than to believe.
None but a Sadducee, who doubts of all
Pertaining to the spiritual world,
Could doubt such manifest and damning proofs!
HATHORNE.
Are you convinced?

MATHER (*to* MARY).

Dear child, be comforted!
Only by prayer and fasting can you drive
These Unclean Spirits from you. An old man
Gives you his blessing. God be with you, Mary!

ACT II.

SCENE I.—GILES COREY'S *farm. Morning. Enter* COREY, *with a horseshoe and a hammer.*

COREY.

The Lord hath prospered me. The rising sun
Shines on my Hundred Acres and my woods
As if he loved them. On a morn like this
I can forgive mine enemies, and thank God
For all his goodness unto me and mine.
My orchard groans with russets and pear-mains;
My ripening corn shines golden in the sun;
My barns are crammed with hay, my cattle thrive;
The birds sing blithely on the trees around me!
And blither than the birds my heart within me.
But Satan still goes up and down the earth;
And to protect this house from his assaults,
And keep the powers of darkness from my door,
This horseshoe will I nail upon the threshold.

Nails down the horseshoe.

There, ye night-hags and witches that torment
The neighborhood, ye shall not enter here!—
What is the matter in the field?—John Gloyd!
The cattle are all running to the woods!—
John Gloyd! Where is the man?

Enter JOHN GLOYD.

Look there!
What ails the cattle? Are they all bewitched?
They run like mad.

GLOYD.

They have been overlooked.

COREY.

The Evil Eye is on them sure enough.
Call all the men. Be quick. Go after them!

Exit GLOYD *and enter* MARTHA.

MARTHA.

What is amiss?

COREY.

The cattle are bewitched.
They are broken loose and making for the woods.

MARTHA.

Why will you harbor such delusions, Giles?
Bewitched? Well, then it was John Gloyd bewitched them;
I saw him even now take down the bars
And turn them loose! They 're only frolicsome.

COREY.

The rascal!

MARTHA.

I was standing in the road,
Talking with Goodwife Proctor, and I saw him.

COREY.

With Proctor's wife? And what says Goodwife Proctor?

MARTHA.

Sad things indeed; the saddest you can hear
Of Bridget Bishop. She 's cried out upon!

COREY.

Poor soul! I 've known her forty year or more.
She was the widow Wasselby; and then
She married Oliver, and Bishop next.
She 's had three husbands. I remember well
My games of shovel-board at Bishop's tavern
In the old merry days, and she so gay
With her red paragon bodice and her ribbons!
Ah, Bridget Bishop always was a Witch!

MARTHA.

They 'll little help her now,—her caps and ribbons,
And her red paragon bodice, and her plumes,
With which she flaunted in the Meeting-house!
When next she goes there, it will be for trial.

COREY.

When will that be?

MARTHA.

This very day at ten.

COREY.

Then get you ready. We will go and see it.
Come; you shall ride behind me on the pillion.

MARTHA.

Not I. You know I do not like such things.
I wonder you should. I do not believe
In Witches nor in Witchcraft.

COREY.

Well, I do.
There 's a strange fascination in it all,
That draws me on and on, I know not why.

MARTHA.

What do we know of spirits good or ill,
Or of their power to help us or to harm us?

COREY.

Surely what 's in the Bible must be true.
Did not an Evil Spirit come on Saul?
Did not the Witch of Endor bring the ghost
Of Samuel from his grave? The Bible says so.

MARTHA.

That happened very long ago.

COREY.

With God
There is no long ago.

MARTHA.

There is with us.

COREY.

And Mary Magdalene had seven devils,
And he who dwelt among the tombs a legion!

MARTHA.

God's power is infinite. I do not doubt it.
If in His providence He once permitted
Such things to be among the Israelites,
It does not follow He permits them now,
And among us who are not Israelites.
But we will not dispute about it, Giles.
Go to the village, if you think it best,
And leave me here; I 'll go about my work.

[*Exit into the house.*

COREY.

And I will go and saddle the gray mare.
The last word always. That is woman's nature.
If an old man will marry a young wife,
He must make up his mind to many things.
It 's putting new cloth into an old garment,
When the strain comes, it is the old gives way.

Goes to the door.

O Martha! I forgot to tell you something.
I 've had a letter from a friend of mine,
A certain Richard Gardner of Nantucket,
Master and owner of a whaling-vessel;
He writes that he is coming down to see us.
I hope you 'll like him.

MARTHA.

I will do my best.

COREY.

That 's a good woman. Now I will be gone.
I 've not seen Gardner for this twenty year;
But there is something of the sea about him,—
Something so open, generous, large, and strong,
It makes me love him better than a brother.

[*Exit.*

MARTHA *comes to the door.*

MARTHA.

Oh these old friends and cronies of my husband,
These captains from Nantucket and the Cape,
That come and turn my house into a tavern
With their carousing! Still, there 's something frank
In these seafaring men that makes me like them.
Why, here 's a horseshoe nailed upon the doorstep!
Giles has done this to keep away the Witches.
I hope this Richard Gardner will bring with him
A gale of good sound common-sense, to blow
The fog of these delusions from his brain!

COREY (*within*).

Ho! Martha! Martha!

Enter COREY.

Have you seen my saddle?

MARTHA.

I saw it yesterday.

COREY.

Where did you see it?

MARTHA.

On a gray mare, that somebody was riding
Along the village road.

COREY.

Who was it? Tell me.

MARTHA.

Some one who should have stayed at home.

COREY (*restraining himself*).

I see!
Don't vex me, Martha. Tell me where it is.

MARTHA.

I 've hidden it away.

COREY.

Go fetch it me.

MARTHA.

Go find it.

COREY.

No. I 'll ride down to the village
Bare-back; and when the people stare and say,
"Giles Corey, where 's your saddle?" I will answer,
"A Witch has stolen it." How shall you like that?

MARTHA.

I shall not like it.

COREY.

Then go fetch the saddle.

[*Exit* MARTHA.

If an old man will marry a young wife,
Why then—why then—why then—he must spell Baker!

Enter MARTHA *with the saddle, which she throws down.*

MARTHA.

There! There 's the saddle.

COREY.

Take it up.

MARTHA.

I won't!

COREY.

Then let it lie there. I 'll ride to the village,
And say you are a Witch.

MARTHA.

No, not that, Giles.

She takes up the saddle.

COREY.

Now come with me, and saddle the gray mare
With your own hands; and you shall see me ride
Along the village road as is becoming
Giles Corey of the Salem Farms, your husband!

[*Exeunt.*

SCENE II.—*The Green in front of the Meeting-house in Salem Village. People coming and going. Enter* GILES COREY.

COREY.

A melancholy end! Who would have thought
That Bridget Bishop e'er would come to this?
Accused, convicted, and condemned to death
For Witchcraft! And so good a woman too!

A FARMER.

Good morrow, neighbor Corey.

COREY (*not hearing him*).

Who is safe?
How do I know but under my own roof
I too may harbor Witches, and some Devil
Be plotting and contriving against me?

FARMER.

He does not hear. Good morrow, neighbor Corey!

COREY.

Good morrow.

FARMER.

Have you seen John Proctor lately?

COREY.

No, I have not.

FARMER.

Then do not see him, Corey.

COREY.

Why should I not?

FARMER.

Because he 's angry with you.
So keep out of his way. Avoid a quarrel.

COREY.

Why does he seek to fix a quarrel on me?

FARMER.

He says you burned his house.

COREY.

I burn his house?
If he says that, John Proctor is a liar!
The night his house was burned I was in bed,
And I can prove it! Why, we are old friends!
He could not say that of me.

FARMER.

He did say it.
I heard him say it.

COREY.

Then he shall unsay it.

FARMER.

He said you did it out of spite to him
For taking part against you in the quarrel
You had with your John Gloyd about his wages.
He says you murdered Goodell; that you trampled
Upon his body till he breathed no more.
And so beware of him; that 's my advice!

[*Exit.*

COREY.

By Heaven! this is too much! I 'll seek him out,
And make him eat his words, or strangle him.
I 'll not be slandered at a time like this,
When every word is made an accusation,
When every whisper kills, and every man
Walks with a halter round his neck!

Enter GLOYD *in haste.*

What now?

GLOYD.

I came to look for you. The cattle—

COREY.

Well,
What of them? Have you found them?

GLOYD.

They are dead.
I followed them through the woods, across the meadows;
Then they all leaped into the Ipswich River,
And swam across, but could not climb the bank,
And so were drowned.

COREY.

You are to blame for this;
For you took down the bars, and let them loose.

GLOYD.

That I deny. They broke the fences down.
You know they were bewitched.

COREY.

Ah, my poor cattle!
The Evil Eye was on them; that is true.
Day of disaster! Most unlucky day!
Why did I leave my ploughing and my reaping
To plough and reap this Sodom and Gomorrah?
Oh, I could drown myself for sheer vexation!

[*Exit.*

GLOYD.

He 's going for his cattle. He won't find them.
By this time they have drifted out to sea.
They will not break his fences any more,
Though they may break his heart. And what care I?

[*Exit.*

SCENE III.—COREY'S *kitchen. A table with supper.* MARTHA *knitting.*

MARTHA.

He 's come at last. I hear him in the passage.
Something has gone amiss with him to-day;
I know it by his step, and by the sound
The door made as he shut it. He is angry.

Enter COREY *with his riding-whip. As he speaks he takes off his hat and gloves, and throws them down violently.*

COREY.

I say if Satan ever entered man
He 's in John Proctor!

MARTHA.

Giles, what is the matter?
You frighten me.

COREY.

I say if any man
Can have a Devil in him, then that man
Is Proctor,—is John Proctor, and no other!

MARTHA.

Why, what has he been doing?

COREY.

Everything!
What do you think I heard there in the village?

MARTHA.

I 'm sure I cannot guess. What did you hear?

COREY.

He says I burned his house!

MARTHA.

Does he say that?

COREY.

He says I burned his house. I was in bed
And fast asleep that night; and I can prove it.

MARTHA.

If he says that, I think the Father of Lies
Is surely in the man.

COREY.

He does say that,
And that I did it to wreak vengeance on him
For taking sides against me in the quarrel
I had with that John Gloyd about his wages.
And God knows that I never bore him malice
For that, as I have told him twenty times!

MARTHA.

It is John Gloyd has stirred him up to this.
I do not like that Gloyd. I think him crafty,
Not to be trusted, sullen, and untruthful.
Come, have your supper. You are tired and hungry.

COREY.

I 'm angry, and not hungry.

MARTHA.

Do eat something.
You 'll be the better for it.

COREY (*sitting down*).

I 'm not hungry.

MARTHA.

Let not the sun go down upon your wrath.

COREY.

It has gone down upon it, and will rise
To-morrow, and go down again upon it.
They have trumped up against me the old story
Of causing Goodell's death by trampling on him.

MARTHA.

Oh, that is false. I know it to be false.

COREY.

He has been dead these fourteen years or more.
Why can't they let him rest? Why must they drag him
Out of his grave to give me a bad name?
I did not kill him. In his bed he died,
As most men die, because his hour had come.
I have wronged no man. Why should Proctor say
Such things about me? I will not forgive him
Till he confesses he has slandered me.
Then, I 've more trouble. All my cattle gone.

MARTHA.

They will come back again.

COREY.

Not in this world.
Did I not tell you they were overlooked?
They ran down through the woods, into the meadows,
And tried to swim the river, and were drowned.
It is a heavy loss.

MARTHA.

I 'm sorry for it.

COREY.

All my dear oxen dead. I loved them, Martha,
Next to yourself. I liked to look at them,
And watch the breath come out of their wide nostrils,
And see their patient eyes. Somehow I thought
It gave me strength only to look at them.

And how they strained their necks against the yoke
If I but spoke, or touched them with the goad!
They were my friends; and when Gloyd came and told me
They were all drowned, I could have drowned myself
From sheer vexation; and I said as much
To Gloyd and others.

MARTHA.

Do not trust John Gloyd
With anything you would not have repeated.

COREY.

As I came through the woods this afternoon,
Impatient at my loss, and much perplexed
With all that I had heard there in the village,
The yellow leaves lit up the trees about me
Like an enchanted palace, and I wished
I knew enough of magic or of Witchcraft
To change them into gold. Then suddenly
A tree shook down some crimson leaves upon me,
Like drops of blood, and in the path before me
Stood Tituba the Indian, the old crone.

MARTHA.

Were you not frightened?

COREY.

No, I do not think
I know the meaning of that word. Why frightened?
I am not one of those who think the Lord
Is waiting till He catches them some day
In the back yard alone! What should I fear?
She started from the bushes by the path,
And had a basket full of herbs and roots
For some witch-broth or other,—the old hag!

MARTHA.

She has been here to-day.

COREY.

With hand outstretched
She said: "Giles Corey, will you sign the Book?"
"Avaunt!" I cried: "Get thee behind me, Satan!"
At which she laughed and left me. But a voice
Was whispering in my ear continually:

"Self-murder is no crime. The life of man
Is his, to keep it or to throw away!"

MARTHA.

'T was a temptation of the Evil One!
Giles, Giles! why will you harbor these dark thoughts?

COREY (*rising*).

I am too tired to talk. I 'll go to bed.

MARTHA.

First tell me something about Bridget Bishop.
How did she look? You saw her? You were there?

COREY.

I 'll tell you that to-morrow, not to-night.
I 'll go to bed.

MARTHA.

First let us pray together.

COREY.

I cannot pray to-night.

MARTHA.

Say the Lord's Prayer,
And that will comfort you.

COREY.

I cannot say,
"As we forgive those that have sinned against us,"
When I do not forgive them.

MARTHA (*kneeling on the hearth*).

God forgive you!

COREY.

I will not make believe! I say, to-night
There 's something thwarts me when I wish to pray,
And thrusts into my mind, instead of prayers,
Hate and revenge, and things that are not prayers.
Something of my old self,—my old, bad life,—
And the old Adam in me, rises up,
And will not let me pray. I am afraid
The Devil hinders me. You know I say
Just what I think, and nothing more nor less,
And, when I pray, my heart is in my prayer.
I cannot say one thing and mean another.
If I can't pray, I will not make believe!

[*Exit* COREY. MARTHA *continues kneeling*.

ACT III.

SCENE I.—GILES COREY'S *kitchen. Morning.* COREY *and* MARTHA *sitting at the breakfast-table.*

COREY (*rising*).

Well, now I 've told you all I saw and heard
Of Bridget Bishop; and I must be gone.

MARTHA.

Don't go into the village, Giles, to-day.
Last night you came back tired and out of humor.

COREY.

Say, angry; say, right angry. I was never
In a more devilish temper in my life.
All things went wrong with me.

MARTHA.

You were much vexed;
So don't go to the village.

COREY (*going*).

No, I won't.
I won't go near it. We are going to mow
The Ipswich meadows for the aftermath,
The crop of sedge and rowens.

MARTHA.

Stay a moment.
I want to tell you what I dreamed last night.
Do you believe in dreams?

COREY.

Why, yes and no.
When they come true, then I believe in them;
When they come false, I don't believe in them.
But let me hear. What did you dream about?

MARTHA.

I dreamed that you and I were both in prison;
That we had fetters on our hands and feet;
That we were taken before the Magistrates,
And tried for Witchcraft, and condemned to death!
I wished to pray; they would not let me pray;
You tried to comfort me, and they forbade it.
But the most dreadful thing in all my dream
Was that they made you testify against me!

And then there came a kind of mist between us;
I could not see you; and I woke in terror.
I never was more thankful in my life
Than when I found you sleeping at my side!

COREY (*with tenderness*).

It was our talk last night that made you dream.
I 'm sorry for it. I 'll control myself
Another time, and keep my temper down!
I do not like such dreams.—Remember, Martha,
I 'm going to mow the Ipswich River meadows;
If Gardner comes, you 'll tell him where to find me.
[*Exit.*

MARTHA.

So this delusion grows from bad to worse.
First, a forsaken and forlorn old woman,
Ragged and wretched, and without a friend;
Then something higher. Now it 's Bridget Bishop;
God only knows whose turn it will be next!
The Magistrates are blind, the people mad!
If they would only seize the Afflicted Children,
And put them in the Workhouse, where they should be,
There 'd be an end of all this wickedness. [*Exit.*

SCENE II.—*A street in Salem Village. Enter* MATHER *and* HATHORNE.

MATHER.

Yet one thing troubles me.

HATHORNE.

And what is that?

MATHER.

May not the Devil take the outward shape
Of innocent persons? Are we not in danger,
Perhaps, of punishing some who are not guilty?

HATHORNE.

As I have said, we do not trust alone
To spectral evidence.

MATHER.

And then again,
If any shall be put to death for Witchcraft,
We do but kill the body, not the soul.

The Unclean Spirits that possessed them once
Live still, to enter into other bodies.
What have we gained? Surely, there's nothing gained.

HATHORNE.

Doth not the Scripture say, "Thou shalt not suffer
A Witch to live?"

MATHER.

The Scripture sayeth it,
But speaketh to the Jews; and we are Christians.
What say the laws of England?

HATHORNE.

They make Witchcraft
Felony without the benefit of Clergy.
Witches are burned in England. You have read—
For you read all things, not a book escapes you—
The famous Demonology of King James?

MATHER.

A curious volume. I remember also
The plot of the Two Hundred, with one Fian,
The Registrar of the Devil, at their head,
To drown his Majesty on his return
From Denmark; how they sailed in sieves or riddles
Unto North Berwick Kirk in Lothian,
And, landing there, danced hand in hand, and sang,
"Goodwife, go ye before! goodwife, go ye!
If ye 'll not go before, goodwife, let me!"
While Geilis Duncan played the Witches' Reel
Upon a jews-harp.

HATHORNE.

Then you know full well
The English law, and that in England Witches,
When lawfully convicted and attainted,
Are put to death.

MATHER.

When lawfully convicted;
That is the point.

HATHORNE.

You heard the evidence
Produced before us yesterday at the trial
Of Bridget Bishop.

MATHER.

One of the Afflicted,
I know, bore witness to the apparition
Of ghosts unto the spectre of this Bishop,
Saying, "You murdered us!" of the truth whereof
There was in matter of fact too much suspicion.

HATHORNE.

And when she cast her eyes on the Afflicted,
They were struck down; and this in such a manner
There could be no collusion in the business.
And when the accused but laid her hand upon them,
As they lay in their swoons, they straight revived,
Although they stirred not when the others touched them.

MATHER.

What most convinced me of the woman's guilt
Was finding hidden in her cellar wall
Those poppets made of rags, with headless pins
Stuck into them point outwards, and whereof
She could not give a reasonable account.

HATHORNE.

When you shall read the testimony given
Before the Court in all the other cases,
I am persuaded you will find the proof
No less conclusive than it was in this.
Come, then, with me, and I will tax your patience
With reading of the documents so far
As may convince you that these sorcerers
Are lawfully convicted and attainted.
Like doubting Thomas, you shall lay your hand
Upon these wounds, and you will doubt no more.

[*Exeunt.*

SCENE III.—*A room in* COREY'S *house.* MARTHA *and two Deacons of the church.*

MARTHA.

Be seated. I am glad to see you here.
I know what you are come for. You are come
To question me, and learn from my own lips
If I have any dealings with the Devil;
In short, if I 'm a Witch.

DEACON (*sitting down*).

Such is our purpose.
How could you know beforehand why we came?

MARTHA.

'T was only a surmise.

DEACON.

We came to ask you,
You being with us in church covenant,
What part you have, if any, in these matters.

MARTHA.

And I make answer, No part whatsoever.
I am a farmer's wife, a working woman;
You see my spinning-wheel, you see my loom,
You know the duties of a farmer's wife,
And are not ignorant that my life among you
Has been without reproach until this day.
Is it not true?

DEACON.

So much we 're bound to own;
And say it frankly, and without reserve.

MARTHA.

I 've heard the idle tales that are abroad;
I 've heard it whispered that I am a Witch;
I cannot help it. I do not believe
In any Witchcraft. It is a delusion.

DEACON.

How can you say that it is a delusion,
When all our learned and good men believe it?—
Our Ministers and worshipful Magistrates?

MARTHA.

Their eyes are blinded, and see not the truth.
Perhaps one day they will be open to it.

DEACON.

You answer boldly. The Afflicted Children
Say you appeared to them.

MARTHA.

And did they say
What clothes I came in?

DEACON.

No, they could not tell.
They said that you foresaw our visit here,
And blinded them, so that they could not see
The clothes you wore.

MARTHA.

The cunning, crafty girls!
I say to you, in all sincerity,
I never have appeared to any one
In my own person. If the Devil takes
My shape to hurt these children, or afflict them,
I am not guilty of it. And I say
It 's all a mere delusion of the senses.

DEACON.

I greatly fear that you will find too late
It is not so.

MARTHA (*rising*).

They do accuse me falsely.
It is delusion, or it is deceit.
There is a story in the ancient Scriptures
Which much I wonder comes not to your minds.
Let me repeat it to you.

DEACON.

We will hear it.

MARTHA.

It came to pass that Naboth had a vineyard
Hard by the palace of the King called Ahab.
And Ahab, King of Israel, spake to Naboth,
And said to him, Give unto me thy vineyard,
That I may have it for a garden of herbs,
And I will give a better vineyard for it,
Or, if it seemeth good to thee, its worth
In money. And then Naboth said to Ahab,
The Lord forbid it me that I should give
The inheritance of my fathers unto thee.
And Ahab came into his house displeased
And heavy at the words which Naboth spake,
And laid him down upon his bed, and turned
His face away; and he would eat no bread.
And Jezebel, the wife of Ahab, came

And said to him, Why is thy spirit sad?
And he said unto her, Because I spake
To Naboth, to the Jezreelite, and said,
Give me thy vineyard; and he answered, saying,
I will not give my vineyard unto thee.
And Jezebel, the wife of Ahab, said,
Dost thou not rule the realm of Israel?
Arise, eat bread, and let thy heart be merry;
I will give Naboth's vineyard unto thee.
So she wrote letters in King Ahab's name,
And sealed them with his seal, and sent the letters
Unto the elders that were in his city
Dwelling with Naboth, and unto the nobles;
And in the letters wrote, Proclaim a fast;
And set this Naboth high among the people,
And set two men, the sons of Belial,
Before him, to bear witness and to say,
Thou didst blaspheme against God and the King;
And carry him out and stone him, that he die!
And the elders and the nobles of the city
Did even as Jezebel, the wife of Ahab,
Had sent to them and written in the letters.
And then it came to pass, when Ahab heard
Naboth was dead, that Ahab rose to go
Down unto Naboth's vineyard, and to take
Possession of it. And the word of God
Came to Elijah, saying to him, Arise,
Go down to meet the King of Israel
In Naboth's vineyard, whither he hath gone
To take possession. Thou shalt speak to him,
Saying, Thus saith the Lord! What! hast thou killed
And also taken possession? In the place
Wherein the dogs have licked the blood of Naboth
Shall the dogs lick thy blood,—ay, even thine!

Both of the Deacons start from their seats.

And Ahab then, the King of Israel,
Said, Hast thou found me, O mine enemy?
Elijah the Prophet answered, I have found thee!
So will it be with those who have stirred up
The Sons of Belial here to bear false witness

And swear away the lives of innocent people;
Their enemy will find them out at last,
The Prophet's voice will thunder, I have found thee!

[*Exeunt.*

SCENE IV.—*Meadows on Ipswich River.* COREY *and his men mowing;* COREY *in advance.*

COREY.

Well done, my men. You see, I lead the field!
I 'm an old man, but I can swing a scythe
Better than most of you, though you be younger.

Hangs his scythe upon a tree.

GLOYD (*aside to the others*).

How strong he is! It 's supernatural.
No man so old as he is has such strength.
The Devil helps him!

COREY (*wiping his forehead*).

Now we 'll rest awhile,
And take our nooning. What 's the matter with you?
You are not angry with me,—are you, Gloyd?
Come, come, we will not quarrel. Let 's be friends.
It 's an old story, that the Raven said,
"Read the Third of Colossians and fifteenth."

GLOYD.

You 're handier at the scythe, but I can beat you
At wrestling.

COREY.

Well, perhaps so. I don't know.
I never wrestled with you. Why, you 're vexed!
Come, come, don't bear a grudge.

GLOYD.

You are afraid.

COREY.

What should I be afraid of? All bear witness
The challenge comes from him. Now, then, my man.

They wrestle, and GLOYD *is thrown.*

ONE OF THE MEN.

That 's a fair fall.

ANOTHER.

'T was nothing but a foil!

OTHERS.

You 've hurt him!

COREY (*helping* GLOYD *rise*).

No; this meadow-land is soft.
You 're not hurt,—are you, Gloyd?

GLOYD (*rising*).

No, not much hurt.

COREY.

Well, then, shake hands; and there 's an end of it.
How do you like that Cornish hug, my lad?
And now we 'll see what 's in our basket here.

GLOYD (*aside*).

The Devil and all his imps are in that man!
The clutch of his ten fingers burns like fire!

COREY (*reverentially taking off his hat*).

God bless the food He hath provided for us,
And make us thankful for it, for Christ's sake!

He lifts up a keg of cider, and drinks from it.

GLOYD.

Do you see that? Don't tell me it 's not Witchcraft.
Two of us could not lift that cask as he does!

COREY *puts down the keg, and opens a basket. A voice is heard calling.*

VOICE.

Ho! Corey, Corey!

COREY.

What is that? I surely
Heard some one calling me by name!

VOICE.

Giles Corey!

Enter a boy, running, and out of breath.

BOY.

Is Master Corey here?

COREY.

Yes, here I am.

BOY.

O Master Corey!

COREY.

Well?

BOY.

Your wife—your wife—

COREY.

What 's happened to my wife?

BOY.

She 's sent to prison!

COREY.

The dream! the dream! O God, be merciful!

BOY.

She sent me here to tell you.

COREY (*putting on his jacket*).

Where 's my horse?
Don't stand there staring, fellows. Where 's my horse?

[*Exit* COREY.

GLOYD.

Under the trees there. Run, old man, run, run!
You 've got some one to wrestle with you now
Who 'll trip your heels up, with your Cornish hug.
If there 's a Devil, he has got you now.
Ah, there he goes! His horse is snorting fire!

ONE OF THE MEN.

John Gloyd, don't talk so! It 's a shame to talk so!
He 's a good master, though you quarrel with him.

GLOYD.

If hard work and low wages make good masters,
Then he is one. But I think otherwise.
Come, let us have our dinner and be merry,
And talk about the old man and the Witches.
I know some stories that will make you laugh.

They sit down on the grass, and eat.

Now there are Goody Cloyse and Goody Good,
Who have not got a decent tooth between them,
And yet these children—the Afflicted Children—
Say that they bite them, and show marks of teeth
Upon their arms!

ONE OF THE MEN.

That makes the wonder greater.
That 's Witchcraft. Why, if they had teeth like yours,
'T would be no wonder if the girls were bitten!

GLOYD.

And then those ghosts that come out of their graves
And cry, "You murdered us! you murdered us!"

ONE OF THE MEN.

And all those Apparitions that stick pins
Into the flesh of the Afflicted Children!

GLOYD.

Oh those Afflicted Children! They know well
Where the pins come from. I can tell you that.
And there 's old Corey, he has got a horseshoe
Nailed on his doorstep to keep off the Witches,
And all the same his wife has gone to prison.

ONE OF THE MEN.

Oh, she 's no Witch. I 'll swear that Goodwife Corey
Never did harm to any living creature.
She 's a good woman, if there ever was one.

GLOYD.

Well, we shall see. As for that Bridget Bishop,
She has been tried before; some years ago
A negro testified he saw her shape
Sitting upon the rafters in a barn,
And holding in its hand an egg; and while
He went to fetch his pitchfork, she had vanished.
And now be quiet, will you? I am tired,
And want to sleep here on the grass a little.

They stretch themselves on the grass.

ONE OF THE MEN.

There may be Witches riding through the air
Over our heads on broomsticks at this moment,
Bound for some Satan's Sabbath in the woods
To be baptized.

GLOYD.

I wish they 'd take you with them,
And hold you under water, head and ears,
Till you were drowned; and that would stop your talking,
If nothing else will. Let me sleep, I say.

ACT IV.

SCENE I.—*The Green in front of the village Meeting-house. An excited crowd gathering. Enter* JOHN GLOYD.

A FARMER.

Who will be tried to-day?

A SECOND.

I do not know.
Here is John Gloyd. Ask him; he knows.

FARMER.

John Gloyd,
Whose turn is it to-day?

GLOYD.

It 's Goodwife Corey's.

FARMER.

Giles Corey's wife?

GLOYD.

The same. She is not mine.
It will go hard with her with all her praying.
The hypocrite! She 's always on her knees;
But she prays to the Devil when she prays.
Let us go in.

A trumpet blows.

FARMER.

Here come the Magistrates.

SECOND FARMER.

Who 's the tall man in front?

GLOYD.

Oh, that is Hathorne,
A Justice of the Court, and Quartermaster
In the Three County Troop. He 'll sift the matter.
That 's Corwin with him; and the man in black
Is Cotton Mather, Minister of Boston.

Enter HATHORNE *and other Magistrates on horseback, followed by the Sheriff, constables, and attendants on foot. The Magistrates dismount, and enter the Meeting-house, with the rest.*

FARMER.

The Meeting-house is full. I never saw
So great a crowd before.

GLOYD.

No matter. Come.
We shall find room enough by elbowing
Our way among them. Put your shoulder to it.

FARMER.

There were not half so many at the trial
Of Goodwife Bishop.

GLOYD.

Keep close after me.
I 'll find a place for you. They 'll want me there.
I am a friend of Corey's, as you know,
And he can't do without me just at present.

[*Exeunt.*

SCENE II.—*Interior of the Meeting-house.* MATHER *and the Magistrates seated in front of the pulpit. Before them a raised platform.* MARTHA *in chains.* COREY *near her.* MARY WALCOT *in a chair. A crowd of spectators, among them* GLOYD. *Confusion and murmurs during the scene.*

HATHORNE.

Call Martha Corey.

MARTHA.

I am here.

HATHORNE.

Come forward.

She ascends the platform.

The Jurors of our Sovereign Lord and Lady
The King and Queen, here present, do accuse you
Of having on the tenth of June last past,
And divers other times before and after,
Wickedly used and practised certain arts
Called Witchcrafts, Sorceries, and Incantations,
Against one Mary Walcot, single woman,
Of Salem Village; by which wicked arts
The aforesaid Mary Walcot was tormented,
Tortured, afflicted, pined, consumed, and wasted,
Against the peace of our Sovereign Lord and Lady
The King and Queen, as well as of the Statute
Made and provided in that case. What say you?

MARTHA.

Before I answer, give me leave to pray.

HATHORNE.

We have not sent for you, nor are we here,
To hear you pray, but to examine you

In whatsoever is alleged against you.
Why do you hurt this person?

MARTHA.

I do not.
I am not guilty of the charge against me.

MARY.

Avoid, she-devil! You torment me now!
Avoid, avoid, Witch!

MARTHA.

I am innocent.
I never had to do with any Witchcraft
Since I was born. I am a gospel woman.

MARY.

You are a gospel Witch!

MARTHA (*clasping her hands*).

Ah me! ah me!
Oh, give me leave to pray!

MARY (*stretching out her hands*).

She hurts me now.
See, she has pinched my hands!

HATHORNE.

Who made these marks
Upon her hands?

MARTHA.

I do not know. I stand
Apart from her. I did not touch her hands.

HATHORNE.

Who hurt her then?

MARTHA.

I know not.

HATHORNE.

Do you think
She is bewitched?

MARTHA.

Indeed I do not think so.
I am no Witch, and have no faith in Witches.

HATHORNE.

Then answer me: When certain persons came
To see you yesterday, how did you know
Beforehand why they came?

MARTHA.

I had had speech,
The children said I hurt them, and I thought
These people came to question me about it.

HATHORNE.

How did you know the children had been told
To note the clothes you wore?

MARTHA.

My husband told me
What others said about it.

HATHORNE.

Goodman Corey,
Say, did you tell her?

COREY.

I must speak the truth;
I did not tell her. It was some one else.

HATHORNE.

Did you not say your husband told you so?
How dare you tell a lie in this assembly?
Who told you of the clothes? Confess the truth.

MARTHA *bites her lips, and is silent.*

You bite your lips, but do not answer me!

MARY.

Ah, she is biting me! Avoid, avoid!

HATHORNE.

You said your husband told you.

MARTHA.

Yes, he told me
The children said I troubled them.

HATHORNE.

Then tell me,
Why do you trouble them?

MARTHA.

I have denied it.

MARY.

She threatened me; stabbed at me with her spindle;
And, when my brother thrust her with his sword,
He tore her gown, and cut a piece away.
Here are they both, the spindle and the cloth.

Shows them.

HATHORNE.

And there are persons here who know the truth
Of what has now been said. What answer make you?

MARTHA.

I make no answer. Give me leave to pray.

HATHORNE.

Whom would you pray to?

MARTHA.

To my God and Father.

HATHORNE.

Who is your God and Father?

MARTHA.

The Almighty!

HATHORNE.

Doth he you pray to say that he is God?
It is the Prince of Darkness, and not God.

MARY.

There is a dark shape whispering in her ear.

HATHORNE.

What does it say to you?

MARTHA.

I see no shape.

HATHORNE.

Did you not hear it whisper?

MARTHA.

I heard nothing.

MARY.

What torture! Ah, what agony I suffer!

Falls into a swoon.

HATHORNE.

You see this woman cannot stand before you.
If you would look for mercy, you must look
In God's way, by confession of your guilt.
Why does your spectre haunt and hurt this person?

MARTHA.

I do not know. He who appeared of old
In Samuel's shape, a saint and glorified,
May come in whatsoever shape he chooses.
I cannot help it. I am sick at heart!

COREY.

O Martha, Martha! let me hold your hand.

HATHORNE.

No; stand aside, old man.

MARY (*starting up*).

Look there! Look there!
I see a little bird, a yellow bird,
Perched on her finger; and it pecks at me.
Ah, it will tear mine eyes out!

MARTHA.

I see nothing.

HATHORNE.

'T is the Familiar Spirit that attends her.

MARY.

Now it has flown away. It sits up there
Upon the rafters. It is gone; is vanished.

MARTHA.

Giles, wipe these tears of anger from mine eyes.
Wipe the sweat from my forehead. I am faint.

She leans against the railing.

MARY.

Oh, she is crushing me with all her weight!

HATHORNE.

Did you not carry once the Devil's Book
To this young woman?

MARTHA.

Never.

HATHORNE.

Have you signed it,
Or touched it?

MARTHA.

No; I never saw it.

HATHORNE.

Did you not scourge her with an iron rod?

MARTHA.

No, I did not. If any Evil Spirit
Has taken my shape to do these evil deeds,
I cannot help it. I am innocent.

HATHORNE.

Did you not say the Magistrates were blind?
That you would open their eyes?

MARTHA (*with a scornful laugh*).

Yes, I said that;
If you call me a sorceress, you are blind!
If you accuse the innocent, you are blind!
Can the innocent be guilty?

HATHORNE.

Did you not
On one occasion hide your husband's saddle
To hinder him from coming to the Sessions?

MARTHA.

I thought it was a folly in a farmer
To waste his time pursuing such illusions.

HATHORNE.

What was the bird that this young woman saw
Just now upon your hand?

MARTHA.

I know no bird.

HATHORNE.

Have you not dealt with a Familiar Spirit?

MARTHA.

No, never, never!

HATHORNE.

What then was the Book
You showed to this young woman, and besought her
To write in it?

MARTHA.

Where should I have a book?
I showed her none, nor have none.

MARY.

The next Sabbath
Is the Communion Day, but Martha Corey
Will not be there!

MARTHA.

Ah, you are all against me.
What can I do or say?

HATHORNE.

You can confess.

MARTHA.

No, I cannot, for I am innocent.

HATHORNE.

We have the proof of many witnesses
That you are guilty.

MARTHA.

Give me leave to speak.
Will you condemn me on such evidence,—
You who have known me for so many years?
Will you condemn me in this house of God,
Where I so long have worshipped with you all?
Where I have eaten the bread and drunk the wine
So many times at our Lord's Table with you?
Bear witness, you that hear me; you all know
That I have led a blameless life among you,
That never any whisper of suspicion
Was breathed against me till this accusation.
And shall this count for nothing? Will you take
My life away from me, because this girl,
Who is distraught, and not in her right mind,
Accuses me of things I blush to name?

HATHORNE.

What! is it not enough? Would you hear more?
Giles Corey!

COREY.

I am here.

HATHORNE.

Come forward, then.

COREY *ascends the platform.*

Is it not true, that on a certain night
You were impeded strangely in your prayers?
That something hindered you? and that you left
This woman here, your wife, kneeling alone
Upon the hearth?

COREY.

Yes; I cannot deny it.

HATHORNE.

Did you not say the Devil hindered you?

COREY.

I think I said some words to that effect.

HATHORNE.

Is it not true, that fourteen head of cattle,
To you belonging, broke from their enclosure
And leaped into the river, and were drowned?

COREY.

It is most true.

HATHORNE.

And did you not then say
That they were overlooked?

COREY.

So much I said.
I see; they 're drawing round me closer, closer,
A net I cannot break, cannot escape from! (*Aside.*)

HATHORNE.

Who did these things?

COREY.

I do not know who did them.

HATHORNE.

Then I will tell you. It is some one near you;
You see her now; this woman, your own wife.

COREY.

I call the heavens to witness, it is false!
She never harmed me, never hindered me
In anything but what I should not do.
And I bear witness in the sight of heaven,
And in God's house here, that I never knew her
As otherwise than patient, brave, and true,
Faithful, forgiving, full of charity,
A virtuous and industrious and good wife!

HATHORNE.

Tut, tut, man; do not rant so in your speech;
You are a witness, not an advocate!
Here, Sheriff, take this woman back to prison.

MARTHA.

O Giles, this day you 've sworn away my life!

MARY.

Go, go and join the Witches at the door.
Do you not hear the drum? Do you not see them?
Go quick. They 're waiting for you. You are late.

[*Exit* MARTHA; COREY *following*.

COREY.

The dream! the dream! the dream!

HATHORNE.

What does he say?
Giles Corey, go not hence. You are yourself
Accused of Witchcraft and of Sorcery
By many witnesses. Say, are you guilty?

COREY.

I know my death is foreordained by you,—
Mine and my wife's. Therefore I will not answer.

During the rest of the scene he remains silent.

HATHORNE.

Do you refuse to plead?—'T were better for you
To make confession, or to plead Not Guilty.—
Do you not hear me?—Answer, are you guilty?
Do you not know a heavier doom awaits you,
If you refuse to plead, than if found guilty?
Where is John Gloyd?

GLOYD (*coming forward*).

Here am I.

HATHORNE.

Tell the Court;
Have you not seen the supernatural power
Of this old man? Have you not seen him do
Strange feats of strength?

GLOYD.

I 've seen him lead the field,
On a hot day, in mowing, and against
Us younger men; and I have wrestled with him.
He threw me like a feather. I have seen him
Lift up a barrel with his single hands,
Which two strong men could hardly lift together,
And, holding it above his head, drink from it.

HATHORNE.

That is enough; we need not question further.
What answer do you make to this, Giles Corey?

MARY.

See there! See there!

HATHORNE.

What is it? I see nothing.

MARY.

Look! Look! It is the ghost of Robert Goodell,
Whom fifteen years ago this man did murder
By stamping on his body! In his shroud
He comes here to bear witness to the crime!

The crowd shrinks back from COREY *in horror.*

HATHORNE.

Ghosts of the dead and voices of the living
Bear witness to your guilt, and you must die!
It might have been an easier death. Your doom
Will be on your own head, and not on ours.
Twice more will you be questioned of these things;
Twice more have room to plead or to confess.
If you are contumacious to the Court,
And if, when questioned, you refuse to answer,
Then by the Statute you will be condemned
To the *peine forte et dure*! To have your body
Pressed by great weights until you shall be dead!
And may the Lord have mercy on your soul!

ACT V.

SCENE I.—COREY'S *farm as in Act II., Scene I. Enter* RICHARD GARDNER, *looking round him.*

GARDNER.

Here stands the house as I remember it,
The four tall poplar-trees before the door;
The house, the barn, the orchard, and the well,
With its moss-covered bucket and its trough;
The garden, with its hedge of currant-bushes;
The woods, the harvest-fields; and, far beyond,
The pleasant landscape stretching to the sea.
But everything is silent and deserted!
No bleat of flocks, no bellowing of herds,
No sound of flails, that should be beating now;
Nor man nor beast astir. What can this mean?

Knocks at the door.

What ho! Giles Corey! Hillo-ho! Giles Corey!—
No answer but the echo from the barn,
And the ill-omened cawing of the crow,

That yonder wings his flight across the fields,
As if he scented carrion in the air.

Enter TITUBA *with a basket.*

What woman 's this, that, like an apparition,
Haunts this deserted homestead in broad day?
Woman, who are you?

TITUBA.

I am Tituba.
I am John Indian's wife. I am a Witch.

GARDNER.

What are you doing here?

TITUBA.

I 'm gathering herbs,—
Cinquefoil, and saxifrage, and pennyroyal.

GARDNER (*looking at the herbs*).

This is not cinquefoil, it is deadly night-shade!
This is not saxifrage, but hellebore!
This is not pennyroyal, it is henbane!
Do you come here to poison these good people?

TITUBA.

I get these for the Doctor in the Village.
Beware of Tituba. I pinch the children;
Make little poppets and stick pins in them,
And then the children cry out they are pricked.
The Black Dog came to me, and said, "Serve me!"
I was afraid. He made me hurt the children.

GARDNER.

Poor soul! She 's crazed, with all these Devil's doings.

TITUBA.

Will you, sir, sign the Book?

GARDNER.

No, I 'll not sign it.
Where is Giles Corey? Do you know Giles Corey?

TITUBA.

He 's safe enough. He 's down there in the prison.

GARDNER.

Corey in prison? What is he accused of?

TITUBA.

Giles Corey and Martha Corey are in prison
Down there in Salem Village. Both are Witches.

She came to me and whispered, "Kill the children!"
Both signed the Book!

GARDNER.

Begone, you imp of darkness!
You Devil's dam!

TITUBA.

Beware of Tituba!

[*Exit.*

GARDNER.

How often out at sea on stormy nights,
When the waves thundered round me, and the wind
Bellowed, and beat the canvas, and my ship
Clove through the solid darkness, like a wedge,
I 've thought of him, upon his pleasant farm,
Living in quiet with his thrifty housewife,
And envied him, and wished his fate were mine!
And now I find him shipwrecked utterly,
Drifting upon this sea of sorceries,
And lost, perhaps, beyond all aid of man!

[*Exit.*

SCENE II.—*The prison.* GILES COREY *at a table on which are some papers.*

COREY.

Now I have done with earth and all its cares;
I give my worldly goods to my dear children;
My body I bequeath to my tormentors.
And my immortal soul to Him who made it.
O God! who in thy wisdom dost afflict me
With an affliction greater than most men
Have ever yet endured or shall endure,
Suffer me not in this last bitter hour
For any pains of death to fall from thee!

MARTHA *is heard singing.*

Arise, O righteous Lord!
And disappoint my foes;
They are but thine avenging sword,
Whose wounds are swift to close.

COREY.

Hark, hark! it is her voice! She is not dead!
She lives! I am not utterly forsaken!

MARTHA, *singing.*

By thine abounding grace,
And mercies multiplied,
I shall awake, and see thy face;
I shall be satisfied.

COREY *hides his face in his hands. Enter the* JAILER, *followed by* RICHARD GARDNER.

JAILER.

Here 's a seafaring man, one Richard Gardner,
A friend of yours, who asks to speak with you.

COREY *rises. They embrace.*

COREY.

I 'm glad to see you, ay, right glad to see you.

GARDNER.

And I most sorely grieved to see you thus.

COREY.

Of all the friends I had in happier days,
You are the first, ay, and the only one,
That comes to seek me out in my disgrace!
And you but come in time to say farewell.
They 've dug my grave already in the field.
I thank you. There is something in your presence,
I know not what it is, that gives me strength.
Perhaps it is the bearing of a man
Familiar with all dangers of the deep,
Familiar with the cries of drowning men,
With fire, and wreck, and foundering ships at sea!

GARDNER.

Ah, I have never known a wreck like yours!
Would I could save you!

COREY.

Do not speak of that.
It is too late. I am resolved to die.

GARDNER.

Why would you die who have so much to live for?—
Your daughters, and—

COREY.

You cannot say the word.
My daughters have gone from me. They are married;
They have their homes, their thoughts, apart from me;
I will not say their hearts,—that were too cruel.
What would you have me do?

GARDNER.

Confess and live.

COREY.

That 's what they said who came here yesterday
To lay a heavy weight upon my conscience
By telling me that I was driven forth
As an unworthy member of their church.

GARDNER.

It is an awful death.

COREY.

'T is but to drown,
And have the weight of all the seas upon you.

GARDNER.

Say something; say enough to fend off death
Till this tornado of fanaticism
Blows itself out. Let me come in between you
And your severer self, with my plain sense;
Do not be obstinate.

COREY.

I will not plead.
If I deny, I am condemned already,
In courts where ghosts appear as witnesses,
And swear men's lives away. If I confess,
Then I confess a lie, to buy a life
Which is not life, but only death in life.
I will not bear false witness against any,
Not even against myself, whom I count least.

GARDNER (*aside*).

Ah, what a noble character is this!

COREY.

I pray you, do not urge me to do that
You would not do yourself. I have already
The bitter taste of death upon my lips;
I feel the pressure of the heavy weight

That will crush out my life within this hour;
But if a word could save me, and that word
Were not the Truth; nay, if it did but swerve
A hair's-breadth from the Truth, I would not say it!

GARDNER (*aside*).

How mean I seem beside a man like this!

COREY.

As for my wife, my Martha and my Martyr,—
Whose virtues, like the stars, unseen by day,
Though numberless, do but await the dark
To manifest themselves unto all eyes,—
She who first won me from my evil ways,
And taught me how to live by her example,
By her example teaches me to die,
And leads me onward to the better life!

SHERIFF (*without*).

Giles Corey! Come! The hour has struck!

COREY.

I come!

Here is my body; ye may torture it,
But the immortal soul ye cannot crush!

[*Exeunt.*

SCENE III.—*A street in the Village. Enter* GLOYD *and others.*

GLOYD.

Quick, or we shall be late!

A MAN.

That 's not the way.

Come here; come up this lane.

GLOYD.

I wonder now

If the old man will die, and will not speak?
He 's obstinate enough and tough enough
For anything on earth.

A bell tolls.

Hark! What is that?

A MAN.

The passing bell. He 's dead!

GLOYD.

We are too late.

[*Exeunt in haste.*

SCENE IV.—*A field near the graveyard.* GILES COREY *lying dead, with a great stone on his breast. The Sheriff at his head,* RICHARD GARDNER *at his feet. A crowd behind. The bell tolling. Enter* HATHORNE *and* MATHER.

HATHORNE.

This is the Potter's Field. Behold the fate
Of those who deal in Witchcrafts, and, when questioned,
Refuse to plead their guilt or innocence,
And stubbornly drag death upon themselves.

MATHER.

O sight most horrible! In a land like this,
Spangled with Churches Evangelical,
Inwrapped in our salvations, must we seek
In mouldering statute-books of English Courts
Some old forgotten Law, to do such deeds?
Those who lie buried in the Potter's Field
Will rise again, as surely as ourselves
That sleep in honored graves with epitaphs;
And this poor man, whom we have made a victim,
Hereafter will be counted as a martyr!

Finale

ST. JOHN

SAINT JOHN *wandering over the face of the Earth.*

ST. JOHN.

The Ages come and go,
The Centuries pass as Years;
My hair is white as the snow,
My feet are weary and slow,
The earth is wet with my tears!
The kingdoms crumble, and fall
Apart, like a ruined wall,
Or a bank that is undermined
By a river's ceaseless flow,
And leave no trace behind!
The world itself is old;
The portals of Time unfold

On hinges of iron, that grate
And groan with the rust and the weight,
Like the hinges of a gate
That hath fallen to decay;
But the evil doth not cease;
There is war instead of peace,
Instead of Love there is hate;
And still I must wander and wait,
Still I must watch and pray,
Not forgetting in whose sight,
A thousand years in their flight
Are as a single day.

The life of man is a gleam
Of light, that comes and goes
Like the course of the Holy Stream,
The cityless river, that flows
From fountains no one knows,
Through the Lake of Galilee,
Through forests and level lands,
Over rocks, and shallows, and sands
Of a wilderness wild and vast,
Till it findeth its rest at last
In the desolate Dead Sea!
But alas! alas for me
Not yet this rest shall be!

What, then! doth Charity fail?
Is Faith of no avail?
Is Hope blown out like a light
By a gust of wind in the night?
The clashing of creeds, and the strife
Of the many beliefs, that in vain
Perplex man's heart and brain,
Are naught but the rustle of leaves,
When the breath of God upheaves
The boughs of the Tree of Life,
And they subside again!
And I remember still
The words, and from whom they came,

Not he that repeateth the name,
But he that doeth the will!

And Him evermore I behold
Walking in Galilee,
Through the cornfield's waving gold,
In hamlet, in wood, and in wold,
By the shores of the Beautiful Sea.
He toucheth the sightless eyes;
Before him the demons flee;
To the dead He sayeth: Arise!
To the living: Follow me!
And that voice still soundeth on
From the centuries that are gone,
To the centuries that shall be!

From all vain pomps and shows,
From the pride that overflows,
And the false conceits of men;
From all the narrow rules
And subtleties of Schools,
And the craft of tongue and pen;
Bewildered in its search,
Bewildered with the cry:
Lo, here! lo, there, the Church!
Poor, sad Humanity
Through all the dust and heat
Turns back with bleeding feet,
By the weary road it came,
Unto the simple thought
By the great Master taught.
And that remaineth still:
Not he that repeateth the name,
But he that doeth the will!

from
AFTERMATH

The Haunted Chamber

Each heart has its haunted chamber,
  Where the silent moonlight falls!
On the floor are mysterious footsteps,
  There are whispers along the walls!

And mine at times is haunted
  By phantoms of the Past,
As motionless as shadows
  By the silent moonlight cast.

A form sits by the window,
  That is not seen by day,
For as soon as the dawn approaches
  It vanishes away.

It sits there in the moonlight,
  Itself as pale and still,
And points with its airy finger
  Across the window-sill.

Without, before the window,
  There stands a gloomy pine,
Whose boughs wave upward and downward
  As wave these thoughts of mine.

And underneath its branches
  Is the grave of a little child,
Who died upon life's threshold,
  And never wept nor smiled.

What are ye, O pallid phantoms!
  That haunt my troubled brain?
That vanish when day approaches,
  And at night return again?

What are ye, O pallid phantoms!
   But the statues without breath,
That stand on the bridge overarching
   The silent river of death?

The Meeting

After so long an absence
   At last we meet again:
Does the meeting give us pleasure,
   Or does it give us pain?

The tree of life has been shaken,
   And but few of us linger now,
Like the Prophet's two or three berries
   In the top of the uppermost bough.

We cordially greet each other
   In the old, familiar tone;
And we think, though we do not say it,
   How old and gray he is grown!

We speak of a Merry Christmas
   And many a Happy New Year;
But each in his heart is thinking
   Of those that are not here.

We speak of friends and their fortunes,
   And of what they did and said,
Till the dead alone seem living,
   And the living alone seem dead.

And at last we hardly distinguish
   Between the ghosts and the guests;
And a mist and shadow of sadness
   Steals over our merriest jests.

Vox Populi

When Mazárvan the Magician
  Journeyed westward through Cathay,
Nothing heard he but the praises
  Of Badoura on his way.

But the lessening rumor ended
  When he came to Khaledan,
There the folk were talking only
  Of Prince Camaralzaman.

So it happens with the poets:
  Every province hath its own;
Camaralzaman is famous
  Where Badoura is unknown.

Changed

From the outskirts of the town,
  Where of old the mile-stone stood,
Now a stranger, looking down
I behold the shadowy crown
  Of the dark and haunted wood.

Is it changed, or am I changed?
  Ah! the oaks are fresh and green,
But the friends with whom I ranged
Through their thickets are estranged
  By the years that intervene.

Bright as ever flows the sea,
  Bright as ever shines the sun,
But alas! they seem to me
Not the sun that used to be,
  Not the tides that used to run.

The Challenge

I have a vague remembrance
  Of a story, that is told
In some ancient Spanish legend
  Or chronicle of old.

It was when brave King Sanchez
  Was before Zamora slain,
And his great besieging army
  Lay encamped upon the plain.

Don Diego de Ordoñez
  Sallied forth in front of all,
And shouted loud his challenge
  To the warders on the wall.

All the people of Zamora,
  Both the born and the unborn,
As traitors did he challenge
  With taunting words of scorn.

The living, in their houses,
  And in their graves, the dead!
And the waters of their rivers,
  And their wine, and oil, and bread!

There is a greater army,
  That besets us round with strife,
A starving, numberless army,
  At all the gates of life.

The poverty-stricken millions
  Who challenge our wine and bread,
And impeach us all as traitors,
  Both the living and the dead.

And whenever I sit at the banquet,
  Where the feast and song are high,
Amid the mirth and the music
  I can hear that fearful cry.

And hollow and haggard faces
  Look into the lighted hall,
And wasted hands are extended
  To catch the crumbs that fall.

For within there is light and plenty,
  And odors fill the air;
But without there is cold and darkness,
  And hunger and despair.

And there in the camp of famine,
  In wind and cold and rain,
Christ, the great Lord of the army,
  Lies dead upon the plain!

Aftermath

When the summer fields are mown,
When the birds are fledged and flown,
  And the dry leaves strew the path;
With the falling of the snow,
With the cawing of the crow,
Once again the fields we mow
  And gather in the aftermath.

Not the sweet, new grass with flowers
Is this harvesting of ours;
  Not the upland clover bloom;
But the rowen mixed with weeds,
Tangled tufts from marsh and meads,
Where the poppy drops its seeds
  In the silence and the gloom.

from

THE MASQUE OF PANDORA AND OTHER POEMS

Morituri Salutamus

Poem for the Fiftieth Anniversary of the Class of 1825 in Bowdoin

Tempora labuntur, tacitisque senescimus annis,
Et fugiunt freno non remorante dies.
OVID *Fastorum,* Lib. vi.

"O Cæsar, we who are about to die
Salute you!" was the gladiators' cry
In the arena, standing face to face
With death and with the Roman populace.

O ye familiar scenes,—ye groves of pine,
That once were mine and are no longer mine,—
Thou river, widening through the meadows green
To the vast sea, so near and yet unseen,—
Ye halls, in whose seclusion and repose
Phantoms of fame, like exhalations, rose
And vanished,—we who are about to die,
Salute you; earth and air and sea and sky,
And the Imperial Sun that scatters down
His sovereign splendors upon grove and town.

Ye do not answer us! ye do not hear!
We are forgotten; and in your austere
And calm indifference, ye little care
Whether we come or go, or whence or where.
What passing generations fill these halls,
What passing voices echo from these walls,
Ye heed not; we are only as the blast,
A moment heard, and then forever past.

Not so the teachers who in earlier days
Led our bewildered feet through learning's maze;
They answer us—alas! what have I said?

What greetings come there from the voiceless dead?
What salutation, welcome, or reply?
What pressure from the hands that lifeless lie?
They are no longer here; they all are gone
Into the land of shadows,—all save one.
Honor and reverence, and the good repute
That follows faithful service as its fruit,
Be unto him, whom living we salute.

The great Italian poet, when he made
His dreadful journey to the realms of shade,
Met there the old instructor of his youth,
And cried in tones of pity and of ruth:
"Oh, never from the memory of my heart
Your dear, paternal image shall depart,
Who while on earth, ere yet by death surprised,
Taught me how mortals are immortalized;
How grateful am I for that patient care
All my life long my language shall declare."

To-day we make the poet's words our own,
And utter them in plaintive undertone;
Nor to the living only be they said,
But to the other living called the dead,
Whose dear, paternal images appear
Not wrapped in gloom, but robed in sunshine here;
Whose simple lives, complete and without flaw,
Were part and parcel of great Nature's law;
Who said not to their Lord, as if afraid,
"Here is thy talent in a napkin laid,"
But labored in their sphere, as men who live
In the delight that work alone can give.
Peace be to them; eternal peace and rest,
And the fulfilment of the great behest:
"Ye have been faithful over a few things,
Over ten cities shall ye reign as kings."

And ye who fill the places we once filled,
And follow in the furrows that we tilled,
Young men, whose generous hearts are beating high,

We who are old, and are about to die,
Salute you; hail you; take your hands in ours,
And crown you with our welcome as with flowers!

How beautiful is youth! how bright it gleams
With its illusions, aspirations, dreams!
Book of Beginnings, Story without End,
Each maid a heroine, and each man a friend!
Aladdin's Lamp, and Fortunatus' Purse,
That holds the treasures of the universe!
All possibilities are in its hands,
No danger daunts it, and no foe withstands;
In its sublime audacity of faith,
"Be thou removed!" it to the mountain saith,
And with ambitious feet, secure and proud,
Ascends the ladder leaning on the cloud!

As ancient Priam at the Scæan gate
Sat on the walls of Troy in regal state
With the old men, too old and weak to fight,
Chirping like grasshoppers in their delight
To see the embattled hosts, with spear and shield,
Of Trojans and Achaians in the field;
So from the snowy summits of our years
We see you in the plain, as each appears,
And question of you; asking, "Who is he
That towers above the others? Which may be
Atreides, Menelaus, Odysseus,
Ajax the great, or bold Idomeneus?"

Let him not boast who puts his armor on
As he who puts it off, the battle done.
Study yourselves; and most of all note well
Wherein kind Nature meant you to excel.
Not every blossom ripens into fruit;
Minerva, the inventress of the flute,
Flung it aside, when she her face surveyed
Distorted in a fountain as she played;
The unlucky Marsyas found it, and his fate
Was one to make the bravest hesitate.

Write on your doors the saying wise and old,
"Be bold! be bold!" and everywhere, "Be bold;
Be not too bold!" Yet better the excess
Than the defect; better the more than less;
Better like Hector in the field to die,
Than like a perfumed Paris turn and fly.

And now, my classmates; ye remaining few
That number not the half of those we knew,
Ye, against whose familiar names not yet
The fatal asterisk of death is set,
Ye I salute! The horologe of Time
Strikes the half-century with a solemn chime,
And summons us together once again,
The joy of meeting not unmixed with pain.

Where are the others? Voices from the deep
Caverns of darkness answer me: "They sleep!"
I name no names; instinctively I feel
Each at some well-remembered grave will kneel,
And from the inscription wipe the weeds and moss,
For every heart best knoweth its own loss.
I see their scattered gravestones gleaming white
Through the pale dusk of the impending night;
O'er all alike the impartial sunset throws
Its golden lilies mingled with the rose;
We give to each a tender thought, and pass
Out of the graveyards with their tangled grass,
Unto these scenes frequented by our feet
When we were young, and life was fresh and sweet.

What shall I say to you? What can I say
Better than silence is? When I survey
This throng of faces turned to meet my own,
Friendly and fair, and yet to me unknown,
Transformed the very landscape seems to be;
It is the same, yet not the same to me.
So many memories crowd upon my brain,
So many ghosts are in the wooded plain,
I fain would steal away, with noiseless tread,
As from a house where some one lieth dead.

I cannot go;—I pause;—I hesitate;
My feet reluctant linger at the gate;
As one who struggles in a troubled dream
To speak and cannot, to myself I seem.

Vanish the dream! Vanish the idle fears!
Vanish the rolling mists of fifty years!
Whatever time or space may intervene,
I will not be a stranger in this scene.
Here every doubt, all indecision, ends;
Hail, my companions, comrades, classmates, friends!

Ah me! the fifty years since last we met
Seem to me fifty folios bound and set
By Time, the great transcriber, on his shelves,
Wherein are written the histories of ourselves.
What tragedies, what comedies, are there;
What joy and grief, what rapture and despair!
What chronicles of triumph and defeat,
Of struggle, and temptation, and retreat!
What records of regrets, and doubts, and fears!
What pages blotted, blistered by our tears!
What lovely landscapes on the margin shine,
What sweet, angelic faces, what divine
And holy images of love and trust,
Undimmed by age, unsoiled by damp or dust!

Whose hand shall dare to open and explore
These volumes, closed and clasped forevermore?
Not mine. With reverential feet I pass;
I hear a voice that cries, "Alas! alas!
Whatever hath been written shall remain,
Nor be erased nor written o'er again;
The unwritten only still belongs to thee:
Take heed, and ponder well what that shall be."

As children frightened by a thunder-cloud
Are reassured if some one reads aloud
A tale of wonder, with enchantment fraught,
Or wild adventure, that diverts their thought,

Let me endeavor with a tale to chase
The gathering shadows of the time and place,
And banish what we all too deeply feel
Wholly to say, or wholly to conceal.

In mediæval Rome, I know not where,
There stood an image with its arm in air,
And on its lifted finger, shining clear,
A golden ring with the device, "Strike here!"
Greatly the people wondered, though none guessed
The meaning that these words but half expressed,
Until a learned clerk, who at noonday
With downcast eyes was passing on his way,
Paused, and observed the spot, and marked it well,
Whereon the shadow of the finger fell;
And, coming back at midnight, delved, and found
A secret stairway leading underground.
Down this he passed into a spacious hall,
Lit by a flaming jewel on the wall;
And opposite, in threatening attitude,
With bow and shaft a brazen statue stood.
Upon its forehead, like a coronet,
Were these mysterious words of menace set:
"That which I am, I am; my fatal aim
None can escape, not even yon luminous flame!"

Midway the hall was a fair table placed,
With cloth of gold, and golden cups enchased
With rubies, and the plates and knives were gold,
And gold the bread and viands manifold.
Around it, silent, motionless, and sad,
Were seated gallant knights in armor clad,
And ladies beautiful with plume and zone,
But they were stone, their hearts within were stone;
And the vast hall was filled in every part
With silent crowds, stony in face and heart.

Long at the scene, bewildered and amazed
The trembling clerk in speechless wonder gazed;
Then from the table, by his greed made bold,

He seized a goblet and a knife of gold,
And suddenly from their seats the guests upsprang,
The vaulted ceiling with loud clamors rang,
The archer sped his arrow, at their call,
Shattering the lambent jewel on the wall,
And all was dark around and overhead;—
Stark on the floor the luckless clerk lay dead!

The writer of this legend then records
Its ghostly application in these words:
The image is the Adversary old,
Whose beckoning finger points to realms of gold;
Our lusts and passions are the downward stair
That leads the soul from a diviner air;
The archer, Death; the flaming jewel, Life;
Terrestrial goods, the goblet and the knife;
The knights and ladies, all whose flesh and bone
By avarice have been hardened into stone;
The clerk, the scholar whom the love of pelf
Tempts from his books and from his nobler self.

The scholar and the world! The endless strife,
The discord in the harmonies of life!
The love of learning, the sequestered nooks,
And all the sweet serenity of books;
The market-place, the eager love of gain,
Whose aim is vanity, and whose end is pain!

But why, you ask me, should this tale be told
To men grown old, or who are growing old?
It is too late! Ah, nothing is too late
Till the tired heart shall cease to palpitate.
Cato learned Greek at eighty; Sophocles
Wrote his grand Œdipus, and Simonides
Bore off the prize of verse from his compeers,
When each had numbered more than fourscore years,
And Theophrastus, at fourscore and ten,
Had but begun his "Characters of Men."
Chaucer, at Woodstock with the nightingales,
At sixty wrote the Canterbury Tales;

Goethe at Weimar, toiling to the last,
Completed Faust when eighty years were past.
These are indeed exceptions; but they show
How far the gulf-stream of our youth may flow
Into the arctic regions of our lives,
Where little else than life itself survives.

As the barometer foretells the storm
While still the skies are clear, the weather warm
So something in us, as old age draws near,
Betrays the pressure of the atmosphere.
The nimble mercury, ere we are aware,
Descends the elastic ladder of the air;
The telltale blood in artery and vein
Sinks from its higher levels in the brain;
Whatever poet, orator, or sage
May say of it, old age is still old age.
It is the waning, not the crescent moon;
The dusk of evening, not the blaze of noon;
It is not strength, but weakness; not desire,
But its surcease; not the fierce heat of fire,
The burning and consuming element,
But that of ashes and of embers spent,
In which some living sparks we still discern,
Enough to warm, but not enough to burn.

What then? Shall we sit idly down and say
The night hath come; it is no longer day?
The night hath not yet come; we are not quite
Cut off from labor by the failing light;
Something remains for us to do or dare;
Even the oldest tree some fruit may bear;
Not Œdipus Coloneus, or Greek Ode,
Or tales of pilgrims that one morning rode
Out of the gateway of the Tabard Inn,
But other something, would we but begin;
For age is opportunity no less
Than youth itself, though in another dress,
And as the evening twilight fades away
The sky is filled with stars, invisible by day.

Belisarius

I am poor and old and blind;
The sun burns me, and the wind
    Blows through the city gate,
And covers me with dust
From the wheels of the august
    Justinian the Great.

It was for him I chased
The Persians o'er wild and waste,
    As General of the East;
Night after night I lay
In their camps of yesterday;
    Their forage was my feast.

For him, with sails of red,
And torches at mast-head,
    Piloting the great fleet,
I swept the Afric coasts
And scattered the Vandal hosts,
    Like dust in a windy street.

For him I won again
The Ausonian realm and reign,
    Rome and Parthenope;
And all the land was mine
From the summits of Apennine
    To the shores of either sea.

For him, in my feeble age,
I dared the battle's rage,
    To save Byzantium's state,
When the tents of Zabergan
Like snow-drifts overran
    The road to the Golden Gate.

And for this, for this, behold!
Infirm and blind and old,
    With gray, uncovered head,

Beneath the very arch
Of my triumphal march,
    I stand and beg my bread!

Methinks I still can hear,
Sounding distinct and near,
    The Vandal monarch's cry,
As, captive and disgraced,
With majestic step he paced,—
    "All, all is Vanity!"

Ah! vainest of all things
Is the gratitude of kings;
    The plaudits of the crowd
Are but the clatter of feet
At midnight in the street,
    Hollow and restless and loud.

But the bitterest disgrace
Is to see forever the face
Of the Monk of Ephesus!
The unconquerable will
This, too, can bear;—I still
    Am Belisarius!

Three Friends of Mine

I.

When I remember them, those friends of mine,
  Who are no longer here, the noble three,
  Who half my life were more than friends to me,
  And whose discourse was like a generous wine,
I most of all remember the divine
  Something, that shone in them, and made us see
  The archetypal man, and what might be
  The amplitude of Nature's first design.
In vain I stretch my hands to clasp their hands;

I cannot find them. Nothing now is left
But a majestic memory. They meanwhile
Wander together in Elysian lands,
Perchance remembering me, who am bereft
Of their dear presence, and, remembering, smile.

II.

In Attica thy birthplace should have been,
Or the Ionian Isles, or where the seas
Encircle in their arms the Cyclades,
So wholly Greek wast thou in thy serene
And childlike joy of life, O Philhellene!
Around thee would have swarmed the Attic bees;
Homer had been thy friend, or Socrates,
And Plato welcomed thee to his demesne.
For thee old legends breathed historic breath;
Thou sawest Poseidon in the purple sea,
And in the sunset Jason's fleece of gold!
Oh, what hadst thou to do with cruel Death,
Who wast so full of life, or Death with thee,
That thou shouldst die before thou hadst grown old!

III.

I stand again on the familiar shore,
And hear the waves of the distracted sea
Piteously calling and lamenting thee,
And waiting restless at thy cottage door.
The rocks, the sea-weed on the ocean floor,
The willows in the meadow, and the free
Wild winds of the Atlantic welcome me;
Then why shouldst thou be dead, and come no more?
Ah, why shouldst thou be dead, when common men
Are busy with their trivial affairs,
Having and holding? Why, when thou hadst read
Nature's mysterious manuscript, and then
Wast ready to reveal the truth it bears,
Why art thou silent? Why shouldst thou be dead?

IV.

River, that stealest with such silent pace
  Around the City of the Dead, where lies
  A friend who bore thy name, and whom these eyes
  Shall see no more in his accustomed place,
Linger and fold him in thy soft embrace,
  And say good night, for now the western skies
  Are red with sunset, and gray mists arise
  Like damps that gather on a dead man's face.
Good night! good night! as we so oft have said
  Beneath this roof at midnight, in the days
  That are no more, and shall no more return.
Thou hast but taken thy lamp and gone to bed;
  I stay a little longer, as one stays
  To cover up the embers that still burn.

V.

The doors are all wide open; at the gate
  The blossomed lilacs counterfeit a blaze,
  And seem to warm the air; a dreamy haze
  Hangs o'er the Brighton meadows like a fate,
And on their margin, with sea-tides elate,
  The flooded Charles, as in the happier days,
  Writes the last letter of his name, and stays
  His restless steps, as if compelled to wait.
I also wait; but they will come no more,
  Those friends of mine, whose presence satisfied
  The thirst and hunger of my heart. Ah me!
They have forgotten the pathway to my door!
  Something is gone from nature since they died,
  And summer is not summer, nor can be.

Chaucer

An old man in a lodge within a park;
  The chamber walls depicted all around
  With portraitures of huntsman, hawk, and hound,
  And the hurt deer. He listeneth to the lark,

Whose song comes with the sunshine through the dark
Of painted glass in leaden lattice bound;
He listeneth and he laugheth at the sound,
Then writeth in a book like any clerk.
He is the poet of the dawn, who wrote
The Canterbury Tales, and his old age
Made beautiful with song; and as I read
I hear the crowing cock, I hear the note
Of lark and linnet, and from every page
Rise odors of ploughed field or flowery mead.

Shakespeare

A vision as of crowded city streets,
With human life in endless overflow;
Thunder of thoroughfares; trumpets that blow
To battle; clamor, in obscure retreats,
Of sailors landed from their anchored fleets;
Tolling of bells in turrets, and below
Voices of children, and bright flowers that throw
O'er garden-walls their intermingled sweets!
This vision comes to me when I unfold
The volume of the Poet paramount,
Whom all the Muses loved, not one alone;—
Into his hands they put the lyre of gold,
And, crowned with sacred laurel at their fount,
Placed him as Musagetes on their throne.

Milton

I pace the sounding sea-beach and behold
How the voluminous billows roll and run,
Upheaving and subsiding, while the sun
Shines through their sheeted emerald far unrolled,
And the ninth wave, slow gathering fold by fold
All its loose-flowing garments into one,

Plunges upon the shore, and floods the dun
Pale reach of sands, and changes them to gold.
So in majestic cadence rise and fall
The mighty undulations of thy song,
O sightless bard, England's Mæonides!
And ever and anon, high over all
Uplifted, a ninth wave superb and strong,
Floods all the soul with its melodious seas.

Keats

The young Endymion sleeps Endymion's sleep;
The shepherd-boy whose tale was left half told!
The solemn grove uplifts its shield of gold
To the red rising moon, and loud and deep
The nightingale is singing from the steep;
It is midsummer, but the air is cold;
Can it be death? Alas, beside the fold
A shepherd's pipe lies shattered near his sheep.
Lo! in the moonlight gleams a marble white,
On which I read: "Here lieth one whose name
Was writ in water." And was this the meed
Of his sweet singing? Rather let me write:
"The smoking flax before it burst to flame
Was quenched by death, and broken the bruised reed."

The Galaxy

Torrent of light and river of the air,
Along whose bed the glimmering stars are seen
Like gold and silver sands in some ravine
Where mountain streams have left their channels bare!
The Spaniard sees in thee the pathway, where
His patron saint descended in the sheen
Of his celestial armor, on serene
And quiet nights, when all the heavens were fair.
Not this I see, nor yet the ancient fable
Of Phaeton's wild course, that scorched the skies

Where'er the hoofs of his hot coursers trod;
But the white drift of worlds o'er chasms of sable,
The star-dust, that is whirled aloft and flies
From the invisible chariot-wheels of God.

The Sound of the Sea

The sea awoke at midnight from its sleep,
And round the pebbly beaches far and wide
I heard the first wave of the rising tide
Rush onward with uninterrupted sweep;
A voice out of the silence of the deep,
A sound mysteriously multiplied
As of a cataract from the mountain's side,
Or roar of winds upon a wooded steep.
So comes to us at times, from the unknown
And inaccessible solitudes of being,
The rushing of the sea-tides of the soul;
And inspirations, that we deem our own,
Are some divine foreshadowing and foreseeing
Of things beyond our reason or control.

A Nameless Grave

"A soldier of the Union mustered out,"
Is the inscription on an unknown grave
At Newport News, beside the salt-sea wave,
Nameless and dateless; sentinel or scout
Shot down in skirmish, or disastrous rout
Of battle, when the loud artillery drave
Its iron wedges through the ranks of brave
And doomed battalions, storming the redoubt.
Thou unknown hero sleeping by the sea
In thy forgotten grave! with secret shame
I feel my pulses beat, my forehead burn,
When I remember thou hast given for me
All that thou hadst, thy life, thy very name,
And I can give thee nothing in return.

from

KÉRAMOS AND OTHER POEMS

Kéramos

Turn, turn, my wheel! Turn round and round
Without a pause, without a sound:
So spins the flying world away!
This clay, well mixed with marl and sand,
Follows the motion of my hand;
For some must follow, and some command,
Though all are made of clay!

Thus sang the Potter at his task
Beneath the blossoming hawthorn-tree,
While o'er his features, like a mask,
The quilted sunshine and leaf-shade
Moved, as the boughs above him swayed,
And clothed him, till he seemed to be
A figure woven in tapestry,
So sumptuously was he arrayed
In that magnificent attire
Of sable tissue flaked with fire.
Like a magician he appeared,
A conjurer without book or beard;
And while he plied his magic art—
For it was magical to me—
I stood in silence and apart,
And wondered more and more to see
That shapeless, lifeless mass of clay
Rise up to meet the master's hand,
And now contract and now expand,
And even his slightest touch obey;
While ever in a thoughtful mood
He sang his ditty, and at times
Whistled a tune between the rhymes,
As a melodious interlude.

Turn, turn, my wheel! All things must change
To something new, to something strange;
Nothing that is can pause or stay;
The moon will wax, the moon will wane,
The mist and cloud will turn to rain,
The rain to mist and cloud again,
To-morrow be to-day.

Thus still the Potter sang, and still,
By some unconscious act of will,
The melody and even the words
Were intermingled with my thought,
As bits of colored thread are caught
And woven into nests of birds.
And thus to regions far remote,
Beyond the ocean's vast expanse,
This wizard in the motley coat
Transported me on wings of song,
And by the northern shores of France
Bore me with restless speed along.

What land is this that seems to be
A mingling of the land and sea?
This land of sluices, dikes, and dunes?
This water-net, that tessellates
The landscape? this unending maze
Of gardens, through whose latticed gates
The imprisoned pinks and tulips gaze;
Where in long summer afternoons
The sunshine, softened by the haze,
Comes streaming down as through a screen;
Where over fields and pastures green
The painted ships float high in air,
And over all and everywhere
The sails of windmills sink and soar
Like wings of sea-gulls on the shore?
What land is this? Yon pretty town
Is Delft, with all its wares displayed;
The pride, the market-place, the crown
And centre of the Potter's trade.

See! every house and room is bright
With glimmers of reflected light
From plates that on the dresser shine;
Flagons to foam with Flemish beer,
Or sparkle with the Rhenish wine,
And pilgrim flasks with fleurs-de-lis,
And ships upon a rolling sea,
And tankards pewter topped, and queer
With comic mask and musketeer!
Each hospitable chimney smiles
A welcome from its painted tiles;
The parlor walls, the chamber floors,
The stairways and the corridors,
The borders of the garden walks,
Are beautiful with fadeless flowers,
That never droop in winds or showers,
And never wither on their stalks.

Turn, turn, my wheel! All life is brief;
What now is bud will soon be leaf,
What now is leaf will soon decay;
The wind blows east, the wind blows west;
The blue eggs in the robin's nest
Will soon have wings and beak and breast,
And flutter and fly away.

Now southward through the air I glide,
The song my only pursuivant,
And see across the landscape wide
The blue Charente, upon whose tide
The belfries and the spires of Saintes
Ripple and rock from side to side,
As, when an earthquake rends its walls,
A crumbling city reels and falls.

Who is it in the suburbs here,
This Potter, working with such cheer,
In this mean house, this mean attire,
His manly features bronzed with fire,
Whose figulines and rustic wares

Scarce find him bread from day to day?
This madman, as the people say,
Who breaks his tables and his chairs
To feed his furnace fires, nor cares
Who goes unfed if they are fed,
Nor who may live if they are dead?
This alchemist with hollow cheeks
And sunken, searching eyes, who seeks,
By mingled earths and ores combined
With potency of fire, to find
Some new enamel, hard and bright,
His dream, his passion, his delight?
O Palissy! within thy breast
Burned the hot fever of unrest;
Thine was the prophet's vision, thine
The exultation, the divine
Insanity of noble minds,
That never falters nor abates,
But labors and endures and waits,
Till all that it foresees it finds,
Or what it cannot find creates!

Turn, turn, my wheel! This earthen jar
A touch can make, a touch can mar;
And shall it to the Potter say,
What makest thou? Thou hast no hand?
As men who think to understand
A world by their Creator planned,
Who wiser is than they.

Still guided by the dreamy song,
As in a trance I float along
Above the Pyrenean chain,
Above the fields and farms of Spain,
Above the bright Majorcan isle,
That lends its softened name to art,—
A spot, a dot upon the chart,
Whose little towns, red-roofed with tile,
Are ruby-lustred with the light
Of blazing furnaces by night,

And crowned by day with wreaths of smoke.
Then eastward, wafted in my flight
On my enchanter's magic cloak,
I sail across the Tyrrhene Sea
Into the land of Italy,
And o'er the windy Apennines,
Mantled and musical with pines.

The palaces, the princely halls,
The doors of houses and the walls
Of churches and of belfry towers,
Cloister and castle, street and mart,
Are garlanded and gay with flowers
That blossom in the fields of art.
Here Gubbio's workshops gleam and glow
With brilliant, iridescent dyes,
The dazzling whiteness of the snow,
The cobalt blue of summer skies;
And vase and scutcheon, cup and plate,
In perfect finish emulate
Faenza, Florence, Pesaro.

Forth from Urbino's gate there came
A youth with the angelic name
Of Raphael, in form and face
Himself angelic, and divine
In arts of color and design.
From him Francesco Xanto caught
Something of his transcendent grace,
And into fictile fabrics wrought
Suggestions of the master's thought.
Nor less Maestro Giorgio shines
With madre-perl and golden lines
Of arabesques, and interweaves
His birds and fruits and flowers and leaves
About some landscape, shaded brown,
With olive tints on rock and town.

Behold this cup within whose bowl,
Upon a ground of deepest blue

With yellow-lustred stars o'erlaid,
Colors of every tint and hue
Mingle in one harmonious whole!
With large blue eyes and steadfast gaze,
Her yellow hair in net and braid,
Necklace and ear-rings all ablaze
With golden lustre o'er the glaze,
A woman's portrait; on the scroll,
Cana, the Beautiful! A name
Forgotten save for such brief fame
As this memorial can bestow,—
A gift some lover long ago
Gave with his heart to this fair dame.

A nobler title to renown
Is thine, O pleasant Tuscan town,
Seated beside the Arno's stream;
For Luca della Robbia there
Created forms so wondrous fair,
They made thy sovereignty supreme.
These choristers with lips of stone,
Whose music is not heard, but seen,
Still chant, as from their organ-screen,
Their Maker's praise; nor these alone,
But the more fragile forms of clay,
Hardly less beautiful than they,
These saints and angels that adorn
The walls of hospitals, and tell
The story of good deeds so well
That poverty seems less forlorn,
And life more like a holiday.

Here in this old neglected church,
That long eludes the traveller's search,
Lies the dead bishop on his tomb;
Earth upon earth he slumbering lies,
Life-like and death-like in the gloom;
Garlands of fruit and flowers in bloom
And foliage deck his resting-place;
A shadow in the sightless eyes,

A pallor on the patient face,
Made perfect by the furnace heat;
All earthly passions and desires
Burnt out by purgatorial fires;
Seeming to say, "Our years are fleet,
And to the weary death is sweet."

But the most wonderful of all
The ornaments on tomb or wall
That grace the fair Ausonian shores
Are those the faithful earth restores,
Near some Apulian town concealed,
In vineyard or in harvest field,—
Vases and urns and bas-reliefs,
Memorials of forgotten griefs,
Or records of heroic deeds
Of demigods and mighty chiefs:
Figures that almost move and speak,
And, buried amid mould and weeds,
Still in their attitudes attest
The presence of the graceful Greek,—
Achilles in his armor dressed,
Alcides with the Cretan bull,
And Aphrodite with her boy,
Or lovely Helena of Troy,
Still living and still beautiful.

Turn, turn, my wheel! 'T is nature's plan
The child should grow into the man,
The man grow wrinkled, old, and gray;
In youth the heart exults and sings,
The pulses leap, the feet have wings;
In age the cricket chirps, and brings
The harvest-home of day.

And now the winds that southward blow,
And cool the hot Sicilian isle,
Bear me away. I see below
The long line of the Libyan Nile,
Flooding and feeding the parched lands

With annual ebb and overflow,
A fallen palm whose branches lie
Beneath the Abyssinian sky,
Whose roots are in Egyptian sands.
On either bank huge water-wheels,
Belted with jars and dripping weeds,
Send forth their melancholy moans,
As if, in their gray mantles hid,
Dead anchorites of the Thebaid
Knelt on the shore and told their beads,
Beating their breasts with loud appeals
And penitential tears and groans.

This city, walled and thickly set
With glittering mosque and minaret,
Is Cairo, in whose gay bazaars
The dreaming traveller first inhales
The perfume of Arabian gales,
And sees the fabulous earthen jars,
Huge as were those wherein the maid
Morgiana found the Forty Thieves
Concealed in midnight ambuscade;
And seeing, more than half believes
The fascinating tales that run
Through all the Thousand Nights and One,
Told by the fair Scheherezade.

More strange and wonderful than these
Are the Egyptian deities,
Ammon, and Emeth, and the grand
Osiris, holding in his hand
The lotus; Isis, crowned and veiled;
The sacred Ibis, and the Sphinx;
Bracelets with blue enamelled links;
The Scarabee in emerald mailed,
Or spreading wide his funeral wings;
Lamps that perchance their night-watch kept
O'er Cleopatra while she slept,—
All plundered from the tombs of kings.

Turn, turn, my wheel! The human race,
Of every tongue, of every place,
Caucasian, Coptic, or Malay,
All that inhabit this great earth,
Whatever be their rank or worth,
Are kindred and allied by birth,
And made of the same clay.

O'er desert sands, o'er gulf and bay,
O'er Ganges and o'er Himalay,
Bird-like I fly, and flying sing,
To flowery kingdoms of Cathay,
And bird-like poise on balanced wing
Above the town of King-te-tching,
A burning town, or seeming so,—
Three thousand furnaces that glow
Incessantly, and fill the air
With smoke uprising, gyre on gyre,
And painted by the lurid glare,
Of jets and flashes of red fire.

As leaves that in the autumn fall,
Spotted and veined with various hues,
Are swept along the avenues,
And lie in heaps by hedge and wall,
So from this grove of chimneys whirled
To all the markets of the world,
These porcelain leaves are wafted on,
Light yellow leaves with spots and stains
Of violet and of crimson dye,
Or tender azure of a sky
Just washed by gentle April rains,
And beautiful with celadon.

Nor less the coarser household wares,
The willow pattern, that we knew
In childhood, with its bridge of blue
Leading to unknown thoroughfares;
The solitary man who stares
At the white river flowing through

Its arches, the fantastic trees
And wild perspective of the view;
And intermingled among these
The tiles that in our nurseries
Filled us with wonder and delight,
Or haunted us in dreams at night.

And yonder by Nankin, behold!
The Tower of Porcelain, strange and old,
Uplifting to the astonished skies
Its ninefold painted balconies,
With balustrades of twining leaves,
And roofs of tile, beneath whose eaves
Hang porcelain bells that all the time
Ring with a soft, melodious chime;
While the whole fabric is ablaze
With varied tints, all fused in one
Great mass of color, like a maze
Of flowers illumined by the sun.

Turn, turn, my wheel! What is begun
At daybreak must at dark be done,
To-morrow will be another day;
To-morrow the hot furnace flame
Will search the heart and try the frame,
And stamp with honor or with shame
These vessels made of clay.

Cradled and rocked in Eastern seas,
The islands of the Japanese
Beneath me lie; o'er lake and plain
The stork, the heron, and the crane
Through the clear realms of azure drift,
And on the hillside I can see
The villages of Imari,
Whose thronged and flaming workshops lift
Their twisted columns of smoke on high,
Cloud cloisters that in ruins lie,
With sunshine streaming through each rift,
And broken arches of blue sky.

All the bright flowers that fill the land,
Ripple of waves on rock or sand,
The snow on Fusiyama's cone,
The midnight heaven so thickly sown
With constellations of bright stars,
The leaves that rustle, the reeds that make
A whisper by each stream and lake,
The saffron dawn, the sunset red,
Are painted on these lovely jars;
Again the skylark sings, again
The stork, the heron, and the crane
Float through the azure overhead,
The counterfeit and counterpart
Of Nature reproduced in Art.

Art is the child of Nature; yes,
Her darling child, in whom we trace
The features of the mother's face,
Her aspect and her attitude;
All her majestic loveliness
Chastened and softened and subdued
Into a more attractive grace,
And with a human sense imbued.
He is the greatest artist, then,
Whether of pencil or of pen,
Who follows Nature. Never man,
As artist or as artisan,
Pursuing his own fantasies,
Can touch the human heart, or please,
Or satisfy our nobler needs,
As he who sets his willing feet
In Nature's footprints, light and fleet,
And follows fearless where she leads.

Thus mused I on that morn in May,
Wrapped in my visions like the Seer,
Whose eyes behold not what is near,
But only what is far away,
When, suddenly sounding peal on peal,
The church-bell from the neighboring town

Proclaimed the welcome hour of noon.
The Potter heard, and stopped his wheel,
His apron on the grass threw down,
Whistled his quiet little tune,
Not overloud nor overlong,
And ended thus his simple song:

Stop, stop, my wheel! Too soon, too soon
The noon will be the afternoon,
Too soon to-day be yesterday;
Behind us in our path we cast
The broken potsherds of the past,
And all are ground to dust at last,
And trodden into clay!

Vittoria Colonna

Once more, once more, Inarimé,
I see thy purple halls!—once more
I hear the billows of the bay
Wash the white pebbles on thy shore.

High o'er the sea-surge and the sands,
Like a great galleon wrecked and cast
Ashore by storms, thy castle stands,
A mouldering landmark of the Past.

Upon its terrace-walk I see
A phantom gliding to and fro;
It is Colonna,—it is she
Who lived and loved so long ago.

Pescara's beautiful young wife,
The type of perfect womanhood,
Whose life was love, the life of life,
That time and change and death withstood.

For death, that breaks the marriage band
In others, only closer pressed
The wedding-ring upon her hand
And closer locked and barred her breast.

She knew the life-long martyrdom,
The weariness, the endless pain
Of waiting for some one to come
Who nevermore would come again.

The shadows of the chestnut trees,
The odor of the orange blooms,
The song of birds, and, more than these,
The silence of deserted rooms;

The respiration of the sea,
The soft caresses of the air,
All things in nature seemed to be
But ministers of her despair;

Till the o'erburdened heart, so long
Imprisoned in itself, found vent
And voice in one impassioned song
Of inconsolable lament.

Then as the sun, though hidden from sight,
Transmutes to gold the leaden mist,
Her life was interfused with light,
From realms that, though unseen, exist.

Inarimé! Inarimé!
Thy castle on the crags above
In dust shall crumble and decay,
But not the memory of her love.

The Revenge of Rain-in-the-Face

In that desolate land and lone,
Where the Big Horn and Yellowstone
  Roar down their mountain path,
By their fires the Sioux Chiefs
Muttered their woes and griefs
  And the menace of their wrath.

"Revenge!" cried Rain-in-the-Face,
"Revenge upon all the race
  Of the White Chief with yellow hair!"
And the mountains dark and high
From their crags reëchoed the cry
  Of his anger and despair.

In the meadow, spreading wide
By woodland and river-side
  The Indian village stood;
All was silent as a dream,
Save the rushing of the stream
  And the blue-jay in the wood.

In his war paint and his beads,
Like a bison among the reeds,
  In ambush the Sitting Bull
Lay with three thousand braves
Crouched in the clefts and caves,
  Savage, unmerciful!

Into the fatal snare
The White Chief with yellow hair
  And his three hundred men
Dashed headlong, sword in hand;
But of that gallant band
  Not one returned again.

The sudden darkness of death
Overwhelmed them like the breath
  And smoke of a furnace fire:
By the river's bank, and between
The rocks of the ravine,
  They lay in their bloody attire.

But the foemen fled in the night,
And Rain-in-the-Face, in his flight,
  Uplifted high in air
As a ghastly trophy, bore
The brave heart, that beat no more,
  Of the White Chief with yellow hair.

Whose was the right and the wrong?
Sing it, O funeral song,
  With a voice that is full of tears,
And say that our broken faith
Wrought all this ruin and scathe,
  In the Year of a Hundred Years.

Nature

As a fond mother, when the day is o'er,
  Leads by the hand her little child to bed,
  Half willing, half reluctant to be led,
  And leave his broken playthings on the floor,
Still gazing at them through the open door,
  Nor wholly reassured and comforted
  By promises of others in their stead,
  Which, though more splendid, may not please him more;
So Nature deals with us, and takes away
  Our playthings one by one, and by the hand
  Leads us to rest so gently, that we go
Scarce knowing if we wish to go or stay,
  Being too full of sleep to understand
  How far the unknown transcends the what we know.

Eliot's Oak

Thou ancient oak! whose myriad leaves are loud
With sounds of unintelligible speech,
Sounds as of surges on a shingly beach,
Or multitudinous murmurs of a crowd;
With some mysterious gift of tongues endowed,
Thou speakest a different dialect to each;
To me a language that no man can teach,
Of a lost race, long vanished like a cloud.
For underneath thy shade, in days remote,
Seated like Abraham at eventide
Beneath the oaks of Mamre, the unknown
Apostle of the Indians, Eliot, wrote
His Bible in a language that hath died
And is forgotten, save by thee alone.

The Poets

O ye dead Poets, who are living still
Immortal in your verse, though life be fled,
And ye, O living Poets, who are dead
Though ye are living, if neglect can kill,
Tell me if in the darkest hours of ill,
With drops of anguish falling fast and red
From the sharp crown of thorns upon your head,
Ye were not glad your errand to fulfil?
Yes; for the gift and ministry of Song
Have something in them so divinely sweet,
It can assuage the bitterness of wrong;
Not in the clamor of the crowded street,
Not in the shouts and plaudits of the throng,
But in ourselves, are triumph and defeat.

The Harvest Moon

It is the Harvest Moon! On gilded vanes
And roofs of villages, on woodland crests
And their aerial neighborhoods of nests
Deserted, on the curtained window-panes
Of rooms where children sleep, on country lanes
And harvest-fields, its mystic splendor rests!
Gone are the birds that were our summer guests;
With the last sheaves return the laboring wains!
All things are symbols: the external shows
Of Nature have their image in the mind,
As flowers and fruits and falling of the leaves;
The song-birds leave us at the summer's close,
Only the empty nests are left behind,
And pipings of the quail among the sheaves.

The Broken Oar

Once upon Iceland's solitary strand
A poet wandered with his book and pen,
Seeking some final word, some sweet Amen,
Wherewith to close the volume in his hand.
The billows rolled and plunged upon the sand,
The circling sea-gulls swept beyond his ken,
And from the parting cloud-rack now and then
Flashed the red sunset over sea and land.
Then by the billows at his feet was tossed
A broken oar; and carved thereon he read:
"Oft was I weary, when I toiled at thee";
And like a man, who findeth what was lost,
He wrote the words, then lifted up his head,
And flung his useless pen into the sea.

Haroun Al Raschid

One day, Haroun Al Raschid read
A book wherein the poet said:—

"Where are the kings, and where the rest
Of those who once the world possessed?

"They're gone with all their pomp and show,
They're gone the way that thou shalt go.

"O thou who choosest for thy share
The world, and what the world calls fair,

"Take all that it can give or lend,
But know that death is at the end!"

Haroun Al Raschid bowed his head:
Tears fell upon the page he read.

Venice

White swan of cities, slumbering in thy nest
  So wonderfully built among the reeds
  Of the lagoon, that fences thee and feeds,
  As sayeth thy old historian and thy guest!
White water-lily, cradled and caressed
  By ocean streams, and from the silt and weeds
  Lifting thy golden filaments and seeds,
  Thy sun-illumined spires, thy crown and crest!
White phantom city, whose untrodden streets
  Are rivers, and whose pavements are the shifting
  Shadows of palaces and strips of sky;
I wait to see thee vanish like the fleets
  Seen in mirage, or towers of cloud uplifting
  In air their unsubstantial masonry.

The Three Silences of Molinos

To John Greenleaf Whittier

Three Silences there are: the first of speech,
  The second of desire, the third of thought;
  This is the lore a Spanish monk, distraught
  With dreams and visions, was the first to teach.
These Silences, commingling each with each,
  Made up the perfect Silence that he sought
  And prayed for, and wherein at times he caught
  Mysterious sounds from realms beyond our reach.
O thou, whose daily life anticipates
  The life to come, and in whose thought and word
  The spiritual world preponderates,
Hermit of Amesbury! thou too hast heard
  Voices and melodies from beyond the gates,
  And speakest only when thy soul is stirred!

from
ULTIMA THULE

The Chamber Over the Gate

Is it so far from thee
Thou canst no longer see,
In the Chamber over the Gate,
That old man desolate,
Weeping and wailing sore
For his son, who is no more?
    O Absalom, my son!

Is it so long ago
That cry of human woe
From the walled city came,
Calling on his dear name,
That it has died away
In the distance of to-day?
    O Absalom, my son!

There is no far or near,
There is neither there nor here,
There is neither soon nor late,
In that Chamber over the Gate,
Nor any long ago
To that cry of human woe,
    O Absalom, my son!

From the ages that are past
The voice sounds like a blast,
Over seas that wreck and drown,
Over tumult of traffic and town;
And from ages yet to be
Come the echoes back to me,
    O Absalom, my son!

Somewhere at every hour
The watchman on the tower

Looks forth, and sees the fleet
Approach of the hurrying feet
Of messengers, that bear
The tidings of despair.
O Absalom, my son!

He goes forth from the door,
Who shall return no more.
With him our joy departs;
The light goes out in our hearts;
In the Chamber over the Gate
We sit disconsolate.
O Absalom, my son!

That 't is a common grief
Bringeth but slight relief;
Ours is the bitterest loss,
Ours is the heaviest cross;
And forever the cry will be
"Would God I had died for thee,
O Absalom, my son!"

Jugurtha

How cold are thy baths, Apollo!
Cried the African monarch, the splendid,
As down to his death in the hollow
Dark dungeons of Rome he descended,
Uncrowned, unthroned, unattended;
How cold are thy baths, Apollo!

How cold are thy baths, Apollo!
Cried the Poet, unknown, unbefriended,
As the vision, that lured him to follow,
With the mist and the darkness blended,
And the dream of his life was ended;
How cold are thy baths, Apollo!

Helen of Tyre

What phantom is this that appears
Through the purple mists of the years,
    Itself but a mist like these?
A woman of cloud and of fire;
It is she; it is Helen of Tyre,
    The town in the midst of the seas.

O Tyre! in thy crowded streets
The phantom appears and retreats,
    And the Israelites that sell
Thy lilies and lions of brass,
Look up as they see her pass,
    And murmur "Jezebel!"

Then another phantom is seen
At her side, in a gray gabardine,
    With beard that floats to his waist;
It is Simon Magus, the Seer;
He speaks, and she pauses to hear
    The words he utters in haste.

He says: "From this evil fame,
From this life of sorrow and shame,
    I will lift thee and make thee mine;
Thou hast been Queen Candace,
And Helen of Troy, and shalt be
    The Intelligence Divine!"

Oh, sweet as the breath of morn,
To the fallen and forlorn
    Are whispered words of praise;
For the famished heart believes
The falsehood that tempts and deceives,
    And the promise that betrays.

So she follows from land to land
The wizard's beckoning hand,
    As a leaf is blown by the gust,

Till she vanishes into night.
O reader, stoop down and write
With thy finger in the dust.

O town in the midst of the seas,
With thy rafts of cedar trees,
Thy merchandise and thy ships,
Thou, too, art become as naught,
A phantom, a shadow, a thought,
A name upon men's lips.

Elegiac

Dark is the morning with mist; in the narrow mouth of the harbor
Motionless lies the sea, under its curtain of cloud;
Dreamily glimmer the sails of ships on the distant horizon,
Like to the towers of a town, built on the verge of the sea.

Slowly and stately and still, they sail forth into the ocean;
With them sail my thoughts over the limitless deep,
Farther and farther away, borne on by unsatisfied longings,
Unto Hesperian isles, unto Ausonian shores.

Now they have vanished away, have disappeared in the ocean;
Sunk are the towers of the town into the depths of the sea!
All have vanished but those that, moored in the neighboring roadstead,
Sailless at anchor ride, looming so large in the mist.

Vanished, too, are the thoughts, the dim, unsatisfied longings;
Sunk are the turrets of cloud into the ocean of dreams;
While in a haven of rest my heart is riding at anchor,
Held by the chains of love, held by the anchors of trust!

The Tide Rises, the Tide Falls

The tide rises, the tide falls,
The twilight darkens, the curlew calls;
Along the sea-sands damp and brown
The traveller hastens toward the town,
  And the tide rises, the tide falls.

Darkness settles on roofs and walls,
But the sea, the sea in the darkness calls;
The little waves, with their soft, white hands,
Efface the footprints in the sands,
  And the tide rises, the tide falls.

The morning breaks; the steeds in their stalls
Stamp and neigh, as the hostler calls;
The day returns, but nevermore
Returns the traveller to the shore,
  And the tide rises, the tide falls.

My Cathedral

Like two cathedral towers these stately pines
  Uplift their fretted summits tipped with cones;
  The arch beneath them is not built with stones,
  Not Art but Nature traced these lovely lines,
And carved this graceful arabesque of vines;
  No organ but the wind here sighs and moans,
  No sepulchre conceals a martyr's bones,
  No marble bishop on his tomb reclines.
Enter! the pavement, carpeted with leaves,
  Gives back a softened echo to thy tread!
  Listen! the choir is singing; all the birds,
In leafy galleries beneath the eaves,
  Are singing! listen, ere the sound be fled,
  And learn there may be worship without words.

The Burial of the Poet

Richard Henry Dana

In the old churchyard of his native town,
And in the ancestral tomb beside the wall,
We laid him in the sleep that comes to all,
And left him to his rest and his renown.
The snow was falling, as if Heaven dropped down
White flowers of Paradise to strew his pall;—
The dead around him seemed to wake, and call
His name, as worthy of so white a crown.
And now the moon is shining on the scene,
And the broad sheet of snow is written o'er
With shadows cruciform of leafless trees,
As once the winding-sheet of Saladin
With chapters of the Koran; but, ah! more
Mysterious and triumphant signs are these.

Night

Into the darkness and the hush of night
Slowly the landscape sinks, and fades away,
And with it fade the phantoms of the day,
The ghosts of men and things, that haunt the light.
The crowd, the clamor, the pursuit, the flight,
The unprofitable splendor and display,
The agitations, and the cares that prey
Upon our hearts, all vanish out of sight.
The better life begins; the world no more
Molests us; all its records we erase
From the dull commonplace book of our lives,
That like a palimpsest is written o'er
With trivial incidents of time and place,
And lo! the ideal, hidden beneath, revives.

The Poet and His Songs

As the birds come in the Spring,
  We know not from where;
As the stars come at evening
  From depths of the air;

As the rain comes from the cloud,
  And the brook from the ground;
As suddenly, low or loud,
  Out of silence a sound;

As the grape comes to the vine,
  The fruit to the tree;
As the wind comes to the pine,
  And the tide to the sea;

As come the white sails of ships
  O'er the ocean's verge;
As comes the smile to the lips,
  The foam to the surge;

So come to the Poet his songs,
  All hitherward blown
From the misty realm, that belongs
  To the vast Unknown.

His, and not his, are the lays
  He sings; and their fame
Is his, and not his; and the praise
  And the pride of a name.

For voices pursue him by day,
  And haunt him by night,
And he listens, and needs must obey,
  When the Angel says: "Write!"

from

IN THE HARBOR

The Poet's Calendar

JANUARY.

Janus am I; oldest of potentates;
  Forward I look, and backward, and below
I count, as god of avenues and gates,
  The years that through my portals come and go.

I block the roads, and drift the fields with snow;
  I chase the wild-fowl from the frozen fen;
My frosts congeal the rivers in their flow,
  My fires light up the hearths and hearts of men.

FEBRUARY.

I am lustration; and the sea is mine!
  I wash the sands and headlands with my tide;
My brow is crowned with branches of the pine;
  Before my chariot-wheels the fishes glide.
By me all things unclean are purified,
  By me the souls of men washed white again;
E'en the unlovely tombs of those who died
  Without a dirge, I cleanse from every stain.

MARCH.

I Martius am! Once first, and now the third!
  To lead the Year was my appointed place;
A mortal dispossessed me by a word,
  And set there Janus with the double face.
Hence I make war on all the human race;
  I shake the cities with my hurricanes;
I flood the rivers and their banks efface,
  And drown the farms and hamlets with my rains.

APRIL.

I open wide the portals of the Spring
  To welcome the procession of the flowers,
With their gay banners, and the birds that sing
  Their song of songs from their aerial towers.
I soften with my sunshine and my showers
  The heart of earth; with thoughts of love I glide
Into the hearts of men; and with the Hours
  Upon the Bull with wreathèd horns I ride.

MAY.

Hark! The sea-faring wild-fowl loud proclaim
  My coming, and the swarming of the bees.
These are my heralds, and behold! my name
  Is written in blossoms on the hawthorn-trees.
I tell the mariner when to sail the seas;
  I waft o'er all the land from far away
The breath and bloom of the Hesperides,
  My birthplace. I am Maia. I am May.

JUNE.

Mine is the Month of Roses; yes, and mine
  The Month of Marriages! All pleasant sights
And scents, the fragrance of the blossoming vine,
  The foliage of the valleys and the heights.
Mine are the longest days, the loveliest nights;
  The mower's scythe makes music to my ear;
I am the mother of all dear delights;
  I am the fairest daughter of the year.

JULY.

My emblem is the Lion, and I breathe
  The breath of Libyan deserts o'er the land;
My sickle as a sabre I unsheathe,

And bent before me the pale harvests stand.
The lakes and rivers shrink at my command,
And there is thirst and fever in the air;
The sky is changed to brass, the earth to sand;
I am the Emperor whose name I bear.

AUGUST.

The Emperor Octavian, called the August,
I being his favorite, bestowed his name
Upon me, and I hold it still in trust,
In memory of him and of his fame.
I am the Virgin, and my vestal flame
Burns less intensely than the Lion's rage;
Sheaves are my only garlands, and I claim
The golden Harvests as my heritage.

SEPTEMBER.

I bear the Scales, where hang in equipoise
The night and day; and when unto my lips
I put my trumpet, with its stress and noise
Fly the white clouds like tattered sails of ships;
The tree-tops lash the air with sounding whips;
Southward the clamorous sea-fowl wing their flight;
The hedges are all red with haws and hips,
The Hunter's Moon reigns empress of the night.

OCTOBER.

My ornaments are fruits; my garments leaves,
Woven like cloth of gold, and crimson dyed;
I do not boast the harvesting of sheaves,
O'er orchards and o'er vineyards I preside.
Though on the frigid Scorpion I ride,
The dreamy air is full, and overflows
With tender memories of the summer-tide,
And mingled voices of the doves and crows.

NOVEMBER.

The Centaur, Sagittarius, am I,
Born of Ixion's and the cloud's embrace;
With sounding hoofs across the earth I fly,
A steed Thessalian with a human face.
Sharp winds the arrows are with which I chase
The leaves, half dead already with affright;
I shroud myself in gloom; and to the race
Of mortals bring nor comfort nor delight.

DECEMBER.

Riding upon the Goat, with snow-white hair,
I come, the last of all. This crown of mine
Is of the holly; in my hand I bear
The thyrsus, tipped with fragrant cones of pine.
I celebrate the birth of the Divine,
And the return of the Saturnian reign;—
My songs are carols sung at every shrine.
Proclaiming "Peace on earth, good will to men."

Autumn Within

It is autumn; not without,
But within me is the cold.
Youth and spring are all about;
It is I that have grown old.

Birds are darting through the air,
Singing, building without rest;
Life is stirring everywhere,
Save within my lonely breast.

There is silence: the dead leaves
Fall and rustle and are still;
Beats no flail upon the sheaves,
Comes no murmur from the mill.

Victor and Vanquished

As one who long hath fled with panting breath
  Before his foe, bleeding and near to fall,
  I turn and set my back against the wall,
  And look thee in the face, triumphant Death.
I call for aid, and no one answereth;
  I am alone with thee, who conquerest all;
  Yet me thy threatening form doth not appall,
  For thou art but a phantom and a wraith.
Wounded and weak, sword broken at the hilt,
  With armor shattered, and without a shield,
  I stand unmoved; do with me what thou wilt;
I can resist no more, but will not yield.
  This is no tournament where cowards tilt;
  The vanquished here is victor of the field.

Moonlight

As a pale phantom with a lamp
  Ascends some ruin's haunted stair,
So glides the moon along the damp
  Mysterious chambers of the air.

Now hidden in cloud, and now revealed,
  As if this phantom, full of pain,
Were by the crumbling walls concealed,
  And at the windows seen again.

Until at last, serene and proud
  In all the splendor of her light,
She walks the terraces of cloud,
  Supreme as Empress of the Night.

I look, but recognize no more
  Objects familiar to my view;
The very pathway to my door
  Is an enchanted avenue.

All things are changed. One mass of shade,
The elm-trees drop their curtains down;
By palace, park, and colonnade
I walk as in a foreign town.

The very ground beneath my feet
Is clothed with a diviner air;
While marble paves the silent street
And glimmers in the empty square.

Illusion! Underneath there lies
The common life of every day;
Only the spirit glorifies
With its own tints the sober gray.

In vain we look, in vain uplift
Our eyes to heaven, if we are blind;
We see but what we have the gift
Of seeing; what we bring we find.

Hermes Trismegistus

Still through Egypt's desert places
Flows the lordly Nile,
From its banks the great stone faces
Gaze with patient smile.
Still the pyramids imperious
Pierce the cloudless skies,
And the Sphinx stares with mysterious,
Solemn, stony eyes.

But where are the old Egyptian
Demi-gods and kings?
Nothing left but an inscription
Graven on stones and rings.
Where are Helios and Hephæstus,
Gods of eldest eld?
Where is Hermes Trismegistus,
Who their secrets held?

Where are now the many hundred
    Thousand books he wrote?
By the Thaumaturgists plundered,
    Lost in lands remote;
In oblivion sunk forever,
    As when o'er the land
Blows a storm-wind, in the river
    Sinks the scattered sand.

Something unsubstantial, ghostly,
    Seems this Theurgist,
In deep meditation mostly
    Wrapped, as in a mist.
Vague, phantasmal, and unreal
    To our thought he seems,
Walking in a world ideal,
    In a land of dreams.

Was he one, or many, merging
    Name and fame in one,
Like a stream, to which, converging,
    Many streamlets run?
Till, with gathered power proceeding,
    Ampler sweep it takes,
Downward the sweet waters leading
    From unnumbered lakes.

By the Nile I see him wandering,
    Pausing now and then,
On the mystic union pondering
    Between gods and men;
Half believing, wholly feeling,
    With supreme delight,
How the gods, themselves concealing,
    Lift men to their height.

Or in Thebes, the hundred-gated,
    In the thoroughfare
Breathing, as if consecrated,
    A diviner air;

And amid discordant noises,
    In the jostling throng,
Hearing far, celestial voices
    Of Olympian song.

Who shall call his dreams fallacious?
    Who has searched or sought
All the unexplored and spacious
    Universe of thought?
Who, in his own skill confiding,
    Shall with rule and line
Mark the border-land dividing
    Human and divine?

Trismegistus! three times greatest!
    How thy name sublime
Has descended to this latest
    Progeny of time!
Happy they whose written pages
    Perish with their lives,
If amid the crumbling ages
    Still their name survives!

Thine, O priest of Egypt, lately
    Found I in the vast,
Weed-encumbered, sombre, stately,
    Grave-yard of the Past;
And a presence moved before me
    On that gloomy shore,
As a waft of wind, that o'er me
    Breathed, and was no more.

The Bells of San Blas

What say the Bells of San Blas
To the ships that southward pass
From the harbor of Mazatlan?
To them it is nothing more
Than the sound of surf on the shore,—
Nothing more to master or man.

But to me, a dreamer of dreams,
To whom what is and what seems
Are often one and the same,—
The Bells of San Blas to me
Have a strange, wild melody,
And are something more than a name.

For bells are the voice of the church;
They have tones that touch and search
The hearts of young and old;
One sound to all, yet each
Lends a meaning to their speech,
And the meaning is manifold.

They are a voice of the Past,
Of an age that is fading fast,
Of a power austere and grand;
When the flag of Spain unfurled
Its folds o'er this western world,
And the Priest was lord of the land.

The chapel that once looked down
On the little seaport town
Has crumbled into the dust;
And on oaken beams below
The bells swing to and fro,
And are green with mould and rust.

"Is, then, the old faith dead,"
They say, "and in its stead
Is some new faith proclaimed,

That we are forced to remain
Naked to sun and rain,
Unsheltered and ashamed?

"Once in our tower aloof
We rang over wall and roof
Our warnings and our complaints;
And round about us there
The white doves filled the air,
Like the white souls of the saints.

"The saints! Ah, have they grown
Forgetful of their own?
Are they asleep, or dead,
That open to the sky
Their ruined Missions lie,
No longer tenanted?

"Oh, bring us back once more
The vanished days of yore,
When the world with faith was filled;
Bring back the fervid zeal,
The hearts of fire and steel,
The hands that believe and build.

"Then from our tower again
We will send over land and main
Our voices of command,
Like exiled kings who return
To their thrones, and the people learn
That the Priest is lord of the land!"

O Bells of San Blas, in vain
Ye call back the Past again!
The Past is deaf to your prayer;
Out of the shadows of night
The world rolls into light;
It is daybreak everywhere.

OTHER POEMS

Mezzo Cammin

Half of my life is gone, and I have let
  The years slip from me and have not fulfilled
  The aspiration of my youth, to build
  Some tower of song with lofty parapet.
Not indolence, nor pleasure, nor the fret
  Of restless passions that would not be stilled,
  But sorrow, and a care that almost killed,
  Kept me from what I may accomplish yet;
Though, half-way up the hill, I see the Past
  Lying beneath me with its sounds and sights,—
  A city in the twilight dim and vast,
With smoking roofs, soft bells, and gleaming lights,—
  And hear above me on the autumnal blast
  The cataract of Death far thundering from the heights.

The Cross of Snow

In the long, sleepless watches of the night,
  A gentle face—the face of one long dead—
  Looks at me from the wall, where round its head
  The night-lamp casts a halo of pale light.
Here in this room she died; and soul more white
  Never through martyrdom of fire was led
  To its repose; nor can in books be read
  The legend of a life more benedight.
There is a mountain in the distant West
  That, sun-defying, in its deep ravines
  Displays a cross of snow upon its side.
Such is the cross I wear upon my breast
  These eighteen years, through all the changing scenes
  And seasons, changeless since the day she died.

from
Michael Angelo: A Fragment

DEDICATION.

Nothing that is shall perish utterly,
But perish only to revive again
In other forms, as clouds restore in rain
The exhalations of the land and sea.
Men build their houses from the masonry
Of ruined tombs; the passion and the pain
Of hearts, that long have ceased to beat, remain
To throb in hearts that are, or are to be.
So from old chronicles, where sleep in dust
Names that once filled the world with trumpet tones,
I build this verse; and flowers of song have thrust
Their roots among the loose disjointed stones,
Which to this end I fashion as I must.
Quickened are they that touch the Prophet's bones.

THE LAST JUDGMENT.

MICHAEL ANGELO'S *Studio. He is at work on the cartoon of the Last Judgment.*

MICHAEL ANGELO.

Why did the Pope and his ten Cardinals
Come here to lay this heavy task upon me?
Were not the paintings on the Sistine ceiling
Enough for them? They saw the Hebrew leader
Waiting, and clutching his tempestuous beard,
But heeded not. The bones of Julius
Shook in their sepulchre. I heard the sound;
They only heard the sound of their own voices.

Are there no other artists here in Rome
To do this work, that they must needs seek me?

Fra Bastian, my Fra Bastian, might have done it,
But he is lost to art. The Papal Seals,
Like leaden weights upon a dead man's eyes,
Press down his lids; and so the burden falls
On Michael Angelo, Chief Architect
And Painter of the Apostolic Palace.
That is the title they cajole me with,
To make me do their work and leave my own;
But having once begun, I turn not back.
Blow, ye bright angels, on your golden trumpets
To the four corners of the earth, and wake
The dead to judgment! Ye recording angels,
Open your books and read! Ye dead, awake!
Rise from your graves, drowsy and drugged with death,
As men who suddenly aroused from sleep
Look round amazed, and know not where they are!

In happy hours, when the imagination
Wakes like a wind at midnight, and the soul
Trembles in all its leaves, it is a joy
To be uplifted on its wings, and listen
To the prophetic voices in the air
That call us onward. Then the work we do
Is a delight, and the obedient hand
Never grows weary. But how different is it
In the disconsolate, discouraged hours,
When all the wisdom of the world appears
As trivial as the gossip of a nurse
In a sick-room, and all our work seems useless.

What is it guides my hand, what thoughts possess me,
That I have drawn her face among the angels,
Where she will be hereafter? O sweet dreams,
That through the vacant chambers of my heart
Walk in the silence, as familiar phantoms
Frequent an ancient house, what will ye with me?
'T is said that Emperors write their names in green
When under age, but when of age in purple.
So Love, the greatest Emperor of them all,
Writes his in green at first, but afterwards

In the imperial purple of our blood.
First love or last love,—which of these two passions
Is more omnipotent? Which is more fair,
The star of morning, or the evening star?
The sunrise or the sunset of the heart?
The hour when we look forth to the unknown,
And the advancing day consumes the shadows,
Or that when all the landscape of our lives
Lies stretched behind us, and familiar places
Gleam in the distance, and sweet memories
Rise like a tender haze, and magnify
The objects we behold, that soon must vanish?

What matters it to me, whose countenance
Is like Laocoön's, full of pain? whose forehead
Is a ploughed harvest-field, where threescore years
Have sown in sorrow and have reaped in anguish?
To me, the artisan, to whom all women
Have been as if they were not, or at most
A sudden rush of pigeons in the air,
A flutter of wings, a sound, and then a silence?
I am too old for love; I am too old
To flatter and delude myself with visions
Of never-ending friendship with fair women,
Imaginations, fantasies, illusions,
In which the things that cannot be take shape,
And seem to be, and for the moment are.

Convent bells ring.

Distant and near and low and loud the bells,
Dominican, Benedictine, and Franciscan,
Jangle and wrangle in their airy towers,
Discordant as the brotherhoods themselves
In their dim cloisters. The descending sun
Seems to caress the city that he loves,
And crowns it with the aureole of a saint.
I will go forth and breathe the air a while.

from Part First

I turn for consolation to the leaves
Of the great master of our Tuscan tongue,
Whose words, like colored garnet-shirls in lava,
Betray the heat in which they were engendered.
A mendicant, he ate the bitter bread
Of others, but repaid their meagre gifts
With immortality. In courts of princes
He was a by-word, and in streets of towns
Was mocked by children, like the Hebrew prophet,
Himself a prophet. I too know the cry,
Go up, thou bald head! from a generation
That, wanting reverence, wanteth the best food
The soul can feed on. There 's not room enough
For age and youth upon this little planet.
Age must give way. There was not room enough
Even for this great poet. In his song
I hear reverberate the gates of Florence,
Closing upon him, never more to open;
But mingled with the sound are melodies
Celestial from the gates of paradise.
He came and he is gone. The people knew not
What manner of man was passing by their doors,
Until he passed no more; but in his vision
He saw the torments and beatitudes
Of souls condemned or pardoned, and hath left
Behind him this sublime Apocalypse.
I strive in vain to draw here on the margin
The face of Beatrice. It is not hers,
But the Colonna's. Each hath his ideal,
The image of some woman excellent,
That is his guide. No Grecian art, nor Roman,
Hath yet revealed such loveliness as hers.

VITERBO.

VITTORIA COLONNA *at the convent window.*

VITTORIA.

Parting with friends is temporary death,
As all death is. We see no more their faces,
Nor hear their voices, save in memory.
But messages of love give us assurance
That we are not forgotten. Who shall say
That from the world of spirits comes no greeting,
No message of remembrance? It may be
The thoughts that visit us, we know not whence,
Sudden as inspiration, are the whispers
Of disembodied spirits, speaking to us
As friends, who wait outside a prison wall,
Through the barred windows speak to those within.

[*A pause.*

As quiet as the lake that lies beneath me,
As quiet as the tranquil sky above me,
As quiet as a heart that beats no more,
This convent seems. Above, below, all peace!
Silence and solitude, the soul's best friends,
Are with me here, and the tumultuous world
Makes no more noise than the remotest planet.

[*A pause.*

O gentle spirit, unto the third circle
Of heaven among the blessed souls ascended,
Who, living in the faith and dying for it,
Have gone to their reward, I do not sigh
For thee as being dead, but for myself
That I am still alive. Turn those dear eyes,
Once so benignant to me, upon mine,
That open to their tears such uncontrolled
And such continual issue. Still awhile
Have patience; I will come to thee at last.
A few more goings in and out these doors,
A few more chimings of these convent bells,
A few more prayers, a few more sighs and tears,
And the long agony of this life will end,

And I shall be with thee. If I am wanting
To thy well-being, as thou art to mine,
Have patience; I will come to thee at last.
Ye winds that loiter in these cloister gardens,
Or wander far above the city walls,
Bear unto him this message, that I ever
Or speak or think of him, or weep for him.

By unseen hands uplifted in the light
Of sunset, yonder solitary cloud
Floats, with its white apparel blown abroad,
And wafted up to heaven. It fades away,
And melts into the air. Ah, would that I
Could thus be wafted unto thee, Francesco,
A cloud of white, an incorporeal spirit!

MICHAEL ANGELO, *returning to his work.*

MICHAEL ANGELO.

How will men speak of me when I am gone,
When all this colorless, sad life is ended,
And I am dust? They will remember only
The wrinkled forehead, the marred countenance,
The rudeness of my speech, and my rough manners,
And never dream that underneath them all
There was a woman's heart of tenderness;
They will not know the secret of my life,
Locked up in silence, or but vaguely hinted
In uncouth rhymes, that may perchance survive
Some little space in memories of men!
Each one performs his life-work, and then leaves it;
Those that come after him will estimate
His influence on the age in which he lived.

from Part Second

MONOLOGUE.

Macello de' Corvi. A room in MICHAEL ANGELO'S *house.*
MICHAEL ANGELO, *standing before a model of St. Peter's.*

MICHAEL ANGELO.

Better than thou I cannot, Brunelleschi,
And less than thou I will not! If the thought
Could, like a windlass, lift the ponderous stones
And swing them to their places; if a breath
Could blow this rounded dome into the air,
As if it were a bubble, and these statues
Spring at a signal to their sacred stations,
As sentinels mount guard upon a wall,
Then were my task completed. Now, alas!
Naught am I but a Saint Sebaldus, holding
Upon his hand the model of a church,
As German artists paint him; and what years,
What weary years, must drag themselves along,
Ere this be turned to stone! What hindrances
Must block the way; what idle interferences
Of Cardinals and Canons of St. Peter's,
Who nothing know of art beyond the color
Of cloaks and stockings, nor of any building
Save that of their own fortunes! And what then?
I must then the short-coming of my means
Piece out by stepping forward, as the Spartan
Was told to add a step to his short sword.

[*A pause.*

And is Fra Bastian dead? Is all that light
Gone out? that sunshine darkened? all that music
And merriment, that used to make our lives
Less melancholy, swallowed up in silence
Like madrigals sung in the street at night
By passing revellers? It is strange indeed
That he should die before me. 'T is against
The laws of nature that the young should die,
And the old live; unless it be that some
Have long been dead who think themselves alive,
Because not buried. Well, what matters it,
Since now that greater light, that was my sun,

Is set, and all is darkness, all is darkness!
Death's lightnings strike to right and left of me,
And, like a ruined wall, the world around me
Crumbles away, and I am left alone.
I have no friends, and want none. My own thoughts
Are now my sole companions,—thoughts of her,
That like a benediction from the skies
Come to me in my solitude and soothe me.
When men are old, the incessant thought of Death
Follows them like their shadow; sits with them
At every meal; sleeps with them when they sleep;
And when they wake already is awake,
And standing by their bedside. Then, what folly
It is in us to make an enemy
Of this importunate follower, not a friend!
To me a friend, and not an enemy,
Has he become since all my friends are dead.

IN THE COLISEUM.

MICHAEL ANGELO *and* TOMASO DE' CAVALIERI.

CAVALIERI.

What do you here alone, Messer Michele?

MICHAEL ANGELO.

I come to learn.

CAVALIERI.

You are already master,
And teach all other men.

MICHAEL ANGELO.

Nay, I know nothing;
Not even my own ignorance, as some
Philosopher hath said. I am a school-boy
Who hath not learned his lesson, and who stands
Ashamed and silent in the awful presence

Of the great master of antiquity
Who built these walls cyclopean.

CAVALIERI.

Gaudentius
His name was, I remember. His reward
Was to be thrown alive to the wild beasts
Here where we now are standing.

MICHAEL ANGELO.

Idle tales.

CAVALIERI.

But you are greater than Gaudentius was,
And your work nobler.

MICHAEL ANGELO.

Silence, I beseech you.

CAVALIERI.

Tradition says that fifteen thousand men
Were toiling for ten years incessantly
Upon this amphitheatre.

MICHAEL ANGELO.

Behold
How wonderful it is! The queen of flowers,
The marble rose of Rome! Its petals torn
By wind and rain of thrice five hundred years;
Its mossy sheath half rent away, and sold
To ornament our palaces and churches,
Or to be trodden under feet of man
Upon the Tiber's bank; yet what remains
Still opening its fair bosom to the sun,
And to the constellations that at night
Hang poised above it like a swarm of bees.

CAVALIERI.

The rose of Rome, but not of Paradise;
Not the white rose our Tuscan poet saw,
With saints for petals. When this rose was perfect
Its hundred thousand petals were not saints,
But senators in their Thessalian caps,
And all the roaring populace of Rome;
And even an Empress and the Vestal Virgins,
Who came to see the gladiators die,
Could not give sweetness to a rose like this.

MICHAEL ANGELO.

I spake not of its uses, but its beauty.

CAVALIERI.

The sand beneath our feet is saturate
With blood of martyrs; and these rifted stones
Are awful witnesses against a people
Whose pleasure was the pain of dying men.

MICHAEL ANGELO.

Tomaso Cavalieri, on my word,
You should have been a preacher, not a painter!
Think you that I approve such cruelties,
Because I marvel at the architects
Who built these walls, and curved these noble arches?
Oh, I am put to shame, when I consider
How mean our work is, when compared with theirs!
Look at these walls about us and above us!
They have been shaken by earthquakes, have been made
A fortress, and been battered by long sieges;
The iron clamps, that held the stones together,
Have been wrenched from them; but they stand erect
And firm, as if they had been hewn and hollowed
Out of the solid rock, and were a part
Of the foundations of the world itself.

CAVALIERI.

Your work, I say again, is nobler work,
In so far as its end and aim are nobler;
And this is but a ruin, like the rest.
Its vaulted passages are made the caverns
Of robbers, and are haunted by the ghosts
Of murdered men.

MICHAEL ANGELO.

A thousand wild flowers bloom
From every chink, and the birds build their nests
Among the ruined arches, and suggest
New thoughts of beauty to the architect.
Now let us climb the broken stairs that lead
Into the corridors above, and study
The marvel and the mystery of that art
In which I am a pupil, not a master.

All things must have an end; the world itself
Must have an end, as in a dream I saw it.
There came a great hand out of heaven, and touched
The earth, and stopped it in its course. The seas
Leaped, a vast cataract, into the abyss;
The forests and the fields slid off, and floated
Like wooded islands in the air. The dead
Were hurled forth from their sepulchres; the living
Were mingled with them, and themselves were dead,—
All being dead; and the fair, shining cities
Dropped out like jewels from a broken crown.
Naught but the core of the great globe remained,
A skeleton of stone. And over it
The wrack of matter drifted like a cloud,
And then recoiled upon itself, and fell
Back on the empty world, that with the weight
Reeled, staggered, righted, and then headlong plunged
Into the darkness, as a ship, when struck
By a great sea, throws off the waves at first
On either side, then settles and goes down
Into the dark abyss, with her dead crew.

CAVALIERI.

But the earth does not move.

MICHAEL ANGELO.

Who knows? who knows?
There are great truths that pitch their shining tents
Outside our walls, and though but dimly seen
In the gray dawn, they will be manifest
When the light widens into perfect day.
A certain man, Copernicus by name,
Sometime professor here in Rome, has whispered
It is the earth, and not the sun, that moves.
What I beheld was only in a dream,
Yet dreams sometimes anticipate events,
Being unsubstantial images of things
As yet unseen.

THE OAKS OF MONTE LUCA.

MICHAEL ANGELO, *alone in the woods.*

MICHAEL ANGELO.

How still it is among these ancient oaks!
Surges and undulations of the air
Uplift the leafy boughs, and let them fall
With scarce a sound. Such sylvan quietudes
Become old age. These huge centennial oaks,
That may have heard in infancy the trumpets
Of Barbarossa's cavalry, deride
Man's brief existence, that with all his strength
He cannot stretch beyond the hundredth year.
This little acorn, turbaned like the Turk,
Which with my foot I spurn, may be an oak
Hereafter, feeding with its bitter mast
The fierce wild-boar, and tossing in its arms
The cradled nests of birds, when all the men
That now inhabit this vast universe,
They and their children, and their children's children,
Shall be but dust and mould, and nothing more.
Through openings in the trees I see below me
The valley of Clitumnus, with its farms
And snow-white oxen grazing in the shade
Of the tall poplars on the river's brink.
O Nature, gentle mother, tender nurse!
I, who have never loved thee as I ought,
But wasted all my years immured in cities,
And breathed the stifling atmosphere of streets,
Now come to thee for refuge. Here is peace.
Yonder I see the little hermitages
Dotting the mountain side with points of light,
And here St. Julian's convent, like a nest
Of curlews, clinging to some windy cliff.
Beyond the broad, illimitable plain
Down sinks the sun, red as Apollo's quoit,
That, by the envious Zephyr blown aside,
Struck Hyacinthus dead, and stained the earth
With his young blood, that blossomed into flowers.

And now, instead of these fair deities,
Dread demons haunt the earth; hermits inhabit
The leafy homes of sylvan Hamadryads;
And jovial friars, rotund and rubicund,
Replace the old Silenus with his ass.

Here underneath these venerable oaks,
Wrinkled and brown and gnarled like them with age,
A brother of the monastery sits,
Lost in his meditations. What may be
The questions that perplex, the hopes that cheer him?—
Good-evening, holy father.

MONK.

God be with you.

MICHAEL ANGELO.

Pardon a stranger if he interrupt
Your meditations.

MONK.

It was but a dream,—
The old, old dream, that never will come true;
The dream that all my life I have been dreaming,
And yet is still a dream.

MICHAEL ANGELO.

All men have dreams.
I have had mine; but none of them came true;
They were but vanity. Sometimes I think
The happiness of man lies in pursuing,
Not in possessing; for the things possessed
Lose half their value. Tell me of your dream.

MONK.

The yearning of my heart, my sole desire,
That like the sheaf of Joseph stands upright,
While all the others bend and bow to it;
The passion that torments me, and that breathes
New meaning into the dead forms of prayer,
Is that with mortal eyes I may behold
The Eternal City.

MICHAEL ANGELO.

Rome?

MONK.

There is but one;
The rest are merely names. I think of it
As the Celestial City, paved with gold,
And sentinelled with angels.

MICHAEL ANGELO.

Would it were.
I have just fled from it. It is beleaguered
By Spanish troops, led by the Duke of Alva.

MONK.

But still for me 't is the Celestial City,
And I would see it once before I die.

MICHAEL ANGELO.

Each one must bear his cross.

MONK.

Were it a cross
That had been laid upon me, I could bear it,
Or fall with it. It is a crucifix;
I am nailed hand and foot, and I am dying!

MICHAEL ANGELO.

What would you see in Rome?

MONK.

His Holiness.

MICHAEL ANGELO.

Him that was once the Cardinal Caraffa?
You would but see a man of fourscore years,
With sunken eyes, burning like carbuncles,
Who sits at table with his friends for hours,
Cursing the Spaniards as a race of Jews
And miscreant Moors. And with what soldiery
Think you he now defends the Eternal City?

MONK.

With legions of bright angels.

MICHAEL ANGELO.

So he calls them;
And yet in fact these bright angelic legions
Are only German Lutherans.

MONK, *crossing himself.*

Heaven protect us!

MICHAEL ANGELO.

What further would you see?

MONK.

The Cardinals.
Going in their gilt coaches to High Mass.

MICHAEL ANGELO.

Men do not go to Paradise in coaches.

MONK.

The catacombs, the convents, and the churches;
The ceremonies of the Holy Week
In all their pomp, or, at the Epiphany,
The feast of the Santissimo Bambino
At Ara Cœli. But I shall not see them.

MICHAEL ANGELO.

These pompous ceremonies of the Church
Are but an empty show to him who knows
The actors in them. Stay here in your convent,
For he who goes to Rome may see too much.
What would you further?

MONK.

I would see the painting
Of the Last Judgment in the Sistine Chapel.

MICHAEL ANGELO.

The smoke of incense and of altar candles
Has blackened it already.

MONK.

Woe is me!
Then I would hear Allegri's Miserere,
Sung by the Papal choir.

MICHAEL ANGELO.

A dismal dirge!
I am an old, old man, and I have lived
In Rome for thirty years and more, and know
The jarring of the wheels of that great world,
Its jealousies, its discords, and its strife.
Therefore I say to you, remain content
Here in your convent, here among your woods,
Where only there is peace. Go not to Rome.
There was of old a monk of Wittenberg

Who went to Rome; you may have heard of him;
His name was Luther; and you know what followed.
[*The convent bell rings.*

MONK, *rising.*

It is the convent bell; it rings for vespers.
Let us go in; we both will pray for peace.

THE DEAD CHRIST.

MICHAEL ANGELO'S *Studio.* MICHAEL ANGELO *with a light, working upon the Dead Christ. Midnight.*

MICHAEL ANGELO.

O Death, why is it I cannot portray
Thy form and features? Do I stand too near thee?
Or dost thou hold my hand, and draw me back,
As being thy disciple, not thy master?
Let him who knows not what old age is like
Have patience till it comes, and he will know.
I once had skill to fashion Life and Death
And Sleep, which is the counterfeit of Death;
And I remember what Giovanni Strozzi
Wrote underneath my statue of the Night
In San Lorenzo, ah, so long ago!
Grateful to me is sleep! More grateful now
Than it was then; for all my friends are dead;
And she is dead, the noblest of them all.
I saw her face, when the great sculptor Death,
Whom men should call Divine, had at a blow
Stricken her into marble; and I kissed
Her cold white hand. What was it held me back
From kissing her fair forehead, and those lips,
Those dead, dumb lips? Grateful to me is sleep!

Enter GIORGIO VASARI.

GIORGIO.

Good-evening, or good-morning, for I know not
Which of the two it is.

MICHAEL ANGELO.

How came you in?

GIORGIO.

Why, by the door, as all men do.

MICHAEL ANGELO.

Ascanio
Must have forgotten to bolt it.

GIORGIO.

Probably.
Am I a spirit, or so like a spirit,
That I could slip through bolted door or window?
As I was passing down the street, I saw
A glimmer of light, and heard the well-known chink
Of chisel upon marble. So I entered,
To see what keeps you from your bed so late.

MICHAEL ANGELO, *coming forward with the lamp.*

You have been revelling with your boon companions,
Giorgio Vasari, and you come to me
At an untimely hour.

GIORGIO.

The Pope hath sent me.
His Holiness desires to see again
The drawing you once showed him of the dome
Of the Basilica.

MICHAEL ANGELO.

We will look for it.

GIORGIO.

What is the marble group that glimmers there
Behind you?

MICHAEL ANGELO.

Nothing, and yet everything,—
As one may take it. It is my own tomb
That I am building.

GIORGIO.

Do not hide it from me.
By our long friendship and the love I bear you,
Refuse me not!

MICHAEL ANGELO, *letting fall the lamp.*

Life hath become to me
An empty theatre,—its lights extinguished,
The music silent, and the actors gone;
And I alone sit musing on the scenes

That once have been. I am so old that Death
Oft plucks me by the cloak, to come with him;
And some day, like this lamp, shall I fall down,
And my last spark of life will be extinguished.
Ah me! ah me! what darkness of despair!
So near to death, and yet so far from God.

from Part Third

TRANSLATIONS

The Celestial Pilot

And now, behold! as at the approach of morning,
  Through the gross vapors, Mars grows fiery red
  Down in the west upon the ocean floor,
Appeared to me,—may I again behold it!
  A light along the sea, so swiftly coming,
  Its motion by no flight of wing is equalled.
And when therefrom I had withdrawn a little
  Mine eyes, that I might question my conductor,
  Again I saw it brighter grown and larger.
Thereafter, on all sides of it, appeared
  I knew not what of white, and underneath,
  Little by little, there came forth another.
My master yet had uttered not a word,
  While the first whiteness into wings unfolded;
  But, when he clearly recognized the pilot,
He cried aloud: "Quick, quick, and bow the knee!
  Behold the Angel of God! fold up thy hands!
  Henceforward shalt thou see such officers!
See, how he scorns all human arguments,
  So that no oar he wants, nor other sail
  Than his own wings, between so distant shores!
See, how he holds them, pointed straight to heaven,
  Fanning the air with the eternal pinions,
  That do not moult themselves like mortal hair!"
And then, as nearer and more near us came
  The Bird of Heaven, more glorious he appeared,
  So that the eye could not sustain his presence,
But down I cast it; and he came to shore
  With a small vessel, gliding swift and light,
  So that the water swallowed naught thereof.
Upon the stern stood the Celestial Pilot!
  Beatitude seemed written in his face!
  And more than a hundred spirits sat within.
"In exitu Israel de Ægypto!"

Thus sang they all together in one voice,
With whatso in that Psalm is after written.
Then made he sign of holy rood upon them,
Whereat all cast themselves upon the shore,
And he departed swiftly as he came.

Dante, *Purgatorio*, II.13–51

The Terrestrial Paradise

Longing already to search in and round
The heavenly forest, dense and living-green,
Which tempered to the eyes the new-born day,
Withouten more delay I left the bank,
Crossing the level country slowly, slowly,
Over the soil, that everywhere breathed fragrance.
A gently-breathing air, that no mutation
Had in itself, smote me upon the forehead
No heavier blow than of a pleasant breeze,
Whereat the tremulous branches readily
Did all of them bow downward towards that side
Where its first shadow casts the Holy Mountain;
Yet not from their upright direction bent
So that the little birds upon their tops
Should cease the practice of their tuneful art;
But, with full-throated joy, the hours of prime
Singing received they in the midst of foliage
That made monotonous burden to their rhymes,
Even as from branch to branch it gathering swells,
Through the pine forests on the shore of Chiassi,
When Æolus unlooses the Sirocco.
Already my slow steps had led me on
Into the ancient wood so far, that I
Could see no more the place where I had entered.
And lo! my further course cut off a river,
Which, tow'rds the left hand, with its little waves,
Bent down the grass, that on its margin sprang.
All waters that on earth most limpid are,
Would seem to have within themselves some mixture,

Compared with that, which nothing doth conceal,
Although it moves on with a brown, brown current,
Under the shade perpetual, that never
Ray of the sun lets in, nor of the moon.

Dante, *Purgatorio*, XXVIII.1–33

Beatrice

Even as the Blessed, at the final summons,
Shall rise up quickened, each one from his grave,
Wearing again the garments of the flesh,
So, upon that celestial chariot,
A hundred rose *ad vocem tanti senis*,
Ministers and messengers of life eternal.
They all were saying, "*Benedictus qui venis*,"
And scattering flowers above and round about,
"*Manibus o date lilia plenis.*"
Oft have I seen, at the approach of day,
The orient sky all stained with roseate hues,
And the other heaven with light serene adorned,
And the sun's face uprising, overshadowed,
So that, by temperate influence of vapors,
The eye sustained his aspect for long while;
Thus in the bosom of a cloud of flowers,
Which from those hands angelic were thrown up,
And down descended inside and without,
With crown of olive o'er a snow-white veil,
Appeared a lady, under a green mantle,
Vested in colors of the living flame.

. . . .

Even as the snow, among the living rafters
Upon the back of Italy, congeals,
Blown on and beaten by Sclavonian winds,
And then, dissolving, filters through itself,
Whene'er the land, that loses shadow, breathes,
Like as a taper melts before a fire,
Even such I was, without a sigh or tear,
Before the song of those who chime forever

After the chiming of the eternal spheres;
But, when I heard in those sweet melodies
Compassion for me, more than had they said,
"Oh wherefore, lady, dost thou thus consume him?"
The ice, that was about my heart congealed,
To air and water changed, and, in my anguish,
Through lips and eyes came gushing from my breast.

. . . .

Confusion and dismay, together mingled,
Forced such a feeble "Yes!" out of my mouth,
To understand it one had need of sight.
Even as a cross-bow breaks, when 't is discharged,
Too tensely drawn the bow-string and the bow,
And with less force the arrow hits the mark;
So I gave way beneath this heavy burden,
Gushing forth into bitter tears and sighs,
And the voice, fainting, flagged upon its passage.

Dante, *Purgatorio*, XXX.13–33, 85–99,
XXXI.13–21

The Good Shepherd

(El Buen Pastor)

Shepherd! who with thine amorous, sylvan song
Hast broken the slumber that encompassed me,
Who mad'st thy crook from the accursed tree,
On which thy powerful arms were stretched so long!
Lead me to mercy's ever-flowing fountains;
For thou my shepherd, guard, and guide shalt be;
I will obey thy voice, and wait to see
Thy feet all beautiful upon the mountains.
Hear, Shepherd! thou who for thy flock art dying,
Oh, wash away these scarlet sins, for thou
Rejoicest at the contrite sinner's vow.
Oh, wait! to thee my weary soul is crying,
Wait for me! Yet why ask it, when I see,
With feet nailed to the cross, thou 'rt waiting still for me!

Lope de Vega

To-morrow

(Mañana)

Lord, what am I, that, with unceasing care,
  Thou didst seek after me, that thou didst wait,
  Wet with unhealthy dews, before my gate,
  And pass the gloomy nights of winter there?
Oh, strange delusion! that I did not greet
  Thy blest approach! and oh, to Heaven how lost,
  If my ingratitude's unkindly frost
  Has chilled the bleeding wounds upon thy feet.
How oft my guardian angel gently cried,
  "Soul, from thy casement look, and thou shalt see
  How he persists to knock and wait for thee!"
And, oh! how often to that voice of sorrow,
  "To-morrow we will open," I replied,
  And when the morrow came I answered still, "To-morrow."

Lope de Vega

Santa Teresa's Book-Mark

(Letrilla que llevaba por Registro en su Breviario)

Let nothing disturb thee,
Nothing affright thee;
All things are passing;
God never changeth;
Patient endurance
Attaineth to all things;
Who God possesseth
In nothing is wanting;
Alone God sufficeth.

Teresa de Avila

Let Me Go Warm

Let me go warm and merry still;
And let the world laugh, an' it will.

Let others muse on earthly things,—
The fall of thrones, the fate of kings,
  And those whose fame the world doth fill;
Whilst muffins sit enthroned in trays,
And orange-punch in winter sways
The merry sceptre of my days;—
  And let the world laugh, an' it will.

He that the royal purple wears
From golden plate a thousand cares
  Doth swallow as a gilded pill:
On feasts like these I turn my back,
Whilst puddings in my roasting-jack
Beside the chimney hiss and crack;—
  And let the world laugh, an' it will.

And when the wintry tempest blows,
And January's sleets and snows
  Are spread o'er every vale and hill,
With one to tell a merry tale
O'er roasted nuts and humming ale,
I sit, and care not for the gale;—
  And let the world laugh, an' it will.

Let merchants traverse seas and lands,
For silver mines and golden sands;
  Whilst I beside some shadowy rill,
Just where its bubbling fountain swells,
Do sit and gather stones and shells,
And hear the tale the blackbird tells;—
  And let the world laugh, an' it will.

For Hero's sake the Grecian lover
The stormy Hellespont swam over:
  I cross, without the fear of ill,

The wooden bridge that slow bestrides
The Madrigal's enchanting sides,
Or barefoot wade through Yepes' tides;—
   And let the world laugh, an' it will.

But since the Fates so cruel prove,
That Pyramus should die of love,
   And love should gentle Thisbe kill;
My Thisbe be an apple-tart,
The sword I plunge into her heart
The tooth that bites the crust apart,—
   And let the world laugh, an' it will.

Luis de Góngora y Argote

The Sea Hath Its Pearls

The sea hath its pearls,
   The heaven hath its stars;
But my heart, my heart,
   My heart hath its love.

Great are the sea and the heaven,
   Yet greater is my heart;
And fairer than pearls and stars
   Flashes and beams my love.

Thou little, youthful maiden,
   Come unto my great heart;
My heart, and the sea, and the heaven
   Are melting away with love!

Heinrich Heine

Retribution

Though the mills of God grind slowly, yet they grind
exceeding small;
Though with patience he stands waiting, with exactness
grinds he all.

Friedrich von Logau

The Grave

For thee was a house built
Ere thou wast born,
For thee was a mould meant
Ere thou of mother camest.
But it is not made ready,
Nor its depth measured,
Nor is it seen
How long it shall be.
Now I bring thee
Where thou shalt be;
Now I shall measure thee,
And the mould afterwards.

Thy house is not
Highly timbered,
It is unhigh and low;
When thou art therein,
The heel-ways are low,
The side-ways unhigh.
The roof is built
Thy breast full nigh,
So thou shalt in mould
Dwell full cold,
Dimly and dark.

Doorless is that house,
And dark it is within;
There thou art fast detained
And Death hath the key.

Loathsome is that earth-house,
And grim within to dwell.
There thou shalt dwell,
And worms shall divide thee.

Thus thou art laid,
And leavest thy friends;
Thou hast no friend,
Who will come to thee,
Who will ever see
How that house pleaseth thee;
Who will ever open
The door for thee,
And descend after thee;
For soon thou art loathsome
And hateful to see.

from the Anglo-Saxon

Rondel

Love, love, what wilt thou with this heart of mine?
Naught see I fixed or sure in thee!
I do not know thee,—nor what deeds are thine:
Love, love, what wilt thou with this heart of mine?
Naught see I fixed or sure in thee!

Shall I be mute, or vows with prayers combine?
Ye who are blessed in loving, tell it me:
Love, love, what wilt thou with this heart of mine?
Naught see I permanent or sure in thee!

Jean Froissart

The Artist

Nothing the greatest artist can conceive
  That every marble block doth not confine
  Within itself; and only its design
  The hand that follows intellect can achieve.
The ill I flee, the good that I believe,
  In thee, fair lady, lofty and divine,
  Thus hidden lie; and so that death be mine,
  Art, of desired success, doth me bereave.
Love is not guilty, then, nor thy fair face,
  Nor fortune, cruelty, nor great disdain,
  Of my disgrace, nor chance nor destiny,
If in thy heart both death and love find place
  At the same time, and if my humble brain,
  Burning, can nothing draw but death from thee.

Michelangelo

To Vittoria Colonna

Lady, how can it chance—yet this we see
  In long experience—that will longer last
  A living image carved from quarries vast
  Than its own maker, who dies presently?
Cause yieldeth to effect if this so be,
  And even Nature is by Art surpassed;
  This know I, who to Art have given the past,
  But see that Time is breaking faith with me.
Perhaps on both of us long life can I
  Either in color or in stone bestow,
  By now portraying each in look and mien;
So that a thousand years after we die,
  How fair thou wast, and I how full of woe,
  And wherefore I so loved thee, may be seen.

Michelangelo

Dante

What should be said of him cannot be said;
  By too great splendor is his name attended;
  To blame is easier those who him offended,
  Than reach the faintest glory round him shed.
This man descended to the doomed and dead
  For our instruction; then to God ascended;
  Heaven opened wide to him its portals splendid,
  Who from his country's, closed against him, fled.
Ungrateful land! To its own prejudice
  Nurse of his fortunes; and this showeth well,
  That the most perfect most of grief shall see.
Among a thousand proofs let one suffice,
  That as his exile hath no parallel,
  Ne'er walked the earth a greater man than he.

Michelangelo

A Neapolitan Canzonet

One morning, on the sea-shore as I strayed,
My heart dropped in the sand beside the sea;
I asked of yonder mariners, who said
They saw it in thy bosom,—worn by thee.
And I am come to seek that heart of mine,
For I have none, and thou, alas! hast two;
If this be so, dost know what thou shalt do?—
Still keep my heart, and give me, give me thine.

from the Italian

SELECTED PROSE

Kavanagh

A Tale

The flighty purpose never is o'ertook,
Unless the deed go with it.
SHAKSPEARE.

Who ne'er his bread in sorrow ate,
Who ne'er the mournful midnight hours
Weeping upon his bed has sate,
He knows you not, ye Heavenly Powers.
GOETHE.

I.

GREAT men stand like solitary towers in the city of God, and secret passages running deep beneath external nature give their thoughts intercourse with higher intelligences, which strengthens and consoles them, and of which the laborers on the surface do not even dream!

Some such thought as this was floating vaguely through the brain of Mr. Churchill, as he closed his school-house door behind him; and if in any degree he applied it to himself, it may perhaps be pardoned in a dreamy, poetic man like him; for we judge ourselves by what we feel capable of doing, while others judge us by what we have already done. And moreover his wife considered him equal to great things. To the people in the village he was the schoolmaster, and nothing more. They beheld in his form and countenance no outward sign of the divinity within. They saw him daily moiling and delving in the common path, like a beetle, and little thought that underneath that hard and cold exterior lay folded delicate golden wings, wherewith, when the heat of day was over, he soared and revelled in the pleasant evening air.

To-day he was soaring and revelling before the sun had set; for it was Saturday. With a feeling of infinite relief he left behind him the empty school-house, into which the hot sun of a September afternoon was pouring. All the bright young faces were gone; all the impatient little hearts were gone; all the fresh voices, shrill, but musical with the melody of childhood were gone; and the lately busy realm was given up to silence, and the dusty sunshine, and the old gray flies, that buzzed and bumped their heads against the window-panes. The sound of the outer door, creaking on its hebdomadal hinges, was like a sentinel's challenge, to which the key growled responsive in the lock; and the master, casting a furtive glance at the last caricature of himself in red chalk on the wooden fence close by, entered with a light step the solemn avenue of pines that led to the margin of the river.

At first his step was quick and nervous; and he swung his cane as if aiming blows at some invisible and retreating enemy. Though a meek man, there were moments when he remembered with bitterness the unjust reproaches of fathers and their insulting words; and then he fought imaginary battles with people out of sight, and struck them to the ground, and trampled upon them; for Mr. Churchill was not exempt from the weakness of human nature, nor the customary vexations of a schoolmaster's life. Unruly sons and unreasonable fathers did sometimes embitter his else sweet days and nights. But as he walked, his step grew slower, and his heart calmer. The coolness and shadows of the great trees comforted and satisfied him, and he heard the voice of the wind as it were the voice of spirits calling around him in the air. So that when he emerged from the black woodlands into the meadows by the river's side, all his cares were forgotten.

He lay down for a moment under a sycamore, and thought of the Roman Consul Licinius, passing a night with eighteen of his followers in the hollow trunk of the great Lycian plane-tree. From the branches overhead the falling seeds were wafted away through the soft air on plumy tufts of down. The continuous murmur of the leaves and of the swift-running stream seemed rather to deepen than disturb the pleasing solitude and silence of the place; and for a moment he imagined himself far away in the broad prairies of the West, and lying beneath the luxuriant trees that overhang the banks of the Wabash and the Kaskaskia. He saw the sturgeon leap from the river, and flash for a moment in the sunshine. Then a flock of wild-fowl flew across the sky towards the sea-mist that was rising slowly in the east; and his soul seemed to float away on the river's current, till he had glided far out into the measureless sea, and the sound of the wind among the leaves was no longer the sound of the wind, but of the sea.

Nature had made Mr. Churchill a poet, but destiny made him a schoolmaster. This produced a discord between his outward and his inward existence. Life presented itself to him like the Sphinx, with its perpetual riddle of the real and the ideal. To the solution of this dark problem he devoted his days and his nights. He was forced to teach grammar when he would fain have written poems; and from day to day, and from year to year, the trivial things of life postponed the great designs, which he felt capable of accomplishing, but never had the resolute courage to begin. Thus he dallied with his thoughts and with all things, and wasted his strength on trifles; like the lazy sea, that plays with the pebbles on its beach, but under the inspiration of the wind might lift great navies on its outstretched palms, and toss them into the air as playthings.

The evening came. The setting sun stretched his celestial rods of light across the level landscape, and, like the Hebrew in Egypt, smote the rivers and the brooks and the ponds, and they became as blood.

Mr. Churchill turned his steps homeward. He climbed the hill with the old windmill on its summit, and below him saw the lights of the village; and around him the great landscape sinking deeper and deeper into the sea of darkness. He passed an orchard. The air was filled with the odor of the fallen fruit, which seemed to him as sweet as the fragrance of the blossoms in June. A few steps farther brought him to an old and neglected graveyard; and he paused a moment to look at the white gleaming stone, under which slumbered the old clergyman, who came into the village in the time of the Indian wars, and on which was recorded that for half a century he had been "a painful preacher of the word." He entered the village street, and interchanged a few words with Mr. Pendexter, the venerable divine, whom he found standing at his gate. He met, also, an ill-looking man, carrying so many old boots that he seemed literally buried in them; and at intervals encountered a stream of strong tobacco smoke, exhaled from the pipe of an Irish laborer, and pervading the damp evening air. At length he reached his own door.

II.

When Mr. Churchill entered his study, he found the lamp lighted, and his wife waiting for him. The wood fire was singing on the hearth like a grasshopper in the heat and silence of a summer noon; and to his heart the chill autumnal evening became a summer noon. His wife turned towards him with looks of love in her joyous blue eyes; and in the serene expression of her face he read the Divine beatitude, "Blessed are the pure in heart."

No sooner had he seated himself by the fireside than the door was swung wide open, and on the threshold stood, with his legs apart, like a miniature colossus, a lovely, golden boy, about three years old, with long, light locks, and very red cheeks. After a moment's pause, he dashed forward into the room with a shout, and established himself in a large armchair, which he converted into a carrier's wagon, and over the back of which he urged forward his imaginary horses. He was followed by Lucy, the maid of all work, bearing in her arms the baby, with large, round eyes, and no hair. In his mouth he held an India-rubber ring, and looked very much like a street-door knocker. He came down to say good night, but after he got down, could not say it; not being able to say anything but a kind of explosive "Papa!" He was then a good deal kissed and tormented in various ways, and finally sent off to bed blowing little bubbles with his mouth,—Lucy blessing his little heart, and asseverating that nobody could feed him in the night without loving him; and that if the flies bit him any more she would pull out every tooth in their heads!

Then came Master Alfred's hour of triumph and sovereign sway. The fire-light gleamed on his hard, red cheeks, and glanced from his liquid eyes, and small, white teeth. He piled his wagon full of books and papers, and dashed off to town at the top of his speed; he delivered and received parcels and letters, and played the post-boy's horn with his lips. Then he climbed the back of the great chair, sang "Sweep ho!" as from the top of a very high chimney, and, sliding down upon the cushion, pretended to fall asleep in a little white bed, with white curtains; from which imaginary slumber his father awoke him by crying in his ear, in mysterious tones,—

"What little boy is this!"

Finally he sat down in his chair at his mother's knee, and listened very attentively, and for the hundredth time, to the story of the dog Jumper, which was no sooner ended, than vociferously called for again and again. On the fifth repetition, it was cut as short as the dog's tail by Lucy, who, having put the baby to bed, now came for Master Alfred. He seemed to hope he had been forgotten, but was nevertheless marched off without any particular regard to his feelings, and disappeared in a kind of abstracted mood, repeating softly to himself his father's words,—

"Good night, Alfred!"

His father looked fondly after him as he went up stairs, holding Lucy by one hand, and with the other rubbing the sleep out of his eyes.

"Ah! these children, these children!" said Mr. Churchill, as he sat down at the tea-table; "we ought to love them very much now, for we shall not have them long with us!"

"Good heavens!" exclaimed his wife, "what do you mean? Does anything ail them? Are they going to die?"

"I hope not. But they are going to grow up, and be no longer children."

"Oh, you foolish man! You gave me such a fright!"

"And yet it seems impossible that they should ever grow to be men, and drag the heavy artillery along the dusty roads of life."

"And I hope they never will. That is the last thing I want either of them to do."

"Oh, I do not mean literally, only figuratively. By the way, speaking of growing up and growing old, I saw Mr. Pendexter this evening, as I came home."

"And what had he to say?"

"He told me he should preach his farewell sermon to-morrow."

"Poor old man! I really pity him."

"So do I. But it must be confessed he is a dull preacher; and I dare say it is as dull work for him as for his hearers."

"Why are they going to send him away?"

"Oh, there are a great many reasons. He does not give time and attention enough to his sermons and to his parish. He is always at work on his farm; always wants his salary raised; and insists upon his right to pasture his horse in the parish fields."

"Hark!" cried his wife, lifting up her face in a listening attitude.

"What is the matter?"

"I thought I heard the baby!"

There was a short silence. Then Mr. Churchill said,—

"It was only the cat in the cellar."

At this moment Lucy came in. She hesitated a little, and then, in a submissive voice, asked leave to go down to the village to buy some ribbon for her bonnet. Lucy was a girl of fifteen, who had been taken a few years before from an Orphan Asylum. Her dark eyes had a gypsy look, and she wore her brown hair twisted round her head after the manner of some of Murillo's girls. She had Milesian blood in her veins, and was impetuous and impatient of contradiction.

When she had left the room, the schoolmaster resumed the conversation by saying,—

"I do not like Lucy's going out so much in the evening. I am afraid she will get into trouble. She is really very pretty."

Then there was another pause, after which he added,—

"My dear wife, one thing puzzles me exceedingly."

"And what is that?"

"It is to know what that man does with all the old boots he picks up about the village. I met him again this evening. He seemed to have as many feet as Briareus had hands. He is a kind of centipede."

"But what has that to do with Lucy?"

"Nothing. It only occurred to me at the moment; and I never can imagine what he does with so many old boots."

III.

When tea was over, Mr. Churchill walked to and fro in his study, as his custom was. And as he walked, he gazed with secret rapture at the books, which lined the walls, and thought how many bleeding hearts and aching heads had found consolation for themselves and imparted it to others, by writing those pages. The books seemed to him almost as living beings, so instinct were they with human thoughts and sympathies. It was as if the authors themselves were gazing at him from the walls, with countenances neither sorrowful nor glad, but full of calm indifference to fate, like those of the poets who appeared to Dante in his vision, walking together on the dolorous shore. And then he dreamed of fame, and thought that perhaps hereafter he might be in some degree, and to some one, what these men were to him; and in the enthusiasm of the moment he exclaimed aloud,

"Would you have me be like these, dear Mary?"

"Like these what?" asked his wife, not comprehending him.

"Like these great and good men,—like these scholars and poets,—the authors of all these books!"

She pressed his hand and said, in a soft, but excited tone,—

"Oh, yes! Like them, only perhaps better!"

"Then I will write a Romance!"

"Write it!" said his wife, like the angel. For she believed that then he would become famous forever; and that all the vexed and busy world would stand still to hear him blow his little trumpet, whose sound was to rend the adamantine walls of time, and reach the ears of a far-off and startled posterity.

IV.

"I was thinking to-day," said Mr. Churchill a few minutes afterwards, as he took some papers from a drawer scented with a quince, and arranged them on the study table, while his wife as usual seated herself opposite to him with her work in her hand,—"I was thinking to-day how dull and prosaic the study of mathematics is made in our school-books; as if the grand science of numbers had been discovered and perfected merely to further the purposes of trade."

"For my part," answered his wife, "I do not see how you can make mathematics poetical. There is no poetry in them."

"Ah, that is a very great mistake! There is something divine in the science of numbers. Like God, it holds the sea in the hollow of its hand. It measures the earth; it weighs the stars; it illumines the universe; it is law, it is order, it is beauty. And yet we imagine—that is, most of us—that its highest end and culminating point is book-keeping by double entry. It is our way of teaching it that makes it so prosaic."

So saying, he arose, and went to one of his book-cases, from the shelf of which he took down a little old quarto volume, and laid it upon the table.

"Now here," he continued, "is a book of mathematics of quite a different stamp from ours."

"It looks very old. What is it?"

"It is the Lilawati of Bhascara Acharya, translated from the Sanscrit."

"It is a pretty name. Pray what does it mean?"

"Lilawati was the name of Bhascara's daughter; and the book was written to perpetuate it. Here is an account of the whole matter."

He then opened the volume, and read as follows:—

"It is said that the composing of Lilawati was occasioned by the following circumstance. Lilawati was the name of the author's daughter, concerning whom it appeared, from the qualities of the Ascendant at her birth, that she was destined to pass her life unmarried, and to remain without children. The father ascertained a lucky hour for contracting her in marriage, that she might be firmly connected, and have children. It is said that, when that hour approached, he brought his daughter and his intended son near him. He left the hour-cup on the vessel of water, and kept in attendance a time-knowing astrologer, in order that, when the cup should subside in the water, those two precious jewels should be united. But as the intended arrangement was not according to destiny, it happened that the girl, from a curiosity natural to children, looked into the cup to observe the water coming in at the hole; when by chance a pearl separated from her bridal dress, fell into the cup, and, rolling down to the hole, stopped the influx of the water. So the astrologer waited in expectation of the promised hour. When the operation of the cup had thus been delayed beyond all moderate time, the father was in consternation, and examining, he found that a small pearl had stopped the course of the water, and the long-expected hour was passed. In short, the father, thus disappointed, said to his unfortunate daughter, I will write a book of your name, which shall remain to the latest times,—for a good name is a second life, and the groundwork of eternal existence."

As the schoolmaster read, the eyes of his wife dilated and grew tender, and she said,—

"What a beautiful story! When did it happen?"

"Seven hundred years ago, among the Hindoos."

"Why not write a poem about it?"

"Because it is already a poem of itself,—one of those things of which the simplest statement is the best, and which lose by embellishment. The old Hindoo legend, brown with age, would not please me so well if decked in gay colors, and hung round with the tinkling bells of rhyme. Now hear how the book begins."

Again he read:—

"Salutation to the elephant-headed Being who infuses joy into the minds of his worshippers, who delivers from every difficulty those that call upon him, and whose feet are reverenced by the gods!—Reverence to Ganesa, who is beautiful as the pure purple lotos, and around whose neck the black curling snake winds itself in playful folds!"

"That sounds rather mystical," said his wife.

"Yes, the book begins with a salutation to the Hindoo deities, as the old Spanish Chronicles begin in the name of God and the Holy Virgin. And now see how poetical some of the examples are."

He then turned over the leaves slowly and read,—

"One third of a collection of beautiful water-lilies is offered to Mahadev, one fifth to Huri, one sixth to the Sun, one fourth to Devi, and six which remain are presented to the spiritual teacher. Required the whole number of water-lilies."

"That is very pretty," said the wife, "and would put it into the boys' heads to bring you pond-lilies."

"Here is a prettier one still. One fifth of a hive of bees flew to the Kadamba flower; one third flew to the Silandhara;

three times the difference of these two numbers flew to an arbor; and one bee continued flying about, attracted on each side by the fragrant Ketaki and the Malati. What was the number of the bees?"

"I am sure I should never be able to tell."

"Ten times the square root of a flock of geese"—

Here Mrs. Churchill laughed aloud; but he continued very gravely,—

"Ten times the square root of a flock of geese, seeing the clouds collect, flew to the Manus lake; one eighth of the whole flew from the edge of the water amongst a multitude of water-lilies; and three couple were observed playing in the water. Tell me my young girl with beautiful locks, what was the whole number of geese?"

"Well, what was it?"

"What should you think?"

"About twenty."

"No, one hundred and forty-four. Now try another. The square root of half a number of bees, and also eight ninths of the whole, alighted on the jasmines, and a female bee buzzed responsive to the hum of the male enclosed at night in a water-lily. Oh, beautiful damsel, tell me the number of bees."

"That is not there. You made it."

"No, indeed I did not. I wish I had made it. Look and see."

He showed her the book, and she read it herself. He then proposed some of the geometrical questions.

"In a lake the bud of a water-lily was observed, one span above the water, and when moved by the gentle breeze, it sank in the water at two cubits' distance. Required the depth of the water."

"That is charming, but must be very difficult. I could not answer it."

"A tree one hundred cubits high is distant from a well two hundred cubits; from this tree one monkey descends and goes to the well; another monkey takes a leap upwards, and then descends by the hypothenuse; and both pass over an equal space. Required the height of the leap."

"I do not believe you can answer that question yourself, without looking into the book," said the laughing wife, laying her hand over the solution. "Try it."

"With great pleasure, my dear child," cried the confident schoolmaster, taking a pencil and paper. After making a few figures and calculations, he answered,—

"There, my young girl with beautiful locks, there is the answer,—forty cubits."

His wife removed her hand from the book, and then, clapping both in triumph, she exclaimed,—

"No, you are wrong, you are wrong, my beautiful youth with a bee in your bonnet. It is fifty cubits!"

"Then I must have made some mistake."

"Of course you did. Your monkey did not jump high enough."

She signalized his mortifying defeat as if it had been a victory, by showering kisses, like roses, upon his forehead and cheeks, as he passed beneath the triumphal archway of her arms, trying in vain to articulate,—

"My dearest Lilawati, what is the whole number of the geese?"

V.

After extricating himself from this pleasing dilemma, he said,—

"But I am now going to write. I must really begin in sober earnest, or I shall never get anything finished. And you know I have so many things to do, so many books to write, that really I do not know where to begin. I think I will take up the Romance first."

"It will not make much difference, if you only begin!"

"That is true. I will not lose a moment."

"Did you answer Mr. Wainwright's letter about the cottage bedstead?"

"Dear me, no! I forgot it entirely. That must be done first, or he will make it all wrong."

"And the young lady who sent you the poetry to look over and criticise?"

"No; I have not had a single moment's leisure. And there is Mr. Hanson, who wants to know about the cooking-range. Confound it! there is always something interfering with my Romance. However, I will despatch those matters very speedily."

And he began to write with great haste. For a while nothing was heard but the scratching of his pen. Then he said, probably in connection with the cooking-range,—

"One of the most convenient things in house-keeping is a ham. It is always ready and always welcome. You can eat it with anything, and without anything. It reminds me always of the great wild boar Scrimner, in the Northern Mythology, who is killed every day for the gods to feast on in Valhalla, and comes to life again every night."

"In that case, I should think the gods would have the nightmare," said his wife.

"Perhaps they do."

And then another long silence, broken only by the skating of the swift pen over the sheet. Presently Mrs. Churchill said,—as if following out her own train of thought, while she ceased plying her needle to bite off the thread, which women will sometimes do in spite of all that is said against it,—

"A man came here to-day, calling himself the agent of an extensive house in the needle trade. He left this sample, and said the drill of the eye was superior to any other, and they are warranted not to cut the thread. He puts them at the wholesale price; and if I do not like the sizes, he offers to exchange them for others, either sharps or betweens."

To this remark the abstracted schoolmaster vouchsafed no reply. He found his half-dozen letters not so easily answered, particularly that to the poetical young lady, and worked away busily at them. Finally they were finished and sealed, and he looked up to his wife. She turned her eyes dreamily upon him. Slumber was hanging in their blue orbs, like snow in the heavens, ready to fall. It was quite late, and he said to her,—

"I am too tired, my charming Lilawati, and you too sleepy, to sit here any longer to-night. And, as I do not wish to begin my Romance without having you at my side, so that I can read detached passages to you as I write, I will put it off till to-morrow or the next day."

He watched his wife as she went up stairs with the light. It was a picture always new and always beautiful, and like a painting of Gherardo della Notte. As he followed her, he paused to look at the stars. The beauty of the heavens made his soul overflow.

"How absolute," he exclaimed, "how absolute and omnipotent is the silence of the night! And yet the stillness seems almost audible! From all the measureless depths of air around us comes a half-sound, a half-whisper, as if we could hear the crumbling and falling away of earth and all created things, in the great miracle of nature, decay and reproduction, ever beginning, never ending,—the gradual lapse and running of the sand in the great hour-glass of Time!"

In the night, Mr. Churchill had a singular dream. He thought himself in school, where he was reading Latin to his pupils. Suddenly all the genitive cases of the first declension began to make faces at him, and to laugh immoderately; and when he tried to lay hold of them, they jumped down into the ablative, and the circumflex accent assumed the form of a great moustache. Then the little village school-house was transformed into a vast and endless school-house of the world, stretching forward, form after form, through all the generations of coming time; and on all the forms sat young men and old, reading and transcribing his Romance, which now in his dream was completed, and smiling and passing it onward from one to another, till at last the clock in the corner struck twelve, and the weights ran down with a strange, angry whirr, and the school broke up; and the schoolmaster awoke to find this vision of fame only a dream, out of which his alarm clock had aroused him at an untimely hour.

VI.

Meanwhile, a different scene was taking place at the parsonage. Mr. Pendexter had retired to his study to finish his farewell sermon. Silence reigned through the house. Sunday had already commenced there. The week ended with the setting of the sun, and the evening and the morning were the first day.

The clergyman was interrupted in his labors by the old sexton, who called as usual for the key of the church. He was gently rebuked for coming so late, and excused himself by saying that his wife was worse.

"Poor woman!" said Mr. Pendexter; "has she her mind?"

"Yes," answered the sexton, "as much as ever."

"She has been ill a long time," continued the clergyman. "We have had prayers for her a great many Sundays."

"It is very true, sir," replied the sexton, mournfully; "I have given you a great deal of trouble. But you need not pray for her any more. It is of no use."

Mr. Pendexter's mind was in too fervid a state to notice the extreme and hopeless humility of his old parishioner, and the unintentional allusion to the inefficacy of his prayers. He pressed the old man's hand warmly, and said, with much emotion,—

"To-morrow is the last time that I shall preach in this parish, where I have preached for twenty-five years. But it is not the last time I shall pray for you and your family."

The sexton retired also much moved; and the clergyman again resumed his task. His heart glowed and burned within him. Often his face flushed and his eyes filled with tears, so that he could not go on. Often he rose and paced the chamber to and fro, and wiped away the large drops that stood on his red and feverish forehead.

At length the sermon was finished. He rose and looked out of the window. Slowly the clock struck twelve. He had not heard it strike before, since six. The moonlight silvered the distant hills, and lay, white almost as snow, on the frosty roofs of the village. Not a light could be seen at any window.

"Ungrateful people! Could you not watch with me one hour?" exclaimed he, in that excited and bitter moment; as if he had thought that on that solemn night the whole parish would have watched, while he was writing his farewell discourse. He pressed his hot brow against the window-pane to allay its fever, and across the tremulous wavelets of the river the tranquil moon sent towards him a silvery shaft of light, like an angelic salutation. And the consoling thought came to him that not only this river, but all rivers and lakes, and the great sea itself, were flashing with this heavenly light, though he beheld it as a single ray only; and that what to him were the dark waves were the dark providences of God, luminous to others, and even to himself should he change his position.

VII.

The morning came—the dear, delicious, silent Sunday; to the weary workman, both of brain and hand, the beloved day of rest. When the first bell rang, like a brazen mortar, it seemed from its gloomy fortress to bombard the village with bursting shells of sound, that exploded over the houses, shattering the ears of all the parishioners, and shaking the consciences of many.

Mr. Pendexter was to preach his farewell sermon. The church was crowded, and only one person came late. It was a modest, meek girl, who stole silently up one of the side aisles,—not so silently, however, but that the pew-door creaked a little as she opened it; and straightway a hundred heads were turned in that direction, although it was in the midst of the prayer. Old Mrs. Fairfield did not turn round, but she and her daughter looked at each other, and their bonnets made a parenthesis in the prayer, within which one asked what that was, and the other replied,—

"It is only Alice Archer. She always comes late."

Finally the long prayer was ended, and the congregation sat down, and the weary children—who are always restless during prayers, and had been for nearly half an hour twisting and turning, and standing first on one foot and then on the other, and hanging their heads over the backs of the pews, like tired colts looking into neighboring pastures—settled suddenly down, and subsided into something like rest.

The sermon began,—such a sermon as had never been preached, or even heard of before. It brought many tears into the eyes of the pastor's friends, and made the stoutest hearts among his foes quake with something like remorse. As he announced the text, "Yea, I think it meet as long as I am in this tabernacle to stir you up, by putting you in remembrance," it seemed as if the apostle Peter himself, from whose pen the words first proceeded, were calling them to judgment.

He began by giving a minute sketch of his ministry and the state of the parish, with all its troubles and dissensions, social, political, and ecclesiastical. He concluded by thanking those ladies who had presented him with a black silk gown, and had been kind to his wife during her long illness; by apologizing for having neglected his own business, which was to study and preach, in order to attend to that of the parish, which was to support its minister,—stating that his own shortcomings had been owing to theirs, which had driven him into the woods in winter and into the fields in summer; and finally by telling the congregation in general that they were so confirmed in their bad habits, that no reformation was to be expected in them under his ministry, and that to produce one would require a greater exercise of Divine power than it did to create the world; for in creating the world there had been no opposition, whereas, in their reformation, their own obstinacy and evil propensities, and self-seeking, and worldly-mindedness, were all to be overcome!

VIII.

When Mr. Pendexter had finished his discourse, and pronounced his last benediction upon a congregation to whose spiritual wants he had ministered for so many years, his people, now his no more, returned home in very various states of mind. Some were exasperated, others mortified, and others filled with pity.

Among the last was Alice Archer,—a fair, delicate girl, whose whole life had been saddened by a too sensitive organization and by somewhat untoward circumstances. She had a pale, transparent complexion and large gray eyes, that seemed to see visions. Her figure was slight, almost fragile; her hands white, slender, diaphanous. With these external traits her character was in unison. She was thoughtful, silent, susceptible; often sad, often in tears, often lost in reveries. She led a lonely life with her mother, who was old, querulous, and nearly blind. She had herself inherited a predisposition to blindness, and in her disease there was this peculiarity, that she could see in Summer, but in Winter the power of vision failed her.

The old house they lived in, with its four sickly Lombardy poplars in front, suggested gloomy and mournful thoughts. It was one of those houses that depress you as you enter, as if many persons had died in it,—sombre, desolate, silent. The very clock in the hall had a dismal sound, gasping and catching its breath at times, and striking the hour with a violent, determined blow, reminding one of Jael driving the nail into the head of Sisera.

One other inmate the house had, and only one. This was Sally Manchester, or Miss Sally Manchester, as she preferred to be called; an excellent chambermaid and a very bad cook, for she served in both capacities. She was, indeed, an extraordinary woman, of large frame and masculine features;—one of those who are born to work, and accept their inheritance of toil as if it were play, and who consequently, in the language of domestic recommendations, are usually styled "a treasure, if you can get her." A treasure she was to this family; for she did all the housework, and in addition took care of the cow and the poultry,—occasionally venturing into the field of veterinary practice, and administering lamp-oil to the cock, when she thought he crowed hoarsely. She had on her forehead what is sometimes denominated a "widow's peak,"—that is to say, her hair grew down to a point in the middle; and on Sundays she appeared at church in a blue poplin gown, with a large pink bow on what she called "the congregation side of her bonnet." Her mind was strong, like her person; her disposition not sweet, but, as is sometimes said of apples by way of recommendation, a pleasant sour.

Such were the inmates of the gloomy house,—from which the last-mentioned frequently expressed her intention of retiring, being engaged to a travelling dentist, who, in filling her teeth with amalgam, had seized the opportunity to fill a soft place in her heart with something still more dangerous and mercurial. The wedding-day had been from time to time postponed, and at length the family hoped and believed it never would come,—a wish prophetic of its own fulfilment.

Almost the only sunshine that from without shone into the dark mansion came from the face of Cecilia Vaughan, the school-mate and bosom-friend of Alice Archer. They were nearly of the same age, and had been drawn together by that mysterious power which discovers and selects friends for us in our childhood. They sat together in school; they walked together after school; they told each other their manifold secrets; they wrote long and impassioned letters to each other in the evening; in a word, they were in love with each other. It was, so to speak, a rehearsal in girlhood of the great drama of woman's life.

IX.

The golden tints of Autumn now brightened the shrubbery around this melancholy house, and took away something of its gloom. The four poplar trees seemed all ablaze, and flickered in the wind like huge torches. The little border of box filled the air with fragrance, and seemed to welcome the return of Alice, as she ascended the steps, and entered the house with a lighter heart than usual. The brisk autumnal air had quickened her pulse and given a glow to her cheek.

She found her mother alone in the parlor, seated in her large arm-chair. The warm sun streamed in at the uncurtained windows, and lights and shadows from the leaves lay upon her face. She turned her head as Alice entered, and said,—

"Who is it? Is it you, Alice?"

"Yes, it is I, mother."

"Where have you been so long?"

"I have been nowhere, dear mother. I have come directly home from church."

"How long it seems to me! It is very late. It is growing quite dark. I was just going to call for the lights."

"Why, mother!" exclaimed Alice, in a startled tone; "what do you mean? The sun is shining directly into your face!"

"Impossible, my dear Alice. It is quite dark. I cannot see you. Where are you?"

She leaned over her mother and kissed her. Both were silent,—both wept. They knew that the hour, so long looked forward to with dismay, had suddenly come. Mrs. Archer was blind!

This scene of sorrow was interrupted by the abrupt entrance of Sally Manchester. She, too, was in tears; but she was weeping for her own affliction. In her hand she held an open letter, which she gave to Alice, exclaiming amid sobs,—

"Read this, Miss Archer, and see how false man can be! Never trust any man! They are all alike; they are all false—false—false!"

Alice took the letter and read as follows:—

"It is with pleasure, Miss Manchester, I sit down to write you a few lines. I esteem you as highly as ever, but Providence has seemed to order and direct my thoughts and affections to another,—one in my own neighborhood. It was rather unexpected to me. Miss Manchester, I suppose you are well aware that we, as professed Christians, ought to be resigned to our lot in this world. May God assist you, so that we may be prepared to join the great company in heaven. Your answer would be very desirable. I respect your virtue, and regard you as a friend.

"Martin Cherryfield.

"P. S. The society is generally pretty good here, but the state of religion is quite low."

"That is a cruel letter, Sally," said Alice, as she handed it back to her. "But we all have our troubles. That man is unworthy of you. Think no more about him."

"What is the matter?" inquired Mrs. Archer, hearing the counsel given and the sobs with which it was received. "Sally, what is the matter?"

Sally made no answer; but Alice said,—

"Mr. Cherryfield has fallen in love with somebody else."

"Is that all?" said Mrs. Archer, evidently relieved. "She ought to be very glad of it. Why does she want to be married? She had much better stay with us; particularly now that I am blind."

When Sally heard this last word, she looked up in consternation. In a moment she forgot her own grief to sympathize with Alice and her mother. She wanted to do a thousand things at once; to go here; to send there; to get this and that; and particularly to call all the doctors in the neighborhood. Alice assured her it would be of no avail, though she finally consented that one should be sent for.

Sally went in search of him. On her way, her thoughts reverted to herself; and, to use her own phrase, "she curbed in like a stage-horse," as she walked. This state of haughty and offended pride continued for some hours after her return home. Later in the day, she assumed a decent composure, and requested that the man—she scorned to name him—might never again be mentioned in her hearing. Thus was her whole dream of felicity swept away by the tide of fate, as the nest of a ground-swallow by an inundation. It had been built too low to be secure.

Some women, after a burst of passionate tears, are soft, gentle, affectionate; a warm and genial air succeeds the rain. Others clear up cold, and are breezy, bleak, and dismal. Of the latter class was Sally Manchester. She became embittered against all men on account of one, and was often heard to say that she thought women were fools to be married, and that, for one, she would not marry any man, let him be who he might,—not she!

The village doctor came. He was a large man, of the cheerful kind; vigorous, florid, encouraging, and pervaded by an indiscriminate odor of drugs. Loud voice, large cane, thick boots—everything about him synonymous with noise. His presence in the sick-room was like martial music,—inspiriting, but loud. He seldom left it without saying to the patient, "I hope you will feel more comfortable to-morrow," or, "When your fever leaves you, you will be better." But, in this instance, he could not go so far. Even his hopefulness was not sufficient for the emergency. Mrs. Archer was blind,—beyond remedy, beyond hope,—irrevocably blind!

X.

On the following morning, very early, as the schoolmaster stood at his door, inhaling the bright, wholesome air, and beholding the shadows of the rising sun, and the flashing dew-drops on the red vine-leaves, he heard the sound of wheels, and saw Mr. Pendexter and his wife drive down the village street in their old-fashioned chaise, known by all the boys in town as "the ark." The old white horse, that for so many years had stamped at funerals, and gnawed the tops of so many posts, and imagined he killed so many flies because he wagged the stump of a tail, and, finally, had been the cause of so much discord in the parish, seemed now to make common cause with his master, and stepped as if endeavoring to shake the dust from his feet as he passed out of the ungrateful village. Under the axle-tree hung suspended a leather trunk; and in the chaise, between the two occupants, was a large bandbox which forced Mr. Pendexter to let his legs hang out of the vehicle, and gave him the air of imitating the Scriptural behavior of his horse. Gravely and from a distance he saluted the schoolmaster, who saluted him in return, with a tear in his eye, that no man saw, but which, nevertheless, was not unseen.

"Farewell, poor old man!" said the schoolmaster within himself, as he shut out the cold autumnal air, and entered his comfortable study. "We are not worthy of thee, or we should have had thee with us forever. Go back again to the place of thy childhood, the scene of thine early labors and thine early love; let thy days end where they began, and, like the emblem of eternity, let the serpent of life coil itself round and take its tail into its mouth, and be still from all its hissings forevermore! I would not call thee back; for it is better thou shouldst be where thou art, than amid the angry contentions of this little town."

Not all took leave of the old clergyman in so kindly a spirit. Indeed, there was a pretty general feeling of relief in the village, as when one gets rid of an ill-fitting garment, or old-fashioned hat, which one neither wishes to wear, nor is quite willing to throw away.

Thus Mr. Pendexter departed from the village. A few days afterwards he was seen at a fall training, or general muster of the militia, making a prayer on horseback, with his eyes wide open; a performance in which he took evident delight, as it gave him an opportunity of going quite at large into some of the bloodiest campaigns of the ancient Hebrews.

XI.

For a while the schoolmaster walked to and fro, looking at the gleam of the sunshine on the carpet, and revelling in his day-dreams of unwritten books and literary fame. With these day-dreams mingled confusedly the pattering of little feet, and the murmuring and cooing of his children overhead. His plans that morning, could he have executed them, would have filled a shelf in his library with poems and romances of his own creation. But suddenly the vision vanished, and another from the actual world took its place. It was the canvas-covered cart of the butcher, that, like the flying wigwam of the Indian tale, flitted before his eyes. It drove up the yard and stopped at the back door; and the poet felt that the sacred rest of Sunday, the God's-truce with worldly cares, was once more at an end. A dark hand passed between him and the land of light. Suddenly closed the ivory gate of dreams, and the horn gate of every-day life opened, and he went forth to deal with the man of flesh and blood.

"Alas!" said he with a sigh; "and must my life, then, always be like the Sabbatical river of the Jews, flowing in full stream only on the seventh day, and sandy and arid all the rest?"

Then he thought of his beautiful wife and children, and added, half aloud,—

"No; not so! Rather let me look upon the seven days of the week as the seven magic rings of Jarchas, each inscribed with the name of a separate planet, and each possessing a peculiar power;—or, as the seven sacred and mysterious stones which the pilgrims of Mecca were forced to throw over their shoulders in the valleys of Menah and Akbah, cursing the devil and saying at each throw, 'God is great!' "

He found Mr. Wilmerdings, the butcher, standing beside his cart, and surrounded by five cats, that had risen simultaneously on their hind legs, to receive their quotidian morning's meal. Mr. Wilmerdings not only supplied the village with fresh provisions daily, but he likewise weighed all the babies. There was hardly a child in town that had not hung beneath his steelyards, tied in a silk handkerchief, the movable weight above sliding along the notched beam from eight pounds to twelve. He was a young man with a very fresh and rosy complexion, and every Monday morning he appeared dressed in an exceedingly white frock. He had lately married a milliner, who sold "Dunstable and eleven-braid, openwork and colored straws," and their bridal tour had been to a neighboring town to see a man hanged for murdering his wife. A pair of huge ox-horns branched from the gable of his slaughter-house, and near it stood the great pits of the tannery, which all the school-boys thought were filled with blood!

Perhaps no two men could be more unlike than Mr. Churchill and Mr. Wilmerdings. Upon such a grating iron hinge opened the door of his daily life—opened into the school-room, the theatre of those life-long labors, which theoretically are the most noble, and practically the most vexatious in the world. Toward this, as soon as breakfast was over, and he had played a while with his children, he directed his steps. On his way, he had many glimpses into the lovely realms of Nature, and one into those of Art, through the medium of a placard pasted against a wall. It was as follows:—

"The subscriber professes to take profiles, plain and shaded, which, viewed at right-angles with the serious countenance, are warranted to be infallibly correct.

"No trouble of adorning or dressing the person is required. He takes infants and children at sight, and has frames of all sizes to accommodate.

"A profile is a delineated outline of the exterior form of any person's face and head, the use of which when seen tends to vivify the affections of those whom we esteem or love.

"WILLIAM BANTAM."

Erelong even this glimpse into the ideal world had vanished; and he felt himself bound to the earth with a hundred invisible threads, by which a hundred urchins were tugging and tormenting him; and it was only with considerable effort, and at intervals, that his mind could soar to the moral dignity of his profession.

Such was the schoolmaster's life, and a dreary, weary life it would have been, had not poetry from within gushed through every crack and crevice in it. This transformed it, and made it resemble a well, into which stones and rubbish have been thrown; but underneath is a spring of fresh, pure water, which nothing external can ever check or defile.

XII.

Mr. Pendexter had departed. Only a few old and middle-aged people regretted him. To these few, something was wanting in the service ever afterwards. They missed the accounts of the Hebrew massacres, and the wonderful tales of the Zumzummims; they missed the venerable gray hair, and the voice that had spoken to them in childhood, and forever preserved the memory of it in their hearts, as in the Russian Church the old hymns of the earliest centuries are still piously retained.

The winter came, with all its affluence of snows, and its many candidates for the vacant pulpit. But the parish was difficult to please, as all parishes are; and talked of dividing itself, and building a new church, and other extravagances, as all parishes do. Finally it concluded to remain as it was, and the choice of a pastor was made.

The events of the winter were few in number, and can be easily described. The following extract from a school-girl's letter to an absent friend contains the most important:—

"At school, things have gone on pretty much as usual. Jane Brown has grown very pale. They say she is in a consumption, but I think it is because she eats so many slate-pencils. One of her shoulders has grown a good deal higher than the other. Billy Wilmerdings has been turned out of school for playing truant. He promised his mother, if she would not whip him, he would experience religion. I am sure I wish he would; for then he would stop looking at me through the hole in the top of his desk. Mr. Churchill is a very curious man. To-day he gave us this question in arithmetic: 'One fifth of a hive of bees flew to the Kadamba flower; one third flew to the Silandhara; three times the difference of these two numbers flew to an arbor; and one bee continued flying about, attracted on each side by the fragrant Ketaki and the Malati. What was the number of bees?' Nobody could do the sum.

"The church has been repaired, and we have a new mahogany pulpit. Mr. Churchill bought the old one, and had it put up in his study. What a strange man he is! A good many candidates have preached for us. The only one we like is Mr. Kavanagh. Arthur Kavanagh! is not that a romantic name? He is tall, very pale, with beautiful black eyes and hair! Sally—Alice Archer's Sally—says 'he is not a man; he is a Thaddeus of Warsaw!' I think he is very handsome. And such sermons! So beautifully written, so different from old Mr. Pendexter's! He has been invited to settle here, but he cannot come till Spring. Last Sunday he preached about the ruling passion. He said that once a German nobleman, when he was dying, had his hunting-horn blown in his bedroom, and his hounds let in, springing and howling about him; and that so it was with the ruling passions of men; even around the death-bed, at the well-known signal, they howled and leaped about those that had fostered them! Beautiful, is it not? and so original! He said in another sermon, that disappointments feed and nourish us in the desert places of life, as the ravens did the Prophet in the wilderness; and that as, in Catholic countries, the lamps lighted before the images of saints, in narrow and dangerous streets, not only served as offerings of devotion, but likewise as lights to those who passed, so, in the dark and dismal streets of the city of Unbelief, every good thought, word, and deed of a man, not only was an offering to heaven, but likewise served to light him and others on their way homeward! I have taken a good many notes of Mr. Kavanagh's sermons, which you shall see when you come back.

"Last week we had a sleigh-ride, with six white horses. We went like the wind over the hollows in the snow;—the driver called them 'thank-you-ma'ams,' because they made everybody bow. And such a frantic ball as we had at Beaverstock! I wish you had been there! We did not get home till two o'clock in the morning; and the next day Hester Green's minister asked her if she did not feel the fire of a certain place growing hot under her feet, while she was dancing!

"The new fashionable boarding-school begins next week. The prospectus has been sent to our house. One of the regulations is, 'Young ladies are not allowed to cross their benders in school'! Papa says he never heard knees called so before.

Old Mrs. Plainfield is gone at last. Just before she died, her Irish chambermaid asked her if she wanted to be buried with her false teeth! There has not been a single new engagement since you went away. But somebody asked me the other day if you were engaged to Mr. Pillsbury. I was very angry. Pillsbury, indeed! He is old enough to be your father!

"What a long, rambling letter I am writing you!—and only because you will be so naughty as to stay away and leave me all alone. If you could have seen the moon last night! But what a goose I am!—as if you did not see it! Was it not glorious? You cannot imagine, dearest, how every hour in the day I wish you were here with me. I know you would sympathize with all my feelings, which Hester does not at all. For, if I admire the moon, she says I am romantic, and, for her part, if there is anything she despises, it is the moon! and that she prefers a snug, warm bed (oh, horrible!) to all the moons in the universe!"

XIII.

The events mentioned in this letter were the principal ones that occurred during the winter. The case of Billy Wilmerdings grew quite desperate. In vain did his father threaten and the schoolmaster expostulate; he was only the more sullen and stubborn. In vain did his mother represent to his weary mind, that, if he did not study, the boys who knew the dead languages would throw stones at him in the street; he only answered that he should like to see them try it. Till, finally, having lost many of his illusions, and having even discovered that his father was not the greatest man in the world, on the breaking up of the ice in the river, to his own infinite relief and that of the whole village, he departed on a coasting trip in a fore-and-aft schooner, which constituted the entire navigation of Fairmeadow.

Mr. Churchill had really put up in his study the old white pulpit, shaped like a wine-glass. It served as a play-house for his children, who, whether in it or out of it, daily preached to his heart, and were a living illustration of the way to enter into the kingdom of heaven. Moreover, he himself made use of it externally as a note-book, recording his many meditations with a pencil on the white panels. The following will serve as a specimen of this pulpit eloquence:—

Morality without religion is only a kind of dead-reckoning, —an endeavor to find our place on a cloudy sea by measuring the distance we have run, but without any observation of the heavenly bodies.

Many readers judge of the power of a book by the shock it gives their feelings,—as some savage tribes determine the power of muskets by their recoil; that being considered best which fairly prostrates the purchaser.

Men of genius are often dull and inert in society; as the blazing meteor, when it descends to earth, is only a stone.

The natural alone is permanent. Fantastic idols may be worshipped for a while; but at length they are overturned by the continual and silent progress of Truth, as the grim statues of Copan have been pushed from their pedestals by the growth of forest-trees, whose seeds were sown by the wind in the ruined walls.

The every-day cares and duties, which men call drudgery, are the weights and counterpoises of the clock of time, giving its pendulum a true vibration, and its hands a regular motion; and when they cease to hang upon the wheels, the pendulum no longer swings, the hands no longer move, the clock stands still.

The same object, seen from the three different points of view,—the Past, the Present, and the Future,—often exhibits three different faces to us; like those sign-boards over shop doors, which represent the face of a lion as we approach, of a man when we are in front, and of an ass when we have passed.

In character, in manners, in style, in all things, the supreme excellence is simplicity.

With many readers, brilliancy of style passes for affluence of thought; they mistake buttercups in the grass for immeasurable gold mines under ground.

The motives and purposes of authors are not always so pure and high as, in the enthusiasm of youth, we sometimes imagine. To many the trumpet of fame is nothing but a tin horn to call them home, like laborers from the field, at dinner-time; and they think themselves lucky to get the dinner.

The rays of happiness, like those of light, are colorless when unbroken.

Critics are sentinels in the grand army of letters, stationed at the corners of newspapers and reviews, to challenge every new author.

The country is lyric,—the town dramatic. When mingled, they make the most perfect musical drama.

Our passions never wholly die; but in the last cantos of life's romantic epos, they rise up again and do battle, like some of Ariosto's heroes, who have already been quietly interred, and ought to be turned to dust.

This country is not priest-ridden, but press-ridden.

Some critics have the habit of rowing up the Heliconian rivers with their backs turned, so as to see the landscape precisely as the poet did not see it. Others see faults in a book much larger than the book itself; as Sancho Panza, with his eyes blinded, beheld from his wooden horse the earth no larger than a grain of mustard-seed, and the men and women on it as large as hazel-nuts.

Like an inundation of the Indus is the course of Time. We look for the homes of our childhood, they are gone; for the friends of our childhood, they are gone. The loves and animosities of youth, where are they? Swept away like the camps that had been pitched in the sandy bed of the river.

As no saint can be canonized until the Devil's Advocate has exposed all his evil deeds, and showed why he should not be made a saint, so no poet can take his station among the gods until the critics have said all that can be said against him.

It is curious to note the old sea-margins of human thought! Each subsiding century reveals some new mystery; we build where monsters used to hide themselves.

XIV.

At length the Spring came, and brought the birds, and the flowers, and Mr. Kavanagh, the new clergyman, who was ordained with all the pomp and ceremony usual on such occasions. The opening of the season furnished also the theme of his first discourse, which some of the congregation thought very beautiful, and others very incomprehensible.

Ah, how wonderful is the advent of the Spring!—the great annual miracle of the blossoming of Aaron's rod, repeated on myriads and myriads of branches!—the gentle progression and growth of herbs, flowers, trees,—gentle, and yet irrepressible,—which no force can stay, no violence restrain, like love, that wins its way and cannot be withstood by any human power, because itself is divine power. If Spring came but once a century, instead of once a year, or burst forth with the sound of an earthquake, and not in silence, what wonder and expectation would there be in all hearts to behold the miraculous change!

But now the silent succession suggests nothing but necessity. To most men, only the cessation of the miracle would be miraculous, and the perpetual exercise of God's power seems less wonderful than its withdrawal would be. We are like children who are astonished and delighted only by the second-hand of the clock, not by the hour-hand.

Such was the train of thought with which Kavanagh commenced his sermon. And then, with deep solemnity and emotion, he proceeded to speak of the Spring of the soul, as from its cheerless wintry distance it turns nearer and nearer to the great Sun, and clothes its dry and withered branches anew with leaves and blossoms, unfolded from within itself, beneath the penetrating and irresistible influence.

While delivering the discourse, Kavanagh had not succeeded so entirely in abstracting himself from all outward things as not to note in some degree its effect upon his hearers. As in modern times no applause is permitted in our churches, however moved the audience may be, and, consequently, no one dares wave his hat and shout,—"Orthodox Chrysostom! Thirteenth Apostle! Worthy the Priesthood!"—as was done in the days of the Christian Fathers; and, moreover, as no one after church spoke to him of his sermon, or of anything else, he went home with rather a heavy heart, and a feeling of discouragement. One thing had cheered and consoled him. It was the pale countenance of a young girl, whose dark eyes had been fixed upon him during the whole discourse with unflagging interest and attention. She sat alone in a pew near the pulpit. It was Alice Archer. Ah! could he have known how deeply sank his words into that simple heart, he might have shuddered with another kind of fear than that of not moving his audience sufficiently!

XV.

On the following morning Kavanagh sat musing upon his worldly affairs, and upon various little household arrangements which it would be necessary for him to make. To aid him in these, he had taken up the village paper, and was running over the columns of advertisements,—those narrow and crowded thoroughfares, in which the wants and wishes of humanity display themselves like mendicants without disguise. His eye ran hastily over the advantageous offers of the cheap tailors and the dealers in patent medicines. He wished neither to be clothed nor cured. In one place he saw that a young lady, perfectly competent, desired to form a class of young mothers and nurses, and to instruct them in the art of talking to infants so as to interest and amuse them; and in another, that the firemen of Fairmeadow wished well to those hostile editors who had called them gamblers, drunkards, and rioters, and hoped that they might be spared from that great fire which they were told could never be extinguished! Finally, his eye rested on the advertisement of a carpet warehouse, in which the one-price system was strictly adhered to. It was farther stated that a discount would be made "to clergymen on small salaries, feeble churches, and charitable institutions." Thinking that this was doubtless the place for one who united in himself two of these qualifications for a discount, with a smile on his lips, he took his hat and sallied forth into the street.

A few days previous, Kavanagh had discovered in the tower of the church a vacant room, which he had immediately determined to take possession of, and to convert into a study. From this retreat, through the four oval windows, fronting the four corners of the heavens, he could look down upon the streets, the roofs and gardens of the village,—on the winding river, the meadows, the farms, the distant blue mountains. Here he could sit and meditate, in that peculiar sense of seclusion and spiritual elevation, that entire separation from the world below, which a chamber in a tower always gives. Here, uninterrupted and aloof from all intrusion, he could pour his heart into those discourses, with which he hoped to reach and move the hearts of his parishioners.

It was to furnish this retreat, that he went forth on the Monday morning after his first sermon. He was not long in procuring the few things needed,—the carpet, the table, the chairs, the shelves for books; and was returning thoughtfully homeward, when his eye was caught by a sign-board on the corner of the street, inscribed "Moses Merryweather, Dealer in Singing Birds, foreign and domestic." He saw also a whole chamber-window transformed into a cage, in which sundry canary-birds, and others of a gayer plumage, were jargoning together, like people in the market-places of foreign towns. At the sight of these old favorites, a long slumbering passion awoke within him, and he straightway ascended the dark wooden staircase, with the intent of enlivening his solitary room with the vivacity and songs of these captive ballad-singers.

In a moment he found himself in a little room hung round with cages, roof and walls; full of sunshine; full of twitterings, cooings, and flutterings; full of downy odors, suggesting nests, and dovecots, and distant islands inhabited only by birds. The taxidermist—the Selkirk of the sunny island—was not there; but a young lady of noble mien, who was looking at an English goldfinch in a square cage with a portico, turned upon him, as he entered, a fair and beautiful face, shaded by long light locks, in which the sunshine seemed entangled, as among the boughs of trees. That face he had never seen before, and yet it seemed familiar to him; and the added light in her large, celestial eyes, and the almost imperceptible expression that passed over her face, showed that she knew who he was.

At the same moment the taxidermist presented himself, coming from an inner room;—a little man in gray, with spectacles upon his nose, holding in his hands, with wings and legs drawn close and smoothly together, like the green husks of the maize ear, a beautiful carrier-pigeon, who turned up first one bright eye and then the other, as if asking, "What are you going to do with me now?" This silent inquiry was soon answered by Mr. Merryweather, who said to the young lady,—

"Here, Miss Vaughan, is the best carrier-pigeon in my whole collection. The real Columba Tabullaria. He is about three years old, as you can see by his wattle."

"A very pretty bird," said the lady; "and how shall I train it?"

"Oh, that is very easy. You have only to keep it shut up for a few days, well fed and well treated. Then take it in an open cage to the place you mean it to fly to, and do the same thing there. Afterwards it will give you no trouble; it will always fly between those two places."

"That, certainly, is not very difficult. At all events, I will make the trial. You may send the bird home to me. On what shall I feed it?"

"On any kind of grain; barley and buckwheat are best; and remember to let it have a plenty of gravel in the bottom of its cage."

"I will not forget. Send me the bird to-day, if possible."

With these words she departed, much too soon for Kavanagh, who was charmed with her form, her face, her voice; and who, when left alone with the little taxidermist, felt that the momentary fascination of the place was gone. He heard no longer the singing of the birds; he saw no longer their gay plumage; and having speedily made the purchase of a canary and a cage, he likewise departed, thinking of the carrier-pigeons of Bagdad, and the columbaries of Egypt, stationed at fixed intervals as relays and resting-places for the flying post. With an indefinable feeling of sadness, too, came wafted like a perfume through his memory those tender, melancholy lines of Maria del Occidente:—

And as the dove, to far Palmyra flying,
  From where her native founts of Antioch beam,
Weary, exhausted, longing, panting, sighing,
  Lights sadly at the desert's bitter stream;

So many a soul, o'er life's drear desert faring,—
  Love's pure, congenial spring unfound, unquaffed,—
Suffers, recoils, then, thirsty and despairing
  Of what it would, descends and sips the nearest draught.

Meanwhile, Mr. Merryweather, left to himself, walked about his aviary, musing, and talking to his birds. Finally he paused before the tin cage of a gray African parrot, between which and himself there was a strong family likeness, and, giving it his finger to peck and perch upon, conversed with it in that peculiar dialect with which it had often made vocal the distant groves of Zanguebar. He then withdrew to the inner room, where he resumed his labor of stuffing a cardinal grossbeak, saying to himself between whiles,—

"I wonder what Miss Cecilia Vaughan means to do with a carrier-pigeon!"

Some mysterious connection he had evidently established already between this pigeon and Mr. Kavanagh; for, continuing his revery, he said, half aloud,—

"Of course she would never think of marrying a poor clergyman!"

XVI.

The old family mansion of the Vaughans stood a little out of town, in the midst of a pleasant farm. The county road was not near enough to annoy, and the rattling wheels and little clouds of dust seemed like friendly salutations from travellers as they passed. They spoke of safety and companionship, and took away all loneliness from the solitude.

On three sides, the farm was enclosed by willow and alder hedges, and the flowing wall of a river; nearer the house were groves clear of all underwood, with rocky knolls, and breezy bowers of beech; and afar off the blue hills broke the horizon, creating secret longings for what lay beyond them, and filling the mind with pleasant thoughts of Prince Rasselas and the Happy Valley.

The house was one of the few old houses still standing in New England,—a large, square building, with a portico in front, whose door in Summer time stood open from morning until night. A pleasing stillness reigned about it, and soft gusts of pine-embalmed air, and distant cawings from the crow-haunted mountains, filled its airy and ample halls.

In this old-fashioned house had Cecilia Vaughan grown up to maidenhood. The travelling shadows of the clouds on the hillsides,—the sudden Summer wind, that lifted the languid leaves, and rushed from field to field, from grove to grove, the forerunner of the rain,—and, most of all, the mysterious mountain, whose coolness was a perpetual invitation to her, and whose silence a perpetual fear,—fostered her dreamy and poetic temperament. Not less so did the reading of poetry and romance in the long, silent, solitary winter evenings. Her mother had been dead for many years, and the memory of that mother had become almost a religion to her. She recalled it incessantly, and the reverential love which it inspired completely filled her soul with melancholy delight. Her father was a kindly old man, a judge in one of the courts; dignified, affable, somewhat bent by his legal erudition, as a shelf is by the weight of the books upon it. His papers encumbered the study table,—his law books, the study floor. They seemed to shut out from his mind the lovely daughter, who had grown up to womanhood by his side, but almost without his recognition. Always affectionate, always indulgent, he left her to walk alone, without his stronger thought and firmer purpose to lean upon; and though her education had been, on this account, somewhat desultory, and her imagination indulged in many dreams and vagaries, yet, on the whole, the result had been more favorable than in many cases where the process of instruction has been too diligently carried on, and where, as sometimes on the roofs of farm-houses and barns, the scaffolding has been left to deform the building.

Cecilia's bosom-friend at school was Alice Archer; and, after they left school, the love between them, and consequently the letters, rather increased than diminished. These two young hearts found not only a delight, but a necessity, in pouring forth their thoughts and feelings to each other; and it was to facilitate this intercommunication, for whose exigencies the ordinary methods were now found inadequate, that the carrier-pigeon had been purchased. He was to be the flying post; their bedrooms the dovecots, the pure and friendly columbaria.

Endowed with youth, beauty, talent, fortune, and, moreover, with that indefinable fascination which has no name, Cecilia Vaughan was not without lovers, avowed and unavowed;—young men, who made an ostentatious display of their affection;—boys, who treasured it in their bosoms, as something indescribably sweet and precious, perfuming all the chambers of the heart with its celestial fragrance. Whenever she returned from a visit to the city, some unknown youth of elegant manners and varnished leather boots was sure to hover round the village inn for a few days,—was known to visit the Vaughans assiduously, and then silently to disappear, and be seen no more. Of course, nothing could be known of the secret history of such individuals, but shrewd surmises were formed as to their designs and their destinies; till finally, any well-dressed stranger, lingering in the village without ostensible business, was set down as "one of Miss Vaughan's lovers."

In all this, what a contrast was there between the two young friends! The wealth of one and the poverty of the other were not so strikingly at variance, as this affluence and refluence of love. To the one, so much was given that she became regardless of the gift; from the other, so much withheld, that, if possible, she exaggerated its importance.

XVII.

In addition to these transient lovers, who were but birds of passage, winging their way, in an incredibly short space of time, from the torrid to the frigid zone, there was in the village a domestic and resident adorer, whose love for himself, for Miss Vaughan, and for the beautiful, had transformed his name from Hiram A. Hawkins to H. Adolphus Hawkins. He was a dealer in English linens and carpets—a profession which of itself fills the mind with ideas of domestic comfort. His waistcoats were made like Lord Melbourne's in the illustrated English papers, and his shiny hair went off to the left in a superb sweep, like the hand-rail of a banister. He wore many rings on his fingers, and several breastpins and gold chains disposed about his person. On all his bland physiognomy was stamped, as on some of his linens, "Soft finish for family use." Everything about him spoke the lady's man. He was, in fact, a perfect ring-dove; and, like the rest of his species, always walked up to the female, and, bowing his head, swelled out his white crop, and uttered a very plaintive murmur.

Moreover, Mr. H. Adolphus Hawkins was a poet,—so much a poet, that, as his sister frequently remarked, he "spoke blank verse in the bosom of his family." The general tone of his productions was sad, desponding, perhaps slightly morbid. How could it be otherwise with the writings of one who had never been the world's friend, nor the world his? who looked upon himself as "a pyramid of mind on the dark desert of despair"? and who, at the age of twenty-five, had drunk the bitter draught of life to the dregs, and dashed the goblet down? His productions were published in the Poet's Corner of the Fairmeadow Advertiser, and it was a relief to know, that, in private life, as his sister remarked, he was "by no means the censorious and moody person some of his writings might imply."

Such was the personage who assumed to himself the perilous position of Miss Vaughan's permanent lover. He imagined that it was impossible for any woman to look upon him and not love him. Accordingly, he paraded himself at his shop-door as she passed; he paraded himself at the corners of the streets; he paraded himself at the church-steps on Sunday.

He spied her from the window; he sallied from the door; he followed her with his eyes; he followed her with his whole august person; he passed her and repassed her, and turned back to gaze; he lay in wait with dejected countenance and desponding air; he persecuted her with his looks; he pretended that their souls could comprehend each other without words; and whenever her lovers were alluded to in his presence, he gravely declared, as one who had reason to know, that, if Miss Vaughan ever married, it would be some one of gigantic intellect!

Of these persecutions Cecilia was for a long time the unconscious victim. She saw this individual, with rings and strange waistcoats, performing his gyrations before her, but did not suspect that she was the centre of attraction,—not imagining that any man would begin his wooing with such outrages. Gradually the truth dawned upon her, and became the source of indescribable annoyance, which was augmented by a series of anonymous letters, written in a female hand, and setting forth the excellences of a certain mysterious relative,—his modesty, his reserve, his extreme delicacy, his talent for poetry,—rendered authentic by extracts from his papers, made, of course, without the slightest knowledge or suspicion on his part. Whence came these sibylline leaves? At first Cecilia could not divine; but, erelong, her woman's instinct traced them to the thin and nervous hand of the poet's sister. This surmise was confirmed by her maid, who asked the boy that brought them.

It was with one of these missives in her hand that Cecilia entered Mrs. Archer's house, after purchasing the carrier-pigeon. Unannounced she entered, and walked up the narrow and imperfectly lighted stairs to Alice's bedroom,—that little sanctuary draped with white,—that columbarium lined with warmth, and softness, and silence. Alice was not there; but the chair by the window, the open volume of Tennyson's poems on the table, the note to Cecilia by its side, and the ink not yet dry in the pen, were like the vibration of a bough, when the bird has just left it,—like the rising of the grass, when the foot has just pressed it. In a moment she returned. She had been down to her mother, who sat talking, talking, talking, with an old friend in the parlor below, even as these young friends were talking together, in the bedroom above. Ah, how different were their themes! Death and Love,—apples of Sodom, that crumble to ashes at a touch,—golden fruits of the Hesperides,—golden fruits of Paradise, fragrant, ambrosial, perennial!

"I have just been writing to you," said Alice; "I wanted so much to see you this morning!"

"Why this morning in particular? Has anything happened?"

"Nothing, only I had such a longing to see you!"

And, seating herself in a low chair by Cecilia's side, she laid her head upon the shoulder of her friend, who, taking one of her pale, thin hands in both her own, silently kissed her forehead again and again.

Alice was not aware, that, in the words she uttered, there was the slightest shadow of untruth. And yet had nothing happened? Was it nothing, that among her thoughts a new thought had risen, like a star, whose pale effulgence, mingled with the common daylight, was not yet distinctly visible even to herself, but would grow brighter as the sun grew lower, and the rosy twilight darker? Was it nothing, that a new fountain of affection had suddenly sprung up within her, which she mistook for the freshening and overflowing of the old fountain of friendship, that hitherto had kept the lowland landscape of her life so green, but now, being flooded by more affection, was not to cease, but only to disappear in the greater tide, and flow unseen beneath it? Yet so it was; and this stronger yearning—this unappeasable desire for her friend—was only the tumultuous swelling of a heart, that as yet knows not its own secret.

"I am so glad to see you, Cecilia!" she continued. "You are so beautiful! I love so much to sit and look at you! Ah, how I wish Heaven had made me as tall, and strong, and beautiful as you are!"

"You little flatterer! What an affectionate, lover-like friend you are! What have you been doing all the morning?"

"Looking out of the window, thinking of you, and writing you this letter, to beg you to come and see me."

"And I have been buying a carrier-pigeon, to fly between us, and carry all our letters."

"That will be delightful."

"He is to be sent home to-day; and after he gets accustomed to my room, I shall send him here, to get acquainted with yours;—an Iachimo in my Imogen's bedchamber, to spy out its secrets."

"If he sees Cleopatra in these white curtains, and silver Cupids in these andirons, he will have your imagination."

"He will see the book with the leaf turned down, and you asleep, and tell me all about you."

"A carrier-pigeon! What a charming idea! and how like you to think of it!"

"But to-day I have been obliged to bring my own letters. I have some more sibylline leaves from my anonymous correspondent, in laud and exaltation of her modest relative, who speaks blank verse in the bosom of his family. I have brought them to read you some extracts, and to take your advice; for, really and seriously, this must be stopped. It has grown too annoying."

"How much love you have offered you!" said Alice, sighing.

"Yes, quite too much of this kind. On my way here, I saw the modest relative, standing at the corner of the street, hanging his head in this way."

And she imitated the melancholy Hiram Adolphus, and the young friends laughed.

"I hope you did not notice him?" resumed Alice.

"Certainly not. But what do you suppose he did? As soon as he saw me, he began to walk backward down the street only a short distance in front of me, staring at me most impertinently. Of course, I took no notice of this strange conduct. I felt myself blushing to the eyes with indignation, and yet could hardly suppress my desire to laugh."

"If you had laughed, he would have taken it for an encouragement, and I have no doubt it would have brought on the catastrophe."

"And that would have ended the matter. I half wish I had laughed."

"But think of the immortal glory of marrying a poet!"

"And of inscribing on my cards, Mrs. H. Adolphus Hawkins!"

"A few days ago, I went to buy something at his shop; and, leaning over the counter, he asked me if I had seen the sun set the evening before,—adding, that it was gorgeous, and that the grass and trees were of a beautiful Paris green!"

And again the young friends gave way to their mirth.

"One thing, dear Alice, you must consent to do for me. You must write to Miss Martha Amelia, the author of all these epistles, and tell her very plainly how indelicate her conduct is, and how utterly useless all such proceedings will prove in effecting her purpose."

"I will write this very day. You shall be no longer persecuted."

"And now let me give you a few extracts from these wonderful epistles."

So saying, Cecilia drew forth a small package of three-cornered billets, tied with a bit of pink ribbon. Taking one of them at random, she was on the point of beginning, but paused, as if her attention had been attracted by something out of doors. The sound of passing footsteps was heard on the gravel walk.

"There goes Mr. Kavanagh," said she, in a half-whisper.

Alice rose suddenly from her low chair at Cecilia's side, and the young friends looked from the window to see the clergyman pass.

"How handsome he is!" said Alice, involuntarily.

"He is, indeed."

At that moment Alice started back from the window. Kavanagh had looked up in passing, as if his eye had been drawn by some secret magnetism. A bright color flushed the cheek of Alice; her eyes fell, but Cecilia continued to look steadily into the street. Kavanagh passed on, and in a few moments was out of sight.

The two friends stood silent, side by side.

XVIII.

Arthur Kavanagh was descended from an ancient Catholic family. His ancestors had purchased from the Baron Victor of St. Castine a portion of his vast estates, lying upon that wild and wonderful sea-coast of Maine, which, even upon the map, attracts the eye by its singular and picturesque indentations, and fills the heart of the beholder with something of that delight which throbbed in the veins of Pierre du Gast, when, with a royal charter of the land from the Atlantic to the Pacific, he sailed down the coast in all the pride of one who is to be prince of such a vast domain. Here, in the bosom of the solemn forests, they continued the practice of that faith which had first been planted there by Rasle and St. Castine; and the little church where they worshipped is still standing, though now as closed and silent as the graves which surround it, and in which the dust of the Kavanaghs lies buried.

In these solitudes, in this faith, was Kavanagh born, and grew to childhood, a feeble, delicate boy, watched over by a grave and taciturn father, and a mother who looked upon him with infinite tenderness, as upon a treasure she should not long retain. She walked with him by the seaside, and spake to him of God, and the mysterious majesty of the ocean, with its tides and tempests. She sat with him on the carpet of golden threads beneath the aromatic pines, and, as the perpetual melancholy sound ran along the rattling boughs, his soul seemed to rise and fall, with a motion and a whisper like those in the branches over him. She taught him his letters from the Lives of the Saints,—a volume full of wondrous legends, and illustrated with engravings from pictures by the old masters, which opened to him at once the world of spirits and the world of art; and both were beautiful. She explained to him the pictures; she read to him the legends,—the lives of holy men and women, full of faith and good works,—things which ever afterward remained associated together in his mind. Thus holiness of life, and self-renunciation, and devotion to duty, were early impressed upon his soul. To his quick imagination, the spiritual world became real; the holy company of the saints stood round about the solitary boy; his guardian angels led him by the hand by day, and sat by his pillow at night. At times, even, he wished to die, that he might see them and talk with them, and return no more to his weak and weary body.

Of all the legends of the mysterious book, that which most delighted and most deeply impressed him was the legend of St. Christopher. The picture was from a painting of Paolo

Farinato, representing a figure of gigantic strength and stature, leaning upon a staff, and bearing the infant Christ on his bending shoulders across the rushing river. The legend related, that St. Christopher, being of huge proportions and immense strength, wandered long about the world before his conversion, seeking for the greatest king, and willing to obey no other. After serving various masters, whom he in turn deserted, because each recognized by some word or sign another greater than himself, he heard by chance of Christ, the king of heaven and earth, and asked of a holy hermit where he might be found, and how he might serve him. The hermit told him he must fast and pray, but the giant replied that if he fasted he should lose his strength, and that he did not know how to pray. Then the hermit told him to take up his abode on the banks of a dangerous mountain torrent, where travellers were often drowned in crossing, and to rescue any that might be in peril. The giant obeyed, and tearing up a palm-tree by the roots for a staff, he took his station by the river's side, and saved many lives. And the Lord looked down from heaven and said, "Behold this strong man, who knows not yet the way to worship, but has found the way to serve me!" And one night he heard the voice of a child, crying in the darkness and saying, "Christopher! come and bear me over the river!" And he went out, and found the child sitting alone on the margin of the stream; and taking him upon his shoulders, he waded into the water. Then the wind began to roar, and the waves to rise higher and higher about him, and his little burden, which at first had seemed so light, grew heavier and heavier as he advanced, and bent his huge shoulders down, and put his life in peril; so that, when he reached the shore, he said, "Who art thou, O child, that hast weighed upon me with a weight, as if I had borne the whole world upon my shoulders?" And the little child answered, "Thou hast borne the whole world upon thy shoulders, and Him who created it. I am Christ, whom thou by thy deeds of charity wouldst serve. Thou and thy service are accepted. Plant thy staff in the ground, and it shall blossom and bear fruit!" With these words, the child vanished away.

There was something in this beautiful legend that entirely captivated the heart of the boy, and a vague sense of its hidden meaning seemed at times to seize him and control him. Later in life it became more and more evident to him, and remained forever in his mind as a lovely allegory of active charity and a willingness to serve. Like the giant's staff, it blossomed and bore fruit.

But the time at length came, when his father decreed that he must be sent away to school. It was not meet that his son should be educated as a girl. He must go to the Jesuit college in Canada. Accordingly, one bright summer morning, he departed with his father, on horseback, through those majestic forests that stretch with almost unbroken shadows from the sea to the St. Lawrence, leaving behind him all the endearments of home, and a wound in his mother's heart that never ceased to ache,—a longing, unsatisfied and insatiable, for her absent Arthur, who had gone from her perhaps forever.

At college he distinguished himself by his zeal for study, by the docility, gentleness, and generosity of his nature. There he was thoroughly trained in the classics, and in the dogmas of that august faith, whose turrets gleam with such crystalline light, and whose dungeons are so deep, and dark, and terrible. The study of philosophy and theology was congenial to his mind. Indeed, he often laid aside Homer for Parmenides, and turned from the odes of Pindar and Horace to the mystic hymns of Cleanthes and Synesius.

The uniformity of college life was broken only by the annual visit home in the summer vacation; the joyous meeting, the bitter parting; the long journey to and fro through the grand, solitary, mysterious forest. To his mother these visits were even more precious than to himself; for ever more and more they added to her boundless affection the feeling of pride and confidence and satisfaction,—the joy and beauty of a youth unspotted from the world, and glowing with the enthusiasm of virtue.

At length his college days were ended. He returned home full of youth, full of joy and hope; but it was only to receive the dying blessings of his mother, who expired in peace, having seen his face once more. Then the house became empty to him. Solitary was the sea-shore, solitary were the woodland walks. But the spiritual world seemed nearer and more real. For affairs he had no aptitude; and he betook himself again to his philosophic and theological studies. He pondered with fond enthusiasm on the rapturous pages of Molinos and Madame Guyon; and in a spirit akin to that which wrote, he read the writings of Santa Theresa, which he found among his mother's books,—the Meditations, the Road to Perfection, and the Moradas, or Castle of the Soul. She, too, had lingered over those pages with delight, and there were many passages marked by her own hand. Among them was this, which he often repeated to himself in his lonely walks: "O Life, Life! how canst thou sustain thyself, being absent from thy Life? In so great a solitude, in what shalt thou employ thyself? What shalt thou do, since all thy deeds are faulty and imperfect?"

In such meditations passed many weeks and months. But mingled with them, continually and ever with more distinctness, arose in his memory from the days of childhood the old tradition of St. Christopher,—the beautiful allegory of humility and labor. He and his service had been accepted, though he would not fast, and had not learned to pray! It became more and more clear to him, that the life of man consists not in seeing visions, and in dreaming dreams, but in active charity and willing service.

Moreover, the study of ecclesiastical history awoke within him many strange and dubious thoughts. The books taught him more than their writers meant to teach. It was impossible to read of Athanasius without reading also of Arius; it was impossible to hear of Calvin without hearing of Servetus. Reason began more energetically to vindicate itself; that Reason, which is a light in darkness, not that which is "a thorn in Revelation's side." The search after Truth and Freedom, both intellectual and spiritual, became a passion in his soul, and he pursued it until he had left far behind him many dusky dogmas, many antique superstitions, many time-honored observances, which the lips of her alone, who first taught them to him in his childhood, had invested with solemnity and sanctity.

By slow degrees, and not by violent spiritual conflicts, he became a Protestant. He had but passed from one chapel to another in the same vast cathedral. He was still beneath the same ample roof, still heard the same divine service chanted in a different dialect of the same universal language. Out of his old faith he brought with him all he had found in it that was holy and pure and of good report. Not its bigotry, and fanaticism, and intolerance; but its zeal, its self-devotion, its heavenly aspirations, its human sympathies, its endless deeds of charity. Not till after his father's death, however, did he become a clergyman. Then his vocation was manifest to him. He no longer hesitated, but entered upon its many duties and responsibilities, its many trials and discouragements, with the zeal of Peter and the gentleness of John.

XIX.

A week later, and Kavanagh was installed in his little room in the church-tower. A week later, and the carrier-pigeon was on the wing. A week later, and Martha Amelia's anonymous epistolary eulogies of her relative had ceased forever.

Swiftly and silently the summer advanced, and the following announcement in the Fairmeadow Advertiser proclaimed the hot weather and its alleviations:—

"I have the pleasure of announcing to the Ladies and Gentlemen of Fairmeadow and its vicinity, that my Bath House is now completed, and ready for the reception of those who are disposed to regale themselves in a luxury peculiar to the once polished Greek and noble Roman.

"To the Ladies I will say, that Tuesday of each week will be appropriated to their exclusive benefit; the white flag will be the signal; and I assure the Ladies, that due respect shall be scrupulously observed, and that they shall be guarded from each vagrant foot and each licentious eye.

"EDWARD DIMPLE."

Moreover, the village was enlivened by the usual travelling shows,—the wax-work figures representing Eliza Wharton and the Salem Tragedy, to which clergymen and their families were "respectfully invited, free on presenting their cards"; a stuffed shark, that had eaten the exhibitor's father in Lynn Bay; the menagerie, with its loud music and its roars of rage; the circus, with its tan and tinsel,—its faded Columbine and melancholy Clown; and, finally, the standard drama, in which Elder Evans, like an ancient Spanish Bululú, impersonated all the principal male characters, and was particularly imposing in Iago and the Moor, having half his face lamp-blacked, and turning now the luminous, now the eclipsed side to the audience, as the exigencies of the dialogue demanded.

There was also a great Temperance Jubilee, with a procession, in which was conspicuous a large horse, whose shaven tail was adorned with gay ribbons, and whose rider bore a banner with the device, "Shaved in the Cause!" Moreover, the Grand Junction Railroad was opened through the town, running in one direction to the city, and in the other into unknown northern regions, stringing the white villages like pearls upon its black thread. By this, the town lost much of its rural quiet and seclusion. The inhabitants became restless and ambitious. They were in constant excitement and alarm, like children in story-books hidden away somewhere by an ogre, who visits them regularly every day and night, and occasionally devours one of them for a meal.

Nevertheless, most of the inhabitants considered the railroad a great advantage to the village. Several ladies were heard to say that Fairmeadow had grown quite metropolitan; and Mrs. Wilmerdings, who suffered under a chronic suspension of the mental faculties, had a vague notion, probably connected with the profession of her son, that it was soon to become a seaport.

In the fields and woods, meanwhile, there were other signs and signals of the summer. The darkening foliage; the embrowning grain; the golden dragon-fly haunting the blackberry-bushes; the cawing crows, that looked down from the mountain on the cornfield, and waited day after day for the scarecrow to finish his work and depart; and the smoke of far-off burning woods, that pervaded the air and hung in purple haze about the summits of the mountains,—these were the vaunt-couriers and attendants of the hot August.

Kavanagh had now completed the first great cycle of parochial visits. He had seen the Vaughans, the Archers, the Churchills, and also the Hawkinses and the Wilmerdingses, and many more. With Mr. Churchill he had become intimate. They had many points of contact and sympathy. They walked together on leisure afternoons; they sat together through long summer evenings; they discoursed with friendly zeal on various topics of literature, religion, and morals.

Moreover, he worked assiduously at his sermons. He preached the doctrines of Christ. He preached holiness, self-denial, love; and his hearers remarked that he almost invariably took his texts from the Evangelists, as much as possible from the words of Christ, and seldom from Paul, or the Old Testament. He did not so much denounce vice, as inculcate virtue; he did not deny, but affirm; he did not lacerate the hearts of his hearers with doubt and disbelief, but consoled, and comforted, and healed them with faith.

The only danger was that he might advance too far, and leave his congregation behind him; as a piping shepherd, who, charmed with his own music, walks over the flowery mead, not perceiving that his tardy flock is lingering far behind, more intent upon cropping the thymy food around them, than upon listening to the celestial harmonies that are gradually dying away in the distance.

His words were always kindly; he brought no railing accusation against any man; he dealt in no exaggerations nor overstatements. But while he was gentle, he was firm. He did not refrain from reprobating intemperance because one of his deacons owned a distillery; nor war, because another had a contract for supplying the army with muskets; nor slavery, because one of the great men of the village slammed his pew-door, and left the church with a grand air, as much as to say, that all that sort of thing would not do, and the clergy had better confine themselves to abusing the sins of the Hindoos, and let our domestic institutions alone.

In affairs ecclesiastical he had not suggested many changes. One that he had much at heart was, that the partition wall between parish and church should be quietly taken down, so that all should sit together at the Supper of the Lord. He also desired that the organist should relinquish the old and pernicious habit of preluding with triumphal marches, and running his fingers at random over the keys of his instrument, playing scraps of secular music very slowly to make them sacred, and substitute instead some of the beautiful symphonies of Pergolesi, Palestrina, and Sebastian Bach.

He held that sacred melodies were becoming to sacred themes; and did not wish, that, in his church, as in some of the French Canadian churches, the holy profession of religion should be sung to the air of "When one is dead 't is for a long time,"—the commandments, aspirations for heaven, and the necessity of thinking of one's salvation, to "The Follies of Spain," "Louisa was sleeping in a grove," or a grand "March of the French Cavalry."

The study in the tower was delightful. There sat the young apostle, and meditated the great design and purpose of his life, the removal of all prejudice, and uncharitableness, and persecution, and the union of all sects into one church universal. Sects themselves he would not destroy, but sectarianism; for sects were to him only as separate converging roads, leading all to the same celestial city of peace. As he sat alone, and thought of these things, he heard the great bell boom above him, and remembered the ages when in all Christendom there was but one Church; when bells were anointed, baptized, and prayed for, that, wheresoever those holy bells should sound, all deceits of Satan, all danger of whirlwinds, thunders, lightnings, and tempests might be driven away,—that devotion might increase in every Christian when he heard them,—and that the Lord would sanctify them with his Holy Spirit, and infuse into them the heavenly dew of the Holy Ghost. He thought of the great bell Guthlac, which an abbot of Croyland gave to his monastery, and of the six others given by his successor,—so musical, that, when they all rang together, as Ingulphus affirms, there was no ringing in England equal to it. As he listened, the bell seemed to breathe upon the air such clangorous sentences as,

> Laudo Deum verum, plebem voco, congrego clerum,
> Defunctos ploro, nimbum fugo, festaque honoro.

Possibly, also, at times, it interrupted his studies and meditations with other words than these. Possibly it sang into his ears, as did the bells of Varennes into the ears of Panurge,—"Marry thee, marry thee, marry, marry; if thou shouldst marry, marry, marry, thou shalt find good therein, therein, therein, so marry, marry."

From this tower of contemplation he looked down with mingled emotions of joy and sorrow on the toiling world below. The wide prospect seemed to enlarge his sympathies and his charities, and he often thought of the words of Plato: "When we consider human life, we should view as from a high tower all things terrestrial; such as herds, armies, men employed in agriculture, in marriages, divorces, births, deaths; the tumults of courts of justice; desolate lands; various barbarous nations; feasts, wailings, markets; a medley of all things, in a system adorned by contrarieties."

On the outside of the door Kavanagh had written the vigorous line of Dante,

Think that To-day will never dawn again!

that it might always serve as a salutation and memento to him as he entered. On the inside, the no less striking lines of a more modern bard,—

Lose this day loitering, 't will be the same story
To-morrow, and the next more dilatory;
For indecision brings its own delays,
And days are lost, lamenting o'er lost days.
Are you in earnest? Seize this very minute!
What you can do or think you can, begin it!
Boldness has genius, power, and magic in it!
Only engage, and then the mind grows heated:
Begin it, and the work will be completed.

Once, as he sat in this retreat near noon, enjoying the silence, and the fresh air that visited him through the oval windows, his attention was arrested by a cloud of dust, rolling along the road, out of which soon emerged a white horse, and then a very singular, round-shouldered, old-fashioned chaise, containing an elderly couple, both in black. What particularly struck him was the gait of the horse, who had a very disdainful fling to his hind legs. The slow equipage passed, and would have been forever forgotten, had not Kavanagh seen it again at sunset, stationary at Mr. Churchill's door, towards which he was directing his steps.

As he entered, he met Mr. Churchill, just taking leave of an elderly lady and gentleman in black, whom he recognized as the travellers in the old chaise. Mr. Churchill looked a little flushed and disturbed, and bade his guests farewell with a constrained air. On seeing Kavanagh, he saluted him, and called him by name; whereupon the lady pursed up her mouth, and, after a quick glance, turned away her face; and the gentleman passed with a lofty look, in which curiosity, reproof, and pious indignation were strangely mingled. They got into the chaise, with some such feelings as Noah and his wife may be supposed to have had on entering the ark; the whip descended upon the old horse with unusual vigor, accompanied by a jerk of the reins that caused him to say within himself, "What is the matter now?" He then moved off at his usual pace, and with that peculiar motion of the hind legs which Kavanagh had perceived in the morning.

Kavanagh found his friend not a little disturbed, and evidently by the conversation of the departed guests.

"That old gentleman," said Mr. Churchill, "is your predecessor, Mr. Pendexter. He thinks we are in a bad way since he left us. He considers your liberality as nothing better than rank Arianism and infidelity. The fact is, the old gentleman is a little soured; the vinous fermentation in his veins is now over, and the acetous has commenced."

Kavanagh smiled, but made no answer.

"I, of course, defended you stoutly," continued Mr. Churchill; "but if he goes about the village sowing such seed, there will be tares growing with the wheat."

"I have no fears," said Kavanagh, very quietly.

Mr. Churchill's apprehensions were not, however, groundless; for in the course of the week it came out that doubts, surmises, and suspicions of Kavanagh's orthodoxy were springing up in many weak but worthy minds. And it was ever after observed, that, whenever that fatal, apocalyptic white horse and antediluvian chaise appeared in town, many parishioners were harassed with doubts and perplexed with theological difficulties and uncertainties.

Nevertheless, the main current of opinion was with him; and the parish showed their grateful acknowledgment of his zeal and sympathy, by requesting him to sit for his portrait to a great artist from the city, who was passing the summer months in the village for recreation, using his pencil only on rarest occasions and as a particular favor. To this martyrdom the meek Kavanagh submitted without a murmur. During the progress of this work of art, he was seldom left alone; some one of his parishioners was there to enliven him; and most frequently it was Miss Martha Amelia Hawkins, who had become very devout of late, being zealous in the Sunday School, and requesting her relative not to walk between churches any more. She took a very lively interest in the portrait, and favored with many suggestions the distinguished artist, who found it difficult to obtain an expression which would satisfy the parish, some wishing to have it grave, if not severe, and others with "Mr. Kavanagh's peculiar smile." Kavanagh himself was quite indifferent about the matter, and met his fate with Christian fortitude, in a white cravat and sacerdotal robes, with one hand hanging down from the back of his chair, and the other holding a large book with the fore-finger between its leaves, reminding Mr. Churchill of Milo with his fingers in the oak. The expression of the face was exceedingly bland and resigned; perhaps a little wanting in strength, but on the whole satisfactory to the parish. So was the artist's price; nay, it was even held by some persons to be cheap, considering the quantity of background he had put in.

XX.

Meanwhile, things had gone on very quietly and monotonously in Mr. Churchill's family. Only one event, and that a mysterious one, had disturbed its serenity. It was the sudden disappearance of Lucy, the pretty orphan girl; and, as the booted centipede, who had so much excited Mr. Churchill's curiosity, disappeared at the same time, there was little doubt that they had gone away together. But whither gone, and wherefore, remained a mystery.

Mr. Churchill, also, had had his profile, and those of his wife and children, taken, in a very humble style, by Mr. Bantam, whose advertisement he had noticed on his way to school nearly a year before. His own was considered the best, as a work of art. The face was cut out entirely; the collar of the coat velvet; the shirt-collar very high and white; and the top of his head ornamented with a crest of hair turning up in front, though his own turned down,—which slight deviation from nature was explained and justified by the painter as a license allowable in art.

One evening, as he was sitting down to begin, for at least the hundredth time, the great Romance,—subject of so many resolves and so much remorse, so often determined upon but never begun,—a loud knock at the street-door, which stood wide open, announced a visitor. Unluckily, the study-door was likewise open; and consequently, being in full view, he found it impossible to refuse himself; nor, in fact, would he have done so, had all the doors been shut and bolted,—the art of refusing one's self being at that time but imperfectly understood in Fairmeadow. Accordingly, the visitor was shown in.

He announced himself as Mr. Hathaway. Passing through the village, he could not deny himself the pleasure of calling on Mr. Churchill, whom he knew by his writings in the periodicals, though not personally. He wished, moreover, to secure the coöperation of one, already so favorably known to the literary world, in a new Magazine he was about to establish, in order to raise the character of American literature, which, in his opinion, the existing reviews and magazines had entirely failed to accomplish. A daily increasing want of something better was felt by the public, and the time had come for the establishment of such a periodical as he proposed. After explaining, in rather a florid and exuberant manner, his plan and prospects, he entered more at large into the subject of American literature, which it was his design to foster and patronize.

"I think, Mr. Churchill," said he, "that we want a national literature commensurate with our mountains and rivers,—commensurate with Niagara, and the Alleghanies, and the Great Lakes!"

"Oh!"

"We want a national epic that shall correspond to the size of the country; that shall be to all other epics what Banvard's Panorama of the Mississippi is to all other paintings,—the largest in the world!"

"Ah!"

"We want a national drama in which scope enough shall be given to our gigantic ideas, and to the unparalleled activity and progress of our people!"

"Of course."

"In a word, we want a national literature altogether shaggy and unshorn, that shall shake the earth, like a herd of buffaloes thundering over the prairies!"

"Precisely," interrupted Mr. Churchill; "but excuse me!—are you not confounding things that have no analogy? Great has a very different meaning when applied to a river, and when applied to a literature. Large and shallow may perhaps be applied to both. Literature is rather an image of the spiritual world, than of the physical, is it not?—of the internal, rather than the external. Mountains, lakes, and rivers are, after all, only its scenery and decorations, not its substance and essence. A man will not necessarily be a great poet because he lives near a great mountain. Nor, being a poet, will he necessarily write better poems than another, because he lives nearer Niagara."

"But, Mr. Churchill, you do not certainly mean to deny the influence of scenery on the mind?"

"No, only to deny that it can create genius. At best, it can only develop it. Switzerland has produced no extraordinary poet; nor, as far as I know, have the Andes, or the Himalaya mountains, or the Mountains of the Moon in Africa."

"But, at all events," urged Mr. Hathaway, "let us have our literature national. If it is not national, it is nothing."

"On the contrary, it may be a great deal. Nationality is a good thing to a certain extent, but universality is better. All that is best in the great poets of all countries is not what is national in them, but what is universal. Their roots are in their native soil; but their branches wave in the unpatriotic air, that speaks the same language unto all men, and their leaves shine with the illimitable light that pervades all lands. Let us throw all the windows open; let us admit the light and air on all sides; that we may look towards the four corners of the heavens, and not always in the same direction."

"But you admit nationality to be a good thing?"

"Yes, if not carried too far; still, I confess, it rather limits one's views of truth. I prefer what is natural. Mere nationality is often ridiculous. Every one smiles when he hears the Icelandic proverb, 'Iceland is the best land the sun shines upon.' Let us be natural, and we shall be national enough. Besides, our literature can be strictly national only so far as our character and modes of thought differ from those of other nations. Now, as we are very like the English,—are, in fact, English under a different sky,—I do not see how our literature can be very different from theirs. Westward from hand to hand we pass the lighted torch, but it was lighted at the old domestic fireside of England."

"Then you think our literature is never to be anything but an imitation of the English?"

"Not at all. It is not an imitation, but, as some one has said, a continuation."

"It seems to me that you take a very narrow view of the subject."

"On the contrary, a very broad one. No literature is complete until the language in which it is written is dead. We may well be proud of our task and of our position. Let us see if we can build in any way worthy of our forefathers."

"But I insist upon originality."

"Yes; but without spasms and convulsions. Authors must not, like Chinese soldiers, expect to win victories by turning somersets in the air."

"Well, really, the prospect from your point of view is not very brilliant. Pray, what do you think of our national literature?"

"Simply, that a national literature is not the growth of a day. Centuries must contribute their dew and sunshine to it. Our own is growing slowly but surely, striking its roots downward, and its branches upward, as is natural; and I do not wish, for the sake of what some people call originality, to invert it, and try to make it grow with its roots in the air. And as for having it so savage and wild as you want it, I have only to say, that all literature, as well as all art, is the result of culture and intellectual refinement."

"Ah! we do not want art and refinement; we want genius,—untutored, wild, original, free."

"But, if this genius is to find any expression, it must employ art, for art is the external expression of our thoughts.

Many have genius, but, wanting art, are forever dumb. The two must go together to form the great poet, painter, or sculptor."

"In that sense, very well."

"I was about to say also that I thought our literature would finally not be wanting in a kind of universality. As the blood of all nations is mingling with our own, so will their thoughts and feelings finally mingle in our literature. We shall draw from the Germans, tenderness; from the Spaniards, passion; from the French, vivacity,—to mingle more and more with our English solid sense. And this will give us universality, so much to be desired."

"If that is your way of thinking," interrupted the visitor, "you will like the work I am now engaged upon."

"What is it?"

"A great national drama, the scene of which is laid in New Mexico. It is entitled Don Serafin, or the Marquis of the Seven Churches. The principal characters are Don Serafin, an old Spanish hidalgo, his daughter Deseada, and Fra Serapion, the Curate. The play opens with Fra Serapion at breakfast; on the table a game-cock, tied by the leg, sharing his master's meal. Then follows a scene at the cockpit, where the Marquis stakes the remnant of his fortune—his herds and hacienda—on a favorite cock, and loses."

"But what do you know about cock-fighting?" demanded, rather than asked, the astonished and half-laughing schoolmaster.

"I am not very well informed on that subject, and I was going to ask you if you could not recommend some work."

"The only work I am acquainted with," replied Mr. Churchill, "is the Reverend Mr. Pegge's Essay on Cock-fighting among the Ancients, and I hardly see how you could apply that to the Mexicans."

"Why, they are a kind of ancients, you know. I certainly will hunt up the essay you mention, and see what I can do with it."

"And all I know about the matter itself," continued Mr. Churchill, "is, that Mark Antony was a patron of the pit, and that his cocks were always beaten by Cæsar's; and that, when Themistocles the Athenian general was marching against the

Persians, he halted his army to see a cock-fight, and made a speech to his soldiery, to the effect, that those animals fought, not for the gods of their country, nor for the monuments of their ancestors, nor for glory, nor for freedom, nor for their children, but only for the sake of victory. On his return to Athens, he established cock-fights in that capital. But how this is to help you in Mexico I do not see, unless you introduce Santa Anna, and compare him to Cæsar and Themistocles."

"That is it; I will do so. It will give historic interest to the play. I thank you for the suggestion."

"The subject is certainly very original, but it does not strike me as particularly national."

"Prospective, you see!" said Mr. Hathaway, with a penetrating look.

"Ah, yes; I perceive you fish with a heavy sinker,—down, far down in the future,—among posterity, as it were."

"You have seized the idea. Besides, I obviate your objection, by introducing an American circus company from the United States, which enables me to bring horses on the stage and produce great scenic effect."

"That is a bold design. The critics will be out upon you without fail."

"Never fear that. I know the critics root and branch,—out and out,—have summered them, and wintered them,—in fact, am one of them myself. Very good fellows are the critics, are they not?"

"Oh, yes; only they have such a pleasant way of talking down upon authors."

"If they did not talk down upon them, they would show no superiority; and, of course, that would never do."

"Nor is it to be wondered at, that authors are sometimes a little irritable. I often recall the poet in the Spanish fable, whose manuscripts were devoured by mice, till at length he put some corrosive sublimate into his ink, and was never troubled again."

"Why don't you try it yourself?" said Mr. Hathaway, rather sharply.

"Oh," answered Mr. Churchill, with a smile of humility, "I and my writings are too insignificant. They may gnaw and welcome. I do not like to have poison about, even for such purposes."

"By the way, Mr. Churchill," said the visitor, adroitly changing the subject, "do you know Honeywell?"

"No, I do not. Who is he?"

"Honeywell the poet, I mean."

"No, I never even heard of him. There are so many poets nowadays!"

"That is very strange indeed! Why, I consider Honeywell one of the finest writers in the country,—quite in the front rank of American authors. He is a real poet, and no mistake. Nature made him with her shirt-sleeves rolled up."

"What has he published?"

"He has not published anything yet, except in the newspapers. But, this autumn, he is going to bring out a volume of poems. I could not help having my joke with him about it. I told him he had better print it on cartridge-paper."

"Why so?"

"Why, to make it go off better; don't you understand?"

"Oh, yes, now that you explain it. Very good."

"Honeywell is going to write for the Magazine; he is to furnish a poem for every number; and as he succeeds equally well in the plaintive and didactic style of Wordsworth, and the more vehement and impassioned style of Byron, I think we shall do very well."

"And what do you mean to call the new Magazine?" inquired Mr. Churchill.

"We think of calling it The Niagara."

"Why, that is the name of our fire-engine! Why not call it the Extinguisher?"

"That is also a good name; but I prefer The Niagara, as more national. And I hope, Mr. Churchill, you will let us count upon you. We should like to have an article from your pen for every number."

"Do you mean to pay your contributors?"

"Not the first year, I am sorry to say. But after that, if the work succeeds, we shall pay handsomely. And, of course, it will succeed, for we mean it shall; and we never say fail. There is no such word in our dictionary. Before the year is out, we mean to print fifty thousand copies; and fifty thousand copies will give us, at least, one hundred and fifty thousand readers; and, with such an audience, any author might be satisfied."

He had touched at length the right strings in Mr. Churchill's bosom; and they vibrated to the touch with pleasant harmonies. Literary vanity!—literary ambition! The editor perceived it; and so cunningly did he play upon these chords, that, before he departed, Mr. Churchill had promised to write for him a series of papers on Obscure Martyrs,—a kind of tragic history of the unrecorded and life-long sufferings of women, which hitherto had found no historian, save now and then a novelist.

Notwithstanding the certainty of success,—notwithstanding the fifty thousand subscribers and the one hundred and fifty thousand readers,—the Magazine never went into operation. Still the dream was enough to occupy Mr. Churchill's thoughts, and to withdraw them entirely from his Romance for many weeks together.

XXI.

Every State, and almost every county, of New England, has its Roaring Brook,—a mountain streamlet, overhung by woods, impeded by a mill, encumbered by fallen trees, but ever racing, rushing, roaring down through gurgling gullies, and filling the forest with its delicious sound and freshness; the drinking-place of home-returning herds; the mysterious haunt of squirrels and blue-jays; the sylvan retreat of schoolgirls, who frequent it on summer holidays, and mingle their restless thoughts, their overflowing fancies, their fair imaginings, with its restless, exuberant, and rejoicing stream.

Fairmeadow had no Roaring Brook. As its name indicates, it was too level a land for that. But the neighboring town of Westwood, lying more inland, and among the hills, had one of the fairest and fullest of all the brooks that roar. It was the boast of the neighborhood. Not to have seen it was to have seen no brook, no waterfall, no mountain ravine. And, consequently, to behold it and admire was Kavanagh taken by Mr. Churchill as soon as the summer vacation gave leisure and opportunity. The party consisted of Mr. and Mrs. Churchill, and Alfred, in a one-horse chaise; and Cecilia, Alice, and Kavanagh, in a carryall,—the fourth seat in which was occupied by a large basket, containing what the Squire of the Grove, in Don Quixote, called his "fiambreras,"—that magniloquent Castilian word for cold collation. Over warm uplands, smelling of clover and mint; through cool glades, still wet with the rain of yesterday; along the river; across the rattling and tilting planks of wooden bridges; by orchards; by the gates of fields, with the tall mullen growing at the bars; by stone walls overrun with privet and barberries; in sun and heat, in shadow and coolness,—forward drove the happy party on that pleasant summer morning.

At length they reached the Roaring Brook. From a gorge in the mountains, through a long, winding gallery of birch, and beech, and pine, leaped the bright, brown waters of the jubilant streamlet; out of the woods, across the plain, under the rude bridge of logs, into the woods again,—a day between two nights. With it went a song that made the heart sing likewise—a song of joy, and exultation, and freedom; a continuous and unbroken song of life, and pleasure, and perpetual youth. Like the old Icelandic Scald, the streamlet seemed to say,—

"I am possessed of songs such as neither the spouse of a king, or any son of man, can repeat; one of them is called the Helper; it will help thee at thy need, in sickness, grief, and all adversity."

The little party left their carriages at a farm-house by the bridge, and followed the rough road on foot along the brook; now close upon it, now shut out by intervening trees. Mr. Churchill, bearing the basket on his arm, walked in front with his wife and Alfred. Kavanagh came behind with Cecilia and Alice. The music of the brook silenced all conversation; only occasional exclamations of delight were uttered,—the irrepressible applause of fresh and sensitive natures, in a scene so lovely. Presently, turning off from the road, which led directly to the mill, and was rough with the tracks of heavy wheels, they went down to the margin of the brook.

"How indescribably beautiful this brown water is!" exclaimed Kavanagh. "It is like wine, or the nectar of the gods of Olympus; as if the falling Hebe had poured it from her goblet."

"More like the mead or metheglin of the northern gods," said Mr. Churchill, "spilled from the drinking-horns of Valhalla."

But all the ladies thought Kavanagh's comparison the better of the two, and in fact the best that could be made; and Mr. Churchill was obliged to retract and apologize for his allusion to the celestial ale-house of Odin.

Erelong they were forced to cross the brook, stepping from stone to stone, over the little rapids and cascades. All crossed lightly, easily, safely; even "the sumpter mule," as Mr. Churchill called himself, on account of the pannier. Only Cecilia lingered behind, as if afraid to cross. Cecilia, who had crossed at that same place a hundred times before,—Cecilia, who had the surest foot, and the firmest nerves, of all the village maidens,—she now stood irresolute, seized with a sudden tremor; blushing, and laughing at her own timidity, and yet unable to advance. Kavanagh saw her embarrassment and hastened back to help her. Her hand trembled in his; she thanked him with a gentle look and word. His whole soul was softened within him. His attitude, his countenance, his voice, were alike submissive and subdued. He was as one penetrated with tenderest emotions.

It is difficult to know at what moment love begins; it is less difficult to know that it has begun. A thousand heralds proclaim it to the listening air; a thousand ministers and messengers betray it to the eye. Tone, act, attitude and look,—the signals upon the countenance,—the electric telegraph of touch; all these betray the yielding citadel before the word itself is uttered, which, like the key surrendered, opens every avenue and gate of entrance, and makes retreat impossible!

The day passed delightfully with all. They sat upon the stones and the roots of trees. Cecilia read, from a volume she had brought with her, poems that rhymed with the running water. The others listened and commented. Little Alfred waded in the stream, with his bare white feet, and launched boats over the falls. Noon had been fixed upon for dining, but they anticipated it by at least an hour. The great basket was opened; endless sandwiches were drawn forth, and a cold pastry, as large as that of the Squire of the Grove. During the repast, Mr. Churchill slipped into the brook, while in the act of handing a sandwich to his wife, which caused unbounded mirth; and Kavanagh sat down on a mossy trunk, that gave way beneath him, and crumbled into powder. This, also, was received with great merriment.

After dinner, they ascended the brook still farther,—indeed, quite to the mill, which was not going. It had been stopped in the midst of its work. The saw still held its hungry teeth fixed in the heart of a pine. Mr. Churchill took occasion to make known to the company his long cherished purpose of writing a poem called "The Song of the Saw-Mill," and enlarged on the beautiful associations of flood and forest connected with the theme. He delighted himself and his audience with the fine fancies he meant to weave into his poem, and wondered nobody had thought of the subject before. Kavanagh said it had been thought of before; and cited Kerner's little poem, so charmingly translated by Bryant. Mr. Churchill had not seen it. Kavanagh looked into his pocket-book for it, but it was not to be found; still he was sure that there was such a poem. Mr. Churchill abandoned his design. He had spoken,—and the treasure, just as he had touched it with his hand, was gone forever.

The party returned home as it came, all tired and happy, excepting little Alfred, who was tired and cross, and sat sleepy and sagging on his father's knee, with his hat cocked rather fiercely over his eyes.

XXII.

The brown autumn came. Out of doors, it brought to the fields the prodigality of the golden harvest,—to the forest, revelations of light,—and to the sky, the sharp air, the morning mist, the red clouds at evening. Within doors, the sense of seclusion, the stillness of closed and curtained windows, musings by the fireside, books, friends, conversation, and the long, meditative evenings. To the farmer, it brought surcease of toil,—to the scholar, that sweet delirium of the brain which changes toil to pleasure. It brought the wild duck back to the reedy marshes of the south; it brought the wild song back to the fervid brain of the poet. Without, the village street was paved with gold; the river ran red with the reflection of the leaves. Within, the faces of friends brightened the gloomy walls; the returning footsteps of the long-absent gladdened the threshold; and all the sweet amenities of social life again resumed their interrupted reign.

Kavanagh preached a sermon on the coming of autumn. He chose his text from Isaiah, "Who is this that cometh from Edom, with dyed garments from Bozrah? this that is glorious in his apparel, travelling in the greatness of his strength? Wherefore art thou red in thine apparel, and thy garments like him that treadeth in the wine-vat?"

To Mr. Churchill, this beloved season—this Joseph with his coat of many colors, as he was fond of calling it—brought an unexpected guest, the forlorn, forsaken Lucy. The surmises of the family were too true. She had wandered away with the Briareus of boots. She returned alone, in destitution and despair; and often, in the grief of a broken heart and a bewildered brain, was heard to say,—

"Oh, how I wish I were a Christian! If I were only a Christian, I would not live any longer; I would kill myself! I am too wretched!"

A few days afterwards, a gloomy-looking man rode through the town on horseback, stopping at every corner, and crying into every street, with a loud and solemn voice,—

"Prepare! prepare! prepare to meet the living God!"

It was one of that fanatical sect who believed the end of the world was imminent, and had prepared their ascension robes to be lifted up in clouds of glory, while the worn-out, weary world was to burn with fire beneath them, and a new and fairer earth to be prepared for their inheritance. The appearance of this forerunner of the end of the world was followed by numerous camp-meetings, held in the woods near the village, to whose white tents and leafy chapels many went for consolation and found despair.

XXIII.

Again the two crumbly old women sat and talked together in the little parlor of the gloomy house under the poplars, and the two girls sat above, holding each other by the hand, thoughtful, and speaking only at intervals.

Alice was unusually sad and silent. The mists were already gathering over her vision,—those mists that were to deepen and darken as the season advanced, until the external world should be shrouded and finally shut from her view. Already the landscape began to wear a pale and sickly hue, as if the sun were withdrawing farther and farther, and were soon wholly to disappear, as in a northern winter. But to brighten this northern winter there now arose within her a soft, auroral light. Yes, the auroral light of love, blushing through the whole heaven of her thoughts. She had not breathed that word to herself, nor did she recognize any thrill of passion in the new emotion she experienced. But love it was; and it lifted her soul into a region which she at once felt was native to it,—into a subtler ether, which seemed its natural element.

This feeling, however, was not all exhilaration. It brought with it its own peculiar languor and sadness, its fluctuations and swift vicissitudes of excitement and depression. To this the trivial circumstances of life contributed. Kavanagh had met her in the street, and had passed her without recognition; and, in the bitterness of the moment, she forgot that she wore a thick veil, which entirely concealed her face. At an evening party at Mr. Churchill's, by a kind of fatality, Kavanagh had stood very near her for a long time, but with his back turned, conversing with Miss Hawkins, from whose toils, he was, in fact, though vainly, struggling to extricate himself; and, in the irritation of supposed neglect, Alice had said to herself,—

"This is the kind of woman which most fascinates men!"

But these cruel moments of pain were few and short, while those of delight were many and lasting. In a life so lonely, and with so little to enliven and embellish it as hers, the guest in disguise was welcomed with ardor, and entertained without fear or suspicion. Had he been feared or suspected, he would have been no longer dangerous. He came as friendship, where friendship was most needed; he came as devotion, where her holy ministrations were always welcome.

Somewhat differently had the same passion come to the heart of Cecilia; for as the heart is, so is love to the heart. It partakes of its strength or weakness, its health or disease. In Cecilia, it but heightened the keen sensation of life. To all eyes, she became more beautiful, more radiant, more lovely, though they knew not why. When she and Kavanagh first met, it was hardly as strangers meet, but rather as friends long separated. When they first spoke to each other, it seemed but as the renewal of some previous interrupted conversation. Their souls flowed together at once, without turbulence or agitation, like waters on the same level. As they found each other without seeking, so their intercourse was without affectation and without embarrassment.

Thus, while Alice, unconsciously to herself, desired the love of Kavanagh, Cecilia, as unconsciously, assumed it as already her own. Alice keenly felt her own unworthiness; Cecilia made no comparison of merit. When Kavanagh was present, Alice was happy, but embarrassed; Cecilia, joyous and natural. The former feared she might displease; the latter divined from the first that she already pleased. In both, this was the intuition of the heart.

So sat the friends together, as they had done so many times before. But now, for the first time, each cherished a secret, which she did not confide to the other. Daily, for many weeks, the feathered courier had come and gone from window to window, but this secret had never been intrusted to his keeping. Almost daily the friends had met and talked together, but this secret had not been told. That could not be confided to another, which had not been confided to themselves; that could not be fashioned into words, which was not yet fashioned into thoughts, but was still floating, vague and formless, through the mind. Nay, had it been stated in words, each, perhaps, would have denied it. The distinct apparition of this fair spirit, in a visible form, would have startled them; though, while it haunted all the chambers of their souls as an invisible presence, it gave them only solace and delight.

"How very feverish your hand is, dearest!" said Cecilia. "What is the matter? Are you unwell?"

"Those are the very words my mother said to me this morning," replied Alice. "I feel rather languid and tired, that is all. I could not sleep last night; I never can, when it rains."

"Did it rain last night? I did not hear it."

"Yes; about midnight, quite hard. I listened to it for hours. I love to lie awake, and hear the drops fall on the roof, and on the leaves. It throws me into a delicious, dreamy state, which I like much better than sleep."

Cecilia looked tenderly at her pale face. Her eyes were very bright, and on each cheek was a crimson signal, the sight of which would have given her mother so much anguish, that, perhaps, it was better for her to be blind than to see.

"When you enter the land of dreams, Alice, you come into my peculiar realm. I am the queen of that country, you know. But, of late, I have thought of resigning my throne. These endless reveries are really a great waste of time and strength."

"Do you think so?"

"Yes; and Mr. Kavanagh thinks so, too. We talked about it the other evening; and afterwards, upon reflection, I thought he was right."

And the friends resolved, half in jest and half in earnest, that, from that day forth, the gate of their day-dreams should be closed. And closed it was, erelong;—for one, by the Angel of Life; for the other, by the Angel of Death!

XXIV.

The project of the new Magazine being heard of no more, and Mr. Churchill being consequently deprived of his one hundred and fifty thousand readers, he laid aside the few notes he had made for his papers on the Obscure Martyrs, and turned his thoughts again to the great Romance. A whole leisure Saturday afternoon was before him,—pure gold, without alloy. Ere beginning his task, he stepped forth into his garden to inhale the sunny air, and let his thoughts recede a little, in order to leap farther. When he returned, glowing and radiant with poetic fancies, he found, to his unspeakable dismay, an unknown damsel sitting in his arm-chair. She was rather gayly yet elegantly dressed, and wore a veil, which she raised as Mr. Churchill entered, fixing upon him the full, liquid orbs of her large eyes.

"Mr. Churchill, I suppose?" said she, rising, and stepping forward.

"The same," replied the schoolmaster, with dignified courtesy.

"And will you permit me," she continued, not without a certain serene self-possession, "to introduce myself, for want of a better person to do it for me? My name is Cartwright,—Clarissa Cartwright."

This announcement did not produce that powerful and instantaneous effect on Mr. Churchill which the speaker seemed to anticipate, or at least to hope. His eye did not brighten with any quick recognition, nor did he suddenly exclaim,—

"What! Are you Miss Cartwright, the poetess, whose delightful effusions I have seen in all the magazines?"

On the contrary, he looked rather blank and expectant, and only said,—

"I am very glad to see you; pray sit down."

So that the young lady herself was obliged to communicate the literary intelligence above alluded to, which she did very gracefully, and then added,—

"I have come to ask a great favor of you, Mr. Churchill, which I hope you will not deny me. By the advice of some friends, I have collected my poems together,"—and here she drew forth from a paper a large, thin manuscript, bound in crimson velvet,—"and think of publishing them in a volume. Now, would you do me the favor to look them over, and give me your candid opinion, whether they are worth publishing? I should value your advice so highly!"

This simultaneous appeal to his vanity and his gallantry from a fair young girl, standing on the verge of that broad, dangerous ocean, in which so many have perished, and looking wistfully over its flashing waters to the shores of the green Isle of Palms,—such an appeal, from such a person, it was impossible for Mr. Churchill to resist. He made, however, a faint show of resistance,—a feeble grasping after some excuse for refusal,—and then yielded. He received from Clarissa's delicate, trembling hand the precious volume, and from her eyes a still more precious look of thanks, and then said,—

"What name do you propose to give the volume?"

"Symphonies of the Soul, and other Poems," said the young lady; "and, if you like them, and it would not be asking too much, I should be delighted to have you write a Preface, to introduce the work to the public. The publisher says it would increase the sale very considerably."

"Ah, the publisher! yes, but that is not very complimentary to yourself," suggested Mr. Churchill. "I can already see your Poems rebelling against the intrusion of my Preface, and rising like so many nuns in a convent to expel the audacious foot that has dared to invade their sacred precincts."

But it was all in vain, this pale effort at pleasantry. Objection was useless, and the soft-hearted schoolmaster a second time yielded gracefully to his fate, and promised the Preface. The young lady took her leave with a profusion of thanks and blushes, and the dainty manuscript, with its delicate chirography and crimson cover, remained in the hands of Mr. Churchill, who gazed at it less as a Paradise of Dainty Devices than as a deed or mortgage of so many precious hours of his own scanty inheritance of time.

Afterwards, when he complained a little of this to his wife,—who, during the interview, had peeped in at the door, and, seeing how he was occupied, had immediately withdrawn,—she said that nobody was to blame but himself; that he should learn to say "No!" and not do just as every romantic girl from the Academy wanted him to do; adding, as a final aggravation and climax of reproof, that she really believed he never would, and never meant to, begin his Romance!

XXV.

Not long afterwards, Kavanagh and Mr. Churchill took a stroll together across the fields, and down green lanes, walking all the bright, brief afternoon. From the summit of the hill, beside the old windmill, they saw the sun set, and, opposite, the full moon rise, dewy, large, and red. As they descended, they felt the heavy dampness of the air, like water, rising to meet them,—bathing with coolness first their feet, then their hands, then their faces, till they were submerged in that sea of dew. As they skirted the woodland on their homeward way, trampling the golden leaves underfoot, they heard voices at a distance, singing; and then saw the lights of the camp-meeting gleaming through the trees, and, drawing nearer, distinguished a portion of the hymn:—

Don't you hear the Lord a-coming
To the old churchyards,
With a band of music,
With a band of music,
With a band of music,
Sounding through the air?

These words, at once awful and ludicrous, rose on the still twilight air from a hundred voices, thrilling with emotion, and from as many beating, fluttering, struggling hearts. High above them all was heard one voice, clear and musical as a clarion.

"I know that voice," said Mr. Churchill; "it is Elder Evans's."

"Ah!" exclaimed Kavanagh,—for only the impression of awe was upon him,—"he never acted in a deeper tragedy than this! How terrible it is! Let us pass on."

They hurried away, Kavanagh trembling in every fibre. Silently they walked, the music fading into softest vibrations behind them.

"How strange is this fanaticism!" at length said Mr. Churchill, rather as a relief to his own thoughts, than for the purpose of reviving the conversation. "These people really believe that the end of the world is close at hand."

"And to thousands," answered Kavanagh, "this is no fiction,—no illusion of an over-heated imagination. To-day, to-morrow, every day, to thousands, the end of the world is close at hand. And why should we fear it? We walk here as it were in the crypts of life; at times, from the great cathedral above us, we can hear the organ and the chanting of the choir; we see the light stream through the open door, when some friend goes up before us; and shall we fear to mount the narrow staircase of the grave, that leads us out of this uncertain twilight into the serene mansions of the life eternal?"

They reached the wooden bridge over the river, which the moonlight converted into a river of light. Their footsteps sounded on the planks; they passed without perceiving a female figure that stood in the shadow below on the brink of the stream, watching wistfully the steady flow of the current. It was Lucy! Her bonnet and shawl were lying at her feet; and when they had passed, she waded far out into the shallow stream, laid herself gently down in its deeper waves, and floated slowly away into the moonlight, among the golden leaves that were faded and fallen like herself,—among the water-lilies, whose fragrant white blossoms had been broken off and polluted long ago. Without a struggle, without a sigh, without a sound, she floated downward, downward, and silently sank into the silent river. Far off, faint, and indistinct, was heard the startling hymn, with its wild and peculiar melody,—

Oh, there will be mourning, mourning, mourning,
    mourning,—
Oh, there will be mourning, at the judgment-seat of Christ!

Kavanagh's heart was full of sadness. He left Mr. Churchill at his door, and proceeded homeward. On passing his church, he could not resist the temptation to go in. He climbed to his chamber in the tower, lighted by the moon. He sat for a long time gazing from the window, and watching a distant and feeble candle, whose rays scarcely reached him across the brilliant moon-lighted air. Gentler thoughts stole over him; an invisible presence soothed him; an invisible hand was laid upon his head, and the trouble and unrest of his spirit were changed to peace.

"Answer me, thou mysterious future!" exclaimed he; "tell me,—shall these things be according to my desires?"

And the mysterious future, interpreted by those desires, replied,—

"Soon thou shalt know all. It shall be well with thee!"

XXVI.

On the following morning, Kavanagh sat as usual in his study in the tower. No traces were left of the heaviness and sadness of the preceding night. It was a bright, warm morning; and the window, open towards the south, let in the genial sunshine. The odor of decaying leaves scented the air; far off flashed the hazy river.

Kavanagh's heart, however, was not at rest. At times he rose from his books, and paced up and down his little study; then took up his hat as if to go out; then laid it down again, and again resumed his books. At length he arose, and, leaning on the window-sill, gazed for a long time on the scene before him. Some thought was laboring in his bosom, some doubt or fear, which alternated with hope, but thwarted any fixed resolve.

Ah, how pleasantly that fair autumnal landscape smiled upon him! The great golden elms that marked the line of the village street, and under whose shadows no beggars sat; the air of comfort and plenty, of neatness, thrift, and equality, visible everywhere; and from far-off farms the sound of flails, beating the triumphal march of Ceres through the land;—these were the sights and sounds that greeted him as he looked. Silently the yellow leaves fell upon the graves in the church-yard, and the dew glistened in the grass, which was still long and green.

Presently his attention was arrested by a dove, pursued by a little king-bird, who constantly endeavored to soar above it, in order to attack it at greater advantage. The flight of the birds, thus shooting through the air at arrowy speed, was beautiful. When they were opposite the tower, the dove suddenly wheeled, and darted in at the open window, while the pursuer held on his way with a long sweep, and was out of sight in a moment.

At the first glance, Kavanagh recognized the dove, which lay panting on the floor. It was the same he had seen Cecilia buy of the little man in gray. He took it in his hands. Its heart was beating violently. About its neck was a silken band; beneath its wing a billet, upon which was a single word, "Cecilia." The bird, then, was on its way to Cecilia Vaughan. He hailed the omen as auspicious, and, immediately closing the window, seated himself at his table, and wrote a few hurried words, which, being carefully folded and sealed, he fastened to the band, and then hastily, as if afraid his purpose might be changed by delay, opened the window and set the bird at liberty. It sailed once or twice round the tower, apparently uncertain and bewildered, or still in fear of its pursuer. Then, instead of holding its way over the fields to Cecilia Vaughan, it darted over the roofs of the village, and alighted at the window of Alice Archer.

Having written that morning to Cecilia something urgent and confidential, she was already waiting the answer; and, not doubting that the bird had brought it, she hastily untied the silken band, and, without looking at the superscription, opened the first note that fell on the table. It was very brief—only a few lines, and not a name mentioned in it; an impulse, an ejaculation of love; every line quivering with electric fire,—every word a pulsation of the writer's heart. It was signed "Arthur Kavanagh."

Overwhelmed by the suddenness and violence of her emotions, Alice sat for a long time motionless, holding the open letter in her hand. Then she read it again, and then relapsed into her dream of joy and wonder. It would be difficult to say which of the two emotions was the greater,—her joy that her prayer for love should be answered, and so answered,—her wonder that Kavanagh should have selected her! In the tumult of her sensations, and hardly conscious of what she was doing, she folded the note and replaced it in its envelope. Then, for the first time, her eye fell on the superscription. It was "Cecilia Vaughan." Alice fainted.

On recovering her senses, her first act was one of heroism. She sealed the note, attached it to the neck of the pigeon, and sent the messenger rejoicing on his journey. Then her feelings had way, and she wept long and bitterly. Then, with a desperate calmness, she reproved her own weakness and selfishness, and felt that she ought to rejoice in the happiness of her friend, and sacrifice her affection, even her life, to her. Her heart exculpated Kavanagh from all blame. He had not deluded her; she had deluded herself. She alone was in fault; and in deep humiliation, with wounded pride and wounded love, and utter self-abasement, she bowed her head and prayed for consolation and fortitude.

One consolation she already had. The secret was her own. She had not revealed it even to Cecilia. Kavanagh did not suspect it. Public curiosity, public pity, she would not have to undergo.

She was resigned. She made the heroic sacrifice of self, leaving her sorrow to the great physician, Time,—the nurse of care, the healer of all smarts, the soother and consoler of all sorrows. And, thenceforward, she became unto Kavanagh what the moon is to the sun, forever following, forever separated, forever sad!

As a traveller, about to start upon his journey, resolved and yet irresolute, watches the clouds, and notes the struggle between the sunshine and the showers, and says, "It will be fair; I will go,"—and again says, "Ah, no, not yet; the rain is not yet over,"—so at this same hour sat Cecilia Vaughan, resolved and yet irresolute, longing to depart upon the fair journey before her, and yet lingering on the paternal threshold, as if she wished both to stay and to go, seeing the sky was not without its clouds, nor the road without its dangers.

It was a beautiful picture, as she sat there with sweet perplexity in her face, and above it an immortal radiance streaming from her brow. She was like Guercino's Sibyl, with the scroll of fate and the uplifted pen; and the scroll she held contained but three words,—three words that controlled the destiny of a man, and, by their soft impulsion, directed forevermore the current of his thoughts. They were,—

"Come to me!"

The magic syllables brought Kavanagh to her side. The full soul is silent. Only the rising and falling tides rush murmuring through their channels. So sat the lovers, hand in hand; but for a long time neither spake,—neither had need of speech!

XXVII.

In the afternoon, Cecilia went to communicate the news to Alice with her own lips, thinking it too important to be intrusted to the wings of the carrier-pigeon. As she entered the door, the cheerful doctor was coming out; but this was no unusual apparition, and excited no alarm. Mrs. Archer, too, according to custom, was sitting in the little parlor with her decrepit old neighbor, who seemed almost to have taken up her abode under that roof, so many hours of every day did she pass there.

With a light, elastic step, Cecilia bounded up to Alice's room. She found her reclining in her large chair, flushed and excited. Sitting down by her side, and taking both her hands, she said, with great emotion in the tones of her voice,—

"Dearest Alice, I have brought you some news that I am sure will make you well. For my sake, you will be no longer ill when you hear it. I am engaged to Mr. Kavanagh!"

Alice feigned no surprise at this announcement. She returned the warm pressure of Cecilia's hand, and, looking affectionately in her face, said very calmly,—

"I knew it would be so. I knew that he loved you, and that you would love him."

"How could I help it?" said Cecilia, her eyes beaming with dewy light; "could any one help loving him?"

"No," answered Alice, throwing her arms around Cecilia's neck, and laying her head upon her shoulder; "at least, no one whom he loved. But when did this happen? Tell me all about it, dearest!"

Cecilia was surprised, and perhaps a little hurt, at the quiet, almost impassive manner in which her friend received this great intelligence. She had expected exclamations of wonder and delight, and such a glow of excitement as that with which she was sure she should have hailed the announcement of Alice's engagement. But this momentary annoyance was soon swept away by the tide of her own joyous sensations, as she proceeded to recall to the recollection of her friend the thousand little circumstances that had marked the progress of her love and Kavanagh's; things which she must have noticed, which she could not have forgotten; with questions interspersed at intervals, such as, "Do you recollect when?" and "I am sure you have not forgotten, have you?" and dreamy little pauses of silence, and intercalated sighs. She related to her, also, the perilous adventure of the carrier-pigeon; how it had been pursued by the cruel king-bird; how it had taken refuge in Kavanagh's tower, and had been the bearer of his letter, as well as her own. When she had finished, she felt her bosom wet with the tears of Alice, who was suffering martyrdom on that soft breast, so full of happiness. Tears of bitterness,—tears of blood! And Cecilia, in the exultant temper of her soul at the moment, thought them tears of joy, and pressed Alice closer to her heart, and kissed and caressed her.

"Ah, how very happy you are, Cecilia!" at length sighed the poor sufferer, in that slightly querulous tone to which Cecilia was not unaccustomed; "how very happy you are, and how very wretched am I! You have all the joy of life, I all its loneliness. How little you will think of me now! How little you will need me! I shall be nothing to you,—you will forget me."

"Never, dearest!" exclaimed Cecilia, with much warmth and sincerity. "I shall love you only the more. We shall both love you. You will now have two friends instead of one."

"Yes; but both will not be equal to the one I lose. No, Cecilia; let us not make to ourselves any illusions. I do not. You cannot now be with me so much and so often as you have been. Even if you were, your thoughts would be elsewhere. Ah, I have lost my friend, when most I needed her!"

Cecilia protested ardently and earnestly, and dilated with eagerness on her little plan of life, in which their romantic friendship was to gain only new strength and beauty from the more romantic love. She was interrupted by a knock at the street door; on hearing which, she paused a moment, and then said,—

"It is Arthur. He was to call for me."

Ah, what glimpses of home, and fireside, and a whole life of happiness for Cecilia, were revealed by that one word of love and intimacy, "Arthur"! and for Alice, what a sentence of doom! what sorrow without a name! what an endless struggle of love and friendship, of duty and inclination! A little quiver of the eyelids and the hands, a hasty motion to raise her head from Cecilia's shoulder,—these were the only outward signs of emotion. But a terrible pang went to her heart; her blood rushed eddying to her brain; and when Cecilia had taken leave of her with the triumphant look of love beaming upon her brow, and an elevation in her whole attitude and bearing, as if borne up by attendant angels, she sank back into her chair, exhausted, fainting, fearing, longing, hoping to die.

And below sat the two old women, talking of moths, and cheap furniture, and what was the best remedy for rheumatism; and from the door went forth two happy hearts, beating side by side with the pulse of youth and hope and joy, and within them and around them was a new heaven and a new earth!

Only those who have lived in a small town can really know how great an event therein is a new engagement. From tongue to tongue passes the swift countersign; from eye to eye flashes the illumination of joy, or the bale-fire of alarm; the streets and houses ring with it, as with the penetrating, all-pervading sound of the village bell; the whole community feels a thrill of sympathy, and seems to congratulate itself that all the great events are by no means confined to the great towns. As Cecilia and Kavanagh passed arm in arm through the village, many curious eyes watched them from the windows, many hearts grown cold or careless rekindled their household fires of love from the golden altar of God, borne through the streets by those pure and holy hands!

The intelligence of the engagement, however, was received very differently by different persons. Mrs. Wilmerdings wondered, for her part, why anybody wanted to get married at all. The little taxidermist said he knew it would be so from the very first day they had met at his aviary. Miss Hawkins lost suddenly much of her piety and all her patience, and laughed rather hysterically. Mr. Hawkins said it was impossible, but went in secret to consult a friend, an old bachelor, on the best remedy for love; and the old bachelor, as one well versed in such affairs, gravely advised him to think of the lady as a beautiful statue!

Once more the indefatigable school-girl took up her pen, and wrote to her foreign correspondent a letter that might rival the famous epistle of Madame de Sévigné to her daughter, announcing the engagement of Mademoiselle Montpensier. Through the whole of the first page, she told her to guess who the lady was; through the whole of the second, who the gentleman was; the third was devoted to what was said about it in the village; and on the fourth there were two postscripts, one at the top and the other at the bottom, the first stating that they were to be married in the Spring, and to go to Italy immediately afterwards, and the last, that Alice Archer was dangerously ill with a fever.

As for the Churchills, they could find no words powerful enough to express their delight, but gave vent to it in a banquet on Thanksgiving-day, in which the wife had all the trouble and the husband all the pleasure. In order that the entertainment might be worthy of the occasion, Mr. Churchill wrote to the city for the best cookery-book; and the bookseller, executing the order in all its amplitude, sent him the Practical Guide to the Culinary Art in all its Branches, by Frascatelli, pupil of the celebrated Carême, and Chief Cook to Her Majesty the Queen,—a ponderous volume, illustrated with numerous engravings, and furnished with bills of fare for every month in the year, and any number of persons. This great work was duly studied, evening after evening; and Mr. Churchill confessed to his wife, that, although at first startled by the size of the book, he had really enjoyed it very highly, and had been much pleased to be present in imagination at so many grand entertainments, and to sit opposite the Queen without having to change his dress or the general style of his conversation.

The dinner hour, as well as the dinner itself, was duly debated. Mr. Churchill was in favor of the usual hour of one; but his wife thought it should be an hour later. Whereupon he remarked,—

"King Henry the Eighth dined at ten o'clock and supped at four. His queen's maids of honor had a gallon of ale and a chine of beef for their breakfast."

To which his wife answered,—

"I hope we shall have something a little more refined than that."

The day on which the banquet should take place was next discussed, and both agreed that no day could be so appropriate as Thanksgiving-day; for, as Mrs. Churchill very truly remarked, it was really a day of thanksgiving to Kavanagh. She then said,—

"How very solemnly he read the Governor's Proclamation yesterday! particularly the words 'God save the Commonwealth of Massachusetts!' And what a Proclamation it was! When he spread it out on the pulpit, it looked like a tablecloth!"

Mr. Churchill then asked,

"What day of the week is the first of December? Let me see,—

> 'At Dover dwells George Brown, Esquire,
> Good Christopher Finch and Daniel Friar!'

Thursday."

"I could have told you that," said his wife, "by a shorter process than your old rhyme. Thanksgiving-day always comes on Thursday."

These preliminaries being duly settled, the dinner was given.

There being only six guests, and the dinner being modelled upon one for twenty-four persons, Russian style in November, it was very abundant. It began with a Colbert soup, and ended with a Nesselrode pudding; but as no allusion was made in the course of the repast to the French names of the dishes, and the mutton, and turnips, and pancakes were all called by their English patronymics, the dinner appeared less magnificent in reality than in the bill of fare, and the guests did not fully appreciate how superb a banquet they were enjoying. The hilarity of the occasion was not marred by any untoward accident; though once or twice Mr. Churchill was much annoyed, and the company much amused, by Master Alfred, who was allowed to be present at the festivities, and audibly proclaimed what was coming, long before it made its appearance. When the dinner was over, several of the guests remembered brilliant and appropriate things they might have said, and wondered they were so dull as not to think of them in season; and when they were all gone, Mr. Churchill remarked to his wife that he had enjoyed himself very much, and that he should like to ask his friends to just such a dinner every week!

XXVIII.

The first snow came. How beautiful it was, falling so silently, all day long, all night long, on the mountains, on the meadows, on the roofs of the living, on the graves of the dead! All white save the river, that marked its course by a winding black line across the landscape; and the leafless trees, that against the leaden sky now revealed more fully the wonderful beauty and intricacy of their branches!

What silence, too, came with the snow, and what seclusion! Every sound was muffled, every noise changed to something soft and musical. No more trampling hoofs,—no more rattling wheels! Only the chiming sleigh-bells, beating as swift and merrily as the hearts of children.

All day long, all night long, the snow fell on the village and on the churchyard; on the happy home of Cecilia Vaughan, on the lonely grave of Alice Archer! Yes; for before the winter came she had gone to that land where winter never comes. Her long domestic tragedy was ended. She was dead; and with her had died her secret sorrow and her secret love. Kavanagh never knew what wealth of affection for him faded from the world when she departed; Cecilia never knew what fidelity of friendship, what delicate regard, what gentle magnanimity, what angelic patience, had gone with her into the grave; Mr. Churchill never knew, that, while he was exploring the Past for records of obscure and unknown martyrs, in his own village, near his own door, before his own eyes, one of that silent sisterhood had passed away into oblivion, unnoticed and unknown.

How often, ah, how often, between the desire of the heart and its fulfilment, lies only the briefest space of time and distance, and yet the desire remains forever unfulfilled! It is so near that we can touch it with the hand, and yet so far away that the eye cannot perceive it. What Mr. Churchill most desired was before him. The Romance he was longing to find and record had really occurred in his neighborhood, among his own friends. It had been set like a picture into the frame-work of his life, enclosed within his own experience. But he could not see it as an object apart from himself; and as he was gazing at what was remote and strange and indistinct, the nearer incidents of aspiration, love, and death, escaped him. They were too near to be clothed by the imagination with the golden vapors of romance; for the familiar seems trivial, and only the distant and unknown completely fill and satisfy the mind.

The winter did not pass without its peculiar delights and recreations. The singing of the great wood fires; the blowing of the wind over the chimney-tops, as if they were organ pipes; the splendor of the spotless snow; the purple wall built round the horizon at sunset; the sea-suggesting pines, with the moan of the billows in their branches, on which the snows were furled like sails; the northern lights; the stars of steel; the transcendent moonlight, and the lovely shadows of the leafless trees upon the snow;—these things did not pass unnoticed nor unremembered. Every one of them made its record upon the heart of Mr. Churchill.

His twilight walks, his long Saturday afternoon rambles, had again become solitary; for Kavanagh was lost to him for such purposes, and his wife was one of those women who never walk. Sometimes he went down to the banks of the frozen river, and saw the farmers crossing it with their heavy-laden sleds, and the Fairmeadow schooner imbedded in the ice; and thought of Lapland sledges, and the song of Kulnasatz, and the dismantled, ice-locked vessels of the explorers in the Arctic Ocean. Sometimes he went to the neighboring lake, and saw the skaters wheeling round their fire, and speeding away before the wind; and in his imagination arose images of the Norwegian Skate-Runners, bearing the tidings of King Charles's death from Frederickshall to Drontheim, and of the retreating Swedish army, frozen to death in its fireless tents among the mountains. And then he would watch the cutting of the ice with ploughs, and the horses dragging the huge blocks to the storehouses, and contrast them with the Grecian mules, bearing the snows of Mount Parnassus to the markets of Athens, in panniers, protected from the sun by boughs of oleander and rhododendron.

The rest of his leisure hours were employed in anything and everything save in writing his Romance. A great deal of time was daily consumed in reading the newspapers, because it was necessary, he said, to keep up with the times; and a great deal more in writing a Lyceum Lecture, on "What Lady Macbeth might have been, had her energies been properly directed." He also made some little progress in a poetical arithmetic, founded on Bhascara's, but relinquished it, because the school committee thought it was not practical enough, and more than hinted that he had better adhere to the old system. And still the vision of the great Romance moved before his mind, august and glorious, a beautiful mirage of the desert.

XXIX.

The wedding did not take place till spring. And then Kavanagh and his Cecilia departed on their journey to Italy and the East,—a sacred mission, a visit like the Apostle's to the Seven Churches, nay, to all the Churches of Christendom; he hoping by some means to sow in many devout hearts the desire and prophecy that filled his own,—the union of all sects into one universal Church of Christ. They intended to be absent one year only; they were gone three. It seemed to their friends that they never would return. But at length they came,—the long absent, the long looked for, the long desired,—bearing with them that delicious perfume of travel, that genial, sunny atmosphere, and soft, Ausonian air, which returning travellers always bring about them.

It was night when they reached the village, and they could not see what changes had taken place in it during their absence. How it had dilated and magnified itself,—how it had puffed itself up, and bedizened itself with flaunting, ostentatious signs,—how it stood, rotund and rubicund with brick, like a portly man, with his back to the fire and both hands in his pockets, warm, expansive, apoplectic, and entertaining a very favorable opinion of himself,—all this they did not see, for the darkness; but Kavanagh beheld it all, and more, when he went forth on the following morning.

How Cecilia's heart beat as they drove up the avenue to the old house! The piny odors in the night air, the solitary light at her father's window, the familiar bark of the dog Major at the sound of the wheels, awakened feelings at once new and old. A sweet perplexity of thought, a strange familiarity, a no less pleasing strangeness! The lifting of the heavy brass latch, and the jarring of the heavy brass knocker as the door closed, were echoes from her childhood. Mr. Vaughan they found, as usual, among his papers in the study;—the same bland, white-haired man, hardly a day older than when they left him there. To Cecilia the whole long absence in Italy became a dream, and vanished away. Even Kavanagh was for the moment forgotten. She was a daughter, not a wife;—she had not been married, she had not been in Italy!

In the morning, Kavanagh sallied forth to find the Fairmeadow of his memory, but found it not. The railroad had completely transformed it. The simple village had become a very precocious town. New shops, with new names over the doors; new streets, with new forms and faces in them; the whole town seemed to have been taken and occupied by a besieging army of strangers. Nothing was permanent but the workhouse, standing alone in the pasture by the river; and, at the end of the street, the school-house, that other workhouse, where in childhood we twist and untwist the cordage of the brain, that, later in life, we may not be obliged to pull to pieces the more material cordage of old ships.

Kavanagh soon turned in despair from the main street into a little green lane, where there were few houses, and where the barberry still nodded over the old stone wall;—a place he had much loved in the olden time for its silence and seclusion. He seemed to have entered his ancient realm of dreams again, and was walking with his hat drawn a little over his eyes. He had not proceeded far, when he was startled by a woman's voice, quite sharp and loud, crying from the opposite side of the lane. Looking up, he beheld a small cottage, against the wall of which rested a ladder, and on this ladder stood the woman from whom the voice came. Her face was nearly concealed by a spacious gingham sun-bonnet, and in her right hand she held extended a large brush, with which she was painting the front of her cottage, when interrupted by the approach of Kavanagh, who, thinking she was calling to him, but not understanding what she said, made haste to cross over to her assistance. At this movement her tone became louder and more peremptory, and he could now understand that her cry was rather a warning than an invitation.

"Go away!" she said, flourishing her brush. "Go away! What are you coming down here for, when I am on the ladder, painting my house? If you don't go right about your business, I will come down and"—

"Why, Miss Manchester!" exclaimed Kavanagh; "how could I know that you would be going up the ladder just as I came down the lane?"

"Well, I declare! If it is not Mr. Kavanagh!"

And she scrambled down the ladder backwards with as much grace as the circumstances permitted. She, too, like the rest of his friends in the village, showed symptoms of growing older. The passing years had drunk a portion of the light from her eyes, and left their traces on her cheeks, as birds that drink at lakes leave their footprints on the margin. But the pleasant smile remained, and reminded him of the bygone days, when she used to open for him the door of the gloomy house under the poplars.

Many things had she to ask, and many to tell; and for full half an hour Kavanagh stood leaning over the paling, while she remained among the hollyhocks, as stately and red as the plants themselves. At parting, she gave him one of the flowers for his wife; and, when he was fairly out of sight, again climbed the perilous ladder, and resumed her fresco painting.

Through all the vicissitudes of these later years, Sally had remained true to her principles and resolution. At Mrs. Archer's death, which occurred soon after Kavanagh's wedding, she had retired to this little cottage, bought and paid for by her own savings. Though often urged by Mr. Vaughan's man, Silas, who breathed his soul out upon the air of summer evenings through a keyed bugle, she resolutely refused to marry. In vain did he send her letters written with his own blood,—going barefooted into the brook to be bitten by leeches, and then using his feet as inkstands: she refused again and again. Was it that in some blue chamber, or some little warm back parlor, of her heart, the portrait of the inconstant dentist was still hanging? Alas, no! But as to some hearts it is given in youth to blossom with the fragrant blooms of young desire, so others are doomed by a mysterious destiny to be checked in Spring by chill winds, blowing over the bleak common of the world. So had it been with her desires and thoughts of love. Fear now predominated over hope; and to die unmarried had become to her a fatality which she dared not resist.

In the course of his long conversation with Miss Manchester, Kavanagh learned many things about the inhabitants of the town. Mrs. Wilmerdings was still carrying on her labors in the "Dunstable and eleven-braid, open-work and colored straws." Her husband had taken to the tavern, and often came home very late, "with a brick in his hat," as Sally expressed it. Their son and heir was far away in the Pacific, on board a whale-ship. Miss Amelia Hawkins remained unmarried, though possessing a talent for matrimony which amounted almost to genius. Her brother, the poet, was no more. Finding it impossible to follow the old bachelor's advice, and look upon Miss Vaughan as a beautiful statue, he made one or two attempts, but in vain, to throw himself away on unworthy objects, and then died. At this event, two elderly maidens went into mourning simultaneously, each thinking herself engaged to him; and suddenly went out of it again, mutually indignant with each other, and mortified with themselves. The little taxidermist was still hopping about in his aviary, looking more than ever like his gray African parrot. Mrs. Archer's house was uninhabited.

XXX.

Kavanagh continued his walk in the direction of Mr. Churchill's residence. This, at least, was unchanged,—quite unchanged. The same white front, the same brass knocker, the same old wooden gate, with its chain and ball, the same damask roses under the windows, the same sunshine without and within. The outer door and study door were both open, as usual in the warm weather, and at the table sat Mr. Churchill, writing. Over each ear was a black and inky stump of a pen, which, like the two ravens perched on Odin's shoulders, seemed to whisper to him all that passed in heaven and on earth. On this occasion, their revelations were of the earth. He was correcting school exercises.

The joyful welcome of Mr. Churchill, as Kavanagh entered, and the cheerful sound of their voices, soon brought Mrs. Churchill to the study,—her eyes bluer than ever, her cheeks fairer, her form more round and full. The children came in also,—Alfred grown to boy's estate and exalted into a jacket, and the baby, that was less than two years behind him, and catching all his falling mantles, and all his tricks and maladies.

Kavanagh found Mr. Churchill precisely where he left him.

He had not advanced one step,—not one. The same dreams, the same longings, the same aspirations, the same indecision. A thousand things had been planned, and none completed. His imagination seemed still to exhaust itself in running, before it tried to leap the ditch. While he mused, the fire burned in other brains. Other hands wrote the books he dreamed about. He freely used his good ideas in conversation, and in letters, and they were straightway wrought into the texture of other men's books, and so lost to him forever. His work on Obscure Martyrs was anticipated by Mr. Hathaway, who, catching the idea from him, wrote and published a series of papers on Unknown Saints, before Mr. Churchill had fairly arranged his materials. Before he had written a chapter of his great Romance, another friend and novelist had published one on the same subject.

Poor Mr. Churchill! So far as fame and external success were concerned, his life certainly was a failure. He was, perhaps, too deeply freighted, too much laden by the head, to ride the waves gracefully. Every sea broke over him,—he was half the time under water!

All his defects and mortifications he attributed to the outward circumstances of his life, the exigencies of his profession, the accidents of chance. But, in reality, they lay much deeper than this. They were within himself. He wanted the all-controlling, all-subduing will. He wanted the fixed purpose that sways and bends all circumstances to its uses, as the wind bends the reeds and rushes beneath it.

In a few minutes, and in that broad style of handling in which nothing is distinctly defined, but everything clearly suggested, Kavanagh sketched to his friends his three years' life in Italy and the East. And then, turning to Mr. Churchill, he said,—

"And you, my friend,—what have you been doing all this while? You have written to me so rarely that I have hardly kept pace with you. But I have thought of you constantly. In all the old cathedrals; in all the lovely landscapes, among the Alps and Apennines; in looking down on Duomo d'Ossola; at the Inn of Baveno; at Gaeta; at Naples; in old and mouldy Rome; in older Egypt; in the Holy Land; in all galleries and churches and ruins; in our rural retirement at Fiesoli;—whenever I have seen anything beautiful, I have thought of you, and of how much you would have enjoyed it!"

Mr. Churchill sighed; and then, as if, with a touch as masterly, he would draw a picture that should define nothing, but suggest everything, he said,—

"You have no children, Kavanagh; we have five."

"Ah, so many already!" exclaimed Kavanagh. "A living Pentateuch! A beautiful Pentapylon, or five-gated temple of Life! A charming number!"

"Yes," answered Mr. Churchill, "a beautiful number, Juno's own; the wedding of the first even and first uneven numbers; the number sacred to marriage, but having no reference, direct or indirect, to the Pythagorean novitiate of five years of silence."

"No; it certainly is not the vocation of children to be silent," said Kavanagh, laughing. "That would be out of nature; saving always the children of the brain, which do not often make so much noise in the world as we desire. I hope a still larger family of these has grown up around you during my absence."

"Quite otherwise," answered the schoolmaster, sadly. "My brain has been almost barren of songs. I have only been trifling, and I am afraid, that, if I play any longer with Apollo, the untoward winds will blow the discus of the god against my forehead, and strike me dead with it, as they did Hyacinth of old."

"And your Romance,—have you been more successful with that? I hope it is finished, or nearly finished?"

"Not yet begun," said Mr. Churchill. "The plan and characters still remain vague and indefinite in my mind. I have not even found a name for it."

"That you can determine after the book is written," suggested Kavanagh. "You can name it, for instance, as the old Heimskringla was named, from the initial word of the first chapter."

"Ah! that was very well in the olden time, and in Iceland, when there were no quarterly reviews. It would be called affectation now."

"I see you still stand a little in awe of opinion. Never fear that. The strength of criticism lies only in the weakness of the thing criticised."

"That is the truth, Kavanagh; and I am more afraid of deserving criticism than of receiving it. I stand in awe of my own opinion. The secret demerits of which we alone, perhaps, are conscious, are often more difficult to bear than those which have been publicly censured in us, and thus in some degree atoned for."

"I will not say," replied Kavanagh, "that humility is the only road to excellence, but I am sure that it is one road."

"Yes, humility, but not humiliation," sighed Mr. Churchill, despondingly. "As for excellence, I can only desire it and dream of it; I cannot attain to it, it lies too far from me; I cannot reach it. These very books about me here, that once stimulated me to action, have now become my accusers. They are my Eumenides, and drive me to despair."

"My friend," said Kavanagh, after a short pause, during which he had taken note of Mr. Churchill's sadness, "that is not always excellent which lies far away from us. What is remote and difficult of access we are apt to overrate; what is really best for us lies always within our reach, though often overlooked. To speak frankly, I am afraid this is the case with your Romance. You are evidently grasping at something which lies beyond the confines of your own experience, and which, consequently, is only a play of shadows in the realm of fancy. The figures have no vitality; they are only outward shows, wanting inward life. We can give to others only what we have."

"And if we have nothing worth giving?" interrupted Mr. Churchill.

"No man is so poor as that. As well might the mountain streamlets say they have nothing worth giving to the sea, because they are not rivers. Give what you have. To some one, it may be better than you dare to think. If you had looked nearer for the materials of your Romance, and had set about it in earnest, it would now have been finished."

"And burned, perhaps," interposed Mr. Churchill; "or sunk with the books of Simon Magus to the bottom of the Dead Sea."

"At all events, you would have had the pleasure of writing it. I remember one of the old traditions of Art, from which you may perhaps draw a moral. When Raphael desired to paint his Holy Family, for a long time he strove in vain to express the idea that filled and possessed his soul. One morning, as he walked beyond the city gates, meditating the sacred theme, he beheld, sitting beneath a vine at her cottage door, a peasant woman, holding a boy in her arms, while another leaned upon her knee, and gazed at the approaching stranger. The painter found here, in real life, what he had so long sought for in vain in the realms of his imagination; and quickly, with his chalk pencil, he sketched, upon the head of a wine-cask that stood near them, the lovely group, which afterwards, when brought into full perfection, became the transcendent Madonna della Seggiola."

"All this is true," replied Mr. Churchill, "but it gives me no consolation. I now despair of writing anything excellent. I have no time to devote to meditation and study. My life is given to others, and to this destiny I submit without a murmur; for I have the satisfaction of having labored faithfully in my calling, and of having perhaps trained and incited others to do what I shall never do. Life is still precious to me for its many uses, of which the writing of books is but one. I do not complain, but accept this destiny, and say, with that pleasant author, Marcus Antoninus, 'Whatever is agreeable to thee shall be agreeable to me, O graceful Universe! nothing shall be to me too early or too late, which is seasonable to thee! Whatever thy seasons bear shall be joyful fruit to me, O Nature! from thee are all things; in thee they subsist; to thee they return. Could one say, Thou dearly beloved city of Cecrops? and wilt thou not say, Thou dearly beloved city of God?' "

"Amen!" said Kavanagh. "And, to follow your quotation with another, 'The gale that blows from God we must endure, toiling but not repining.' "

Here Mrs. Churchill, who had something of Martha in her, as well as of Mary, and had left the room when the conversation took a literary turn, came back to announce that dinner was ready, and Kavanagh, though warmly urged to stay, took his leave, having first obtained from the Churchills the promise of a visit to Cecilia during the evening.

"Nothing done! nothing done!" exclaimed he, as he wended his way homeward, musing and meditating. "And shall all these lofty aspirations end in nothing? Shall the arms be thus stretched forth to encircle the universe, and come back empty against a bleeding, aching breast?"

And the words of the poet came into his mind, and he thought them worthy to be written in letters of gold, and placed above every door in every house, as a warning, a suggestion, an incitement:—

> Stay, stay the present instant!
> Imprint the marks of wisdom on its wings!
> Oh, let it not elude thy grasp, but like
> The good old patriarch upon record,
> Hold the fleet angel fast until he bless thee!

The Literary Spirit of Our Country

> The spirit of that day is still awake,
> And spreads itself, and shall not sleep again.
>
> *Bryant.*

I NEVER think of my native land without a feeling of pride in my national ancestry. Our government has passed the ordeal of time, and we have among us, neither the practical atheism of a papal hierarchy, nor that dangerous system of politics, which, in the days of Cardinal Richelieu, made France the terror of Europe. The same spirit that animated our fathers in their great struggle for freedom, still directs the popular mind to honourable enterprise, and whilst

> "Westward the star of empire takes its way,"

the star of mental light still looks cheerfully upon New England. There is throughout our territories a spirit of activity, that will insure success in every honourable undertaking; and this spirit has already directed itself to literature, with an energy that increases with the exercise. What will be done, may be predicted from what has already been done; and as national talent is gradually developed in the walks of literature, and unfolds itself in greater vigor and richness day after day, a national literature will be formed. Revolutions in letters are, indeed, the most gradual of all revolutions. A single day may decide the fate of an empire, the event of an hour sweep a throne from the earth, but years must elapse, ere any sensible changes can be introduced in literature. And yet in this the mind can proceed surely with its reasonings, whilst in the science of politics it will be led into constant error, by the uncertainty of political innovations;—for it is a principle well founded in nature, that those reasonings are most sure, whose subjects are not influenced by individual caprice, but move only with the motion of the popular mind.

Perhaps there never was a better field for the exercise of talent than our own country exhibits at the present day. Whilst there are here but few great minds wholly devoted to letters, the exertions of genius will be far more conspicuous and effectual, than when a larger multitude has gathered around our literary altars. It is not when many have come forth into the ripened harvest, that we are to look for great individual pre-eminence. But it is when competition is limited to the few gifted minds, that are willing to toil in difficult and untrodden paths. Then, if ever, must appear those men, who, like Homer and Shakspeare, will have no imitators; and who, like them, will never become models, that others would think of excelling, or hope to equal. I do not say, that this would advance to any great extent our national literature, nor even so far as it would be advanced by a more moderate, but a more universal excellence in our literary men;—for high excellence in one individual brings with it a hopelessness of success to others, and damps for a season the ardour of competition. But I venture nothing in the assertion, that the opportunity for eminent literary success, which our country now holds out to her sons, is such as can never be given them again. The rapid changes, which are every where going on in our occupations and circumstances as a nation, render this impossible. And when we observe how boldly our country is pressing on in the march of intellect, it is not too much to prophesy,—nay, the conclusion seems almost irresistible, that the nation, whose commerce is overshadowing every ocean with its sails, will ere long enlighten with its own literature, at least, the most distant places of its own territory.

If climate and natural scenery have a powerful influence in forming the intellectual character of a nation, our country has certainly much to hope from them. And that these influences are powerful, the known principles, which regulate the phenomena of mind, render sufficiently obvious. It cannot be, that the eye should always rest upon sublime and beautiful scenery, and thought be always familiar with the grand features of nature, and that we should not receive from such intercourse one deep and long continued impression.

So mind takes colour from the cloud, the storm,
  The ocean, and the torrent: where clear skies
Brighten and purple o'er an earth, whose form
  In the sweet dress of southern summer lies,
  Man drinks the beauty with his gladdened eyes,

And sends it out in music:—where the strand
  Sounds with the surging waves, that proudly rise
To meet the frowning clouds, the soul is manned
To mingle in their wrath and be as darkly grand.
Percival.

It is upon the poetic mind, where sensibility to natural beauty is more exquisite than elsewhere, that the influence of natural scenery is most evident; since it is through the medium of fancy and feeling, that this influence is exerted and felt. Poetry has been correctly defined the language of the imagination and the passions; and perhaps there is nothing which more awakens the former than the sublime in nature,—and nothing which more influences the latter, than the beautiful. And hence, whenever national peculiarities, and the civil and religious institutions of a people have introduced peculiar and appropriate modes of thought, and given an individual character to their poetry, the influence of climate and natural scenery become eminently obvious. Thus the sunny hills and purple vineyards of Italy and South France have given a character of delicate beauty to their poetry, and the wild scenery and severer climate of Scotland have breathed a tone of high sublimity into the writings of its bards. In our own country nature has exhibited her works upon the most beautiful and magnificent scale. And this vast theatre, where she has so finely mingled and varied her scenery, is the school in which the genius of our country is to be trained. As the eye scans the open volume of nature, the lessons that it reads there, pass into the mind; and thus we receive those gradual impressions, which go so far to form the mental character. The sentiments with which nature inspires us—those hallowed and associated feelings—we cherish and revere through life. And it is by this intercourse and long familiarity, that our native scenery comes to exert so strong an influence upon the mind, and that the features of intellect are moulded after those of nature.

It has been often urged against the advancement of a national literature in our country, that America is not classic ground; and that we are not rich in those fine classic allusions, which mould the poetic mind to its most perfect beauty, and give to genius the materials for superior exertion. But this is an objection, to which more weight is given than in reality belongs to it. Those nations that are rich in poetic associations, are not always rich in poetic minds. The Grecian monuments, ancient as they are,—whatever enthusiasm they may have awakened, have never breathed inspiration over the lyres of modern Greeks. And the wandering Improvisatori of Florence and Naples have done little for modern literature in classic Italy. But if the natural scenery of our country, where nature exhibits such various beauty and sublimity, can give strength and vigor to intellect, and with them unite poetic feeling, the lapse of another century will give to us those rich associations, which it is said are now wanting, and will make America in some degree a classic land. Time, indeed, has already hallowed those places of our territory where the people of an ancient race, that has long since ceased to be, have left "a record in the desert;" and the tumuli, that hold their mouldering bones, are mementos of those men, who once peopled our western forests. As population advances westward, the plough-share turns up the wasted skeleton; and happy villages arise upon the sites of unknown burial-places. And when our native Indians, who are fast perishing from the earth, shall have left forever the borders of our wide lakes and rivers, and their villages have decayed within the bosoms of our western hills, the dim light of tradition will rest upon those places, which have seen the glory of their battles, and heard the voice of their eloquence;—and our land will become, indeed, a classic ground.

Perhaps the chief cause which has retarded the progress of poetry in America, is the want of that exclusive cultivation, which so noble a branch of literature would seem to require. Few here think of relying upon the exertion of poetic talent for a livelihood, and of making literature the profession of life. The bar or the pulpit claims the greater part of the scholar's existence, and poetry is made its pastime. This is a defect, which the hand of honourable patronage alone can remedy. I believe it is a remark of Roscoe, that there is no intellectual occupation, which requires such high, peculiar, and exclusive qualifications as the labours of the poet. But we fail in their acquisition, through the want of a rich and abundant patronage. It is the fear of poverty that deters many gifted and poetic minds from coming forward into the arena, and wiping away all reproach from our literature. When the scholar can go on his way prosperous and rejoicing, and poetry no longer holds with us a "bootless reed;" minds of the finest mould will be active to invigorate our literature, and to honour the country, which in its turn shall honour them. Added to this circumstance, so injurious to our literature, is the wide influence which English belles-lettres and poetry exert within our land. The delicately finished model of English taste has always been the model by which we have fashioned our writings; and perhaps it is well, that it must for a time continue to be so. But let our admiration for the excellent literary taste of England stop in the imitation;—at least, let us not cherish it to our own injury and the neglect of our own literature. Let us not esteem our native writers the less, because they are native, nor set too high a value upon those things, whose chief value is, that they came from the classic land of England. But while we admire the exertions of foreign intellect, let us cherish more tenderly that spirit of literature, which belongs to us, and entertain a cheerful and honourable pride in having already done so much as we have done.

THE LAY MONK.

Table-Talk

If you borrow my books, do not mark them; for I shall not be able to distinguish your marks from my own, and the pages will become like the doors in Bagdad marked by Morgiana's chalk.

Don Quixote thought he could have made beautiful bird-cages and toothpicks if his brain had not been so full of ideas of chivalry. Most people would succeed in small things, if they were not troubled with great ambitions.

A torn jacket is soon mended; but hard words bruise the heart of a child.

Authors, in their Prefaces, generally speak in a conciliatory, deprecating tone of the critics, whom they hate and fear; as of old the Greeks spake of the Furies as the Eumenides, the benign Goddesses.

Doubtless criticism was originally benignant, pointing out the beauties of a work, rather than its defects. The passions of men have made it malignant, as the bad heart of Procrustes turned the bed, the symbol of repose, into an instrument of torture.

Popularity is only, in legal phrase, the "instantaneous seisin" of fame.

The Mormons make the marriage ring, like the ring of Saturn, fluid, not solid, and keep it in its place by numerous satellites.

In the mouths of many men soft words are like roses that soldiers put into the muzzles of their muskets on holidays.

We often excuse our own want of philanthropy by giving the name of fanaticism to the more ardent zeal of others.

Every great poem is in itself limited by necessity,—but in its suggestions unlimited and infinite.

If we could read the secret history of our enemies, we should find in each man's life sorrow and suffering enough to disarm all hostility.

As turning the logs will make a dull fire burn, so change of studies a dull brain.

The Laws of Nature are just, but terrible. There is no weak mercy in them. Cause and consequence are inseparable and inevitable. The elements have no forbearance. The fire burns, the water drowns, the air consumes, the earth buries. And perhaps it would be well for our race if the punishment of crimes against the Laws of Man were as inevitable as the punishment of crimes against the Laws of Nature,—were Man as unerring in his judgments as Nature.

Round about what is, lies a whole mysterious world of might be,—a psychological romance of possibilities and things that do not happen. By going out a few minutes sooner or later, by stopping to speak with a friend at a corner, by meeting this man or that, or by turning down this street instead of the other, we may let slip some great occasion of good, or avoid some impending evil, by which the whole current of our lives would have been changed. There is no possible solution to the dark enigma but the one word, "Providence."

The Helicon of too many poets is not a hill crowned with sunshine and visited by the Muses and the Graces, but an old, mouldering house, full of gloom and haunted by ghosts.

"Let us build such a church, that those who come after us shall take us for madmen," said the old canon of Seville, when the great cathedral was planned. Perhaps through every mind passes some such thought, when it first entertains the design of a great and seemingly impossible action, the end of which it dimly foresees. This divine madness enters more or less into all our noblest undertakings.

I feel a kind of reverence for the first books of young authors. There is so much aspiration in them, so much audacious hope and trembling fear, so much of the heart's history, that all errors and short-comings are for a while lost sight of in the amiable self-assertion of youth.

Authors have a greater right than any copyright, though it is generally unacknowledged or disregarded. They have a right to the reader's civility. There are favorable hours for reading a book, as for writing it, and to these the author has a claim. Yet many people think that when they buy a book they buy with it the right to abuse the author.

A thought often makes us hotter than a fire.

Black seals upon letters, like the black sails of the Greeks, are signs of bad tidings and ill success.

Love makes its record in deeper colors as we grow out of childhood into manhood; as the Emperors signed their names in green ink when under age, but when of age, in purple.

Some critics are like chimney-sweepers; they put out the fire below, or frighten the swallows from their nests above; they scrape a long time in the chimney, cover themselves with soot, and bring nothing away but a bag of cinders, and then sing from the top of the house as if they had built it.

When we reflect that all the aspects of Nature, all the emotions of the soul, and all the events of life, have been the subjects of poetry for hundreds and thousands of years, we can hardly wonder that there should be so many resemblances and coincidences of expression among poets, but rather that they are not more numerous and more striking.

The first pressure of sorrow crushes out from our hearts the best wine; afterwards the constant weight of it brings forth bitterness,—the taste and stain from the lees of the vat.

The tragic element in poetry is like Saturn in alchemy,—the Malevolent, the Destroyer of Nature; but without it no true Aurum Potabile, or Elixir of Life, can be made.

Address on the Death of Washington Irving

Delivered to the Massachusetts Historical Society
December 15, 1859

EVERY reader has his first book. I mean to say, one book among all others, which in early youth first fascinates his imagination, and at once excites and satisfies the desires of his mind. To me this first book was the *Sketch Book* of Washington Irving. I was a school-boy when it was published, and read each succeeding number with ever-increasing wonder and delight; spell-bound by its pleasant humor, its melancholy tenderness, its atmosphere of reverie, nay, even by its gray-brown covers, the shaded letters of the titles, and the fair, clear type, which seemed an outward symbol of the style.

How many delightful books the same author has given us, written before and since—volumes of history and fiction, most of which illustrate his native land, and some of which illumine it, and make the Hudson, I will not say as classic, but as romantic as the Rhine! Yet still the charm of the *Sketch Book* remains unbroken: the old fascination still lingers about it; and whenever I open its pages, I open also that mysterious door which leads back into the haunted chambers of youth.

Many years afterwards, I had the pleasure of meeting Mr. Irving in Spain, and found the author, whom I had loved, repeated in the man. The same playful humor; the same touches of sentiment; the same poetic atmosphere; and, what I admired still more, the entire absence of all literary jealousy, of all that mean avarice of fame, which counts what is given to another as so much taken from one's self—

> "And rustling hears in every breeze,
> The laurels of Miltiades."

At this time Mr. Irving was at Madrid, engaged upon his *Life of Columbus*; and if the work itself did not bear ample testimony to his zealous and conscientious labor, I could do so from personal observation. He seemed to be always at work. "Sit down," he would say; "I will talk with you in a moment, but I must first finish this sentence."

One summer morning, passing his house at the early hour of six, I saw his study window already wide open. On my mentioning it to him afterwards, he said: "Yes, I am always at my work as early as six." Since then I have often remembered that sunny morning and that open window, so suggestive of his sunny temperament and his open heart, and equally so of his patient and persistent toil; and have recalled those striking words of Dante:

"Seggendo in piuma,
In fama non si vien, ne sotto coltre:
Senza la qual chi sua vita consuma,
Cotal vestigio in terra di se lascia,
Qual fumo in aere, od in acqua la schiuma."

"Seated upon down,
Or in his bed, man cometh not to fame,
Withouten which, whoso his life consumes,
Such vestige of himself on earth shall leave,
As smoke in air, and in the water foam."

Remembering these things, I esteem it a great though a melancholy privilege, to lay upon his hearse the passing tribute of these resolutions:

Resolved, That while we deeply deplore the death of our friend and associate, Washington Irving, we rejoice in the completeness of his life and labors, which, closing together, have left behind them so sweet a fame, and a memory so precious.

Resolved, That we feel a just pride in his renown as an author, not forgetting that, to his other claims upon our gratitude, he adds also that of having been the first to win for our country an honourable name and position in the History of Letters.

Resolved, That we hold in affectionate remembrance the noble example of his long literary career, extending through half a century of unremitted labors, graced with all the amenities of authorship, and marred by none of its discords and contentions.

Resolved, That as members of this Historical Society, we regard with especial honor and admiration, his Lives of Columbus, the Discoverer, and of Washington, the Father of our Country.

Resolved, That a copy of these resolutions be transmitted to his family, with the expression of our deepest and sincere sympathy.

CHRONOLOGY

NOTE ON THE TEXTS

NOTES

INDEX OF TITLES AND FIRST LINES

Chronology

1807 Henry Wadsworth Longfellow born February 27 in Portland, Maine, second child of Stephen Longfellow and Zilpah Wadsworth Longfellow, and named after uncle Henry Wadsworth, a naval officer who was killed at age 19 fighting the Tripoli pirates in 1804. (Father, born 1776, graduated from Harvard, where he was a classmate of William Ellery Channing, then read law and was admitted to the bar in 1801; he would later serve for one term in Congress, 1823–25. Mother, born 1778, is a daughter of Peleg Wadsworth, a descendant of the Pilgrims John Alden and Priscilla Mullens who served as a general in the Massachusetts militia during the Revolution and as a congressman, 1793–1807. Parents married on January 1, 1804; their first child, Stephen, was born in 1805.)

1808 Sister Elizabeth born.

1810 Sister Anne born.

1813 Begins attending Portland Academy. Spends summers at his paternal grandfather's farm in Gorham and his maternal grandfather's estate in Hiram. Attends Unitarian services with his family.

1814 Brother Alexander born.

1816 Sister Mary born.

1818 Sister Ellen born.

1819 Brother Samuel born.

1820 First published poem appears in the *Portland Gazette* on November 17. Early reading includes Shakespeare, Milton, Pope, Goldsmith, Cowper, Johnson, Gibbon, and Ossian.

1821 Enrolled at Bowdoin College in Brunswick, Maine, but remains at home for his first year because of his youth.

1822 Takes up residence at college with his brother Stephen; classmates include Nathaniel Hawthorne.

1823–25 Publishes poetry and prose. Writes to his father during his senior year: "I most eagerly aspire after future eminence in literature, my whole soul burns most ardently for it, and every earthly thought centres on it." Delivers oration "Our Native Writers" at his commencement in September 1825. Bowdoin offers him its newly established professorship of modern languages on condition that he travel in Europe to prepare himself for the position.

1826 Sails in April for France, where he reads, studies, attends lectures and the theater, and takes lessons in Italian. Visits Rouen, Auteuil, Limoges, and Bordeaux, and undertakes long walking tour of the Loire Valley. Meets in Paris with the Marquis de Lafayette, a friend of his father.

1827 Moves to Madrid in March. Studies Spanish and spends time with Washington Irving, whom he has admired since childhood. Travels to Segovia, La Mancha, Cordova, Seville, Cadiz, and Granada. Meets George Washington Greene in Marseilles, beginning lifelong friendship. Arrives in Italy on December 24.

1828 Settles in Florence; visits Rome, Naples, and Venice. Writes father in December that he is now fluent in French, Spanish, and Italian, and can read Portuguese.

1829 Travels to Vienna, Prague, Dresden, and Göttingen, where he attends lectures at the university and begins work on "a kind of Sketch-Book of scenes in France, Spain and Italy." Sister Elizabeth dies on May 5. Homesick, Longfellow sails for America in July. Takes up his duties at Bowdoin in September, teaching French and Spanish and serving as college librarian.

1830–31 Lectures on French, Spanish, and Italian literature; translates and edits French, Spanish, and Italian textbooks for use by his students. Publishes scholarly articles in *The North American Review,* but writes little poetry. Feeling isolated in rural Brunswick, returns often to Portland. Marries Mary Storer Potter, age 19, a neighbor in Portland and daughter of Judge Barrett Potter, on September 14, 1831.

1832 Begins lecturing on the literary history of the Middle Ages. Writes poem "The Past and the Present" and delivers it at the college commencement in September. Sister Anne marries George Washington Pierce, his friend and Bowdoin classmate, on November 26.

1833 Publishes translation of *Coplas por la muerte de su padre* by 15th-century Spanish poet Jorge Manrique.

1834 Sister Ellen dies on August 12. Longfellow accepts offer from Josiah Quincy, president of Harvard, to become its Smith Professor of Modern Languages. Plans new trip to Europe to improve his German.

1835 *Outre-Mer: A Pilgrimage beyond the Sea,* collection of travel sketches, published anonymously in New York and London. Sails for England in April with his wife and her friends Mary Caroline Goddard and Clara Crowninshield. Calls on Thomas Carlyle, then travels to Hamburg, Copenhagen, and Stockholm. Studies Swedish and Finnish, reads Esaias Tegnér's heroic poem *Frithiofs Saga,* and visits the University of Upsala. Returns to Copenhagen, where he studies Danish and Old Icelandic, then travels to Amsterdam to study Dutch. Mary Longfellow suffers miscarriage on October 5 and dies from an infection in Rotterdam on November 29. Longfellow, Goddard, and Crowninshield travel to Heidelberg, where he forms friendship with William Cullen Bryant. Receives letter on December 24 telling him of the death of his brother-in-law George Washington Pierce.

1836 Writes in letter on January 10: "I have a void in my heart—a constant feeling of sorrow and bereavement, and utter loneliness . . ." Reads Goethe, Tieck, Brentano, Hoffmann, and Richter. Tours southern Germany, the Tyrol, and Switzerland during summer months; shares coach from Munich to Salzburg with poet and playwright Franz Grillparzer. Meets wealthy Boston merchant Nathan Appleton, his son Tom, daughters Frances Elizabeth (Fanny) and Mary, and nephew William, and travels with them from Interlaken to Lucerne, Zürich, and Schaffhausen, where William Appleton dies of consumption. Falls in love with 19-year-old Fanny Appleton, who initially rejects him. Returns to America in the fall. Takes rooms in Cambridge on Kirkland Street, near the Harvard campus. Meets Charles Sumner, then an instructor at Harvard Law School, who becomes a lifelong friend. Prepares courses on medieval and modern European literature.

1837 Longfellow, Sumner, Cornelius Felton, George Hillard, and Henry Cleveland form deep mutual friendship, and eventually call themselves "The Five of Clubs." Begins teaching in May. Publishes "Hawthorne's *Twice Told Tales*" and "Tegnér's *Frithiofs Saga*" in *The North American Review*. Tours the White Mountains during summer. Takes rooms in Craigie House on Brattle Street.

1838 Writes "A Psalm of Life" in July. Lectures at Harvard on Dante, Goethe, and "The Lives of Literary Men." Begins work in September on *Hyperion*.

1839 *Hyperion, A Romance,* published in two volumes in August; its thinly disguised version of their meeting at Interlaken embarrasses Fanny Appleton, prolonging her rejection of his marriage proposal. Sister Mary marries James Greenleaf on October 22. Publishes *Voices of the Night* in December; Hawthorne writes: "I read your poems over and over, and over again. . . . Nothing equal to some of them was ever written in this world."

1840–41 Lectures in January 1840 on Dante and Jean Paul at the Mercantile Library Association in New York. Begins writing ballads, including "The Skeleton in Armor" and "The Wreck of the Hesperus." Lectures on Spanish drama and begins work on verse play *The Spanish Student*. *Voices of the Night* goes into its fifth printing by April 1841. Spends summer in coastal town of Nahant, Massachusetts. Conceives of poem treating aspects of Christianity in the apostolic, middle, and modern ages (eventually published as *Christus*). *Ballads and Other Poems* published in December 1841; Edgar Allan Poe attacks it, charging plagiarism and insisting that Longfellow's "conception of the *aim* of poetry *is all wrong*."

1842 Spends time with Charles Dickens in Boston. Suffering from nervousness and deteriorating health, obtains six-month leave of absence to take the "water-cure" at

Marienberg. Sails for Europe in April and travels through Paris, Antwerp, Ghent, Bruges, and Cologne on his way to Marienberg, where he stays from June to September. Befriends German poet Ferdinand Freiligrath, who later becomes his translator. Visits Charles Dickens in London in October; dines with Walter Savage Landor. Impressed by chapter on slavery in Dickens's *American Notes.* Returns to America in November and publishes *Poems on Slavery,* composed during return voyage, in December.

1843 *The Spanish Student* published in May 1843. Marries Fanny Appleton on July 13. After they return from their wedding journey in the Catskills and the Berkshires, Nathan Appleton purchases Craigie House for them.

1844 Suffers eye trouble that severely restricts reading and writing. Son Charles Appleton Longfellow born June 9. John Greenleaf Whittier, impressed by *Poems on Slavery,* asks Longfellow to run for Congress as Liberty Party candidate, but he declines, writing: "At all times I shall rejoice in the progress of true liberty, and in freedom from slavery of all kinds; but I cannot for a moment think of entering the political arena." *The Waif,* an anthology of favorite poems by other poets, published in December.

1845 Publishes anthology *The Poets and Poetry of Europe* in June and *Poems,* an illustrated collection of his own work, in November. Son Ernest Wadsworth Longfellow born November 23. *The Belfry of Bruges and Other Poems* published in December. Attends lectures by Emerson. Following a suggestion from Hawthorne, works on "Gabrielle," a poem in hexameters eventually titled *Evangeline.* Writes in his journal on December 31: "Peace to the embers of burnt-out things; fears, anxieties, doubts, all gone! I see them now as a thin blue smoke, hanging in the bright heaven of the past year, vanishing away into utter nothingness. Not many hopes deceived, not many illusions scattered, not many anticipations disappointed; but love fulfilled, the heart comforted, the soul enriched with affection!"

1846 Spends summer with family in Portland and Pittsfield, Massachusetts, where he visits Hawthorne. Anthology *The Estray,* a companion to *The Waif,* published in December.

1847 Completes *Evangeline* in February and begins work on novel *Kavanagh.* Lectures on Molière and Dante. Daughter Fanny Longfellow born April 7. *Evangeline, A Tale of Acadie* is published November 1; the book goes through six printings in three months.

1848 Daughter Fanny dies on September 11.

1849 Meets young Ojibway writer Kah-ge-ga-gah-bowh (also known as George Copway). *Kavanagh* published in May and praised by Emerson. Father dies on August 3. After learning of the death in October of Edgar Allan Poe, Longfellow writes: "The harshness of his criticisms I have never attributed to anything but the irritation of a sensitive nature chafed by some indefinite sense of wrong." *The Seaside and the Fireside,* collection of his poetry, published in December.

1850 Criticizes Daniel Webster's speech on March 7 in defense of Fugitive Slave Law. In May visits New York, Philadelphia, and Washington, where he has dinner with President Zachary Taylor and meets with Webster and Henry Clay. Spends summer with family in Nahant (will return there for almost every subsequent summer). Lectures at Harvard on Dante, Petrarch, Boccaccio, and Tasso; attends lectures on geology given by Louis Agassiz. Dismayed by passage of the Fugitive Slave Law. Brother Stephen dies on September 19. Daughter Alice Mary born September 22. Hears Jenny Lind sing—"like the morning star; clear, liquid, heavenly sounds"—and calls on her. Given deed to Oxbow Farm near Stockbridge, Massachusetts, by Nathan Appleton in October.

1851 Mother dies on March 12. Charles Sumner is elected to the U.S. Senate on April 24. Longfellow lectures on Dante and Goethe and attends recitals by Jenny Lind and lectures by Emerson. *The Golden Legend* published in November.

1852 Meets exiled Hungarian leader Lajos Kossuth in May. Spends summer in Newport, Rhode Island, with his family and his brother-in-law Thomas Gold Appleton, Julia Ward Howe, George William Curtis, and others; visits Newport's Jewish cemetery. Becomes friends with English poet Arthur Hugh Clough in November. Begins collecting occasional prose for *Driftwood,* a volume that is partially printed but never published. Attends lecture by William Makepeace Thackeray and has dinner with him in December.

1853 Resumes translation of Dante's *Purgatorio,* which he had set aside in 1843, on February 1. Meets Harriet Beecher Stowe. Completes translation of the *Purgatorio* on February 27, his 46th birthday. Gives a farewell dinner on June 13 for Hawthorne on his departure for England; guests include Emerson, Clough, James Russell Lowell, and Charles Eliot Norton. Suffers from neuralgia, eye problems, and fatigue. Daughter Edith born October 22. Writes in his journal: "How barren of all poetic production, and even prose production, this last year has been! For 1853 I have absolutely nothing to show."

1854 Resigns from Harvard on February 16 and delivers his last lecture on April 19. Reads Finnish epic, the *Kalevala.* Begins work on *The Song of Hiawatha* on June 25.

1855 Sees French actress Rachel—"a great actress; the best I ever saw"—in series of French dramas in October. Daughter Anne Allegra born November 8. *The Song of Hiawatha* published to great acclaim on November 10.

1856 In response to a suggestion by German poet Emmanuel Scherb that he write a poem about Puritans and Quakers, Longfellow begins prose tragedy "The Old Colony" in April (later called "Wenlock Christison," and eventually published as "John Endicott" in *The New England Tragedies*). Sumner is severely caned on the Senate floor by South Carolina congressman Preston Brooks on May 22, two days after delivering a lengthy antislavery speech. Longfellow participates in public protest meeting in Boston on May 24, and writes to Sumner praising his speech as "the greatest voice, on the greatest subject, that has been uttered since we became a nation."

1857 Records in his journal on March 31 the number of copies sold of his books: *Voices of the Night,* 43,500; *Ballads and Other Poems,* 40,470; *The Spanish Student;* 38,400; *The Belfry of Bruges,* 38,300; *Evangeline,* 35,850; *Seaside and*

Fireside, 30,000; *The Golden Legend,* 17,188; *The Song of Hiawatha,* 50,000; *Outre-Mer,* 7,500; *Hyperion,* 14,550; *Kavanagh,* 10,500. Joins the Saturday Club, literary group whose members include Emerson, James Russell Lowell, and Oliver Wendell Holmes, in May.

1858 *The Courtship of Miles Standish and Other Poems* is published on October 16; it sells 25,000 copies in two months, and in London 10,000 copies the first day.

1859 Awarded honorary LL.D. from Harvard in July. Writes in his journal on December 2: "This will be a great day in our history; the date of a new Revolution—quite as much needed as the old one. Even now as I write, they are leading old John Brown to execution in Virginia for attempting to rescue slaves! This is sowing the wind to reap the whirlwind, which will come soon."

1860 Attends several readings from Shakespeare's plays by Fanny Kemble and hears Adelina Patti sing at the opera. Begins "Paul Revere's Ride" on April 6. Meets Edward, Prince of Wales, on October 18. Writes in journal after Lincoln wins presidential election: "It is the redemption of the country. Freedom is triumphant." Buys Wetmore Cottage in Nahant with Thomas Gold Appleton in December.

1861 Follows secession crisis and outbreak of the Civil War, writing in his journal on April 23: "Weary days with wars and rumors of wars, and marching of troops, and flags waving and people talking. No reading but reading of newspapers." On July 9 Fanny accidentally sets her light summer dress on fire at Craigie House while using hot wax to seal a package containing curls she had just cut from her daughters Edith and Anne Allegra; she runs from the library into Longfellow's adjoining study, where he tries to extinguish the flames by wrapping her in a rug. Fanny dies on the morning of July 10 and is buried in Mount Auburn Cemetery July 13; Longfellow is unable to attend the funeral because of his own serious burns. Father-in-law Nathan Appleton dies on July 14. Longfellow writes to his sister-in-law Mary Appleton Macintosh on August 18: "How I am alive after what my eyes have seen, I know not. I am at least patient, if not resigned; and thank God hourly—as I have from the beginning—for the beautiful life we led together, and that I loved her more and more to the end. . . . I never looked at her without a thrill of pleasure; she never came into a room where I was without my heart beating quicker, nor went out without my feeling that something of the light went with her. I loved her so entirely, and I know she was very happy." Grows a beard when his burns prevent him from shaving.

1862 Writes in his journal on January 16: "So one after another the heavy days are rolled over the horizon and disappear in the abyss." Resumes translation of Dante's *Paradiso.* Visits Niagara Falls, Toronto, and Montreal with his sons and mother-in-law, Harriot Appleton, in June. Works on *Tales of a Wayside Inn.*

1863 On January 9 writes in his journal: "Very dark and dreary within me. I am ashamed to lead so useless and listless a life." Son Charles runs away to northern Virginia and joins First Massachusetts Cavalry. Longfellow begins translation of the *Inferno* on March 14 and finishes it on April 16. *Tales of a Wayside Inn* published in November. After Charles is seriously wounded in skirmish near New Hope Church, Virginia, on November 27, Longfellow and his son Ernest travel to Washington and bring him back to Cambridge to recover.

1864 Charles is discharged from the army in February. Longfellow attends the funeral of Nathaniel Hawthorne in Concord on May 23. Visited regularly by Charles Sumner, James Russell Lowell, Louis Agassiz, and Richard Henry Dana.

1865 First volume of his translation of *The Divine Comedy of Dante Alighieri* is privately issued in February. Founds the Dante Club with Lowell and Charles Eliot Norton in October to help with final revisions of his translation.

1866 *Flower-de-Luce* published in November.

1867 *The Divine Comedy of Dante Alighieri* published in three volumes, April–June. Sells Oxbow Farm in September.

Sees Charles Dickens during his visit to Boston in November.

1868 Son Ernest marries Harriet Spelman on May 21. Longfellow sails to England on May 27 with his five children, his daughter-in-law, his brother Samuel and sisters Anne and Mary, his brother-in-law Thomas Gold Appleton, and the family governess, Hannah Davie. Receives honorary LL.D. from Cambridge University on June 16. Visits with William Gladstone, Edward, Prince of Wales, Dickens, and Alfred Lord Tennyson, and calls on Queen Victoria at Windsor Castle. Leaves England in late July and travels through France, Belgium, Germany, Switzerland, and Italy. *The New England Tragedies* published in October. Longfellow arrives in Rome in late December.

1869 Meets Franz Liszt and hears him play. Leaves Rome in late February and travels to Naples, Florence, Venice, Innsbruck, Nuremberg, Dresden, and Paris, where he visits Sainte-Beuve and John Ruskin. Continues on to London and Edinburgh and receives honorary D.C.L. from Oxford University on July 27. Sails from England August 21 and arrives in Cambridge on September 1.

1870 Begins second series of Wayside Inn tales in January. Saddened by the death of Dickens on June 9. Begins work on *The Divine Tragedy* in November.

1871 Revised edition of *The Poets and Poetry of Europe* published in March. Dines with President Ulysses S. Grant in October. *The Divine Tragedy* published in December.

1872 *Three Books of Song* published in May. *Christus: A Mystery* published in September.

1873 *Aftermath* published in September.

1874 Sells poem "The Hanging of the Crane" for $3,000 to the New York *Ledger* in February. Charles Sumner dies on March 11; Longfellow serves as pallbearer at funeral in Boston and as a literary trustee for the estate (will help arrange publication of authorized four-volume biography by Edward L. Pierce). Begins work in May on *Poems of*

1825. Of the poems printed in this volume, only "The Spirit of Poetry," composed in 1825, was written before 1838. It was later published in *The Voices of the Night* (1839), Longfellow's first volume of poems, which also included "Hymn to the Night," "A Psalm of Life," "The Light of Stars," and "Footsteps of Angels," written in 1838 or 1839. "The Skeleton in Armor," "The Wreck of the Hesperus," "The Village Blacksmith," "It Is Not Always May," "The Rainy Day," "God's-Acre," "To the River Charles," "The Goblet of Life," and "Excelsior," poems written between December 1839 and November 1841, were published in *Ballads and Other Poems* (1842). Longfellow wrote "The Slave's Dream," "The Slave Singing at Midnight," "The Witnesses," and "The Warning" at sea in November 1842, while returning from Europe on board the *Great Western.* These poems were published with four other antislavery poems the following month in *Poems on Slavery.*

Poems, published in Philadelphia by Carey and Hart in November 1845, was the first collected edition of Longfellow's poetry. It reprinted *The Voices of the Night* and *Ballads and Other Poems* but also contained poems not previously published in book form: "A Gleam of Sunshine," "The Arsenal at Springfield," "Rain in Summer," "The Occultation of Orion," "The Bridge," "To the Driving Cloud," "Afternoon in February," and "Curfew." These poems appeared the following month in *The Belfry of Bruges and Other Poems* (1845), a volume that also included "The Day Is Done," which had been published as the "Proem" to *The Waif* (Cambridge: John Owen, 1845), an anthology edited by Longfellow. *Poems* was also the first book publication of "Seaweed," later collected in *The Seaside and the Fireside* (1850). *Poems* did not include poems from *Poems on Slavery.*

"Autumn," "Dante," "The Evening Star," "The Old Clock on the Stairs," "To a Child," and "The Arrow and the Song" were first published in book form in *The Belfry of Bruges and Other Poems* (1845), which collected poems written between 1842 and 1845.

Longfellow first heard the legend that he adapted for *Evangeline: A Tale of Acadie* from the Reverend Horace Conolly, an acquaintance of Hawthorne's, in 1840 or 1841. Conolly, who had previously told Hawthorne the story, repeated it while visiting Longfellow in Cambridge with Hawthorne. According to Longfellow's account of the conversation, he then asked Hawthorne, "If you have really made up your mind not to use it for a story, will you give it to me for a poem?" Hawthorne agreed and did not mention the legend in his "The Removal of the Inhabitants of Acadia," published in *Famous Old People: Being the Second Epoch of Grandfather's Chair* (1841).

Places, an anthology that will eventually be published in 31 volumes.

1875 Suffers from neuralgia, headaches, and insomnia. Reads "Morituri Salutamus," poem on the 50th anniversary of the Class of 1825, at Bowdoin College commencement in July. Visited by Anthony Trollope in October. *The Masque of Pandora and Other Poems* published in October.

1876 Visits Centennial Exhibition in Philadelphia and meets Walt Whitman in Camden, New Jersey. First eight volumes of *Poems of Places* published (remaining 23 volumes appear 1877–79).

1877 Longfellow's 70th birthday is occasion for widespread celebration. Attends 70th birthday dinner for John Greenleaf Whittier.

1878 Daughter Edith marries Richard Henry Dana II on January 10. *Kéramos and Other Poems* published in April.

1879 Receives "Village Blacksmith" armchair, carved from chestnut tree memorialized in the poem, from Cambridge schoolchildren on his birthday, February 27. Grandchild Richard Henry Dana III born on September 1.

1880 *Ultima Thule* published in September.

1881 Grandchild Henry Wadsworth Longfellow Dana born January 26. James T. Fields, Longfellow's longtime publisher and friend, dies April 24. Writes in his journal that he is confined to his room from October to December by "a violent attack of vertigo, followed by nervous prostration."

1882 Visited in January by Oscar Wilde. Falls ill with peritonitis on March 17 and dies at home on March 24. Buried at Mount Auburn Cemetery in Cambridge on March 26 following a family funeral service at Craigie House.

Note on the Texts

This volume contains 127 poems and 15 translations of poems published by Henry Wadsworth Longfellow during his lifetime; selections from the long poem *Christus: A Mystery,* first published in 1871; and two poems and selections from the verse drama *Michael Angelo* that were left in manuscript at the time of Longfellow's death in 1882. Following the poems, this volume presents Longfellow's novel *Kavanagh, A Tale* (1849), and three essays composed between 1825 and 1859.

Many of Longfellow's poems were first published in magazines, anthologies, and gift-book editions. If Longfellow revised his poems after their first publication, he would usually do so when preparing one of his own volumes. Longfellow published 12 gatherings of new poetry and five book-length poems between 1839 and 1880: *The Voices of the Night* (Cambridge: John Owen, 1839); *Ballads and Other Poems* (Cambridge: John Owen, 1842); *Poems on Slavery* (Cambridge: John Owen, 1842); *The Belfry of Bruges and Other Poems* (Cambridge: John Owen, 1845); *Evangeline: A Tale of Acadie* (Boston: William D. Ticknor, 1847); *The Seaside and the Fireside* (Boston: Ticknor, Reed and Fields, 1850); *The Golden Legend* (Boston: Ticknor, Reed and Fields, 1851); *The Song of Hiawatha* (Boston: Ticknor and Fields, 1855); *The Courtship of Miles Standish and Other Poems* (Boston: Ticknor and Fields, 1858); *Tales of a Wayside Inn* (Boston: Ticknor and Fields, 1863); *Flower-de-Luce* (Boston: Ticknor and Fields, 1866); *The New England Tragedies* (Boston: Ticknor and Fields, 1868); *The Divine Tragedy* (Boston: James R. Osgood, 1871); *Aftermath* (Boston: James R. Osgood, 1873); *The Masque of Pandora and Other Poems* (Boston: James R. Osgood, 1875); *Kéramos and Other Poems* (Boston: Houghton, Osgood and Company, 1878); and *Ultima Thule* (Boston: Houghton, Mifflin and Company, 1880). *The Golden Legend, The New England Tragedies,* and *The Divine Tragedies* were collected as a single work in *Christus: A Mystery* (Boston: James R. Osgood, 1871). A posthumously published volume, *In the Harbor* (Boston: Houghton, Mifflin and Company, 1882), collected Longfellow's late poems, most of which had previously appeared in periodicals.

In addition to these volumes, Longfellow's poems were reprinted, and in some instances published for the first time in book form, in collected editions, such as *Poems* (Philadelphia: Carey and Hart,

1845); *Poems* (Boston: Ticknor and Fields, 1857), the "Blue and Gold" edition; *Household Poems* (Boston: Ticknor & Fields, 1865); *Poetical Works* (Boston: Ticknor & Fields, 1866); *Three Books of Song* (Boston: Ticknor and Fields, 1872); *The Complete Poetical Works of Henry Wadsworth Longfellow* (Boston: Ticknor & Fields, 1873); *Poetical Works* (Boston: James R. Osgood, 1874), the "Household" edition; and *Complete Poetical Works* (Boston: James R. Osgood and Co., 1876), the "Centennial" edition. Most of these collected editions reprinted all of Longfellow's poetry that had been published up to their time of publication.

There are often variations in wording and punctuation among different editions of Longfellow's poetry; there are also variations among different printings of specific editions. Some of these variations are simply corrections of error, but others are Longfellow's revisions, though he did not revise poems extensively once they had appeared in book form. For example, the version of "The Landlord's Tale: Paul Revere's Ride" that appears in *Tales of a Wayside Inn* (1863) differs from the version published in the 1866 *Poetical Works* in three places: line 31, "Then he climbed to the tower of the church" is revised to "Then he climbed the tower of the Old North Church," and "Up" is changed to "By" at lines 32 and 37. The 1866 version was then reprinted in subsequent collected editions of Longfellow's poetry. These changes are typical of the sorts of revisions made to the poems in collected editions, when any were made at all. In the case of his translations, Longfellow would sometimes make revisions because of new scholarship. When preparing his collection *The Poets and Poetry of Europe* in 1844, a book that included several of his translations, Longfellow wrote to Carey and Hart, his publishers, that he would be "interested in future editions and would make the improvements and additions from time to time which will be required to keep the book up to the level of the new translations, which are constantly appearing."

Shortly after Longfellow's death, Horace E. Scudder edited and published *Works* (Boston: Houghton, Mifflin and Co., 1886), an 11-volume edition that collected Longfellow's original poems, translations, and prose works. In addition to the poems already published, it also included poems that were in manuscript at the time of Longfellow's death. The texts of this "Riverside" edition incorporate Longfellow's final revisions; therefore the texts of all poems printed in the present volume are taken from the 1886 "Riverside" edition.

Although he published more than 30 poems in newspapers and magazines while an undergraduate at Bowdoin, Longfellow wrote few original poems in the eleven years following his graduation in

Hawthorne sent Longfellow a copy of *Famous Old People* early in 1841; Longfellow then had a second conversation with Conolly and Hawthorne and read Thomas Chandler Haliburton's *History of Nova Scotia* (1829) and George Bancroft's essay "The Exiles of Acadia," published in 1841. He did not begin writing the poem, however, until November 1845, using the working title "Gabrielle" at first. He worked on the poem steadily during 1846 and early 1847 and completed *Evangeline,* according to an entry in his journal, on February 27, 1847. The first edition of *Evangeline* was published on October 30, 1847, and met with enormous success; by January 1848 it was in its sixth printing, and it was frequently reprinted throughout Longfellow's career.

"The Building of the Ship," "Chrysaor" (under the title "The Evening Star"), "Twilight," "Sir Humphrey Gilbert," "The Lighthouse," "The Fire of Drift-Wood," "Resignation," "The Builders," "Sand of the Desert in an Hour-Glass," and "The Open Window" were published for the first time in book form in *The Seaside and the Fireside* (1850). These poems were written between 1846 and 1849.

On June 22, 1854, Longfellow wrote in his journal, "I have at length hit upon a plan for a poem on the American Indians, which seems to be the right one, and the only. It is to weave together their beautiful traditions into a whole. I have hit upon a measure, too, which I think the right and only one for such a theme." The "measure" was that of the *Kalevala,* the Finnish epic, which Longfellow was then reading in German translation. Longfellow wrote on June 25 that he was "making a beginning of 'Manabozho' or whatever the poem is to be called." The following day he began reading Henry Rowe Schoolcraft's *Historical and Statistical Information Respecting the History, Conditions, and Prospects of the Indian Tribes of the United States* (6 vols., 1851–57) at the library at Harvard College, and on June 28 he decided to use "Hiawatha" as his working title. After writing steadily through 1854 and early 1855, he finished a draft in March 1855, then copied and revised his manuscript before sending it to the printer in May, remarking that "re-writing a poem so long as Hiawatha is very wearisome; but very profitable, as one can better see it as a whole, and fill up gaps." *The Song of Hiawatha* was published on November 10, 1855; according to an entry in Longfellow's journal of that day, "more than four thousand out of the five of the first edition are sold. They ordered a new edition of three thousand." A letter from his publisher dated January 1, 1856, informed Longfellow that the book was selling "at the rate of three thousand a day." A version containing Longfellow's revisions appeared in 1866 in *Poetical Works.*

Longfellow initially planned to write "The Courtship of Miles Standish" as a verse drama. He wrote the first scene on December 2, 1856, but did not return to the material until December 1857, when he began "a new poem 'Priscilla'; to be a kind of Puritan pastoral; the subject, the courtship of Miles Standish. This, I think, will be a better treatment of the subject than the dramatic one I wrote some time ago." He finished the manuscript, now titled "The Courtship of Miles Standish," on March 22, 1858. It was published in *The Courtship of Miles Standish and Other Poems* (1858), with "Birds of Passage," written in 1845, and several poems written between 1849 and 1857: "The Ladder of St. Augustine," "The Phantom Ship," "The Warden of the Cinque Ports," "Haunted Houses," "In the Churchyard at Cambridge," "The Emperor's Bird's-Nest," "The Two Angels," "Daylight and Moonlight," "The Jewish Cemetery at Newport," "My Lost Youth," "The Ropewalk," "Daybreak," "The Fiftieth Birthday of Agassiz," "Children," and "Sandalphon." Three of these poems, "The Rope Walk," "The Two Angels," and "The Warden of the Cinque Ports," had been published previously in *The Voices of the Night, Ballads, and Other Poems* (London: Routledge and Co., 1857).

"The Children's Hour," "Enceladus," "The Cumberland," "Snow-Flakes," "A Day of Sunshine," "Something Left Undone," and "Weariness" were written between 1859 and 1863 and published in *Tales of a Wayside Inn.* Longfellow wrote several of the tales in *Tales of a Wayside Inn,* including "The Saga of King Olaf" and "Paul Revere's Ride," before deciding to bring them together in a single work. "The Saga of King Olaf," an adaptation of a story in the *Heimskringla,* was begun after Longfellow read a translation of the Icelandic epic in February 1859, although the opening section, "The Challenge of Thor" (which was intended to be part of *Christus: A Mystery*), was written in 1849. In a journal entry dated October 11, 1862, Longfellow records that he wrote "a little upon the Wayside Inn,—a beginning, only." Later that month, he chose "The Sudbury Tales" as a working title, and wrote to James Fields on November 11 that "The Sudbury Tales go on famously. I now have five complete, with a great part of the 'Prelude.'" When the work was announced as "The Sudbury Tales," Longfellow wrote to Fields: "Now that I see it announced I do not like the title." *Tales of a Wayside Inn* was published on November 25, 1863. The volume contained Part First of "Tales of a Wayside Inn"; Part Second was added in *Three Books of Song* (1872); Part Third was first published in *Aftermath* (1873).

"Palingenesis," "Hawthorne," "Christmas Bells," "The Wind Over the Chimney," "Killed at the Ford," "Giotto's Tower," and

"Divina Commedia" were published in *Flower-de-Luce* (1866), which collected poems written between 1864 and 1866. Two poems, "Palingenesis" and "Christmas Bells," had previously appeared in book form in *Household Poems* (1865). The first sonnet of "Divina Commedia" had been published with Longfellow's translation of Dante's *Inferno* in 1865, the second with his translation of *Purgatorio* in 1866. The third sonnet was later reprinted for Longfellow's translation of *Paradiso,* which appeared in 1867.

The three parts of *Christus: A Mystery* were published separately in 1851, 1868, and 1871. *The Golden Legend,* written between 1849 and 1851, was completed first. According to a journal entry dated November 8, 1850, Longfellow had "nearly finished" a draft in blank verse; an entry dated March 28, 1851, recorded that he was revising the poem and "putting the blank verse into rhyme." *The Golden Legend* was published in November 1851. Longfellow worked on "John Endicott," using the tentative titles "The Old Colony" and "Wenlock Christison," periodically between 1856 and 1868. "Giles Corey of the Salem Farms" was written in 1868. The two works first appeared in book form in *The New England Tragedies* (1868). *The Divine Tragedy* was begun in 1870 and completed the following year. "Finale: St. John" was first published in the first edition of *Christus: A Mystery* (1872).

"The Haunted Chamber," "The Meeting," "Vox Populi," "Changed," "The Challenge," and "Aftermath" were published in *Aftermath* (1873), which collected poems written between 1870 and 1873. "Morituri Salutamus," "Belisarius," "Three Friends of Mine," "Chaucer," "Shakespeare," "Milton," "Keats," "The Galaxy," "The Sound of the Sea," and "A Nameless Grave," written between 1873 and 1875, were published in *The Masque of Pandora and Other Poems* (1875). "Morituri Salutamus" was read at Bowdoin College on July 7, 1875. The poem was revised for publication in the August 1875 edition of *Harper's Monthly Magazine,* then revised further for inclusion in *The Masque of Pandora and Other Poems.*

"Kéramos," "Vittoria Colonna," "The Revenge of Rain-in-the-Face," "Nature," "Eliot's Oak," "The Poets," "The Harvest Moon," "The Broken Oar," "Haroun Al Raschid," "Venice," and "The Three Silences of Molinos" were written between 1875 and 1878 and published in *Kéramos and Other Poems* (1878). Longfellow had six copies of "Kéramos" privately printed, then revised the poem for publication in the December 1877 number of *Harper's Monthly Magazine.* It was further revised for publication in *Kéramos and Other Poems.* Excerpts from the poem appeared, under the titles "China Ware," "The Porcelain Tower," "Japan," and "Egypt," in the anthology *Poems of*

Places, edited by Longfellow and published in Boston by James R. Osgood in 1877. *Poems of Places* also included the first book publications of "Castles in Spain," "Venice," and "Victoria Colonna," which appeared under the title "Inarime."

"The Chamber Over the Gate," "Jugurtha," "Helen of Tyre," "Elegiac," "The Tide Rises, The Tide Falls," "My Cathedral," "The Burial of the Poet," "Night," and "The Poet and His Songs," poems written between 1878 and 1880, were published in *Ultima Thule* (1880). "The Poet's Calendar," "Autumn Within," "Victor and Vanquished," "Moonlight," "Hermes Trismegistus," and "The Bells of San Blas" were collected in the posthumous volume *In the Harbor* (1882). Of these poems, "Autumn Within," composed in 1874, was written earliest; the latest, "The Bells of San Blas," was written in 1882.

The selections in the "Other Poems" section of this volume were not published during Longfellow's lifetime. "Mezzo Cammin" was written on August 25, 1842. "The Cross of Snow" was written on July 10, 1879. Both poems were first published in Samuel Longfellow's *Life of Henry Wadsworth Longfellow with Extracts from His Journals and Correspondence* (Boston: Ticknor and Company, 1886). *Michael Angelo: A Fragment* was found among Longfellow's papers after his death in a nearly completed state. The greater part of the poem was written in 1872 but was kept for possible revision. It was first published in the *Atlantic Monthly* in January, February, and March 1883. A newly edited version appeared in 1886 in the "Riverside" edition.

As with his poems, this volume presents Longfellow's translations as they appeared in the "Riverside" edition, which include Longfellow's final revisions. "The Celestial Pilot," "The Terrestrial Paradise," and "Beatrice" were first published in *The Voices of the Night* (1839). These passages, with revisions, were incorporated into Longfellow's translation of *Purgatorio,* published in 1866. "The Good Shepherd" and "To-morrow" first appeared in *Coplas de Don Jorge Manrique* (Boston: Akken and Ticknor, 1833), a volume of translations from the Spanish, and were also included in *The Voices of the Night.* "The Grave" was first published in *The Voices of the Night.* "Retribution" was first published in book form as one of the "Poetic Aphorisms" in *The Belfry of Bruges and Other Poems* (1845). "Let Me Go Warm," "The Sea Hath Its Pearls," "Rondel," "The Artist," "To Vittoria Colonna," "Dante," and "A Neapolitan Canzonet" were first published in book form in Longfellow's anthology *The Poets and Poetry of Europe* (Philadelphia: Carey and Hart, 1844); "Santa Teresa's Book-Mark" was added to an expanded edition of the anthology published in 1871.

Longfellow began writing *Kavanagh* in 1847. A draft of the novel was finished on November 9, 1848, and on February 13, 1849, Longfellow's journal records that "with some doubts and misgivings" he delivered a portion of the manuscript to the printer. He continued to work on it through March and April. *Kavanagh, A Tale* was published in Boston by Ticknor, Reed, and Fields on April 12, 1849. With minor revisions, it was included as part of *The Complete Works of Henry Wadsworth Longfellow* published by Ticknor and Fields in 1866. It was collected in the "Riverside" edition, which is the text printed here.

"The Literary Spirit of Our Country" was published in *The United States Literary Gazette* on April 1, 1824, which is the text printed here, since it was not collected by Longfellow or included in the "Riverside" edition. "Table-Talk" was first published in the "Drift-Wood" section of *Prose Works of Henry Wadsworth Longfellow,* published in Boston by Ticknor and Fields in 1857. The text printed here is taken from the "Riverside" edition. "Address on the Death of Washington Irving" was read as a speech during a meeting at the Massachusetts Historical Society on December 5, 1859, and printed in *Irvingiana: A Memorial of Washington Irving* (New York: Charles B. Richardson, 1860). Since the speech was not included in the "Riverside" edition, the text printed here is taken from *Irvingiana.*

The following is a list of pages where a stanza break coincides with the foot of the page (except where such breaks are apparent from the regular stanzaic structure of the poem: 36, 47, 117, 118, 119, 122, 355, 364, 381, 383, 431, 433, 434, 435, 448, 449, 451, 493, 635, 642, 644, 681.

This volume presents the texts listed here without change except for the correction of typographical errors; it does not attempt to reproduce features of their typographic design. Spelling, punctuation, and capitalization are often expressive, and they are not altered, even when inconsistent or irregular. The following is a list of typographical errors in the source texts that have been corrected, cited by page and line number: 184.37, they.; 787.9, Kavanagh,; 791.34, pay.

Notes

In the notes below, the reference numbers denote page and line of this volume (the line count includes titles and headings). No note is made for material included in standard desk-reference books such as *Webster's Collegiate* and *Webster's Biographical* dictionaries. Biblical quotations are keyed to the King James Version. Quotations from Shakespeare are keyed to *The Riverside Shakespeare*, ed. G. Blakemore Evans (Boston: Houghton Mifflin, 1974). For more detailed notes, references to other studies, and further biographical background than is in the Chronology, see: Newton Arvin, *Longfellow: His Life and Work* (Boston: Little, Brown, 1963); Samuel Longfellow, *Life of Henry Wadsworth Longfellow* (Boston: Ticknor, 1866); Andrew Hilen, editor, *The Letters of Henry Wadsworth Longfellow* (Cambridge, Massachusetts: The Belknap Press of Harvard University Press, six volumes, 1966–82).

2.26 *'Ασπασίη, τρίλλιστος.*] The epigraph, from *Iliad*, Book 8, is translated at line 3.15: "The welcome, the thrice-prayed for."

4.25 *The Light of Stars*] "This poem was written on a beautiful summer night. The moon, a little strip of silver, was just setting behind the groves of Mount Auburn, and the planet Mars blazing in the southeast. There was a singular light in the sky." [Longfellow's note]

6.14 He, the young and strong] The reference is to Longfellow's brother-in-law George Washington Pierce, news of whose death reached the poet in Heidelberg on Christmas Eve, 1835, a month after the death of Longfellow's first wife, Mary, who is referred to from stanza six through the end of the poem.

12.23 *Skoal!*] "In Scandinavia, this is the customary salutation when drinking a health. I have slightly changed the orthography of the word, in order to preserve the correct pronunciation (*skaal*)." [Longfellow's note]

14.20 Norman's Woe] The *Hesperus* was wrecked on Norman's Woe, near Gloucester, Massachusetts, in 1839.

17.2 *No hay pájaros en los nidos antaño*] The epigraph is translated at line 17.27.

20.10 three friends] Charles Sumner (1811–74), a young Boston lawyer when Longfellow first met him in 1836, later a renowned U.S. senator from Massachusetts and a lifelong friend; Charles Folsom (1794–1872), whom Longfellow met in 1832, while Folsom was an editor for the

University Press in Cambridge, and subsequently librarian of the Boston Athenaeum; Charles Amory (1808–98), whom he met in Göttigen in 1829, later studied medicine at Harvard.

21.31 The prayer of Ajax was for light] Cf. *Iliad,* Book 17.

22.16 *Excelsior*] Higher.

25.28 Songs of triumph] Cf. Exodus 15:1.

26.5 Paul and Silas] Cf. Acts 16:19–34.

27.18 Israelite of old] Cf. Judges 14:8–9.

30.8 All the Foresters of Flanders] "The title of Foresters was given to the early governors of Flanders, appointed by the kings of France. Lyderick du Bucq, in the days of Clotaire the Second, was the first of them; and Beaudoin Bras-de-Fer, who stole away the fair Judith, daughter of Charles the Bald, from the French court, and married her in Bruges, was the last. After him the title of Forester was changed to that of Count. Philippe d'Alsace, Guy de Dampierre, and Louis de Crécy, coming later, in the order of time, were therefore rather Counts than Foresters. Philippe went twice to the Holy Land as a Crusader, and died of the plague at St. Jean-d'Acre, shortly after the capture of the city by the Christians. Guy de Dampierre died in the prison of Compiégne. Louis de Crécy was son and successor of Robert de Béthune, who strangled his wife, Yolande de Bourgogne, with the bridle of his horse, for having poisoned, at the age of eleven years, Charles, his son by his first wife, Blanche d'Anjou." [Longfellow's note]

30.12 Stately dames] "When Philippe-le-Bel, king of France, visited Flanders with his queen, she was so astonished at the magnificence of the dames of Bruges, that she exclaimed: 'Je croyais être seule reine ici, mais il paraît que ceux de Flandre qui se trouvent dans nos prisons sont tous des princes, car leurs femmes sont habillées comme des princesses et des reines.' [The queen exclaims: 'I thought I was the only queen here, but it appears that those Flemish in our prisons are all princes, for their women are dressed like princesses and queens.']

"When the burgomasters of Ghent, Bruges, and Ypres went to Paris to pay homage to King John, in 1351, they were received with great pomp and distinction; but, being invited to a festival, they observed that their seats at table were not furnished with cushions; whereupon, to make known their displeasure at this want of regard to their dignity, they folded their richly embroidered cloaks and seated themselves upon them. On rising from table, they left their cloaks behind them, and, being informed of their apparent forgetfulness, Simon van Eertrycke, burgomaster of Bruges, replied, 'We Flemings are not in the habit of carrying away our cushions after dinner.'" [Longfellow's note]

30.12–13 the Fleece of Gold] "Philippe de Bourgogne, surnamed Le Bon, espoused Isabella of Portugal, on the 10th of January, 1430; and on the same day instituted the famous order of the Fleece of Gold." [Longfellow's note]

30.18 the gentle Mary] "Marie de Valois, Duchess of Burgundy, was left by the death of her father, Charles le Téméraire, at the age of twenty, the richest heiress of Europe. She came to Bruges, as Countess of Flanders, in 1477, and in the same year was married by proxy to the Archduke Maximilian. According to the custom of the time, the Duke of Bavaria, Maximilian's substitute, slept with the princess. They were both in complete dress, separated by a naked sword, and attended by four armed guards. Marie was adored by her subjects for her gentleness and her many other virtues.

"Maximilian was son of the Emperor Frederick the Third [. . .] Having been imprisoned by the revolted burghers of Bruges, they refused to release him till he consented to kneel in the public square, and to swear on the Holy Evangelists and the body of Saint Donatus that he would not take vengeance upon them for their rebellion." [Longfellow's note]

30.24–25 the Spurs of Gold] "This battle, the most memorable in Flemish history, was fought under the walls of Courtray, on the 11th of June, 1302, between the French and the Flemings, the former commanded by Robert, Comte d'Artois, and the latter by Guillaume de Juliers, and Jean, Comte de Namur. The French army was completely routed, with a loss of twenty thousand infantry and seven thousand cavalry; among whom were sixty-three princes, dukes, and counts, seven hundred lords-banneret, and eleven hundred noblemen. The flower of the French nobility perished on that day; to which history has given the name of the *Journée des Éperons d'Or*, from the great number of golden spurs found on the field of battle. Seven hundred of them were hung up as a trophy in the church of Notre Dame de Courtray; and, as the cavaliers of that day wore but a single spur each, these vouched to God for the violent and bloody death of seven hundred of his creatures." [Longfellow's note]

30.26 the fight at Minnewater] "When the inhabitants of Bruges were digging a canal at Minnewater, to bring the waters of the Lys from Deynze to their city, they were attacked and routed by the citizens of Ghent, whose commerce would have been much injured by the canal. They were led by Jean Lyons, captain of a military company at Ghent, called the *Chaperons Blancs.* He had great sway over the turbulent populace, who, in those prosperous times of the city, gained an easy livelihood by laboring two or three days in the week, and had the remaining four or five to devote to public affairs. The fight at Minnewater was followed by an open rebellion against Louis de Maele, the Count of Flanders and Protector of Bruges. His superb château of Wondelghem was pillaged and burnt; and the insurgents forced the gates of Bruges, and entered in triumph, with Lyons mounted at their head. A few days afterwards he died suddenly, perhaps by poison.

"Meanwhile the insurgents received a check at the village of Nevèle; and two hundred of them perished in the church, which was burned by the

Count's orders. One of the chiefs, Jean de Lannoy, took refuge in the belfry. From the summit of the tower he held forth his purse filled with gold, and begged for deliverance. It was in vain. His enemies cried to him from below to save himself as best he might; and, half suffocated with smoke and flame, he threw himself from the tower and perished at their feet. Peace was soon afterwards established, and the Count retired to faithful Bruges." [Longfellow's note]

30.28–29 the Golden Dragon's nest] "The Golden Dragon, taken from the church of St. Sophia, at Constantinople, in one of the Crusades, and placed on the belfry of Bruges, was afterwards transported to Ghent by Philip van Artevelde, and still adorns the belfry of that city.

"The inscription on the alarm-bell at Ghent is, '*Mynen naem is Roland; als ik klep is er brand, and als ik luy is er victorie in het land.*' My name is Roland; when I toll there is fire, and when I ring there is victory in the land." [Longfellow's note]

32.15–16 celestial ladder . . . dream] Cf. Genesis 28:12.

33.16 Miserere] The opening of Psalm 51, "Miserere mei, Deus" (Have mercy upon me, O God).

33.23 Cimbric] The Cimbri, a Teutonic tribe, thought to have come originally from the Jutland peninsula.

39.22–24 within these walls . . . dwelt] Craigie House, Longfellow's home from 1837 on, had been George Washington's headquarters during the siege of Boston, 1775–76.

42.32 Acestes' shaft] During the funeral games in Book V of Virgil's *Aeneid*, the Sicilian king Acestes shoots his arrow with such strength that it catches fire and leaves a track of flame.

43.1 *The Occultation of Orion*] "Astronomically speaking, this title is incorrect; as I apply to a constellation what can properly be applied to some of its stars only. But my observation is made from the hill of song, and not from the hill of science; and will, I trust, be found sufficiently accurate for the present purpose." [Longfellow's note]

43.14 The Samian's] Pythagoras'.

43.35 Algebar] The star Rigel in the constellation Orion.

44.22–26 as of yore . . . sun] Orion sought to marry Merope, daughter of Oenopion and granddaughter of Dionysus. Oenopion consented to the marriage on condition that Orion rid his island of all its wild beasts, and Orion duly brought to Merope each night the pelts of the animals he had killed. Because he was himself in love with his daughter, Oenopion refused to give her up to Orion. Subsequently Orion, drunk, raped Merope and in consequence was blinded by Oenopion. An oracle predicted he would regain his sight only if he gazed on the sun at its first rising; he traveled to the smithy of Hephaestus and kidnapped the apprentice Cedalion, who guided him over land and sea to the farthest Ocean, where Eos fell in love with him. Eos' brother Helius restored Orion's sight.

48.4 Who, unharmed, on his tusks] "'A delegation of warriors from the Delaware tribe having visited the governor of Virginia, during the Revolution, on matters of business, after these had been discussed and settled in council, the governor asked them some questions relative to their country, and, among others, what they knew or had heard of the animal whose bones were found at the Saltlicks on the Ohio. Their chief speaker immediately put himself into an attitude of oratory, and, with a pomp suited to what he conceived the elevation of his subject, informed him that it was a tradition handed down from their fathers, "that in ancient times a herd of these tremendous animals came to the Big-bone licks, and began an universal destruction of the bear, deer, elks, buffaloes, and other animals which had been created for the use of the Indians: that the Great Man above, looking down and seeing this, was so enraged, that he seized his lightning, descended on the earth, seated himself on a neighboring mountain, on a rock of which his seat and the print of his feet are still to be seen, and hurled his bolts among them till the whole were slaughtered, except the big bull, who, presenting his forehead to the shafts, shook them off as they fell; but missing one at length, it wounded him in the side; whereon, springing round, he bounded over the Ohio, over the Wabash, the Illinois, and finally over the great lakes, where he is living at this day."'—Jefferson's *Notes on Virginia,* Query VI. [Longfellow's note]

49.1–2 some poem . . . heartfelt lay] This poem was originally written as the proem to Longfellow's anthology *The Waif,* a collection of favorite poems.

51.3 old-fashioned country-seat] The house described is the Gold mansion in Pittsfield, Massachusetts, the homestead of Fanny Appleton, Longfellow's maternal grandfather.

51.8 Forever–never!] In his diary, on November 12, 1845, Longfellow wrote: "Began a poem on a clock, with the words 'Forever, never,' as the burden; suggested by the words of [Jacques] Bridaine, the old French missionary, who said of eternity, *C'est une pendule dont le balancier dit et redit sans cesse ces deux mots seulement dans le silence des tombeaux,—Toujours, jamais! Jamais, toujours! Et pendant ces effrayables révolutions, un réprouvé s'écrie, 'Quelle heure est-il?' et la voix d'un autre misérable lui répond, 'L'Eternité.'*" ["Eternity is a clock, the tick-tock of which repeats incessantly amid the silence of the tombs, these two words only: 'Forever, never—Never, forever.' And during its terrifying revolutions, a reprobate cries out, 'What time is it?' and the voice of another in misery replies, 'Eternity.'"]

54.9 like imperial Charlemagne] "Charlemagne may be called by preëminence the monarch of farmers. According to the German tradition, in seasons of great abundance, his spirit crosses the Rhine on a golden bridge at

Bingen, and blesses the cornfields and the vineyards. During his lifetime, he did not disdain, says Montesquieu, 'to sell the eggs from the farmyards of his domains, and the superfluous vegetables of his gardens; while he distributed among his people the wealth of the Lombards and the immense treasures of the Huns.'" [Longfellow's note]

54.23 Farinata] Cf. *Inferno,* Canto 10, lines 28–51.

61.25 startled the penitent Peter] Cf. Matthew 26:74–75; Mark 14:72; Luke 22:60–61.

63.12–13 Lucky was he . . . swallow!] "'If the eyes of one of the young of a swallow be put out, the mother bird will bring from the sea-shore a little stone, which will immediately restore its sight; fortunate is the person who finds this little stone in the nest, for it is a miraculous remedy.' Pluquet, *Contes Populaires,* quoted by Wright, *Literature and Superstitions of England in the Middle Ages,* I. 128." [Longfellow's note]

63.21 "Sunshine of Saint Eulalie"]
"Si le soleil rit le jour Sainte-Eulalie
Il y aura pommes et cidre à folie.
PLUQUET in WRIGHT, I. 131." [Longfellow's note]

63.37–38 as Jacob of old with the angel] Cf. Genesis 32:24–29.

64.27–28 Flashed . . . mantles and jewels] "See Evelyn's Silva, II. 53." [Longfellow's note] Herodotus tells in his *History* (Book 7) of a plane-tree that the Persian king Xerxes found so beautiful he adorned it in jewels and fine robes.

68.3–4 Louisburg . . . Beau Séjour . . . Port Royal] Forts on Nova Scotia built by the French but captured by the English.

69.14 Loup-garou] Were-wolf.

70.18–71.7 "Once in an ancient . . . was inwoven."] Cf. Rossini's opera, *La Gaza Ladra.*

73.21–22 As out . . . with Hagar!] Cf. Genesis 21:14.

78.4 Elijah] Cf. II Kings 2:11.

79.3–4 like the Prophet . . . Sinai] Cf. Exodus 34:29–30.

83.3 shipwrecked Paul . . . sea-shore] Cf. Acts 27:44–28:1.

84.6 gleeds] Burning coals.

87.39 Thou art too fair . . . tresses] "There is a Norman saying of a maid who does not marry—*Elle restera pour coiffer Sainte Katherine.*" [Longfellow's note]

92.16 ladder of Jacob] Cf. Genesis 28:12.

98.9 ci-devant] Former.

101.13 "Upharsin."] Cf. Daniel 5:25–28.

103.16 amorphas] Wild bean plants, covered with purple flowers.

103.23 Ishmael's children] Cf. Genesis 21:13.

112.6–7 "The poor . . . with you."] Cf. John 12:8.

112.32–33 Swedes . . . Wicaco] Swedes founded Gloria Dei church at Wicaco, in what is now the Southwark section of Philadelphia, as early as 1698.

113.34–36 like the Hebrew . . . pass over] Cf. Exodus 12:3–13.

122.3 Behold, at last] "I wish to anticipate a criticism on this passage, by stating that sometimes, though not usually, vessels are launched fully sparred and rigged. I have availed myself of the exception as better suited to my purposes than the general rule; but the reader will see that it is neither a blunder nor a poetic license. On this subject a friend in Portland, Maine, writes me thus:—

"'In this State, and also, I am told, in New York, ships are sometimes rigged upon the stocks, in order to save time, or to make a show. There was a fine, large ship launched last summer at Ellsworth, fully sparred and rigged. Some years ago a ship was launched here, with her rigging, spars, sails, and cargo aboard. She sailed the next day and—was never heard of again! I hope this will not be the fate of your poem!'" [Longfellow's note]

128.16 *Chrysaor*] Son of Poseidon, who sprang to life with his brother Pegasus from the body of Medusa after she had been slain by Perseus.

128.27 Callirrhoe] One of the daughters of the titan Oceanus.

130.1 *Sir Humphrey Gilbert*] "'When the wind abated and the vessels were near enough, the Admiral was seen constantly sitting in the stern, with a book in his hand. On the 9th of September he was seen for the last time, and was heard by the people of the *Hind* to say, "We are as near heaven by sea as by land." In the following night, the lights of the ship suddenly disappeared. The people in the other vessel kept a good lookout for him during the remainder of the voyage. On the 22nd of September they arrived, through much tempest and peril, at Falmouth. But nothing more was seen or heard of the Admiral.'—Belknap's *American Biography*, i. 203." [Longfellow's note]

132.1 Christopher] Third century A.D. Christian martyr often described allegorically as a giant who carries the young Christ over the river of death.

135.3 one dead lamb] This poem was written in the autumn of 1848, soon after the death of Longfellow's daughter Fanny, aged fifteen months, on September 11.

135.8 Rachel] Cf. Jeremiah 31:15 and Matthew 2:18.

138.10–13 Perhaps the camels . . . son they bore] Cf. Genesis 37:25–36.

141.1 THE SONG OF HIAWATHA] "This Indian Edda—if I may so call it—is founded on a tradition, prevalent among the North American Indians, of a personage of miraculous birth, who was sent among them to clear their rivers, forests, and fishing-grounds, and to teach them the arts of peace. He was known among different tribes by the several names of Michabou, Chiabo, Manabozo, Tarenya-wagon, and Hiawatha. Mr. Schoolcraft gives an account of him in his *Algic Researches,* vol. I. p. 134; and in his *History, Condition, and Prospects of the Indian Tribes of the United States,* Part III. p. 314, may be found the Iroquois form of the tradition, derived from the verbal narrations of an Onondaga chief.

"Into this old tradition I have woven other curious Indian legends, drawn chiefly from the various and valuable writings of Mr. Schoolcraft, to whom the literary world is greatly indebted for his indefatigable zeal in rescuing from oblivion so much of the legendary lore of the Indians.

"The scene of the poem is among the Ojibways on the southern shore of Lake Superior, in the region between the Pictured Rocks and the Grand Sable.

"VOCABULARY

Adjidau'mo, *the red squirrel.*
Ahdeek', *the reindeer.*
Ahkose'win, *fever.*
Ahmeek', *the beaver.*
Algon'quin, *Ojibway.*
Annemee'kee, *the thunder.*
Apuk'wa, *a bulrush.*
Baim-wa'wa, *the sound of the thunder.*
Bemah'gut, *the grapevine.*
Be'na, *the pheasant.*
Big-Sea-Water, *Lake Superior.*
Bukada'win, *famine.*
Cheemaun', *a birch canoe.*
Chetowaik', *the plover.*
Chibia'bos, *a musician; friend of Hiawatha; ruler in the Land of Spirits.*
Dahin'da, *the bull-frog*
Dush-kwo-ne'she, *or* Kwo-ne'she, *the dragon-fly.*
Esa, *shame upon you.*
Ewa-yea', *lullaby.*
Ghee'zis, *the sun.*
Gitche Gu'mee, *the Big Sea-Water, Lake Superior.*
Gitche Man'ito, *the Great Spirit, the Master of Life.*
Gushkewau', *the darkness.*
Hiawa'tha, *the Wise Man, the Teacher; son of Mudjekeewis, the West-Wind, and Wenonah, daughter of Nokomis.*
Ia'goo, *a great boaster and story-teller.*
Inin'ewug, *men, or pawns in the Game of the Bowl.*
Ishkoodah', *fire; a comet.*
Jee'bi, *a ghost, a spirit.*
Joss'akeed, *a prophet.*
Kabibonok'ka, *the North-Wind.*
Kagh, *the hedgehog.*
Ka'go, *do not.*
Kahgahgee', *the raven.*
Kaw, *no.*
Kayoshk', *the sea-gull.*
Kaween', *no indeed.*
Kee'go, *a fish.*
Keeway'din, *the Northwest Wind, the Home-Wind.*
Kena'beek, *a serpent.*
Keneu', *the great war-eagle.*
Keno'zha, *the pickerel.*
Ko'ko-ko'ho, *the owl.*
Kuntasoo', *the Game of Plum-stones.*
Kwa'sind, *the Strong Man.*
Kwo-ne'she, *or* Dush-kwo-ne'she, *the dragon-fly.*
Mahnahbe'zee, *the swan.*
Mahng, *the loon.*
Mahn-go-tay'see, *loon-hearted brave.*
Mahnomo'nee, *wild rice.*
Ma'ma, *the woodpecker.*
Maskeno'zha, *the pike.*
Me'da, *a medicine-man.*
Meenah'ga, *the blueberry.*
Megissog'won, *the great Pearl-Feather, a magician and the Manito of Wealth.*

Meshinau'wa, *a pipe-bearer.*
Minjekah'wun, *Hiawatha's mittens.*
Minneha'ha, *Laughing Water; a waterfall on a stream running into the Mississippi, between Fort Snelling and the Falls of St. Anthony.*
Minneha'ha, *Laughing Water; wife of Hiawatha.*
Minne-wa'wa, *a pleasant sound, as of the wind in the trees.*
Mishe-Mo'kwa, *the Great Bear.*
Mishe-Nah'ma, *the Great Sturgeon.*
Miskodeed', *the Spring Beauty, the Claytonia Virginica.*
Monda'min, *Indian Corn.*
Moon of Bright Nights, *April.*
Moon of Leaves, *May*
Moon of Strawberries, *June.*
Moon of the Falling Leaves, *September.*
Moon of Snow-Shoes, *November.*
Mudjekee'wis, *the West-Wind; father of Hiawatha.*
Mudway-aush'ka, *sound of waves on a shore.*
Mushkoda'sa, *the grouse.*
Na'gow Wudj'oo, *the Sand Dunes of Lake Superior.*
Nah'ma, *the sturgeon.*
Nah'ma-wusk, *spearmint.*
Nee-ba-naw'baigs, *water spirits*
Nenemoo'sha, *sweetheart.*
Nepah'win, *sleep*
Noko'mis, *a grandmother; mother of Wenonah.*
No'sa, *my father.*
Nush'ka, *look! look!*
Odah'min, *the strawberry.*
Okahah'wis, *the fresh-water herring*
Ome'mee, *the pigeon.*
Ona'gon, *a bowl.*
Onaway', *awake.*
Ope'chee, *the robin.*
Osse'o, *Son of the Evening Star.*
Owais'sa, *the bluebird.*
Oweenee', *wife of Osseo.*
Ozawa'beek, *a round piece of brass or copper in the Game of the Bowl.*
Pah'-puk-kee'na, *the grasshopper.*
Pau'guk, *death.*
Pau-Puk-Kee'wis, *the handsome Yenadizze, the Storm-Fool.*
Pauwa'ting, *Sault Sainte Marie.*
Pe'boan, *Winter.*
Pem'ican, *meat of the deer or buffalo dried and pounded.*
Pezheekee', *the bison.*
Pishnekuh', *the brant.*
Pone'mah, *hereafter.*
Pugasaing', *Game of the Bowl.*
Puggawau'gun, *a war-club.*
Puk-Wudj'ies, *little wild men of the woods; pygmies.*
Sah'wa, *the perch.*
Sebowish'a, *rapids.*
Segwun', *Spring.*
Sha'da, *the pelican.*
Shahbo'min, *the gooseberry.*
Shah-shah, *long ago.*
Shaugoda'y, *a coward.*
Shawgashee', *the crawfish.*
Shawonda'see, *the South-Wind.*
Shaw-shaw, *the swallow.*
Shesh'ebwug, *ducks; pieces in the Game of the Bowl.*
Shin'gebis, *the diver or grebe.*
Showain' neme'shin, *pity me.*
Shuh-shuh'gah, *the blue heron.*
Soan-ge-ta'ha, *strong hearted.*
Subbeka'she, *the spider.*
Sugge'ma, *the mosquito.*
To'tem, *family coat of arms.*
Ugh, *yes.*
Ugudwash', *the sun-fish.*
Unktahee', *the God of Water.*
Wabas'so, *the rabbit; the North.*
Wabe'no, *a magician, a juggler.*
Wabe'no-wusk, *yarrow.*
Wa-bun, *the East-Wind.*
Wa'bun An'nung, *the Star of the East, the Morning Star.*
Wahono'win, *a cry of lamentation.*
Wah-wah-tay'see, *the fire-fly.*
Wam'pum, *beads of shell.*
Waubewy'on, *a white skin wrapper.*
Wa'wa, *the wild goose.*
Waw'beek, *a rock.*
Waw-be-wa'wa, *the white goose.*
Wawonais'sa, *the whippoorwill.*
Way-muk-kwa'na, *the caterpillar.*
Wen'digoes, *giants.*
Weno'nah, *Hiawatha's mother, daughter of Nokomis.*
Yenadiz'ze, *an idler and gambler; an Indian dandy."*

[Longfellow's note]

142.6 In the vale of Tawasentha] "This valley, now called Norman's Kill, is in Albany County, New York." [Longfellow's note]

144.3 On the Mountains of the Prairie] "Mr. Catlin, in his *Letters and Notes on the Manners, Customs, and Condition of the North American Indians,* vol. II. p. 160, gives an interesting account of the *Côteau des Prairies,* and the Red Pipestone Quarry. He says:—

"'Here (according to their traditions) happened the mysterious birth of the red pipe, which has blown its fumes of peace and war to the remotest corners of the continent; which has visited every warrior, and passed through its reddened stem the irrevocable oath of war and desolation. And here, also, the peace-breathing calumet was born, and fringed with the eagle's quills, which has shed its thrilling fumes over the land, and soothed the fury of the relentless savage.

"'The Great Spirit at an ancient period here called the Indian nations together, and, standing on the precipice of the red pipe-stone rock, broke from its wall a piece, and made a huge pipe by turning it in his hand, which he smoked over them, and to the North, the South, the East, and the West, and told them that this stone was red,—that it was their flesh,—that they must use it for their pipes of peace,—that it belonged to them all, and that the war-club and scalping-knife must not be raised on its ground. At the last whiff of his pipe his head went into a great cloud, and the whole surface of the rock for several miles was melted and glazed; two great ovens were opened beneath, and two women (guardian spirits of the place) entered them in a blaze of fire; and they are heard there yet (Tso-mec-cos-tee and Tso-me-cos-te-won-dee), answering to the invocations of the high-priests or medicine-men, who consult them when they are visitors to this sacred place.'" [Longfellow's note]

149.15 "Hark you, Bear! . . . coward] "This anecdote is from Heckewelder. In his account of the Indian Nations, he describes an Indian hunter as addressing a bear in nearly these words. 'I was present,' he says, 'at the delivery of this curious invective; when the hunter had despatched the bear, I asked him how he thought that poor animal could understand what he said to it. "Oh," said he in answer, "the bear understood me very well; did you not observe how *ashamed* he looked while I was upbraiding him?"' —*Transactions of the American Philosphical Society,* vol. I. p. 240." [Longfellow's note]

158.4 "Hush! the Naked Bear will hear thee!"] "Heckewelder, in a letter published in the *Transactions of the American Philosophical Society,* vol. IV. p. 260, speaks of this tradition as prevalent among the Mohicans and Delawares.

"'Their reports,' he says, 'run thus: that among all animals that had been formerly in this country, this was the most ferocious; that it was much larger than the largest of the common bears, and remarkably long-bodied; all over (except a spot of hair on its back of a white color) naked. . . .

"'The history of this animal used to be a subject of conversation among the Indians, especially when in the woods a hunting. I have also heard them say to their children when crying: "Hush! the naked bear will hear you, be upon you, and devour you."'" [Longfellow's note]

168.25 Where the Falls of Minnehaha] "'The scenery about Fort Snelling is rich in beauty. The Falls of St. Anthony are familiar to travellers, and to readers of Indian sketches. Between the fort and these falls are the "Little Falls," forty feet in height, on a stream that empties into the Mississippi. The Indians called them Mine-hah-hah, or "laughing waters."' —Mrs. Eastman's *Dacotah, or Legends of the Sioux,* Introd. p. ii." [Longfellow's note]

209.1 Sand Hills of the Nagow Wudjoo!] "A description of the *Grand Sable,* or great sand-dunes of Lake Superior, is given in Foster and Whitney's *Report on the Geology of the Lake Superior Land District,* Part II. p. 131.

"'The Grand Sable possesses a scenic interest little inferior to that of the Pictured Rocks. The explorer passes abruptly from a coast of consolidated sand to one of loose materials; and although in the one case the cliffs are less precipitous, yet in the other they attain a higher altitude. He sees before him a long reach of coast, resembling a vast sand-bank, more than three hundred and fifty feet in height, without a trace of vegetation. Ascending to the top, rounded hillocks of blown sand are observed, with occasional clumps of trees, standing out like oases in the desert.'" [Longfellow's note]

209.24 "Onaway! Awake, beloved!] "The original of this song may be found in *Littell's Living Age,* vol. XXV. p. 45." [Longfellow's note]

212.8 Or the Red Swan floating, flying] "The fanciful tradition of the Red Swan may be found in Schoolcraft's *Algic Researches.* vol. II. p. 9. Three brothers were hunting on a wager to see who would bring home the first game.

"'They were to shoot no other animal,' so the legend says, 'but such as each was in the habit of killing. They set out different ways; Odjibwa, the youngest, had not gone far before he saw a bear, an animal he was not to kill, by the agreement. He followed him close, and drove an arrow through him, which brought him to the ground. Although contrary to the bet, he immediately commenced skinning him, when suddenly something red tinged all the air around him. He rubbed his eyes, thinking he was perhaps deceived; but without effect, for the red hue continued. At length he heard a strange noise at a distance. It first appeared like a human voice, but after following the sound for some distance, he reached the shores of a lake, and soon saw the object he was looking for. At a distance out in the lake sat a most beautiful Red Swan, whose plumage glittered in the sun, and who would now and then make the same noise he had heard. He was within long bow-shot, and, pulling the arrow from the bowstring up to his ear, took deliberate aim and shot. The arrow took no effect; and he shot and shot again till his quiver was empty. Still the swan remained, moving round and round, stretching its long neck and dipping its bill into the water, as if heedless of the arrows shot at it. Odjibwa ran home and got all his own and his brothers' arrows, and shot them all away. He then stood and gazed at the beautiful bird. While standing, he remembered his brothers' saying that in their deceased father's medicine-sack were three magic arrows. Off he started, his anxiety to kill the swan overcoming all scruples. At any other time he would have deemed it sacrilege to open his father's medicine-sack; but now he hastily seized the three arrows and ran back, leaving the other contents of the sack scattered over the lodge. The swan was still there. He shot the first arrow with great precision, and came very near to it. The second came still closer; as he took the last arrow, he felt his arm firmer, and, drawing it up with vigor, saw it pass through the neck of the swan a little above the breast. Still it did not prevent the bird from flying off, which it did, however, at first slowly, flapping its wings and rising gradually into the air, and then flying off toward the sinking of the sun.'—Pages 10–12." [Longfellow's note]

220.28 "When I think of my beloved] "The original of this song may be found in *Oneóta,* p. 15." [Longfellow's note]

221.30 Sing the mysteries of Mondamin] "The Indians hold the maize, or Indian corn, in great veneration. 'They esteem it so important and divine a grain,' says Schoolcraft, 'that their story-tellers invented various tales, in which this idea is symbolized under the form of a special gift from the Great Spirit. The Odjibwa-Algonquins, who call it Mon-da-min, that is, this Spirit's grain or berry, have a pretty story of the kind, in which the stalk in full tassel is represented as descending from the sky, under the guise of a handsome youth, in answer to the prayers of a young man at his fast of virility, or coming to manhood.

"'It is well known that corn-planting and corn-gathering, at least among all the still *uncolonized* tribes, are left entirely to the females and children, and a few superannuated old men. It is not generally known, perhaps, that this labor is not compulsory, and that it is assumed by the females as a just equivalent, in their view, for the onerous and continuous labor of the other sex, in providing meats, and skins for clothing, by the chase, and in defending their villages against their enemies, and keeping intruders off their territories. A good Indian housewife deems this a part of her prerogative, and prides herself to have a store of corn to exercise her hospitality, or duly honor her husband's hospitality in the entertainment of the lodge guests.' —*Oneóta,* p. 82." [Longfellow's note]

223.2 "Thus the fields shall be more fruitful] "'A singular proof of this belief, in both sexes, of the mysterious influence of the steps of a woman on the vegetable and insect creation, is found in an ancient custom, which was related to me, respecting corn-planting. It was the practice of the hunter's wife, when the field of corn had been planted, to choose the first dark or overclouded evening to perform a secret circuit, *sans habillement,* around the field. For this purpose she slipped out of the lodge in the evening, unobserved, to some obscure nook, where she completely disrobed. Then, taking her matchecota, or principal garment, in one hand, she dragged it around the field. This was thought to insure a prolific crop, and to prevent the assault of insects and worms upon the grain. It was supposed that they could not creep over the charmed line.'—*Oneóta,* p. 83." [Longfellow's note]

225.21 With his prisoner-string he bound him] "'These cords,' says Mr. Tanner, 'are made of the bark of the elm-tree, by boiling and then immersing it in cold water. . . . The leader of a war party commonly carries several fastened about his waist, and if, in the course of the fight, any one of his young men takes a prisoner, it is his duty to bring him immediately to the chief, to be tied, and the latter is responsible for his safe keeping.' —*Narrative of Captivity and Adventures,* p. 412." [Longfellow's note]

227.14–15 "Wagemin, the thief. . . the maize-ear!"] "'If one of the young female huskers finds a *red* ear of corn, it is typical of a brave admirer, and is regarded as a fitting present to some young warrior. But if the ear be *crooked*, and tapering to a point, no matter what color, the whole circle is set in a roar, and *wa-ge-min* is the word shouted aloud. It is the symbol of a thief in the cornfield. It is considered as the image of an old man stooping as he enters the lot. Had the chisel of Praxiteles been employed to produce this image, it could not more vividly bring to the minds of the merry group the idea of a pilferer of their favorite mondámin. . . .

"'The literal meaning of the term is, a mass, or crooked ear of grain; but the ear of corn so called is a conventional type of a little old man pilfering ears of corn in a cornfield. It is in this manner that a single word or term, in these curious languages, becomes the fruitful parent of many ideas. And we can thus perceive why it is that the word *wagemin* is alone competent to excite merriment in the husking circle.

"'This term is taken as a basis of the cereal chorus, or corn song, as sung by the Northern Algonquin tribes. It is coupled with the phrase *Paimosaid*,—a permutative form of the Indian substantive, made from the verb *pim-o-sa*, to walk. Its literal meaning is, *he who walks*, or *the walker*; but the ideas conveyed by it are, he who walks by night to pilfer corn. It offers, therefore, a kind of parallelism in expression to the preceding term.'—*Oneóta*, p. 254." [Longfellow's note]

239.23 Pugasaing, with thirteen pieces] "This Game of the Bowl is the principal game of hazard among the Northern tribes of Indians. Mr. Schoolcraft gives a particular account of it in *Oneóta*, p. 85. 'This game,' he says, 'is very fascinating to some portions of the Indians. They stake at it their ornaments, weapons, clothing, canoes, horses, everything in fact they possess; and have been known, it is said, to set up their wives and children, and even to forfeit their own liberty. Of such desperate stakes I have seen no examples, nor do I think the game itself in common use. It is rather confined to certain persons, who hold the relative rank of gamblers in Indian society,—men who are not noted as hunters or warriors, or steady providers for their families. Among these are persons who bear the term of *Ienadizze-wug*, that is, wanderers about the country, braggadocios, or fops. It can hardly be classed with the popular games of amusement, by which skill and dexterity are acquired. I have generally found the chiefs and graver men of the tribes, who encouraged the young men to play ball, and are sure to be present at the customary sports, to witness, and sanction, and applaud them, speak lightly and disparagingly of this game of hazard. Yet it cannot be denied that some of the chiefs, distinguished in war and the chase, at the West, can be referred to as lending their example to its fascinating power.'

"See also his *History, Conditions, and Prospects of the Indian Tribes*, Part II. p. 72." [Longfellow's note]

251.36 To the Pictured Rocks of sandstone] "The reader will find a long description of the Pictured Rocks in Foster and Whitney's *Report on the Geology of the Lake Superior Land District*, Part II. p. 124. From this I make the following extract:—

"'The Pictured Rocks may be described, in general terms, as a series of sandstone bluffs extending along the shore of Lake Superior for about five miles, and rising, in most places, vertically from the water, without any beach at the base, to a height varying from fifty to nearly two hundred feet. Were they simply a line of cliffs, they might not, so far as relates to height or extent, be worthy of a rank among great natural curiosities, although such an assemblage of rocky strata, washed by the waves of the great lake, would not, under any circumstances, be destitute of grandeur. To the voyager, coasting along their base in his frail canoe, they would, at all times, be an object of dread; the recoil of the surf, the rock-bound coast, affording for miles no place of refuge,—the lowering sky, the rising wind,—all these would excite his apprehension, and induce him to ply a vigorous oar until the dreaded wall was passed. But in the Pictured Rocks there are two features which communicate to the scenery a wonderful and almost unique character. These are, first, the curious manner in which the cliffs have been excavated and worn away by the action of the lake, which, for centuries, has dashed an ocean-like surf against their base; and, second, the equally curious manner in which large portions of the surface have been colored by bands of brilliant hues.

"'It is from the latter circumstance that the name, by which these cliffs are known to the American traveller, is derived; while that applied to them by the French voyageurs ("Les Portails") is derived from the former, and by far the most striking peculiarity.

"'The term *Pictured Rocks* has been in use for a great length of time; but when it was first applied, we have been unable to discover. It would seem that the first travellers were more impressed with the novel and striking distribution of colors on the surface than with the astonishing variety of form into which the cliffs themselves have been worn. . . .

"'Our voyageurs had many legends to relate of the pranks of the *Mennibojou* in these caverns, and, in answer to our inquiries, seemed disposed to fabricate stories, without end, of the achievements of this Indian deity.'" [Longfellow's note]

273.35 Toward the sun his hands were lifted] "In this manner, and with such salutations, was Father Marquette received by the Illinois. See his *Voyages et Découvertes,* Section V." [Longfellow's note]

280.32–35 the captives . . . but Angels."] Pope Gregory the Great (540–604) sent St. Augustine on a mission to the Anglo-Saxons; when Augustine returned to Rome and presented several English natives at the papal court, the Pope's play on words was recorded.

282.15 Aspinet . . . Tokamahamon!] Names of Indians mentioned in early New England chronicles.

285.25 "'T is not good . . . alone] Cf. Genesis 2:18.

290.6–7 "Let not him . . . backwards] Cf. Luke 9:62.

294.16 City of God . . . John the Apostle] Cf. Revelation 21:2.

295.9–14 voice of the Prophet . . . the battle!] Cf. II Samuel 11.

299.24 "Not so thought St. Paul] Cf. Acts 2:3–4.

307.24 the river Euphrates] Cf. Genesis 2:14.

311.26 Og, king of Bashan] Cf. Joshua 13:12.

315.2 merestead] A dwelling-house with its land and outbuildings.

316.9–10 virtuous woman . . . in the Proverbs] Cf. Proverbs 31:10–31.

319.22–23 Ruth and of Boaz] Cf. Ruth 4.

323.7–8 valley of Eschol] Cf. Numbers 13:23–24.

323.10–11 Rebecca and Isaac] Cf. Genesis 24:20–21.

324.27 That of our vices we can frame] "The words of St. Augustine are, 'De vitiis nostris scalam nobis facimus, si vitia ipse calcamus.' Sermon III. *De Ascensione.*" [Longfellow's note]

326.12 Mather's Magnalia Christi] Cf. *Magnalia Christi Americana,* book 1, chapter vi.

328.1 *The Warden of the Cinque Ports*] The Duke of Wellington, who died on September 13, 1852. Longfellow's poem was written a month later.

331.2–6 In the village churchyard she lies . . . Lies a slave] According to local legend, Mrs. John Vassal, wife of the first owner of Craigie House, ordered two Negro slaves be buried with her, one at her head, the other at her feet.

332.20 And the Emperor but a Macho!] "*Macho,* in Spanish, signifies a mule. *Golondrina* is the feminine form for *Golondrino,* a swallow, and also a cant name for a deserter." [Longfellow's note]

333.17 Two angels . . . of Death] Longfellow's daughter Edith was born October 22, 1853, five days before the death of Maria White Lowell, the young wife of his friend, the poet James Russell Lowell.

336.3–4 the tablets of the Law . . . mountain's base] Cf. Exodus, 32:19.

336.32 marah] Bitterness.

337.1 Anathema maranatha!] Cf. I Corinthians 16:22.

337.22 beautiful town] Portland, Maine, Longfellow's birthplace.

337.27 a Lapland song] Lapland folksong included in Johann Gottfried von Herder's anthology of popular poetry, *Die Stimmen der Völker in Liedern* (1778–79); Longfellow is remembering the lines, "*Knabenwille ist Windeswille, / Jünglings Gedanken lange Gedanken.*"

338.28 I remember the sea-fight] "This was the engagement between the Enterprise and Boxer, off the harbor of Portland, in which both captains were slain. They were buried side by side in the cemetery on Mountjoy." [Longfellow's note]

339.2 Deering's Woods] Woods near Portland, Maine, which Longfellow roamed as a child.

343.1 *The Fiftieth Birthday of Agassiz*] This poem was read by Longfellow during a dinner to celebrate, on May 28, 1857, the birthday of the Swiss-born naturalist Louis Agassiz (1807–73).

343.28 Ranz des Vaches] Song of the Swiss cowherds.

347.13–14 Alice . . . Edith] Longfellow's three youngest children.

347.29–30 Bishop . . . Rhine!] A medieval watch-tower on the Rhine, supposedly so named because of the tradition that Archbishop Hatto was devoured there by mice in the tenth century; the story is told in Robert Southey's poem "God's Judgment on a Wicked Bishop."

348.13 *Enceladus*] In Greek mythology, the hundred-armed Enceladus, son of Tartarus and Gaea, was one of the titans who attacked the Olympian gods. In punishment, Zeus chained him under Mount Etna. The poem was written in 1859, the year of Italy's uprising against its Austrian occupiers.

349.19 Hampton Roads] On March 8, 1862, on its first day of action, the ironclad *Merrimac* sank two of the Union navy's wooden warships, the *Congress* and the *Cumberland*, commanded by George Upham Morris, and drove the stream frigate *Minnesota* aground, in the waters of Hampton Roads, Virginia. The following day, the Union ironclad *Monitor* engaged the *Merrimac* and forced her to retire for safety back up the Elizabeth River.

354.2 WAYSIDE INN] In a letter to Frances Farrer dated December 28, 1863, Longfellow wrote of this poem: "The Wayside Inn has more foundation in fact than you may suppose. The town of Sudbury is about twenty miles from Cambridge. Some two hundred years ago, an English family, by the name of Howe, built there a country house, which has remained in the family down to the present time, the last of the race dying but two years ago. Losing their fortune, they became inn-keepers; and for a century the Red-Horse Inn has flourished, going down from father to son. The place is just as I have described it, though no longer an inn . . . All the characters are real. The musician is Ole Bull; the Spanish Jew, Israel Edrehi, whom I have seen as I have painted him, etc., etc."

Edrehi's first name was actually Isaac, and the innkeeper's full name Lyman Howe. Other models for Longfellow's characters were Henry Ware Wales, a Harvard graduate with a degree in medicine (the Student), Luigi Monti, a political exile who taught Italian at Harvard (the Sicilian), Daniel Treadwell, professor of physics at Harvard (the Theologian), and Thomas William Parsons, a translator of Dante (the Poet).

355.26 Princess Mary's] Daughter of James II and Anne Hyde; as Mary II (1662–94) assumed the English throne with her husband William of Orange in 1689.

355.38 Major Molineaux] William Molineux (d. 1774) of Boston; he figures in Hawthorne's 1832 short story "My Kinsman, Major Molineux."

358.8 Palermo's fatal siege] The city fell to royalist troops in April 1849 during the suppression of the Sicilian revolution of 1848–49.

358.10 King Bomba's] King Ferdinand II (1810–59) was called "King Bomba" because he had the principal cities in Sicily bombarded during the suppression of the 1848–49 revolution.

358.23–24 Immortal Four / Of Italy] Dante, Petrarch, Ariosto, and Tasso.

358.37 Meli] Giovanni Meli (1740–1815), Sicilian poet noted for his poems in dialect.

359.20 Pierre Alphonse] Pedro Alfonso (also known as Petrus Alfonsi), 11th-century author of *Disciplina Clericalis*; he prepared an edition of Aesop's fables.

359.22 Parables of Sandabar] The *Misklo Sandabar*, a medieval Hebrew collection of stories.

359.23 Pilpay] More commonly Bidpai, supposed author of a version of the Sanskrit collection of tales, the *Panchatantra*.

359.26 Targum] Aramaic paraphrase of the Old Testament.

361.1 Strömkarl] In Norse myth, a water sprite, usually having musical abilities and weeping when it hears the harp.

361.11 Elivagar's river] In Norse mythology, poisonous waters gushing from the center of Niflheim, the land of mist.

367.1 Thus Ariosto says] Cf. *Orlando Furioso,* Canto I, line 1.

367.11 Decameron] Boccaccio's collection (1348–53) of one hundred stories is framed as the entertainment of a group of Florentines who have sought refuge from plague at a country estate.

385.11 'Heimskringla'] A prose history of the kings of Norway to the year 1177, compiled by Snorri Sturluson (1179–1241).

395.12 Witch of Endor] Cf. I Samuel 28:7.

423.17 Regnarock] In Norse mythology, the final catastrophe in which the gods will be destroyed.

439.23–24 merry Night of Straparole . . . Belphagor] The *Piacevoli notti* (1550–54) of Giovan Francesco Straparola was a collection of 74 stories set on the island of Murano; Machiavelli's *Novella di Belfagor* was originally titled *Il demonio che prese moglie* (*The Demon Who Took a Wife*).

441.20 Edwards on the Will] *A Careful and Strict Inquiry into the Modern Prevailing Notions of that Freedom of the Will, Which Is Supposed to Be Essential to Moral Agency, Virtue and Vice, Reward and Punishment, Praise and Blame* (1754) by Jonathan Edwards, commonly known as *Freedom of the Will.*

442.28 as David did for Saul] Cf. I Samuel 16:17–23.

445.8 St. Bartholomew] The St. Bartholomew's Day massacre of French Protestants in Paris took place on August 24, 1572.

450.33 Regenbogen's] A German Meistersinger of the 14th century.

451.7–8 Reynard the Fox . . . Ship of Fools . . . Eulenspiegel] The medieval cycle of beast tales concerning Reynard the Fox circulated in many languages; the German poet Sebastian Brant's satire *Narrenschiff* (*Ship of Fools*) appeared in 1494; the pranks of the legendary 14th-century German clown Tyl Eulenspiegel were recounted in many stories and poems.

464.15 Claudian's Old Man of Verona] Cf. Claudian, *Carmina minores,* 20: "Of an old man of Verona who never left his home." The poem became well-known in English through Abraham Cowley's translation.

472.3 *Palingenesis*] Longfellow explained the significance of this term to him in a letter to Frances Farrer (March 20, 1859): "Spring always reminds of me of the *Palingenesis,* or re-creation, of the old alchemists, who believed that *form* is indestructible, and that out of the ashes of a rose the rose itself could be reconstructed,—if they could only discover the great secret of Nature. It is done every spring beneath our windows and before our eyes; and is always so wonderful and beautiful!"

474.1 *Hawthorne*] Nathaniel Hawthorne was buried in Concord, New Hampshire on May 23, 1864.

474.33 the tale half told] Hawthorne left several novels unfinished at his death.

477.32 Meleager] When Meleager was born to Althea (as recounted in Ovid's *Metamorphoses,* Book 8), the Fates tossed a brand into the fire and declared he would live only as long as the wood lasted. Althea snatched the brand from the fire and hid it; after Meleager killed Althea's brothers, she threw the brand back in the fire, causing his death.

480.1 *Divina Commedia*] These six sonnets were written while Longfellow was translating Dante's poem. When his translation appeared in 1870, the first two sonnets prefaced the *Inferno,* the third and fourth introduced the *Purgatorio,* and the fifth and sixth the *Paradiso.*

481.9–10 "Although . . . the snow."] Cf. Isaiah 1:18.

481.13 She stands before thee] Dante's beloved Beatrice.

481.23 Lethe and Eunoe] Two sides of a stream in Dante's *Purgatorio,* Canto 28, 127–32; the waters called Lethe ("forgetfulness") remove the memory of sin and those called Eunoë ("kindly thoughts, remembrance of good") restore the memory of good deeds.

488.11 Avesta] The Zend Avesta, the scriptures of Zoroastrianism.

488.18–19 the Enchantress . . . ghost of Samuel] Cf. I Samuel 28:7.

488.36 Ahriman] The evil spirit against whom, in the Zoroastrian religion, the deity Ahura Mazda does eternal battle.

489.28 Rahab] Harlot of Jericho who hid Joshua's spies, sometimes identified with an ancestor of David; cf. Joshua 2:1 and Matthew 1:5.

493.11–12 Laws . . . Twelve Tables] Roman code created in the fifth century B.C. by a board of ten patricians known as decemvirs; it was the basis for all subsequent Roman law.

504.10–17 I heard a great . . . adored his image] Cf. Revelation 16:1–2.

504.30 Death is . . . our windows] Cf. Jeremiah 9:21.

507.14–15 that cut . . . the colors of the king] John Endecott (1589–1665), governor of Massachusetts, cut the cross out of the English ensign in 1634 because of its papist associations (in John Winthrop's words, "the red cross was given to the king of England by the pope, as an ensign of victory, and so a superstitious thing, and a relique of antichrist"); the incident is the basis of Nathaniel Hawthorne's story "Endicott and the Red Cross."

507.23–30 The Book of Deuteronomy declares . . . To slay him] Cf. Deuteronomy 13:6–9.

513.35 Ixion's wheel] When Ixion, a Thessalian king, attempted to seduce Hera, Zeus punished him by chaining him to a burning wheel for eternity.

524.18 "Lord, I believe . . . unbelief"] Cf. Mark 9:24.

532.8–9 "Upon my handmaidens . . . shall prophesy"] Cf. Acts 2:18.

533.10 Eleazer] Third son of Aaron, priest and leader of Levites. Cf. Numbers 3:4; Numbers 20:28.

536.18–23 "Blessed are ye . . . been persecuted."] Cf. Matthew 5:11–12.

544.13 Samaria's well] The well of Jacob; cf. John 4:5–15.

546.37 O Absalom, my son!] Cf. II Samuel 18:33.

547.14 the Regicides] Thirteen men executed in 1660 for the murder of Charles I, who was beheaded in 1649.

551.16–19 "In journeyings often . . . in cold and nakedness;"] Cf. II Corinthians 11:26–27.

559.6 the Seven Thunders] Cf. Revelation 10:3–4.

563.26 Scribonius] Scribonius Largus (c. A.D. 1–50), Roman physician, recorded his observations in the work *Compositiones* (Prescriptions).

566.13 "My name is Legion!"] Cf. Mark 5:9.

570.31 hands of Briareus . . . eyes of Argus] Briareus, many-armed monster, the offspring of Gaia and Uranus; Argus, mythological monster with multiple eyes.

587.5–6 "Thou shalt . . . Witch to live?"] Cf. Exodus 22:18.

590.20 a story in the ancient Scriptures] Cf. I Kings 21:1–19.

616.12 The Prophet's . . . berries] Cf. Isaiah 17:6.

620.4 *Morituri Salutamus*] "We who are about to die salute you."

620.6–7 *Tempora labuntur . . . remorante dies.*] Cf. *Fasti,* VI, 477: "Time slips by, and we grow old with the silent years."

621.5 all save one] Alpheus Spring Packard (1798–1884), professor of languages while Longfellow was studying at Bowdoin and for many years afterwards. In his retirement he lived in Brunswick, and attended Longfellow's reading of this poem on July 7, 1875.

621.9 The great Italian poet] For Dante's meeting with his teacher, Brunetto Latini, see *Inferno,* Canto 15, lines 79–87.

621.28 "Here is thy talent . . . napkin laid,"] Cf. Luke 19:20.

622.8 Fortunatus' Purse] Medieval legend of a man who possessed an inexhaustible purse and a wishing cap.

622.16–19 As ancient Priam . . . like grasshoppers] Cf. *Iliad,* Book 3.

622.36 Marsyas] In Greek mythology, Marsyas the satyr learned to play the flute so well he challenged Apollo and his lyre to a musical contest, the victor allowed to inflict any punishment on the loser. Apollo was declared winner and flayed Marsyas alive.

623.2 "Be bold!] Cf. *The Faerie Queene,* Book III, xi, 54.

625.5 In mediæval Rome] A story drawn from Tale 107 of the *Gestae Romanorum,* a collection of moralizing popular tales in Latin, compiled around 1300.

628.1 *Belisarius*] General (c. 505–65) of the Byzantine emperor Justinian (483–565); when accused of conspiring against the emperor, he was imprisoned, but within six months restored to favor. A later story tells of his having been blinded in punishment.

628.21 Ausonian realm] Italy; according to legend, the people of Italy were descendents of Auson, son of Ulysses and Calypso.

628.22 Parthenope] In ancient poetry, a name for Naples; from its founder, the siren Parthenope, who was cast up on its shores.

628.29 Zabergan] Zaberganes, Persian ambassador to Byzantium.

629.6 the Vandal monarch's] Gelimer, whom Belisarius defeated in A.D. 534.

629.18 Monk of Ephesus] Theodosius, adopted son of Belisarius, became the lover of Belisarius's wife, Antonina; according to the *Secret History* of Procopius, he became a monk at Ephesus to avoid danger.

629.22 *Three Friends of Mine*] Cornelius Conway Felton (1807–62), professor of Greek at Harvard, and afterward its president; Louis Agassiz (1807–73), who owned a summer house near Longfellow's at Nahant; and Charles Sumner (1811–74).

632.25 Musagetes] Literally "Leader of the Muses," an epithet of Apollo.

633.5 Mæonides] An epithet for Homer.

635.3 *Kéramos*] Greek word for potter's clay.

638.13 Palissy] Bernard Palissy (c. 1509–89), French potter and enamelist, noted for scientific and technical experiments; he devoted 16 years to developing a process to produce enamels.

639.26 Francesco Xanto] Avelli Xanto, Italian painter and ceramicist of the 16th century, who worked in Urbino 1530–42.

639.30 Maestro Giorgio] Giorgio di Pietro Andreoli (c. 1500), also called "Maestro Giorgio," Italian sculptor and ceramicist, whose pottery motifs were often inspired by Raphael. He developed a carmine tint for which the majolica of Gubbio became famous.

641.9 Ausonian] See note 628.21.

642.9 Thebaid] The Roman province of Upper Egypt.

642.20–21 Morgiana . . . ambuscade] Ali Baba's faithful slave in *Ali Baba and the Forty Thieves,* who discovers the hidden thieves and contrives to kill them all.

642.28 Emeth] Ammit or Ammut; in Egyptian religion, a monster stationed by the scales of judgment in Osiris's hall in the underworld.

643.13 King-te-tching] Jingdezhen, city in northeast Jiangxi (Kiangsi) province, China; its potteries first specialized in a celadon glaze, and later, after the Ming emperors made their capital in Nanking, it supplied ceramic wares to the court.

644.8 Tower of Porcelain] Octagonal tower, about 260 feet high, whose outer walls were cased with porcelain bricks; begun in 1413 by Emperor Yung Lo (1403–28), it was destroyed during the T'ai P'ing rebellion of the 1850s.

646.15 Inarimé] "Vitorria Colonna, on the death of her husband, the Marchese di Pescara, retired to her castle at Ischia (Inarimé), and there wrote the Ode upon his death which gained her the title of Divine." [Longfellow's note]

648.10 White Chief with yellow hair] General George A. Custer.

650.2 Thou ancient oak!] The oak, cut down in 1855, stood in Brighton, under Nonantum Hill, about three miles from Longfellow's Cambridge home.

650.11 Abraham at eventide] Cf. Genesis 18:1.

650.14 a language that hath died] John Eliot's translation of the Bible into the Massachusett language was published in one volume in 1663.

651.17–26 Once upon . . . carved thereon] In his diary for November 13, 1864, Longfellow noted: "I am frequently tempted to write upon my work the inscription found upon an oar cast on the coast of Iceland,—*Oft war ek dasa durek dro thick.* Oft was I weary when I tugged at thee."

654.7 That old man desolate] Cf. II Samuel 18:33.

655.21 How cold are thy baths, Apollo!] Cf. Plutarch, *Marius,* Chapter 12.

656.17 Simon Magus] Samarian sorcerer, whose cult combined Christian and pagan elements. Cf. Acts 8:9.

656.23 Queen Candace] Queen of the Ethiopians; cf. Acts 8:27.

659.1 *The Burial of the Poet*] Richard Henry Dana (1787–1879), poet and literary editor, died in Boston on February 2, 1879.

666.17 *Hermes Trismegistus*] "Thoth the very great," Egyptian god of wisdom and learning, to whom was attributed authorship of the late Hellenic occult writings collected as *Hermetica.*

669.1 *The Bells of San Blas*] Suggested by "Typical Journeys and Country Life in Mexico," by W. H. Bishop, in *Harper's Monthly Magazine,* March 1882.

671.2 *Mezzo Cammin*] Cf. Dante, *Inferno,* Canto 1, line 1. When first published in Samuel Longfellow's *Life of Henry Wadsworth Longfellow* (1886), it appeared with the following note: "Boppard on the Rhine. August 25, 1842."

671.17 *The Cross of Snow*] This poem was written on July 10, 1879, the 18th anniversary of the death of Longfellow's second wife, Fanny, to whom he had been married for 18 years. He never published this poem in his lifetime; it first appeared in Samuel Longfellow's 1886 biography of his older brother.

671.26 a mountain] Mountain of the Holy Cross in Colorado.

674.14 Laocoön] Trojan prince and priest of Poseidon, killed with his sons by sea serpents after he protested acceptance of the Trojan horse; the ancient marble sculpture depicting his death, now in the Vatican, was discovered in Rome in 1506.

675.2 great master] Dante.

676.25–26 third circle / Of heaven] Cf. Dante, *Paradiso,* Cantos 8–9.

679.19 TOMASO DE' CAVALIERI] Young Roman nobleman to whom Michelangelo addressed a series of passionate sonnets.

683.35–38 Apollo's quoit . . . into flowers] The youth Hyacinthus was loved by Apollo and accidentally killed by him with a discus; from his blood sprang the flower of the same name.

685.8–9 beleaguered / By Spanish troops] Rome was sacked in 1527 by Spanish troops in the service of Emperor Charles V.

690.36 *"In exitu Israel de Ægypto!"*] "In Israel's flight from Egypt." Cf. Dante, *Purgatorio,* Canto 2, line 46.

692.11 *ad vocem tanti senis*] "At the voice of so venerable an old man." [Longfellow's translation]; cf. Dante, *Purgatorio,* Canto 30, line 17.

692.13 *"Benedictus qui venis,"*] "Blessed is he who cometh." [Longfellow's translation]; cf. Dante, *Purgatorio,* Canto 30, line 19, quoting Matthew 21:9.

692.15 *"Manibus o date lilia plenis."*] "Give me lilies in handfuls." [Longfellow's translation]; cf. Dante, *Purgatorio,* Canto 30, line 21, quoting *Aeneid* vi.833.

703.3–4 *The flighty purpose . . . go with it.*] Cf. *Macbeth,* IV.i.145–46.

703.7–10 *Who ne'er . . . ye Heavenly Powers.*] Cf. Goethe, *Wilhelm Meister's Apprenticeship,* Book 2, chapter 13.

705.24–25 the Hebrew in Egypt] Cf. Exodus 7:20.

706.14 "Blessed are the pure in heart."] Cf. Matthew 5:8.

708.24 Milesian] Irish.

708.35 Briareus] See note 570.31.

709.11–12 the poets who appeared to Dante] Homer, Horace, Ovid, and Lucan; cf. *Inferno,* Canto 4, lines 82–102.

710.16 Bhascara Acharya] Bhaskaracarya (1114–c. 1185) or Bhaskara the Learned, Indian mathematician and astronomer.

711.24 Ganesa] Ganesha, elephant-headed Hindu god of wisdom and success.

715.3 Gherardo della Notte] The Dutch painter Gerrit van Honthorst (1590–1656).

716.31–32 Could you not . . . one hour?"] Cf. Matthew 26:40; Mark 14:37.

717.35–36 "Yea, I think . . . remembrance,"] II Peter 1:13.

719.7–8 Jael driving . . . Sisera] Cf. Judges 4:21.

724.16 ivory gate of dreams] In Greek legend, false dreams pass through the Gate of Ivory, and those which come true pass through the Gate of Horn.

726.10 Zumzummims] Zamzummims, biblical race of giants; cf. Deuteronomy 2:20.

727.7–8 Thaddeus of Warsaw] Polish patriot Tadeusz Kosciuszko (1746–1817), protagonist of Jane Porter's novel *Thaddeus of Warsaw* (1803).

730.24–27 Sancho Panza . . . as large as hazel-nuts] Cf. *Don Quixote,* Part II, Chapter 41.

734.1 Selkirk] Alexander Selkirk (1676–1721), the model for Defoe's Robinson Crusoe, was put ashore in 1704 on Juan Fernandez Island, west of Valparaiso, after a dispute with the captain of his ship; he lived there alone for four years.

735.8 Maria del Occidente] Pseudonym of the American poet Maria Gowen Brooks (1794?–1845).

736.9 Prince Rasselas] Hero of Samuel Johnson's *The History of Rasselas, Prince of Abissinia* (1759), whose home is the Happy Valley.

741.4 Iachimo in my Imogen's bedchamber] Cf. Shakespeare, *Cymbeline,* II.ii.

747.33 Eliza Wharton] Heroine of Hannah Foster's *The Coquette,* epistolary novel published anonymously in 1797. The plot, concerning seduction and tragic early death, was based on recent events in Massachusetts.

750.31 Ingulphus] Head abbot of Croyland, Lincolnshire, from 1075 to 1101; a chronicle of the abbey, now dated to the 15th century, was formerly attributed to him.

750.34–35 Laude Deum . . . festaque honoro.] I praise the true God, I call upon the congregation, I gather together the clergy, I weep for those that have died, I celebrate the feast day.

750.38 bells . . . Panurge] Cf. Rabelais, *Gargantua and Pantagruel,* Book 3, chapter 9.

751.15 Think that . . . again!] Cf. *Purgatorio,* Canto 12, line 84.

751.19–27 Lose this day loitering . . . work will be completed] Cf. Goethe, *Faust,* "Prologue." The citation is from John Anster's 1835 translation.

753.19 Milo] Greek athlete of the sixth century B.C. According to legend, he attempted in his old age to rip an oak tree apart, but the two halves closed over his hands; while thus trapped, he was devoured by wolves.

754.38–39 Banvard's Panorama of the Mississippi] John Banvard (1815–92), writer and artist, was celebrated for his huge diorama of the Mississippi River; Longfellow had seen it when it was displayed in Boston in December 1846.

762.1 Hebe] In Greek mythology, goddess of youth and cupbearer of the gods.

763.17–18 Kerner's little poem . . . translated by Bryant] William Cullen Bryant's translation from the German of Andreas Kerner's "The Saw-Mill" was published in *Graham's Magazine,* February 1850.

764.8 text from Isaiah] Cf. Isaiah 63:1–2.

764.27 that fanatical sect] The Millerites, followers of William Miller (1782–1849), born in Pittsfield, Massachusetts, leader of a religious awakening based on the imminent second advent of Christ. Miller predicted the world would end in 1843; when that date passed, another was set, October 22, 1844. At the last general conference in Albany, New York, the belief was restated but no specific date set.

777.30–31 the famous epistle . . . to her daughter] The letter, dated December 15, 1670, was in fact addressed to Mme. de Sévigné's cousin Philippe-Emmanuel de Coulanges.

785.26 two ravens] In Norse mythology, the two ravens on Odin's shoulders are called Huginn (Mind) and Munnin (Memory).

787.25 Hyacinth] See note 683.35–38.

787.33 Heimskringla] See note 385.11.

789.22–28 Marcus Antoninus . . . city of God?"] Cf. Marcus Aurelius, *Meditations,* 4.23.

790.7–11 Stay, stay . . . until he bless thee!] Cf. Nathaniel Cotton, "Tomorrow."

791.2–3 The spirit . . . not sleep again] Cf. William Cullen Bryant, "The Ages," stanza 24.

791.13 "Westward . . . its way,"] Cf. George Berkeley, "On the Prospect of Planting Arts and Learning in America" (1952), stanza 6.

793.5 *Percival*] The American poet James Gates Percival (1795–1856), whose work was collected in *Poems* (1821), *Clio I* and *II* (1822), and *The Dream of a Day, and Other Poems* (1843).

796.4–5 doors in Bagdad . . . chalk] See note 642.20–21.

796.6–7 Don Quixote thought . . . toothpicks] Cf. *Don Quixote,* Part II, Chapter 6.

800.31–32 "And rustling . . . of Miltiades."] Cf. *Tales of a Wayside Inn,* Prelude, lines 239–40.

801.11–20 "Seggendo . . . water foam."] Cf. Dante, *Inferno,* Canto 24, lines 47–51.

Index of Titles and First Lines

Library of Congress Cataloging-in-Publication Data

Longfellow, Henry Wadsworth, 1807–1882.
[Selections. 2000]
Poems and other writings / Henry Wadsworth Longfellow.
p. cm. — (The Library of America 118)
Includes index.
ISBN 1–883011–85–X (alk. paper)
I. Title. II. Series.

PS2253 2000
811′.3—dc21 00–026678

THE LIBRARY OF AMERICA SERIES

The Library of America helps to preserve our nation's literary heritage by publishing, and keeping permanently in print, authoritative editions of America's best and most significant writing. An independent nonprofit organization, it was founded in 1979 with seed money from the National Endowment for the Humanities and the Ford Foundation.

1. Herman Melville, *Typee, Omoo, Mardi* (1982)
2. Nathaniel Hawthorne, *Tales and Sketches* (1982)
3. Walt Whitman, *Poetry and Prose* (1982)
4. Harriet Beecher Stowe, *Three Novels* (1982)
5. Mark Twain, *Mississippi Writings* (1982)
6. Jack London, *Novels and Stories* (1982)
7. Jack London, *Novels and Social Writings* (1982)
8. William Dean Howells, *Novels 1875–1886* (1982)
9. Herman Melville, *Redburn, White-Jacket, Moby-Dick* (1983)
10. Nathaniel Hawthorne, *Collected Novels* (1983)
11. Francis Parkman, *France and England in North America*, vol. I (1983)
12. Francis Parkman, *France and England in North America*, vol. II (1983)
13. Henry James, *Novels 1871–1880* (1983)
14. Henry Adams, *Novels, Mont Saint Michel, The Education* (1983)
15. Ralph Waldo Emerson, *Essays and Lectures* (1983)
16. Washington Irving, *History, Tales and Sketches* (1983)
17. Thomas Jefferson, *Writings* (1984)
18. Stephen Crane, *Prose and Poetry* (1984)
19. Edgar Allan Poe, *Poetry and Tales* (1984)
20. Edgar Allan Poe, *Essays and Reviews* (1984)
21. Mark Twain, *The Innocents Abroad, Roughing It* (1984)
22. Henry James, *Literary Criticism: Essays, American & English Writers* (1984)
23. Henry James, *Literary Criticism: European Writers & The Prefaces* (1984)
24. Herman Melville, *Pierre, Israel Potter, The Confidence-Man, Tales & Billy Budd* (1985)
25. William Faulkner, *Novels 1930–1935* (1985)
26. James Fenimore Cooper, *The Leatherstocking Tales*, vol. I (1985)
27. James Fenimore Cooper, *The Leatherstocking Tales*, vol. II (1985)
28. Henry David Thoreau, *A Week, Walden, The Maine Woods, Cape Cod* (1985)
29. Henry James, *Novels 1881–1886* (1985)
30. Edith Wharton, *Novels* (1986)
31. Henry Adams, *History of the U.S. during the Administrations of Jefferson* (1986)
32. Henry Adams, *History of the U.S. during the Administrations of Madison* (1986)
33. Frank Norris, *Novels and Essays* (1986)
34. W.E.B. Du Bois, *Writings* (1986)
35. Willa Cather, *Early Novels and Stories* (1987)
36. Theodore Dreiser, *Sister Carrie, Jennie Gerhardt, Twelve Men* (1987)
37. Benjamin Franklin, *Writings* (1987)
38. William James, *Writings 1902–1910* (1987)
39. Flannery O'Connor, *Collected Works* (1988)
40. Eugene O'Neill, *Complete Plays 1913–1920* (1988)
41. Eugene O'Neill, *Complete Plays 1920–1931* (1988)
42. Eugene O'Neill, *Complete Plays 1932–1943* (1988)
43. Henry James, *Novels 1886–1890* (1989)
44. William Dean Howells, *Novels 1886–1888* (1989)
45. Abraham Lincoln, *Speeches and Writings 1832–1858* (1989)
46. Abraham Lincoln, *Speeches and Writings 1859–1865* (1989)
47. Edith Wharton, *Novellas and Other Writings* (1990)
48. William Faulkner, *Novels 1936–1940* (1990)
49. Willa Cather, *Later Novels* (1990)
50. Ulysses S. Grant, *Memoirs and Selected Letters* (1990)

51. William Tecumseh Sherman, *Memoirs* (1990)
52. Washington Irving, *Bracebridge Hall, Tales of a Traveller, The Alhambra* (1991)
53. Francis Parkman, *The Oregon Trail, The Conspiracy of Pontiac* (1991)
54. James Fenimore Cooper, *Sea Tales: The Pilot, The Red Rover* (1991)
55. Richard Wright, *Early Works* (1991)
56. Richard Wright, *Later Works* (1991)
57. Willa Cather, *Stories, Poems, and Other Writings* (1992)
58. William James, *Writings 1878–1899* (1992)
59. Sinclair Lewis, *Main Street & Babbitt* (1992)
60. Mark Twain, *Collected Tales, Sketches, Speeches, & Essays 1852–1890* (1992)
61. Mark Twain, *Collected Tales, Sketches, Speeches, & Essays 1891–1910* (1992)
62. *The Debate on the Constitution: Part One* (1993)
63. *The Debate on the Constitution: Part Two* (1993)
64. Henry James, *Collected Travel Writings: Great Britain & America* (1993)
65. Henry James, *Collected Travel Writings: The Continent* (1993)
66. *American Poetry: The Nineteenth Century,* Vol. 1 (1993)
67. *American Poetry: The Nineteenth Century,* Vol. 2 (1993)
68. Frederick Douglass, *Autobiographies,* (1994)
69. Sarah Orne Jewett, *Novels and Stories* (1994)
70. Ralph Waldo Emerson, *Collected Poems and Translations* (1994)
71. Mark Twain, *Historical Romances* (1994)
72. John Steinbeck, *Novels and Stories 1932–1937* (1994)
73. William Faulkner, *Novels 1942–1954* (1994)
74. Zora Neale Hurston, *Novels and Stories* (1995)
75. Zora Neale Hurston, *Folklore, Memoirs, and Other Writings* (1995)
76. Thomas Paine, *Collected Writings* (1995)
77. *Reporting World War II: American Journalism 1938–1944* (1995)
78. *Reporting World War II: American Journalism 1944–1946* (1995)
79. Raymond Chandler, *Stories and Early Novels* (1995)
80. Raymond Chandler, *Later Novels and Other Writings* (1995)
81. Robert Frost, *Collected Poems, Prose, & Plays* (1995)
82. Henry James, *Complete Stories 1892–1898* (1996)
83. Henry James, *Complete Stories 1898–1910* (1996)
84. William Bartram, *Travels and Other Writings* (1996)
85. John Dos Passos, *U.S.A.* (1996)
86. John Steinbeck, *The Grapes of Wrath and Other Writings 1936–1941* (1996)
87. Vladimir Nabokov, *Novels and Memoirs 1941–1951* (1996)
88. Vladimir Nabokov, *Novels 1955–1962* (1996)
89. Vladimir Nabokov, *Novels 1969–1974* (1996)
90. James Thurber, *Writings and Drawings* (1996)
91. George Washington, *Writings* (1997)
92. John Muir, *Nature Writings* (1997)
93. Nathanael West, *Novels and Other Writings* (1997)
94. *Crime Novels: American Noir of the 1930s and 40s* (1997)
95. *Crime Novels: American Noir of the 1950s* (1997)
96. Wallace Stevens, *Collected Poetry and Prose* (1997)
97. James Baldwin, *Early Novels and Stories* (1998)
98. James Baldwin, *Collected Essays* (1998)
99. Gertrude Stein, *Writings 1903–1932* (1998)
100. Gertrude Stein, *Writings 1932–1946* (1998)
101. Eudora Welty, *Complete Novels* (1998)
102. Eudora Welty, *Stories, Essays, & Memoir* (1998)
103. Charles Brockden Brown, *Three Gothic Novels* (1998)
104. *Reporting Vietnam: American Journalism 1959–1969* (1998)
105. *Reporting Vietnam: American Journalism 1969–1975* (1998)
106. Henry James, *Complete Stories 1874–1884* (1999)
107. Henry James, *Complete Stories 1884–1891* (1999)

108. *American Sermons: The Pilgrims to Martin Luther King Jr.* (1999)
109. James Madison, *Writings* (1999)
110. Dashiell Hammett, *Complete Novels* (1999)
111. Henry James, *Complete Stories 1864–1874* (1999)
112. William Faulkner, *Novels 1957–1962* (1999)
113. John James Audubon, *Writings & Drawings* (1999)
114. *Slave Narratives* (2000)
115. *American Poetry: The Twentieth Century*, Vol. 1 (2000)
116. *American Poetry: The Twentieth Century*, Vol. 2 (2000)
117. F. Scott Fitzgerald, *Novels and Stories 1920–1922* (2000)
118. Henry Wadsworth Longfellow, *Poems and Other Writings* (2000)
119. Tennessee Williams, *Plays 1937–1955* (2000)
120. Tennessee Williams, *Plays 1957–1980* (2000)

*This book is set in 10 point Linotron Galliard,
a face designed for photocomposition by Matthew Carter
and based on the sixteenth-century face Granjon. The paper is
acid-free Ecusta Nyalite and meets the requirements for permanence
of the American National Standards Institute. The binding
material is Brillianta, a woven rayon cloth made by
Van Heek-Scholco Textielfabrieken, Holland.
The composition is by The Clarinda
Company. Printing and binding by
R.R.Donnelley & Sons Company.
Designed by Bruce Campbell.*